THE VILLAGE

ALL THREE BOOKS IN THE TRILOGY

RACHEL MCLEAN

Catawampus
press

Catawampus Press

catawampus-press.com

JOIN MY BOOK CLUB

If you want to find out more about the characters in *The Village* - how they escaped the floods and arrived at the village - you can read the prequel for free by joining my book club **at rachelmclean.com/underwater.**

Please see the end of this book for full details.

Thanks,
Rachel McLean

THICKER THAN WATER

1

Hurricane Victoria, they called it. Such a British name. So full of history, and patriotism, and shades of Empire.

It won't affect me, thought Jess as she shrugged on her coat for the cinema. Rolling live news channels had to create drama, after all. She flicked off the TV and headed out. She ignored the internal voice that nagged her to turn it off at the wall.

As she strolled into the multiplex, the sky was clear. It would be clear when she left. But as the cinema lights dimmed and muffled hoots rang around the auditorium, the storm clouds built to the east, over the North Sea.

As the trailers ended, the clouds moved south over the English Channel.

As the movie reached its climax, the Thames Barrier finally gave up, relinquishing its thirty-five-year hold over the city.

And as the lights came on and Jess rode the flood of people spilling out of the dark cinema, water breached her ground floor flat. Seeping under the door and darkening the carpets, the tide continued until it lapped around the foot of her bed. The water swelled to blossom across the corners of her duvet, leaving stains she'd later prefer not to identify.

Now, as she headed for the bus stop, she sensed the panic in the air.

The people fleeing the bars she passed on her way to the bus stop. The fellow passengers she ignored as she waited, jabbing at their phones for news and casting panicked glances towards the east. The driver who snapped at her as she fumbled for her Oyster card. The teenagers who jostled her as she touched down from the bus, heels splashing in dirty water.

None would escape. And the next morning, they would all inhabit a different city from the one they knew.

At home, her front door was heavy. As she shouldered it open, her cat fled, brushing her legs. She glanced back at it then turned and gasped. Books floated towards her. Dark tide marks seeped up the wallpaper. And the smell. It was like nothing she'd experienced before. Brackish and heavy, like cooked cabbage mixed with unwashed bodies.

She turned back to the street.

"Rufus?"

But the cat was gone.

She shrugged and waded inside. The flat was devastated. She grabbed her mobile but it was out of battery. The landline was silent.

Mum.

She bundled what dry clothes she could find into a rucksack, shouldered it and headed out.

Outside, pockets of chaos and noise were broken by patches of quiet shattered only by the wind. As she leaned into the night and started walking to her mother's, she wondered where Ben was. Whether he too would be heading home.

2

J ess turned the corner into the Parade and eyed her brother Ben's house ahead of her.

She stared at it, her heart thumping. She walked, head high, praying that he wouldn't emerge. She wasn't ready. Not yet.

As she passed the allotments and reached the halfway point between her house and the village square, she heard a sound from behind the houses to her left. She turned, scanning for signs of movement, signs of children playing.

Nothing.

Her breathing slowed. There it was again. Unmistakable. A child's scream.

She dropped her bag of books and sprinted between the houses, reaching the dilapidated playground in seconds. Asha and Soria, sisters from Jess's class, stood on the grass beyond the wooden climbing frame. Their mouths hung open. On top of the climbing frame, their backs to Jess, were two figures she didn't recognise. Too tall and broad to be pupils in her class yet not grown men. They both wore hoodies; one grey, the other black with an Adidas logo. Stretched taut between them was a bed sheet.

"Oi! You two," she shouted. "Get down from there. That climbing frame is for children under ten."

They swivelled towards her, tangling themselves up in the sheet. Their pale faces, partially obscured by their hoods, weren't ones she recognised. When they managed to unfurl their sheet and she read the text daubed across it, she knew.

Go Home Skum.

She sighed. *Idiots.* She approached the climbing frame and the two girls made a dash for her. Their small hands clutched at her trousers.

"Get down now, please. There's no need to frighten these poor girls, is there?"

"Oh noo!" the one in the Adidas hoody called, his voice a parody of her own. "Poor little girls. Children under ten. Eff off home, you parasites!"

She bent to the girls.

"Run home, quickly. Stay inside until I come and fetch you for school."

Asha nodded and grabbed her sister's hand, dragging her as she ran. Soria looked back as they rounded the first house, curiosity beating fear.

Jess turned to the climbing frame. She'd been joined by three village council members. Colin, the rule-abiding council secretary, her brother's best friend Sanjeev, and her own ally Toni. They moved to position themselves on the other side of the frame.

The boys were surrounded.

"Where's Ben?" Jess called to Sanjeev.

"Right here." Ben appeared next to her, eyeing the boys. Toni shot Jess a worried smile.

"Tell me what to do," Jess muttered, her hands trembling. She didn't need this on her first day as steward.

"It's alright," Ben replied through gritted teeth. "I'll sort it."

He approached the climbing frame. She reached out to put a hand on his arm.

"It's my job now. I just need you to tell me what to do."

He turned to her, eyes flashing. "You don't know what you're doing, sis. Should have thought of that last night."

She followed him. As they neared the climbing frame, the villagers spread out, forming a loose ring.

"Hello there!" Ben called up, raising a hand to shield his eyes from the sun. "And what brings you fine fellows here today?"

Jess eyed them, irritated. She should be doing this.

The boys fidgeted in their eyrie. Adidas nudged Grey Hoody who leaned towards Ben, his face twisted.

"Fuck off back home! We don't want you here!"

Ben sighed. "Oh dear. You boys aren't very clever, are you?"

The boys exchanged nervous glances. Grey Hoody answered in a low growl.

"What do you mean? We're plenty clever enough. Cleverer than you, anyway!" He pointed at Sanjeev. "Cleverer than *your sort*."

Sanjeev stiffened. Ben looked at him; he shook his head. Ben smiled at the boys and cast his arms out wide. "Well, you seem to think you've got some sort of safe vantage point up there, on your climbing frame for little kiddies."

The boys stumbled backwards; Grey Hoody had to grab Adidas to avoid tumbling off. "Yeah!" Adidas shouted. "You can't get us up here! Too big for this climbing frame, aren't you?"

Ben smiled. "OK, gentlemen, you have a point. But in case you haven't noticed, my friend over there–" he nodded towards Colin, who had come to stand next to Jess, "–has taken a photo of you. Plus, you're surrounded. But we don't mean you any harm. We just want you to go away and leave those poor girls alone. The girls you so bravely scared off."

The boys shifted, drawing closer together. They said nothing. Ben continued.

"Now, you see, if you can just come down quietly and be on your way, we won't hold it against you. In fact we'll let you go and we can all carry on with our day. Yes, everyone?"

There were nods and grunts of assent. Sanjeev and Colin drew apart, making space for the boys to pass through. Jess stepped towards her brother.

"Come down now, boys," she said. Grey Hoody looked at her and gave a hoarse laugh. She felt her face grow hot.

Ben turned to her.

"Let me handle this, eh? You've done enough damage already."

Toni stepped between them. "Jess is the steward now. Let her try."

Ben glared at her. For a moment, Jess thought he was going to hit her, something he hadn't done since his teenage years. Finally, he shrugged.

"Have it your way," he said. "But don't come running to me if they hurt someone."

"I won't," Jess said, fighting the tremor in her voice.

He turned away from her, glancing at Sanjeev. Sanjeev looked back through lowered lashes.

Ben walked through the crowd that had gathered towards the village centre and the house he shared with Ruth and their twin boys. As he disappeared beyond the first house, Jess felt the anxiety flow out of her body.

Sanjeev was watching him. "Mind if I go after him?"

"Course not."

He ran off.

Colin and Toni were focused on the boys, while the other villagers exchanged puzzled looks. The boys grinned at her.

"Come on then, bitch!" Grey Hoody called. "Get us down if you can." His friend snorted.

"We've still got you surrounded," she said, approaching the climbing frame. "And there are more of us. You'll be safer if you get down and leave quickly. Come down and leave us alone, please."

"I've got a photo of you boys," said Colin. He held up his phone. "We'll take it to the police. Maybe post it through some doors on your estate. You are from the estate just outside Filey, aren't you?"

Adidas nodded and his companion gave him a sharp prod in the ribs. "Fuckwit," he hissed.

Colin coughed. "Come on down now, sons. I'm going to make some space and you can leave us alone."

"Ha! You shouldn't be here, what kind of an accent is that?"

Colin's nostrils flared. "Essex. And it's you who shouldn't be here. We don't want any trouble. Now come on, lads."

The boys looked from each other to the villagers. Adidas had developed a twitch in his leg. People were staring out now from the surrounding houses. Pale figures, clutching frightened children and waiting for Jess to rid them of these invaders.

Colin moved further away from Toni and gestured with his hand. Jess backed away, her eyes on the boys. The boys slid down off the frame and darted through the space, pulling their arms in tight. They raced towards the village's northern edge.

Jess motioned to Toni and she set off in a slow jog, to check that they'd gone and weren't hiding in the village. Jess's heart pounded in her ears as she waited for her to return. The silent figures watching from their houses didn't move, but the people around the climbing frame started to gather, muttering, some exchanging hugs. Jess wondered what had happened to Ben.

Toni reappeared.

"They've gone," she panted. "Ran off across the fields."

"Thanks."

Jess turned back towards the village hall, remembering her dropped bag of books. She passed through the dispersing villagers, offering reassurances.

As she waved to a family huddled behind the window closest to her, she heard a woman's scream.

"Help! Someone, help me, Quickly!"

B en marched away, anger stirring in his stomach. *How dare she talk to me like that?*

Clenching his fists by his sides and lowering his face to avoid the stares, he rounded the first house and paused to gather his breath.

"Ben? Everything OK?"

He turned to see Sanjeev running up behind him, his face red. He frowned; he didn't need babysitting.

"Fine."

Sanjeev stopped and bent over, his fists balled on his thighs. Finally he straightened and pulled back his shoulders. "It's not her fault, you know."

Ben grunted. Sanjeev owed Ben his life and would never turn his back on him, but last night had felt like something close to it.

"You didn't exactly stop her."

Sanjeev pursed his lips. "There wasn't anything to stop."

Ben squared his shoulders. How could he not see? His own sister, betraying him like that.

"You should have supported me. You said you'd support me."

"I did. But then when Colin said about the—"

"Yeah, whatever. Just leave me be, OK?"

Sanjeev looked at him for a few moments then shrugged and turned away. Ben leaned on the wall of the house. He was tired.

He caught movement out of the corner of his eye. A man had opened the door of the house and was emerging. In the window next to him, a young woman smiled through the glass.

Ben pulled on a smile. "Don't worry. It's all under control."

"What is?"

"The boys. The playground. Isn't that what you wanted to know about?"

"Oh. No." The man looked back at the woman in the window. "No, it's something else?"

The man was biting his lower lip. Ben sighed.

"Go on then. Mark, isn't it?"

"Mark Palfrey. Yes."

"Well?"

Mark looked back at the woman. She was giving him a nervous smile, holding her hand up.

"Sally and me have got engaged. I was hoping you'd officiate. As the steward."

Ben stared at him. "What?"

Mark fidgeted. The woman was behind him now, holding his hand.

"Well, I know the steward normally does weddings. I wanted to ask if you'd—"

"Ask my sister."

Ben's jaw was tight. He stared at the couple, then heaved his weight off the wall. He started walking into the village.

He picked up his pace, heading for the Parade. How was he going to fill the day? Going home to Ruth was obvious, but then what? It wasn't just his job Jess had stolen. His sense of purpose had left him, too.

He was soon on the main road, striding towards the village square. His house was nearby, backing onto the sea. People would wonder why he wasn't at the playground. But his front door was in view now. Sanctuary.

A scream rang out and he jerked his head backwards. He squinted, eyes scanning the blank houses. In the silence left behind the scream, all he could hear was the distant hum of the sea and his own shallow breathing.

There it was again. Another scream and a muffled voice. He broke into a run, glad of something to do.

"Ruth love, we need your help." The surgery door burst open and Ben staggered in, carrying a boy covered in blood. Jess followed with Colin Barker and Toni Stewart.

Ruth dropped the medicine she'd been sorting as the panicked group crowded in. Ben was panting, sweat beading his forehead. The boy in his arms looked about eight years old and he was bleeding from a head wound. Toni was muttering to him and trying to catch his hand. Jess looked pale. Ruth cleared the medicine boxes from the table, placing her precious hoard on the floor. It had taken two months of planning to get her hands on this, to arrange last week's black market trip to Scarborough. She didn't like leaving it out in the open.

"Put him on the table," she told her husband. "Jess, can you get me a towel?"

Jess grabbed two towels from a high shelf and tucked one under the boy's head as Ben laid him on the table. She handed the other one to Ruth.

Ruth gave the boy her warmest smile. "I'm Ruth. What's

your name?"

"Rory." His voice was faint.

"He's my nephew. Susan's youngest." Toni was standing behind him, her hand cradling his. The boy continued to stare at Ruth.

The door opened again and a woman shoved her way in, nearly knocking Jess over.

"Hey, my little man, what's happened?" she wailed, kneeling at his side. He wiped his eyes and nodded at her.

"We're not sure," said Toni. "Ruth's just checking him over."

Susan stood up and twisted a finger into Toni's shoulder. "Right. You can go now." Her voice was hard.

Toni looked at her sister for a moment then headed for the door, shrugging at Jess as she squeezed past her.

Ruth looked at Jess. She hadn't seen her since last night's council meeting but knew what had happened. There were accusations swirling around her head, but now wasn't the time.

The boy blinked up at her. A gash above his eyebrow was bleeding into his eye. It was long and dotted with splinters but, she hoped, not deep. Susan knelt again and muttered into his ear. A smile flickered on his lips and his breathing calmed. Ruth grabbed bandages, tweezers, cotton wool and disinfectant. She turned back to the table, pulling in a deep breath.

"Right," she said to the boy, her voice brighter than she felt. "You look as if you've been in the wars. I've got something here I can use to clean you up, and then we'll take a look at what's happened to you."

She cocked her head and smiled at him. "OK?"

The boy nodded. Tears were mixing with the blood, making it look even worse.

"Now, it's going to sting a bit, but you can be a brave boy, can't you?"

The boy screwed up his eyes. His mother put her hands over his and made shushing sounds. She looked up at Ruth, her eyes wide.

"Can you hold him still for me please?" Ruth asked. "Hold his head? I don't want to get this in his eyes."

Susan stifled a sniff and moved her hands to her son's head.

Ruth opened the disinfectant bottle and held a piece of cotton wool to it. She looked up to see the band of onlookers watching in blinking silence.

"You don't all need to be here. Can everyone except his mum leave us, please?"

Ben threw a look at Jess. Jess was too busy watching the boy to notice. "Let me know if you need anything," she told Ruth.

Ruth grunted, not ready to acknowledge Jess's authority just yet. She looked at Ben. This would be hard for him.

Ben offered a thin smile in return and followed Jess outside. The bell over the door rang as it clapped shut. Colin followed, casting a meaningful look back at Ruth as he left. Ruth wondered why so many of them had come along with the boy.

She took a deep breath and surveyed the wound. She could hear the clock ticking on the wall above the door.

She dabbed at his brow with the disinfectant, feeling him tense beneath her touch. His mother held him still. Ruth eased out the splinters, examining them before dropping them into a metal bowl. Soon his forehead was clear except for the red line of the cut. She turned back to her medicine drawers and found a plaster which she smoothed onto it.

Rory's eyes were fluttering open. Ruth smiled.

"That's better. Now, d'you think you can sit up for me?"

The boy let his mother pull him up to a sitting position, skinny legs dangling over the edge of the table in his over-sized blue shorts.

"Is it bad?" Susan asked. Her voice had lost its panic but was still hollow.

Ruth shook her head. "There were some splinters but I got them out. He's had a nasty bump to the head, so you'll need to keep a close eye on him. Have someone sleep with him."

Susan nodded, her lips tight. "You don't think it'll get infected?"

Ruth felt her face tighten. "No."

"Have you got anything, if it does? Antibiotics?"

"Sorry. They probably wouldn't work, anyway. Not anymore."

Ruth remembered how blithely she'd handed packs of antibiotics to clients in her days as a veterinary nurse. How they'd shovelled them into pets with the slightest risk of infection; dogs with tooth decay, cats with flea infestations, even a rabbit that had been bitten by a squirrel. How she'd struggled to get them on the black market on the journey here, after Ben's mother Sonia had taken ill. Now so many of those medicines she'd taken for granted were lost. If supplies hadn't been wiped out by the floods and their after-math, they'd been defeated by the bacteria, reproducing at breakneck speed and acquiring resistance to drugs that had once been lifesavers.

"Now, Rory," she said, forcing breeziness into her voice. "Let's go into the shop and see if we can find you something that will help make it better."

"Thank you." Rory's voice was pale and reedy. He slid

down from the table under his mother's guiding hand and stood on the hard floor, swaying.

"Ready?" asked Ruth. He nodded and she led them out of the tiny pharmacy that served as village surgery, into the village shop that fronted it. Pam Heston was in there, tallying ration sheets. She looked up at Ruth.

"Everything alright? We had quite a crowd trailing through here."

This shop, in turn, was Pam's dominion. She guarded it jealously, knowing how important it was to maintain control of stock, to ensure everyone got their allocation and nothing more.

Ruth gave Rory's head a tousle. "All fine, thanks Pam. Sorry about the crowd. Rory here cut his head and they were helping out."

Pam grunted. Ruth decided to ignore it.

"But Rory's going to be back here tomorrow, with his mum, so I can check him out. Meanwhile could he have a lollipop? From my rations?"

Pam raised an eyebrow. "Sean and Ollie won't be happy."

"Sean and Ollie will never know. But Rory has been a brave boy and deserves a reward."

"Hmmpf." Pam stooped under the counter, placing a hand on her back. She scraped a box across the floor and took out a lollipop, handing it to Ruth, not Rory. Ruth knew how few sweets were in there: only two per child, per month. Enough to last six months. Pam disapproved of people sharing their rations. But she wouldn't want to anger the woman she still believed to be the wife of the steward.

"Thanks, Pam," Ruth said, handing the lollipop to Rory. "There you are. A reward for a brave little soldier. Now you can go outside with your mum."

5

A crowd had gathered in the village square. As Jess emerged from the shop with Ben and Colin, a red-faced man pushed his way towards them. Michael Walker, Rory's father.

"What's happened to my boy? Where is he?"

Ben stepped forward. "He's going to be fine, Mike. Ruth's taking good care and his mum is with him. He's had a cut on the head but Ruth can clean him up."

The man paled. "What? How the hell?" He lowered his voice. "Is it infected?"

Jess slid in next to Ben. "I don't think there's a risk of that." She looked around the crowd before turning back to Michael. "Please, let's not panic. You'll see him very soon, once Ruth's finished."

"What happened to him?" A voice from the back of the crowd.

"Ben found him between his house and the playground. He was lying on the ground. I didn't see what happened."

There was a hush while people waited for Ben to speak. He nodded but stayed silent.

"I saw!" A woman pushed forward. "It was those thugs. From Filey. What are you going to do about them?"

The woman's face was twisted and she jabbed at the air with a finger. Jess tensed. Next to her, Ben was drawing patterns in the dirt with his shoe, his head hung low. Jess let out an exasperated sigh.

"OK," Jess said, scanning the crowd. Sanjeev, in the centre, was watching Ben, waiting to catch his eye. She looked back at the woman. "We need to find out exactly what happened. D'you mind sitting down with me and telling me what you saw, please? We can get someone to open the JP, have a cup of tea to help us all calm down."

"We don't need to calm down! We need revenge. Those kids have been terrorising our village for weeks!" The woman was advancing through the crowd, jostling people aside. Ben cleared his throat in warning, but Jess ignored him.

"Please, everyone. The important thing now is not to overreact. We all know that our existence here is fragile. If we retaliate, we'll be on the back foot. No one will believe our side of the story. Meeting their aggression with more of the same won't work." Jess could hear a shrill note in her voice.

"So what are you going to do? And why are *you* answering me, not your brother?"

Jess felt heat rise to her cheeks. Ben, still looking at the ground, stilled his foot. She waited a few heartbeats before replying, pushing lightness into her voice.

"Good question. There'll be a village meeting tonight following yesterday's council meeting. I'd rather not be telling you like this, but I've been elected steward. So, I'll be doing my best to—"

"We need *him* right now." The woman thrust her finger towards Ben. "A man who knows what he's doing."

Jess forced the tremor out of her voice. "The steward's term of office is two years. That meant we had to elect a new person."

She looked over the crowd towards the houses opposite, where the other members of the council lived. She was still in the house on the village's edge that they'd been allocated when they arrived, five years ago. The house where her mother died.

There was a movement in the crowd, people muttering as they processed what she'd said.

"So," she continued. "We need to get to the bottom of what happened here today."

The woman was still glaring, but now her hands hung loosely at her sides. Jess swallowed.

"The first thing I'm going to do is ask you and anyone else who saw what happened to come into the JP, one at a time, and tell us what happened. Colin, can you help out?" Colin motioned to the woman to follow him. Sanjeev started threading his way through the crowd to join them. Ben looked up to watch his friend, his face hard.

"Thanks Colin. Sanjeev." Jess's voice was lower now. The crowd was breaking up. "Ben, I'd be grateful if you could come too. Let us know what you saw."

He looked at her, startled. Defiance crossed his face. "I didn't see anything. He was already on the ground. No one else around. Apart from Rita here." He motioned towards the woman who'd been shouting at Jess. "She was standing over him, screaming."

Sanjeev was with them now. He put a hand on Ben's arm. Ben flinched.

"Anything I can do to help, mate?" Sanjeev asked in a low voice. Ben shook his head.

Jess approached her brother. "You sure you didn't see anything else?"

"Nothing," he replied, avoiding her gaze. "What about school?"

"Oh." A weight dropped into her chest. "Er, the school won't be opening for a bit – not until this afternoon." She turned back; most of the remaining villagers had children with them. "Please can I ask parents to keep their children at home for a while while we sort this out?"

More muttering. This was something she'd have to find a better solution for.

"Thanks, everyone," she said. "We need to pull together on this and I appreciate your help."

She sighed and turned towards Ben, ignoring the contempt in his eyes.

6

That afternoon, the children were restless. Jess caught fragments of increasingly outrageous rumours about what had happened to Rory.

Finally, she decided to take control.

"Everyone," she announced. "I want us to talk about this morning."

The twelve children who'd made it into school stared at her in silence. She looked around the group, wondering about their previous lives, the journeys some of the older ones had made to come here. The children under six – more like nine or ten if you counted what they could remember – had never known the luxury of twenty-four-hour power, of so many toys they never had time to play with them all, of so much food that they could afford to throw half of it away.

"I know you've been talking about this," she said. "Asha and Soria were in the playground this morning and saw some boys from outside the village."

All heads turned towards the sisters, who blushed.

"Asha and Soria were very brave." Jess smiled. Asha smiled back but Soria's gaze dropped into her lap. "And you've heard about Rory. Well, again I was there and you'll be pleased to know that Rory's going to be fine. He's got a cut on his forehead, a bit like you did, Paul, that time you tripped on the way to the beach."

The heads turned towards ten-year-old Paul, who puffed out his chest. His cut had been more serious than Rory's. Ruth had needed to send out for surgical glue, and his parents had worn a haunted look for days afterwards.

"Paul, you were fine after a little while, weren't you?" Paul nodded, raising a finger to the faint scar above his eye. "So you all know that Rory will be too."

She sat back in her chair, waiting for questions. A hand shot up.

"Miss, will the boys come back?"

The fear of invasion hung over the village like a permanent fog, threatening them with the prospect of being displaced once again.

"I can't answer that question, Shelley. But the village council took photographs of the boys for the police. The boys won't come back if they think they might be arrested."

The children shared nervous glances. No one here saw what remained of the police, or any authority figure from the outside world, as an ally. They were alone here, and the children knew it.

Another hand shot up. "Will there be guards outside the village again?"

Jess swallowed, remembering the attacks four years ago. Guards had patrolled the village perimeter each night. Ben had been a junior member of the village council, and Sonia had still been alive. Just.

"I don't know, Mandy. But we're doing everything we can to keep you all safe." She paused. "Now, let's go down to the beach, shall we? Have a game of rounders."

The older children groaned and some of the little ones looked nervous. She stood up. Getting the children outside would break the mood. She hoped.

"Come on, everyone, let's make the most of this sunshine."

~

AT LAST THE end of the school day arrived and Jess flung open the schoolroom doors. One of the upsides of this life was the fact that none of the parents felt the need to accompany their children home from school. Instead, the kids were free to spill out into the village, some meandering home while others stopped to play.

Today was different. As she opened the school doors she heard voices outside. Every child, it seemed, had a worried parent here to pick them up. When she emerged, a hush descended. She smiled reassuringly as the children shuffled into waiting arms.

"See you tonight at the meeting," she said, as they started to turn away, shepherding their children home. There were a few nods and murmurs of assent.

Sean and Ollie were the last to leave. As the youngest in the group Jess usually accompanied them home; it made for an excuse to drop in on her brother and sister-in-law. But today their mum was here to pick them up herself.

"Hi Ruth," said Jess, glad to see her.

"Hello." Ruth's voice was hard.

"Come for the boys?"

Ruth gathered her twins to her, ruffling their hair and kissing their foreheads. Ollie looked up at her, puzzled. She gave him a warm smile, a smile that always made Jess melt. Ruth bent to whisper into the boys' ears. Ollie frowned, then shrugged as his brother grabbed him and pulled him towards their house. Jess guessed Ben was in there, licking his wounds.

Ruth turned back to Jess, her eyes lowered.

"How's Ben?" Jess asked.

"We need to talk."

A lump came to Jess's throat. "Of course. Come inside."

Ruth looked over Jess's shoulder into the schoolroom, then back at the house. Ollie was pounding at the front door, Sean not far behind. The door opened and a silhouetted figure greeted them: Ben.

Ruth turned back to her. "No. Come into the pharmacy." She paused. "Please."

Jess trailed behind as Ruth led her to the village shop, throwing Pam a tense hello as she passed through. Once inside the pharmacy, Ruth leaned against the table where Rory had lain earlier. Jess perched next to her.

Ruth pulled a hand through her hair. "How did you get on in the JP? With the investigation?"

Jess thought back to the witnesses she'd spent the morning interrogating, the jumble of information they'd provided.

"Only one person saw anything. Rita."

"What did she say?"

Jess remembered the way Rita had looked at her. *Impostor*, her eyes said. "There were just two boys. The ones at the playground. They started taunting Rory. Then they hit him with something. He went down and she screamed."

She slid down from the bench to face Ruth.

"Have you any idea what they hit him with? Could you tell, from the wound?"

"Judging from the splinters, something wooden. Some

sort of stick. They might have picked it up on the playground, maybe the beach."

Jess thought about her trip to the beach. There had been pieces of driftwood dotted about.

"Did he tell you anything? Rory?" she asked.

"Too shaken."

"Poor thing. I hope he'll be OK."

"He'll be fine."

Jess shuddered, remembering how helpless she'd felt when Sonia had suffered from infection. How it had nearly killed her.

Ruth pulled a cardigan down from a hook and wrapped it around her shoulders. The pale blue wool was threadbare, in need of darning.

"People have been asking me if they're going to station guards again," Ruth said, looking at the floor.

Jess realised that her sister-in-law was scared. Her hair was dishevelled and her face had lost its colour. She was scared herself, too. Not just of the intruders, but of the weight of responsibility.

"We're meeting tonight, to discuss it. I hope you and Ben will be there."

Ruth shrugged.

"Ruth—" Jess began.

"I don't understand."

Jess tried to keep her voice even. "Sorry?"

"Why you did that to Ben."

"It wasn't exactly my idea."

Ruth said nothing. Jess reached out but she shrank back.

"I didn't mean to upset him," Jess said. "But he knew it was time to elect a new steward."

Ruth looked up. "You?"

Jess held her gaze. "Someone has to do it."

"Ben's livid."

"He needs to get some perspective, then." Jess could feel herself shaking. "Did he ask you to speak to me?"

"No. I don't understand, that's all. We're a family. We should pull together."

"Pull together?"

Ruth nodded.

"I don't recall us pulling together when you and Ben moved out of the house. Left me there to watch Mum die."

Ruth's forehead creased. "What?"

Jess waved a hand, already regretting what she'd said. "It wasn't easy."

"You never said so."

"Of course I didn't. Ben had just been elected, you had the boys to think of. I owed it to Mum to take care of her."

"So why now? Why are you accusing me of this, after everything I did for her on the road? Things that maybe you should have done."

Jess's vision blurred. "How dare you."

"I'm sorry." Ruth's voice softened. "I didn't mean that. You were with her at the end, when she needed you."

"But not earlier?"

Ruth said nothing. But Jess knew she'd neglected Sonia when they'd been in London. Wasted all that time she could have spent with her. And Ruth had been like a daughter to Sonia, nursing her on the journey, risking her own safety to find medicine.

Jess wiped the tears from her face. Ruth moved away and busied herself at the cupboards where she kept her supplies under lock and key. Jess felt numb.

Finally Ruth broke the silence. "You've really hurt your brother."

Jess closed her eyes. "I know. I'm sorry, I really am. It

didn't turn out quite like I thought it would. The council meeting, I mean."

"No? So how was it supposed to turn out, Jess? Tell me that."

Jess swallowed.

7

The meeting had started innocently enough, the first two agenda items purely procedural. In fact, it wasn't until the third item that anyone other than Colin spoke.

"So. Item three on the agenda." said Colin. "Election of a new steward."

Normally Ben would chair these meetings but this time he had to listen while Colin led the meeting as council secretary. Colin was a perfect fit for the role as a natural upholder of rules and procedure, a man who had been active on committees in his old life: golf club, rotary club, Neighbourhood Watch. Jess knew that Colin would resist what Ben was planning.

"Do we have any nominations?" Colin looked up from his notebook and peered through his smeared glasses.

They were in the space that functioned as schoolroom during the day and village hall in the evenings and at weekends. Tomorrow morning there would be a yoga class in here, middle-aged women heaving their way through stretches and contortions in the hope of staving off ill health. Anything to avoid getting sick.

Low-powered lights cast an ugly yellow glow on the tops of their heads. Being limited to an hour of electricity gave the meetings focus.

There was a cough from Jess's right: Sanjeev.

"I'd like to nominate Ben," he said, folding his arms across his chest.

Colin hooked a finger beneath his collar and tugged it loose. "Ben's already had two years as steward. Surely you're aware, Sanjeev, that he can't stand again."

"Two years isn't long. And Ben's a good steward. I think we should amend the rules so that the steward can be in post for up to four years."

Colin exhaled. "This is not the normal process."

"Four years. No more. With elections every year just as they are now. It seems reasonable to me."

Ted Evans was sitting across from Jess. He was staring at his sidekick Harry Mills, his eyebrows raised. Harry realised he was expected to speak.

"This is daft!" he spluttered. "The constitution says a maximum of two years. That's a long time when we've only been here six. Some of us much less. Ben here took over from Murray when his two years were up, and Murray in turn took over from you, Colin, after your two years."

Colin nodded. "Thank you, Harry. Now isn't the time to start suggesting changes to the council's constitution. Can I ask for nominations please—"

"Hang on a minute!" It was Sanjeev. "You can't just ignore my suggestion. I move that we take a vote on an amendment to the constitution before we hold the election."

Colin's handwriting on the pad between him and Ben had morphed into a scrawl. He turned to Ben.

"What do you say about this?"

Ben shrugged. "I don't think it's for me to get involved. Nor anyone else who wants to stand for election. But I do think we should ask members what they think." He looked at Sanjeev, who nodded.

Ted was glaring at Ben, so hard that Jess thought her brother might disintegrate under his stare.

Harry coughed. "This is all highly irregular. If we're going to talk about an amendment to the constitution, we need to hold a special meeting and then elect a steward afterwards."

"We can't do that, Harry," said Toni. "Ben's term of office expires tomorrow."

Colin sighed. "I have to admit Toni does have a point. We can't be without leadership."

Jess watched Colin and thought of his brother, of the past he'd kept hidden from most of the people around this table. Rules and procedure were probably what kept him afloat.

Colin straightened and gazed around the table. "I move that we take a vote. All those in favour of an amendment to the constitution, allowing the steward a maximum four years in post, with annual elections."

There was a shuffling sound as hands went up, some fast, others more hesitant. Five hands, including Ben, Toni and Sanjeev. Jess shifted in her seat as Ben glared at her.

"Those against," Colin muttered, writing names into his notebook in tiny text. Paper was expensive and couldn't be squandered.

Again, the rustling sound of arms being raised. Ben was still staring at Jess, but she held her hands in her lap. He raised an eyebrow. Six hands this time, including Colin, Harry and Ted.

"Abstention," said Colin. Jess raised an arm, avoiding Ben's eye.

More shuffling, accompanied this time by the sound of Colin clearing his throat and smoothing the paper of his book. His voice was edged with relief.

"I'm sorry, Ben," he said. "But that means our next agenda item is electing your successor."

Jess could hear Ben's breathing across the table, slow and deliberate. He nodded.

"I nominate Ted," said Harry. Ted sat up in his chair. Colin and Sanjeev frowned. Toni looked from face to face.

"Thank you," said Colin. "Any other nominations?"

Toni sniffed, looked at Ben and then Jess, and cleared her throat. "Yes," she said. "Jess."

Jess stared at Toni. Panic slid over her, making her short of breath. Sanjeev was watching Ben, who was still. Toni was nodding, a smile playing on her lips.

Colin looked towards Jess, a mix of surprise and relief in his face. "Jess," he asked. "That OK with you?"

She nodded, her mind racing. She tried to ignore Ben's eyes drilling into her across the table. Had she just agreed to take her brother's job?

8

J ess sat in the grass on the cliff top. Far below, she could hear the waves crashing down the coast from the north, but tonight's clouds cloaked the ocean in grey. Power-down had begun hours ago, and now only the occasional gas lamp or candle illuminated the houses.

She lay back in the grass, staring at the clouds that dragged across the sky, watching the moon's ghostly outline break through them. The grass beneath her head was wiry and cold. She soon sat up again, digging her hands beneath her thighs. She stamped her feet slowly, wriggling stiffness out of her body.

Today hadn't been easy. The villagers were agitated, and she had no easy answers. Sure, they had photographs of the boys on the climbing frame. Evidence. But the police were almost as hostile towards this little community as those boys were, and had no interest in tracking down their attackers. They would have to look after themselves.

Ruth had turned quiet after Jess had recounted the details of the council meeting. Jess had tried to explain that it had never been her plan to take over her brother's job. But no one believed her.

At the village meeting tonight she'd announced they would be posting sentries, teams of two with the honour of staying up all night, blowing on their hands against the cold and trying to spot anyone entering the village. She hoped that the dark night and threatening rain would put any intruders off.

She wondered what Ben would have done today. More than once she'd tried to take him to one side, ask his advice. But he'd refused to speak to her.

They'd had intruders during his tenure. Once there was even a protest at the main entrance to the village. But that had run its course, the villagers staying indoors and no confrontation taking place. Ben had never been called on to deal with a violent attack inside the village boundaries.

From the corner of her eye, she glimpsed a movement and swivelled round. The light of a torch was bobbing up and down to the beat of its owner's footsteps. She watched the beam, feeling her heart rise in her chest.

FROM THE EDGE of the village, Ben could see the grass fanning out in front of him. In the narrow beam of torch-light it was impossible to tell if it went on forever, or stopped just beyond his feet. Beyond the cliff, he knew, was the long sweep of the beach, beautiful on clear nights but hazy tonight. Like his own mood.

Jess was out on the clifftop. He could see her silhouette, arms raised against the wind that pushed in from the North Sea. He guessed that she'd come out here to be alone or to remember their mother. Or to hide from him.

He picked his way towards her, tension tightening his chest. The torch beam bobbed in the air before him, the yellow ellipse of light shifting over the grass.

Finally, the beam lit up Jess's long red hair. She swivelled round, squinting and raising a hand to protect her eyes.

"Hello, Jess."

Her hand fell. "Ben."

He snapped the torch off and they were plunged into darkness. The only sound was the thrum of the waves.

"How did you know I was out here?" she asked, her body a dim silhouette against the sky.

"Do you really need me to answer that?"

His voice was rough, shot through with the shock of the past twenty-four hours. Jess tightened her shoulders and went back to staring at the sea. *Coward*, he thought.

"What the hell was all that about?" he demanded.

She turned again. A brief, guilty image of her falling backwards shot through his mind. He blinked it away.

"You know I didn't mean—"

"You didn't mean? *You didn't mean?* What exactly didn't you mean to do, Jess? Undermine me in front of everyone? Steal my job from under me?"

She pulled up the hood of her coat and climbed to her feet. She extended a hand towards his shoulder.

"Don't," he snapped, pulling away.

He looked past her towards the sea. A gap had formed in the clouds, letting in a chink of moonlight. He could see waves breaking on the Brigg End rocks, just beyond Filey. He thought back to the look on her face in the community room, her feigned surprise last night and then her smooth assurance this evening.

"You've got a nerve, Jess. I thought you supported me.

You know how important this job has been to me, how much I love it. I'm bloody good at it, too."

"Ben, please—"

"No." He could feel his eyes prickling. "I expected trouble from Ted. Even Harry. But I never thought *you'd* be the one to stab me in the back."

She inhaled, a tremor in her breath.

"I'm sorry," she pleaded. "I promise you. It was as much of a shock to me as it was to you." She paused. "But Ben..."

"What?"

"Maybe it's right that the steward job is only for two years. Maybe the village does need someone new."

"Someone new? *Someone new? You?*"

She put her hands on her hips. "Why don't you think I can do it? Why am I not good enough, and you are?"

"What?"

"You always let me play second fiddle."

He tightened his grip on the torch. It was one thing that she'd got his job, but another entirely that she thought she deserved it. That he didn't.

She held his gaze, her eyes shadowed by her hood. Sonia's coat. *How come she ended up with all Mum's stuff?*

She had no idea how lost he'd felt, how he'd clung to the steward job after Sonia's death. Without it, there was nothing between him and his grief.

"You're a selfish bitch, sis."

She plunged her hands into her pockets.

"I'm sorry. I really am. I swear I didn't expect Toni to nominate me. I didn't ask anyone to vote for me."

He glared at her.

"You made a right mess of what happened this morning. Those boys. You don't know what you're dealing with."

There was a pause. The sea felt as if it was creeping closer, hissing in the darkness.

"Look, think what you want," said Jess. "I can't make you believe me. But I can promise you that I never meant for this to happen and I never meant to hurt you. You're my brother."

"Not any more, I'm not," he snapped, and turned back towards the village.

He strode into the wind. It buffeted against his body, slowing him down.

"Ben, please come back!" she called over the sound of the waves.

He dug his hands into his pockets and pushed on.

JESS WATCHED Ben's silhouette recede into the darkness. She turned back to the empty night, feeling hollow.

She froze. There was something out there, moving with the waves.

She spun back towards the spot where her brother had disappeared.

"Ben? Ben!"

No answer: not surprising. She felt her heart quicken.

"Ben! You need to see this! Please!" She flung the words into the night. When there was still no reply she started to run after her brother.

"Ben, there's a light! Ben, please, come and look!"

"Ow! Shit, Jess."

He appeared suddenly out of the darkness, the torch still extinguished, and they smashed into each other.

"Sorry," she panted. "But please, you need to see this."

He scrambled for his torch.

"No! Keep the light off. Look out to sea."

He put the torch away. Darkness sank over them. She turned towards the sound of the waves and felt him do the same.

"What is it?" he asked.

She pointed out to sea, a hesitant finger aiming into the darkness.

"That. Right there, Ben!"

"What?" He was quiet, scanning the darkness.

"That light," she said.

Ahead of them, about halfway towards the horizon, a light was flashing intermittently. Near the Brigg End rocks.

"That's odd," he said.

She nodded, shivering. No boats came down this stretch of coast at night. There was no decent fishing any more and they had long since passed the time when those people who did own boats (and the fuel to power them) attempted to cross the sea in search of sanctuary.

"It's flashing," she said.

"Is that normal?" he asked.

"I don't know." Her voice was strained. "But I think it's morse code."

9

"How do you know?"

"I did it at Guides," Jess replied. "Well, I had a go. Didn't get my badge but I do remember enough to know what that is."

"Which is?" He felt a gnawing sensation in the pit of his stomach. Today had been hard enough without mysterious boats signalling to them from the North Sea.

She leaned on his arm. He stiffened but didn't pull away.

"SOS. Dot dot dot, dash, dash dash. They're signalling SOS, again and again. Pausing between each one."

He rubbed his neck. "What are we supposed to do about it?"

"There isn't a coastguard along this stretch of coast anymore, at least not one you could rely on," she replied. "It's up to us to help them out."

Ben didn't like this. He'd worked hard to create a refuge in this village, a place for people to rebuild their lives despite the power shortages and the rationing. A community that had learned self-reliance. When they'd arrived, the place had been barely inhabited, just a few other families and two officials from the county council allocating houses. They'd been given the house Jess now occupied, ideal for Sonia thanks to its privacy. The officials were harassed and reluctant, and the villagers had soon taken over their job.

And it had worked. Despite the hardships, and the attacks from outside, they had drawn in on themselves and defied those who would send them back to what remained of London.

But now Jess was telling him to reach outside that bubble.

The sky was darkening, clouds thickening over the sea. Somewhere beyond the light he saw two quick flashes. Lightning. The thunder wasn't far behind.

He swallowed. "I'm not so sure."

Jess's face was pale. "We can't just stand here and watch a boat in trouble. People could be drowning."

"I know, but look—"

"We'll need the boat," she shouted over the wind. Her gaze was fixed on the sea. "And people to sail it."

"What? Jess, it's the middle of the night."

"They'll be dead by the morning. We have to help. Either come with me or don't."

It was a slap in the face.

"OK," he finally muttered.

They ran to the JP, where the key to the boathouse was kept. They hammered on the door. Jess pressed her face to the glass, peering inside to find Clyde, the landlord.

Ben placed a hand on her back. "You tell Clyde what's happened. I'll get some more people."

He raced towards his home between the village square and the cliffs, hoping Ruth had gone to bed. He started knocking on doors. Sanjeev first, followed by Colin, Toni and – reluctantly – Harry.

Sanjeev threw open an upstairs window and stuck his head out.

"What the—?"

"It's me. Ben," he called up. Rain fell into his mouth. "There's a boat out at sea, a distress call. We should help them."

"What? It's gone ten o'clock, Ben! It's too dangerous."

"They're in trouble, San. This village is all about helping people who are in trouble, isn't it?" He wasn't about to admit that Jess had overruled him.

"Where's Jess?"

Ben gritted his teeth. "At the JP. Getting Clyde. Don't worry, San, I'm not mounting a coup." He could hear the sarcasm in his voice.

"I didn't say that."

His friend disappeared back inside. Moments later he appeared at his front door, shrugging on his waterproof.

10

Ruth gazed at her shadowy reflection in the window. Ben had gone out looking for Jess nearly an hour ago. They would be at the beach, she was sure: Jess's place of refuge. She shuddered.

She wanted to go and find him, but didn't trust her knowledge of the dunes. Despite growing up near the coast, she'd avoided the beach and had never been a confident swimmer. Ben's family had grown up in cities, never understanding how the sea could dominate a landscape, how you could smell its mood changing. How the weather it ushered in could hit you with raw force.

They'd learned the hard way, six years earlier. Storms pounding the east coast for weeks. Flood water making half of London homeless. Power down, trains stuck. They'd had no choice but to walk to Leeds, to Ben's aunt. Ben had begged her to come, to marry him even. It was a while before she'd accepted his proposal, but she'd been happy to have a place to go.

But right now, there was no way she could leave the boys. She'd checked on them twice since negotiating the bedtime routine, quarrels and refusals mixed in with cuddles and the calm of the bedtime story. Sean and Ollie were too young and too wrapped up in each other to dwell on what had happened to Rory, but it worried her. Until now she'd often let them play in the streets between the village houses, knowing the older kids would keep a watchful eye over them. But that had changed when she'd seen the fear on Susan Walker's face.

There was little to see beyond the window. Hers was one of the last houses before you reached the cliffs, in a row of former holiday cottages occupied by council members and their families.

So she was surprised to see a flash of movement out towards the clifftop.

She stepped closer to the window, not daring to touch the glass. There it was again. A figure, running across the grass.

She froze, wishing she'd turned out the light in the hallway behind her. Ben always took the path and there weren't many others who liked to go near the sea at night. Those boys from this morning would never dare to come here after sundown. And the guards Jess had stationed at the edges of the village would soon see them off. It couldn't be them.

But if it wasn't Ben, or the boys... who?

A shiver ran through her and she glanced back towards the stairs. As she turned back to the window, her heart leapt in her chest. Someone was there. Right outside, waving their arms in the darkness.

She scrambled back. She wanted to flee up the stairs, to throw herself across the boys' bodies. To protect them. But she couldn't take her eyes off the person on the grass.

The figure came closer and she cried out in relief. Ben.

He knocked on the window and made a circular gesture with his arm, then darted towards the front door. She raced to fling it open.

"Ben! What's happened? What are you doing? Where's Jess?" She was scared, but also annoyed that he'd managed to frighten her.

He leaned over, hands on his knees, panting. His hair was dripping. "Don't worry about that. There's a boat. Out in the bay. Distress signal. We need to get our boat out. Help them."

Her eyes widened. "What?"

His breathing was settling now but his face was dark with exertion. Behind him, people ran between houses, calling to each other.

"I'm sorry to disturb you, love, I know the boys are in bed. But there might be people injured. Clyde's down at the boathouse, getting the boat ready. He and Harry are going to take it out with a couple of the Golder lads. They're strong swimmers."

"Swimmers? You don't want anyone swimming out there in the dark. Do you know what the currents—"

"I know. But Jess says we have to help whoever's on that boat. They could be injured. We might need you, in the pharmacy."

"OK." Jess was right. They couldn't stoop to the level of the outside world, however badly it treated them. "Is Colin with you?"

Ben nodded. "He is. I'll stay with the boys." A pause. "They need you more than me."

She felt her shoulders drop. "Don't, Ben.."

He shook his head and pushed past her. She watched him creep upstairs. This wasn't the time.

She grabbed her coat.

11

W hen Jess arrived at the boathouse, Samuel and Zack Golder were busy untying ropes and hauling tarpaulins off the boat. Clyde folded them and lifted them up to a high shelf.

Jess hadn't been down here for a while. The boat was only kept for emergencies and critical trips down the coast past Hull, still impassable. Diesel was in short supply and so Clyde limited boat trips to once a month or so, giving its engine a quick blast to keep it from seizing up.

Sometimes Clyde would have dolphins for company, smooth grey outriders whose backs glinted in the sunshine. Jess would spot them from the beach, watching them bounce in front of the boat through her binoculars. But there weren't enough fish in these waters for the dolphins to stay long. And the ocean here was often freezing cold and polluted. Debris would wash up on the beach: lengths of rope, empty bottles and cans, sheets of plastic mixed in with toys and clothes sometimes, a sight that made Jess shudder. No wonder the dolphins didn't hang around.

Harry arrived as Clyde was directing Jess to the life-jackets kept in a metal storage unit at the back of the boathouse. Now was as good a time as any to build some bridges with Ted's right hand man. Maybe Harry would be less hostile on his own.

"Hi, Harry," Jess called over the hiss of the rain. "Thanks for coming."

Harry grunted. The wind blew his hood off and he yanked it back up again, swearing under his breath. "Fool's errand, this. Why the hell we're going out there at this time of night, I don't know."

Jess drew in a long breath, remembering her conversation with Ben. She glanced at her watch. Was it only half an hour ago they'd spotted the light? It was going to be a long night.

"I guess that's why they've got into trouble. We can't just abandon them."

Harry said nothing, but reluctantly took the lifejacket she offered him. He was a heavy man and it wasn't easy for him to squeeze it on. Jess shrugged hers on with ease, taking her eyes off Harry to fasten it correctly.

Clyde passed between them, checking each lifejacket in turn. The Golder boys – not boys anymore, but young men – lifted their arms for Clyde to check the fastenings at the side of their jackets. Jess followed suit, watching Harry's disgruntled expression as he waited for the final checks to be made. Once Clyde had given them the all clear, Jess spoke again.

"I appreciate your help, Harry. We need your experience tonight."

Harry grunted again. "No place for a woman, this," he said.

She shrugged. "I'm the steward. I saw the boat. I think I should go."

She placed a hand on her chest, feeling her heartbeat through the thick wadding of the lifejacket. She was more scared than she let on, and glad to have Harry here.

As a former trawlerman, he was the best placed to navigate these waters at night. He'd worked somewhere along the North Sea coast. There was a good chance he'd fished further out than they were going tonight, and in far worse conditions. She knew he was contemptuous of this tiny dayboat, a frivolous leisure craft. It would have to do.

Clyde and the Golder boys released the ropes securing the boat's trailer to hooks on the boathouse wall and started dragging it down the beach. The off-white boat floated over the dark sand. A flash of lightning reflected off its sides, illuminating the name painted in scrawling letters. *Mary Jane*. She wondered what had become of its original owners.

Jess paused to close and secure the boathouse doors then followed the others onto the beach. A small crowd had gathered. In the dark she couldn't make out faces, and wondered if Ben or Ruth might be among the villagers. The crowd was silent. No farewells or well wishes tonight, just a quiet acceptance and dread.

"Hang on a minute," said Jess. As the boat neared the water she was struck by how tiny it seemed. "We can't all go out, not if we're going to have room for passengers."

"You're right," said Clyde. "I'll stay here. Harry can pilot the boat, and he'll be more use once they get there. The lads are strong – they should go with him."

Jess frowned. She didn't want Harry out there without her, and the boys were heavy. They didn't need both of them. "No," she replied. I'll go with Harry and one of Sam or Zack."

She turned to the brothers. "I don't mind which one of you comes with us. You decide, quick."

Zack lifted a hand. "I can go." The pair exchanged glances. "I'm a better swimmer than Sam." Sam shrugged and took a step backwards. Jess nodded at his brother.

"Good. Now, let's get going."

They edged their way out to the distress signal, still flashing across the waves. Jess pulled at her lifejacket, wishing she'd stopped to put on an extra layer. The rain needled into her flimsy waterproof, and as they left the shore the wind accelerated to a full-blown gale. They stared ahead, fixated on the light as if it might disappear. Their silence was punctuated only by the drum of rain on the fibreglass hull and the rasp of the outboard motor. Harry sat at the front of the boat, peering over the open cabin's low roof. Jess huddled on the bench behind him, her knees rubbing against Zack's every time the waves rocked them.

The light drew closer, its reflection bobbing in the water. Jess swallowed, pushing down nausea, and turned to Zack. His face was pale, his jaw set. She closed her eyes and took a deep breath. The rain was icy against her cheeks and her body felt constricted by the lifejacket, as if she might suffocate.

Breathe, she told herself. She clenched and unclenched her fists, one at a time. Her hands were shaking.

The light approached and beneath it the outline of a boat. Much larger than theirs, it looked like a small trawler. Harry gave a grunt of recognition and Jess tapped him on the back. Realising he couldn't feel anything through the lifejacket, she placed a hand on his arm.

"Do you recognise it, Harry?" she shouted.

He nodded. "It's an outrigger. Type of trawler."

This meant nothing to Jess, but his calm was reassuring.

The boat didn't look as if it was in trouble; its keel rode high above the waves and it was coping with the rising and falling of the sea better than their own tiny craft was. She wondered why they had sent out a distress signal.

As they neared the trawler, she made out a movement on its deck.

"Ahoy there!" a voice called.

"Hello!" Harry called back. His voice was carried off by the wind. He repeated himself, louder this time.

"We saw your distress signal!" Jess yelled, hoping the silhouetted figure above would hear. Rain was running down her neck, soaking into her sweater. The nausea was swelling.

She swallowed and wiped the rain from her eyes. "Are you in trouble?" she shouted.

"We're taking on water," the voice called back, the words rising and falling with the waves. "Our engine has flooded and we can't move. We need to abandon ship."

Jess looked at Harry, whose face was impassive. "What do you think?" she shouted into his ear. Opposite her Zack was still and silent. Their boat lurched to the right and she grabbed the hull behind her. He put out a hand to steady her, throwing her a grim smile.

She turned back to Harry.

"Well?" Her throat was sore.

Harry shrugged. "Not sure. Their boat looks OK, but that might be deceptive."

She felt Zack slam into her as their boat tilted again. Water filled her eyes; spray or rain, she couldn't tell. They needed to hurry, or their small boat would come out of this worse than the trawler.

"How many of you are there?" she called.

"Just three!"

Jess looked at Harry and Zack, glad that she'd left the others behind. The dayboat's engine was low now, inaudible against the roar of the sea. The trawler's engine was silent. A wave crashed into them, slamming their boat into the side of the trawler. She yelped.

She nodded to Harry, feeling her stomach protest. "We've got to help them."

"OK!" Harry called. "We're coming up alongside." He adjusted the boat's angle next to the trawler, making it feel even smaller. "We'll throw you a rope."

Zack stood, spreading his legs wide and tossing a rope up towards the darkened figure. Jess had a moment of panic. They knew nothing about this boat and its occupants, yet here they were, offering them the sanctuary of their tiny boat and their village. Maybe Ben – or Harry – had been right.

She pushed her fears down into her churning gut. "Got it?" she called.

"Got it," the voice called back. She felt the boat braking as it came alongside the trawler. It swayed as Zack moved across the deck towards the trawler.

Jess stood up, feeling her legs wobble. She looked up to see the man descending over the side of the trawler. He was placing his feet on footholds on its side. *Hurry*, she thought.

Jess and Zack held their arms out to help him into their

boat, but he leapt down nimbly. He turned to face them as his weight made their boat dip further towards the trawler.

"Thanks."

The man was breathing hard. His face was dark, his wild, ragged hair silhouetted by the bright light that flashed down at them from the trawler. Jess shielded her eyes, trying to make out his face.

"Move to the other side, now!" Harry snapped as the boat dipped threateningly. The man pushed past Jess and slumped down on the bench across from her. Jess felt the boat level itself.

The man stared at her. "Don't look at me, then! Help the others!"

Jess blushed despite her cold cheeks, and turned back to the trawler. Zack was guiding a second man down, his boots nearly at the level of their hull. The boat shifted again as his weight hit the deck and he followed his companion to the far bench, saying nothing. The two of them huddled together, muttering. A cold fist of panic clutched at Jess's stomach.

She looked back to see the final man slip as his foot came into contact with the hull. There was a scraping sound and a splash as he missed his footing and disappeared between the two boats.

"Man overboard!" yelled Harry. Behind her the two strangers went quiet; she felt them lean towards her.

Zack stretched over the side of the boat as he leaned down. Jess grabbed the back of his lifejacket. She could sense his muscles working as he strained to rescue the man.

After what felt like a lifetime Zack straightened up, dragging the third man into the boat. He fell onto the deck, his body slamming into her legs. She stumbled onto the bench opposite the other men.

Harry twisted round to look at them. "He's OK," he gasped. "But we need to get him back to the village, quickly."

She looked down at the man, whose face was blue in the dim light. His eyelashes were tipped with icy water and his lips trembled. She pulled him up onto the bench and sat next to him, taking his weight on her shoulder.

"You're going to be OK," she muttered to him. "We've got you now."

His head lolled. To her relief he was slight, his weight against her barely more than that of Ben's boys when they cuddled up to their Aunty Jess.

Harry snapped at them again.

"Everybody sit down! Time to go home."

Zack threw Jess a worried look then sat on the other side of the man, sandwiching him between them. Harry turned the boat round in the water, heading for home. They rode the tide, which made progress quicker this time. She watched Zack, who watched the two men opposite, who occasionally whispered into each other's ears. The third man shivered against her. She stared at the dark shape of the trawler as they left it behind; it was still riding high on the waves, with no apparent lean. They'd said it was letting in water. Wouldn't it be starting to sink by now?

13

Ruth stood at the front of a crowd of villagers. She stared out to sea, and the flashing light. From the voices behind her, she sensed that the crowd was growing; word must have travelled. She glanced back over her shoulder. Some of the villagers were bundled up in coats, hats and sensible shoes against the chilly March night; others had headed out in their night clothes.

Toni came to stand beside her, stamping feet and blowing into her hands.

"How long are they going to be?"

"No idea," said Ruth, squinting. It was twenty minutes since the darkness had sucked up the small boat. The rain had stopped here but she had no way of knowing what it was like out at sea.

"Jeez. It looks rough. Who's out there?"

"Jess, Harry and Zack Golder."

Toni stopped blowing. She squinted out to sea. "Does she know boats?"

"No more than the rest of us."

"God. Poor Jess."

Ruth nodded. She wished she'd had a chance to dissuade Jess from going out, to let Clyde take her place.

Clyde stood a little way ahead of them, on the beach. Next to him was a pile of lifejackets and blankets, the lifejackets carried down from the boathouse and the blankets brought by those villagers who could spare them. Blankets were valuable here; with the restrictions on heating and power use, people relied on them as a source of warmth in the evenings and sometimes the daytime too.

A hum was working its way through the crowd: speculations about what had happened to the crew. Ruth kept her gaze trained on the sea, praying for her sister-in-law to reappear.

Clyde let out a shout. "I can see them!" he called, grabbing a couple of lifejackets and hurrying across the sand to the shore. He gasped as the cold waves flowed over his feet. She rushed forwards to join him, holding a pile of blankets high in her arms to keep them dry. She waded into the shallows, calling out to the boat which loomed out of the darkness.

"Jess! Over here! Can you see me?" she called, but the wind whipped away her voice. She clutched the blankets to her. Finally, she heard voices from the boat.

"Three extra men aboard!" It was Zack Golder.

Clyde splashed past her, seemingly oblivious to the icy water. The end of a rope curled through the air towards him, its movement like a whip. He grabbed it, trying to pull the boat in towards the beach. He looked back over his shoulder to the crowd on the beach.

"I need help here!"

Samuel Golder came to grasp the rope, soon joined by three other young men. Between them they heaved the boat onto the sand, a job made easier when Jess and Zack jumped out and helped to push. Two men whose faces Ruth couldn't distinguish leaped out after them and added their weight to the effort until the boat was safely on dry land.

Ruth rushed towards them, holding a blanket out towards Jess. Jess took it and let Ruth lean into her, hugging.

"Jess, I'm so glad you're OK," she breathed. Jess felt cold; her skin was like jelly.

Jess pulled back to look at Ruth. "Thanks," she smiled. "Where's Ben?"

"With the boys."

Jess nodded. "Say thanks to him, please. He helped us get out there quickly. He was with me when I – we – spotted the SOS."

Ruth allowed herself to smile. "Will do. I'm sorry, Jess." She hugged her again, feeling Jess's weight pulling down on her.

"You're soaked through," she said, "We need to get you and the others up to the pharmacy, check you out."

Jess shook her head and looked back at the boat. There was a dark shape next to it, two men standing over a third, who lay on the sand. He was moaning.

"He needs help, Ruth."

Jess looked back at her, her eyes wild. Ruth nodded and put a hand on her sister-in-law's arm.

"Seriously. He fell in the sea."

Ruth hesitated then approached the man – boy, really. He was convulsing with shivers, his skin pale. She stiffened. *Hypothermia*. No choice, then. She had to help.

She started to move closer but Zack Golder was already beside the boy, lifting him. She threw a blanket over him and ran ahead to the pharmacy, hoping she'd have everything ready before they arrived. Hoping she could save him.

14

There was a heavy drizzle in the air. Often on days like this, a dark mood would settle over the village, the weather reminding everyone of the days they'd spent walking here, tramping across sodden ground.

But today, despite the damp, people were outside, curious. As Jess passed the allotments where food for the village was grown, people unbent from their work and called questions to her. In the village square, a woman rushed out of the bakery and started asking about the boy, the one who'd fallen overboard. And if they weren't approaching her they were speculating among themselves.

She didn't have any answers. The younger man had been in no fit state for an interrogation and the other two had been allocated a place to stay by Colin before she had a chance to speak to them. When she'd left the pharmacy at 1am the village had been deserted, rainwater washing down the Parade, the downpour enveloping the houses in a blanket of silence.

She still didn't know who these men were, or how they

had come to be out at sea late at night. She had no idea whose trawler it was, or what had happened to it. *I don't even know where they are right now*. The thought made the skin on the back of her neck prickle.

As she approached the school, she saw that a crowd had gathered in the square. Rain-hooded people formed small groups as they talked, gossip passing through the crowd. Ben was nowhere to be seen, nor were any of the newcomers, but other council members were arriving. As they pushed through the crowds, villagers grabbed at them, desperate for news.

She approached the crowd, readying herself to push through to Ben's house.

A woman at the back turned.

"You!"

Jess felt a weight fall over her. "Rita. Hello."

"First you let those boys in, and now this!"

"This is different."

People were turning, mutters building to shouts.

"How is it different? Why did you let these strangers in? Who's to say they won't attack our children?"

Jess pushed her shoulders back. "There was a distress signal, out at sea. You know there's no Coastguard any more. We couldn't just leave them."

"Yes, you could." A man, standing next to Rita. Mark Palfrey.

"Mark. Congratulations. I hear you and Sally have—"

"Don't change the subject. Who are you to bring strangers into our village without consulting anyone?"

"We didn't have time."

"You should've waited," Rita said. "Called a meeting. That's how it works. Or are you planning on grabbing power for yourself?"

Jess felt like she'd been punched. "Of course not. We were all strangers once. All looking for refuge This village gave it to us. That's what we do."

"Not like this, we don't."

"Hey, gorgeous."

Jess turned to see Clyde approaching, the doors to the JP banging shut.

A friendly face. At last.

~

HE LOOKED tired and his clothes were dishevelled, as if he'd retrieved them from where he'd dropped them on the bedroom floor last night.

"Clyde. Let's go into the JP."

He looked puzzled, but turned back to the pub. Inside, he scanned the main room then went behind the bar to turn on a single light.

She slumped into a chair. "Thanks. How are you?"

He smiled. "Glad you stopped me going out in that boat, I have to admit. Damn freezing out there it was, according to Harry. My old Jamaican bones creak in the cold."

Harry. She looked out of the window. People were outside. Would the *closed* sign hold them out there?.

"Do you know where they are?"

"Two of them are enjoying the hospitality of the JP," he said, jerking his head towards the Gents toilets. "They're in there, getting washed up. I made a couple of beds up in the lounge bar."

"Is that wise?"

"The stock's all under lock and key. I know we can't spare anything, shipwrecks or not."

"How are they doing?"

"They're fine. They seem less affected by their ordeal than any of our people who went out there. Unlike their friend."

She frowned. "Is he with them?"

"Ruth was worried about him so she moved him into hers and Ben's house. Keep a weather eye on him."

She couldn't imagine Ben wanting village business intruding on his family right now. "How d'you know that?" she asked.

"Ruth came and told me, when she went back to the pharmacy to get the boy. Man. Not sure how old he is. She left him in there, but then she got worried. She wanted me to tell the other men."

"OK. I need to go."

"Anything I can help with?"

She shook her head and pushed the door open, anxious to speak to her brother.

SHE HAMMERED on Ben and Ruth's door.

"Ben! Ruth! It's Jess! Let me in, please."

Ruth appeared, her face pale above her bright pink dressing gown. She looked over Jess's shoulder and shrank back when she glimpsed the crowd.

"Quick, get inside," she hissed, pulling Jess by the arm.

Inside, Ben sat at the kitchen table with a young man who couldn't be more than twenty years old. He had mousy brown hair and skin so pale it was almost translucent. His cheekbones protruded in a way that would be elegant if he had a bit more meat on him. He was wearing Ben's clothes, at least a size too large despite Ben's slender build.

The man glanced up at her, his eyes bloodshot. She tried to give him a reassuring smile.

"Hello, I'm Jess. Ben's sister. You might remember me from the boat. You've had quite an ordeal."

The man nodded. "Martin," he whispered.

Ben looked up at her. He had dark circles under his eyes and his skin had lost some of its colour, but his smile was calm.

"Martin's been filling me in on what happened to their boat."

The man licked his lips nervously, and shifted his grip on the steaming mug that rested on the table before him.

Jess took a seat opposite Ben, next to Martin. Ruth put a chipped teacup in front of her and poured tea from the pot in the middle of the table. Behind her in the living room, Sean and Ollie were playing a noisy game of Snap! Every time one of them shouted their victory with a slap of the cards, Martin flinched.

She let out a long breath. "So?"

Ben scratched his head. "First off, Martin here is alright now. Ruth was worried about him last night—" he glanced up at Ruth, who gave his shoulder a squeeze, "—but he's doing fine. She's been giving him energy drinks. From her rations."

Jess detected a flicker of tension.

"What about the other two?" Jess asked.

Ben shrugged. "I haven't met them yet. They're in the JP, with Clyde." He paused. "People aren't happy."

"I know." She looked at Martin. "So what happened? To your boat?"

Martin fidgeted with his mug. "We went out yesterday afternoon. Do some fishing. We got into trouble when it was getting dark. The engine was fine at first, and then it stopped. I think it took on water." His voice was flat and pale.

Jess wondered why this boy who knew nothing about boats had been out there on the North Sea in the first place.

"OK," she said. "I need to go and speak to the other men before the rest of the village does." She ignored Ben's frown.

Ben eased himself up from the chair. Ruth stepped back to let him pass.

"I'll come with you," he said. "Find some council members."

"Thanks."

They headed for the front door. Outside she could hear the rising chatter of the crowd.

"Take care, both of you," Ruth called after them. Sean leapt up from his game of cards and hurled himself at his dad, who made an 'oof' noise as his son's face hit him in the stomach.

"Where are you going, Daddy?" he asked.

"Just out, Sean. Just like any other day. See you later, big man." He gave Sean's head a rub then turned to the living room. "You too, Ollie. Be good!"

Sean ran back to his brother. As Ben turned the door handle, Jess realised it had gone quiet outside.

THE CROWD HAD TURNED to watch the two men approaching the house. People stepped aside to let them through.

The men's heads were bowed. They didn't have coats and Jess could see the damp settling across the shoulders of the one in front, his T-shirt stained with moisture. She wondered what had happened to their clothes from last night.

As they passed through, the crowd shifted to face Jess. She heard a woman hiss *hush* at a small boy.

The two men ignored the muttering that rose around

them. Next to her Ben stood motionless. She steeled herself, ready to do her job.

As the men approached she could make out their hard, angular features and their weather-worn skin. It looked as though they'd had a tough life. One had a single scar snaking from the wrist of his right arm to the elbow. His companion brought up the rear and wore a white shirt, one of Clyde's. He was slimmer than his companion, and shorter.

She heard the door behind her open and then slam shut. She turned to see the boy cowering behind her.

"Robert," he whispered.

The men stopped in front of Jess and Ben. The heavier man at the front stood to one side as his companion pushed past him.

As his eyes met Jess's, she gasped.

Robert, the boy had called him. Martin was so close she could feel his breath on her neck.

She knew this man.

15

"I don't like them being here," said Harry, his face dark with anger. "There was nothing wrong with that boat as far as I could tell, and now we've got three strangers pawning off us with no idea where they're from or how long they're going to be here."

Voices rose as council members fought to be heard – to support Harry or shout him down. Ben rubbed his eyes, tired still from last night's broken sleep and troubled by his secret. He'd spoken to nobody about recognising one of the men, not even Jess. But standing on the doorstep, he'd sensed her sharing the same flash of recognition.

By contrast, Robert had shown no sign of remembering them. The four of them had exchanged curt greetings, Ben struggling to find his usual warmth, distracted by memories.

Sanjeev's voice rose above the others. Ben stared at his hands, twisting in his lap. He still couldn't look his friend in the eye.

"Listen, everyone. Jess is right. This village has been offering sanctuary to people in trouble since before even we arrived here. It's right that we've done the same now. But we need to know more about these men. What state is their boat in? Do we need to go out and make repairs? How long are they planning to stay?"

Voices rose again. Ben dug deep inside himself. He had to find the energy to keep up with the emotions playing out around him. He watched Jess lead the meeting, her brow furrowing as she concentrated on giving everyone a chance to speak. He gritted his teeth at the memory of what he'd said to Sanjeev, how he'd gone along with Jess's insistence that they rescue the men. Had it only been last night?

"OK," Jess exhaled. "First things first, I propose that we find them somewhere better to stay, see if there's an empty house somewhere. Colin?"

"Hang on a minute—" Ted interrupted. Jess raised a hand.

"Bear with me, Ted. I'm just trying to get all the facts before we make a decision. Don't worry, you'll all have a say."

Ted grunted and stared at Colin, who was studying a plan of the village, one he'd annotated with the names of the people who lived in each house or flat.

"There's a couple of flats, in the centre of the village," Colin said. "They're designed for two, but one of them could take three."

Jess nodded. Across the table, Toni raised a hand.

"Wouldn't it be better to separate them? Then they can't plot anything."

"What makes you think they would?" asked Sanjeev. Ben felt his stomach tighten and risked a glance at Jess. Her face gave nothing away.

Toni shrugged. "I don't know. But after what Harry said—"

Ben closed his eyes as voices rose around the table. He

stood up suddenly, his chair scraping across the faded wooden floor.

"Shut up, everyone! Please. Let Jess speak."

He sat down, his heart pounding. Jess glared at him. Heat rushed into his face.

"We can't spare two flats and besides, we don't want to make them too comfortable," Jess said.

Please Jess, make them very uncomfortable, Ben thought.

"I propose that we put them all in the one flat together," Jess continued. "There are folding beds stored in the back room of the JP, we can move one of them into the flat."

"Jess is right," said Sanjeev. "What do you think, Ben?"

Ben raised his head to see everyone looking at him. Sanjeev offered him a smile and a shrug. Jess was smiling too, but her eyes were hard.

He shrugged. There was silence while they waited to hear what he had to say; he couldn't help feeling gratified, but didn't trust himself to speak.

"Ben?" Jess asked, her voice clipped.

"I guess keeping them together makes sense," he finally muttered.

Jess sighed. "It'll be tight for three grown men but they'll cope," she said. "Until we know how long they're staying, and whether they have people who'll be joining them."

Jess clasped her hands together; her nails were bitten to the quick. "Now, I'll take contributions from Ted, Toni, Sanjeev, then Colin. After that, we'll put it to a vote."

16

Martin sat on Ruth and Ben's sofa, looking at the same view Ruth had gazed at the night before. It wasn't dark now, not yet, and the grey sea was visible across the grass behind the house.

There were a few shadows on the horizon; the smudged outlines of distant rainclouds, obscuring any boats that might be out there. That was good.

He ran Robert's plan through his head again, the hurried instructions before setting off in the trawler the previous day. Robert knew about this community north of them along the coast, about the way it still welcomed the occasional refugee from the floods even now, six years after they had ravaged the country. Martin had lived further south back then, near the Norfolk coast. The sea had crashed in on them that night, his grandmother panicking and phoning his mum to babble incoherences about 1953. He knew about 1953 of course, the great storm that had hammered at so much of the east coast, wrecking acres of farmland and altering the coastline forever. 1953 still haunted his village, but they'd learned their lesson and built defences to prevent it recurring.

What they couldn't have known was just how ineffective those defences would prove to be in a modern world that insisted on building houses, factories and power stations on flood plains. The authorities built their coastal defences and erected the Thames Barrier, ploughing in millions as the years passed and the storms worsened. But then when times got hard the defences were neglected, and the influx of Londoners to the vast plains around Peterborough and Norfolk were welcomed as a boost to the local economy.

None of this had concerned him. He had his own life to lead, earning what little he could from casual farm labour and the occasional job in a holiday village or working security at a festival. Keeping his dad's temper at bay with packets of cash accompanied by bottles of beer in brown paper bags when he had the money to spare. And the weather was a given on this stretch of coast. Harsh winters and wet summers were to be expected, and people barely commented when they found themselves repairing boundary walls and moving livestock further from the sea and the rivers each winter.

When the water had hit his parents' farm they had sat tight, rummaging in the eaves of the barn for sandbags and shoring themselves up, proud of their self-sufficiency. They passed ten days hunkered indoors, peering through the rain at the sandbags outside, dreading the moment when the lapping water would breach them. A couple of times his dad shouted him out of his chair, urging him to venture out and secure their teetering flood wall. When the water finally burst through he was prepared, his valuables packed in a rucksack on a high shelf in his bedroom, wrapped in plastic bags.

His mum panicked, crossing from room to room and staring outside, eyes bloodshot. His dad continued drinking, staring at the TV as the water swirled at the base of his armchair. Martin pulled his mum up the stairs, resisting her efforts to grab the cheap ornaments on the mantelpiece, dragging her heavy frame up to the relative safety of his parents' bedroom.

When the TV exploded in a shower of wet sparks, his dad still stayed put. His back was to the stairs so Martin had no idea if he was awake, asleep, or worse. He knew he should wade through to help the old bastard, find out how he was. Or he could take his chances, abandon this man who'd never shown any care for him, and escape.

"I'll get help, Mum," he promised, after pulling the crumpled dinghy down the ladder from their tiny attic, leaping back when it landed in a cloud of dust. He had no idea if it would hold, but he was prepared to risk it. He entreated his mum to come with him but she refused.

"I'll tell someone you're here. Fire Brigade, Army. Whoever."

The army were out in force, criss-crossing the region with boats and food supplies, pulling people from upstairs windows and ferrying them to safety. But their farm was isolated and so far there was no sign of any rescuers.

He'd folded his mum in a hug, trying not to cry, and lowered the dinghy through the window, inflated with the tiny pump he'd found at the bottom of a trunk full of junk. It had taken what seemed like hours to blow it up but finally it floated on the murky water that was halfway up the kitchen windows by now, its bright yellow sides dazzling against the grey and brown landscape.

He'd straddled the windowsill, throwing a last smile at his mum, who stayed calm as she waved to him. It was as if she was pretending he was heading out for a day's work, not leaving her forever.

AND NOW HERE HE WAS, the first time in six years he'd slept under clean sheets and rested his tired legs on something as decadent as a sofa. Ruth and Ben were good people, kind to take him in. Ruth had spent the day clucking around him, coming in from the pharmacy every couple of hours to check his temperature and lung capacity. She'd even found him clothes from the back of Ben's cupboard. They hung loose on him but it was good to wear something without holes. In a previous life he would have been irritated but now the ministrations of a woman filled him with gratitude.

Thinking about Ruth, he remembered Robert's plan, the one that he was expected to help carry out. Guilt gnawed at his insides.

17

R uth was relieved when Martin went to bed early. He was a nice enough lad, but once Ollie and Sean were in bed, the silence between them was almost chewable. She sat alone for a few moments, listening to him preparing for bed; water running in the bathroom, floorboards creaking overhead. When all she could hear was the whistling of the wind around the kitchen window – she must get Ben to fix that – she lit the gas lamp and placed it on the kitchen table. She turned it down as low as she could while still having enough light to read her book, one she'd picked up from the library shelf in the JP.

Fifty or so pages later, her eyelids felt heavy and her legs itched. She cast around for a bookmark, sandwiching a scrap of paper between the pages, and slid the book onto the shelf above the kettle. Books were scarce now, and precious. She turned the gas off, watching the lamp flicker, and let the shadows guide her towards the stairs.

As her bare toes felt for the bottom step, she heard a key turn in the front door.

"Ben?"

"What!" Ben slammed the door behind him. "Sorry, I thought you'd gone to bed. You made me jump."

She retraced her steps to the table and relit the gas lamp, Ben watching. His chin was dark with stubble. She gave him a sympathetic smile.

"You look terrible, love. Why don't you go to bed?"

He groaned. "In a bit."

He clattered into the living room and slumped onto the sofa, staring out of the darkened back window. She sat next to him.

"How did council go?"

He said nothing.

"Ben?"

She tried to take his hand but he didn't respond. She headed back to the kitchen and started tidying up, washing mugs and plates and sorting through their food rations for tomorrow.

After ten minutes he still hadn't spoken. She moved the kettle and tins of tea and coffee, the battered bread bin and the jug of flowers she'd picked from the dunes, and cleaned under them. When the kitchen was gleaming she heard Ben moving. He stumbled into the kitchen, poured a glass of water and slumped into a chair. She tried not to look at the ring his glass left on the table.

She eased into the chair next to him. "Ben? What happened? Was it the council meeting?"

He frowned. "Hmm? No. We agreed to—" He paused and looked around the room. "Where is he?" he whispered.

"Martin?" She found herself whispering in response. "He's upstairs, in bed. Been up there for a couple of hours."

She glanced towards the stairs. She'd watched Martin through the open door as Ben and Jess met the two other men. He'd cowered behind Jess, as if hiding from his friends. She'd assumed he was embarrassed, but now she wasn't so sure. In fact, she now remembered something in Ben's stance when the men arrived, a stiffening. Why was he so nervous?

Ben nodded. "Has he said anything to you about why they're here? Where they're from?"

"He hardly speaks. Blushes whenever I go near him. Good manners, though. Please and thank you for everything."

"You sure? No clue at all? You haven't heard him talking to the others?"

She could smell coffee on his breath; no beer tonight. She shook her head.

"What's wrong?" she asked. "Why can't you ask them yourself?"

"I haven't had the chance, that's all. Thought he might have said something to you."

His voice was too casual.

"Ben, what's wrong? What did they say to you, after you left the house this morning?"

He shook his head.

"You can tell me, love," she said. "Whatever it is. Please."

"I don't know, Ruth."

She tightened her grip on his arm. "What do you mean, you don't know? This kid has been in our house all day and all night and now you're worried about him?"

He looked down at the table, his face under lit by the gas lamp. Her stomach tightened.

"Are we safe? Are the boys safe?"

His head shot up. "Yes. Yes, I'm pretty sure of it."

"*Pretty sure?* Is that the best you can offer me?"

"Sorry. Yes, it's fine. Martin seems OK. You don't need to worry."

"That's Martin. What about the others? What did they tell you?"

He paused, breathing heavily.

"Not much. We took them to the JP to talk, it was amicable enough. They told us they'd come from down the coast, had been moving around since the flooding made them homeless."

"All that time? Six years is a lot of diesel, for a boat that size."

"I don't know. But the council is happy to have them here. The two others are already in the flat the council has allocated them, across from the school. We'll move Martin there tomorrow. Promise."

Behind Ben the clock ticked in the darkness. Above their heads the boys slept, with this stranger in the room next to them. She felt her skin prickling.

"You've got me worried. I'm going to sleep in with the boys tonight, just in case."

Ben didn't argue, but turned out the gas lamp and gave her a stiff hug. "I'm sorry about all this, Ruth. Sorry about everything."

She let herself relax into him, remembering his promises when he had asked her to flee London with him. Little did she know she'd find herself in a place like this, hundreds of miles from home as the *de facto* doctor to nearly two hundred people. She stroked his cheek then pulled away, anxious to start making herself a temporary bed on the boys' floor.

18

As Jess reached the Parade she was approached by a group of men, in hats and heavy jackets. They were little more than boys, lads she'd chaperoned through their teenage years until their makeshift school system spat them out at the other end. No one mentioned that an education was pointless without prospects.

Now, they were heading out of the village – she guessed in search of casual work. Saturday usually meant that the waged men working on the land reclamation around Hull would be at home, so there were more pickings for them. The gangers who ran the work crews didn't stop at the weekend, and nor did the work, which meant that the group leaving today was larger than it was on weekdays.

She had no idea what the salaried men were paid but she knew how little these lads received for their labours. Twelve hours of back-breaking work and no more to show for it than they'd have earned in a couple of hours in the old days. But that cash was a lifeline to the village, letting them buy what they couldn't grow, rear or make themselves. And the men who brought it home received extra rations for their pains.

They muttered greetings as they passed her. She noticed the Golder boys, and thanked them for their help with the boat. Samuel blushed but Zack treated her to a wide grin, showing the gaps in his teeth.

She strolled towards the village centre and past the school-room. Voices rang out from inside, the Saturday morning yoga group that some of the women had established. The village was quiet as she made her way up Ben's front path and knocked at his door, before shoving her chilled fingers under her armpits.

There was no answer. She knocked again, puzzled. Ben and Ruth were larks. On a Saturday morning one of them would be out working while the other had long since tidied away breakfast.

She leaned in to the door. "Ben? Ruth? It's Jess!"

She wondered if they were both out, moving their temporary lodger to his new accommodation. As she turned back towards the village centre, the door opened.

She spun round, her smile falling. Ben stood in the doorway, his hair bed-rough and still wearing his pyjamas. Behind him she could hear the screams of a boyhood game or maybe a quarrel.

"Jess. Come in," he breathed. She shrugged past him as he held the door open.

Inside, dirty crockery littered the table and the work-tops, there was toast jam-side down on the rug, and a spreading damp patch in front of the back doors.

"You OK?" she asked.

It was the first time they'd been alone since the recue. Had he recognised Robert too?

"Where's Ruth?" she asked.

He plunged a hand into his hair. "That's just it. I don't know. She slept with the boys last night. We— She was—" He swallowed. "She was worried about them. They came down without her this morning and when I went upstairs, there was no sign of her."

"Surely she's at the pharmacy? She gets up early at the weekend."

Ben was shifting from one foot to the other and scratching his chin. He hadn't shaved since the men had arrived and was showing the beginnings of a beard. He smelt musty.

He shook his head, his eyes bright. "Her clothes are still there. On the floor next to the bed she made up for herself. Neatly folded, just the same as she would have left them last night."

Jess felt a shiver crawl down her arms. "OK," she said, trying to stay calm. "Can I have a look? Please?"

Ben nodded and headed for the stairs. In the living area the boys had stopped fighting and were watching them, their mouths jam-ringed Os. She waved at them and followed her brother upstairs, the treads creaking beneath their feet. She realised how quiet the house was; Ruth had a radio and allowed herself to use it at breakfast time only, giving the house a bustling, lived-in feel in the mornings.

She hurried up the stairs and followed Ben into the first bedroom. The two beds were unmade, duvets screwed up like soft mountains, and pillows slung on the floor. At the foot of the beds was a heap of blankets and a pillow, also dishevelled. Beyond that was a neat pile of clothes, T-shirt and sweater folded on top of a pair of faded jeans.

"That's what she was wearing, last night," Ben said. Jess turned to him.

"She couldn't have come into your room, got some clothes out?"

He shook his head again. His eyes were red-rimmed. "No. She wasn't here when I woke up. Even if I didn't hear her, I've checked, and there's nothing gone. Her coat's on the hook downstairs. It's cold today."

She took two deep breaths, her mind racing. She walked out of the bedroom and looked around the landing. The door to Ben and Ruth's room was flung open but the other one was closed. She dropped her voice to a whisper.

"What about him? Martin. Has he appeared yet this morning?"

Ben clutched his hair again. "I don't know," he whispered. "I haven't—"

She nodded towards the door. "Why don't you ask him if he heard her go out?" she asked, trying to convince herself as much as Ben that Ruth had left the house as normal.

He bit his lip and knocked quietly on the door. Then more loudly when there was no reply.

"Martin?" he called softly. "Sorry to disturb you, but I was wondering if you'd seen Ruth this morning?"

Still no answer.

"Go in," Jess said.

Ben stared at her. "Should I?"

"It's your house."

Ben shuddered and grasped the doorknob, knocking quietly as he turned it. His shoulders blocked her view as he eased the door open and peered into the darkened room.

He turned back to her, his face pale.

"He's gone too."

19

J ess grabbed the stair rail. "Are you sure?" she asked. "Maybe he's gone to the flat, got out from under your feet."

Ben felt bile rise in his gut. Downstairs, he could hear the boys.

Jess's hand was on his arm.

"Look," she said. "You go out and look for her. Check where Martin is. See if he's at the flat. I'll stay here, keep an eye on the boys."

He nodded. This wasn't like Ruth; she would never go out without giving the boys a kiss, without telling him where she was. He realised how much more solid than him she was.

He breathed in again and turned away from Jess, closing the bedroom door behind him. He tore open the wardrobe doors and worked his hands through the clothes, his mind numb.

"Jess?" he called, his voice plaintive.

She was still outside the door. "Ben? You OK?"

He plunged his head into his hands. "Can you help me, please? I can't think straight."

She pushed open the door, suddenly brusque, and frowned at him as she shoved a clean shirt, a blue sweater and a pair of trousers into his outstretched arms. He took them from her, letting them hang in his hands.

"Do you need me to help you put them on?" she asked, her voice shifting from annoyance to concern.

He shook his head. "No," he replied. "But stay here for a moment, will you? While I get ready?"

She sat on the bed and bowed her head; it had been nearly fifteen years since she'd last seen him dress. He dragged the clothes onto his thin body and laid his pyjamas on the bed.

Jess took his hand. "Come on, bro. She'll turn up, you just wait and see. Do you want me to go and look?"

He shook his head again.

"OK then," she said as she stood up and pulled him towards the door. "Let's get started. You go and check the pharmacy and the men's flat. If she's not there, check the school – I heard voices coming from there on my way over."

He grabbed his coat.

PAM WAS ALREADY in the village shop, stocking shelves.

"Is Ruth here?" he panted.

"And good morning to you too. No, she's not."

"Has she been in?"

"No. What's this about?"

He shook his head. "Nothing." He ran out.

The flat was in the village centre, along the Parade. Ben felt his chest tighten as he approached it. He still hadn't spoken to Robert since his arrival. Not alone.

Ruth, where are you?

He reached the door to the flat. He took a deep breath, raising his fist.

He knocked, once. His head felt light and his breathing was shallow.

No answer.

He knocked again, louder this time.

Still nothing.

He leaned against the door. He placed his ear to it. The flat was on the first floor, up a flight of stairs immediately behind that door. He wouldn't be able to hear them if they were shouting. This village had been built with the needs of holidaymakers in mind, people who valued their privacy.

He hammered on the door with both fists. "Is there anyone in there?"

Silence.

"Everything alright?"

He turned to see Sanjeev standing in the road behind him.

"San. You made me jump. I'm trying to get hold of the men. The ones who came in on the boat. You haven't seen them, have you?"

"No. Sorry."

Sanjeev walked up the path towards Ben.

"Right," said Ben. He swallowed. "Have you seen Ruth?"

"Ruth?"

"She's not at home. Or the pharmacy. I was thinking..."

"You think she's in there? Is the young guy with them now, then?"

"No. It's just..."

Sanjeev cocked his head. "Is this important, Ben?"

Ben stiffened. "Yes."

"Well, in that case, let's go see Colin. He'll have a key."

Ben nodded.

"You want me to go?" said Sanjeev. "You can stay here, keep trying."

"Yes. Please."

Sanjeev walked away. When he reached the road, he turned.

"Be careful, Ben."

Ben clenched his fists. "Yes."

He turned and pounded on the door, not stopping until Sanjeev returned. By now, he knew the men were either not in there, or deliberately ignoring him.

Sanjeev had Colin with him.

"What's going on?" asked Colin.

"I need to speak to the men," Ben panted. "They're not opening the door."

"This is very irregular."

"I know. But I can't find Ruth. I thought they might have her."

"Why would you think that?"

Ben avoided Colin's eye. "Maybe she's checking them over. Signs of hypothermia, or something."

"Wouldn't she answer the door?"

"I don't know. Colin, please will you just let me in? Or go in yourself, if you must."

"Right." Colin dug a bunch of keys from his coat pocket. He frowned at Ben as he put one in the lock.

Before turning it, he hit the door with the flat of his hand. "Hello? Anyone in?"

No answer. *I could have told you that*, thought Ben.

Colin turned the key then eased the door open.

"Hello?"

Ben followed him inside. Colin stopped at the bottom of the stairs.

"It's Colin, and Ben. From the village council. Can we talk to you, please?"

Nothing. *Get a move on.*

Ben pushed past Colin and clattered up the stairs. At the top was an open plan living area. Dirty mugs littered the coffee table, and a plate sat on the countertop next to the sink. There was no one there.

He ran into the bedroom, flinging open cupboard doors. They were all empty. No sign of the clothes they'd lent the men. Or of their own clothes, laundered for them last night.

Colin and Sanjeev were behind him, staring around the main room. Colin looked puzzled. Sanjeev cast a wary glance towards Ben.

"They've gone," Ben said. "And they've taken Ruth."

20

J ess watched Ben stumble towards the village square. A few people were out and about now; a couple greeted him and he grunted, alarmed. He picked up his pace and ran towards the schoolroom, disappearing behind the houses that blocked her view. That was good; at last he had some purpose.

Jess closed the door and shot a bright grin at her nephews.

"Now, who wants to help tidy up? There's a lolly in it for you!" she said, hoping Ruth had a stash somewhere.

She threw herself into the task of getting the house back into shape. As she worked she talked with the boys, pushing away any creeping worry.

After twenty minutes by the kitchen clock, she was getting impatient.

"Come on, boys," she said, trying to sound breezy. "Let's go out. Find your dad."

She tossed the boys' coats at them, regretting it when they turned it into a game of throw the coat.

"Stop it!" she shouted. "We need to go out. Get our coats on."

Ollie's lip quivered. Sean gave him a punch then flung his coat on.

"Sorry." She crouched down to Ollie. "I didn't mean it."

He sniffed. She put an arm around him.

"Let's go!" cried Sean.

She placed Ollie's coat over his shoulders. He let her ease it on and button it up.

"Jess! Jess, they've gone!"

She stood, pushing the boys behind her. Ben had flung the door open.

She glared at him, motioning towards the boys.

"The men, all of them!" Ben gasped.

She pulled him to her. "What about Ruth?" she hissed into his ear.

He turned his face to her, eyes wide above blotchy cheeks.

"Nowhere. Not in the pharmacy. Not in the school, or the JP, or at Pam's, or Sanjeev's, or anywhere. The men's flat is empty – no men, no clothes, nothing."

"Oh hell."

"And Jess?"

"Yes?"

"I saw Toni. She told me there are other women gone. Ted's daughter. One of the Murray girls. Sally Angus."

BEN SLID DOWN THE WALL. His legs splayed onto the floor. He felt limp. "Where is she, Jess? What have they done to her?"

Jess crouched down to squeeze his hand. She nodded through the open front door.

"Let me go out there, Ben. Talk to people, find out what they know. That's the only way we'll find her."

She was right, of course.

"Can I stay in here?" he whispered.

"Of course you can."

He looked back at the boys, who were arguing over who had helped the most with the tidying up.

"D'you think they heard?"

"I don't know. But they need to be told something. I can do it, if you want."

"Yes, please. No, I should do it." A pause. "Oh, I don't know."

He blinked, his eyes prickling.

"Ben, do you think you can hold it together just for a bit? Until I've spoken to a few people, tried to find out some more."

He made the effort to smile. "I'll watch from the door," he croaked.

Ben watched his sister advance on the square. People approached her, calling out questions. She came to a halt and a group huddled round her, anxious voices piercing the air.

"You bloody idiot! What do you think you were doing, letting those men in? My girl has gone!"

The crowd turned; it was Ted Evans, bowling towards them from his house a few doors along from Ben's. His wife Dawn stood in the doorway, her face grey.

The crowd parted around Jess.

"I'm sorry, Ted."

"What was that?" Ted demanded. "I didn't hear you!"

Ben flinched. His sons' game had got louder. Hopefully they wouldn't hear.

"I said, I'm sorry," Jess repeated, raising her face towards Ted.

"Sorry. You're *sorry*. How the fuck is that going to get my Sarah back?"

On her doorstep, Dawn was wailing, a desperate keening sound. Ted turned back to her.

"Shut up, you bloody woman! Crying ain't going to get us nowhere, is it?"

Dawn gasped. She seemed to hold her breath, transfixed by this public display of contempt from her husband. Ben had his suspicions about Ted and the way he treated the women in his life; the grey, taciturn Dawn and the quiet, luminous Sarah, both of them cowed in a way that suggested more than just insults were traded behind that front door.

Jess approached Ted and said something Ben couldn't make out.

"I don't bloody know, do I?" Ted shouted in response. "I woke up this morning and the girl were gone. These men, the ones you let in here, the ones you insisted on rescuing, they took her. I knew it from the first time we saw that light, from when Harry told me about the state of their boat. They were con artists, you stupid woman, and you were too damn thick to know it!"

As Jess spoke again, Sanjeev appeared from behind the school building. He picked up speed, heading for the crowd. As he closed on them Ted turned to him, his face contorted with rage.

"And you!" he shouted. The crowd gave a collective intake of breath and drew back. Ben shrank back behind his door.

"Ted," said Sanjeev, louder than Jess. "We know Sarah has gone. She's not the only one. Ruth has gone too."

Ben swayed and put a hand on his chest.

"We've already started talking to people," Sanjeev continued. "Finding out where the men went, where they came from. We'll find them, Ted. We're just as motivated as you are. We all need to keep calm and work together."

Ted cackled. "Don't give me that, you bloody Paki! You and me ain't gonna *work together*, not in a month of Sundays. My daughter's been taken and I'm gonna bloody well find her."

Sanjeev's mouth was wide. Jess put a hand on his arm and whispered something that made Sanjeev collapse into himself, all the fight gone. Jess drew herself up and spoke to Ted, just a few words making their way to Ben. *Search – questions – promise.*

"Pah!" Ted thrust his scowling, twisted face into Jess's and then pulled back, spitting on the ground. He turned and strode towards his house, Dawn shifting on her feet as he approached.

"Get inside, woman!" She shrank into the house and he followed her in, slamming the door behind him.

21

J ess dropped her head in her hands, closing her eyes in concentration.

Four women had gone.

Ruth.

Sarah Evans.

Roisin Murray.

Sally Angus.

Ruth.

She turned back towards the house. Ben was staring at her, his ghostly form silhouetted in the doorway.

She let out a long slow breath. The crowd grew quiet, waiting for her to react to Ted's words.

Sanjeev squinted at her. He looked calmer than she felt.

"What do you want me to do?"

Jess looked at him. The crowd was drawing closer, eager for answers. Beyond it, she spotted Toni running towards them, her face white.

"Jess, have you heard?" she panted, pushing through the crowd. "Roisin Murray and Sally Angus have disappeared."

Flo Murray ran after Toni, dragging a small child behind her. "My girl, my girl, she's gone!"

Jess turned to Toni. "It's not just them. Sarah Evans and Ruth, too."

Toni's eyes widened. "Shit."

Jess tried to keep her voice steady. "Everyone, calm down please. There are four women missing. We're going to find them. Start a search of the village. See if anyone heard anything last night."

Jess looked past the crowd. She couldn't see Ben now but she could feel his presence.

Toni turned to Sanjeev. "I'll head back up the Parade, you do the square and the houses by the beach." She ran off.

Sanjeev looked at Jess. "You alright?"

Jess nodded, then caught herself and shook her head. "You won't find anything," she croaked.

Robert Cope. She should have told them when she recognised him.

Sanjeev gripped her shoulder, as if holding her to the ground. "Someone might have heard something. They might be hiding out in the village."

Jess pushed away a mental image of Robert, staring at her and Ben outside the house. "OK," she said. "You're right. Can you find some people?"

Sanjeev smiled. "No problem. We'll have volunteers coming out of our ears."

He dipped his head to look into Jess's eyes. "You coming?"

"I need to talk to Ben first," she replied. "But yes, I'll be right with you."

"Yep. Give him my... tell him we're all thinking of him, won't you? That we'll find her for him?"

She nodded again.

Sanjeev headed into the crowd, pointing and pulling people out to help with the search: four council members and six others. The group closed in to hear him better and as they moved away, Jess caught sight of Ben's house.

The front door was closed.

22

R uth prised her eyes open. Her head was throbbing in a way that reminded her of student hangovers from a long time ago. In front of her, a flaky patch of damp stained the wall.

She pushed herself onto her back, feeling the mattress bow beneath her. There was a dank, musty smell. She sat up stiffly, her legs curled beneath her and a cold draught at her back.

She touched her face, fingering her jawbone, cheeks and forehead. There was no swelling, and when she dared to prod harder no pain came, no top notes to join the drum beat that hammered at the nape of her neck. She turned her attention to her body. A band of pain encircled her upper arms. She eased up the sleeves of the T-shirt she'd slept in. Red marks were starting to show signs of blue: fresh bruises. She hadn't been here long, then.

Somewhere outside, a bird was singing. No voices.

She leaned against the wall and released her breath, realising she'd been holding it. She wiped tears away with her sleeve.

The room was small and cell-like. The grey mattress almost filled the entire space. On the floor beneath a small metal-legged table was a tray, embellished with pink flowers and brown stains. It held a metal flask and an unopened packet of oatcakes. Beyond that was a black metal bucket. Next to her on the mattress was a navy blanket pockmarked with loose threads; she imagined it had slipped off her when she sat up, too drowsy to notice.

She grabbed the metal flask and twisted off its lid, its contents swishing. Without pausing to check the contents, she threw her head back and swallowed gratefully. The water was brackish but cold.

When the flask was empty she replaced the lid and pushed it back onto the tray, startled by the clattering noise it made as it slipped from her hands. She looked up at the door, her panicked breathing the only sound. When no one came she reached for the oatcakes and tore open the packet, eating the first of them in one bite.

She eased her feet off the mattress and lifted herself, fighting the cramp that gripped her legs. Finally she was upright, leaning on the table. The table was sticky and its touch made her stomach heave. She stretched her arms above her head, her fingertips nearly touching the sloping ceiling, and looked around again.

Over the table was a window, its faded blue paint peeling and the glass covered in a film of grime. Beyond it was a wire mesh, bolted on from the outside.

Behind her was a wooden door, the kind you'd find on a shed. There was a gap where one of the boards had warped, covered on the other side so she couldn't see out.

She shuffled towards the door, hardly daring to breathe, her bare feet cold on the rough floor. When she reached it she leaned against it. Listening.

All she could hear was her own heartbeat, throbbing in her ears. If there was someone out there, keeping guard, they were silent. She twisted the doorknob and leaned into the door.

Nothing.

She pushed her other hand against the door. It shifted, straining against the lock, but it still wasn't budging.

She let go and stumbled backwards, falling onto the mattress and groaning as her arm hit the table. She pulled her knees up to her chest and folded her arms around them, her lank hair falling into her face.

Finally she let the tears come.

23

Ben waited for news, stranded on his sofa. Trying his best to answer Sean's questions.

The boys were burrowed in either side of him. He had offered them a story about Mummy going away to get medicine. She would be back soon. *Promise.* Ollie was whimpering into Ben's lap. Jess sat across from them, her face crumpled.

Jess had been a part of their silent vigil for over an hour now. Toni's search along the Parade had proved fruitless and Sanjeev was still out on the beach with his party. Jess had returned after getting the search started. She helped him calm the boys, distracting them with games and stories, and ferried cups of hot tea back and forth from the kitchen. Ben couldn't eat but she'd made the boys sandwiches at teatime. It wouldn't be long before they'd need feeding again, followed by bedtime.

When the door banged open Jess leapt from her seat. Sanjeev stepped into the room. He opened his mouth to speak and then noticed the boys.

Jess bustled past him. "Come on now, boys. Let's see if

we can find you both a treat in the kitchen? Come on, both of you up!"

She stood over the sofa, her arms outstretched.

"Go on, now. There's good boys," Ben muttered. They groaned and heaved themselves up, letting him give them a push.

Sanjeev took Ollie's spot next to Ben.

"So?" Ben's skin felt clammy.

"I'm sorry, mate." He sighed, looking up at Ben. "No sign of them. The women or the men. And we can't find anyone who heard anything."

Ben glanced at the kitchen. Jess was opening and closing cabinets, encouraging the boys to pick something nice to eat. A challenge, with their scant supplies. He pictured Ruth, sitting at that table the night before. Questioning him. *Are we safe?*

"You sure you spoke to everyone?" he asked.

"Everyone," Sanjeev replied. "We started out by knocking on doors but then when word started travelling through the village people came out to find out what had happened. We opened up the school room, spoke to each family one by one." He breathed in and out a few times. "Colin found a list, checked everyone was covered. We didn't speak to every individual, but we did get every household—"

"Hang on," muttered Ben. "Who didn't you speak to? Where were they?"

Sanjeev smoothed his palms down his trousers, leaving a faint trail of sweat.

"Some of the young men went out looking for work this morning. Saturday's a good day for—"

"But what if they saw something? They were up early, right? When do they get back?"

Sanjeev looked past Ben at the clock on the kitchen wall. "Not long I guess."

Ben glared at Sanjeev. "Sanjeev, why are you—?"

"Can you keep your voice down, please?" Jess stood behind him.

"They haven't found her, sis. Haven't found them. But there are men still out there, gone out to work. They might have seen something."

"I know who you mean," she said. "I saw them, on my way into the village this morning. Not long before I got here."

She turned to Sanjeev.

"There were ten of them," she told him. "Including the Golder boys. Zack Golder saw the men, when we rescued them. They were up early, they might have heard something."

She held her breath.

"We need to check the boathouse. They came in our boat, they might have left that way."

Sanjeev cleared his throat.

"You think they left another way?" Jess asked.

"No," he replied.

"Well? Did you..."

Sanjeev nodded. "Clyde already checked it."

"And?"

"And it's gone."

"The boat? The village boat?"

"Yes. It's gone, Jess. That's how they left."

24

T he men's feet and shins flickered in the firelight, the rest of their bodies receding into the darkness. From time to time the flames caught on the flask that worked its way from hand to hand, glinting amber in the shadows.

They were full of talk tonight. Robert's eyes shone as he surveyed the group, and Bill was pumped up with bravado and tall tales. *Nearly drowned – tiny dinghy rescued us – Martin here had hypothermia – those women didn't know what hit 'em*. There were scraps of truth in his words, coloured by the whisky fumes. Robert let Bill do the talking, content simply to correct him now and then.

The thought of the women in the outhouse nagged at Martin. He pictured the dingy rooms they'd been manhandled into in the early hours of this morning. They would be awake now, staring into the darkness.

He had no idea how Robert and Bill had selected the women. Ruth had always been a target, but the other three appeared out of nowhere. Chosen for their youth, he guessed. He stared into the flames, remembering Ruth's kindness, her friendly goodnight when he'd bumped into her outside her sons' room the night before.

And now here he was, back at the farm with Ruth and her companions shut away behind him. Bill was still bragging.

"The young one, the blonde one, she was easy," he bragged. "I didn't even have to break in. She walked right out of that bloody great house, looking for a cat or something."

Robert smiled. "She'll regret that."

The men laughed, some slapping their knees and one spluttering on the whisky. Martin tried to join in.

"Crept up behind her, I did," Bill continued. "Whipped the rag out of my pocket and bam! Like putty in my hands. So light I carried her onto the boat like she were a bag o' sugar."

"What about the dark one, Robert's woman?" one of the men asked, stifling a belch.

The men stopped laughing and looked at Robert. None of them knew why, but this woman was serious business to him. He frowned.

"We have young Martin to thank for Ruth's presence here," he said. Martin flinched under his glaze.

"Oh yes," said Bill. "Did exactly as he was told. Bottle of chloroform, dry rag, put her out of her misery for hours. She's only just woken up, poor bitch."

Robert flashed Bill a look.

Martin wished he had the hip flask so he could swig it and hide the colour in his cheeks. He felt pressure on his arm as someone nudged him with it. He grabbed it and took a swig.

"Would you like to see her again?" asked Robert, leaning over the fire. "Tomorrow?"

Sniggers flowed around the circle.

There was a cough from beyond the fire: Leroy. The man who'd told Robert about the village.

Robert tipped a finger to his forehead in recognition. "Leroy, you deserve thanks. A happy coincidence that Ben Dyer should be so close to us."

There was muttering: men pretending they knew who Ruth's husband was or why he was important. Martin watched the sparks float up into the sky and tried to forget that he was still wearing Ben's trousers.

25

"OK," said Jess, her mind ticking over. "So at least that means we have some idea of where they've gone."

"Do we?" Sanjeev looked unsure.

"Yes. Along the coast. In the village boat they won't have made much progress."

A keening sound came from Ben. He'd doubled over into himself, his arms folded around his shoulders. Jess glanced at the boys to see Sean watching. She tried to give him a reassuring smile.

"Ben, please hold it together," she muttered. "The boys can hear."

Ben nodded. He gave her a long look. "The men," he whispered.

He mouthed one word. *Robert.*

She sighed. "It's not your fault," she said, not sure if she meant it.

He said nothing, his keening fading to a whimper.

She stood up. "Where do you keep your binoculars?"

Sean was next to Ben now, but Ben hadn't noticed the

small hand on his arm. "Top shelf, on the wall," he muttered.

She walked into the kitchen, fumbling on the top shelf. She grabbed the handle of the binoculars case and pulled, bringing it slamming down.

Sanjeev was watching her. "It's been hours, Jess. I don't think we'll—"

"I know that," she snapped. "But I want to check if their trawler is still out there."

Three heavy knocks sounded at the door. Ben didn't move.

Jess went to answer. Zack Golder was outside, panting. He smelt of tar and dirt, and his clothes were stained orange.

"Oh," he said. "I was expecting Ben."

She gave him a tight smile. "That's OK. He's here. Did your mum send you?"

"She told me what's happened. I think I might be able to help."

She threw the door back, letting him push past.

"Ben, San," she called over him. "Zack's here. He says he can help."

Zack headed towards Ben, who raised his head from his hands. His eyes were red and his face stained with tears. Zack hesitated.

"It's OK," Jess said, following him into the kitchen. "He's upset. If you can help us find Ruth that will be a big help."

"Sit down, Zack," Sanjeev said. "Tell us what you know."

Zack dragged a chair over. "I've got an idea where the men came from. Where they took them."

Jess held her breath, leaning in.

"Go on," said Sanjeev. Ben was silent.

"On the flood defence works down by Hull, where me and the other lads go to work?"

"We know it. Go on." Sanjeev's voice was edged with impatience.

Zack shot Jess a nervous look.

"Some of the men who work there. They come from a farm past Withernsea. Where the land's nearly blocked off."

Jess knew the area. It led down towards Hull, which was a ghost town these days. Since the floods it was connected by just one bridge near the coast at Withernsea. It had been evacuated years ago.

There was another silence.

Zack coughed. "We overheard something today. One of those men saying something about getting some women, how much they were looking forward to it. Sam asked him what women he meant, assuming it was family coming to join them. But he wouldn't say. Just grinned and said they were women from up the coast."

Jess shivered. Ben was staring at Zack.

Jess pulled her chair closer in. "Did he know where you were from, this man? Could he have made the connection?"

Zack shook his head. "We know not to talk about the village, not down there."

"Good. Do you know where their farm is?"

"Not really, no. Somewhere past Withernsea. I thought it was ruined, though. The land. Can't see why anyone'd want a farm there."

"Is it near where you go to work? Can we get there by road?"

Another shake. "Don't think so. Where we go is inland from there, the other side of Hull. They're shifting earth from somewhere, bringing it in on trucks, trying to reclaim some of the city. But it's marshy down there, not safe. That's what the men say."

"Thanks Zack," Sanjeev said. "That's helpful. What do you want us to do, Jess? Ben?"

The three of them turned towards Ben, who had unfurled himself and was staring through the window, towards the sea. He shook his head, squeezing his eyes shut.

Jess scratched her neck, thinking.

"OK," she said. "They either know how to get over that bridge or they've gone in the boat. Unless the bridge is safe now. We can't be sure that what Zack's been told is entirely accurate."

Sanjeev and Zack said nothing.

"So," she continued. "If they've gone by sea, they'll be slow in our boat. Unless..."

"What?" asked Sanjeev.

She remembered the trawler, riding high as they'd left it behind. She stood up. "They've gone back to their trawler. That's how they'll get down the coast."

Sanjeev whistled. "Shit."

She nodded. "We'll have to go after them by land. How far is it, Zack?"

"Um, not sure. It takes about an hour by truck to where we go and the roads are pretty bad, so I guess it's about 30 miles? Withernsea's further down the coast, about 40 miles away?"

Damn. It would take two days to walk that far, longer if the roads were difficult. By then, who knew what might have happened to Ruth?

A shadow passed over Ben's face.

"We need to get moving," Jess said. "Head out first thing, as soon as it's light."

Ben shook his head. "We can't do that."

She put her hands on her hips. "Why not?"

"The village has to agree."

"What?"

Sanjeev looked at her. "He's right, Jess. You know how it works. We need to call a meeting."

She stifled a yell of frustration. "OK. Tomorrow morning. We do it then. Ben?"

Ben was staring out of the back window again, ignoring her.

"Ben?" she repeated. "We'll need you there. There could be resistance, you know what people are like about leaving the village."

"OK," he replied, not sounding convinced.

She stared at him, resisting the urge to shake him. "I need to do something," she said. "I'm going to the beach."

The beach was deathly quiet, the pale circle of the moon reflected in the waves. Jess pulled her coat tighter, wishing she'd brought something more substantial out with her. She hadn't set foot inside her own house for more than twelve hours now and was surprised to find herself missing it, or at least missing the connection with Sonia that it gave her. Sonia had loved Ruth, accepted her rushed admission into their little family without comment, and leaned on Ruth's growing medical skills as her illness had progressed.

Jess listened to the swish of the waves pounding on the beach, relieved that the night wasn't as wild as when she had – foolishly – launched the rescue. Would she and Ben have done it without the steady drip of Ruth's strength and decency seeping into them over the past six years? Would that frightened, nervous boy she'd seen grow up into a prickly adult have taken such risks?

She'd come across Toni on her way to the beach, heading home herself, and her friend had joined her. Toni held the binoculars up, scanning the sea for signs of life.

This was futile: the binoculars wouldn't make an unlit boat visible, even under this moon. Jess put her hands up to her face, blocking out the moon to see better.

Eventually Toni lowered the binoculars.

"Nothing," she said. "No sign of a boat or a light." Her voice was flat.

"You OK?" asked Jess.

Toni nodded, pursing her lips. "I'm fine."

"You don't look it."

Toni forced a smile. "It's Roisin."

"She's your friend. I forgot."

"Not friends. More than friends."

Jess's throat ached. "I'm sorry."

Another nod. "How's Ben holding up?"

"Don't ask."

Toni raised an eyebrow. "That bad?"

Jess shrugged. "He's lost without her. I didn't see it before, but she's the core of our family. The only one of us that's solid."

Toni turned to her. "Ben isn't the rock everyone thinks he is, you know."

"What's that supposed to mean?"

"Nothing. Just that I'm glad you're steward now, and not him."

"Well, I'm not."

Toni squeezed her arm. "I am. And not just because you're my friend. We'll find them. With you in charge, we'll pull together."

"I hope so. I really do."

~

THE NEXT MORNING, Jess woke early and hurried towards the

beach. People were already up; it was Monday and the weekday routines were still necessary. No one knew yet that there was going to be a meeting, and Jess would be expected in the schoolroom.

Not many people here had business outside the village. Only the young men went out for work, ferried away on trucks early most mornings in search of cash. But everyone else had tasks. Self-sufficiency, it turned out, made for a lot of work. Jobs had been created that had seemed archaic just a few short years ago; there were people who tended the land, others who reared livestock for milk, eggs and occasional meat. A small, trusted group of people, none from the same family, handled the food, collecting milk and eggs and delivering them to Pam in the store. Toni headed this team and she and Pam held combined but opposed power, each a check on the other.

Then there were those that tended the village itself, keeping the roadways tidy and carrying out repairs to the public buildings in the village centre: the former restaurant that served as school room and village hall, the store and pharmacy and the JP. Then there was the bakery, the old restaurant kitchen where a team of five sweaty women churned out pies and bread with black market flour. It was the kind of heavy bread that would once have been expensive, *artisan*. And for fish there was the smokehouse, sending its fumes inland from along the beach.

She passed the shop, imagining Pam in there. Wondering who would be minding the pharmacy.

She was answered by the ring of the bell over the shop door as Pam emerged.

"Jess."

"Pam. How's the shop?"

"It's fine. The pharmacy isn't."

"No."

"I'm keeping an eye on things. Dispensing medicine. But I'm not qualified. It can't carry on like this."

"It won't. We'll get her back. All of them."

"Why did you do it, Jess?"

Jess took a step back. "Sorry?"

"Why did you go out there? Bring those men here? It was clear they were trouble."

Jess took a breath. "How long have you been here, Pam?"

"Five years and one month. A month less than you. You know that."

"I do. And I also know you'd been walking for a week before you arrived."

"You can't compare me to those men."

"I can. They were in need of help. We took them in, just like the village took all of us in. It's what we do."

"Well maybe we should stop."

Pam turned to clatter into the shop. Jess watched her, feeling her chest rise and fall. Was this all her fault? Had she been naïve?

Should she have told them?

Slowly, she turned for Ben's house. It was lifeless, no sign of movement.

She spotted Dawn Evans shuffling towards her with a lopsided, slippered gait. Jess stopped. She rarely saw Dawn away from her own threshold. She didn't even attend village meetings, represented instead by her sharp-eyed husband. Dawn's front door faced the village hall and Jess did try to greet her from time to time. But she never received more than a tight smile, often followed by a hasty glance back into the house.

Jess smiled, raising her palms upwards in a friendly gesture.

"Woman!"

Dawn froze as if hit by a tranquiliser dart. Ted was behind her in their open doorway. His feet were bare and he wore trousers whose braces hung at his sides topped by a greying T-shirt, his skinny neck protruding over bony shoulders.

Jess looked between the two of them.

"Where do you think you're going?"

Dawn still had her back to her husband. She gave Jess a tiny shake of her head. *Stay out of this.*

"Everything OK?" Jess asked, searching Dawn's face.

"Is there any news of Sarah?" A whisper.

Jess cursed herself. She'd forgotten that their daughter had been taken.

"Sorry. We're doing everything we can. To look for them." Jess flushed. "I'm sorry, Dawn. I feel responsible."

Dawn shook her head. "No. It's not your fault." She looked over her shoulder. Ted was still in the doorway, his legs planted wide on the doorstep and his face hard.

"I'll let you know if I hear anything. How can I get news to you?" Jess whispered.

"The bins outside our back door. Leave me a note."

Jess looked past Dawn to see Ted approaching.

Dawn lowered her head. "Please."

Dawn turned towards the house. Ted stopped as she passed him, jostling her. She said nothing. Ted didn't follow her but stood glaring at Jess for a few moments. She held her ground but said nothing, knowing that if she angered him it would be Dawn who paid for it. Finally he made a hawking noise and spat on the pavement between them, then turned on his heel and strode back toward his house, slamming the door behind him.

27

B en reached out across the mattress, his hand coming to rest on a cold pillow.

He rolled onto his back and blinked up at the ceiling. Last night he had sat up late, staring through the glass pane of the back door in the vain hope he might spot something out there, some sort of clue. Jess had returned from the beach with her eyes lowered and her body drained of the energy from earlier on. By then the boys were in bed, exhausted, and Ben and Jess had sat at the kitchen table together, talking. Or Jess had talked while Ben gazed at his hands, turning his wedding ring round on his finger.

They weren't really married of course, not in the eyes of the law. After their flight north, registrars hadn't been easy to find, and the village council was all that remained of officialdom by the time Ruth had been ready. A simple ceremony on the beach, with Colin officiating. Ruth held flowers that Jess had picked from the scrubland behind the village and wore Sonia's wedding ring – *I don't need it, your dad's long gone*, Sonia had insisted. On his own finger was a ring from a long-dead relative of Sanjeev, one of the family heirlooms he'd been trying to rescue when Ben had first met him. When Ben had rescued him and his younger brother from a house fire on their journey north.

The ceremony had shades of earlier times, when couples would travel thousands of miles to celebrate barefoot on tropical sands. But the rush of the grey waves at their backs and the threatening rain had the guests shivering and stamping their feet on the sand even in July. Colin hurried through proceedings, anxious to seek refuge in the JP. Pickings from the last few weeks' rations had been saved up for a makeshift wedding breakfast.

Of course there was no honeymoon, but they enjoyed a few days together in the house they shared with Jess and Sonia, who made themselves as scarce as possible. That didn't last long; Sonia's illness brought her quickly home, and the sound of her coughing in her downstairs room quashed any remaining ardour.

But it wasn't the novelty of marriage he valued about life with Ruth, or the extra attention they enjoyed as newlyweds, or even the shock when she agreed to come north with him after the floods. The best thing about Ruth was the everyday, the humdrum reality of existence with this woman who became the bright centre of his life, giving him energy and helping him find calm at the same time.

The challenges of life here brought something out in Ruth that he hadn't seen in London. Sure, she'd had a steadiness about her then, but it was nothing out of the ordinary.

He'd loved her for the sparkle in her eyes, the way she'd tease him for his seriousness, how she'd brush his leg with her foot under the table. But life as a refugee had matured her. It gave her an outlet to become something more, without losing the sense of fun that she directed at the boys these days, sharing private jokes and tickling them until they laughed so hard they couldn't breathe.

He turned now as the boys tumbled into the room. They hurled themselves onto the bed as if nothing was new, as if Mummy had just gone out to work early. Ollie landed on Ben's full bladder and he groaned, then pulled them down onto the bed, kissing each one on the forehead.

Ollie put a hand on Ben's face, *Daddy tickly!* Ben rubbed his stubble: he hadn't shaved yesterday.

Sean pulled back. "Daddy, where's Mummy?"

Ben snuggled in between them, avoiding eye contact. "She's had to go away for a few days, boys. Get some supplies for the pharmacy. Like she did just before your birthday, do you remember?"

Ollie's head moved against his chest as the boy nodded. Sean jumped up to a sitting position, leaning painfully into Ben's chest. He had a birthmark on his chin that Ruth loved to kiss.

"I want her back, Daddy. She hasn't seen my drawing. I want to give her my drawing, today."

Ben ruffled Sean's hair, his throat tight.

Why didn't I warn her?

"She'll be home soon, Sean. Let's put the drawing somewhere safe in the meantime, eh?"

Sean nodded, his blue eyes huge.

"Why don't you go and get it and I can put it in Mummy's wardrobe? Then when she gets back she'll find it. It will be a lovely surprise for her."

28

Ruth was woken by the sound of a key turning in the lock.

Heaving her body into a sitting position, she remembered where she was. Truth was, she had no idea where she was. Or who was turning that key.

She shrank back against the wall, clutching her knees to her chest. Her heartbeat thudded in her ears.

She watched as the handle turned and the door opened, revealing two men. The first was small and slim, smirking at her. The second was taller and just as thin. His shoulders were stooped and his eyes on the ground.

The one at the back she knew – or thought she had. Martin. And in front, one of his companions, the one who seemed to be in charge.

They shuffled into the room and closed the door. The older man turned to Martin and told him to stand by it.

"We can't have you running out on us, can we, Mrs Dyer?" he said, turning to her. His voice was gentle, almost melodic.

"Where am I?" she demanded, climbing stiffly to her feet. "And why have you got me imprisoned in here?"

"Now, now," he said, smiling. "Let's not rush things, shall we?"

"Where are my kids?"

He stepped towards her, ignoring the question. She shrank back. She could smell him: musky aftershave mixed with mint.

He laughed and put his hands on his hips. He was pale, with neat dark hair. His jeans were clean, unlike her own. Just as he had in the village, he was wearing a clean shirt. "I'd say introductions are in order, don't you?"

She met his gaze but said nothing. He looked back at Martin.

"Martin here I believe you've met. Very kind of you to take him in." He turned back to her. "Stupid, but kind." Her jaw clenched with anger: at him, at herself.

"Let me out. Take me back to my family," she hissed.

The man shook his head and put a finger to his lips. "Hush now," he said. "Where was I? Oh yes, introductions. I'm Robert. Your husband may have told you about me."

She scrolled through her memory. Nothing.

"No?" he said. "Forgetful of him, considering everything we went through together."

He frowned. "Martin, lock the door please."

Martin hesitated, then Ruth heard the lock snap into place. "This isn't right," he muttered. "We should let her go."

She glared at him. *A bit late for that now.*

Robert swivelled to face him. "Mrs Dyer is our guest now. You played your part, and you'll get your reward." He looked back at Ruth, eyes narrowing. "We both will."

She felt her fists clench. He was slight, and Martin might not stop her. Maybe if she...

He gave a little laugh. It was high pitched and loose. "I can see what you're thinking, Mrs Dyer. You want to escape, and you're hatching a plan to take those lovely fists of yours and do me some damage with them." He raised an eyebrow. "Am I right?"

She said nothing, but loosened her fists.

"I wouldn't advise it," he said, reaching into his pocket and bringing out a cylindrical object. A flick-knife.

He brought it between them and applied pressure, flipping the blade up in front of his face. He smiled again, cocking his head to one side. A lock of hair fell over his forehead. He reached up and pushed it away.

"Best not, don't you think?" he said.

She swallowed. The rusty blade was inches away from her face. She thought of Rory in the pharmacy, of his mother's fear of infection. Of Sonia.

He lowered the blade to his side. "It's not in the best condition. I apologise for that. Maybe Martin can clean it up for me later."

Martin's head jolted up. Robert laughed.

"Only joking. This doesn't leave my sight." He flicked the blade shut and pushed it back into his pocket.

"Now, if you'd be so good as to sit down."

She looked around, calculating. The mattress was too low, too vulnerable. She perched on the table, legs swinging.

"Very good," he said. "Move up."

He motioned with his hand and she pushed herself along so that she was almost falling onto the floor. He put a hand out to touch hers on the table. She flinched.

He smiled. "It's alright, Mrs Dyer. I'm not going to hurt you."

He heaved himself up to join her on the table, laying his

hand on hers. He stroked her wedding ring. She squeezed her eyes shut.

"Nice," he said.

She nodded, unable to speak. His body was millimetres away from hers, heat emanating from him. Her flesh felt as if hot ants were crawling all over her.

"Take it off."

She felt her body go rigid. "What?"

"Your husband's ring. Take it off."

She looked down at her left hand, at the simple band Ben had placed on her finger, not long after they'd arrived at the village. It had been raining – it was always raining, back then – but they'd darted outside for just long enough to say their vows in front of Colin, who was steward at the time.

He stopped stroking and pushed at the ring with his forefinger. She felt it dig into her knuckle.

"Please." His voice was low.

She looked at Martin, who was staring down at his feet. *Coward*, she thought. *Liar*.

Robert moved his forefinger, sliding it around the ring. Her hand was trembling.

"Martin," said Robert. "Help Mrs Dyer with her ring."

Martin shuffled towards her. He was still wearing Ben's trousers, hanging from his hips, too big for him. Ruth drew in a trembling breath.

Martin stared at Ruth. She returned his gaze. Did he know how much she hated him?

"I asked you to help Mrs Dyer with her ring," Robert said. He moved his hand away and put it in his lap. It was smooth and pale, in contrast to Martin's which was bony and calloused.

Martin grabbed Ruth's hand. She pulled it away. "I can do it."

Muttering a silent apology to Ben and Sonia, she pulled the ring off, struggling to get it past the timeworn ridges in her skin. She palmed it, her grip tight.

Robert coughed. "Hand it over, please."

Tears stabbed her eyes. She mustn't cry.

He plucked the ring from her open palm. With effort, she kept her hand still.

Robert examined the ring. He placed it in the top pocket of his shirt. He patted it.

"There, that wasn't so bad, was it?"

She said nothing. He gave another one of his tight, short laughs and stood up.

"Now, we'll leave you alone. I'll be back later. I'm sure we have lots to catch up on."

"I doubt it," she said, relieved to find her voice.

He placed a hand on her shoulder. She drew back, tensing.

"Welcome, Mrs Dyer. We're very pleased to have you here."

"I can't say I'm pleased to be here."

"Well, no. But you'll learn. The truth about your husband. Maybe then you'll be glad we brought you here."

"Never."

He smiled again, his eyes dancing. Martin was fumbling with the door key.

"Adieu, my dear. Until later."

Martin slid out first and then Robert followed him, backing through the door and blowing Ruth a kiss as he did. She grimaced.

The door closed and the air grew still. All she could hear was her own heavy breathing. She slid down from the table, blinking against the daylight that sparked in her eyes.

29

J ess hurried along the coast path towards the beach. The sky to the north, where the weather came from at this time of year, was dark, ominous clouds reaching down towards the sea. Blurred shadows painted the air above the water: rain. Not the weather for a rescue mission.

She reached the beach and turned to the south where the sky was brighter, the morning's sunshine receding into the past. Near the shore, four figures were moving across the sand, stooped as if looking for something. They were making slow progress, each of them stopping to reach down from time to time.

She ran towards them. As she drew closer, she could make out Colin, Sanjeev, Toni and Harry. They were scouring the sand, sifting through it and pocketing things. As she got closer she spotted flecks of colour scattered around the shoreline. Tiny scraps of red fabric.

She picked up her pace. As she approached them, her breath fast and hard, she called out.

"What's that? What have you found?"

"Jess!"

She turned. Ben was sitting alone, huddled on the cold sand. His face was grey and his chin shadowed with stubble. He wore a faded blue T-shirt and a threadbare grey hoody, no coat. He looked like a man who'd seen a ghost.

She changed tack to approach him but stopped when she spotted movement out of the corner of her eye, along the beach.

"What's that?"

Colin straightened, shielding his eyes with his hand. "The little bastards!"

Along the shore, level with the boat house, two figures were wading in the shallows, dragging the village boat between them. They both wore hoodies, raised against the wind.

Colin broke into a run, gesticulating at them and shouting. Jess looked at Ben, then ran after him.

As they got closer, one of the boys spotted them. He grabbed his friend's arm, shaking it violently. The other one fell backwards, splashing in the waves. They started to run.

By the time Jess and Colin made it to the boat, the boys had got away. They ground to a halt at the water's edge, panting.

"When I get hold of them!" Colin grunted.

Jess bent over, pressing her hands into her thighs for support. "That was them, wasn't it? The ones from the playground."

Colin looked after them, his face scarlet. "None other."

She looked at the boat. "How the hell did they get hold of the boat?"

"No idea." He looked out to sea. "One thing's for sure, though."

"What?"

"If those men left the village boat behind, then they're definitely using their trawler. No point looking for it."

Harry ran up to join them. "Did those kids have the boat?"

Jess nodded. "It must have washed back in. How come you didn't see it?"

Harry shrugged.

"It wasn't there when I got here," said Colin.

Jess stared at it, puzzled. Were the boys connected to Robert and his men, somehow? She doubted it. It must have just washed up and they thought they'd try their luck.

"Does it look damaged to you?" she asked Harry.

He heaved it further onto the sand. "Looks OK."

Jess allowed herself a moment's relief. This would make going after Ruth easier. She looked over Colin's shoulder. Sanjeev and Toni were still moving around the beach, picking things up.

"What's all that, on the beach?"

Colin followed her gaze. "We're not sure. Looks like clothing, but we don't know where it came from. We've been going through it, trying to find some clues."

"Is it all the same?" she asked. All she'd seen was red. She and Colin started walking back to the others, leaving Harry to secure the boat.

Colin shook his head. "No. The red scraps are the most obvious, but there are others. The red fabric is thick, seems to be part of a sweater. Then there are thin scraps of yellow; maybe a T-shirt. And we've found a couple of white socks."

Jess felt her stomach churn. "How clean is it?"

"Clean? Why? It's all clean, I suppose. But if it came out of the sea..."

Jess shrugged; she could be wrong. But it felt as if

clothes that had been out there for longer than a day would be dirty, maybe stiffened by salt.

They reached Ben. Jess squatted next to him on the sand and he leaned against her.

"Ben?" she asked softly. "What was Ruth wearing, when she went to bed on Friday night?"

He closed his eyes. "Grey T-shirt. Old. Black jogging bottoms. At least, that's what she'd laid out on the bed, earlier on. I didn't see her get ready, because I – she—"

He collapsed into her, sobs shuddering through her body.

"She slept with the boys," Jess said, remembering what he'd told her. "That night."

He wailed, the sound echoing across the sand.

"Jess, why did I let her? Why did I let that bastard in? I told her I'd keep her safe, Jess! *I told her I'd keep her safe!*"

30

B en sat in the front row with his boys, the hum of
gossip rising behind him. Jess and Colin sat at the
top table, waiting for everyone to arrive.

Once they'd returned from the beach, Colin had joined
Toni, already out speaking to the families of the missing
women, asking if they recognised those clothes. First the
Murrays, then Ted Evans, with Dawn nowhere to be seen
during the brief moments Colin had spent at the doorstep.
And finally Mark Palfrey, Sally Angus's boyfriend. Mark said
that Sally had some white T-shirts, but normally wore one
under a shirt and he couldn't be sure if she had that night.
There was no owner for the red sweater.

And now, two hours later, they were waiting for Jess, the
new steward, to reassure her community.

Ben was glad it wasn't him.

The voices died down and Pam shut the doors at the
back of the room, Ben checked the clock above Jess's head.
9.05am and the space was full, with people standing at the
back. Tables had been cleared to one side and some people
sat on those, legs swinging. Every household seemed to be

here, including children. No one wanted to stay behind to babysit.

Jess looked at Sean and Ollie before lifting her eyes up to the rest of the room.

The room was so quiet Ben could hear the clock ticking high on the wall, almost muffled by the sound of his own breathing in his ears. He waited for Jess to speak.

"Hello, everyone."

Ben felt himself overcome by coughing, bringing his hand up and wiping spittle on his trousers. He thought of the clothes that Ruth had been wearing two nights ago, and nearly slid off his chair.

Jess glanced at him. He sent her a nod, moving his gaze up to the clock to break eye contact.

"Thank you for coming," Jess said, her voice carrying over their heads. Behind him, a chair scraped on the parquet floor.

"We wanted to bring everyone together to update you on what we know about the disappearances."

The silence broke at the use of the word, whispers stuttering through the room. Colin raised his hands.

"Please," said Colin. "Let the steward speak."

Jess frowned at him. Village meetings weren't usually that formal.

Jess looked down at her notes. Ben knew that Jess had three lists: the men's names, the women's names and the clothes they'd found. He steeled himself for the sound of Ruth's name.

"Let's start with the men," she said. "The three men we rescued were Robert, Bill and Martin. Or those are the names they gave us."

He watched Jess. Did Jess remember Robert? Did she remember what happened between them?

"We believe they came from a farm on the land south of here near Hull," she continued. "A piece of land that's almost waterlocked, south of Withernsea."

Along from him in the front row Zack Golder was nodding furiously, and a few people leaned towards him and his brother for confirmation of what Jess had said. More muttering.

"The women—" Jess swallowed. "The women were Sarah Evans, Sally Angus, Roisin Murray and Ruth Dyer." She looked at Ben.

He willed himself to breathe. How would Ruth be behaving now, if it was he who had disappeared?

"We believe they were taken in the early hours of Saturday morning," said Jess, her eyes scanning the crowd. "We think the men stole our boat and used it to sail out to their trawler, which it turns out wasn't damaged."

"What are you doing to get them back?"

A man was standing, immediately behind Ben. Around him people turned to see. Ben hunched low in his seat.

"We've been scouring the beach for clues. This morning," Jess checked her third list, "we found the boat – our boat – washed up on the beach."

Colin cleared his throat. Ben looked at him. Was she going to say anything about those boys?

"And we found the remains of some clothes," Jess continued. "Something red, a sweater. And what we think was a white T-shirt."

Above the hum of the crowd he heard a loud sob: Mark Palfrey, sitting in the second row with his hands over his face. There was a ripple of voices and movement as people craned their necks to see. A woman placed a comforting hand on his arm. Mark was only twenty-two and this wouldn't be easy for him.

Colin was speaking now, letting Jess gather her breath.

"Please, we know this is hard for everyone to take in. But please show some respect for the families affected. We all want to know what's happened, to find the women, but they have a greater need than the rest of us."

"Why aren't you idiots doing anything? Why hasn't anyone gone to get my girl?"

Ted Evans was standing up in the front row, jabbing a finger at Colin.

"Ted," Jess said. "I'm very sorry about Sarah being taken. We all are. I assure you that the council is doing its best—"

"Doing its best? *Doing its best?* You fuckers wouldn't know what doing your best was if it hit you with a ten pound sledgehammer!"

"Ted, you're a member of this council too, please can you—"

Shouts came from the back of the room. *Yeah, what are you doing? Be quiet, sit down! Listen to Jess! Get a bloody move on!*

Ted paced the short distance across the floor to Jess and Colin's table. He leaned over Jess, ignoring Colin's protests. Harry had stood up and was calling to him, trying to calm his friend. Dawn was nowhere to be seen.

"Look at me, you stupid woman." His voice was low and menacing. Jess turned to Ted and returned his gaze. Their faces were inches apart.

"Know this," he hissed. "If my girl dies or never comes back, it'll be your fault. If your brother never sees his wife again, it'll be your fault."

"Ted, please." Colin's hand was on Ted's shoulder, trying to ease him away from Jess. Harry was behind Ted now, shaking his arm and pleading with him to sit down. Ted pushed Harry's hand away. He stormed through the crowd, shouting expletives at anyone who got in his way. The doors at the back of the room clattered open and Ted turned round to send one last threat across the hall.

"If you won't sort this out, I will. You're a godawful steward." Then he marched out of the building.

31

"I'll go after him," said Jess.

"No," said Harry. "I'll go. Trust me, it's better coming from me."

"Thanks," said Colin. "Everyone!" He called over the heads of the people who were moving around the room now. "Please sit down. The meeting isn't over yet."

Jess stared towards the back wall, watching the doors. They swung open as Harry chased Ted outside.

"Sorry about that," Colin said. Jess nodded and took a few shallow breaths. Had he been right? Was she a godawful steward?

"It's OK, Colin," she said, pushing her doubts away. "He's angry. I'm not surprised." She glanced at Ben. "We need to get those women back."

She turned to the room.

"We came together today to discuss how we're going to respond to this as a community, and that's what we're going to do. We've got an idea where the men have gone and now our boat's back, we can go looking for them. The council is proposing we put together a group of people who'll leave as soon as possible, head down the coast and look for signs of this trawler. If no one's on it, they'll put ashore and look for the women."

Jess paused to glance at Colin who nodded, giving her a smile.

"But we need to get the village's agreement," she continued. "So I'll take your questions first."

Hands shot up, and Jess steeled herself to give what answers she could.

AFTER THE MEETING ENDED, with the villagers agreeing to the council's plans, Jess went straight to Ben. His skin was sallow and his clothes dirty from the beach earlier, and he looked ready to collapse.

"Let's take you home."

Ben sighed. "Thanks, sis." He extricated himself from a conversation with Sanjeev and followed her out.

Outside the square was empty, the only sound a bird calling from beyond the flats where they'd billeted the men. She left Ben at home with the boys then hurried back towards the village hall, casting a wary eye at Dawn and Ted's as she passed. The curtains were drawn and no sound came from inside. Jess shuddered as she imagined Dawn in there, hostage to Ted's anger after the meeting. She stopped at the end of their path and wondered if she should knock on the door, offer help.

Then she remembered her promise to Dawn. She delved into her coat pockets and found a scrap of paper and a pencil; *ever the teacher*. She pulled them out, picking off the accumulated lint. She squatted on the path to write, the tip of the pencil pressing into her thigh. The paper was crumpled and coffee-stained but it would do.

Village boat washed up on beach. No one aboard, she wrote. *We found the remains of clothes. A red sweater or hoody and a white T-shirt. Please leave note if these sound familiar. Sorry.*

She resisted an impulse to write Dawn's or her own name and folded the paper up, slipping it into her pocket as she made her way around the house.

She took a circuitous route, passing Sanjeev's next door to reach the back of the row of houses.

She peered around the wall, hoping no one was watching. The Evans's house wall stared back at her, its bulk looming in the mist rising from the sea. There was no window on this side and the bins, thankfully, were at the corner closest to her.

She hurried across the damp grass and reached into her pocket for the note. She slid it beneath the bin closest to her. She would have to hope that Dawn would check soon.

Once the paper was safely concealed she backed away, keeping her eyes on Dawn's wall. Reaching the shelter of Sanjeev's house, she turned and dashed back to the village hall. They needed to move fast.

As SHE REACHED THE SQUARE, she was stopped by Clyde coming the other way. Sanjeev was with him.

"Clyde!" she panted. "Just the person. We need to get the boat ready as quickly as possible."

Clyde shook his head. Sanjeev let out a low-pitched moan.

"What?" asked Jess. "What is it? Is the boat not ready?"

"It's not that," said Sanjeev.

"What, then?"

"It's gone, Jess," said Clyde. "The goddamn boat's gone."

32

Sleep was impossible. Every time Ruth closed her eyes, she could feel the empty space on her ring finger, cold and bare. She thought about the band of gold in Robert's pocket, wondered if it was still there now.

She lay still for a while, staring at the blank wall, willing her mind clear. She tried to think about Ben and the boys, but the rough ache that left in her stomach just made her feel worse.

Eventually she gave up and propped herself against the wall, eyes scanning the room. Perhaps they'd been forgetful. Perhaps there was something in here she could use.

The room was gloomy, with no light showing under the door. Dull light filtered through the window's film of green. It felt like being underwater. The smell of mildew mixed with the heaviness of her own unwashed body.

She moved to the farthest wall, examining the plaster-work. There were cracks, scuffs and red patches, eczema attacking the walls. She traced them with her hands, looking for imperfections. She traced those to their ends, at the corners and towards the ceiling. She poked a finger into a hole, hoping it might give way, might give her something to work with. But it held firm.

She reached the corner next to the window and turned to face the outside wall. She brought her ear to the side wall.

A faint whimper, beyond the wall.

She froze, her breathing as low as she could make it. She listened. There it was again.

There was a person beyond that wall, crying.

She narrowed her eyes, squinting at the fogged-over window, and sent her mind back to the night she'd been taken.

Martin had gone to bed early. Ben had come home and they'd argued about the men, about how safe it was to let them stay in the village. *Amicable*, he'd said. *Happy to have them here.* Martin had been coming out of the bathroom when she went to bed, prompting an awkward moment as they said goodnight. He'd watched as she slipped into the boys' room.

If she'd slept in her own bed, with her husband, could he – or they – have taken her? Would Ben have woken? Or would the boys, alone in their room at the top of the stairs, have been the ones at risk?

She shivered. She had no reason to believe her boys were here too, not from anything that had been said. But then, she couldn't be sure they weren't.

She leaned into the wall, numb. There it was again, the crying. *Who is it?*

33

J ess felt herself crumple. *Is it never going to stop?* One thing after another.

"You've got it wrong. The boat came back. Harry said it was OK to use. We need to get it ready, go after—"

Clyde bit his thumbnail. "I'm sorry. But the boat house has been opened. It's empty."

"Are you sure?" she asked Clyde, her voice dull. Finding Ruth and the other women felt impossible now.

He nodded. Next to him, Sanjeev pulled at the skin on his face. This wasn't easy for any of them.

A lump rose in her throat as she thought of Ruth tending to Sonia on their journey, of the awful decision they'd taken to walk here from Leeds. She couldn't know if the effort had killed her. But she did know that she could have tried harder to convince Sonia to stay behind, with her sister.

Aunt Val's face swam in front of her vision now, announcing what she'd heard about the village. *Just opened – accepting refugees – jobs – food supplies – only option.* She was right, they knew. Val and Liz's flat was cramped and they couldn't stay there and eat all their rations. Sonia had insisted, despite Jess and Ruth's protests. The coughing was persistent by then and they knew they were taking a risk.

But Sonia was her mother, and she couldn't defy her. Now it was Ruth who would be sacrificed to this village, to the desperation they'd all felt since leaving London.

No. I won't allow that, she thought.

"When did this happen?"

"During the meeting. Or maybe just after."

Jess pulled herself in and tried to picture the community hall during the village meeting, the sea of uneasy faces. But she hadn't been able to see everyone, couldn't know who might have been missing.

"Right," she whispered. "Ben's too much of a mess to do anything." *And I'm not risking him too*, she thought. "We need to let him be with his boys and get on with doing what we can to find the boat, find the women."

Clyde nodded, buttoning up his coat. "Let's go."

JESS SENT CLYDE to the village shop, to start gathering provisions for their rescue mission. She needed to speak to the council members, to tell them what had happened. As far as she knew they were still in the village hall.

The mist was settling into a thick fog now that shrouded the houses and plunged the village into silence. There was no sign of the birds she'd heard earlier. As she and Sanjeev passed the row of council members' houses, she spotted a light at a front door: Ted's. She grimaced. Was he waiting for her?

She tapped Sanjeev on the arm and gestured towards

the light. The faint glow of a gas lamp flickered in front of a shadowed human figure. Sanjeev pursed his lips.

"Ted?" he suggested.

"Probably best to leave him," she replied, and picked up her pace.

But as they neared the house she heard a female voice.

"Jess?" Dawn stood in front of her front door, holding that flickering light. Her hair was stuck to her face, her grey cardigan darkened by the damp.

Jess walked hesitantly up Dawn's path.

"Dawn? Are you OK?" She lowered her voice to a whisper. "Did you get my note?"

Dawn nodded, her eyes huge above cheeks so translucent it was as if Jess could see the blood flowing beneath.

"The red sweater. It's hers," she sniffed.

"Oh Dawn," Jess gasped, not knowing what else to say.

Dawn drew into herself.

"Are you OK?" asked Jess, cursing herself. Of course she wasn't.

"Have you seen Ted?" Dawn muttered.

"Ted? Didn't he come home after the meeting?"

"No."

Jess wouldn't have thought it possible, but Dawn paled even more. Her skin was grey now, with veins showing on her forehead. She sensed Sanjeev waiting behind her, soundless in the darkness.

"Dawn, does that mean you don't know what happened at the meeting?"

Dawn shook her head. Jess felt a lump form in the pit of her stomach.

"He stormed out. He was angry with us, for not doing enough." She paused, wondering how much Ted might have told Dawn. The woman was probably as much in the dark as Jess was. "Apparently, he was intent on taking matters into his own hands."

Dawn nodded. "What was he like? His mood?"

"Angry."

Dawn glanced over her shoulder, towards Harry's house.

"Dawn? Is there anything I should know? Something Ted might have told you?"

Dawn pulled at the rough wool of her cardigan.

"Dawn? You can trust me, I promise. I won't tell anyone it was you who told me."

Dawn looked up at Jess, searching her face. "I don't know, Jess. I'm not sure what I heard, but—"

"Yes?"

"I... I overheard something between Ted and Harry. They were whispering. Ted didn't want me to hear. He doesn't like me knowing about his council business, normally sends me upstairs when Harry comes round."

Jess waited.

"Ted said he was going to get a boat, head down the coast and get Sarah himself. Harry tried to talk him out of it, at least I think he did, I could only hear Ted. He was quite angry."

Jess wondered what *quite angry* meant, for Ted. "Please Dawn, what did you hear? Which boat?"

Dawn looked up at her, puzzled. "The village boat, of course. What other boat is there?"

Grey light filtered through the thin curtains of the room Martin shared with two other men. He yawned and stretched his arms, grimacing at a twinge in his back.

This room was at the back of the farmhouse, one of the few not ravaged by damp. The wallpaper that peeled off the walls next to Martin's mattress carried images of Buzz Lightyear. He often wondered about the child who'd slept in this room when that paper was hung. They would be a teenager now. Where could they be? Did they wonder about the house they used to live in, dream of returning?

The blue curtains were threadbare and rough to the touch, sunlight glinting through holes. Curtain hooks were missing and the fabric slumped on its rail, leaving looping gaps that let the light – and the cold – in. Martin turned onto his back, fingers entwined behind his head, and watched as the ceiling brightened. Any time now the peace would be shattered by the morning wake up call. He readied himself to move as soon as the door opened, knowing that if he didn't, two things would happen. The door would hit his head as it swung open, and he would feel a sharp kick as Bill woke him for the day's tasks.

Next to him, Leroy snored gently beneath his mop of curly black hair. Beyond him, Dave was quiet. He might be asleep still, or waiting for the day to begin, like Martin. The three old mattresses they slept on almost filled the floor and the only other piece of furniture was a battered chest of drawers under the window that hit their feet if it was opened while they slept. The chest was made from flimsy particleboard, covered in white laminate except for the places where it had peeled off.

He sat up just as the door swung open, sending a draught of air rushing through the room.

"Wake up!" yelled Bill, just like every other day.

Martin wondered what Bill did before he woke them, whether he had just woken himself or if he had his own responsibilities earlier in the morning. By the time they were dressed – a brief process that consisted of nothing more than grabbing yesterday's grubby jeans from where he'd dropped them at the foot of his mattress and pulling them back on – the kitchen would be warming up. The aroma of cheap coffee would be curling up the stairs and, if they were lucky, the accompanying smell of bread being toasted or maybe some sort of meat being grilled. If one of their raiding parties had got lucky yesterday.

He knew there wasn't much hope of this today. Efforts were focused on their new arrivals and no one had left the farm since he, Bill and Robert had come back with the women, bundling them into outhouses at the back of the farm. It would be a breakfast of weak coffee, eked out for as long as possible. For some of them, accompanying slugs of vodka would soften the edges.

Leroy grunted and muttered something under his

breath. He leaned forwards and lifted his legs to pull his trousers on, all without opening his eyes. Dave was standing and dressed; he'd already been awake. Martin quickly followed suit, pulling on jeans and socks that he preferred not to sniff or even handle that much, and staggering down the narrow stairs.

He was last into the kitchen. Four men were huddled over the coffee pot, helping themselves to the morning pick-me-up. Robert sat at the table, reading a book.

"Good morning, young man!" he smiled at Martin.

Martin knew to be wary of Robert's good moods just as much as the bad ones.

"Morning," he mumbled.

"That's not the spirit. We've got a treat in store for you this morning."

The men at the table turned towards them. Bill knelt on the floor, rummaging in a cupboard under the sink. Martin shivered. Being involved in the raid on the village had been a 'treat'. He thought of Ruth in the pharmacy, the calm way in which she'd checked him over and treated his hypothermia. He reddened.

"That's good. I can see you're keen." Robert leaned back, bestowing a broad smile on his audience. Bill raised his head and barked out a laugh before his head disappeared back into the cupboard. He would be repairing the plumbing again.

"And well you should be," Robert continued, fixing him with his dark eyes. "You're going to be meeting someone new. Not Ruth today, I'll be visiting her alone."

Martin breathed again, guilty at his relief.

"The young one, the girl," said Robert. "She's timid, hasn't said a word since she arrived. Maybe you can bring her out of her shell."

Martin felt cold. This younger woman – Sarah – was the last to be loaded onto the boat, lifeless over Bill's shoulder as he carried her down to the beach from the village. Martin had noticed her long white-blonde hair and her smooth complexion. She had looked calm and unsullied, hanging in Bill's arms.

Robert stood up, sending his chair toppling back. "Come on. Let's pay her a visit. We don't have all day, you know."

He followed Robert out and eased the back door shut behind him, knowing it hung loosely on its hinges. A few metres from the back of the farmhouse was a row of outbuildings, probably used as storage back when this had been a working farm. Robert strode on ahead of him, pulling a fistful of keys from his pocket. He picked out a large, old-fashioned key and turned it in the lock of the door ahead of them. The door swung open and Robert motioned for Martin to go on ahead.

Martin ducked his head to pass through the doorway and stood inside the narrow corridor that ran across the front of the building. The room closest – Ruth's room – he had already been in. He listened, trying to make out signs of movement in there, but there was nothing. She was either asleep, or trying not to attract attention.

He felt Robert's hand on his back pushing him down the corridor, locking the outside door behind them.

"Second door," he said, his voice firm. Martin stopped to face it. He tried to imagine what the girl was doing inside, whether she had heard them.

Robert frowned. "You really don't need to look so miserable. I'll give you twenty minutes with her. Get her to talk, please, I don't like silent women. Up to you how you do it. I have things to do."

Robert cast a sideways glance towards Ruth's cell and

Martin shivered, imagining his 'things to do'. Robert took another key and unlocked Sarah's cell, heaving the door open and pushing Martin in. He didn't follow but pulled the door shut again and locked it.

"Get on with it," he hissed.

35

Jess heard footsteps at her back and turned: it was Toni.

"What's up?"

"It's Ted," said Jess. "He's taken the boat."

"*Shit.*"

"Mm-hmm."

Jess looked back at Dawn. "Dawn, are you sure about what you heard? Sure Harry didn't manage to talk him out of it?"

Dawn shook her head.

"Harry?" said Toni. "What's he got to do with it?"

Jess turned to her. "We need to speak to him. Now."

They crossed to Harry's house. Toni started hammering on the door.

"Harry! We need to speak to you!" Jess called.

No answer. The house was in darkness, but that was nothing unusual.

"Let's look round the back," suggested Toni.

Jess sped round the side of the house. Her earlier mission at the back of Dawn's house felt like a lifetime ago.

Harry's curtains were open but the room was dark. Jess cupped her hands to the glass, forming a seal between them and her face. She peered through the gloom. There were discarded clothes on the sofa. No sign of any light or movement.

"Harry!" she called again. "Are you in there?"

Nothing.

Sanjeev and Toni were skidding to a halt next to her on the wet grass.

"Maybe he went with Ted," Toni suggested.

Jess shrugged. "I guess that would be a good thing. Ted's likely to sink that boat if he's on his own."

"S'pose so."

Sanjeev leaned into the glass, making it vibrate. "We need to talk to Clyde, find out how long the boat's been gone, if anything else was taken. We need to let Ben know, too."

Jess pulled at the back of her neck. Beyond the dark hedge opposite she could hear the sea pounding against the shoreline. She didn't have the stomach for Ben again. She knew he was struggling but irritation with his apathy was starting to overtake sibling sympathy.

"No, San," she said. "We need to stop talking and bloody well do something."

Toni smiled. "Attagirl."

Sanjeev didn't look impressed. "You can't do that. Ben needs to know what's going on. And if you're planning on heading off to find Ruth and the others, you'll get nowhere in this fog."

Damn. He was right. About the fog, if nothing else. And he did owe Ben a huge debt.

"OK. We spend tonight getting ready. Let's gather a

search party, dig out some tents – there are some that people brought with them when they first got here – and then we'll head out at first light tomorrow. The fog'll have lifted by then, I'm sure it will."

Toni smiled. "Count me in."

36

Robert's smile made Ruth shiver. She'd overheard his conversation with Martin in the corridor and was torn between relief that it wasn't her boys next door, and fear. How exactly was Martin expected to make the other woman talk?

"Good morning, Mrs Dyer. How are you today?"

She held his gaze and focused on her breathing, keeping it as steady as she could. She glanced at the bucket under the table. It stank.

He watched her for a moment, as if coming to a decision. She fidgeted, touching her ring finger.

He patted the pocket of his shirt. "You'll get it back eventually. When you're ready."

She glared at him, wondering what *ready* meant.

"But we won't worry about that for now," he said. "You need to earn your keep. This place stinks. You can start by cleaning out that bucket."

She looked at it and resisted an urge to retch. "Where?" she asked.

"There's an old privy, outside this building," he said. "Then there's work for you in the main house."

Her eyes widened. Whatever the 'main house' was, it might afford a means of escape.

He gave one of those tight laughs. "And don't go getting any ideas, my dear." He approached, making her flinch. "Young Sammy will be watching you. He doesn't like women very much, not really *his type*. So watch out for him. No escape back to your doting husband."

She met his gaze, unflinching.

"Nothing to say to me, Mrs Dyer?"

"What do I have to do?"

"Get that bucket sorted first, I can't bear it. And then you can clean the bathrooms in the house. The men don't like doing it themselves, don't make as good a job of it as I'm sure you will."

He motioned towards the bucket and she dragged it out, aware of his breathing behind her as she turned away. She heaved it up and headed out of her cell behind him, her eyes scouring the walls of the corridor, scanning for an escape route.

THE GIRL STOOD opposite Martin near the window, her back so firmly against the wall that he thought it might swallow her up. She stared at him, pale grey-blue eyes in a white face stained with dirt and tears.

As the key turned in the lock behind him she pulled into herself, cowering. He offered his most reassuring smile. "Hello. I'm Martin."

She said nothing, just carried on staring at him and

trembling. He tried taking a step forward. She let out a sound, something between a sob and a wail.

He raised a hand in reassurance, but she wrapped her arms around herself and turned her body sideways, her eyes still trained on him. The spotlight of her terrified stare didn't dim for a moment. He stepped back towards the door and placed his hands against it. They were as far away from each other as they could get.

She dared to take her eyes off his face and look him up and down. Assessing his strength, he imagined. He wondered who had been in here already, if Robert had paid a similar visit to all of the women as the one he'd invited Martin to yesterday. Had Robert brought other men here? Despite her grubbiness and tang of fear, the girl had an ethereal beauty. It would have an effect on men who'd been starved of female presence for so long.

He turned his head to place an ear at the door, listening for Robert. A door closed along the corridor, the bolt clattering. Robert was in with Ruth.

They were alone.

"I'm not going to hurt you," he whispered, his voice echoing. She continued staring at him. He wondered if she could speak. He tried stepping forwards again. She made no sound this time, but her body stiffened.

He stuffed his hands inside his pockets and pulled at the fabric, turning them inside out.

"I've nothing on me. No weapons. I'm not going to hurt you," he said, wondering if the repetition made his words more or less convincing.

"I'm Martin," he said, blushing. "I live here." More blushing: *Stop stating the bloody obvious.*

He hunched up his shoulders in an attempt to release

the tension he'd felt since leaving the kitchen. Maybe if he made himself smaller...

He slid down to the floor, his back rubbing against the rough slats of the door. Finally he was on the floor, his legs splayed out across the concrete. He took care to avoid touching her mattress with his shoe.

He threw her another smile and motioned with his head for her to slide down too, to come down to his level. She shook her head, the first sign of communication. He put his arms out to his sides, placing his palms where she could see them on the floor. He straightened his back against the door, feeling it shift beneath his weight.

"I was in your village," he said. "Ruth and Ben were kind to me, they let me stay in their house."

Her eyelids relaxed a little and some colour returned to her face.

He decided to continue. Robert expected him to fill twenty minutes, after all. Maybe talking would calm her fear.

"Do you know where you are?"

She shook her head slowly, as if expecting some sort of trick.

"You're in an outbuilding at the back of a farmhouse. I've been living here for about four years with a group of men. There are thirteen of us here, all men."

Her eyes widened.

"We're about thirty miles down the coast from your village, on a piece of land that's almost water locked. It was abandoned after the flooding but Robert brought us back here to find a patch of land we could make our own." He lowered his eyes. "It's not much of a patch, though. The crops were ruined by the floods, and what wasn't washed away or waterlogged rotted in the end."

He looked up to see her wiping her eyes with her sleeve. He carried on talking to cover his unease. His mum hadn't been one for displaying emotion, and it was nearly five years since he'd been in the company of a girl his own age.

"We've made a sort of home here. More of a camp, really. Some of us – the ones who got here first – sleep in those rooms in the farmhouse that aren't too damp. Others sleep in the barns. There were men in this building until last week, but Robert told them to clear out before we left for your village."

She watched him steadily. He tried gesturing downwards with his head again and she eased herself to the mattress, not taking her eyes off him for a heartbeat. He smiled but stayed absolutely still.

"What about your village?" he asked. "How long have you been there?"

She shook her head. His openness wasn't about to be reciprocated. They sat for a few moments, staring at each other in silence. From outside he heard birdsong. She cast a brief glance up at the window.

The silence was making him uneasy and his legs were cramping. He stood up, keeping his back against the door. She pulled back as he moved. When he was upright he stood still, arms at his sides, the flapping pockets of his jeans brushing against his palms.

"I don't know what I'm expected to be doing here with you," he said.

He thought of Ruth the previous morning, of the look on her face when Robert had opened up the knife. Of the tension that had overwhelmed her body when he'd sat next to her.

"I just want to talk to you," he said. "I'll try to keep Robert, keep the others from hurting you, if I can."

At Robert's name her eyes flicked from him to the door. So Robert had been here.

He felt the door vibrate behind him.

"Finished?" It was Robert's voice. Sarah bolted upwards, standing against the wall. Trying to let it suck her in again.

Martin tried to give her a reassuring smile, and was rewarded with the same silent stare.

"Sorry," he whispered, turning to the door.

"Finished!" he called, standing back as the door opened. Robert put his head round, looking between his captives.

"Very good," he said, smiling, and opened the door further so that Martin could follow him out.

37

The glass pane shuddered as someone pounded the door

Ben heaved himself off his chair. *Why can't Jess use the front door, for Christ's sake?* He unhitched the latch and slid the door open, surprised to see Sanjeev. His damp hair stood up and his face was pale with cold.

"Ben, it's Ted!" He half walked, half fell into the room. Ben slipped behind him to check outside then latch the door.

"Where's Jess?"

Sanjeev ignored the question. "Ben, it's Ted. He took the boat. Harry's gone with him. They must have stolen it after the meeting, when Harry went after Ted."

"Harry?" Ben was confused. Harry had been helping out all day, joining in with the search on the beach, checking the boat.

Sanjeev nodded. "He tried to talk Ted out of it. But he's not at home, so he must have gone with him. Keep him from killing himself, I suppose. Keep him from wrecking the boat."

Ben's mind raced. Ted and Harry were out there in the fog, trying to make their way south along the coast. They had no chance. But then... Harry was a good sailor, experienced. He knew what he was doing. And the tide was with them.

They could be there by morning. Ted and Harry, the world's worst rescue party. What on earth would happen to Ruth, if Ted was introduced to the mix?

How will Robert and Ted react to each other?

He blushed, remembering that Sanjeev knew nothing about Robert. Only he knew what Robert could be like. But they all knew what Ted could be like. Two fireworks, ready to go off. Getting closer to each other.

He grabbed Sanjeev's arm, his fingernails digging in. Sanjeev shook him off.

"We have to do something."

"I know." It was Jess, coming through the front door. Had he left it open?

Sanjeev looked from Ben to Jess, rubbing his arm.

"Like what?" Sanjeev asked. "We can't go after them in this weather."

Jess shook her head. "We follow them. At first light. Gather together a group."

Sanjeev's eyes flashed. "Yes. If we set out tomorrow morning we might beat Ted, if we're lucky. If he gets lost on the way, maybe. Or if Harry slows him down." He hesitated. "If we can find transport and work out exactly where we're going." Another pause. "It's worth a try, surely?"

"I want to go," Ben interrupted.

"No," said Sanjeev. Ben frowned at him.

"San's right," said Jess.

Ben's chest felt tight. "She's my wife, and I want to get her." He sighed. "If only I had a bike."

Ben had been a championship cyclist as a teenager, winning local contests and one regional one, until financial struggles had put a stop to it.

"Ben," Jess said slowly. "I'm not sure that going off on a search is the best thing for you right now."

"But I need to get her back. Who are you, to tell me what to do?"

Sanjeev put a hand on his shoulder. He shook it off.

"The boys," said Jess. "They can't be without their dad as well as their mum."

He felt his frame sagging. "Yes." He pulled himself up. "But you could look after them for me."

"No, Ben. I love those boys but I'm not their mum. They need a parent right now. And I need to be in the search party."

"Jess is right," said Sanjeev. "I don't think it's a good idea for you to go there."

Ben glared at his friend. "Are you telling me you won't help me?"

"No, Ben," said Jess. "That's the exact opposite of what we're saying."

Sanjeev was looking into his eyes. "We'll get her back. Promise."

Ben nodded, then marched into the living area, where he sank onto the sofa.

"Thanks Ben," Jess called over. "This is for the best, I promise."

38

Ruth could feel her guard's eyes boring into her as she scrubbed at the kitchen floor with a grubby rag. There was no sign of any cleaning products here, something she was used to, but nor were there any of the makeshift concoctions from salt, baking powder and vinegar that she used back at the village to keep the pharmacy and her own house clean.

Bent to her task, she felt vulnerable, as if he might grab her from behind at any moment. But she felt safer here in the farmhouse than in the confines of her cell. This man was younger than Robert or Bill, and had watched her in silence since Bill had left her with him.

When she was finished, she stood up. Her back ached but it felt good to have tired muscles.

She looked at her guard. "What now?"

He sniffed. He was tall and lanky with black skin tainted grey by dirt. His hair was like a bush of tangles and one of his front teeth was missing.

"Bogs," he said.

"Sorry?"

"Clean the bogs. The *toilets*."

"Show the way."

He narrowed his eyes then led her out of the kitchen into a hallway beyond. She stared at the front door, her heart pounding.

"'S locked," he said.

She shrugged.

"You can't get out. Door's locked."

She said nothing.

He led her up a set of creaky stairs. At the top was a musty corridor, its walls patched with damp. She could smell sweat and stale urine, all overlaid by the heaviness of damp.

He gestured towards a door at the end of the corridor. "In there."

He folded his arms across his chest, waiting. She crept towards the door, glancing from side to side. There were three doors to the sides. Two were closed but the third was open. As she approached she heard low voices.

She swallowed.

She slowed, quietening her footsteps. She held her breath and peered into the room.

A man had his back to her, and one more sat on a scruffy single bed. The man with his back to her had greying hair that snaked around his ears: Bill. The other man had black hair and a deeply lined face.

She darted past the doorway and stopped, her senses straining to hear.

"He can't," Bill hissed. "You know that."

Bill's voice was low but Ruth's ears were good.

The other man's voice had the sandpaper tones of a heavy smoker. "What did her husband do to him anyway?"

"I can't talk about it, Eddie. You know that."

"You can trust me."

A sigh. Ruth held her breath.

"You know Robert was in prison, before the floods."

"Yeah."

"It was his fault."

"Whose?"

"The husband's, stupid."

"How?"

"That's all I'm saying. He'll fucking kill me."

Ruth heard footsteps. She put her hand on the toilet door.

"Sammy? What the fuck's going on? What's *she* doing up here?"

"I was told to get her to clean the bogs." Her guard, Sammy, sounded like a little boy now. Not the man he was pretending to be around her.

"Bloody well give us some warning first, you fuckwit."

She pulled at the door handle. The door opened away from her. The toilet's lid was up, the bowl crusted with limescale.

She threw an arm to her face.

Bill had a hand on her arm. "Didn't hear anything, did you?"

"No."

"Hmm. Get on with your cleaning. And then get back to your room. Hear that, Sam?"

"Yes, Bill. Sorry."

39

They had already started gathering in the JP when Ben arrived with his boys. Sanjeev was with Colin, checking the food and equipment they'd need for the journey. Toni was talking to Clyde, debating how far they could walk each day. No sign of Jess yet.

He pulled Sanjeev to one side.

"Alright, mate?" Sanjeev looked worried.

"Why did you say I shouldn't go with you? She's my wife."

"You know why."

"That's got nothing to—"

"Ben. Can you give us a hand with this food, please?'

Colin was behind them, holding up a pack of oatmeal. Jess was next to him, eying Ben.

Ben glared at Sanjeev and shuffled towards Colin. He ignored Jess. "Go on then." Maybe being useful would fill the hole in his mind.

He started sorting through food. They needed things that were light and non-perishable. It felt like packing for a scout trip. Not that he'd know. His hadn't been that kind of childhood.

The boys were restless, flitting between adults and getting in the way. More than once he had to remind them to keep quiet.

"Thanks, Ben." Jess was at his elbow, looking at the four piles he'd made. He turned to her, anxious.

"Here! I've found a map."

Jess turned to Toni, who was clutching a dog-eared Ordnance Survey map. Sam and Zack approached and the four of them huddled over it, muttering.

How dare she treat me like just another helper? He clenched his fists but then spotted Sanjeev giving him a look that said *calm down*. He gritted his teeth and returned to his task.

He watched Jess with the Golder boys out of the corner of his eye, envying their ease with her. Zack was flirting, he was sure. He snorted. *Fat chance, mate.*

In the centre of the floor were two small tents from the storage rooms at the back of the community hall, tents that had arrived with villagers who'd used them on their journey here. As Ben watched Zack strap them to the rucksacks, he thought back to the last time he'd carried a rucksack, to the journey they'd made here. To the day he'd met Sanjeev. *I owe you my life*, Sanjeev had said, after Ben rescued him from his blazing house. A gas explosion, one of plenty they saw on their way here.

Now it was time for Sanjeev to repay that debt.

"All ready," said Jess. Ben shrank into the pub's shadows as the others pushed outside into the bright morning. He was torn when Sanjeev stopped to give him a tight hug.

"We'll get her for you," he said.

40

The key rattled in the lock. Ruth sat up on her mattress, alert.

"Good morning, Mrs Dyer."

She squared her shoulders. *I won't let him frighten me.*

Robert closed the door behind him. He flashed her a smile.

"I won't bite."

She pushed herself up, her back against the wall. When she was standing on the mattress, he nodded.

"Sorry about the facilities. Not very nice, I know. Not what you're used to."

How much did he know about her home? Had Martin let him into the house, when she and Ben had been out?

"Not going to speak?"

"Of course." Her voice was hoarse. She cleared her throat. "I've got nothing to say to you."

"Don't you? Not *why are you doing this? Please let me go?*" He cocked his head. "*Who else have you got here?*"

She stiffened. He approached her, his footsteps light.

"You want to know, don't you? You've heard."

"Heard what?"

He smiled. "You aren't going to trick me, Ruth."

It was the first time he'd used her first name. She felt the skin on her face tighten.

"Anyway, sit down. I just want to get to know you better."

"I don't want to get to know you."

"No? You don't want to know who I am? Why I took you?"

She pulled up her chest. "Go on then."

"Just because you want to know doesn't mean I'm going to tell you. I want to know more about you, Mrs Dyer. About you and your husband."

"None of your business."

"Now, that's not very polite, is it? Here you are enjoying my hospitality and you won't answer my questions."

"If you think this is hospitality, you—"

He raised a hand. "It will get better. When you're ready to join me in the main house."

"I'm not joining you anywhere."

"Not right now. Of course not. We need to get to know each other better. Now sit down."

His voice was firm. She slid to the mattress. He nodded and sat beside her. She pulled away, glad he was closer to the corner.

"That's better," he said. "Now, talk to me. Tell me about your village. Your lovely family."

She said nothing.

"Not going to talk?"

She stared ahead. "No."

He pushed himself up. He looked down at as he opened the door. She stared at it. Could she run past him, escape?

No. His hand was on the latch.

"Silly move, Ruth," he said. "You'll regret this."

41

Clyde was first out of the JP, slapping his hands together to brush off dust as the doors swung behind him. Jess thought about the equipment they'd gathered, equipment that had been in storage for years. Dust would be the least of their troubles.

A crowd was gathering: gawkers and well-wishers wanting to see them off as well as those who knew the future of their community was at stake. In the five years since the authorities had left they'd been entirely self-managed. Electing their own council, growing their own food, carrying out repairs and pooling their scarce resources.

Jess emerged behind him and stopped to look around, raising a hand to shield her eyes from the glare. Clyde shuffled into place next to her with his customary grin.

"Hello, gorgeous," he said. As always, she ignored the flirtation but offered a friendly smile in response.

"Have we got everything we need?" she muttered.

"Seems so," he replied. "Two tents between you, sleeping bags, as much dry food as you can carry, a couple of flasks of water each." He fell quiet. "I don't know about you, but that's a lot more than I had when I came here."

She nodded. Everyone here had experience of difficult journeys, some harder than others. The Evans family, she knew, had walked all the way from Somerset, with no guaranteed shelter on the way and no tent or sleeping bags. Ted's sheer force of will must have got them the three hundred miles. Either that or dishonesty and intimidation.

A hush descended over the crowd as Colin emerged from the JP, followed by the others who'd volunteered for this mission. There was Toni, doing this for Roisin; Ben's ambassador Sanjeev, and finally Zack Golder. He and Sam had decided between them that one should stay behind and the other should go.

The low sun illuminated them as if they were coming out on stage, the world's most unlikely rock band. Each of them squinted and raised a hand against the light as it hit them.

Jess looked around the crowd and then cleared her throat.

"Good morning, everyone."

The crowd quietened, letting her voice catch on the buildings opposite.

"We know you're all worried about Ruth, Sarah, Sally and Roisin." She scanned the crowd for the families of the missing women. "Some of you more than others. And I know you're concerned about Ted and Harry too. We all want to know that they're safe, and we want to bring them home."

The silence was broken by a hum of assent, pierced by the sobbing of Flo Murray, face buried in her husband's chest. Around them, the three younger girls clung to each other, a forlorn huddle in the centre of the crowd. Jess searched for Dawn Evans, but there was no sign of her. Sally's fiancé Mark was at the front, arms folded across his chest. He'd tried to talk them into letting him come along but she'd said no. He was highly strung and she didn't need him slowing them down.

"As soon as we've found them," Jess continued, "we'll send back word. One or two of us will come back as quickly as possible to let you all know that our family members and friends are safe."

She swallowed, aware that the news might not be so positive.

"And while that happens," she continued, "we'll be working on bringing everyone home as quickly as we can. We don't know why the men have taken them; we don't know for sure they have done so. But whatever we need to do to reunite us all and bring everyone home, we'll do it. I promise you that."

She bent to her rucksack, gathering things together and conferring with Colin and Toni.

"Who'll be in charge while you're gone?" a voice called from the crowd. At the end of the front row, Ben straightened, his eyes on Jess.

She shielded her eyes with a hand and peered into the crowd. She glanced at Ben.

"Colin. If you've got questions or concerns while we're gone, talk to him."

She looked at her brother. His cheeks were flushed, his fists clenched at his sides. He was in no state for leadership right now.

"What if you don't find them?" The same voice.

"We will," called Jess. "Zack and Sam have given us good information on the men and we think we know where they are."

"What about Ted?" called someone else.

"We intend to find Ted and Harry too. Hopefully they can help us make sure everyone gets home safely." She felt Colin's hand on her arm. "Now if you don't mind, we need to get started."

Sanjeev and Toni moved into the crowd, clearing a path for them to pass. Sanjeev gave Ben's shoulder a squeeze as he passed him and they exchanged some words, Ben's face hard. The crowd turned inwards, watching them thread their way through.

As they proceeded along the Parade to the village's edge, people followed as if participating in a marriage or a wake. Others stood at their open doors, clutching their children. Some waved and wished them luck, but most were quiet. As they reached the low wall bordering the western edge of the village, Flo Murray ran forward and grabbed Jess by the arm.

"Get her back home safe, please," she whispered, tears rolling down her face.

Jess nodded, and gave her a hug.

"We will," Toni assured her.

Flo trembled, her weight dragging on Jess. She nodded at Toni then lowered her eyes.

Jess pulled back and held Flo at arm's length, memorising her features in anticipation of seeing them in her daughter's face. "You'll hear from us soon."

Flo gulped in a shuddering breath and fell back into her husband's arms. Her children gathered in a tight circle around them. Jess swallowed the lump in her throat.

Ben had moved to the front of the crowd. She gave him a feeble wave. He approached her.

"I hope you know what you're doing."

"You need to be here. With the boys."

"But not in charge."

"Focus on Sean and Ollie. They need you more than the village does." She grabbed his hand. "I'll find her. She'll be back soon."

He pulled his hand away and sank back into the crowd. She searched for him but he was gone.

After one last wave she turned and walked out of the village, Toni next to her and Sanjeev and Zack close behind. She looked back for a final time to see Colin and Clyde at the front of the villagers, watching them leave. As they reached the main road and turned left, the village disappeared out of sight.

There was nowhere to go but south.

42

Robert visited Ruth again the next night.

"Sit down," he told her. "Tell me about Ben."

She thought of the conversation she'd overheard. *It was his fault*. "What did he do to you?"

"Just sit down, woman. Tell me when you met."

She crouched on the mattress while he perched on the table next to her.

"Go on then. Unless you want me to join you down there."

Talking was better than having him next to her. She took a deep breath, remembering Ben as a young man.

"We met in a pub."

"Which pub?"

"I don't know."

"Yes, you do. You met your future husband in a pub and you claim not to remember its name?"

"It was the Dove."

"Where?"

"Hammersmith. On the river."

"Nice. Who was he with?"

"He was on his own."

"And you?"

"A friend. From work."

He leaned back on the table. "What work?"

"The vet's."

"You're a vet?"

"A veterinary nurse. Was."

"So. You met in a picturesque riverside pub. Then what?"

"What d'you mean?"

"Did he ask you out? Did you take him home and shag his brains out? What?"

"He asked me out for pizza. The next weekend."

"A pizza. How dull."

"It wasn't about the food."

"When was this?"

"March."

"I don't mean the month. How many years? How long have you and your beloved husband been together?"

"2017."

"Six months before the floods. A whirlwind romance, then."

"I wouldn't say that."

"Surely you were married before leaving London."

"We married at the village."

Robert stood up. "A village wedding. How sweet." He paced the room.

Ruth watched him, wishing she hadn't said so much.

He turned to her. "Who officiated?"

"Sorry?"

"Your wedding. The marriage of Mr and Mrs Ben Dyer. Registrar, vicar? Who?"

She blushed. "Murray."

"Who the hell is Murray?"

"The village steward. He was then. He left."

"And was he a priest?"

"No."

He crouched down, bringing his face level with hers.

"So you aren't really Mrs Dyer."

"Of course I am."

"Your wedding wasn't legal. You're still single."

"I'm married. To Ben."

He stood up and laughed. "That makes me so happy. Adultery is a sin, you know. This takes a weight off my mind."

He raised his hands above his head, clicking the joints. She looked past him at the door.

He brought his hands back down.

"Stop looking at that door, my dear."

She glared back at him.

He cocked his head. "You won't be in here forever. When you're ready you can join me in the house. Especially now I know you're available."

"I don't think so."

"We'll see. When you've heard all I have to tell you about your so-called husband, you'll thank me."

"Never."

He gave one of his tight laughs and moved towards the door. "Stand up."

She stayed where she was on the mattress.

"Oh, heaven save us from disobedient women."

She scowled.

"Please," he said. "Stand up."

She pushed herself up. He reached out a hand and she pulled back, almost stumbling onto the mattress.

He shook his head. "I only want to hold your hand."

She stood still. He sighed and reached into his pocket,

drawing out the knife he'd shown her on his first visit. He didn't open it but instead turned it over in his hands, admiring the floral pattern on the hilt.

He smiled and plunged the knife back into his pocket. "Well?"

She took a deep breath and held out her hand, her arm quivering.

"Thank you," he said. He took her hand and raised it to his face. She stared, horrified, as he brushed it with his lips.

"Delighted, Ruth," he said, letting go. Her arm fell limp at her side.

He laughed again, his eyes creasing, and turned to the door.

"I know you've heard them."

"Heard who?"

"The others. The woman next door. You listen to her at night, I imagine. Wondering who she might be."

"Who is she? Is she from the village?"

"She's someone you know. They all are. Three of them, a door each. They're your responsibility now."

She said nothing. Instead she looked at the wall, wondering if the woman beyond could hear Robert talking.

He stood in the open doorway. "Behave yourself, and they'll be unharmed. Remember that, next time you see me."

43

The four of them made quick progress at first. The road passing the village was still used by trucks carrying earth down to Hull for the land reclamation, along with a team of labourers, and the road surface was maintained as well as could be expected. There were potholes, but plenty had been patched up. They walked in silence, each of them deep in memories and fears.

Jess thought about the walk from Leeds, and to Leeds from London. Watching Ben with Ruth, the way she had changed him. The excitement on his face the morning after the floods had hit. *She's coming with us! She said she'd marry me.* Jess had only met her the previous night, this quiet woman who'd already been at Sonia's when she arrived. Ben had been unable to take his eyes off her.

Jess hoped he could keep it together while she was gone. With herself, Sanjeev and Toni in this party, plus Harry and Ted ahead of them, not much more than half of the village council was left, and that half had a community of frightened people to watch over. Even with Colin there, they would be looking to Ben.

After six or seven miles and a couple of hours, their progress slowed. The main road continued to the south west, to the flood-ravaged town of Hull.

"We need to turn off here," said Toni. "Towards the coast."

"Right," said Jess. "Let's stop for a bit, get our breath. Sanjeev, can you grab a couple of apples out of your pack?"

"It's too soon."

"They're heavy. We might as well eat them first."

"We've only been walking two hours. We carry on."

Jess folded her arms across her chest. "OK. What does everyone else think?"

"I say we rest," said Zack. "Food will keep our strength up."

"I don't mind," said Toni.

"In that case, we rest. Ten minutes. Sanjeev, an apple please?"

Sanjeev muttered to himself as he pulled two apples out of his rucksack. He held one out to Jess, not making eye contact.

"San? What's up?"

"Nothing." He turned away and sat at the opposite side of the road, sifting through his rucksack to redistribute the load.

Ten minutes later, he approached Jess.

"Time to move. We need to make up for lost time."

"It's only ten minutes, San."

"It's all time."

She resisted the urge to argue with him. They were all tense.

The old coast road was torn up in places, ravaged by misuse and the tide. From time to time they left it to find a smoother way across fields. Leaving the road was risky: the ground was marshy here and would only get wetter, and a misstep might mean a sprained ankle or a tumble into the sodden ground with the heavy rucksack pinning you down once you were there.

After another two hours, they stopped to reconsider their route and share a loaf of bread from Toni's pack. Sanjeev reluctantly took a hunk, his eyes on his watch. Jess hoped he would calm down as they walked further from the village.

Toni had an old Ordnance Survey map in her rucksack. The changing shape of the coast meant it couldn't be relied upon, but at least it showed them where the roads had been.

The map told them that their road followed the coastline a mile inland. As they approached Withernsea it would hug the coast and the fields inland would become impassable. Given this, and the difficulty of identifying which fields were safe to cross, Toni suggested that they walk along the beach.

"Walking on sand will slow us down," complained Sanjeev. "And get sand or water in our shoes. I haven't brought a spare pair."

Jess squinted at the map and looked across the dunes.

"We could take our shoes and socks off," she suggested. "Tie the laces and drape them around our necks, keep our hands free."

Toni nodded. "That could work. I just think the beach is more predictable."

Jess looked at Zack. "What do you think?"

"Beach makes sense. We can see anyone who might be coming. Keeps us clear of any critters too."

"That means anyone can see us," said Sanjeev. "Makes us vulnerable."

Sanjeev had a point. Making quick progress was important, but so was stealth, or what they could approximate of it in a group of four bickering people. She didn't want to give Robert any more notice of their arrival than absolutely necessary.

"Sanjeev's right," she said, consulting the map again. "We don't want them to know we're coming. We have no idea how many of them there are or if they've got weapons. We stick to the road. Where we can, we move through the trees and vegetation, places we're less obvious."

She scanned the landscape: patches of trees and some scrubby grass leading down to the beach. Cover wouldn't be easy to come by. Still, they had to do what they could.

Toni nodded and traced a line on the map. "Let's follow this route. There's a green patch five or six miles ahead. When we get there, we can rest. Hopefully there are still trees there."

They continued along the disused road, finding detours around collapsed sections, and taking care to avoid the wettest ground. They learned the tell-tale signs of boggy ground: dark green, jagged spikes above brown, matted grass that sometimes glistened in the low sun.

As dusk fell, the promised patch of trees was getting nearer. They reached its shelter gratefully and struck camp in a silence broken by groans as their unaccustomed limbs complained at the walking. Only Zack was unaffected. No stranger to physical labour, he erected his and Sanjeev's tent with deft movements, and then helped Jess and Toni with theirs. The four of them sat in a tight group between the tents as they ate some more of the bread with some cheese from the village goats, and took swigs from a flask of water they passed between them.

While they ate, the woods descended into darkness. The

air was closing in on them, damp smells of night rising with the sound of the distant sea.

"We don't know who could be out here," said Zack. "Or if they're looking for us. I think we should keep a lookout, take it in turns."

"OK," sighed Jess, longing for sleep. "I'll take the first watch with Sanjeev. Zack and Toni can take the second half of the night. That gives us six hours sleep each before it gets light. OK with everyone?"

She was answered with low murmurs as they prepared themselves for the night, Sanjeev brewing coffee over the camping stove and the others half crawling, half falling into their tents.

44

Martin stood at the kitchen door. Robert was at the table, deep in conversation with Bill and Eddie.

Martin cleared his throat. "Alright to join you?"

Robert looked up at him. He smiled. "Of course, lad. Sit next to me."

Martin grabbed the chair next to Robert, pulling it away as surreptitiously as he could.

"How was the girl?" Robert asked.

"Scared."

"But you put her mind at rest.'

"I tried."

"I bet you did!"

Robert looked round the men, his eyes flashing.

"No," said Martin. "Not like—"

Silence. Robert turned to him. "Don't tell me you're trying to make friends with these bitches, son."

"No. That's not..." He licked his lips. "We cleared the back field this morning. Me and Leroy."

"Well done. Hard work. Keeps the mind pure. There's

more to do this afternoon."

Robert had only recently agreed to start growing food here. For years he'd been satisfied with stealing it: sending raiding parties to Filey, Scarborough or what remained of Hull each month. Scavenging from allotments, looting warehouses, or using stolen cash to buy black market alcohol. But now those supplies were running out.

Martin nodded. He wolfed down his meal of bread and soup and all but ran out to the fields when he was finished.

His work done, Martin had a makeshift wash in the tin bath full of salty water that sat at the back door of the farmhouse. His senses were alert for voices or movement coming from the outhouse where the women were kept. He hadn't seen Ruth, Sarah or either of the other captives, but their presence was unmistakeable. He could smell tonight's dinner: a fish stew cooked with tomatoes and wild garlic.

As he ate it he listened to the men's conversations, wondering which of them had had contact with the women today and hoping they hadn't been hurt. The kitchen was cleaner than usual: Ruth's handiwork.

When the meal was over, plates wiped clean, chairs pushed back and appreciative belches echoing around the room, the hip flask emerged, passing from hand to hand. Robert was the first to drink and when it returned to him he took another swig and raised it.

"Here's to the women," he said. Martin shuddered. "Damn good cooks and cleaners."

"The women," came the chorus of voices.

"Not bad looking either," added Robert.

Martin clenched his fists, digging his fingernails into his

palms and struggling to breathe. He forced a smile with the others.

"Will they be staying in the outhouses, Robert, or will you be moving them in here with us?" asked Dave, to Martin's left.

Robert glared at him. "That's none of your business."

There was a hush, broken by nervous coughs and the scrape of Dave's chair on the floor as he shrank into it.

Robert laughed. "Oh, don't worry. I won't bite. They'll be staying where they are for now."

Dave blushed and pursed his lips. Bill was silent next to Robert, watching Dave.

"But I might consider moving the lovely Ruth in with me when she's ready," Robert continued, knocking back another tot of brandy. The men said nothing.

"I expect you all to take good care of them though. There are just four of them – well, three – to go around and we need them fit and healthy for work."

The men watched Robert. Martin wondered how many of them had encountered the women, if more of them had been allowed in the cells.

"They're our guests, aren't they? We have to make them feel welcome," Robert said. "Show them some love." He winked. Some of the men laughed, but others looked sheepish, their smiles forced. Martin thought of Sarah, of her delicate features so incongruous in the cramped cell, and made a private vow to get her away from here.

45

J ess blew on her hands. The scrubby woodland felt denser in the dark, as if it might swallow them up.

Sanjeev was beside her, his back to her. He'd dragged his sleeping bag out of his and Zack's tent and was huddled in it for warmth.

They'd been out here together for over two hours and Sanjeev hadn't spoken. He was avoiding her eye.

"Everything alright, San?" she asked.

He shrugged.

She turned to him. "You've been off with me since we left the village. What's up?"

"Nothing."

"Come on. This isn't like you. Tell me what's wrong. Please."

"We should keep quiet. Toni and Zack are asleep."

"We're whispering. It'll be fine."

A shrug.

"Is it something Ben said to you?"

Another shrug.

"I can handle it, you know. I'm his sister. I've seen it all."

"I don't want to talk about it."

"Whatever it is, it's making you jumpy."

"Of course I'm jumpy. I want to get Ruth back. And the others. Don't you?"

"Of course I bloody do. But that's no reason for you not to tell me what Ben's done." She sighed. "Is this about the steward vote? Is he still pissed off with me about that? Are *you* pissed off with me?"

"It's nothing like that."

"Then what?"

Jess was startled by a rustling sound. She and Sanjeev span round. Their fire was all but extinguished now and the forest was plunged in a grey gloom.

She relaxed. It was just a squirrel, scavenging the left-overs of their bread.

"We all want them back, San. But we have to work together."

"It isn't as simple as that."

"It is."

"No. It isn't."

Her leg was cramping. She pushed it out in front of her and rubbed it.

"I'm tired, San. We need to be alert. Let's not argue, please? Whatever it is, it isn't worth it."

"You don't know, do you?" Sanjeev hissed.

"Know what?"

"That man. Robert Cope."

She tensed. She'd never used his full name with other villagers. Had Ben?

"What about him?"

"I know why he did it, Jess. I know why he took Ruth."

46

Martin stared across the room at Sarah. She sat on the floor, her arms around her knees and her eyes lowered. Behind him, he heard the key turn in the lock: Bill this time, not Robert. He hadn't seen Robert yet this morning.

"Hello again," he said, running a hand through his hair. She looked up at him through narrowed eyes, saying nothing.

"Look," he whispered. He crouched down to her level then pulled back as she flinched. "I don't know what's happened to you since I was here last. I dunno if you've been allowed out at all." He swallowed. "Or if anyone else has been in here. Any of the other men."

He felt his cheeks flush. She looked down, her gaze on his chest, and nodded. He didn't know which of his questions she was answering.

He lowered himself to the floor. Her eyes tracked his movements. He looked at the door and listened for a moment. Not a sound from the corridor or the neighbouring rooms.

"I know I've said this before," he continued, still whispering, "but I feel bad about what's happened to you. I want to help make it better."

Her eyes darted up to his. He couldn't tell if it was a question he could see in them, or fear.

"I want to get you out of here. To help you escape."

She nodded, more vehemently this time.

"But I need your help," he said, "I need to know if they let you out of here, and when. I know that some of the women—"

"Women?"

He started at the sound of her voice: it was gentle, like silk.

He nodded.

"There are other women here. Four of you. All from your village. Ruth is in the room through that wall."

He pointed. She reached out and held her palm against the brickwork, spreading her fingers wide.

"And two other women on the other side, each in their own rooms. I don't know their names. Sorry."

"How did I get here?" she asked.

He closed his eyes, ashamed. "We took you. In a boat. You were drugged and carried to your village's boat. We stole it. Then we took you to our trawler. Brought you here."

He wondered how much she'd taken in the last time he was here. "Do you remember what I told you about where you are?" he asked. "About this farm? The men?"

She nodded and looked down again, her pale cheeks darkening. He risked another question. "Who else has been in here? Apart from me?"

Her nails dug into the pads of her fingers, making the flesh white. "Just one," she muttered. "Leroy."

Martin shuddered. Suddenly the man he'd been working so easily alongside became a different person.

"Did he – did he hurt you?" he asked.

"He tried."

His stomach clenched.

"We've got to get you out," he whispered. "Soon as possible. Have they let you out to work? Housework, cooking, anything like that?"

She looked at him again. "Yes. An older man came yesterday afternoon. At first I thought..." She shuddered. "He took me to the house. Made me scrub floors."

"Did he say what else they want you to do? Anything that gets you outside?"

"There was something about bins. Pig food, scraps. I don't know. He didn't say it to me, but I overheard."

He grinned. The pigs were kept around the back of this outhouse, out of sight of the farmhouse. Within reach of the woods that flanked the farm's boundary, about 200 yards away. Running distance.

"Brilliant. That's perfect."

She was watching him, her face creased. She probably thought he was mad.

"One last thing. D'you know what time they normally let you out?"

Her face fell. "No."

"No worry. We can get round that. The pigs are fed late afternoon before we eat. They get peelings and rind."

He'd grown quite attached to the pigs, but she didn't need to know that.

"I'll get you out of here," he whispered, daring to move closer. "This afternoon. I'll make sure you're sent out to feed the pigs and I'll come for you. Wait for me."

She blinked at him. Her eyes were rimmed with red, her hair wild around her face and her skin streaked with dirt. But her smile was beautiful.

47

"Ow!"

Jess threw her arms out to the sides, knowing it was no good. The weight of the rucksack pulled her backwards, sending her tipping into a ditch.

She ran over her body in her mind. She'd taken a bump to the backs of her legs, and her head felt dull, but otherwise nothing hurt.

Zack's face appeared above her. "Need a hand?"

She nodded, feeling foolish. "Please."

He grabbed her hand and hauled her up. She dusted herself down and flashed him a smile. "Thanks."

"No problem. Did you trip?"

She looked at the tree root that had caught her unawares. "I need to look where I'm going."

"Easily done."

She smiled back at him.

"You alright, Jess?" Toni appeared next to Zack, her face pale.

"Just a bit bruised, that's all. Don't stop walking."

They picked up pace, Jess taking care to watch the

ground as well as the sky. Sanjeev lagged behind, having hardly spoken all morning. He'd refused to tell her what he knew last night, and had been visibly relieved to end their shared vigil and crawl back into his tent. The dark circles under his eyes spoke of little sleep.

The road was almost non-existent now, with the route blocked by marshy patches and dense vegetation. The boggy ground was worst: they had no means of getting dry and if they stepped into a deep patch, the least they could hope for was a damp night shivering in thin sleeping bags. But that was the least of it. Zack had heard stories of ground around here that could swallow a person up to their waist. No one relished the idea of pulling someone out, let alone being the one pulled.

As they stumbled onwards Jess listened to the hum of the sea and the birdsong. Zack walked ahead, his footsteps sure. She couldn't believe this was the boy she'd taught for the last year of his school career. He was a man now, nearly twice her size.

When they stopped for lunch, she waited until Sanjeev was settled on a rock and approached him.

"Didn't sleep?" she asked.

He shook his head.

"Me neither."

He flashed her a look then returned to his bowl. The remains of the porridge they'd cooked last night.

"I need you to tell me what you know," she said.

He shook his head.

"It's important. You can't expect me to go in there not knowing everything. This isn't just about Ben."

Sanjeev's eyes were rimmed with red. "He made me promise."

"Of course he did." *Bloody Ben.* "You have to break that promise. It's for Ruth's sake."

"No. It won't help her." He stood up, plunging his bowl into his rucksack. "Let's get moving."

AFTER TWO HOURS, they'd not made more than a few miles' progress and stopped again to assess their route. The land bore little resemblance to the map now, with areas marked as fields just as likely to be marshland, and streams wider and trickier to pass than the thin blue lines suggested.

Toni squatted on a dry patch of earth and unfolded the map in her lap, tracing the route with a finger. Her hands were swollen with the cold and damp.

"I reckon the beach is less than two miles away, just over that rise." She raised a finger eastwards then placed it back on the map. "We should leave the road and take the most direct route. I know there's the risk of being seen from along the coast, but if we carry on like this it'll take us days to get there."

"And we need to catch up with Ted and Harry," Sanjeev said. "I don't like thinking about what Ted could do when he gets there."

Jess gave him a tight smile, relieved he was speaking at last.

"There's another thing," said Zack. "If we're on the beach we'll see if their boat has come ashore."

"Our boat," corrected Jess. "It belongs to the village."

Zack shrugged. Jess looked between the group for signs of objection, but this time there were none.

"OK," she said. "The beach it is. Toni, lead the way."

48

Bill opened Ruth's cell door and motioned her out, grunting. She followed him, carrying the bucket – she knew the routine by now – and headed towards the farmhouse to empty it and then continue with her cleaning jobs. She hoped he'd take her to the rooms at the front of the house. There she could get her bearings, work out how far from the sea she was.

But today was different.

"Leave it there," said Bill, pointing. "By the door. One of the others will clean it."

She placed her bucket next to the door, taking a moment to look inside and note that the kitchen was empty. Silently she apologised to the nameless person who would have to clean out her mess.

"Follow me," snapped Bill, heading around the side of the outbuilding.

She trailed a few paces behind. Bill looked to be in his late forties and was developing a bald patch on the back of his head, whirls of black and grey hair surrounding sun-darkened skin. The skin on his arms and face was leathery, almost obscuring the tattoo that snaked upwards from his right wrist. The men here were weathered by the outdoors, not unlike many of them back at the village. What was it that separated the kind of men who ended up here from the people at the village, she wondered. Did the two groups attract different personality types or was it blind luck? She considered Martin, and his behaviour. She shivered.

They rounded the outhouse, picking their way through muddy patches, and came out onto an area which stretched out for about three hundred yards. To the right was a pigsty. She could smell their muck and make out pink flesh moving between the two pig houses, upside down U-shapes of corrugated iron. That would explain the pork she'd cooked for the men's dinner last night. Next time she'd steal some.

Beyond the pigsties and a patch of nettles was an expanse of ground. Bill pointed to the bare earth.

"You're working here today. Sowing potatoes."

"On my own?"

"On your own. Got any complaints, Lady Muck?"

He headed towards the outhouses and grabbed a hessian sack, one of three propped against its back wall.

"Know how to sow potatoes?"

If it meant a few hours outdoors, then she knew how to do anything.

"Good. Three sacks. Sow them all. Young Martin will be keeping an eye on you."

She bristled and looked around, but Martin was nowhere to be seen. Bill walked to the side of the outhouse and cupped his hands to his mouth.

"Martin! Back field!" he hollered.

Back field. So the farm had more than one of them. She wondered if the others were already cultivated, or if she would be required to do those as well.

Bill had dropped the bulging sack again and some of its contents spilled on the floor: chitted potatoes.

"Well, go on then. We don't have all day."

She walked to the sack and tried to lift it. She recognised the markings on the hessian: stolen from her village.

"Let me help you with that."

She looked up to see Martin standing a few paces behind her. Bill had gone. She drew back.

He lifted the sack, scooping up the potatoes that had fallen out. Not looking at her, he carried it to the first trench.

"There you go," he muttered. "I've been told to watch you. I'm not supposed to help."

He withdrew to perch on the upended crate between her and the pigsty.

She gathered up a handful of potatoes, holding out the hem of her T-shirt to use it as a makeshift carrier. She made her way along the trench, placing potatoes at an interval of a foot or so. She'd never planted potatoes before, but she'd seen it done on TV and she remembered them being pushed into the soil so that they weren't completely covered. The spacing was pure guesswork.

After five minutes or so she'd done the first row and trudged back to the sack to pick up more. After half a dozen rows the sack became lighter and she was able to drag it along the edge of the field. Martin stayed where he was, drawing in the packed earth with a stick and occasionally looking back towards the farm.

The constant bending and lifting made her shoulders ache and she knew her back would hurt later. But it was good to be outdoors. She sucked in the heavy scent of the earth each time she bent to it, followed by the sharpness of the salty air when she stood up again. It felt like she was cleaning the fetid stink of her cell out of her lungs.

Each time she returned to the sack she would take a moment to survey the edges of the field, pretending to stretch her back or her arms. On two sides it was flanked by trees. At the end where Martin sat, there was a wire fence. Some of the wires were barbed and others were straight, possibly electrified. Maybe they had a generator.

It wasn't long before she'd emptied the first sack. She approached Martin, pointing to the second one.

"Can you bring that one over for me, please?"

It felt wrong being polite to him, still behaving as though he was the well-mannered young man that she'd invited to sleep in her spare room.

He stood up, clicking his fingers behind his back, and lifted the sack. He placed it a couple of rows along, further up than she'd asked him to. He was being helpful.

"Thanks," she said. He shrugged.

She continued with her task. When she had reached the point where she could lift the sack she looked back towards the farmhouse, to see what Martin was doing. She was nearly halfway along the field now, and he would need to move if he was going to keep a close eye on her.

The crate where he had been sitting was empty.

She scanned the field, her heart racing. Maybe he was in the pigsty, or nearer the outhouse. But he was nowhere to be seen.

She dropped the sack, wincing as it fell on her foot. She looked over to the woods at the field's far end. How long would it take for her to reach them?

Deciding on stealth, she grabbed a handful of potatoes and turned along the next row, placing them haphazardly without pushing them into the soil. She kept her eyes on the trees she was approaching, scanning for a fence.

Then she saw it: a barbed wire fence, not at the edge of

the trees but set back, snaking its way through thick bushes. It wasn't high. As long as it wasn't electrified, she could climb over, or even leap it.

She was disturbed by voices behind her: two men, distant.

Damn.

She turned to see Martin and Bill again, near the back of the outhouse. But they weren't looking at her, and they weren't alone: a slight, blonde woman stood between them, her hair in messy tangles.

Sarah Evans.

Ruth crouched down, pretending to be placing the last potato in the row. She watched them. Bill was speaking: she could distinguish the rough tones of his voice but couldn't hear what he was saying. He pointed at Sarah, then at the pigsty. Sarah held a bucket in front of her, gripping it in both hands.

Ruth stood and made her way back to the beginning of the row and the sack of potatoes, throwing furtive glances in the others' direction. Bill walked around the outhouse, leaving Martin to guard both women. Martin stayed close to Sarah but kept glancing at Ruth, and back at the outhouses.

When she reached the sack she stopped to watch them. Sarah was in the pigsty now, emptying the contents of her bucket. Martin stood behind her, watching. He was ignoring Ruth. She turned back to look up the field, at the woods. She was closer to them now than she was to the outhouse. She might reach them before anyone reached her.

She glanced back to check where Martin was, fighting her guilt at taking flight without Sarah. She could come back for the girl, bring help, she told herself.

But there was no one in the pigsty and no one watching. Martin and Sarah had disappeared.

49

I n her bedside drawer, Jess had kept an old sweet tin. Now, it was in her rucksack, plunged deep into an inside pocket. Bringing the tin gave her courage.

When they stopped for lunch in the shelter of some trees, she found a spot away from the others and delved into her rucksack for it, her fingers pushing clothes and rations aside. Pulling it out, she slowly twisted the lid, revealing her mother's rings, given to her when they became too loose for the dying woman's fingers.

Nestled in cotton wool that still smelt of Sonia, they taunted her. Her mother had wanted her to wear them.

"Take these, Jess. Wear them. They should be seen, shown off on your lovely young hand." But once Sonia's body had been returned to the earth Jess had put them away, unable to stomach the pain of looking at them.

Until now.

She raised the tin to her face and breathed in its heady scent; her mother's perfume.

"Jess? You alright?" Zack was behind her.

She snapped the tin shut. The scent of the trees hit her nostrils again, undercut by the salt of the sea.

"I'm fine."

"I heard you talking to Sanjeev last night. I hope you don't mind."

She shook her head, distracted. "Did we keep you awake?"

"Don't worry about that. Is everything alright?"

"I hope so."

"Anything I can help with?"

She looked over her shoulder. Toni and Sanjeev were sitting in silence twenty yards away, each focused on eating.

"I just hope I can do this," she murmured.

"Do what?"

"Get them all back. Keep you safe."

"Why should you worry about keeping me safe?"

She smiled. "Not just you. All of us. You're my responsibility."

"We're a team. We'll keep each other safe."

She looked at Sanjeev. He was watching her, his eyes narrowed. *What are you hiding?*

"I do hope so, Zack. I really do."

She pushed the tin back into its hiding place and heaved herself to her feet, remembering how Ben had refused to let Sonia meet Robert when they were young. She shivered.

50

"Now, run!" Martin hissed at Sarah's back. "Straight ahead, there's a hole in the fence behind the pigsty."

She stared back at him, wide-eyed, still clutching the bucket.

"Go! I'm right behind you!"

He knew that Bill might be back at any moment, that they had to take their chance. He also knew that Ruth was in sight across the field.

Sarah dropped the bucket, stumbling over it and nearly falling into the pigs' muck. She ran across the pigsty and vaulted the low wall, landing with a thud.

Martin ran around the sty: it was firmer ground and he was with her before she reached the fence. She looked at him as he drew level with her. Her face was flushed and she was panting.

"Here, quick." He pulled the wire to make the hole bigger. She shrugged her way through and he followed.

On the other side, he grabbed her hand and she pulled it away.

"Sorry," he panted. "But we need to stick together. I know the best way."

She stared at him. Her hair had been made even wilder by being dragged through the fence. He looked back at it and saw a clump of hair caught in a twist of wire. *That must have hurt.*

"Please," he said.

She nodded and he took her hand again, pulling her into the woods and taking a diagonal course away from the farm.

The going wasn't easy: low branches snapped at his face and the undergrowth threatened to trip him with every step. Having only one free hand didn't help but if he let go he might lose her. He thought of Ruth, working her way through those potatoes. What would she do when she saw them gone? Should he have found a way to bring her too?

After a few minutes he heard a whistle from behind.

He froze and stared at Sarah then back towards the farm. But the foliage completely obscured them now. Surely, no one had spotted them? Still, there was no point in hanging around.

"Hurry," he whispered.

They ran. At last they came to the other edge of the woods. Empty land opened out in front of them. They would be vulnerable out there.

"This way," he urged, and pulled her sideways, following the edge of the wood. He could hear noises behind, distant shouting and the crashing of large men struggling through the thick vegetation. The sound made him go cold.

They reached the point where this wood met another at the far end of the field they had skirted. He knew this wood was flanked by a ditch. He led her into the dense tree cover, dry leaves rustling beneath their feet. They were soon at the ditch.

He let go of her hand and jumped in. He turned back and motioned for her to follow. She leapt down into his outstretched arms.

They collapsed onto the ground, breathing heavily. She pushed her hair out of her face and, for the first time, he saw that she was laughing.

51

A stillness descended over the village after Jess and the others left. People retreated to their homes. Clyde closed the JP after the first day and when only Sean and Ollie turned up at school on the morning of the departure, Sheila decided to close that too. Instead she took over Ruth's responsibilities in the pharmacy, sending Ben's boys home with him.

It wasn't easy to keep the boys amused at home so Ben crept into the school room on the first afternoon, using the steward's key he still had. He borrowed books and writing materials, and set the boys up on the kitchen table. Anything to keep them from asking when Jess would return with Ruth.

Every morning he walked to the outskirts of the village and stayed there for as long as he could, scanning the horizon. But all he ever saw were trucks taking men and supplies south to Hull, and the occasional individual or group walking towards Filey. He ducked behind a hedge when people passed close by, wary of being seen.

On the second night he made his way down to the beach

while the boys were playing at a friend's house, thinking of all the times he had come here with Jess. It was one of those rare clear evenings when the vast sky made him think of a Van Gogh painting. He gazed out to sea. His wife was out there, somewhere.

The image of Ruth invaded his thoughts day and night, sending a shooting hollowness through him that would settle in his stomach and make him want to cry out. Ruth knew nothing about Robert, about their past, and had no idea what Robert wanted. He wondered what Robert had told her. There was a version of their story that would horrify Ruth, could even make her refuse to come back. She had to know the whole truth, to understand how much he'd changed.

Tonight the breaking waves hummed under a sky full of stars. He turned his torch off, not spotting the silent figure approaching.

"Ben."

He turned to see Dawn silhouetted against the starlit sky. She sat next to him with a stillness Ben hadn't noticed before. She gazed out to sea.

"I need to speak to you about Sarah and Ted." Her voice rang out in the cold air.

Ben gazed ahead. "Go on."

Dawn shifted her hands in her lap.

"I won't tell him anything that you tell me, if that makes it easier," Ben said. He knew enough about the Evans family to understand that Dawn had secrets.

A sad smile flickered across Dawn's face. "I'm worried about them both. If there's any way of getting a message to your sister, of contacting her."

"I'm sorry," he sighed. "We don't have any way of communicating while they're gone. They said they'd send a messenger back, let us know what's happening. Once they find them."

Dawn said nothing, continuing to look out to sea. She brushed a stray wisp of grey-brown hair away from her face.

"I'm sorry, Ben," she said. "You've got enough to worry about, with Ruth."

Ben pushed down the knot that rose from his stomach. "That doesn't mean you can't talk to me."

Dawn took a deep breath and put both hands up to her hair, gripping it at the sides and pulling it behind her neck and down her back. She still didn't look at Ben.

"Ted isn't a happy man. He finds life in this community challenging." A pause. "I try to make it easier for him. To smooth the way, as you might say. Sarah does her best too. But it isn't easy. He – he gets angry. Sometimes."

Ben resisted the urge to tell her he already knew this. Everyone knew that Ted had a temper.

"I don't worry for myself," she continued. "Ted and I have been together for thirty-two years. A wife comes to know her husband, to anticipate his needs. I know how to manage things, to help him find calm. I have help. I pray every day and God shows me how to be a good wife, how to stay constant."

Ben blinked, surprised. To him the floods had proved there was no benevolent god, but he knew there were others for whom religion was a source of support. That it gave them hope, helped them believe there was a purpose to all they'd suffered, that they would be rewarded at some point.

"But I worry for Sarah."

Sarah was nineteen now, with none of the independence of the other village girls her age. She should be a productive member of the community, allocated some useful role. She should have friends, a boyfriend maybe. But instead she stayed at home with her parents.

"Any mother would worry for her daughter," said Ben, feeling inadequate.

Dawn's sigh was edged with a high note. "Sarah's different. She's lived her whole life in Ted's shadow. I don't imagine I've been the best role model." Her voice rasped. "She's got no fight in her, Ben. If those men threaten her she won't know how to resist them."

Her body convulsed. She raised her hands to her face. "I'm so scared of what they might do to her."

Ben put a tentative hand on Dawn's back. He was scared too.

She turned to him.

"I don't understand," she muttered.

He frowned. "Sorry?"

"Why aren't you going after her?"

He stiffened. "Sorry?"

"I'm surprised you're still here."

The cold damp of the rock suddenly made him shiver.

"I don't think—"

"Sorry," she said, her voice low. "I shouldn't have."

No, I—"

But she was on her feet, making her way across the sand and back towards the village.

52

R uth scanned the field for Martin and Sarah. A whistle shrieked behind her.

"You! Stay right where you are!"

She turned to see Bill running from the outhouse with three other men. She hesitated, wondering whether she had time to run too, but then Bill stopped and stared at her. She felt her muscles slump.

There was a commotion near the pigsty; the men were shouting at each other. Bill pointed to the trees beyond and the others headed in that direction. They ducked one by one through the fence, and Ruth cursed herself for not noticing a hole there earlier.

Bill ran to her. He grabbed her arm.

"There's no need for that. I'm not going anywhere."

At least, not yet.

"Shut up," he barked. "What did you see? Where did they go?"

"I don't know. I was sowing potatoes." She gestured along the row she was working on. "I heard shouting. I looked up and you were there."

His eyes narrowed and his grip tightened.

"Are you sure?"

She nodded. He yanked at her arm, pulling her back towards the farm.

"Robert won't be happy if you're lying," he said, panting with the effort of dragging her across the rough soil. She stumbled after him, kicking potatoes out of place.

"Stop!" she cried. "What about the potatoes?"

"Forget the fucking potatoes. You've got far more to worry about."

She matched his pace. "Where are you taking me?"

He said nothing.

When they were near the outbuildings she looked at the spot where she had last seen Sarah. Sure enough, there was a hole in the fence. Beyond it she could hear the men crashing through the undergrowth, cursing at each other. Bill tugged on her arm again and led her round to the front of the outhouses. The sounds of voices died away behind them.

Bill unlocked the door. There were men in the farmhouse kitchen now, shadowy figures whose conversation stopped when they spotted her. Her bucket was still at the back door. Ben grabbed her arm and shoved her inside.

As she stumbled into her cell, Bill gave her a look of contempt.

"Wait there," he said. As if she could do any different.

"What about my bucket?" she asked. "What if I need to go?"

"You just focus on telling Robert the truth when he gets here."

He slammed the door, leaving her crouching on her mattress, heart pounding.

53

Jess's group reached Withernsea at dusk. It was a bottleneck: the River Humber had flooded inland, making the land between here and the estuary all but an island.

Jess had no idea if the town was inhabited or if that bridge was guarded, but she wanted to be careful.

They found some trees within sight of the bridge and took cover. They settled in to wait. Sanjeev fished in his rucksack for a bag of apples. Jess drew Ben's binoculars from her own rucksack, kneeling to get a better view of the deserted bridge. No vehicles, no sign of recent habitation, nothing.

She handed the binoculars to Sanjeev, trading them for an apple.

"Thanks," she said, looking at the apple.

He curled his lip. "You've got no idea."

"Stop it, San. I know you're scared. I know there's something you're not telling me. But you know what? I don't care. I'm just going to get us over that bridge so we can find the others."

Sanjeev blushed. "Sorry. I've been a bit of a prick, haven't I?"

"I'm not answering that question. So, are you going to tell me, or not?"

"Not. I promised him."

She blew out a breath between her teeth. "Have it your way. But let's work together, huh?"

He nodded.

"There's no one here," said Toni. "The place is deserted."

Jess shook her head. "It's hard to believe a place this big hasn't got anyone living here. Not even somewhere this badly affected by the floods. Somebody always comes back."

She crouched down to get closer to Zack. "What have you heard about this place? From the earth works?"

He shrugged. "I've heard talk of the men camped out in a farmhouse past here. The ones we're looking for. But nobody really says anything 'bout Withernsea."

"You sure?" asked Toni. "You've never seen vehicles heading this way? With groups of men? Or even just one person."

"Nothing."

Jess frowned. "Still. Best to be safe."

Zack nodded and smiled at her. His eyes were dark, boring into her.

They sat in silence, watching the bridge as if it would give up its secrets to them in the blue dusk.

"Must be a ghost town," said Toni. She stood to get a better look.

"Get down!" hissed Zack. "Just because we can't see anyone doesn't mean they're not here."

"True," said Jess. "We wait here till dark."

Toni slumped down, giving Zack a pained look and hunting through the rucksacks for a flask of water.

uth couldn't stop thinking about Sarah and Martin, wondering if they'd got away or if the men had caught them. From her gloomy cell she couldn't hear much: occasional footsteps and voices passing outside her window. She went to stand at the window, sliding in behind the table and getting as close as she could to the glass. She tried wiping the film of dirt from the pane of glass with her sleeve but it was no use: the fabric came away with black marks but the green remained, coating the outside of the window.

After a while the noises increased. There was a sudden crashing sound, followed by raw shouting.

"What the fuck!" came a voice. There was a splintering sound and a crash, followed by muttered curses.

She retreated from the window and slid the table back into place. She slumped onto the mattress, leaning against the wall in the hope of hearing something. She was rewarded with the clatter of the outside door being opened, followed by footsteps in the corridor. No voices, though.

She watched the lock turn, the handle being pushed up, hoping it wouldn't be Robert.

It was.

His face was dark with anger and his blue eyes flashed.

"Where are they?"

She drew back, protecting her chest with her knees. He advanced, leaning over her.

"Get up," he ordered.

She staggered to her feet, sliding her back up against the rough wall and feeling her T-shirt catch on a worn patch.

"Speak to me, Ruth. You were out there. What aren't you telling me?"

He grabbed her wrist. She yelped, pulling away. But he was stronger and she found herself toe to toe with him, trying not to stumble forwards into his grip. He smelt of smoke and sulphur: it made her gag.

She drew her head back. He had her by both wrists now. If he let go she would fall backwards and hit her head on the wall. But the alternative was pulling closer to him.

"Tell me," he hissed into her face. "What did you see? Where did they go?"

She held his gaze. "No idea."

He let go, sending her off balance. She managed to stay upright, throwing an arm out. He was scowling. He eyed her for a few moments as if weighing up what to do next. She stared back.

Finally, he smiled. "I really hope you're not lying to me."

She said nothing. Her eyes stung from the effort of not blinking.

"Don't worry, my darling."

She felt bile rise in her stomach and swallowed heavily.

"It won't be long before you choose to talk. I'll find out where they went, and whether you had a hand in it." He leaned in. She shuddered. "You'll be singing like a canary, once you know the truth."

She felt her breathing shorten.

"He hasn't told you, has he? Of course not. Purer than snow, your *husband*."

He barked a laugh. Ruth pulled herself in to the wall, her muscles tight.

He glared at her. "What did you do, Ruth? Did you help them escape?"

"I didn't, you bastard."

His eyes sparkled. "Talking now?" He cocked his head to one side. "I believe you, thousands wouldn't."

He reached his hand out and placed it on her cheek. "I wonder if it's time." He raised an eyebrow.

She clenched her teeth. He moved his hand down to her neck.

His hand was inside her T-shirt now, stroking the skin below the neckline. She pushed down the urge to hit him.

He smiled. "Tonight. No, tomorrow. We'll need to get things ready. Your new home, Mrs Dyer."

She clenched her toes, willing herself to stay upright. Her face was hot.

He smiled. "You'll be very happy with me in the farmhouse. You'll find me much more attentive than your so-called husband."

"Never."

He leaned forward, his eyes inches from hers. "Not your decision."

"I won't let you touch me."

His eyes flashed and he grabbed her wrist, locking it in his hand.

"You damn well will." He pulled her towards him. His breath was heavy on her cheek. "And you'll enjoy it."

He let go, sending her tumbling back to the mattress.

"Well, get up then. There's work to do."

She pushed herself up while he waited, his nostrils flaring. She slid past him to the door, desperate not to make contact. His breathing was heavy and she could sense his arousal. She swallowed, nauseous.

When she was out of the cell she paused, wondering if the outside door was open. If she too could make a run for it. There were voices outside. But if Martin and Sarah could do it, then so could she.

His finger jabbed her shoulder. "And no thinking of escaping," he muttered in her ear. "We'll be watching you."

55

Ben shivered as he watched dusk descend over the sea, looming over Ollie and Sean as they played on the beach. They were bright flashes of colour, bundled up in coats and scarves. He had on his warmest jacket, but still the damp penetrated his bones.

He'd been calculating walking speeds and distances, and had decided that the group had to be past Withernsea by now. If they'd got past the town safely, then they might reach the farm soon. Ruth could be within his grasp. He tried not to think of her with Robert.

Ben had known Robert at school, as a lonely, troubled figure who generally sat apart from the other kids and seemed to have no friends. He'd watched him from afar, wondering about the acts of petty rebellion he staged against the teachers, acts that seemed to result in more trouble for him than they could possibly be worth. Until the day when Ben had been sent to detention, and had caught Robert's eye.

Ben pushed himself upwards, turning to look down the

coast, where the sand disappeared into the mist. Jess, Sanjeev and the others were along there somewhere.

Fifteen years and two hundred miles weren't enough. Robert had found him.

He yelled Ruth's name at the sky. His voice was swallowed up by the sky. Below him, his sons chased each other, oblivious.

He let out a shaky breath.

'I'm sorry," he whispered.

56

Sarah crouched in front of him, her back rising and falling with each breath. Her head was cocked and she had her eyes softly closed. Concentrating.

"Sarah? What is it?" he whispered.

"Ssh." She raised a finger to quiet him then placed her hand back down to the earth: fingertips, not palms.

Martin shuffled towards her, taking care to keep his body low in the ditch. He stopped just short of touching her. She was calming her breathing, her nostrils flaring with each carefully drawn breath.

After a few moments, she opened her eyes. The proximity startled him: those clear, milky-blue eyes, just centimetres from his own.

"Can you hear it?" she murmured.

He shook his head.

He tried to still his body, slow his breath, quieten his heart, but it was impossible with her so close.

The fingers to her lips again. Eyes wider now.

"There it is again," she said, her eyes scanning his face.

Martin shrugged, raising his eyebrows. Worried.

"Footsteps," she whispered. "It's like drumming, coming through the soil."

He tensed himself to listen, lowering his ear to the ground, feeling foolish. Nothing.

"How on earth can you hear anything?"

With anyone else, he'd assume they were imagining things. But there was something about Sarah that made him believe every word she said.

"On the journey north. After the floods," she murmured. "I picked up some skills. Survival skills."

Her face clouded. "And at home..." She dropped her gaze to the ground. "I learned to listen for trouble."

He could hear it now. Not footsteps, but voices. And breathing.

They stared at each other, wide-eyed.

"Run?" he suggested.

"Where's the sea?"

"Up ahead. That way."

She craned her neck to look round, but at this angle there was nothing to see. She started to shuffle along the ditch and he followed. He could hear those voices again, off to the left.

They crawled, hands and knees pushing forwards through the dirt as quietly as possible. Martin hoped he was right about the ditch. That it led to the sea.

57

The farm felt different. It was as if someone had draped an invisible blanket over it, smothering sound but lending a thickness to the air.

Ruth crept from her cell to the farmhouse, Robert storming along in front of her. He muttered under his breath. She scanned the yard for activity, and strained to hear voices. But there was nothing. In a scraggy tree, a robin sang in defiance of the tension. The sharp smell of the pigs crept around the outhouse behind her, overlaid with the cloying stench of a toilet bucket that had been deposited at the back door. It wasn't hers, and it hadn't been there earlier so it wasn't Sarah's. Once again, she wondered how many prisoners were here.

Robert stopped at the back door, toeing the bucket with a sneer of distaste.

"First thing, sort that out," he snapped. "Then there's a meal to cook. Food's in the kitchen."

Cooking was easier than cleaning, and with luck she could steal some food, quieten the roaring emptiness in her stomach. Her mouth felt dry from the oatcakes that were still being left under her table. A packet a day was nothing to survive on.

She heard movement in the kitchen. A young man emerged, no more than twenty-five. She'd spotted him before, perched on a bed with two others, playing cards. When she'd passed he'd stopped, card frozen in his hand. He and his companions had stared at her, open-mouthed. It was a stare that told her just how long it was since these men had encountered women, or strangers of any kind.

The man's gaze travelled slowly up and down her body, alighting on her hot face. Then he gave a low grunt. Robert glared at him.

"No nonsense from you, Dave. Watch her. She needs to empty her mess out first." He narrowed his eyes. "But don't touch her."

The man's gaze dropped to his hands, which were large and rough, with blurred letters tattooed onto the knuckles. The grey ink was mixed with dirt and crossed by deep-set scars.

"No, boss."

"I mean it, Dave. You cause me problems again, you'll be out of here."

Dave cocked his head, defiant. Ruth wondered if Robert's authority was often challenged, and if she could use it to her advantage.

Robert pushed past him and disappeared into the darkness of the farmhouse. Dave looked at the bucket and then at Ruth.

"Where d'you empty this?"

She shrugged. If he didn't know, she wasn't about to tell him. If he took her somewhere else, it might give her an opportunity.

His face darkened. There was a sound behind her, past

the outhouses. She glanced back before turning back to Dave, reluctant to take her eyes off him. The yard was as still as it had ever been. Even the robin was quiet.

"In there, huh?" His voice was sharp now Robert had gone, and he had a strong London accent.

Her eyes widened. Was there a toilet in the outbuilding? If there was, why was she using the damn bucket? She nodded.

"Right," he grunted.

She picked up the bucket and its contents shifted. She closed her eyes and turned her face away for a couple of gasping breaths.

He was watching her, waiting for her to move. She set off in the direction of the outhouse but had no idea where to go. He sat down on the step, pushing his large feet out in front of him and clicking his fingers. He wore battered Adidas trainers, one with a hole so wide she could see his naked big toe.

"Aren't you supposed to come with me?" she asked.

"What?" He grunted, then heaved himself upright. "Fuck this." He headed for the side of the outhouse, the opposite end from the door. She followed, the bucket banging against her thigh as she walked.

When he reached the side wall he stopped and faced her. "Go on, then."

There was another door at the end of the building. Like the door to her cell, it was made from wooden slats. Shavings of paint indicated that it had once been blue, but now it was faded and warped. One of the slats was torn at eye level, leaving a large gap. The smell from behind it was thick and ripe.

She grabbed the latch and pulled. It didn't budge. She pulled again. Nothing

"It's locked."

Dave pushed her aside, making the bucket jerk ominously. He tugged at the door but it held firm.

"Leave that and come wi' me," he huffed.

She placed the bucket on the ground, glad to be rid of it, and followed as he ambled back to the farmhouse. He had a slow, lopsided gait. He stepped inside the back door and reached around it, half closing it. His hand emerged with a rattling set of keys.

Her heart raced. Was it really as easy as this? A simple hook, hidden behind the open back door to the farmhouse?

The keys looked familiar: a bundle of different types, some rusted but others worn from repeated use. They were clustered on a pair of key rings joined by a fob in the shape of a London bus. A relic.

He passed her again and strolled back to the outhouse, still in no rush. She followed. He fumbled with four keys before finding the right one and yanking the door open.

The stench gusted out and he ducked away from it.

"Get a bloody move on, then," he urged.

She put one hand up to her face and picked up the bucket with the other.

Ahead of her was the foulest toilet she'd ever seen. It had no lid or seat and its sides were smeared in black. Holding her breath, she hurled the contents of the bucket into it, then took a lurching step backwards and dropped the bucket. She sucked in a deep breath then tiptoed back to the toilet, grabbing the chain between thumb and forefinger and pulling it to flush. She jumped back as the toilet gurgled. She leaned on the door to close it, preferring not to check if it had flushed successfully.

As her hip met the wood, she felt cold metal dig into her. The key was still in the lock.

She glanced at Dave then down at the keys, mind racing. If she took them now, even he would spot what she'd done and take them straight back. And next time – if there was a next time – his guard would be up.

No. It was enough to know where the keys were kept, and that they weren't careful with them. She was bound to find a better opportunity. All she needed to do was wait, and watch. Closely.

58

An hour later Jess was cold and stiff, and itched to get moving. The sun had set and a gibbous moon was illuminating the waterlogged fields around them, making the ground glisten.

Jess eased herself to standing, stretching her stiff limbs while scrutinising the bridge. There was still no sign of life, even through the binoculars.

She looked down at the three expectant faces in the moonlight.

"OK," she whispered. "Time to go. I'll go first with Sanjeev. Then Toni and Zack. We'll walk in pairs. Leave a gap just in case. Follow me and no talking till we're over the bridge and we've found shelter on the other side."

The others nodded and joined her on their feet, groaning as the blood rushed back to their legs. They took a few moments to stretch, then Jess put a finger to her lips and gestured towards the bridge. The group stilled, waiting for her move.

She turned and picked her way through the under-growth. She kept low and moved as fluidly as possible, aware of the rucksack rustling on her back. She watched the bridge, and the town on the other side.

She could hear movement behind: the others were following. She turned to see them hunched, focusing on the dark ground. Only Zack was looking up at her. He gave her a thumbs-up. Nobody spoke.

Soon she was out in the open, where the ground rose to the road. She quickened her pace, leading the group as they flowed up the muddy bank and onto the bridge. As she stepped onto tarmac, the bridge was lit up by the moon, its low stone walls casting shadows. She could hear the lapping of the water beneath her feet and smell the saltiness of the sea which the river met to her left, mixed with the sulphuric smell of drains somewhere. Her senses bristled, wondering if drains meant current human activity. But there was no sound except the eddying water, and the quiet slap of foot-steps behind her.

Halfway across she heard a clattering sound ahead, and froze. Sanjeev stumbled into her.

"What's up?" he whispered.

Jess pointed towards the sound. It came again, a metallic clang echoing off the buildings ahead. Beyond the bridge was a crossroads and at the far side was a row of houses, with dustbins outside. One of them had fallen over in the wind. She hoped...

She brought the binoculars up to her eyes and peered at the bins. Another clatter. A bin tottered and fell onto its side.

Sanjeev gasped. She could feel a stillness behind her, as if everyone was holding their breath. She pulled the binocu-lars away from her face. Suddenly there was a flash of move-ment as someone darted out from behind the bin, streaming across the road and disappearing behind a building.

"What was that?" whispered Sanjeev, his voice tight.

Jess heard laughter at the back of the group and spun round, glaring. Zack was laughing hoarsely, his hands on his thighs.

"Sshh!" she hissed. "What the hell—?"

Zack raised a hand, shaking his head between gasps.

"Oh dear god," he laughed. "We were all so scared. Look at us!"

Jess raised an arm. Sanjeev placed a hand on it.

"Shh," whispered Sanjeev. "Zack, what are you on about?"

"It was a fox!" gasped Zack. "Just a stupid, bloody fox!"

Toni started laughing with him. Jess felt stupid. Sanjeev was looking at her, a question on his face.

Jess nodded, remembering the flash of movement, the colours illuminated in the moonlight. Orange and white. Small, quick.

She looked back at the group, irritated.

"OK," she said. "So it was a fox. But that doesn't mean we shouldn't be careful. Let's get a bloody move on."

Toni and Zack fell into step at the back. Jess started moving again, trying to regain the fluidity of movement she had been striving for. They were soon across the bridge and standing next to the bins; one upright, the other overturned. Its lid lay on the floor, still rattling.

They scanned the surrounding buildings. Still no sign of activity. What rubbish was in those bins was old and long since rotted.

"OK everyone. Let's get through here as quickly as we can and find somewhere to set up camp. Those men could be anywhere," she said.

59

M artin recoiled as his hand sank into the mud at the bottom of the ditch. They'd been shuffling along on hands and knees for about ten minutes now, Sarah casting glances at him over her shoulder but saying nothing. The sound of their pursuers had grown fainter now, despite a moment's panic five minutes earlier when they had heard a close rustling sound accompanied by short, panting breaths. Martin and Sarah had frozen in their tracks, too scared to look at each other or barely to breathe, only to collapse in relief when a fox had picked its way across the ditch just feet ahead. Startled by their reaction, the animal had stared at them with unblinking, beady eyes, before leaping out of the ditch and slipping away under a low hedge.

But now it was quiet, the only sounds accompanying their progress the warbling of a chiffchaff in the trees and the dim, distant sound of the sea.

Martin could almost taste it now, a salty heaviness on the air that promised an eventual end to this ditch, and some respite for his tired limbs.

"Mud," she whispered, looking back at him. Her cheeks were red. "You were right."

She put up a hand for him to stop and eased herself around to face him. She grabbed a fistful of mud and daubed herself with it, motioning for him to copy. He squeezed a lump of mud between his thumb and forefinger. It was cold and gritty. Feeling foolish, he reached in for a handful and started plastering it onto his skin: face, hands, hair, anywhere that was exposed. Once he'd done that he followed her lead and started to smear it onto his clothes too, wondering if his threadbare jeans would survive the ordeal.

She smiled at him, her eyes even more wide and blue in her muddy face.

"What now?" he whispered. "Make a run for it?"

He looked up at the darkening sky. If they stayed out here till nightfall, they would freeze.

"Is there any shelter around here?" she breathed. "Anywhere we can spend the night?"

"Not here. But there's huts up by the beach. Falling apart, but they'll do."

"Let's wait till it's nearly dark. Can you find your way?"

He nodded. He'd been roaming this barren patch of land for the last four years, conducting ever widening sorties for Robert in search of food, building materials, livestock, anything they could use at the farm. He'd been organised about it, using a spiralling route to enlarge his search area each time. His forays had taken him as far as Withernsea to the north and almost to Hull in the west. Both were desolate, abandoned by humanity but not by the wildlife that was slowly feasting on what the people had left behind.

Here, not more than two miles from the farm, was part of his territory, land that he had mapped in his head with a detail worthy of any cartographer. This ditch ran alongside a set of fields belonging to a farm long since abandoned, flooded as badly as his own home had been. On the other side was thin, scrubby woodland only a couple of trees deep in places but enough to shield them from the men. He was confident now that they hadn't been followed, but there was always the chance that they lurked there, on the far side of the trees...

"It'll be dark in an hour," she whispered. "Let's rest, get our breath back?"

He slumped onto the ground, flattening himself in the bottom of the ditch and trying to ignore the stench of decaying vegetation mixed with fox dung. He rubbed his aching calves then rolled onto his back and watched the sky dim.

60

Ruth was woken by thumps and voices in the corridor outside. She blinked herself awake, waiting for the key to turn in the lock.

The cell was starting to lighten. As her eyes adjusted to the gloom, charcoal gave way to silver. She sat up, not wanting to be laid out on the mattress when Robert came in.

The cell door next to hers was being opened. A clattering sound echoed along the corridor, accompanied by an angry male voice.

"Get your hands off me, you fuckin' idiot! You can't do this!"

She knew that voice.

Ruth stilled her breathing. She had to be wrong. It could be any one of the men. Anger and foul language were commonplace here.

"Calm down, man." Robert's voice was unmistakeable.

"No, I will not bloody calm down! Get yer 'ands off me, right now!"

She heard scuffling and muffled thuds followed by the sound of a door rattling on its hinges.

"Come on mate, get a grip. We're only leaving you here for a short time. So we can talk to you." Bill's voice, lower than Robert's.

"Talk to me! More like keep me bloody prisoner, you mean! Nobody locks me up against my will. What have you done with my daughter, you bastard?"

Ruth gasped.

She was right; it *was* Ted. Being thrown into the cell that Sarah had vacated just yesterday.

There were more shouts and bangs, followed by the rasp of tape being torn from a roll. More thuds and voices, lower now and coming through the wall between her cell and the next.

"Now stay there and don't move!" Robert snapped, his anger making the hairs on her arms bristle.

"Here's your friend," he continued, his voice level now. She could hear a smile in it. "You'll be sharing."

She heard another slam and felt a draught billow under her door. More scuffling in the corridor outside and another voice.

"Ted, I think we need to calm down a—"

The voice was interrupted. A blow, more tape being applied over its owner's mouth, or the shock of being thrown into a stinking cell: Ruth couldn't be sure. But she could be sure of one thing.

Ted Evans and Harry Mills were in the cell next to hers.

She threw herself at the door and pounded on it with her fists, her voice wild.

"Ted! Harry! Ted! It's me, Ruth! Ruth Dyer! Is Ben with you? Have you come to rescue—"

She fell back as her door was flung open.

"Be quiet! Nobody told you to speak."

Robert loomed over her, framed by the doorway,

fingering the pocket where he kept his knife. She pulled back then staggered upright, meeting his eye.

"Who's that next door, Robert? Who else is with them? Ben?"

"Shut up about your precious husband!"

He slapped her across the face. She cried out and a hand flew up to her cheek; she could feel it throbbing.

"Damn it, Ruth." He lowered his hands. His cheeks were inflamed. "If you knew half the truth about your husband you wouldn't be holding out for any kind of rescue."

Her mind racing, she glanced at the open doorway then barrelled into him. He was taller than her but slim, and she was surprised to find her weight knocked him into the door. She brought her knee up and he crashed to the floor, clutching his groin.

She leapt over his prone body. He made a lunge for her, howling in pain. She was too quick for him, and threw herself through the doorway into the corridor outside.

Panting, she looked from side to side. At the far end, Bill was coming out of the furthest of the four doors. *Who's in there?*

She snatched a wide-eyed glance at Sarah's cell – now Ted and Harry's. Should she try to rescue them? A moment's hesitation, then she threw herself in the opposite direction – towards the door to the outside world.

It was unlocked.

61

Martin was woken by sunlight slanting through the window onto his face. He raised a hand, cursing his hard mattress. His room-mate's breathing was lighter than usual, less laboured.

His eyes shot open.

Above him wasn't the patchy, damp-infested ceiling of his bedroom in the farmhouse, but instead the pitched roof of the hut he and Sarah had hidden in last night, curls of brittle paint floating down over them like flakes of snow.

He pushed up on his elbows, feeling the floorboards shift.

He looked up at the bench above him, more of a glorified shelf really, where he had persuaded Sarah to sleep.

She was staring down at him.

"Morning," she said. His heart lurched. "It's a lovely day out there. Good escaping weather."

He drew his feet up, scraping his heels along the floor, then stretched as he hauled himself upright. He clicked his knuckles behind his back to wake them. She grimaced. He resolved to break the habit.

The floor shuddered as he moved towards the window, imagining someone out there watching.

"Are you alright?" He sat beside her on the bench as she swept her feet round and onto the floor. "How are you not hurt?"

"I'm fine." She brushed a wisp of hair away from her eyes. It caught the sunlight, glistening. "Better than I have been for days."

There was a moment's stillness between them. His heart was pounding, sending blood rushing to his face.

"Thank you," she whispered.

His chest tightened. He wondered what had happened to her back in that cell. Which of his companions had paid visits during the night.

He shook his head and looked out to the beach. The waves sparkled for once, brightening the loneliness of this stretch of coast. In the shallows seagulls paddled, dipping their beaks into the water. Patches of seaweed littered the sand, ribbons of kelp interspersed with green clumps that took him back to swimming in the sea as a boy, his father mocking his yelps when his legs had been tickled by the fronds.

He scanned the coastline, pondering their next move. Should they head up the coast, follow the beach? Or should they go inland, take cover where they could?

Further up the beach, surrounded by a group of gulls, was a low shape, silhouetted by the reflections off the sea. It was squat and hunched, like a mound of earth or a small boat.

A boat!

He turned to Sarah. "Can you see that?"

"What?" she muttered. "The birds?"

"No, not the birds." Impatience made him sound shrill. "That shape, halfway up the beach. Looks like a boat."

She leaned on the glass, her hands smearing the condensation. "Where?"

"Right there!" He grabbed her hand and pulled her off the bench. "Come outside and look."

He bounded out of the door, his feet suddenly light. She dragged on his arm.

"Martin, slow down. We don't know what or who's out there."

"Shit," he breathed. He threw himself against the wall of the hut. "You're right."

He peered up and down the beach but it was deserted, their only companions the wading birds.

"It's OK," he said. "No one's here. You can come out."

She emerged from the hut, squinting up and down the beach and keeping her movements small.

"Up there," he said.

He pulled himself in behind her so they had the same view. He bent to bring his eyes to her level and pointed up the beach, his arm reaching over her shoulder.

She gasped. "The boat."

"What do you mean, *the* boat?"

She span towards him. Her eyes danced. "The village boat," she said. "It has to be – they've sent someone to get us!"

"Us?"

She blushed. "Me and Ruth." She lowered her gaze. "Not you."

He thought about Ben and Jess, about the kindness the villagers had shown him. Ruth's gentle touch in the pharmacy. The warmth of her spare room duvet. What would Ben do, if he found him here?

He cleared his throat. "Sarah, there's something I need to tell you."

"Yes?" Her face was flushed and pupils dilated.

"Nothing. I'll tell you later. Let's investigate that boat."

"Are you sure?"

He nodded. She started towards the boat, pulling him along, her hand cool over his.

62

Ruth paused in the yard, panting. Outside, a low morning sun was emerging over the hedge Sarah and Martin had escaped through yesterday.

She tossed options around in her head. She could follow Sarah's escape route, run round the side of the outhouse and squeeze through the hedge. But there was a good chance Robert and his men had blocked it off.

She could run across the fields. But she'd be more vulnerable on open ground.

Maybe she could skirt the farmhouse; head for the coast that way. If Ted and Harry had made it this far, they must have brought a boat. And there would be others with them. Maybe Ben. They would be near the beach, hiding or guarding the boat. She looked back at the outhouse and sighed. *Ted and Harry.* She couldn't leave without them. And three of them stood a better chance in a fight.

Which left only one course of action.

She darted across the farmyard, keeping watch for any sign of the men. The yard was quiet. A magpie clattered its morning call somewhere in the hedge and she could hear the pigs snuffling in their sty. Beyond the stench of the toilet, the warm aroma of coffee floated from the kitchen door. The doorway itself was dark, with no movement or sounds.

She slowed as she reached the door. She shot a quick glance inside. Empty. A rough pile of dirty dishes was piled up in the sink.

She risked taking a step inside. She reached an arm around the back of the door, groping for the keys. Hoping that this was a spare set, not the one that hung from Robert's belt.

Cold metal brushed her fingers. She closed her eyes in relief.

She eased the keys off the hook, palming them so they wouldn't jangle.

"Get back here, you bitch!"

She turned to see Robert stumbling from the outhouse, his face red. She'd done him more damage than she thought.

Good.

The only way was forwards. She stepped into the kitchen, scanning for a hiding place. Nothing.

The door on the other side of the room was closed but wouldn't be locked. She thundered towards it and threw it open, hoping there was no one on the other side.

There wasn't.

She took a deep, whistling breath, her senses sharp. Behind her, in the yard, she could hear Robert calling for help. She had to hope that all of the men were out working, or that anyone still inside wouldn't hear his strangled cries.

In front of her was a dingy hallway, brown patches seeping up the walls. And a door. The house's front door, which led to the beach. To safety. To Ben...

She slammed into the door, yanking its handle. It was locked.

She leaned back and tugged, muttering under her breath. Behind her, Robert's voice was joined by the shouts of other men.

She opened her hand and studied the keys. The skin of her palm was patterned with the white imprints of the sharp metal.

Six keys. Which one matched this door? She grabbed one at random and fumbled it into the lock, her fingers trembling. It didn't budge.

She glanced round to see that the kitchen had darkened. The silhouetted figure of a man filled the doorway.

There wasn't time to try them all.

She threw herself at the staircase behind her, grabbing the balustrade and swinging herself round. The stairs were uncarpeted and her clattering steps reverberated around the house, but that was the least of her worries now.

At the top of the stairs she paused, glad that she'd paid attention last time she was here. Ahead of her were bedrooms, inhabited by some of the men. At the far end of a side corridor, overlooking that hedge, was a stinking bathroom and a separate toilet, both of which she'd had the pleasure of cleaning yesterday. Behind her was another hallway and more bedrooms, unused rooms that still smelt of damp. Through one of those was a small doorway leading to more stairs and an attic room.

She had two options. The furthest from her pursuers was that attic room, full of junk she could hide behind. She squeezed her eyes shut, trying to remember if there was a lock on that door. Nothing came to her.

The other option was the toilet. It did have a lock, a

flimsy thing high up on the doorframe, easily broken. But it would give her time.

The toilet it was. She slowed her pace and crept along the hallway, hoping the men downstairs wouldn't hear. Below her, doors were being thrown open and the men were calling to each other between rooms.

Then she heard it: the creak of a foot on the bottom stair. She forced herself to stay quiet and not break into a run. The beating of her heart, loud in her ears, was accompanied by the wooden creak of someone ascending the staircase behind her.

When she reached the toilet, she shut the door behind her and slid the bolt, then slumped down on the toilet lid to catch her breath. As the air hit her lungs the room blurred and swayed. Sparkling lights danced like dust captured in sunlight.

She blinked three times and bowed her head, her hands on her knees. She didn't have time for this. Pushing away the dizziness, she stood and turned to kneel on the toilet lid, exploring the window frame with her hands.

"What are you doing?"

She froze.

"Shut up! I don't want her hearing us."

There was a locked door between her and them, for now: she had to move. She returned to the window. One pane of glass was cracked but even if she broke it, she couldn't squeeze through. She had to open it.

She pushed at the wood. The frame was warped and reluctant to move, but she managed to shift it a little, jolting the bottom part of the sash window upwards. The gap was big enough to reach through and get purchase against the bottom of the frame. The air outside warmed her fingertips and made her heart race.

The door behind her rattled as it caught on the lock. There was a pause then a thud as her pursuers leaned into it.

She turned and stared, watching the flimsy lock rattling. She tensed.

Robert's voice came through the door, making her blood run cold.

"I know you're in there, my dear."

63

Martin stumbled after Sarah. She raced across the sand towards the silhouetted boat, her hair streaming behind her .

The first time Sarah had seen him had been in that cell, he was sure. No flicker of recognition had passed over her face when he'd entered, no clue that she might have seen him before.

In the boat – that boat she was running towards right now – she had been unconscious. And he had been gripped by horror at what he'd done.

He paused for breath, scanning the beach for people. If that was the villagers' boat, it meant they had retrieved it somehow, or it had washed back to shore. That it had still been seaworthy. And that they'd sent out a rescue party. At least one of Jess and Ben would be in that party. Possibly both of them.

He dropped to the ground, ignoring Sarah's cries to keep up. He scrutinised the beach and dunes behind. The sand itself was deserted, but there were patches of rough vegetation inland behind which a person could hide, as well as mounds of sand, sculpted by the tides. And the boat. Who could say they wouldn't be behind that, poised for an ambush?

Sarah was on the edge of the shallows now, her shoes dangling from her fingertips. A braver man, a more honest man, would be out there with her, prepared to face whatever was coming for him.

Could he be that man?

AT THE SOUND of Robert's voice, Ruth felt her heart squeeze. No longer needing to be quiet, she heaved at the window frame with all her weight, grimacing as the strain shuddered through her wrists and elbows.

On the first heave it budged an inch or so, dislodging a few dry flakes that sprinkled the black toilet lid. She pushed again and almost fell out as the window shuddered upwards, the sound reverberating in the tight space.

"What are you doing in there? Get out here, right now!"

She ignored him and leaned forward to push the window up as far as it would go. The frame shook and splinters of glass broke free, plummeting to the ground below.

The top pane held a single jagged shard of glass, piercing the space she needed to push herself through.

"There's nowhere for you to go, you know."

There was a splintering sound behind her as the door pushed against the lock. She glanced back to see the wood around the handle crack but not give way. Yet.

She yanked off her grimy t-shirt and wrapped her hand in it. She pulled the tightest fist she could and punched the remaining glass, close to the frame. It came away whole, sailing down to shatter on the pockmarked tarmac below.

She stuck her head out to check her landing site. Below her, shards of glass were strewn across a rough path that bordered the side of the house. Beyond that, about four feet away, was the hedge. It was tall here, almost at the level of the window.

"Now!" There was a cry behind her as the door shook once again. The lock was almost gone: two of the screws holding it in place had flown off and it would only need one more heave.

Biting her tongue, she pulled herself onto the top of the cistern and pushed her legs through the window frame. She hunched her shoulders and squeezed her upper body through, hooking her arms around the frame at the sides, her palms flat on the wall.

She looked down but instantly regretted it. Her head swam.

She looked back up towards the horizon. Beyond the hedge were fields and ditches, interspersed with patches of water that sparkled in the sunlight. To her right, past the front of the house, was a neglected road, the remains of a stile, and a ridged field, maybe one that the men cultivated.

Beyond that were the low hummocks of sand dunes, the flat, dark beach and the shimmering beauty of the sea.

Moving across the field were dark human shapes.

Four men, about to thwart her attempt at escape.

A crash echoed behind her as the door finally gave way, followed by breathless shouting and recriminations.

"Get down, now!" Robert screamed.

She took a deep breath and found a target in the hedge, about two thirds of the way up. As she steeled herself to jump she took one last look at the figures in the field.

One of them was watching her, hand lifted to shield their eyes. There was something about the silhouette... Was that a woman?

64

Ben was woken by insistent knocking on his front door. He fumbled for the T-shirt he'd dropped on the floor the previous night.

Yanking it over his head and glancing at the boys' closed door, he shuffled downstairs.

"Alright, it's alright." He yanked his keys off the hook next to the door. "I'm coming."

He opened the door to a bright, sunlit morning. He threw an arm to his face to ward off the glare.

In front of him was Colin. His face was red and glistening.

Ben took a deep breath. "Colin. What is it?"

Colin spotted the hope in Ben's eyes. He shook his head.

"Not what you think, Ben. Sorry."

Ben's shoulders slumped.

Colin looked at his watch. "Sorry to wake you. You're normally up by now."

Ben shrugged, aware of the mist of sleep and despair that had settled over him. Last night he had sat up late poring through the few photos of Ruth that he owned, gorging himself on her image. Before that he'd taken the boys out to the beach for a dusk game of rounders, then treated them to chocolate from the village shop on the way home, Ruth's keys heavy in his pocket.

"Sorry," he sighed. "There doesn't seem much point. What's with the pounding on my door?"

Colin's face dropped. "We've had another visit."

Ben felt a chill wash over him.

"The men?"

He looked past Colin into the square, expecting to see agitated villagers. But there was nothing. Every house had their door closed despite the brightness of the day, and there was a heavy silence.

Colin shook his head. "No, not that." He coughed. "Come with me."

MARTIN SHOOK himself out and pushed up to his feet, sprinting after Sarah. He had to face whatever was coming to him.

As he reached the boat, panting, she was already exploring it. There was nobody hidden in or behind it, no assailants waiting to spring him.

She was inside the boat now, opening hatches and looking for clues.

"This is the village boat alright," she said, her eyes shining. "But there's nothing to show who brought it here."

She rummaged through coiled ropes and neat boxes of supplies, before giving up and slumping onto the bench seat at the boat's rear. He climbed on board and sat down too, looking around the empty boat. Remembering the last time he'd been in it.

He took a deep breath.

"There is a chance it wasn't brought here by the village," he muttered.

"What d'you mean? How can anyone else have—"

Her hand shot up to her cheek. "Oh. Do you think the men brought it? That they stole it?"

Her face was creasing, a dimple forming in her chin.

"How much do you remember of when you were brought here?" He tried to keep his voice steady. "Of when... they took you?"

She stared at him. "Nothing," she replied. "I was out looking for Snowy – my cat – and then suddenly I felt hands on me from behind, then... nothing. The next thing I knew I was in that cell." Her voice went quiet. "With Robert."

He shivered. She was twisting her hands together on her lap, staring at her fingers.

She looked up at him.

"Martin, is there anything you're not telling me? Do you know what happened?"

He held her gaze, resisting the urge to leap out of the boat and run.

She narrowed her eyes. "*Were you there?*"

en followed Colin to the boathouse, growing more and more puzzled. As they neared it he had a moment of panic.

"The boys! I left them in bed. On their own, in the house."

Colin sighed with exasperation.

"Oh, Christ." He licked his cracked lips. "Right, let's make this quick."

Ben stopped in his tracks. "But what if they—?"

Colin sighed again. He looked towards the boathouse and his face darkened.

"All right," he said. "I'll run back and get Sheila to watch them. Stay here."

Ben's objections hung in the air as Colin ran off. He watched him head back to the houses, puzzled. He'd never seen Colin run before. And he'd certainly never seen him behave so oddly.

As Colin disappeared between the houses, Ben shook the sand off his shoes and turned to the boathouse. The sun might be out but there was still a chill in the air. He shuffled towards the shelter of the building, feeling last night's bottle of whisky pulling at his limbs.

As he approached the building the rear door opened and he froze. Colin hadn't told him to expect anyone.

He darted to the side of the path, trying to flatten himself against the hedge. But at six foot four he couldn't use a low gorse hedge to conceal himself.

A man backed out of the door, locking it behind him.

He breathed a sigh of relief. It was Clyde, probably checking on the supplies inside.

He peeled himself away from the hedge, relieved Clyde hadn't witnessed his foolishness, and strode towards him, raising a hand.

"Clyde," he said, "Hi there. What's up with Colin?"

Clyde stiffened, the key still in the lock, then turned. His face was thunder.

"Ben," he said. "What the hell is going on?"

66

Ruth ran across the road, picking bits of greenery out of her hair and straightening the T-shirt she'd thrown back on as soon as she'd regained her balance. Her arms and chest were covered in scratches. It would smart later but there were no serious injuries.

The road was empty and there was no sign of the people from the field; maybe they'd headed into the house. But that woman watching her so intently, surely she'd have worked out where Ruth was going, known where to look for her?

She crashed into the wall separating the road from the field, wincing as her knee dragged on the rough brickwork. She poked a finger through the tear that had formed in her trousers, then regretted it as a jolt of pain shot through her knee. She was overwhelmed by a desire to stop, to give up – to lie down on this grass verge and let the day wash over her.

She looked back at the farmhouse, its windows dark against the glare of the sun, and imagined Robert's reaction as he saw her disappear out of the window. She smiled. But she had to keep moving.

A short distance away, there was a gate leading onto the

field. It was either that or chance her luck on the road. If the men had transport, they would easily catch her that way. Across the fields, it would be more difficult – for her, but for them, too. And beyond the fields, lay the sea.

She paused, listening. The air was still, only the distant hum of the sea for company. She shook her head and heaved herself up to standing.

Cautiously, she peered over the wall. A pair of eyes gazed back at her. A face split into a smile.

"Jess?"

67

M artin stared at Sarah, unable to reply.

"Were you? Did you come to our village?" Her eyes narrowed. "Tell me, Martin."

He opened his mouth to speak but nothing came out. She threw a glance over his shoulder, scanning the beach.

"Is this a set up? Are they following us now?"

"No. I—" he stammered.

"Why did you take me, only to rescue me again?"

She pushed past him and scanned the beach. He put a hand on her shoulder.

"Leave me alone!" she hissed. "You're leading them here, aren't you? Lulling me into a false sense of security then springing me just as I thought I was safe."

"No. That's not it at all." He licked his lips.

She pulled back, her face twisted in horror.

"What were you going to do to me, in that hut?"

He stepped forward. She flinched and threw a punch at him, hitting him on the jaw. He gasped but did nothing to retaliate. He spread out his hands, desperate for her to listen to him.

"Leave me alone, you lying – you lying – you liar!" She ran past him down the beach, towards the hut.

He watched as she sped along the sand, trying not to trip on her full skirt each time she threw a terrified look over her shoulder. He could hear the thwack of her bare feet on the sand and the whimpering of her voice, rising and falling each time she looked back.

He stood helpless for a few moments, torn between letting her go and running to catch up, to explain himself. Dragging in a trembling breath, he raced towards her across the sand, calling her name.

"Sarah, please! I can explain!"

But it was useless. His words were whipped away by the wind.

She continued running, her skirt gathered in one hand and her bare legs pumping across the beach. When she reached the dunes she stopped, looking between the fields beyond and the two huts – three if you counted the far one with no roof and a missing wall.

He didn't break stride, thundering across the sand towards her, muttering under his breath, rehearsing what he would say when he caught up with her. He wasn't sure the words existed that would convince her to forgive him.

Spotting him, she headed onto the scrubby grass behind her. His laboured breath and pounding heart rushed through his head. He willed himself to keep going, to speed up.

Running like this was something he had only needed to do a few times since leaving his first pursuer, his father, in their flooded house.

A few steps into the dunes she paused and bent to grab her foot. He remembered her shoes, placed together on the damp sand next to the boat. She looked back at him and put her foot down, stumbling. She pulled herself up and started moving through the dunes again, her earlier sprint reduced to a hobble.

He slowed a little. Catching up with her was a certainty now. The huts were little more than a few strides away and she wasn't far past them. But he couldn't hurl himself at her like this.

When he reached the huts he paused, jogging on the spot. "Please! I can explain, I promise!"

She turned and cried out as she lost her footing and stumbled to the ground. He resisted the urge to run after her, to help her up. Instead he sat on the ground, close enough for her to hear him but not so close that he could rush her.

"I'm sorry. I really am. Yes, I was at your village. I was involved, but it was someone else who grabbed you." He took a deep breath, placing a hand to his pounding chest. "I regret it. I wish I'd never gone along with it."

She sat cross-legged, cradling her foot in her hand.

"I want to make it right," he called across the dunes. "I want to help you get back to your village. You, and Ruth, and the others."

"Others?" Her eyes were wide; she stopped massaging her foot. "What others?"

68

Clyde stood with his back to the boathouse, staring at Ben. Damp patches of sweat soaked his T-shirt. Tight-lipped, he opened his eyes wide, daring Ben to reply.

Ben shrugged. "Clyde. I've got no idea what you're on about. Colin told me to come here—"

"Colin?" Clyde placed his fists on his hips. Behind him, a mountain bike lay next to the boathouse, its back wheel spinning in the breeze. Ben felt his heart lurch at the sight of it.

"Clyde! I didn't know you were here." Colin ran up behind Ben, panting. He put a hand on Ben's shoulder. "The boys are fine, Ben. Still asleep. Sheila's at your house."

Clyde didn't move. "Colin. Does this have anything to do with you?" His voice was rough and he was clearly trying not to shout.

Colin took his hand off Ben's shoulder. "Does what have to do with me?"

Clyde waved a hand back at the building. "The boy, Colin. The boy in the boat house."

Ben frowned. "What boy?"

He weighed the possibilities. *Martin?*

Colin took a deep breath. "He's one of the yobs that were here the other day. The ones in the playground. The ones that tried to take the boat."

Ben stepped forward. "So it's not Martin?"

Colin turned back to him. "No, Ben. Not Martin. The boys that hurt young Rory Stewart. Remember them?"

Ben nodded, irritated at Colin's tone. "But what's he doing in the boat house?"

"He's imprisoned in there," said Clyde. "Tied up."

Ben felt lightheaded. "What?"

Colin turned to him, his voice calm. "We found him. Attacking a girl. Roisin Murray's little sister, to be precise. He needs to be punished."

"Hang on a minute." Ben raised a hand to his forehead. "You found this kid attacking a girl so you brought him in here and locked him up? Just you, Colin?"

Colin shook his head. "I had help."

"Who?" Ben asked.

Since when did individual council members take the law into their own hands? Since when did Colin, of all people, ignore the law?

"No one you need trouble yourself with. We've had enough trouble from outsiders these past days. It's time we fought back."

"Fought back?" Clyde stepped towards Colin, his jaw set. "And what d'you think's gonna happen to us if we do that, eh? If the people up the coast get wind that we're imprisoning their kids? If they tell the police?" He jabbed at Colin's shoulder. "You think we'll be allowed to stay here with this sort of thing going on?"

Colin blushed. "I don't know. I guess I – I just snapped."

Ben tried to compose himself, looking between the other two men. A muffled shout came from the boat house. He shuddered, glancing at Clyde.

"Right, Colin," Ben said. "I know this sort of thing's hard for you, after what happened to your brother." Colin had started his journey to the village with his younger brother. But after a confrontation with some pumped up kids – kids just like this one – the brother had been left behind. Ben didn't know why, but he had his theories.

Colin glared at him. He raised a hand. "Sorry. But look, tell us what happened. Where did you find this kid?"

Colin relaxed a little, smoothing his hands down his trousers. He let out a long, rattling breath. "Behind the boat house here. He was with Sinead. He'd grabbed her. If I hadn't got here when I did, I don't know what would have happened."

"So where's she now? Sinead?" asked Ben.

"She ran off. She's with her family, I hope."

"So do I," said Ben. "Look, Colin, I think you should get away from this boy before you do any more harm. Why don't you go back to the village and check that she got home safely? Give her parents some sort of explanation?"

"But—"

He raised a hand. "No. I don't think you're in a position to argue right now. Don't tell them we've got the boy. We can think of what we'll tell the village later. Just reassure them, see if she'll tell you what happened."

Colin sighed. He glared at Clyde. "He should be punished."

Ben closed his eyes and prayed for strength. They watched Colin retreat in silence. Ben knew his cheeks were flushed. But it felt good to take charge again.

When Colin's footsteps had been swallowed up by the wind, Ben turned to Clyde.

"Well?" said Clyde.

"Well, what?"

"What are we going to do about him?"

Ben drew in a long breath, thinking of Robert and what he might be doing to Ruth. Of this boy, a younger version of Robert. *What would I have done, if I'd had the chance to change his ways years ago?*

69

The walk from Withernsea hadn't been an easy one. Wary of the open shoreline, they'd picked their way through a maze of narrow lanes alongside waterlogged, impregnable hedgerows. By the time they came upon the farmhouse and the cultivated field in front of it, Jess's feet ached and her calves were tight.

They crouched in the tangled hedge separating the field from the dunes, hissing plans and questions to each other. Jess longed to look over the hedge but couldn't shake off a nagging dread that someone would be on the other side, listening. The sea was calm now and she could hear birds singing further along the hedgerow.

They decided to risk crossing the field, keeping low and making fast, quiet progress. When she was near to the wall on the far side she spotted movement in a side window of the house.

She waved at Toni behind her.

"Look up there," she hissed, raising a finger. Toni stopped moving.

A rattling sound came from a small window at the side of the house, followed by scrapes and squeaks as it grated its way open. A slender arm – a woman's? – pushed it up. Jess watched, open-mouthed.

First one leg and then another emerged, as the figure started to climb out. Jess's heart picked up its pace. Someone heaving themselves feet-first out of an upstairs window could only be attempting one thing. Escape.

When a head appeared she shot a hand out to grasp Toni's shoulder.

Ruth. It was Ruth.

She watched as Ruth cast her eyes about the landscape. She waited for her to jump.

When Ruth finally threw herself into the air, Jess held her breath. There were muffled shouts as Ruth hit the hedge and tumbled down it, the sound of her body dragging against the branches.

Then there was silence. Jess ducked down next to the wall and the others followed suit. She paused to catch her breath then raised her head to see over the wall. There was shouting coming from inside the house but the windows were dark and the door closed.

Then as if from nowhere, Ruth's face appeared right in front of her. It was all she could do to keep herself from crying out with joy.

Ruth was less guarded. "Jess!" she cried, and burst into noisy tears.

Jess looked past her at the farmhouse: more shouts, and banging from behind that door. She beamed at Ruth.

"Oh my god! Am I glad to see you! Get over here, quick."

Ruth heaved herself over the wall, Jess dragging her body across the rough brickwork. The two of them tumbled onto the ground, clasping each other. Ruth was shaking, tears shuddering through her body. She pulled back and covered Jess's face in kisses.

"Thank you, thank you!" she cried. "I knew you'd come for me. Where's Ben?"

Toni and Sanjeev were at Jess's back now, Sanjeev patting Ruth's arm over Jess's shoulder. Zack stood behind, half crouching, eyes roaming over their surroundings.

"We've got company," he said.

Jess looked up; two men were emerging from the farm-house. More followed, shouting.

"There's no time. We have to run," she told Ruth.

Ruth looked back at the house. "Aren't you going to go straight in there and get them?"

Jess put a hand on Ruth's arm. "We need to be able to get away. All of us. We have no idea if anyone's injured."

Ruth looked at her. For the first time, Jess noticed a yellowing bruise on her cheek.

"Did they hurt you?"

Ruth closed her eyes. "I don't want to talk about it."

"Run, now!" Toni hissed.

The men were reaching the wall now. Jess grabbed Ruth's hand and started running across the rutted field. It was hard going, but the relief of finding her sister-in-law gave her fuel.

Zack was ahead of them. At the far end of the field, he turned.

"Wait," he panted. "They've stopped."

Jess turned back. Sure enough, the men had stopped running. They stared across the field at them. Behind them stood Robert. He had a hand raised and was staring at Ruth.

Jess stared back, her chest rising and falling. What had he said to them? Why had they stopped?

Ruth turned to her.

"Jess," she whispered. "Did Ben know them? The man called Robert? Did he do something to him?"

70

FIFTEEN YEARS EARLIER

After his first encounter with Robert in detention, Ben had started to drift away from his loose group of school friends, spending more and more time with his new pal. Over time, a couple of the others had followed him, becoming part of Robert's group without anything ever being acknowledged. Bored by looming exams and the inevitable futile search for a job, he'd neglected his studies and started to miss the odd day, not enough to get him into trouble with Sonia but enough to provide the thrill of rebellion. He'd even skipped training sessions, knowing his mum couldn't afford to support the cycling much longer.

At first they'd hung around the local shopping centre, whistling at passing girls and muttering amongst themselves on benches, laughing at the glares they got from adults. Jayden, one of the boys who had transferred groups with him, had a good line in impressions and he would mimic the people who passed them once they were safely out of earshot, mincing past the bench, contorting his face into hilarious expressions and adopting imagined voices that make the boys collapse into a pile of laughter and gangly limbs.

As exams drew closer, the new group shrank again, leaving just him and Robert. Robert, despite being cleverer than Ben, had no intention of getting any qualifications and skipped every day of GCSEs, but Ben was too cowed by Sonia's nagging and too worried about his future to risk missing them. But on those days when he had no exams in the afternoon he would join Robert for a celebratory rampage around town, relief at getting through one more exam making him throw caution to the wind and risk shoplifting in the shopping centre or trespassing on the railway lines to daub obscene graffiti for the entertainment of the evening's commuters.

On the day of his last exam, he careered out of school. Robert was watching from the other side of the street, standing in the shadow of a tree. He wore ripped jeans and a Bowie T shirt, teamed with black fingerless gloves in spite of the sunshine.

Ben sped across the road, ignoring the shouts of the boys behind, inviting him to join them in the pub. He grinned as he approached his friend. An afternoon in the Dog and Duck was tempting, but he hadn't brought a change of clothes and knew he wouldn't get served in his uniform. So when Robert raised an eyebrow and turned to lead him along the street, he followed.

He found himself tripping over his feet to keep up with Robert's determined stride. When Robert suddenly came to a halt, he crashed into him, nearly sending the two of them tumbling to the pavement.

"Stop it!" hissed Robert. "Don't be a dumbass." Robert was into Americanisms, that week.

Ben mumbled an apology then looked around. They

were on the edge of an industrial estate about two miles from the school. A single road snaked its way up a low hill, with feeder roads leading off.

At the far end was a high fence with electric wire buzzing across the top. As a kid he'd come here often, riding his bike around the quiet, unkempt roads and cycling away as fast as he could every time someone called hello from the units that flanked his makeshift racetrack. At the far end was an open area where trucks loaded up mornings and evenings. This was a great place to practise tricks, twirling his bike on the tarmac to get up enough speed to lift his wheels off the ground. At the weekends, when there were no cars, he'd arranged makeshift ramps, dragging sheets of metal and abandoned planks of wood into piles and whooping in delight as his bike flew through the air.

Today was a Friday and the place was starting to empty. Robert pulled him into a ditch behind a litter-strewn hedge and put a finger to his mouth as they watched workers leave one by one in their cars, calling to each other to enjoy their weekends.

Fat chance, thought Ben. These idiots would all be heading home to identical boxes with screaming kids and nagging partners, the prospect of a football match or film on TV the greatest excitement the weekend had to offer.

He thought of himself in the same place in ten years' time, shackled by a job and family, and shuddered.

"OK," whispered Robert. By now there were just a few scattered cars left: shift workers, security guards or keen bosses staying on late, hands in the till maybe. "You see that unit up there? With the red sign on the roof?"

Ben followed Robert's finger. At the far end of one of the short, dead end roads that flanked the main drag was a unit two or three times bigger than most, with a large red sign dominating its roof. *Arley Logistics*.

Ben nodded, hearing his heart thumping against the quiet of the afternoon.

Robert threw him a confident smile. "We're going to steal from it."

71

Martin approached Sarah as she rubbed her foot. He swallowed the lump rising in his throat.

"Don't come near me," she snapped, her eyes slits. She dragged a hand across her face and took a breath.

He stopped at the edge of the sand and stared across the beginnings of the scrubby dunes towards her.

"Sorry," he muttered. Behind him a seagull cawed out a greeting which was echoed by another.

"What others?" she repeated. "What else haven't you told me?"

He lowered himself to the ground and knelt, ignoring the damp of the sand through his trousers. His face was level with hers. "There were – are – two other women, as well as you and Ruth. I don't know their names. But they were taken at the same time as you, from your village."

"Were they in the other rooms? In that outhouse?"

"Yes."

"How come I never saw them? Never heard them?"

He shrugged. He hadn't seen the other two women since leaving the boat, and could only assume that they'd not been let out of their cells, or that he hadn't been around when they had. He closed his eyes, imagining what they might be going through back there. What Robert's reaction to Sarah's escape might be, and how he could take it out on the others.

"We have to go back for them." She pulled herself up, wincing as her weight fell onto her foot. He reached out as she stumbled.

She glared. "Don't touch me."

"Sorry."

"Where do they keep the keys? How are we going to get them all out?"

He sat back on the sand, its cold seeping through his torn jeans.

"I don't know whether that's such a—"

"What are you, some sort of coward?"

"No, I just—"

A heavy spot of rain landed on his arm. He looked up to see that the sky had clouded over. Dark dots clustered on the sand, growing to become wet patches.

"We can't go now," he said, standing up. "Let's shelter in the hut."

She looked from him to the huts. The rain was starting to soak through her shirt. She gathered her arms around herself and nodded.

"Only until the rain stops," she said.

He nodded and started running for the hut, the sludgy sand trying to swallow his feet. He turned to see that she was struggling. He went back to her.

"Your foot," he said. "Let me help you. Please."

She scrunched her face up then nodded tersely, reaching up to him. She let him take her weight as they hobbled towards the hut, the rain turning to hail.

72

J ess held her breath. Behind her, Toni's breathing
had slowed.

"They knew each other," Jess whispered. "At
school."

Ruth's face turned grey. "And? What did Ben do to
Robert? He hates him, you know."

Jess sighed. "I don't know all the details. Ben didn't..."
She raked her fingers through her hair, cursing the younger
version of her brother. "Look, we need to get you home. Get
the others home. I think it's for Ben to tell you about
Robert."

"Where is he? Why isn't he with you?"

Jess swallowed. "We agreed it was best for him to stay
with the boys."

Ruth paled. "Are they alright?"

"They're fine. They think you're on one of your trips to
get medical supplies.

Ruth said nothing.

"Ruth?"

"So what do we do now? How did you get here?"

Jess looked back at the farmhouse. The men had retreated inside. She stared at it, its windows giving nothing away.

"We walked," she said. "You can't possibly..."

We'll send word, she'd promised. Ben would be worrying.

Sanjeev was squatting on the ground. His face was flushed.

"Ted and Harry are here." He pushed himself upright. His eyes flitted between her and Ruth, the house, and the beach beyond the field. "That means the boat. We need to secure it. Get some rest, think about what to do next."

Jess sighed. "You're right. We need to get away from that farmhouse. Let's try the beach."

They started to run. Jess opened her mouth to call to Ruth but her voice was drowned out by a clap of thunder. Not breaking stride, she scanned the sky. Up ahead, it was an inky blue-grey, smudged with rain clouds. Huge drops fell on her upturned face.

As she reached the end of the last field, her feet growing heavy with mud, there was a cry from ahead, where Zack was at the beach.

"The huts!" he called. "And a boat!"

She felt her chest fill. She bit her lip to suppress her own answering yell. Now she could send back word, to Ben. She could only hope the boat was in a seaworthy state, and that the rain would let up.

"Into the huts!" she cried, as Sanjeev reached the dunes with Toni. Zack was already on the beach, sprinting for the boat; she would leave him to inspect it. Next to her, Ruth matched her pace, wheezing with the effort.

"We've made it," Jess gasped. "You're going to be alright."

73

S arah huddled in a corner of the hut, flashing him wary glances. Martin hung back, not wanting to startle her, but desperate to explain himself.

She was breathing heavily, her cheeks flushed. She raised a fist to her nose and held it there as she sniffed, trying to compose herself. He waited for her to speak.

"Tell me everything," she breathed. "How you took us. Who else is here. What you've done to the others."

"I haven't seen the others, I—"

"Stop lying to me!"

She was on her feet now, hands on her hips. "You were in the boat, weren't you? When you took us?"

He said nothing.

"Tell me, Martin," she pleaded, her voice cracking.

He swallowed the lump in his throat. "I'm sorry."

She grasped at her hair. "I don't want to hear your puny apologies! Just tell me."

He closed his eyes and cast his mind over the events of the past few days. The fog in his head cleared as he understood what he had to tell her. *Robert*. She had to know about the hold Robert had over him, the type of man he was.

74

The first time Martin had clapped eyes on Robert, he had been lying on the cold concrete floor of a deserted car park somewhere outside Sheffield.

Looming grey shapes swam before his eyes, indistinct patches of blurry nothingness. He had no idea where he was. As he dragged himself into consciousness, he pieced together what he could remember.

He had been making his way north, in search of a place to live, maybe Scotland or the Pennines, away from the floods in the south and east. He wasn't sure how long he'd been on the road; two weeks at least. Two weeks in which he'd travelled not much more than he might have managed in two days back when public transport was functioning and the roads weren't blocked by water, police roadblocks or crowds of refugees.

He could remember a group of boys, around his own age, gathering in front of him in the roadway. He blinked, recalling their shimmering shapes with the sun at their backs. He squeezed his eyes shut to try to remember more but nothing came. Just rough, angry shouts and a sharp pain in the back of his head.

He lay still, knowing that his attackers could still be near. He could hear the sound of breathing nearby.

Wait, he told himself. *Take your time, get your bearings. Maybe then you can lash out, get away.*

He let his head slump back onto the tarmac, feeling the rough ground meet the spot on his head where he had been hit. His hair was matted and his skin cold. Was that blood he could taste? He moved the tip of his tongue around his mouth, feeling his teeth, making sure they were all there. All present and correct.

He resisted the urge to bring his hand to his face and check his jawbone. He tensed his jawline and moved the muscles a little. Everything still worked.

He took a few breaths, not too deep. His chest hurt with each rise and fall and there was a sharp pain under his ribs. Once he was confident he could breathe normally he let out a long slow breath through pursed lips.

"Wake up, my friend."

He stiffened. The voice was male, with a lightness that spoke of comfort and sufficient sleep, not of long days and nights on the road. He brought his arms up to his chest, ready to protect himself.

The man laughed. "You don't need to worry. You're safe now." He muttered something, but not at Martin. *How many other people are here?*

Martin opened his eyes. The man standing above him was lean, with three-day stubble and blue eyes. He wore a neat leather jacket over jeans and a white shirt.

Martin blinked, letting the surroundings come into focus. Past the man's shoulder, he could make out four more silhouettes. He pulled his arms up to protect himself, waiting for a repeat of the previous night.

"Don't hurt me, please," he whimpered.

The man put a hand on Martin's chest. He flinched. The man laughed. "I'm not going to hurt you, you fool." The stranger was smiling, his white teeth incongruous next to the stubble.

"Come on, get up now. There's a good lad." The man grabbed his hand.

Martin was too tired to resist. He allowed himself to be pulled up to standing. Groaning at the pain that seared through his body, he was led across the tarmac and lowered to sit in an abandoned car seat. He let himself melt into its comfort.

"So," said the man. "How d'you get here?"

"I was beaten up," he murmured. "Must have been dumped here."

The man laughed. "Well, I can tell that. But who by? And why?"

Dread shot through Martin as he remembered the rucksack he'd been carrying, the cash he'd managed to steal two days after leaving his parents. He'd crept into an empty cottage at night and helped himself to food and more, leaving a note for the owners in his shame.

He scanned the car park: no sign of the rucksack. He slumped down into the seat.

"They took my stuff," he said. "Rucksack."

The man exhaled. "No surprise there."

Martin nodded and closed his eyes. *What am I going to do now?*

The man crouched down so he was level with Martin. "I'm Robert," he said. "What's your name?"

"Martin."

"Where you from, Martin?"

"Down south. Near the coast. Nowhere you'd know."

He wondered what had happened to his parents, if they were still in that house. If the rescue team he'd spoken to had found his mum.

Robert nodded. "You got any skills?"

"I worked on a farm. Know my way around machinery, and livestock."

Martin's vision was clearing now and he could make out the other figures approaching. Men.

"Today's your lucky day." Robert folded his arms across his chest. "We're looking for an empty farm to make our own. We'll need someone like you."

Martin grimaced as pain shot through his temples.

"But before we get moving we'll need to deal with those thugs who attacked you." Robert held out an arm and some other men appeared. They dragged two boys over, hands tied behind their backs. Martin's attackers.

Robert pulled a knife from his pocket and leaned in to the closer of the two boys, placing the blade against his cheek. He turned to Martin.

"Are these the ones that hit you?"

Martin blanched. The boy closest to Robert was whimpering and the other stared at the blade, his eyes wide. Martin smelt urine.

Robert was smiling at Martin now, twisting the knife gently against the boy's face. Firm enough to pucker the skin but not to pierce it. Martin swallowed hard.

"Yes."

"Good. Take them away, lads. Sort them out."

"No!" cried one of the boys. He was rewarded with a fist in his gut.

After a while, Martin heard screams from a way off,

followed by silence. He shut his eyes. He was safe now, at
least...

75

J ess watched Ruth leaning on the outside wall of the beach hut. She looked frail and her forehead was swollen around the bruise. Jess wanted to touch it, to make it better.

"Ben," Ruth muttered. "Why didn't he come? Why didn't he come for me?"

"I told you. The boys."

"I want Ben. I want my boys." She slid down the side of the hut, landing on the sand.

"I'm sorry. We came for you." Jess smiled at Ruth, worried. Behind her, Toni was trying to unlock the door to the hut.

Ruth wiped the back of her hand across her face. She was covered in scratches, and bits of hedge littered her hair. She smelt of greenery mixed with the mustiness of the unwashed.

"Is Ben alright?" she asked.

"Yes," Jess lied. "He's fine."

"Did they—?"

"Who?" Jess looked back towards the farmhouse. "Oh.

No. The men didn't do anything to Ben. Or to the boys.
They're OK, Ruth."

Another nod.

Jess licked her lips. "I'm so sorry."

Ruth took a deep breath. "It's not your fault."

A lump rose in Jess's throat as she thought of the night
they'd rescued the men. Her second night as steward.

Ruth cleared her throat. "Have you seen Sarah?"

Jess frowned. "Sarah?"

"She escaped. Yesterday." A pause. "With Martin."

"Martin?"

"They went through a gap in the hedge, the other side of
the farm." Ruth pointed back towards the farm. "They must
have gone another way."

"What about Sally and Roisin?" Jess asked. "Did you see
them? Are they still in there?"

Ruth looked surprised. "Sally and Roisin? Surely you
mean Harry and Ted?"

Jess's stomach lurched. "You've seen them?"

"They were in the cell next to me. Sarah's cell. I should
have got them out, too."

She opened her hand to reveal a set of keys nestled in
her palm. Jess looked down at them, marvelling at her
sister-in-law.

"You've got *keys*?"

"I didn't know about Sally and Roisin. Sorry. I just saw
Sarah and Martin, and heard Ted and Harry come in this
morning. Were they with you?"

SARAH STARED AT MARTIN. He hadn't told her everything,
but maybe what he had said was too much. He moved

towards her but she shook her head tightly and he pulled back.

"Look," he began, but was interrupted by a voice outside. Sarah's eyes widened.

He crept to the window. Outside the next hut along was Sanjeev, with a woman he didn't recognise. They were huddled by the door to the hut, the woman tugging on the handle.

Sarah stood up. "Who is it?"

He blinked. "The villagers. They've come for you."

76

Ben and Clyde stood outside the boathouse and watched as the boy sprinted off towards the beach, not so much as glancing back at them.

Clyde let out a long, whistling breath.

"Jesus," he said. "What on earth came over Colin? Has he any idea what'd happen to us if the world knew we'd started locking up their kids?"

Ben continued watching the boy run. Beyond his retreating figure, the sea was changing colour, ominous breakers topping darkening waves. He glanced up at the sky, also growing dark. "Rain coming."

Clyde followed his gaze.

"Uh-huh," he grunted, folding his arms over his ample stomach. The boy skirted a sand dune, disappearing from view. "Let's just hope he's scared of getting into trouble," Clyde continued. "Then he won't tell anyone."

Ben's chest felt hollow.

Clyde started for the boathouse. "Let's get shelter, man."

He stopped walking. The bike was still lying on the

ground, its wheels spinning madly in the rising wind. Clyde leaned over and pulled it upright, facing the beach.

The two men looked from each other to the bike and back again. Ben had a flashback of hurtling around a velodrome, blurred crowds cheering him on, Sonia and Jess in there somewhere.

"I'll put it in the boathouse," said Clyde. "Keep it dry."

Neither of them suggested who they would be keeping it dry for.

Ben shook his head. "It's not secure. I'll take it back to the village. We can store it in the hall."

"Fair enough. I'm getting indoors."

The rain was coming heavily, great spots of water peppering the sand.

Ben shivered as water tricked beneath his collar. Why hadn't he put on a coat? Ruth would have reminded him to.

"Best get back to the boys," he said, turning for the village. Clyde shrugged and headed for the boathouse.

He shook his feet to dry his shoes a little then mounted the bike. The sensation of riding it was both strange and familiar, and made him feel brighter than he had in days. He allowed himself a smile as he sped to the village square, not caring that his shirt was plastered to his skin.

The square was deserted, with no lights showing from the windows. He hitched his sleeve up to see his watch: nine thirty. There would normally be people moving about now, getting on with their tasks for the day. But the rain hung over the village like a shroud. It bounced off puddles, splashing up over his shoes and soaking through his socks. He held his arm out and lifted his face to the sky, enjoying the cool of the water on his cheeks.

A voice called his name. He glanced over at his house, expecting Sheila to be waiting for him in the doorway. But the building was dark, the upstairs curtains still drawn and no light showing through the window in the front door. No surprise: the power would be off at this time of day.

"Ben!"

There it was again, a woman's voice. His heart quickened. *Ruth?*

He climbed off the bike, looking around.

"Ben, over here!"

He turned to see Dawn standing in the front door of the Evans house, her body in shadow.

Dropping the bike and shaking himself, he ran towards her.

"Dawn!" he panted. "Sorry, I thought it was—"

She gave him a tight smile: she understood. He blushed and she pulled back into the house, beckoning him in. He hesitated, startled. He'd never been inside this house.

Inside, the layout was identical to his own but that was where the similarity ended. The only objects in the kitchen were a toaster and kettle. The sink was empty, with no waiting dishes, and there were none of the items pushed against the wall that there were at home: spice pots, old tin cans holding cooking utensils, a makeshift bread bin.

The living room was even more spartan. The only sign of human habitation was on the coffee table: a solitary mug and a book placed squarely next to it, its edge parallel with the table's edge and a bookmark peeking out.

She spotted him looking around and followed his gaze to the coffee table, blanching.

"Sorry about the mess," she muttered, swooping down to transfer the cup to the sink and the book to a nearby bookcase. On one shelf was a row of books, sorted alphabetically by author. No ornaments or photos. Nothing personal.

Her eyes darted around the room, searching for anything else out of place.

"Has there been any news?" she asked.

He frowned and shook his head. "Sorry."

Her shoulders slumped. "Oh."

He cleared his throat. "I'd best be getting along," he said. "The boys."

As he reached for the door knob he felt the air stir behind him. A hand brushed his arm. He flinched and she pulled it back as if she had touched hot coals.

"Do you miss her?" she asked.

"Of course I do. Every minute," he replied, his voice strangled.

She nodded. "That's good."

He stiffened, considering what to say, how much he was ready to know about Ted. She shrank under his gaze, like Sean when he was in trouble.

"I'm sorry, I really need to get back." He pushed the door open, not waiting for a response. As soon as he was outside he pulled the door shut behind him and leaned on it, his head swimming.

Do you miss her? she had asked. But it was more than that. Ruth's absence was like a part of him had been cut away, like a creature was on his back. Whispering in his ear: *It's all your fault.*

In front of him, the boy's bike lay in the grass, speckled with raindrops. It was a cheap thing, just a kid's toy. Nothing like the sleek machines he'd had the joy of riding. But it was a bike.

The rain had stopped now and the village was brightening, the contrasting brickwork of the houses glowing in the heavy orange light that only came after a storm. He could smell the moisture in the grass as the sun warmed it: a heady smell that made him think of his old life, of parks and freshly mown lawns, of walking past damp privet hedges on his way to work.

He strode over to the bike and picked it up, suddenly determined.

77

"I don't understand. So you're saying he helped you escape?" said Jess.

Sarah had asked that only Jess and Ruth come with her to the second hut along. She wanted to talk to the two of them in private. Back in the first hut, the others were with Martin.

Sarah smiled bit her lip. "He got me out of there. He's not like the others."

Beside her Ruth was silent. Her features had set like iron as she'd listened to Sarah recounting her escape from the farmhouse. Jess looked between the two of them, confused.

"It wasn't his idea to take us," Sarah garbled, stumbling over her words, her eyes shifting between the other two women. "Robert made him go along with it."

Ruth gave an involuntary sound. Her skin was pale and damp. Jess reached out and placed a hand on her knee. "You OK, Ruth?"

She gave a tight nod. Jess looked back at Sarah.

"This is what he told you?" she asked.

Sarah nodded again. "I didn't believe him at first," she said. "But he explained."

Ruth folded her arms across her chest.

"He's going to help us," Sarah continued. "He knows the area, and the farmhouse. He can help get the others out, and get us home. We found your boat."

Jess raised an eyebrow. "Our boat?"

"The village boat. It's further up the beach. That's how you got here, isn't it?"

Ruth turned to Jess.

"No," said Jess. "We didn't bring the boat. We walked."

"You *walked*?" Ruth exclaimed. Then she fell back, remembering something. A shadow passed over her face. "Of course," she said.

"Ted and Harry came in the boat. They took it," said Jess.

"My dad's here?" whispered Sarah. Her cheeks had lost their colour and her voice was quiet and childlike.

"Mm-hmm," nodded Jess. "Ruth's seen him."

"Heard him," corrected Ruth. "They've got him and Harry locked up."

"Oh." The life left Sarah's face.

"It's OK," said Jess. "We're going to get them out. Ruth's got keys."

Sarah stood up, her voice breaking. "Don't, please don't," she wailed. "I can't face him!" Sarah pushed past Jess, heading for the door. Outside the rain had stopped.

Sarah turned to them, her hand on the door. Her face was creased and she was close to tears. "I need to see Martin." She pushed her way outside.

Jess stared at Ruth, open-jawed.

78

R uth stared at the door to the hut, trying to get her breath back. She knew Ted was volatile, but surely his presence shouldn't send Sarah running into Martin's arms?

"You OK?" Jess asked her, in a voice that made Ruth suppose she looked anything but.

She nodded, her lips pursed. "I'll be fine. Aren't you going to go after her?"

"I'm worried about you. I'm sorry to say this but you look terrible. What did they do to you?"

She shook her head. *Not now.* She blinked the tears away. "Let's focus on getting home, shall we? And on getting the others out."

The door rattled as Sanjeev knocked on it, entering without waiting for a reply. Jess rose from her squatting position on the floor.

"Sanjeev," said Jess, putting up a hand to stop him speaking. "Sarah went to find Martin, I know. Is she with him?"

"She came barging in when we were trying to get him to

tell us what happened. They took off together. They've headed inland."

Ruth tensed. *Surely they haven't gone back to the farmhouse?*

"Well, he helped her escape," said Jess, breathing slowly. "So surely she'll be OK with him."

"No." Ruth pushed herself up so she was level with the others. "He's not what you think he is."

Jess pushed both hands into her hair. "Jesus," she breathed. "This is all I need."

"Sorry," muttered Ruth. "But Martin isn't to be trusted." She thought of him with Robert, that first day. Locking the door; doing as he was told.

"What?" asked Jess. "He got her out. Why can't we trust him?"

Ruth closed her eyes, stilling her hands. "We just can't." She touched the dent on her finger where her wedding ring had been. "Jess, when am I going to see Ben?"

At the mention of Ben's name Jess turned to Sanjeev.

"We need to get word back to Ben," she said.

Sanjeev nodded. "I can start walking back."

"We've got the boat now. Take that. Tell the village what's going on, let Ben know Ruth's safe, and send someone back to get us."

"Shall I take Ruth with me?"

Ruth felt her body lighten.

"No," said Jess. "I'm really sorry Ruth, but you're the only person we've got who knows their way around that farm. We need you with us."

Ruth's shoulders slumped.

"Is that OK, Ruth? Will you help us get the others?"

Ruth pushed down the lump in her throat. "OK," she whispered.

"Thanks. Come on then."

Ruth looked around the hut. She was desperately in need of rest, but knew they were relying on her.

"I need a moment."

Jess turned. "You OK?"

Ruth's vision was blurring. Could she face going back to the farm? She thought of Ben, waiting for her at home. Of her boys. *Do you miss me?*

"Just give me a few minutes. I need to get my breath."

Jess nodded. "Of course. Shout if you need me, huh?"

"Mmm."

Jess flashed her a worried look then followed Sanjeev outside.

JESS AND SANJEEV headed for the other hut. The rain had stopped now and the sky was clearing. She looked inland for signs of Sarah and Martin. Nothing.

As they approached the hut, the door opened and Toni emerged with Zack.

"How's the boat?" Jess asked.

"Good," replied Zack. "More than able to get home tonight." He smiled at her, his eyes intense. She gave him a nervous smile back.

She looked out to sea; the water looked calm for now and the dark clouds above were moving northwards. But the sun was already setting – they didn't have much time.

"We promised the village we'd send word and that's what we're going to do. San's going to go. How quickly can you get the boat ready?"

Zack shrugged. "Half an hour?"

"Good."

Zack turned back to the boat.

Jess looked at the others. "Let's get some rest. Then we'll head back to the farmhouse when it's dark."

"Should he go on his own?" said Toni. "Sanjeev, I mean?"

Jess looked from her to Sanjeev.

"OK. Can you go?"

Toni frowned. "I want to be here for Roisin."

Jess sighed.

"What about Zack?" said Toni. "He can go."

Jess looked at Zack. She'd come to rely on him; his presence made her feel safer. He was moving around the boat, tying up ropes.

"No," she said. "We'll need Zack's strength."

Zack pointed out to sea. "It's getting dark. It's not safe, going that far in our tiny boat."

Jess followed his gaze. The sky was turning a yellowy grey. She thought of Ben, waiting for them. Of his anger at her.

"I promised Ben," she said. "I can't go back on that. We've taken the boat out at night before, it'll be fine."

Zack opened his mouth to protest but Sanjeev frowned at him. "No problem," he said, and hauled himself up to walk over to the boat.

79

R uth listened to the others' voices outside. What was she doing? Why had she told Jess to leave her?

She slumped onto the floor and pulled her legs in, thinking of that dingy mattress in her cell. She shivered.

She took three deep breaths, her eyes closed. *Come on, you can do this.* She had to, for Roisin and Sally's sakes. For Ted and Harry.

Ted. What would he do when he learned that Sarah had run away? That she was with Martin?

She fingered the swelling on her temple and winced. She was lucky she didn't have concussion. Lucky she wasn't throwing up on the floor.

At the thought of it, a wave of nausea swept through her gut.

She rushed to the door and flung it open, leaning out. She retched but nothing came.

She held the doorframe, panting. This was no good. They needed her.

She looked up. Jess was outside one of the other huts,

talking with Zack. Toni and Sanjeev were walking towards the boat.

Where was Sarah? Martin?

She looked the other way, back towards the farm. The fields were empty.

She was about to step outside when she caught movement from the corner of her eye. There was someone at the side of this hut. Hiding. Waiting?

She took a deep breath then stepped forward. If it was Sarah, maybe she could talk some sense into the girl. They'd both been taken, after all.

The shadow shifted. It was one person, not two. So Sarah hadn't found Martin. Or she'd come back without him.

Good.

As she opened her mouth to speak, the shadow shifted forwards, into the light. It wasn't Sarah.

He stood up, his eyes boring into her face. She stared back, mesmerised. She couldn't breathe.

He stepped towards her. He put a finger on her chest, pushing her round the side of the hut.

"Found you, Mrs Dyer."

JESS WATCHED Toni and Sanjeev head towards the boat.

"Will the boat make it OK?" she asked Zack.

"Course it will. I'll go and help him set off, report back."

"Thanks." She put a hand on his arm. He smiled.

"No problem."

He ran across the sand. She watched until he reached the boat. His gait was strong and confident, his arms pumping as he ran. She smiled, glad he'd come with them.

He reached the boat. Toni and Sanjeev looked up to speak to him. They all looked back at Jess. She waved. They waved in acknowledgment then turned back to the boat.

She scanned the beach, listening. A gaggle of gulls side-stepped across the sand a short way from her and the wind whistled in the scrubby bushes behind the dunes. There was no sign of human life.

Sarah, where the hell did you go?

She raised a hand to her face, squinting at the horizon. They couldn't have gone back to the farmhouse. They could only have gone the other way.

But first, she needed to check on Ruth. She felt bad for not sending her back on the boat. But only Ruth could tell them how the farm was laid out.

80

Ruth looked back at the beach. She'd outrun Robert before; she could do it again.

"Grab her, lads. One arm each."

She felt hands close over her wrists. She turned to see Dave, her guard from before, and another man she didn't recognise. They stepped out of the shadow of the beach hut, grasping her arms.

She struggled, staring at them. "Why are you doing this? Why don't you tell him to fuck off?"

Dave met her stare. The other man flinched and glanced at Robert.

"Go on then," Robert said. "Tell me to fuck off. Good luck finding a place to sleep, and food."

Dave blanched and looked away from Ruth. She scowled at him.

"Let's go," Robert snapped.

Ruth looked past him. Jess was almost at the boat, watching the others. They were intent on preparing it.

"Jess!" she yelled. "Jess! Over here!"

Jess pushed her hair away from her face, still looking out to sea.

"Shout all you want, Ruth," Robert said. "They won't hear you."

He was right. The wind was pushing inland, taking her voice with it. *Jess, turn around*, she thought.

Jess didn't move.

"Come on then," snapped Robert. "Before they come back for her."

The men tightened their grip on her wrists and dragged her round the back of the beach hut. She dug her feet in, but the sand gave no traction.

"No use struggling," said Robert. "Save your energy."

She yanked her arm back, trying to pull it out of Dave's grip. He muttered under his breath but held firm.

She felt Robert's hand on her shoulder.

She stiffened. "Don't touch me."

He pushed her in the back. "Co-operate, and things will be a lot easier for you."

She felt her feet leave the ground as the two men hauled her up into the dunes. Her legs flailed.

"Put me down!" she screamed. Her foot hit something. Her second captor grimaced; she'd caught his leg.

She smiled.

She kicked out again, this time in both directions, sideways. Both men tightened their jaws.

Something hit her leg. Her calf exploded in pain.

"What the—?" she gasped.

Robert rounded the younger men to face her. He held his knife between them. "Just a scratch. But I'd start behaving if I were you."

She spat at him. He shook his head. "Missed."

"Let me go, you bastard! Whatever sick idea you've got about Ben, I don't care. Just let me go!"

He sighed. "You'll find out. Now, move!"

The men picked up pace, dragging her across the rutted field beyond the dunes. She felt blood trickle down her leg. She tried to push the pain away but it was too much, too sharp.

She closed her eyes and focused on drawing all her strength inside of her. She'd need it if she was ever going to escape.

JESS TURNED to look at Ruth's hut. The door was closed, the window next to it glinting in the low sun.

She pushed her shoulders back and walked to it. Her legs felt heavy and her head ached. The sooner this was over, the better. For everyone's sake. But she couldn't go home without Sarah. And she hardly dared return to the farm without her, for fear of Ted's reaction.

First things first. Sanjeev hadn't left yet. It wasn't too late for Ruth to join him. She could tell Jess about the layout of the farm. That would be enough.

Yes. Get Ruth to safety, then worry about the others.

She knocked on the door of the hut and opened it without waiting.

"Ruth?"

She ran back outside, her heart hammering in her chest.

"Ruth!"

She searched the beach. Zack, Toni and Sanjeev were at the boat. They couldn't hear her.

"Ruth! Ruth where are you?"

It was no good. She had gone.

81

"Get in there!"

Robert pushed Ruth into the room. She knew this room; she'd cleaned it. It was at the rear of the house, overlooking the yard. It was the largest of the rooms, the only one with a double bed. When she'd cleaned it two days ago, Bill had been watching her. She'd searched it as best she could, looking for keys, a map, a weapon. Any clue to Robert and Ben's history together.

But the room had been all but bare. The only furniture was the high, old-fashioned bed, a simple chair and a low wooden wardrobe. Inside it were three pairs of jeans and five white shirts. All clean, all hanging neatly.

She walked inside, keeping her face impassive and her stance calm. Her gaze slid over the bed and the chair next to it, to the window. Thin blue curtains hung at it, faded and torn. She crossed to it and reached for the handle.

"It's locked."

She turned. "Worth a try."

"Don't bother."

She folded her arms across her chest. "It doesn't matter

how long you keep me here. Eventually, I'll get the better of you."

"You're a fool, Ruth Dyer. Or maybe I should call you by another surname?"

"Dyer will do."

"Ruth Cope. That has a ring to it."

"Never."

He followed her to the window. She ducked past him, heading for the door.

"It's locked."

She turned. "It won't always be."

He advanced on her. Once again, she shifted past him, heading for the bed this time. She cursed herself; this was the wrong place to be trapped.

He stood with his back to the door, eyeing her. He looked dirty and dishevelled. His brown jacket had a rip in the shoulder and his white shirt was grass-stained. She wondered who washed his clothes. Whether she could concoct some sort of topical poison, offer to wash them for him.

"Do you like your new room?" he asked.

"It's your room," she replied.

"Very observant of you." A pause. "It's yours now, too. I had them make it ready for you. I've even added flowers."

He gestured towards the cast iron fireplace. On the mantelpiece was a cracked jug holding a spray of corn-flowers.

Ruth walked over to it. She pulled the flowers from the jug and let them fall to the floor. She kicked them into the empty grate.

"I didn't ask for flowers. Take me back to my cell."

"Really? You want to go back to that fetid bucket? There's a bathroom through there. Our own."

She followed his gaze to a half-open door. She hadn't been in there before. She said nothing; she'd search in there later, for a means of escape. A pipe pulled away from the wall might make a weapon.

She turned to him. Her hands were shaking; she clenched her fists to still them. "I'm not staying here, with you."

He approached her. He smelled of the sea; salt and sand, mixed with the aftershave she'd smelled on him before. *Where does he get this stuff?*

He reached for her face. "You'll come round. I'm a catch."

She pulled back. "You repulse me."

His hand stilled. Then it moved quickly as he slapped her cheek. She threw her own hand up to it, eyes wide.

"I'll get out," she said, struggling to keep her voice even. "I've done it before and I'll do it again."

He jabbed a finger into her chest. "Forget it, Ruth. Make the best of it. You're better off here, with me. Not with Ben."

"I know why you did this."

He stepped back. "Really?"

"You and Ben. I know."

"Your sister-in-law told you, then?"

She said nothing.

"Well, in that case, you know you're better off." He turned to the door. "Get changed. There's a nightdress under the pillow. I'll see you later."

He strode to the door and yanked it open. He looked back at her and then closed it behind him. She ran to it but it was locked.

She stared at it. *What now?*

82

The farmyard was too quiet.

Jess looked up at the farmhouse, its blank upstairs windows reflecting the moonlight. It looked so normal, as if the events of the last week had never happened.

Ruth, where are you?

She looked over her shoulder. Behind her, Toni and Zack followed in silence. Zack flashed her a supportive smile.

She heard a scratching noise. In a ramshackle kennel under the house's back windows, a dog was curled up. She put a hand up to warn the others, then motioned towards the dog. It was asleep.

"What do we do?" she whispered. "Can we drug it? Knock it out?"

Zack put a hand on her shoulder. "It's injured. Look."

She shielded her eyes from the moonlight, and focused on the dark shape. Zack was right; its paw was bandaged.

"Still," she whispered. "We don't know..."

"Look at the kennel. The wood."

She edged forwards, daring to approach the dog. The base of the kennel was dark with blood.

"And there's a chain," Zack whispered. "It's not going anywhere."

"OK," she conceded. "But we need to be quiet."

"Where is everybody?" he whispered.

She stopped. She was level with the door to the outhouse now, Toni and Zack next to her.

She took a few deep breaths, her heart thumping. They were level with an outhouse behind the main building. The stench of human waste filled the air. Jess held her breath as they passed, her eyes watering.

Ruth had mentioned an outhouse. Ted and Harry, in the next cell. This had to be it.

RUTH LOOKED AROUND THE ROOM. There had to be something in here, something she could use.

She hurried to the bed and fell to the floor, searching under it. She lifted the bedspread. The floor was bare.

She jumped up to examine the walls. There were pale patches where pictures had once hung. Darker, less even patches where damp had done its worst. She pressed herself against the wall, fingers feeling for sunken nails, fixings that might once have held those pictures.

She made her way quickly but quietly around the room, glancing at the door from time to time. There was nothing. She looked at the jug, back on the mantelpiece now.

Yes.

She grabbed it then hurried to the bathroom. It had white tiled walls and a large bathtub, stained with years of use. The toilet had a high cistern and long chain, and the sink was large and solid.

She closed the door behind her. She had to do this quietly. He'd probably left someone outside the door.

She ran back into the bedroom and pushed her hand under the pillow. She searched for the nightdress but found nothing. Her stomach lurched at the thought of Robert climbing into bed with her; her dressed in a nightgown and him naked.

She fought a wave of nausea and panic. *No. I'll die before I let him touch me.*

She leaned over and felt under the other pillow. Her hand hit something soft and lacy. She pulled it out, not caring that the pillow fell to the floor.

She dashed into the bathroom and closed the door. She picked up the jug and wrapped it in the nightdress.

She held it up in front of her. The toilet, or the sink?

She wrapped her hand around the jug, making sure that the layers of fabric were thick where her skin made contact. She brought it down on the sink's edge.

It made a thudding sound. She pushed out a trembling breath.

It hadn't broken.

Again. Harder this time.

She lifted it again and brought it down more heavily, squeezing her eyes shut.

Break, dammit.

She felt it loosen in her grip. She swallowed and opened the door. The bedroom was empty. She hurried to the outer door and placed her ear against it. She held her breath. She heard the creak of floorboards outside.

She crossed to the bed and unwrapped her parcel. The

jug had broken into three pieces. One had a sharp, jagged edge. Perfect.

She slipped it under the mattress. She looked at the remaining pieces. She slipped those under too. Then she shook out the nightdress and folded it. She placed it on the bed and put the pillow back on top.

She sat on the bed, her hands in her lap. The shards of pottery were directly beneath her.

Come and get me.

J ess picked a key, careful not to rattle any of the others on the key ring. She bent down to insert it into the lock and turned.

Nothing.

She pulled it back out. Behind her Toni shifted her weight.

She worked her way through the keys, making sure to take them in order. On the third attempt, the key turned.

"Yes," she hissed. Toni gave her a congratulatory thump on the shoulder. She pushed at the door, waiting for a scrape or a squeaking hinge. But it was quiet.

She looked back at Toni, unable to suppress a grin. Toni smiled back. Her breathing was coming fast and her cheeks were flushed.

Jess eased herself upright and crept forward, reaching out in the darkness. The only source of light was the open doorway behind her, and the obscured moonlight was barely enough to see by. But as her eyes adjusted she began to get a sense of her surroundings.

They were at one end of a narrow corridor, flanked on

one side by a row of four doors and on the other by the outside wall. The floor was concrete and the walls were pale in the dim moonlight that cast a blue haze through the solitary window in the outside wall. There were vague patches on the walls, damp interspersed with the jagged edges of peeling paint, and as her eyes adjusted further she spotted dry white flakes on the floor.

She looked at the doors. Ruth had described the layout: she had been behind the closest door, at Jess's elbow, then Ted and Harry in the next cell. That meant that Sally and Roisin must be behind the other two doors.

She looked at the first door. Cold ran down her back.

She put a hand to it and pushed, fumbling with the keys.

The door gave way. She almost fell through as it gaped open to reveal an empty cell.

She looked back at Toni. "Where's Ruth?"

"Maybe in one of the other cells."

This made no sense. They were all occupied. She pushed her worry to one side and gestured along the corridor; they would start with the farthest door and work backwards.

They crept to the last door. Jess pushed it; it didn't budge. She gave it a quiet knock then put an ear to the wood. Could she hear breathing?

She moved her mouth to the door and spoke through it.

"Hello? It's Jess. Who's in there?"

The door shuddered with the weight of someone landing against it on the other side. Jess held her breath, waiting.

"Jess? Jess from the village?"

"Yes. Who's that?"

"Sally Angus."

Jess felt Toni's body slacken beside her. She leaned into the door.

"Hi Sally," she said. "Give me a minute and I'll let you out."

Toni had moved along the corridor and was in front of the second door, her mouth against the wood. Jess could hear a voice from inside. Toni turned to Jess.

"It's Roisin! We have to let her out."

"Sally first. Keep talking to Roisin."

Toni pushed a clenched fist against the door. "Are you alright?"

Roisin said something Jess couldn't make out. She focused on Sally's door, working her way through the keys again. Inside, Sally was silent.

Toni grabbed her arm, almost making her lose her balance. "Roisin's hurt. We have to get her out."

"Shhh. Please. I've almost got this one. Roisin's next."

"No."

Jess peeled her eyes away from the lock and stared at Toni. *This isn't like you*, she thought.

"Toni, please. Let me do this."

"Roisin's younger. She's hurt. Let her out." A pause. "Please."

Jess clenched her teeth. She almost had Sally now, but maybe if Roisin was injured…

"OK."

She pushed past Toni to stand next to Roisin's door. Toni mouthed a *thank you* but Jess just glared at her. All of the captives were important. Then she caught herself, realising she'd prioritised Ruth. *Ruth, where are you?*

"Let me out, please," wailed Roisin.

Jess bent to the lock, willing herself to focus. The key she had used for the outside door was still pinched between her thumb and forefinger, so she knew which one not to use. She crouched down and looked at the lock: it was similar to the one she'd already opened. That helped.

The second key she tried slid in and turned, the door shuddering on its hinges as she pushed it open.

84

R uth stared at the door, counting in her head. He'd been gone fifteen minutes.

It felt like hours.

She reached under the mattress and fumbled for the shards of crockery. They were still there.

Stop it, she told herself. She didn't need to cut herself on them while she waited.

She stared back at the door. Her skin itched. *Where are you?*

She reached down and grabbed one of the shards, the jagged one. She shoved it into the waistband of her trousers. She was still in the tracksuit bottoms she'd worn for bed, what, four, five days ago?

She went to the window, keeping her footsteps light. It was night now, the moon bright over the yard. She thought of the haze of light that had filtered into her cell, the mesh beyond the window. Then she thought of Roisin and Sally, still out there. Of Harry and Ted.

She peered out of the window. It was misted and blurred. She raised a sleeve to wipe it, and pressed her forehead to the glass. Clouds passed in front of the moon, plunging the yard into gloom. She held her breath, squinting at the outhouse. Could she get the other women out? When would Jess and the others come back for them? Would the men intercept them?

She spotted movement; the door to the outhouse, opening. She held her breath. Robert or one of his men, checking on their prisoners?

The door opened and she saw the silhouette of a man. He was heavily built but otherwise impossible to make out in the dark. It wasn't Robert.

The clouds shifted, brightening the yard. She could see another person now, inside the outhouse, through the solitary window on this side.

She stifled a shout. It was Jess. Her profile was illuminated by the moon. Ruth put a hand to the window just as Jess disappeared.

The door behind her rattled. She turned. She felt for the shard in her waistband but it had fallen. *Please be caught in my trousers and not on the floor.*

The door opened. Robert pushed inside, smiling at her. "Missed me?"

She yanked the curtains closed, her heart hammering at her ribs.

His face fell. "What is it? What were you looking at?

85

The first thing that hit Jess was the smell: the dull scent of an unwashed human being in a confined space, mixed with the sharp tang of urine. Under it was a heavier, metallic scent – blood?

Roisin sat hunched against the wall, her face streaked with dirt and her thick brown hair matted. The thin sweater she wore was torn, the sleeve almost hanging off, and her grey skirt had an unmistakeable bloom of stale brown blood on its front.

Jess looked into Roisin's face, her mind creased with worry. What had they done to this girl?

Toni stumbled into the room, falling on Roisin. "What have they done to you?"

Roisin gave her a weak smile. "I'll be OK."

Jess reached out a hand. "Come quickly." The girl came easily, her frailness nothing against Jess's strength.

She clutched Roisin's arm as they fell into the corridor. "You're not the only one imprisoned here," she explained gently. "We need to get the others out too. Then we'll get you all away from here."

The girl stared back at her, unblinking. Toni put an arm around her and Roisin huddled into her, trembling.

Jess turned back to the other cell, wondering what was going through Sally's mind. She tried the key that had opened Roisin's door. It worked.

Sally was behind the door and fell out as soon as Jess pulled it open. She looked in a better state that Roisin. Her face was dirty and there was a thin cut on her cheek that was starting to yellow, but there was no blood.

Jess gave her a nervous smile. "You OK?"

Sally blinked and nodded. "Is Mark here?"

Jess frowned. *Mark?*

"My fiancée."

Jess remembered Mark Palfrey, pestering her to bring him along with them. After Toni's outburst on seeing Roisin, she was grateful she hadn't listened.

"He's back at the village. Waiting for you. He sent his love."

Sally's face broke into a smile. She was pale and blonde, and suddenly pretty when she smiled.

Next to them, Toni was muttering into Roisin's ear.

"We need to get a move on," Jess said. "Just one more door."

She felt a knot form in her stomach as she approached the third door. She pulled out the key again.

"Harry? Ted? You in there?"

There was relieved laughter inside. "Yes. Who's that?"

"Jess Dyer. I'm with some of the others. We've come to get you out."

She slid the key in the lock.

"Jess Dyer?" said another voice, its tone sharp. "Where's my girl?"

She took a deep breath, the key motionless in her hand.

She couldn't tell him the truth. "She's OK. She got out already. I left her on the beach, in a hut, to wait for us. She's OK."

She closed her eyes as she turned the key and pushed the door open, hoping the lie wouldn't show on her face. Inside, Ted and Harry were both kneeling behind the door. Harry looked tired and pale while Ted had a pinched, angry look to him.

"Those bastards took my girl," he snapped. "Thank you for getting her back for me."

She shrugged, unable to meet his eye.

"Come on, quick," she said. She looked at Roisin, who was deathly pale. "We need to get back to the beach."

86

"It's dark," she said. "I closed the curtains." She swallowed. "I thought you might like some privacy."

She stepped between him and the window, grabbing his hand. He looked down at it then into her face. She held his gaze, despite every bone in her body aching to run.

"Really?" he said.

She shrugged. "It makes the room nicer. Cosy."

He smiled. "I agree."

He tugged on her hand. She glanced back at the window then followed him. *Not the bed. Not the bed.*

He pulled her to the bed. As they reached it, he turned and flicked his wrist, sending her falling onto it.

She threw her hands out behind her and landed in a seated position. She sprang up. "Not yet. I want to talk to you."

"About Ben."

"About you. How did you find this place? How did you find *us*?"

He cocked his head. "Interested, now?"

She nodded.

He sat on the bed. He patted the space next to him. She stayed where she was, standing in front of him. The height of the bed brought his eyes almost level with hers.

She could hear her breath, short and heavy. She resisted an ache to look at the door. Had he locked it?

"Tell me," she said. "Please."

He patted the bed again. "Sit down."

"I'm fine here."

His face darkened. "I said, sit down."

She thought of Jess and the others. With luck, they would be here soon. She had to stall him.

She sat on the bed, a foot away from him.

"Closer." He grabbed her arm, digging his fingers into her flesh. He pulled her next to him. Their thighs were touching now. He smelt of whisky. She swallowed the bile rising in her throat.

"How did you get here? After the floods?" she whispered. She shuffled, releasing the contact.

He stood up, turned to face her and bent over her in one fluid motion. He cupped her face in his hands. She pulled back but he held tight.

"Stop fighting me, woman!"

"I'm not fighting you. I just need time. Talk to me. Please."

He tugged at her face, bringing it closer to his. She tried not to blink.

He frowned. "What is it?"

"What?"

"You looked at the window. What's out there?"

"Nothing. I was just checking."

"Checking what?"

"The curtains. Privacy."

"Privacy? For talking?"

She shrugged.

"OK," he said. He sat back on the bed, the mattress sinking under his weight. He was pressed up against her. She held his stare, her leg against his feeling like it was being bathed in acid.

He leaned in. His breath was sharp, his aftershave heavy. "Prove it, Ruth," he said. "Prove you're not lying to me."

"How?" she breathed.

"Kiss me."

She felt her stomach hollow out. "What?"

"I'm prepared to give you time. I know you're not a whore. Just one kiss."

She pulled back. He held her firm. She glanced at the door, then the window.

He let go of her, sending her falling backwards. He stood and crossed to the window.

"There's someone out there, isn't there?" He pulled the curtains, tearing one of the panels. "Is it your beloved husband?"

"There's no one there. Come back. I'll kiss you."

He leaned into the window. "Fucking bitch!"

He darted to the door and banged on it. "Let me out!"

The door opened. He stormed through, muttering at the man outside to follow him.

Ruth dashed to the window. Jess was in the doorway to the outhouse, Zack its other end. She looked back at the bedroom door. It was hanging open.

87

The corridor was crowded now. Toni was all but carrying Roisin, Ted and Harry were like coiled bags of energy and Sally shuffled behind them all. Jess pushed past them all to the open door. She peered round it into the farmyard.

There was no sign of Zack.

She looked at the farmhouse. The back door was closed.

Harry put a hand on her arm. "Everything alright?"

She shrugged her shoulders. *Where is he?*

A shout rent the air, coming from the farmhouse. Her heart raced.

Harry tightened his grip on her arm, keeping her from bounding across the farmyard. "Look," he said, his breath rising.

Jess looked up to see Robert standing in a window, staring at them.

"Shit," she breathed.

He leaned on the glass then pulled back, disappearing.

She looked at Harry. "We have to find Ruth."

She looked back at the window. There was a new face at it. Ruth.

88

Ruth raced for the door then stopped, listening. Had there been two of them outside?

She had to risk it.

She pulled in a deep breath then stepped out. There was no one there.

There might still be men in the other rooms; she had to take care. This room was along a corridor that ran at right angles to the main hallway. She was as far from the stairs as she could be.

But she knew her way.

She crept along the corridor, holding her breath to hear. There was a door ahead, open. It led to a bedroom where she'd seen two men the day before. They'd been sitting on a dirty mattress, playing gin rummy. They'd looked surprised to see her. Bill had pulled her away, telling them to get downstairs.

If they were in there now, they might think she was up here cleaning again.

She pulled away from the wall and walked down the corridor as casually as she could, her eyes ahead. As she passed the open doorway, she fought the temptation to look inside. She held her stride, strolling past as if everything was normal.

No sound came from within.

When she was out of sight of the door she allowed herself a brief rest, slumping against the wall. She was sweating.

Next, a corner.

She approached it as calmly as she could, once again pretending she was up here doing chores. Eventually she would meet one of the men, and she had no idea how many of them knew she'd been imprisoned in Robert's room.

As she approached the corner, she heard a noise behind her. Voices.

She froze. She cast around, looking for a place to hide.

The room she'd just passed, the bedroom. It was empty, she was sure of it.

She darted back and ducked inside, pushing the door closed. She turned, half expecting to see a roomful of men staring at her.

There was no one. She leaned on the door, her chest rising and falling. Her heart beat so loud she was sure Jess would hear it out in the farmyard.

She heard footsteps outside, and the sound of two men in conversation. She pressed her ear against the door.

"Dave got any of that homebrew left?"

"You don't want that. It stinks."

"Better than nothing."

"Not as good as Robert's stash."

"As if I'd ever get any of that."

"Work harder, mate. Then you'll get some."

"Yeah, right."

The voices receded.

Ruth counted to ten then pulled the door open. She peered out. The corridor was empty. Hoping they hadn't stopped beyond the corner, she headed back towards the stairs. She had to be quick, to get to Jess.

She arrived at the corner. There were no sounds ahead, but she knew that an open door was immediately around it.

She had to take the risk.

She pushed her shoulders back and strode around the corner, trying to look confident. She reached the door. It was open. Voices came from inside. As she passed, they stopped.

"Aren't you supposed to be with Robert?"

She turned and smiled. "I'm going down to cook dinner. Any of you boys fancy stew?"

"Too right." One of the men stood up and placed his hands on his hips. He was bare-chested, wearing nothing but a pair of stained jeans that were at least two sizes too large.

"Yeah Joe, you need some meat on you," said one of his companions. Joe turned and swiped at the other man, who laughed.

Ruth feigned a laugh then carried on walking.

"Does he know you're on your own?"

She turned to see the man who'd insulted Joe leaning out of the door.

She smiled. "Of course. He's waiting for me, in the kitchen."

"Lucky bastard." The man pulled his head back inside.

She allowed herself to breathe again. *No time to stop.* She all but ran for the stairs, pulling herself around the banister at the top and clattering down. The front door was immediately ahead. Robert had brought her in that way; maybe it would still be unlocked.

The hall was empty. Thankfully, the light was off. She sped down the stairs, staring at the door.

As she reached the bottom, it opened. She stopped, almost falling.

She pulled back. Could she get upstairs in time?

A face appeared around the door.

Ruth stepped forward. "Sarah?"

89

Jess stared up at the empty window. She couldn't be sure if Ruth had seen her.

Where's Zack?

She looked at the door to the farmhouse. Robert had spotted them; he would be in there, waiting.

Should they go in and get Ruth, or wait out here? He would be unable to resist the urge to come out and confront her.

She stepped forwards, eyeing the door. Was it locked?

"Jess!"

She turned to see Toni behind her. Roisin leaned against her, breathing heavily.

"We need to get out of here. Roisin's in a bad way."

"We can't." Jess pointed up at the empty window. "Ruth's in there."

Roisin moaned and Toni staggered under her weight. Zack appeared from the side of the outhouse. He rushed to Roisin and took her from Toni, gathering her in his arms.

Jess approached them. Roisin wasn't the only one who looked bad. Both Ted and Harry were pale, with deep circles under their eyes, and Sally's skin had whitened in the moonlight.

"What happened to you?" she asked Zack.

"I wanted to check for more outbuildings. For Ruth."

"She's in there. Upstairs."

Toni grabbed Jess's arm, pulling her down. She put a hand on Roisin's cheek. She was cold and her eyes were closed, dark lashes brushing her cheeks as if asleep.

Jess lowered her face to Roisin's, to check if she was still breathing. Toni held her breath.

Jess exhaled and relaxed. The warmth of Roisin's breath, though feeble, brushed her cheek.

"She's OK," she told Toni, who was pale herself.

She pulled back to let Toni stroke Roisin's face with her fingertips.

"Roisin? Wake up, sweetie."

"She going to be alright?" Zack muttered.

"Her skirt," she whispered. "It's soaked in blood. She needs Ruth." She looked towards the door.

Toni stood up. "She can't stay here. I'll take her back to the beach. Sally too. We'll wait for the boat. And there's food we left in those huts. Look at her: she needs it."

"OK," said Jess. She looked at Roisin and Sally again. "Take them. Go back to the beach. I'll go after Ruth."

"Not on your own," said Zack.

He was right. "Harry, can you help Toni get Roisin to the boat?"

Harry nodded.

"Where's Sarah?"

Jess sighed. She'd been waiting for this. She turned to Ted. "I'm so sorry, Ted. She ran off."

"She did what?"

"We found her. She'd already got away. But then she got scared. The last time I saw her was at the beach hut."

"I was right about you. Fucking awful steward. You lied to me."

"I know. I'm sorry, Ted. We will find her."

She looked at the farmhouse. "It's dark. She hurt her foot – nothing serious – so she won't have got far. Let me get Ruth, then I'll help you find Sarah."

90

Bill had Martin's hands tied behind his back with twine. He pushed him across the dark field. Martin, in turn, pushed Sarah. He whispered in her ear.

"Run."

"No. My foot, remember?"

"Shut up," muttered Bill. He jabbed a thumb into Martin's back.

When they arrived at the farmhouse door, Sarah stopped and Martin barrelled into her.

"Wait," said Bill.

He pushed past, not letting go of Martin.

"Don't move, you little bugger. Got me into no end of trouble, you did."

Martin looked at Sarah. It was his fault that they'd been found. He'd spotted her running from the beach hut and disappearing into the dunes. He'd followed, calling her name. She'd heard him; she'd turned towards him. But Bill had heard him too. And in his surprise at seeing Sarah limping towards him, Martin had dropped his guard, allowing Bill and Leroy to grab him.

And now she was about to be thrown back into that cell. He'd probably be in the one next to her. Or worse.

Bill pushed the door open. "Ladies first."

Sarah narrowed her eyes at him. She looked at Martin. He shrugged.

"Go on," urged Bill. "We haven't got all day."

She stepped into the farmhouse. Then she stopped.

"Ruth!"

Bill stumbled into Martin, pushing him through the door. "What?"

Ruth was standing on the stairs, looking down at Sarah. Sarah's cheeks had regained some colour and she was smiling up at the other woman.

"Is Jess with you?"

Ruth looked past Sarah, at Bill. "No. Just me."

"How?" asked Martin.

"How d'you think?"

The door to the kitchen opened. It was Robert.

He beamed up at Ruth.

"Ruth, my love. Why are you out of our room?"

Martin stared up at Ruth, confused.

"Let her go," Ruth said. "Let her go and I'll do what you want."

Robert's eyes danced. "Not quite yet. We have quite a party going on here. Come into the kitchen."

He glanced at Martin then turned to Bill. "And don't let that little shit out of your sight."

91

Jess looked at the farmhouse door. Zack stood next to her, his face impassive.

What now?" he asked.

"She's in there. So's he."

"We go in then?"

She scanned the back of the house. The rooms were in darkness except one two windows away from where she'd seen Ruth. That one had curtains drawn but a dim light on inside.

Where was Ruth? Would Robert be behind that door, waiting for them?

"He expects us to come in that way," she said. "Maybe we should go round the front."

"Right." Zack started moving towards the side of the house, where Ruth had jumped earlier.

"That's it," breathed Jess. "The window. Maybe she'll..."

She was disturbed by movement around the other side of the house, where Toni and the others had gone.

"Zack!" she whispered. "Wait."

A shadow crossed the yard; a tall, thin man's shape

outlined by the moonlight. He was pushing a bike. She pulled back, her mouth falling open.

She crouched down low, sensing Zack do the same.

The figure moved towards the house, then leaned the bike against its back wall and paused at the door. He placed a hand on the door, paused a few seconds, then opened it. Suddenly the door was illuminated, the man's outline caught in its yellow glow.

She squinted, not trusting her eyes. She looked back at Zack.

"What's he doing here?" she whispered.

uth eyed the door. Could she escape, alert Jess? Should she leave Sarah alone with Robert?

Robert looked up at her, understanding crossing his face. He stepped forwards and grabbed Sarah by the arm. In one swift movement, he had his knife in front of her face.

Ruth closed her eyes.

"In the kitchen. Now," Robert said. Ruth opened her eyes to find him looking at her. She nodded and descended the stairs. Her legs felt weak and her head hollow.

"Sit at the table," he said. She slipped past him and took a seat. She placed her hands on the table. Her fingers trembled.

Robert watched her from the doorway, framed by the kitchen door. He flicked a switch and the kitchen was bathed in yellow light. His face was red and beaded with sweat. It was the first time she'd seen him look anything other than immaculate.

In front of him, her eyes wide and the knife to her throat, was Sarah.

Ruth reached out towards Sarah. Her cheeks were ashen and her clothes even dirtier than before, with fresh tears in the fabric of her blouse.

Nobody spoke. All Ruth could hear was her own laboured breathing and the shuffling of Sarah's feet against the tiles as she struggled to gain her footing. Robert had lifted her in the air, and the tips of her shoes danced across the floor.

Finally Robert broke the silence. "So, here we are."

Ruth willed herself to meet his gaze, her stomach churning. She pushed her chair back and began to rise.

Robert yanked Sarah's head back, his fingers entwined in her knotted hair.

"Sit down," he snapped. Sarah stared at her, eyes pleading.

Beyond her, she saw Martin shuffle closer. Robert's gaze slid to him.

"And you can stay right where you are."

Martin hardened his jaw but stopped moving

Coward.

"Where did you find them?" Ruth asked. She thought of Jess in the outhouse. *Please don't come in here.*

He chuckled. "She was along the beach. Hiding in a ditch. He was running after her, like the pathetic runt he is."

Ruth looked from Martin to Sarah and back again.

"Did Martin bring you back here?" she asked.

Sarah gave a tiny shake of her head. "No."

Ruth pursed her lips and placed a steadying hand on the table. She took a few deep breaths.

"You too," Robert said, looking at Martin. "Get in here. Sit down."

Bill pushed Martin into the room. He shoved him at the table. Martin stumbled then sat heavily down next to Ruth.

Bill tugged at the twine, bringing Martin's hands up above his head.

"The prodigal son returns," said Robert, looking at Martin. Martin ignored him, focussing on Sarah. She closed her eyes.

Robert waved his hands around the room expansively. "Well this is nice, isn't it? All of us back home together."

Martin made a lunge for Robert but was jolted back by Bill, who grunted.

"Bad boy," said Robert. "You behave yourself."

Martin spat in his direction. Robert laughed. "You missed! So..." He looked back at Ruth. "Seeing as you're back for good now, I think it's time you knew a few home truths about your beloved Mr Ben Dyer."

Ruth felt her heart pick up pace.

Robert pushed Sarah onto the chair opposite her.

"Stay there," he breathed into her face. She squeezed her eyes shut.

He stood behind Sarah, the knife still in his hand, so that he was facing Ruth across the table.

"I imagine you'll want to know what your husband did to me."

"Are you talking about me?"

Ruth shot her head towards the back door as the light flicked on.

There, looming in the doorway, was Ben.

93

Jess stared at the silhouetted figure in the farmhouse door. Tall and thin, with scruffy hair. Stooping as he ascended the steps into the house. It was Ben.

Zack was motionless next to her. "What the hell?"

She screwed up her face, holding in her anger. She scanned the farmyard, wondering if he was alone. She looked at the bike, leaning against the farmhouse. Had he cycled here? Whose bike was that?

"Typical bloody Ben," she muttered.

"Huh?" replied Zack.

"I told him not to come but here he is. He never trusts me."

Zack frowned. "I don't think it's like—"

"I've known Ben all my life and this is just the sort of stunt he'd pull. He's going to fuck this up for us. Big time."

"Jess. Go easy on him. He just wants to get Ruth back."

She turned to him. "I love Ruth. Yes, I was pissed off when all of a sudden she had to leave London with us, but she's Ruth, and it wasn't her fault. I came here to get her back, and I don't need Ben butting in."

Zack reddened. "I don't think you're being fair on him."

"Will you two shut up? Someone's going to hear you!"

They turned to see Ted marching back round the side of the house, his face dark.

94

Ruth stared at Ben. Across the table Robert tightened his grip on Sarah and pulled the knife to her face. She stared at it through lowered lashes, her chest rising and falling.

Ben looked from Robert to Ruth. "Ruth?" he whispered. "How are you? What have they..."

He turned back to Robert. "You took my wife, you bastard."

Ruth blinked. "The boys, Ben? Where are the boys?"

"Well done, super sleuth," said Robert. "She's mine now."

"Yours?" cried Ben. "She's not yours and she never will be."

"You haven't answered my question," Ruth said quietly. "About the boys."

Ben looked back at his wife, and stepped towards her.

"Stop!" shouted Robert. "No one moves!"

He twisted his wrist and a spot of blood appeared at the tip of the blade, on Sarah's cheek. She gasped.

"Leave her alone!" shouted Martin. "This isn't about Sarah."

"Shut up, boy," Robert sneered. "You should have had her when you had the chance. You owe me, so just keep your mouth shut and remember where your loyalties lie."

"I don't care about any fucking loyalties! I love her!"

Sarah's eyes widened.

"Oh yes! This is priceless. Don't be so stupid, Martin. You just want to shag her." Robert lifted the knife from Sarah's face and brushed it through her hair. "If it weren't for the lovely Ruth here I'd be tempted myself."

Ben stepped towards Ruth. "If you've touched her—"

"Oh, don't worry, Dyer. I've far too much respect for her." He paused. "You have no idea what you did to me, do you?"

Ruth could hear Ben's breathing, his voice rising in pitch.

"I did nothing and well you know it."

"I went to prison because of you."

"You went to prison because you stabbed that man. And all for a poxy cash tin."

"You're still sticking to that story? Look at her, Ben. Tell your woman the truth."

Ruth looked at Ben. "Tell me, Ben. What did you do to him that was so awful he's prepared to do this?"

95

FIFTEEN YEARS EARLIER

Ben's eyes widened as he took in what Robert had said. He looked back at the building: surely it would have a state of the art alarm, even a security guard. Sure, this wasn't the most glamorous of industrial estates, but businesses protected their property. Didn't they?

"Steal?" he breathed.

"Scared, are you?" mocked Robert.

"But what if there's a guard? An alarm?"

Robert's smile grew. "Don't be stupid, dumbass." He gave Ben a gentle slap on the back of the head. Ben winced but smiled, knowing this was the expected response.

Robert looked back at the building, his eyes narrow. "I've been watching it. There's one man in there this time of day. All the others have headed home now, see?" He gave Ben a patronising smile and Ben nodded again. "He comes out at 4pm, doesn't want to get home early to his adorable wife and kids. Can't blame him. But this is the best bit."

Robert lowered his head towards Ben so that their foreheads were touching. Ben could hear the two boys' breath mingling in the confined space behind the hedge.

Robert gave him another slap. "He comes out with a cashbox. Bold as brass, the twat. Carries it under his arm."

"Has it got cash in it?" Ben whispered.

"*Has it got cash in it?* Yes, of course it's got damn cash in it. It's a cash box." Another slap. "And we're going to take it from him. When he comes out we'll run up and grab it."

"But it can't be as simple as that, can it? To rob someone?"

"Let's see, shall we?" Robert nodded towards the building. Sure enough, a stocky man was emerging, his buttoned-up suit straining against his gut. Under his arm was a large red cash box, its colour echoing the sign on the roof.

Ben scanned the roads. Two cars sat outside nearby units, but there was no sign of life. "What about those cars?" he asked. "What if someone comes out?"

Robert grabbed his arm, pinching the skin under his blazer. "Don't be dumb," he said. "I've been doing my research. Casing the joint. They won't come out for ages."

Ben swallowed.

"Time to go, coward. Now!" Robert hissed. He tightened his grip on Ben's arm and heaved him up to standing. He pulled him through a gap in the hedge and dragged him across the concrete towards the man.

Ben stumbled on a broken patch of road. Robert scrabbled to keep hold of his blazer but Ben fell backwards, landing on his back. He felt a jolt through his head as it slammed into the concrete.

He closed his eyes. Behind his eyelids, the world was orangey-red, like a sunset. He could hear ringing in his ears and feel the hard scratch of gravel on his neck. When he opened his eyes there was nothing except a bright patch of blue sky above him.

There was a shout in the distance. "Hurry up, dumbass!"

He eased himself upwards, fighting nausea. He managed to prop up on his elbows and, blinking, saw Robert running away from him, towards the man. The man had stopped. Ben could hear shouting but couldn't make out the words.

The world went quiet. He let his head fall back. Above him was the sky again, flanked by the low branches of a tree. Somewhere, a bird sang. At least his ears still worked.

He rolled onto his front and pushed himself up, rubbing at the back of his neck. He turned to face the spot where he'd last seen Robert, and the man beyond him. He blinked, struggling to focus in the sunlight.

Across the concrete space, nearly at the door of the unit, two figures merged together, struggling. Someone was shouting but he couldn't tell who.

He had to stop this.

He clenched his fists and ran, pumping his arms as he flew across the car park towards Robert.

As he neared them, the man's eyes flicked off Robert's face and onto him. He was short and fat, his hair bouncing as he tugged at the cashbox.

Ben saw Robert's hand go to his trouser pocket. He saw the flash of steel as he withdrew his knife.

"No!" he shouted.

He picked up pace. He barrelled into them, sending Robert hurtling into the man. Robert screamed and the man made a noise that sounded like a tyre being emptied.

Ben sprang back. He was panting and his hands were slick with sweat.

He bent over and prodded the man.

"Hello?" he muttered.

Robert turned to him. The knife came into Ben's view, sticking out of the man's chest.

Robert's face was red.

"You dumb fuck!" he screamed. "What have you done?"

"What? Nothing! I was trying to..."

"You killed him, you shit. You fucking killed him!"

96

R uth stared at Ben, her mind racing.

"It wasn't my fault," he said.

Robert laid the side of the blade on Sarah's cheek. He placed a finger on it, holding it in place. "I was just going to wave it at him. Get the cash. Then you bloody come and crash into us and push it into his chest. You killed him."

"I wasn't holding the knife."

Robert leaned over Sarah. His hair was slick with sweat and his cheeks glowed. "If it wasn't for you, he wouldn't have died. We'd have got that cash and been out of there. It was your fault and you know it."

"That's not what the police said."

"Police? Once you'd woven your tapestry of lies, they were eating out of your hand. My word against yours. Ben Dyer and his respectable family against me, and my fucked-up alcoholic mother. I didn't stand a chance."

Ruth eased her chair back. "Ben, is this true? Why didn't you tell me?"

Ben's eyes were wild. "Because it was in the past. I'd put it behind me."

"Is it true? Did you have a hand in killing the man? Did you lie about it?"

"Ruth, it wasn't my fault. It wasn't me who pulled the—"

"Watch it, Dyer," Robert admonished. "Don't lie to her. She's better than that."

Ruth shivered.

"Don't talk bollocks, Robert," said Ben. "I don't know how you found us, but—"

"Be quiet!" Robert thundered. "Just stop arguing with me! You lost the right to do that when you shopped me to the police."

Ruth looked at her husband. *Get rid of him, Ben*, she thought. *Sort it. Apologise, if you need to.*

Ben stiffened. "I didn't."

Robert pointed his blade at Ben. "Don't lie to me again."

Sarah's body relaxed as the blade left her skin. She looked across the table at Martin.

Ben shrugged. "There were other witnesses, remember? In the unit opposite. They saw what you did. They told the police."

"Liar," breathed Robert.

"Believe it or don't."

"I've spent years looking for you," hissed Robert. "Thinking about how I'd get you back. And now here we are. You, me, and Ruth. I found you, I tricked you and I took her."

Robert looked at Ruth, a smile playing on his lips. She flinched and looked at his shirt pocket. Could her ring still be in there?

Robert pointed the knife at her, waving it in the air. She

felt Ben stiffening in the doorway, heard his intake of breath. Robert looked back at Ben.

"She's my revenge, don't you see?" he said. "Taking her from you."

97

Jess turned to Ted. "You're supposed to be at the beach. Looking for Sarah."

"She's not there, and you know it. She's in that house somewhere."

"She ran off, at the beach. She won't have come back here."

She exchanged glances with Zack. He looked as worried as she felt.

"Please, Ted," she said. "Let us deal with this. Sarah is somewhere in the fields, if she's not at the beach."

"I don't believe a word you say, Jess. I'm going in there, and I'm going to get her."

She swallowed. "In that case, you'd better come with us. We're going around the front."

"What, with your brother charging into the kitchen like that?"

"We don't want to draw attention to ourselves."

"Bollocks. He'll fuck it up and so will you. I'm going after him."

"Ted, please—"

"Maybe he's right," said Zack. "We need to find out what Ben's up to."

She turned to him. "We need to do the exact opposite. He's drawn attention to himself. We use that as a diversion."

"Let's get moving then."

"Good. Ted, come with us."

She looked towards the farmhouse doorway. Ben was still standing there, gesticulating. Ted was looking at it too. *Don't go in there.*

Ben shifted, disappearing into the house. Beyond him, Jess could just make out a figure, sat at a table. Sarah – and someone else. Behind her, a figure she recognised.

Robert.

She felt the air move. She turned to see Ted spring from their hiding spot. He ran for the farmhouse door, his face contorted in rage.

98

Ben looked from Robert to Ruth, anger rising in his stomach.

"What did he do to you?" he whispered.

She shook her head. In the harsh overhead light her skin was sallow and her hair seemed to have thinned. Ben felt an urge to cry.

"Nothing," she whispered. "Not really." She didn't meet his gaze.

He turned back to Robert, who tightened his grip on Sarah.

"Leave her! This is nothing to do with her!" cried Martin.

Contempt darkened Robert's his face. "Please be quiet, you stupid boy." He drew the blade lightly across Sarah's forehead. A line of red formed, blood dripping into her eyes.

Ben looked at Ruth, more closely now. A bruise was blossoming on her temple. Her hands looked scarred, and there were scratches on her arms. Her T-shirt was torn.

"What did you do to her?"

"I haven't done anything, not yet. Not yet." He gestured upwards, towards the bedrooms.

Ruth tightened her jaw. She stared ahead, at Sarah. Ben wanted to cling to her and not let go, but there was a brittleness to her, like a *keep out* sign.

Robert looked around at them all. "Martin, it's not too late. Now you're back we can keep your girl here. Have her, if you want. If you don't mind sharing. I'm sure Bill won't mind…"

Ben looked at Martin, still tethered to Bill like a dog. Bill clenched his fists, while Martin stared at the floor.

"No," said Bill. "We're not all like you."

"But I let you have the pretty one," said Robert. "The one with the blonde curls."

"Sally. I know," replied Bill.

"What stopped you then?"

Bill stared at Robert, his upper lip trembling. "I'm not like you. The others aren't either. Why d'you think none of them are here?" He gestured towards the doorway. "They're all upstairs, keeping out of it."

Robert's eyes glittered. The blue was just as bright as it had been when they were at school. "Such a hypocrite."

"No," said Bill.

"Nor me!" shouted Martin, struggling against his bindings. "I never touched Sarah!"

Ben looked past Martin, to the kitchen counter. Behind him, next to the sink, was a block of knives. If he could just…

He was disturbed by a groan, and looked back at Ruth. She was hunched over the table now, her head in her hands. Her body shook.

Forgetting Sarah, he stumbled towards his wife and folded his arms around her shoulders, muttering into her ear. She stiffened and he loosened his embrace.

"Ruth," he whispered. "He can't hurt you now. Let's go home."

She shrugged her shoulders, pushing him away. He stared at the top of her head, confused.

"Sarah!"

He looked up to see a man rush through the door and hurl himself at Robert. He lunged for Robert's hands, trying to pull the knife from them. The blade slipped. Sarah screamed and clapped a hand to her eye.

"Leave my daughter alone, you bastard!" the man cried. *Ted?*

Sarah raised her head, blood seeping between her fingers. "Daddy?"

Martin stepped forwards. "Sarah!" he cried. She ignored him, her eyes on her father.

Robert and Ted were scrabbling at each other, Ted desperately trying to snatch the knife. There was a shout as they hit the wall and pulled themselves upright again.

Ben lunged forwards, trying to grab Robert, but he was out of reach. Robert pulled back, the knife dark in his hand. Sarah screeched something unintelligible.

Ted fell to the floor, blood darkening his chest.

99

M artin listened as Robert and Bill argued. As Bill's anger grew, his grip loosened on the twine holding Martin's wrists. He pulled a hand away to remonstrate with Robert, his finger jabbing at the air. The twine grew slack.

Martin pulled on it. Amazingly, Bill didn't pull back.

He looked at Sarah across the table. Dried blood lay on her cheek and her fingers were pushing at her forehead, smeared with blood. She pulled her hands away from her face and looked back at him. She smiled weakly and his heart skipped a beat.

Ruth was bent over the table, her head on her arms.

A man tumbled through the door, screaming Sarah's name. Robert cried out and the man fell on him.

Martin freed his hands and scanned the room, looking for a weapon. He pushed past Bill, reaching out for the knife block next to the sink. He plunged his hand between the handles and pulled one out at random, drawing it in front of his face.

A chef's knife. Perfect.

There was a scream behind him and he spun to find Robert standing over his attacker. His knife was raised in his hand, dark with blood. Sarah shot up from her chair and pushed past Robert, throwing her body over the man on the floor.

"Daddy!" she cried.

"I love you, Sarah," Martin whispered. Then he leapt over the table and hurled himself at Robert, keeping his own knife concealed.

Robert turned towards him. "You bloody idiot."

Momentum carried Martin over the blood-smeared table. His leading shoulder barrelled into Robert, sending him crashing against the wall. He brought his concealed hand forward to lunge with the knife.

"No," he replied, his voice steady. "Not anymore."

"Martin, stop!"

He craned his neck to see Sarah staring at him, her eyes wild. He leaned back, attempting to halt his momentum.

It was no good. He carried on going until he almost hit the wall, Robert's body stopping him in his tracks. The two of them were eye to eye.

He felt heat spreading on his chest and looked down. His arm was stuck, the knife still in his hand, plunged into Robert's neck.

100

J ess stared after Ted. Zack placed a hand on her shoulder.

"You want me to go?"

"No. I mean, yes. We both go."

She clutched his hand, holding it for a moment. She heard a shout from the farmhouse.

She dropped his hand, then ran.

She thundered through the door, grabbing at its frame to stop herself tripping over Ted, who lay on the floor. Zack ran in behind her, sending her crashing to the floor.

Her hands landed on Ted's arm. He groaned, a long, quivering sound that made her stomach turn. His jacket was warm and sticky. Next to her, Sarah was wailing and clutching at Ted.

"Help me, Jess," she pleaded. "My dad."

Jess put her hand on Ted's chest, prodding gently. The wound was to the side, beneath his armpit. Hopefully he would survive it.

"Jess!"

Ben was kneeling beside an ashen Ruth. He had his arm

around her shoulders and was rocking her. She was unresponsive, staring ahead.

Jess pushed herself up to see what Ruth was looking at. Martin and Robert were locked together, Robert sandwiched between Martin and the wall. Robert was making a spluttering sound. Martin's hands were on his neck and blood poured between his fingers.

"What the—?" she exclaimed.

Martin turned towards her, letting go of Robert who slumped to the ground. He grabbed the table to steady himself. His hands slid through the blood on its top as he eased round to Sarah.

"I'm so sorry, I'm so sorry," he cried, kneeling and pushing an arm around her shoulders. She didn't react, but bent over her father, her hands on his wound. She pushed against him with her fists, whimpering.

A faint smile lit up Ted's face. "I'm sorry, love," he whispered.

"Help me stop the blood someone, please!" Jess cried. Bill and Zack moved towards her, crashing into each other. Bill dropped to the floor next to Ted, putting a hand to his chest. He stood up and moved quickly to a drawer next to the sink. He pulled out some cloths and took them back to Ted. Sarah pulled away, giving him room to fashion a tourniquet.

Sarah watched, sobbing and wailing *Daddy* over and over.

Jess turned to Ruth. "Ruth, are you OK?"

Ruth lifted herself from the table and eased round to where Robert lay on the floor, edging past Sarah and Ted, close enough that Jess could hear her sister-in-law's breathing. Ben stood up and watched her.

Ruth stopped as she reached Robert. She looked back at Ben. "What you said about him... Was it true?" she asked.

Ben nodded.

"You lied to the police?"

Another nod. Ben closed his eyes briefly but then opened them again, meeting his wife's steady gaze.

"But it was him who pulled the knife?"

Ben closed his eyes. "The man died two months later. Robert went to prison."

She looked from him and then down at Robert, whose legs were spasming. Jess pinched her nose and took a deep breath.

"He was going to make me live with him," Ruth said. "Sleep with him. But instead he did this." She touched her face. Ben reached out a hand, but she shook it off.

"Bastard," she said, and drew up a foot. Everyone except Sarah stopped to watch her.

She clenched her teeth and pushed the foot down onto Robert's chest, twisting it as it made contact. Blood spluttered from his mouth onto her trousers but she didn't flinch.

She bent over, reaching her hand towards his chest. Jess drew back, her heart in her throat. Ruth pulled Robert's shirt pocket open and drew out a ring. She wiped it clean on her own grubby T-shirt and slid it onto her finger.

Jess looked at Ben: he was staring, holding his breath. His hand had gone to his own ring finger.

Robert's eyes widened. Ruth straightened up, her face expressionless. She twisted her foot again. His eyes rolled back and he stopped moving.

Jess put her hands to her mouth as Ben rose from his chair, the scrape of its legs on the floor breaking the silence. He reached out to Ruth. She looked into his face then shook her head. She sat at the table, shifting her chair away from him.

Ben's face crumpled. He stared at his wife then sank to the floor.

Jess took a deep breath. Above her head, she heard footsteps. Ice ran down her back.

"We need to get moving," she said. "Zack, can you lift Ted?"

"I'll need help."

"Right. Ben, please. Help Zack."

Ben continued staring at Ruth.

"I'll help." Bill stepped forward.

"What about—?"

"I'll help you get Ted out of here, then I'll sort Robert out. The other men will help me."

"What will they do?"

"I think they'll be relieved to be rid of him, if I'm honest."

She swallowed. "Right."

"But we need to get a move on."

"Right." She looked at Sarah. The girl was kneeling over Ted, her eyes wide and her hands covered in blood. She was hyperventilating.

"I'll look after Sarah," said Martin.

Jess eyed him. "No. She's coming home."

"That's what I mean. I'll help you get her to the boat. Get her home, if you'll let me."

"Looks like I don't have much choice."

Zack and Bill heaved Ted up off the floor. He groaned. *Good.*

Sarah followed, oblivious to the people around her. Martin took her arm and let her lean on him as she walked.

Jess crouched to bring herself level with Ruth. There was just the three of them now.

She heard voices again, moving around upstairs.

"We need to get out of here, quick. Ruth, I'll help you. Ben, you need to move."

Ben nodded silently. Ruth looked up at Jess and smiled.

Jess returned the smile. "Lean on me. I'll get you home."

J ess looked out of the beach hut window, listening to Ruth's voice behind her. Roisin was stretched out on the raised bench, wrapped in a blanket they'd taken from the farmhouse. Her clothes were piled on the floor next to them, the heavy smell of stale urine mixing with the metallic tang of blood.

"You're going to be alright, my love," Ruth murmured as she cleaned Roisin's skin, lifting sections of the blanket as she worked. It was cold and they wanted to keep the girl covered.

"Is she?" asked Toni. She was perched on the bench next to Roisin, clasping her hand.

Ruth looked up and nodded. "The bleeding's stopped. It's not as bad as it looked – the urine made it look like there was a lot more."

Jess sighed and looked outside. Ben was leaning on the hut's wall, waiting for his wife to emerge. He stared out to sea, fidgeting with his wedding ring. Watching him, Jess came to a decision.

She picked her way across the hut and pulled her rucksack from the pile of supplies in a corner. Ruth ignored her, focused on her patient.

Deep inside the rucksack, hidden in an internal compartment, was the tin. Sonia's tin. She pulled it out, smoothing her fingers across its hard surface. For a moment she tightened her grip on it, reluctant. But then she turned and held it out to Ruth.

"You should have this."

Ruth looked at the tin. She frowned and then her eyes widened as she realised what it was. "I can't," she said, her voice shaking.

Jess pushed it into her hand. "Yes. You'll wear them. I don't." She pulled in a breath. "And I need to let go."

Ruth searched Jess's face. "I'm not sure... After what he did."

"This isn't about Ben. It's about family."

She closed Ruth's fingers around the tin. Ruth pocketed it, then moved back to Roisin.

The door opened and Ben all but fell inside. "The boat's back."

Jess felt her body fill with relief. She looked out of the window: sure enough, their boat was heading for the beach. The low morning sun filtered through the clouds behind it.

Zack and Harry ran to the water's edge, waving their arms. Zack was laughing. Behind them, Sarah sat on the sand next to Ted, who'd refused to come into the hut. Bill's tourniquet had worked and the blood had stopped. Sarah and Ted sat a few inches apart, not touching.

Sarah kept glancing back towards the farm, probably wondering if Martin would appear. He'd gone back with Bill to bury Robert. Jess shuddered at the thought of it.

She flashed Ruth a look and then ran outside, following Ben. They joined Zack, jumping up and down in the shallows. A silhouetted figure waved back.

She turned to Ben. "I didn't know. About the man. Robert."

"I'm sorry."

"We thought... You told us..."

"I know. It was an accident. But I shouldn't have lied."

"No."

"Do you think Ruth will ever forgive me?"

"Give her time."

"Right."

He turned to her and gripped her arms. His eyes were red.

"Well done, sis. Thank you."

She swallowed the lump in her throat. "Thanks."

The boat approached slowly, its engine becoming louder against the sound of the waves. Harry came up behind them, pulling Sally with him. She'd been silent since their return to the beach huts. Jess wondered what had happened to her, in that cell. What she would tell her fiancé.

The boat's hull dragged onto the sand and Clyde jumped out. Jess felt her spirits lift.

"Clyde! It's good to see you."

He winked at her. "Hello gorgeous." She let herself smile back, spotting Zack watching them. She laughed and Clyde's face fell.

Zack and Harry ran to the boat, joining Clyde in pulling it onto the beach and tying it to a rock. She followed, wrapping Clyde in a hug. Zack moved in and grabbed her hand. She let him hold it, feeling it warm her own.

"Is Sanjeev OK?" she breathed.

Clyde's shoulders heaved. "He's fine." He looked around the others. "Everyone here?"

Jess looked back. Ruth was emerging from the hut, she and Toni supporting Roisin between them. Sally stood at the edge of the water, shivering. Ben was behind Ruth, and Zack was next to her, still holding her hand.

"Yes."

"Stop! Wait for me!"

She turned to see a figure advancing from the dunes: Martin. Sarah stood up shakily and after glancing at Ted, ran towards him. They hugged and Ted spat into the sand.

"I'm not going with that little shit," he muttered.

Jess bit her lip, resisting the urge to tell him just how grateful he should be.

"We won't all fit anyway," she said.

Clyde nodded. "I can do two runs."

"Thanks. Roisin, Sally, Sarah and Ted need to go first. Take them, with Ruth. I'll wait here with Ben, Zack, Toni and Harry." She paused. "And Martin."

Sarah and Martin were with them now. Sarah mouthed a *thank you* to Jess and crossed to her father, pulling him up by the arm. He leaned into her and muttered something unintelligible. His face was pale.

Clyde, Zack and Harry helped the first group onto the boat. It wasn't easy; there were more of them than the boat was built for and Roisin needed to lie across Ruth, Sarah and Sally's laps. Ted brushed off Harry's attempts to help him.

"Leave me alone, mate!" he snapped. "I'm fine by meself."

Harry shrugged, smiling. Ted was going to be fine.

As the boat headed out to sea, Jess drew back towards the huts. "We may as well take shelter," she told Ben.

He followed her, Zack falling in with them. Martin stayed outside, staring out to sea. Toni stood at the edge of the water, her arm shielding her face.

In the beach hut Ben slumped onto the bench, pummelling his legs.

"Haven't ridden a bike for years," he said. "Felt good."

Jess smiled.

"I didn't mean anything by it, you know," he said. She frowned. Zack was next to her, listening quietly, his hand brushing hers.

"Following you," Ben continued. "I knew you'd get her. But it was something Dawn said – I just had to find her. I couldn't stay behind another minute."

She brushed his sleeve with her hand. "I know. She'll be home soon. We all will be."

"What are you going to do about him?"

She looked out of the window at Martin. Could they accept him in the village, after everything he'd done?

"It won't be easy, persuading them to let him in," she said. "I'll need your help."

He nodded.

She took his hand. He looked tired and drawn.

"Ben?"

"Hmm?"

"We'll deal with it together. Family."

He gave her a sad smile. "Family."

<<<<>>>>

FIND out what happens to the villagers next in *Thicker Than Water*'s sequel, *Sea of Lies*.

And you can join the Rachel McLean book club to read

about the floods and how the Dyer family got to North Yorkshire at rachelmclean.com/underwater.

SEA OF LIES

PROLOGUE

Sarah slid the patio doors open quietly, careful not to wake her parents. She'd seen him out there, a flash of white on the grass behind the house. She had no idea how he'd got out.

"Snowy!" she hissed, pulling the door shut. She wrapped her arms around her chest; the wind was rough on the clifftop in September, especially this early in the morning.

She peered back up at the bedroom windows, checking that her parents' curtains were closed. Nineteen years old and still treated like a child. But it was nothing compared to the way her father treated her mother.

Satisfied, she rounded the side of the house, heading for the village square. Snowy liked to head for the bins at the back of the pub in search of scraps. He rarely got lucky; their isolated refugee community was obsessed with minimising waste.

"Snowy!" she called again, wishing the cat would reappear. She wanted her bed. The air was damp and the thin blouse she'd dragged on to come outside – it wouldn't do to risk being seen in her nightclothes – was getting soaked.

She reached the front of her house and stopped. Someone was coming out of the Dyers' front door, four houses along.

She pulled into the shelter of the wall and watched, her heart pounding. There was a reason she only came out here early in the morning or late at night. They stared at her, she knew they did. They gossiped about her. She was a freak, the only girl her age who didn't play a useful role in the village. Her father rarely let her leave the house, so she had little choice.

A figure backed out of the Dyers' door. Tall and lean, struggling with something he pulled behind him. What was Ben Dyer doing dragging things around at this time of day? She shrank back into the wall, her breaths shallow. Could it be something to do with the men that his sister Jess had insisted on rescuing from their stricken trawler two nights ago? Her father had been raging about tit, full of disdain for the actions of Jess Dyer, their new steward. The village had taken the men in, temporarily at least. Ted didn't trust them, but he was powerless against Jess and the rest of the village council members. It was what this community did; take in the dispossessed, the desperate. They'd all been that way once.

The man had mousy blonde hair that looked like it hadn't seen a comb for a very long time. He wore a pair of jogging bottoms that were a couple of sizes too large. He turned and heaved his burden up, supporting it against his side.

Sarah gasped. He was dragging Ruth Dyer, Ben's wife. She leaned on him precariously, her arms flopping at her sides.

But Ben Dyer had dark hair.

Sarah took a step forwards, her heart hammering

against her ribs. She opened her mouth but nothing came out.

She heard footsteps behind her. She closed her eyes. Her father had caught her.

She turned, ready to face the tongue-lashing. Snowy would have to make his own way home.

A man advanced on her. He was heavily built with dark, greasy hair and wore a creased blue shirt with the sleeves rolled up. No coat. He had a tattoo that snaked from his wrist into the folds of his shirt.

This wasn't her father.

"Who are you?" she breathed. She looked back towards Ruth. Another man had joined the first now. They were hauling her away, towards the beach. Sarah felt a cry stick in her throat.

She felt movement and turned to see the man close to her, his face hard. He pushed his hand towards her face and she let out a whimper.

"Shut up, lass," he said. He sounded impatient, irritated. She'd caught him and his friends taking Ruth. Would they punish her, silence her?

He had something in his hand. A cloth. It smelt sharp, medical. She pulled back as he shoved it into her mouth.

She felt his arms go round her as she collapsed, the sound of birds above her head echoing in her ears. Then there was nothing.

1

FIVE DAYS LATER

S arah stared at the approaching beach, her heart thumping in her chest. She could make out dim figures waiting for them.

She raised a hand to wave then dropped it. She was tired. More tired than she could ever remember. The adrenaline had got her out of that festering cell and to the beach with Martin, then back again after her second capture. Now all she wanted to do was sleep.

She felt her father's weight shift next to her. He was clutching his wounded shoulder, muttering under his breath. She looked at him and felt ice run down her back.

She looked back at the beach, searching for her mother. *Mum, have you come out? Did you dare?*

The boat was nearing the shore now, its occupants shifting, preparing for landing. Ruth was sitting in the boat in front of Sarah. She stood up, her face pale as the sea and her lips trembling. She smoothed her hands on her blood-stained trousers and sniffed the air.

Ruth had been in the cell next to her, and Sarah hadn't even known it. Sarah had even run off without taking her.

Ruth was the wife of the village steward – former steward, Sarah corrected herself – and the doctor to their village of refugees. Sarah was nobody.

She hoped the village would forgive her. Their community had been through enough; each of them making their way here after the floods six years earlier, and demonised and attacked by the residents of nearby Filey ever since.

Ruth turned. "Sarah, can you help me with Roisin?" Roisin had been imprisoned in another cell; she'd lost blood.

Sarah nodded. She wasn't used to being asked for help, but her ordeal made her one of them now.

She leaned over Roisin and, together with Ruth, took her weight. The boat's keel scraped on sand, slowing as they crept up the beach. People came forwards, arms outstretched. No one spoke.

She saw a pair of hands reach for Roisin and looked up. The girl's mother.

"Oh my God, my poor girl. Michael, come here. Help her."

A tall stocky man pushed his wife out of the way and leaned into the boat.

"Sweetheart. What have they done to you?"

"It's not as bad as it looks," said Ruth.

The man looked at Ruth and nodded. His lips were tight and his face lined with worry.

"Thank you," he whispered.

Ruth nodded. She helped him manhandle his daughter out of the boat, Sarah flailing to help.

Ruth turned to Sarah. "I need to check you over too. Your face. And your foot."

Sarah put a hand to the knife wound on her forehead.

Her foot throbbed but she'd managed to ignore it for the last few hours.

"My dad first," she said.

"Of course. Ted, can you stand?"

Sarah's father grunted and pushed himself upright. His dark coat was stained with blood and his face was ashen.

"Will he be alright?" Sarah whispered.

"Shut up, girl. I'll be fine."

Ruth threw her a sympathetic smile. "Can't argue with that. I'll need to take you up to the pharmacy though, Ted."

"Can't be doing with that. Fussing's for women."

"It's also for a man who's been stabbed in the shoulder. You'll need antibiotics."

"Then bring 'em to the house." He put a hand on Sarah's shoulder and stumbled out of the boat, all but falling onto the sand. No one came forward to help him.

"Where's your mother?" Ted muttered.

Sarah clambered out of the boat, ignoring the pain in her foot, and went to his side.

"She'll be at home, Dad. Waiting for us."

"Good. Let's go."

Sarah looked up to see the crowd parting to let them through. A few people threw her awkward smiles but no one spoke. In contrast, behind her Ruth was being thronged by well-wishers wanting to welcome her home.

Sarah shrugged and pushed on. She was used to this.

"Stop." Ted stopped walking.

"What?"

"Wait."

"Come on, Dad. Mum will be worried."

"No. The boat's going back out. I need to wait."

She felt her stomach dip. "No, Dad. Let's get home."

He glared at her, panting. "I need to talk to that little bastard. Find out what he did to you."

She looked out to sea. The boat was heading south again, silhouetted by the reflection of the low sun on the waves. It would return soon, with the rest of the villagers who'd gone to the farm, their rescue party. Plus one extra passenger.

"Dad, can't this wait?"

He shrugged off her hand. "Go home. See your mother. Tell her we're back."

He turned to the beach. Harry would be on that second boat, her father's friend. Would he restrain him? Did she want him to?

Ruth was level with them now. "Sarah. Come to the pharmacy, will you? Bring Ted."

"I've already told you," said Ted. "I'm fine."

Ruth put her hands on her hips. "You can intimidate my husband, Ted Evans, but it won't work on me. Your wound needs cleaning up. You need drugs."

"Talk to Dawn. Give her the drugs. She can clean me up, too."

"Very well. Can you ask her to come to the pharmacy, when you get home?"

He grunted and walked past her towards the sea, not making eye contact.

She turned. "Ted, you're going the wrong way."

He waved a hand in dismissal. "Stop telling me what to do, woman. I can look after meself."

Ruth looked at Sarah, her expression one of exasperation. "You'll come?"

Sarah nodded. "Will it be quick?"

"I have to see to Roisin first."

"In that case, I'll wait with my dad. Come on later."

Ruth shook her head. "You need rest, Sarah. Your forehead could get infected."

Sarah raised her fingers to the welt on her forehead, remembering. The knife. Ted hurtling through the door, throwing himself on her attacker. Martin coming at him, plunging a knife into the man's throat. The sucking, gurgling sound of blood leaving his body.

She swallowed a wave of nausea and spread her arms to steady herself. "Alright."

"Thanks."

Ruth picked up pace, catching up with Roisin's family who were almost at the village square and the pharmacy beyond. Sarah looked back at Ted. He stood at the shoreline, fifty feet from the crowd that had stayed behind to wait for the second group. He stared out to sea.

Don't hurt him, Dad, she thought. *Let me deal with him.*

2

The boat dipped under the weight of the five men and one woman. It wasn't built for a load like this; a family craft, it would have been designed for a couple of adults and two kids, four adults at a push.

It wasn't the first time Martin had sailed in it. The first, he had been barely conscious, hardly aware of the storm raging around them. The second – well, best not to think about the second.

Across from him, Ben stared at the sea, his eyes dark. Ben Dyer. The reason all this had happened. In the farmhouse kitchen, there'd been shouts and recriminations. Robert, the leader of the men Martin had been living with until a few hours ago; he and Ben had history, and Robert had taken his revenge by snatching Ben's wife Ruth. Three others, too, including Sarah.

From what Martin could see, Ruth didn't belong to anyone. She'd managed to get herself out of her cell and to the beach with no one's help. When she'd been recaptured, she'd retaliated in the most definitive of ways. He blinked, putting the memory out of his mind.

The sun was high in the sky now, or as high as it got off the North Yorkshire coast at the end of September. It pulsed down weakly, as if aware of how little he deserved its warmth. He shifted to face it, hoping he would dry out. Not much chance of that, with the constant spray.

They rounded a dark, heather-clad cliff and the village came into view. He held his breath. The windows of the houses at the cliff edge glinted in the sun. He wondered if one of them belonged to Sarah's family.

The group at the front of the boat – two men, one young with pale weather-worn skin, the other plump with dark skin, along with Jess, the village steward – had stopped talking. They spotted him watching and looked away. Ben, sitting at the back, was staring at the village now, muttering under his breath. And Harry, next to Ben, was staring at Martin, his disdain undisguised. All Martin knew of Harry was that he was an ally of Sarah's father. And that Robert had locked him and Ted up together when they'd attempted to rescue Sarah.

Was he thinking about what Martin had done, or about what might happen to him when they arrived?

"Nearly there," said the dark-skinned man. The boat leaned and turned for the shore.

They made for the boathouse, passing a crowd on the beach. The villagers watched, some running after them. No sign of Sarah. Ted was there though, looking like he wanted to disintegrate Martin with the force of his stare. Martin stared back, his heart pounding.

This was a bad idea. He should have stayed behind with Bill and the other men. Without Robert, the men would be directionless, but there was a chance they'd change their ways. That was where he belonged, not here. Bill would be in charge now; would things be different?

Then he remembered the way they'd crept up on him as he followed Sarah back through the dunes, intent on fleeing with her. The twine that Bill had tied round his wrists to restrain him.

Martin didn't belong anywhere.

The boathouse doors were pulled open and they chugged in. The dark-skinned man grabbed a rope and Harry jumped out to tie the boat up. One by one, he guided his fellow passengers out of the boat. Each of them headed out of the boathouse at speed, looking for someone from the first boat no doubt.

Harry and the other man stayed behind, securing the boat and unfolding a cover they pulled out of a hatch. They left Martin in the boat.

He watched them, his mouth dry.

"Where should I go?" he asked. His voice echoed in the empty space. Water lapped at the boat and reflected green and blue off the roof.

Harry shrugged. "Back to your mates, if I were you."

"They won't take me back. You saw what happened."

Harry tensed. "I was at the beach, helping the women. The women you took. I saw nothing."

"I helped Sarah. I helped her escape. They came after us, tied me up with twine."

"If you say so."

"It's true. Honest."

"Don't waste your breath. It's Ted you need to convince."

"I want to talk to Sarah first."

Harry let out a low laugh. "Fat chance, mate."

Martin hardened his jaw and put a hand on the side of the boat. He heaved himself out, half expecting one of the other men to jump him. They didn't.

"I'm going to find her."

"Good luck with that."

He slid past them to the boathouse door and eased it open. Outside, the air was cold and still, the only sound a flock of gulls above his head. A path led to the left. To the village.

He clenched his fists and started walking. The sea thrummed to his left and a bird cawed in the hedge to his other side. Clouds scudded overhead, pushed southward by the wind.

It was a climb up to the village, but he could see houses ahead, facing out to sea like a rebuke to the elements. Which one was Sarah's?

He tried to remember what Bill had said, the night after the abduction. *She walked right out of that bloody great house, looking for a cat or something.*

Sarah lived in a large house, then. Probably near the sea, if taking her had been so easy.

The houses were close now. He couldn't go knocking on all of them. Maybe he'd find the pharmacy. Would Ruth help him?

"Oi, you little fucker!"

Ted appeared out of nowhere, his left shoulder in a sling. Blood seeped through it. Martin let himself be distracted by it; it gave Ted the chance to swing at him with his good arm.

Ted grabbed Martin's neck with his hand and dug his fingers in. Martin cried out.

He brought his hands up and prised Ted's fingers off his flesh. The older man's hand was shaking but his grip was firm. He was panting.

"I helped her!" Martin grunted. Ted shrieked and pulled his hand free. He dug his fingers into the flesh of Martin's cheek.

Martin was ready this time. After his experiences on the road as a younger man, he'd learned to defend himself. He was taller than Ted, and uninjured. He shifted his weight back and sideways, sending Ted tumbling to the ground. Ted's grip loosened. Martin grunted and caught Ted as he fell. *Don't hurt him*, he told himself. *However much he wants to hurt you*. This was Sarah's father, after all.

Ted pushed himself up, arm flailing. He threw Martin a look of pure fury and launched himself again.

Martin side-stepped. Ted threw his good arm out to grab Martin's waist but it wasn't enough to stop him crashing to the ground. He landed on his shoulder, screeching in pain. He turned and heaved himself up, prodding at his bandage with a tentative finger.

Martin turned to him, waiting. His breathing was shallow and his senses on fire. Above him, a gull cried out.

Ted stood up. "You bastard. What did you do to my girl?"

"I helped her escape."

"You were with them. The distress call, that trawler you had. The one that weren't in distress at all."

"I had nothing to do with that."

Ted leaned in. His eyes were dark green with flecks of yellow. His breath was sharp and pungent. "Don't lie to me!"

"What's going on?"

Martin turned at the sound of the voice. *Sarah?*

It was Jess, hurrying towards them from the village. She'd led the rescue party the village had sent to find the women. She'd told Martin he could come back with them.

Martin relaxed for a moment, giving Ted an opening to swing at him, catching his chin with his fist.

"Aay!" Martin threw his hand up to his chin. It was bleeding.

"Ted!" Jess shouted. "Stop it. We have ways of dealing with this sort of thing."

Ted stood between them, his chest rising and falling. He looked like a man possessed. "You're not dealing with me, you bitch."

"I don't mean *that*. I mean Martin here." Jess glanced at Martin then approached Ted. "He was involved in the abductions. Just because I let him come back with us doesn't mean I don't recognise that."

"So what you going to do about it? Set an example, I hope."

Martin watched her. How much was she going to tell the village, about what had happened? "The village council will have to meet," she said. "Come to a decision."

"You're not going to call the police?" said Martin.

She eyed him. "If you know anything about this community, you'll know that we don't trust the authorities. They haven't helped us in the past, and I don't expect them to now. But surely you knew that, or why else would you have come here?"

He shrugged. "I just did what I was told."

"Seriously? That's your defence?"

"I'm no—"

She threw up a hand. "Save it. You're badly cut. You need to come to the pharmacy. I'll take you. And Ted, you need Ruth to take another look at that shoulder."

"Bugger that," said Ted.

"Thanks," said Martin.

Jess stared at Martin for a moment, as if sizing him up. She nodded and turned to Ted. "I can't force you to get treatment. But please, keep the law out of your own hands for a while eh?"

"Why should I?"

"Because that's the way we do things round here. If you want to stay in this village, you stick to the rules."

"Fat lot of bloody good the rules have done so far."

"Save it, Ted. There'll be a council meeting tonight. You'll have plenty of chance to raise objections there. And go and see Ruth. Please. At least ask Dawn to get you clean bandages."

She turned for the village, throwing a *come with me* over her shoulder to Martin. He followed, half wishing for and half dreading the prospect of finding Sarah at the pharmacy.

3

Sarah watched as Ruth helped Roisin out of her blood-stained skirt. The girl was shivering, her teeth chattering despite the relative warmth of the pharmacy. Her mother Flo stood next to her, a hand on her shoulder. She took the skirt off Ruth and slid it over her arm.

The door burst open and two small boys ran in in a jumble of voices, limbs and tangled blond heads. Ruth's mouth widened.

"Sean! Ollie!" She bent to clasp them in a tight hug. She planted a kiss on each boy's cheek.

The boys huddled into their mother. One of them started to cry while the other stared at his mum, unblinking. Ruth smiled back at them through tears.

"I'm sorry, my loves. But Mummy has to work for a bit. You know how I help people who are poorly?"

The boy who'd been staring into his mother's eyes nodded. His brother burrowed further into Ruth, whimpering.

Ruth's eyes were gleaming. Sarah stepped forward. "I'll watch them, if you want."

Ruth looked up. "Just into the shop, please. Wait out there till I'm ready for you."

"I'm fine. I promise."

"I just want to check you over."

"Isn't it more important for you to be with your boys?"

"Sarah. Please, just let me do my job."

Ruth wiped a hand across her face. Her hands were scrubbed clean now, free of the blood that had stained them on the journey back.

Sarah shrugged. "Come on, boys. Let's play in the square."

"Sarah."

"We'll be just outside, Ruth. Promise."

Ruth frowned at her but didn't object. Sarah bundled the boys through the village shop that fronted the pharmacy, then into the cold air outside. She was glad to be away from the claustrophobia of the Murray family's worry over Roisin, the smell of blood and stale urine.

Outside, the air was fresh and salt-tanged, but dry. She could hear the sea beyond the village hall and smell cooking from a house just across the road. Her mouth watered. When was the last time she ate?

"How about a game of tag?" she said to the boys. They jumped up and down, each clamouring to be 'it'.

"You go first, Ollie," she said.

"I'm Sean."

"Sorry. You go first, Sean. This bench is den."

She lowered herself to the bench, glad to be off her feet. She hadn't slept for over eighteen hours and that had been on a filthy mattress in a dingy cell.

"That's cheating."

"Not for grown-ups, it isn't. Look, your brother's started running. Go after him. And don't leave my sight!"

She looked past them to see a door open in one of the houses. Her own house. She stiffened.

A figure appeared in the door. Sarah stood and started running.

"Mum!"

Dawn's face broke into a smile. She looked around the square then started to run. They collided not far from where Sean and Ollie had fallen into a squabbling heap on the tarmac.

Dawn held Sarah so tight she almost lifted her off the ground. "I never thought I'd see you again."

"I know, Mum. I'm sorry."

Dawn stood back. She wiped her eyes. "It wasn't your fault, sweetheart. Those men. They should never have gone out to that distress call."

"I know, Mum. But it's not as simple as that."

Dawn clasped her again. "Why isn't it as simple, love? What happened?" She pulled back and her voice darkened. "They didn't – do anything to you, did they?"

Sarah swallowed. "No." She tried to push out the thought of the man who'd visited her cell on the second night. He'd been young, and enthusiastic. But she'd held him off, upturning the table next to her mattress and using it as a shield.

"You're home," Dawn said. "That's what counts. Come inside. I'm never letting you out of my sight again."

"Sarah! I need you in here! Oh."

Sarah turned to see Ruth at the door of the shop. Flo Murray, Roisin's mother, was leading the girl away. Roisin wore a clean blue dress and looked older than she had at the farm. Sarah watched her, wishing she could ask her if the men had visited her, if they'd threatened her too.

"I'm taking Sarah home," said Dawn, her voice so quiet the breeze almost carried it away.

"I only need her for a moment," said Ruth. "Check on that wound. Boys, come into the shop for a minute."

The twins groaned before righting themselves and sprinting over to their mother. She hugged them again before bundling them inside.

Sarah clutched Dawn's arm and looked into her eyes. "It'll be alright, Mum."

Her mother seemed to have aged ten years since she'd last seen her. She wondered how her father had reacted to her disappearance; would he have taken his anger out on his wife?

Dawn nodded and let go.

"Have you told her about Martin?" Ruth asked as Sarah reached the doorway.

"Not yet."

"He'll be back soon, with Ben. God knows what'll happen."

"I know."

Ruth motioned for Sarah to sit on the pharmacy's solitary chair. She took a thermometer out of a metal container and shook it. She put it into Sarah's mouth.

"I hope you know what you're doing."

So do I, thought Sarah. *So do I.*

4

———

"Wait there."

Jess pushed the pharmacy door open and Martin hung behind, doing as he was told.

This wasn't the first time he'd been here; Ruth had brought him to the village pharmacy on the night he'd first arrived. He'd fallen off the trawler, the boat that Robert, Bill and he had convinced the villagers was in trouble. Jess and some others had saved him then Ruth had brought him here to treat him for hypothermia. That was before they had taken Ruth and Sarah, and the other two he'd never met. Before Ruth had let him stay in her and Ben's house, where he'd taken advantage of her hospitality by drugging her and taking her away in the villagers' own boat.

The pharmacy was in a room off the village shop. Behind the counter of the shop, a large woman with a prominent mole above her lip and a disapproving frown watched him.

"Ruth, I've got Martin," said Jess, out of sight. "Ted's split his chin open."

"He did *what*?"

"It was going to happen sooner or later. Better sooner."

The frowning woman pulled some vegetables out of a box and placed them on a shelf, but Martin knew her attention was on him. He listened to Jess and Ruth's conversation, wishing he could disappear.

Jess emerged. "She's busy. Wait here."

He shrugged and bent his head. His shoes were torn and full of wet sand and his clothes were stained with grass and mud. He thought of Ben's trousers that Ruth had given him when he'd fallen overboard, his first night here. He'd still been wearing them when he drugged Ruth and dragged her from her bedroom to the waiting boat.

He stared at the door, his chest tight. Ruth would have to be some sort of saint to treat him. Regardless of what he'd done for Sarah.

"I have to go and deal with... never you mind what I have to do. Just wait there," said Jess.

He nodded.

"Don't move a muscle, OK?"

He nodded again. She screwed up her mouth, glanced at the woman behind the counter then thought better of speaking. With a sigh she pushed the shop door open and disappeared outside. Martin watched her through the glass, the incongruous ting of the shop bell ringing in his ears.

He took a deep breath and waited.

SARAH WANTED TO BE HOME, to check that her mother was all right, to know if her father had arrived yet. If he'd gone home. If he'd found Martin.

She fidgeted as Ruth dabbed at the cut on her forehead. The disinfectant stung but it was nothing to what was going on inside her head. She'd asked Jess to let Martin come back with them. She'd convinced them to trust him, recounting the story of how he'd helped her escape. But what she hadn't told them was how she felt when he'd admitted to being there when she was taken. That he'd been a part of it.

She'd seen the look in his face after Robert, the ring-leader, had fought with her father. She'd heard him shout that he loved her, and listened to him careering across the table towards Robert. He did it for her; at least that was what he believed.

Robert was dead. There was no way Martin could stay at the farm after that. On impulse, she'd told him to come back here, with her.

And now they were home. Had she made the right choice?

The door opened and Jess appeared.

"I've got Martin."

Sarah felt like her heart would stop. *Don't bring him in. Not here. Not now.*

Her hands were clammy and her face hot. She stared between Jess and Ruth, listening to their conversation.

I have to face up to him sometime.

But not yet. She wanted to go home. She wanted her mother.

Jess closed the door – what had they decided? – and Ruth smoothed the dressing on Sarah's forehead.

"There. Just a surface wound. It'll be fine. But let me know if you start feeling off-colour."

"Off-colour?"

"I want to be sure you haven't got an infection. You spent three days in filth. Heaven knows what you've come into contact with."

Sarah resisted the urge to remind Ruth that she too had spent three days in filth, on the other side of the wall.

"Is there another way out of here?"

Ruth frowned. "What?" She looked at the door. "Oh. I see. I'm sorry, you're going to have to go past him. But he helped you, didn't he?"

Sarah nodded. "He took you," she said.

Ruth's face darkened. "I know. I don't think it was his fault though."

"Really?"

Ruth's throat shifted as she swallowed. "Not entirely, anyway. It was Robert Cope. He forced them to do it."

"All of them? Even the other older one?"

"Bill?" Ruth let out a shaky breath. "Who knows. I'm glad he stayed behind, anyway."

"He buried Robert's body. With Martin."

Ruth put a hand on Sarah's arm. "If you need anything, I'm always here."

"I'll be fine."

"I don't mean just physical. It'll be hard talking to your mum about what's happened, I imagine."

Sarah felt her cheeks warm. She blinked back tears. Ruth squeezed her arm.

"Come on. I'll take you out. You can ignore him, if you want. You're going to have to speak to him at some point though. It was you who wanted him with us."

"I know. Thank you."

She stood up. As Ruth put a hand on the door, Sarah stopped her.

"How can you forgive him?"

"Martin?"

"Mm."

"Like I said," Ruth replied. "It wasn't his idea. That was all on Robert. I certainly don't forgive *him*."

Sarah dropped her gaze to the floor.

"Come on then, let's get you out of here." Ruth pushed the door open. "Wait there, Martin. Sarah is just leaving."

Martin stood up. Sarah could smell him; sea and sand mixed with the mud they'd crawled through together. She clenched her eyes shut.

"Sarah?"

She ignored him and bustled past, letting Ruth guide her to the door.

"Hello, Dawn," said Ruth.

Sarah opened her eyes to see her mother entering the shop. She looked worried.

"Is she going to be alright? That cut?"

Sarah's fingers went to the dressing on her forehead. She could feel Martin's stare behind her. Did her mother know who he was?

"She'll be fine," said Ruth. "Just a surface wound."

"Are you coming home then, love?"

Sarah nodded. She felt the air shift behind her. Martin cleared his throat.

No. Stay quiet. Don't speak to her. Please.

"Hello." Another cough. "I'm Martin. You must be Sarah's mum."

Sarah felt her legs weaken. Dawn turned to Martin, puzzled.

"I wanted to apologise, for what happened to her. I helped her escape. I hope she'll recover."

Dawn shrank back. "Oh. Thank you. Who are you?"

"Martin."

"Do you... do you live here?"

"I hope to."

"Oh." Recognition crossed Dawn's face. Sarah felt as if her stomach was turning itself inside out. She grabbed her mother's arm.

"Come on, Mum. Take me home."

"Of course."

Ruth flashed Martin a look then held the door open. Behind the counter, Pam looked on, not even pretending to be working. Sarah wondered if the whole village would be talking about her within the hour.

If they weren't already.

She shoved her mother out of the door and hurried towards the house.

"Slow down, love. You'll do yourself an—"

"Come on. Please. I want to get home."

She kept her head down, unsure if there was anyone around to watch them. Dawn hurried to catch up. They reached the path outside their house and her mother put a hand on her arm to stop her.

Sarah looked up. Dawn was looking at the house, her face pale. Was she scared?

"What did they do to you, Sarah? Did they hurt you? Did they – oh, I don't know how to say this – did they force themselves on you?"

"I don't want to talk about it, Mum."

"Please, love. I want to help you. That Martin lad. Back there. Was he one of them?"

Sarah stiffened. "Yes."

"Did he hurt you? Why is he here?"

"He told you, Mum. He helped me escape. He came back with us."

"He came back with you? Why?"

"He wasn't safe, there."

"Why ever not?"

"Mum! I've told you I don't want to talk about it." Sarah let out a shaky breath. "I'm sorry. I didn't mean to shout. Let's go inside, yes?"

Dawn cast a worried glance at the house. Sarah wondered if her father was home yet.

"Yes. Let's," said her mother.

Dawn hurried along the path, leaving Sarah behind, and turned her key in the lock.

awn pulled Sarah into the house and closed the door behind them. She was like a startled animal, breathing in sharp bursts and looking around her with small, quick movements.

"Mum? What's wrong?"

"Did your father come back with you? Did he find you?"

"Yes. Yes, he caught up with us. He didn't find me though. Jess and the others, they had to let him out."

"*What?*"

"Robert and his men. They found Dad and Harry on the beach, coming after us. They put them in the cell I'd escaped from." She backed into the wall, her limbs heavy. "Dad's injured, Mum."

Dawn paled. "Dear God." She crossed herself.

"His shoulder. But he's going to be alright. He's already shouting at people." Sarah tried to laugh.

"You're making no sense," said Dawn.

"I'm sorry. Look, I need a lie down. Can I talk about it later?"

"I've got someone to see you first."

"Who?"

Sarah pushed past her mother into the living room, wondering who might be there. They never had visitors.

As usual, the room was tidy to the point of sparseness, the sound of the sea faint through the tall windows at the back.

She turned to Dawn. "Who?"

"He's outside. On the grass."

Sarah crossed to the window and peered outside. The sun had disappeared behind thick clouds now and the sky above the sea was blurred. It was going to rain.

There was no one out there.

"Who, Mum?"

"Wait."

Dawn pushed the sliding door open a crack. "We're here. Come in."

Sarah watched, frowning, as a shape appeared from beside the window where it had been huddled unseen against the wall.

He stepped inside, shaking himself out and glancing down at his shoes as if worried he'd bring mud in.

"Sam?"

It was Sam Golder, one of the Golder twins. His brother Zack had gone out in the boat with Jess a week ago, to answer a distress call. The mission that had brought the men to their village. He'd gone with Jess on the walk south to find Sarah and the other women, too. Leaving Sam behind. She wondered how Sam felt about that.

"Hi, Sarah." He ran a hand through his messy hair. He was almost a foot taller than her, and similarly broad. A stranger would never know there were only four years between them.

She turned to Dawn. "Why is Sam here?"

"I thought you might want to see him. After what you've been through."

"Sam?"

"He's your friend, isn't he?"

"Yes, but..." She turned to Sam, aware she was being rude. *Friend* was hardly the word she'd use. She'd spoken to Sam on a few occasions, on the beach. They both liked to go down there for early morning solitude. She had no idea they'd been spotted.

She turned to Dawn. "Have you been spying on me?"

"I just saw you talking. He's a nice boy."

Sarah blushed. She blinked at Sam. Was her mother trying to play Cupid?

"It's good to see you home," said Sam. He looked down at his feet again. He hadn't moved them since stepping inside.

"Close the door," said Sarah. "It's freezing." She reached round him to pull it shut. They both jumped as her arm touched his back.

"Nice house," he said.

She looked around them. The living room was dull in this light, with nothing except her mother's crucifix on the wall. The coffee table was bare except for a single spray of flowers picked from the dunes, in a cracked cup. The kitchen, beyond, was equally bare; nothing on the surfaces except a teapot.

Dawn hurried into the kitchen. She picked up the teapot and put it in a cupboard. "Excuse the mess."

Mum, it's spotless, Sarah wanted to say. But she'd lived with this all her life. It was as if her mother was scared to leave her mark on the world in any way than through her faith.

"Have you been out there for long?" she asked Sam.

"Not long. Twenty minutes or so."

"That's ages, in this cold."

A shrug. "I'm used to it."

She knew he was. Sam was one of several young men who regularly left the village in search of work. It was their community's only way of getting cash for those things they couldn't grow or make themselves. They worked on the land reclamation near Hull, trying to grab back land the sea had taken in the floods six years ago. Floods that had made Sarah's family homeless and forced them to make the journey north to this village. Everyone here was like them, a refugee from the floods, provided with temporary accommodation in this former holiday village but not, as yet, able to leave. She doubted they ever would; the authorities seemed to have abandoned them.

"Why did you come?"

"To see if you were OK, I guess." He shifted his weight without moving his feet. She longed to tell him to step inside, to ignore the mud on the carpet. But her mother would be horrified.

"Well, I am. Thanks for coming."

She put a hand on the door, ready to open it again. He gave her a shy smile as she did. She blushed.

"Quick, out!"

She turned to see her mother advancing on them, her face full of horror.

"What?"

"It's your father. He's outside." Dawn's eyes were wide. "He looks cross."

Cross would be an understatement. In the last few days, Ted had seen his daughter abducted, had gone after her, been locked up himself, and then almost killed the man responsible. Yes, he would be *cross*.

Sarah had the door open. Dawn pushed her and Sam through it. Sarah grabbed her arm, not wanting to go out herself. Surely only Sam needed to leave?

The pressure made Dawn stumble into her. They tumbled to the grass, Dawn gasping in surprise.

Sarah turned back to the glass door. Through it, she could see the front door to their house opening. Without thinking, she yanked the door closed then pushed her mother and Sam to one side, out of sight of the interior.

"What are you doing?" breathed Sam. "Are you coming with me?"

"No, silly." Sarah looked at Dawn. "I don't know what I'm doing. But can you leave me and my mother alone, please. We need to talk."

Sam threw her a sheepish smile then shook his boots out and slipped around the side of the house. Sarah assumed he would head home, to see his brother Zack, who would only just be back himself. She realised she had no idea where he lived.

She turned to Dawn.

"What was all that about?"

"Why did you pull me outside? It's starting to rain." Dawn moaned and tugged her pale blue cardigan up over her head. It was threadbare at the elbows and there was a thin trace of black cotton where she'd sewn up a tear in the hem.

"Sorry. It was an accident. Let's get back inside."

"Yes."

Dawn reached for the door. "It's locked."

"What?"

"You closed it from the outside. I can't open it."

"Damn."

"I *beg* your pardon?"

"Sorry, Mum. Let's go round the front. Dad'll let us in."

Dawn peered round the door. "No."

"It's raining. We have to get inside."

Dawn turned to her. Heavy drops of rain fell, darkening the village and the view out to sea. "I don't want to alarm him."

"Mum, please. He'll let us in. We can tell him we just got back from the pharmacy."

"No, love. We'll shelter for a bit, wait for him to go out."

"What good will that do? We still can't get in."

"Do you have your key?"

"Mum, I just got back from three days being locked up in an outhouse. Of course I don't have my—"

She fumbled in the pocket of her skirt. She had taken her key, on the morning she'd been snatched. Her parents had been asleep and she hadn't wanted to disturb them. She'd been looking for her cat, Snowy. She hadn't seen him since returning.

"I've got it," she breathed. Dawn looked like she might cry with relief.

"Mum, what's he been like? While I've been gone?"

Dawn shook her head. "He's hardly been here. He came after you, remember."

"Dad does things like that when he's angry." She lowered her voice. "Did he take it out on you?"

Dawn looked away. "He shouted at me a bit, that's all. Nothing I can't handle."

"You shouldn't have to handle him, Mum."

Dawn leaned in close. Her eyes flashed at Sarah, the pupils dilated. "With God's help, I handle him. I always have and I always will. It's what I do."

"It's not right."

"Sarah. This is not for you to judge. Now let's get inside. You're the one complaining about the rain."

"I'm not complaining." But Sarah's body *was* complaining. About the wet, and the cold, and the aches deep inside as well as her throbbing head. She wanted to sleep for a year.

They rounded the house to the front. The village square was deserted, rain chasing everyone inside. Sarah slipped past Dawn to get to the front door.

She raised her key to the lock. Theirs was one of few houses that were locked in the daytime.

She paused. "What was all that with Sam?"

Dawn shook her head. Beads of water sprayed into Sarah's eyes. "He's a nice boy."

"I know he's a nice boy, but why did you bring him here?"

"He'd be good for you."

"He'd be *what*? Mum, I don't need a matchmaker."

"You need to lead your own life. Sam could give you that."

"I don't. I'm nineteen years old. I'm not leaving you. Not with him."

She looked back at the door, imagining Ted inside. Would he be pacing the room? Watching from an upstairs window, wondering where his women had got to? Listening to them through the door?

"Just let me make my own decisions, please Mum," she said, as she turned her key in the lock. "I can look after myself."

6

Martin could barely bring himself to look Ruth in the eye as she patched up his chin. She bustled around the pharmacy, grabbing surgical glue, disinfectant and cotton wool, then tending to his wound without looking into his eyes.

At last she was finished. She stood back and wiped her hands on her apron. He jumped down from the table on which he'd been sitting.

"Thanks."

She shrugged.

"I'm sorry."

Her eyes moved upwards to meet his gaze. "Yes."

"If I'd known you, if I'd known what you were like, I'd never have—"

"But given that I was a stranger to you, you were happy to go along with it?"

"Not happy. I was scared. Scared of Robert." His hands were sweating. He hated himself. "I'm sorry, is all. If I can make it up to you in any way…"

"Go home."

"Sorry?"

"I have no idea what possessed you to tag along with the boat. I think the best thing is for you to go back to your friends, at the farm."

"You saw what they did to me. They'll never take me back."

"That's hardly my concern."

"And Sarah wants me here."

Ruth arched an eyebrow. "Does she?"

He thought of Sarah shuffling out of the pharmacy, refusing to look at him. "Maybe I should go back."

"Sensible boy. Just take care of that chin. Keep it clean."

"I will."

He pushed the door to find Jess outside, making stilted conversation with the woman running the shop. Martin knew that she'd only become village steward a few days before he and his friends had taken Sarah and the other women. He'd seen her struggling to assert her authority. Especially with her brother Ben, who'd held the job before her.

She turned at the sound of the door.

"All fixed?"

"Yes. Thanks." He ignored the puzzled stare of the other woman. "I think I'd best be on my way now."

"On your way where?"

"I'm not welcome here. It was stupid of me to think I might be."

Jess shook her head. She opened the shop door and guided him outside.

"That's better," she said. "Pam does like to listen in." She smiled. "Don't tell her I said that."

"I can't if I'm leaving."

"About that. Are you sure?"

He looked around the square in front of the shop. Heavy drops of rain were falling, and there was no one in sight. The air was dark and heavy and he could barely make out the houses beyond.

"Yes," he said. "I should go back to the farm."

"I saw what you did, back there."

"I didn't do anything."

"Yes, you did. You stopped that man in his tracks. And you did it for Sarah."

"If by that man, you mean Robert, well it wasn't me who stopped him. Not in the end."

She shook her head. "Not a word about that. Ruth is the beating heart of my family, and indispensable to this village. If anyone found out what she did..."

"I won't tell."

"Good. Now, the flat your fr— that Robert and Bill were in. After we rescued you from your boat that wasn't really sinking."

He blushed. "Sorry."

"Stop saying that. The flat's still empty. I'm putting you in it for twenty-four hours, while we come to a decision."

"You really don't need to do that."

She stopped walking. A gust of wind blew her red hair in front of her face and she shoved it to one side. "I said you could come. I've only been steward here for a week. If I change my mind, I'll look weak. I'm sticking up for you, whether you like it or not."

"Err—"

"Come with me."

She started walking. He followed, unaware now which direction they were going in. Towards the sea, or away from it? Towards the road back to the farm, or away from it?

"Where are we going?"

She didn't break stride. "I told you. The flat. One night. Then you'll either stay, or you'll go."

They reached a low red brick building. She handed him a key. "Here you are. That door there. It's upstairs, first on the left, once you get inside. It's basic, but it'll do."

"I don't deserve this."

"That's for the village council to decide."

"Thank you."

She hesitated, as if about to say something, then decided against it. She turned away from him and started walking back towards the square. He realised he had no idea where in the village he was, no idea how to get back to the farm even if he wanted to.

When she was twenty yards away, she turned. "Sit tight," she called. "Stay in the flat. And lock your door."

7

S arah sat against her bedroom door, listening to the
voices downstairs. Ted had been irritable when she
and Dawn came in, snapping about the fact that his
lunch wasn't ready and the house was cold. Dawn had
fussed about his shoulder but he'd pushed her away. So
she'd slipped into her usual mode of attempting to reach
him through his stomach. They couldn't be too fussy about
food here, not with the rationing and the limitations on
power. Soup, made from carrots grown in the allotments,
wouldn't have been Ted's preferred meal. But he'd learned
to live with it.

Sarah had slipped upstairs as soon as she and Dawn had
finished the washing up, anxious to get away from her
father. And she was tired. She'd spent over an hour lying on
her bed, blinking up at the ceiling, thinking about Dawn,
and Sam, and Martin. She didn't understand why her
mother was trying to hook her up with Sam. Dawn needed
her here, to help ward off Ted's moods.

Now they were talking about the village council. It
would be meeting in the morning to rule on whether Martin

could be allowed to stay in the village. Ted would fight Jess's decision hard.

But where was Martin now? He deserved to know that his future was in the balance.

She closed the door and crept to the window. It was set into the eaves, with a sloping roof she could jump off.

She reached into her wardrobe for a warm sweater. Her coat was downstairs, on the hook by the door. She would have to do without.

Wrapped up in the sweater and two scarves, she opened the window. Cold air blew in; it had stopped raining but the evening was a bitter one, with a harsh wind coming in off the sea. She wrapped the scarves more tightly around her neck.

She pushed the window as wide as it would go then felt outside, her fingers searching for a place to stand or sit. There was a flat section immediately below the window. It would be somewhere to start.

She took her book from the chair next to her bed and put it on the bed. She picked up the chair and placed it under the window.

She stepped back and put one foot on the chair, then the other. She was next to the window now, nothing between her and the drop.

Downstairs, she heard Ted's voice raised.

"I'm going to bed."

She stared at the door. He never checked on her, but tonight, after everything that had happened...

Quickly, she closed the window and stepped down from the chair. She pushed it back to its spot and dived under her duvet, pulling it up to her neck. She lay there, watching the door, her heart pounding.

The window swung open. She hadn't secured it. She heard footsteps making their way up the stairs.

Did she have time?

The footsteps arrived outside her door. No. She could claim she wanted fresh air while she slept.

The footsteps stopped. She imagined her father outside, listening. She bit her lip.

The window swung to and fro, rattling softly. She stared at it, her heart pounding. *Shut up.*

There was a creak from outside the door, then another door opening and closing. He'd gone to his and Dawn's room.

She put her hand on her chest, breathing heavily. She was no good at this.

She pushed back the duvet and crossed to the window. With Ted in bed, Dawn would be sitting in the living room, staring out to sea through the darkened glass doors. She went into a kind of trance at this time of night, as if reaching into herself for the will to go up and join her husband in bed.

She wouldn't notice Sarah leaving via the front door.

She closed the window, checking the catch, and padded to her bedroom door. She leaned on it for a moment, listening. Nothing.

She turned the handle and pushed the door open, peering into the dark hallway. No light filtered up the stairs; Dawn was sitting in darkness.

At the bottom of the stairs, she grabbed her coat and opened the front door. She slipped outside and pulled the door behind her, twisting the handle to make it close silently. Her key was still in the pocket of her skirt; by the time she returned, both Dawn and Ted would be asleep.

She surveyed the village square. The only light was from

a half moon shrouded by fast-moving clouds. Lights-out was hours ago and not one house was illuminated.

Where would he be? In the JP, maybe? At Ruth and Ben's house again?

No. Last time Martin had slept there, he had taken Ruth in the night.

She headed for the JP. The pub was dark, no sign of movement through the windows. She leaned on the glass, trying to make out shapes.

"Sarah?"

She turned to see a shape heading towards her. She closed her eyes, searching for a story. An excuse for being out here at night.

"Sarah, what are you doing out?"

"Sam?"

He joined her next to the window. His eyes were hooded and he looked puzzled.

"What are you doing here?" she asked him.

"Can't sleep. Thought I'd take a walk. You?"

"Looking for my cat."

She cast around them as if searching for the creature she knew was curled up on a chair at home.

"Is that wise?" Sam asked. "Zack told me you were out looking for it when they took you."

She resisted the urge to tell him not to pry. "He's probably over by our house. See you in the morning."

She started walking.

"Can I help you?"

She turned. "No. No, its fine. Look, there he is." She turned towards her house. "Snowy!" she hissed.

"Where?" he asked. The cat was all-white and would have been distinctive in the darkness.

"He's gone round the side of our house. Probably trying to get in."

"Oh."

She gave him a smile. "Thanks, then. See you around."

He looked dejected. *Don't be hard on him*, she told herself. *It's not his fault.*

"You're working tomorrow, right?" she asked.

"Yes."

"You need your sleep then. Maybe I'll see you when you get back."

His face brightened. She cursed herself for leading him on but held her ground. "See you tomorrow."

"Yes," he said. "Yes, of course."

She watched him run away, towards the northern edge of the village. He must live over there, with Zack.

If Martin wasn't in the JP, then maybe Jess had put him up at her house. She had plenty of space, after all. Jess lived in the last house before you reached the main road, as far from the centre of the village as possible. Sarah's family lived in the big houses overlooking the cliffs, the houses allocated to council members, handy for the village square and community centre. Jess still hadn't moved out of the house where her mother had died, before Jess was elected. Not long after the Dyer family had arrived here.

Sarah squared her shoulders and set off along the Parade.

8

_____

Dawn watched the dark clouds flowing across the sky out to sea. It was windy tonight; mild by the standards of this coastline but a howler compared to the breezes where she'd grown up in Somerset.

She could hear Ted moving around above her, his heavy tread unmistakable. She always knew who was on the move in this house, who was coming down the stairs and who was entering the room. Sarah's footsteps were light and quick; she tried to disguise them but Dawn could always hear. Ted's, by contrast, were heavy and slow. He would lumber down the stairs each morning, prolonging the agony of anticipation as she waited for him to appear in the kitchen.

It was only when Ted was angry that his gait changed. His steps would lighten and he would be fast, nimble even. She dreaded the sound of that tread.

Beneath the creak of Ted's footsteps, Dawn heard a second, lighter tread, so pale as to almost be a whisper. Sarah, coming down the stairs. This was how she sounded when Ted was in one of his moods; wary, hesitant. Scared.

Dawn drew in breath then held still, listening. The

sound stopped as Sarah reached the bottom of the stairs. Dawn pictured the girl watching her, waiting to speak. She prepared herself for conversation.

Sarah didn't head her way. Instead, she pulled the front door open and slid outside. Dawn listened, her heart pounding, as her daughter eased the door closed again.

She turned. The door was closed. Everything was as it had been except for Sarah's coat missing from its peg.

There was a creak above her head; Ted falling into bed. She swallowed the lump in her throat. She would wait half an hour, as always. Until she heard his first snores.

She went to the hallway, running her fingers through the coats. She eased the door open. Outside, Sarah was crossing the square.

She toyed with the idea of running after her daughter, calling her back. But people would see. How many of them were watching Sarah from their darkened windows?

She closed the door again. Sarah would return in her own time. She wasn't stupid.

"What's going on? Why are you going outside?"

She turned to see Ted at the top of the stairs, rubbing his eyes with his good arm. His sling was tangled and spotted with blood. It made her feel queasy.

"Ted! You startled me. I was just locking up for the night. Go back to bed, please."

He rumbled down the stairs, almost tripping in his haste. She pulled back.

"What is it?" He yanked the front door open and stared outside. Dawn held her breath. There were a few seconds of agony as he stared onto the square, then relief as he closed the door.

He turned to her. "What's going on?"

"Nothing. I was locking up."

"I already locked up. I always lock up. You know that."

"I was just checking."

"You saying I didn't do it properly?"

"Of course not."

He pushed past her into the kitchen. He grabbed a glass and turned the tap on, splashing water on his sling. Then he leaned against the counter and took a long drink. Dawn watched, resisting an itch to look towards the door, to check that Sarah wasn't returning.

Ted slammed the glass on the counter and marched to the stairs. "Sarah! Sarah, get down here!"

Dawn stepped in behind him. "Don't wake her, Ted. Not tonight. Not after everything she's been through."

He turned, his eyes dark. His greying hair was messed up from being in bed and a strand leapt up from the top of his head.

"You're acting strange. She'll tell me why."

"She won't. She—"

He raised his hand and she flinched. "Thought I was asleep, didn't you?" His eyes widened. "Were you out there with that boy?"

He tugged the front door open. Dawn tried to look over his shoulder; there were no sounds coming from the square.

He slammed the door shut. "Where is that girl?"

Dawn put a hand on his arm. "Please Ted, just calm down. She needs her sleep."

He shrugged her off and bounded up the stairs, his footsteps light. He flung open Sarah's door, the first one at the top.

Dawn squeezed her eyes shut.

Ted disappeared into Sarah's room then emerged. Dawn couldn't see his face; he was nothing but a dark shadow at the top of the stairs. But she could imagine his expression.

"Where is she?"

He thundered down the stairs. Dawn stumbled back into the living room. She hit the back of the sofa and all but fell over it. Ted followed her.

"Where is she?"

"I—I don't know."

He leaned in. His eyes gleamed and spittle ringed his mouth. "Tell me!"

He rounded the sofa and grabbed the jug of flowers she'd placed there two days ago, while he was gone. She normally kept the surfaces free of anything sharp or heavy. She cursed herself for not removing it when he returned.

He turned the jug upside down and shook it out. The flowers fell to the floor in a spray of water. Ted raised the jug and wielded it over his head. His eyes were bright with pain and anger.

"Tell me!"

"She went outside. I heard her. I don't know why—" Dawn's voice was shrill.

"Why didn't you stop her?"

She shook her head. Her body felt cold, like she had frostbite, all sensation in her fingers and toes gone. "I—I don't know. I'm sorry."

He dropped the jug and stepped towards her. She backed away. He grabbed her wrist and pulled her towards him.

"There," he breathed. "That's better. Tell me the truth, Dawn."

She closed her eyes. She knew better than to meet his gaze when he was like this.

"Maybe she was looking for Snowy," she suggested.

Ted pointed towards the living room. "That cat there, on the sofa?"

Dawn felt her chest dip. "Oh."

Ted glared at her. She shrank back, not meeting his stare. After a few moments, he dropped her arm. He turned and yanked his coat from its peg, thrusting his good arm into a sleeve. He draped the other side of it over his shoulder.

"You stay here. I'm going after her."

9

Sarah strode along the Parade, her eyes on the bend in the road where it led out of the village to the outside world.

It was a route that scared and fascinated her in equal measure.

She'd lived here for almost six years, since she was thirteen and the floods had forced her family from its home in Somerset. She had vague memories of a cottage by a stream, of being nestled against a hillside, hidden away from the world.

Here, she was just as hidden. Not only from the world outside the village, but from the village itself. Ted made sure of that.

And she would never leave the family home, never abandon her mother. Dawn had to know that. All her efforts with Sam were an irrelevance.

Tonight, for the first time since arriving five years ago, she walked towards the village entrance. She slid along the Parade, the main artery of their village, imagining people watching her through their windows. The village was quiet and dark; power was rationed here, like everything else, and lights-out had long since passed. And the people who lived here needed their sleep in preparation for the hard physical work they would be doing in the morning. Tending livestock; digging the allotments; baking bread; smoking fish.

Her steps felt heavy, as if she was being pushed back. She glanced from side to side, checking for movement in the darkened windows. An owl hooted somewhere and she nearly jumped out of her skin.

But she had to know how much involvement Martin had in the plan to snatch her. He'd pretended to be something he wasn't – her rescuer, her knight in shining armour. He'd helped her escape from the farm, and they'd fled together to the beach. But then he'd told her that he'd played a part in taking her. She struggled to reconcile that version of him with the one who had screamed out his love for her and thrown himself on Robert in the farmhouse kitchen, claiming he was defending her.

She had to understand. She had to know what he'd done voluntarily, and what he'd been forced to do. After that, he could leave the village. His presence only led to trouble.

She kept to the shadows and tucked her arms in at her sides, trying to be as inconspicuous as possible. When she heard a scraping sound, she ducked into the shadow of a bush.

"Sarah!" a voice hissed.

She looked back. The road was empty.

"Sarah! Up here!"

She pulled out of the shadows and looked up. A head was poking out of a first floor window above her.

"Shush," she hissed.

"Were you looking for me?"

She frowned; the arrogance. But he was right.

"Yes."

"Wait a minute."

The window closed and he disappeared. Moments later, a door opened below it. The tall, willowy shape of the man who'd abducted her, then helped her escape.

Her stomach contracted.

"Quick, come inside," he whispered.

It was too late to back out now. She approached the door, waiting for him to move out of her way. He obliged, disappearing up a flight of stairs ahead of her. She followed, half intrigued and half terrified.

No one knew she was here.

The flat's main room was lit by a solitary candle. It flickered off the walls, casting ghoulish shadows that only heightened her sense of dread.

"They put you in here," she said.

He gestured around the room, as if welcoming her to his luxurious home. "Just for one night. Then they decide if I can stay."

She nodded but said nothing. There was a small table in one corner and two hard chairs. She took one of them.

Martin took the other one, at right angles to her. She shifted away, the chair legs scraping against the wooden floor. She wondered who lived in the flat below.

"Will you vouch for me?" he asked. "Tell them I helped you get out?"

"I don't know."

Sarah had never even been to a village meeting, let alone a council meeting. The thought of standing in front of them, her father among them, filled her with dread.

"It would help, you know. Only if you want me to stay though."

"I don't know."

He nodded. "I understand."

She sniffed. How long before she could leave? But then she remembered; she'd come here for a reason.

"What happened, the night you took me?" she said.

"Sorry?"

"You heard. I want to know it all."

"Oh." He rubbed his nose. "Of course you do." He placed his hands on the table, fingers laced together. They were long and pale. He huddled over them. She leaned back in her chair.

He spotted her unease and withdrew his hands, placing them on his lap. She made herself relax, wondering if he could hear her heartbeat.

"Where do you want me to start?" he said.

"At the beginning."

"The distress signal?"

"No. Before that. When you agreed to take part."

"I didn't have much choice."

"Everyone has a choice."

"Sarah, you have to understand. Robert Cope, he had a hold over me. I owed him."

"You owed him? What for?"

"He—he helped me, after the floods." He shifted his weight; she watched him, unforgiving. "You know that. I owed him."

"I can't believe you got yourself indebted to that man."

"I know. But it's like I told you after we escaped. He saved me. From those kids who beat me up, took my rucksack. If it wasn't for Robert, I'd probably have died."

"Did that sort of thing happen to you a lot, on the road?" She felt cold, pricked by her own memories of the floods and their aftermath.

Martin bowed his head. "Nothing like that. I managed to

get as far north as Lincoln, before that happened. After that, things were OK. Safety in numbers. And then he told me that if I helped him with this mission, I wouldn't be in his debt anymore."

"*Mission*? That's what you called it?"

"That's what he called it. Not me."

"It's the word you just used."

"Sorry."

"Go on."

His Adam's apple bobbed in the candle light as he swallowed. "He didn't tell me much. Said there was a village, north of us. A family there, that he knew, from before. He said the man had lied about him to the police. That he'd gone to prison."

"And you trusted him, despite knowing he'd been in prison?"

"He said it wasn't his fault. It was this man's fault. That he should have been the one arrested."

"And you believed him."

"I had no reason not to."

"So what did he tell you to do?"

"We'd found a trawler, washed up to the south. Near Hull. A couple of the men knew their way around boats, they'd got it working."

She looked towards the door. "Get to the point."

"Sorry. We were going to go out in it, raise a distress signal. Get ourselves brought to the village."

"And then?"

"Then one of us had to take Ruth. Just Ruth, that's all I knew about."

"Why should I believe that?"

"Its up to you, Sarah. Believe me, or don't. I won't lie to you."

"So why was it you who took her?"

"It was supposed to be Robert. Maybe Bill. But I was closer, in the end."

"Ruth and Ben took you in, after you fell in the sea."

Martin rested his hands on the table again. Sarah didn't move.

"Ruth was kind to me," he said. "She treated me for my hypothermia, gave me a comfortable bed. Clothes. Food. You have no idea how I—"

"I get it. So why didn't you stop at Ruth? What about the rest of us?"

He slumped in his chair. "I don't know. Maybe they planned it, maybe they didn't. But I knew nothing about it until we were on the boat. I promise you."

She stood up. "So you think that exonerates you? That it's fine to do that to Ruth, even if it isn't to the rest of us?"

"No. I wish I could go back, Sarah. I really do. I wish to God I'd never got involved."

She shook her head and headed for the door. She'd heard enough. Tomorrow he would be judged, and she wouldn't be there to vouch for him. Never mind that he'd helped her get away from them. Never mind what he'd told her he felt for her.

"Goodbye, Martin."

"Sarah, please—"

She ignored him and trudged down the stairs. Her feet felt heavy. She was home now, but she had the memory of all that had happened to deal with. She had her mother's insistence on Sam to dismiss.

She pulled open the outer door. Outside, a figure was standing in the road, looking up at Martin's window.

She pulled inside and closed the door. "He's found us."

"Who?"

"My dad."

Martin backed up the stairs. "Shit."

She clenched her fists. Why had she crept out? Coming here had been pointless. She'd known what he was going to tell her, in her heart. He was bad news, and she'd been mad to ever think otherwise.

"You have to hide," Martin said. "He can't find you here."

The door rattled behind her. She felt her legs turn to lead.

"Sarah! Martin! Are you in there?"

Martin stopped at the top of the stairs. "That isn't Ted."

She sighed. "It's Sam."

"Who's Sam?"

"Long story. Be quiet, and he'll leave us alone."

She imagined what Sam would be thinking, standing outside, watching the window. The flickering candle, her alone up here with Martin.

It didn't matter. Sam didn't matter.

"I'll get rid of him," she said. "I'm going."

She opened the door again. Sam fell through.

"Sam, what are you doing here?"

He righted himself, glancing up at Martin. She sensed Martin shifting from foot to foot above her.

"Your dad's on the warpath."

"You've been spying on us."

"No. I was worried about you, when I saw you outside the JP. I went back, I saw him leave your house."

"How did you find me?"

He blushed. "I heard Jess talking to my brother."

She pushed him aside. Despite his bulk, he moved easily. "Don't follow me, Sam. I'm going home."

If Ted was out looking for her, she could slip into the

house without him seeing. She had her key. And she had her lightness, her quietness.

"Sarah!"

She turned to see both young men standing in the doorway. She hissed at them to be quiet.

She ran for home, not caring what they thought.

10

The next morning, Martin sat in his bare flat and waited. Sarah didn't want him here, so there was no reason to stay. But he felt he owed it to Jess to at least wait for the outcome of the council meeting.

The only food in the cupboard was a half-empty tin of biscuits. He'd worked his way through most of them in the night, struggling to sleep. Now he polished the rest off. Robert had told him that the villagers were self-sufficient, which meant someone had baked these biscuits. Did they know they'd been left here? He suddenly felt guilty for eating them.

He'd lost his watch years ago and there was no clock in this flat, so he couldn't be sure what time it was or how long he'd been awake. Judging by the low sun hitting the houses opposite, it was about eight o'clock.

He thought of the look on Sarah's face last night, when she'd thought Ted was outside. He fingered the plaster on his chin, already curling at the edges. Did Ted ever do that to her?

He took one last look out of the window. Two men

passed, deep in conversation. One carried a garden fork and the other a wooden crate which looked heavy.

He came to a decision.

He waited for the men to pass, then unlocked the door and slipped downstairs, keeping quiet in case of curious neighbours.

He headed towards the village square. Sarah's house was that way; he'd watched her run off last night. And if Ted was a member of the village council, then he probably had one of the large houses that looked out to sea, on the same row as Ben and Ruth.

Ben and Ruth. He pushed down a pang of guilt.

He ran as stealthily as he could, passing under an archway next to a pub, his mouth watering at the thought of freshly-pulled ale. He found himself in an open space and remembered watching Robert and Bill walk across it, the morning before they took the women. He'd been standing in the doorway to Ruth and Ben's house, after they'd taken him in because of his hypothermia.

There was no sign of movement at their house. He scanned all the house fronts, looking for clues. The houses were identical, all having solid front doors and no windows facing the front. They'd be at the back, for the views. This had been a holiday village once and views were everything.

A door opened. He pulled back into the shadows, watching. The air was still, the sea beyond the cliff the only sound.

A woman emerged. She was in her early fifties, wearing a pink cardigan over blue trousers and an old-fashioned floral blouse.

Sarah's mum. He remembered her from the pharmacy.

He darted forwards.

"Hello."

Her eyes widened.

"Can you tell me where Sarah is please?"

She looked from side to side. "You can't be here!"

He approached her, being careful not to get too close. Her face was heavily lined and she had purple marks under her eyes. Tiredness, or bruises?

"We met in the pharmacy. Yesterday."

She stiffened. "Go. Now, please. Go."

She looked up at the house behind her.

"I just want to speak to her. Before they tell me to leave."

She folded her arms across her chest. "As well they should."

She took another look around the square then pulled the door closed behind her. "I shouldn't be talking to you."

"Is she in there?"

She squared her shoulders. "If she is, she's not coming out." A pause. "My husband's in there too. He did that to you, didn't he?"

He touched his chin. "Nothing I didn't deserve."

"Sarah's asleep. I suggest you go."

"Let me say goodbye to her first."

"She's not interested in you. She's engaged."

Sarah had said nothing about this. But then, she hadn't had much chance to speak, after he'd answered her questions.

"Engaged? To who?"

"None of your business." She pulled the door open just a crack and took a step backwards.

"Tell me who she's engaged to and I'll leave you alone."

Her eyes were hard now, glinting in the low sunlight. "Sam Golder."

"I met him."

"When?"

"Last night. When I... nothing. He seems nice."

"He is. Quiet. Dependable."

"In that case, I won't cause any trouble. Tell her I said goodbye."

She said nothing. He stared at her for a few moments, breathing heavily. He felt like his legs had been ripped from under him.

"Go on then."

He turned for the clifftop and started walking. He'd rather take the long route than be spotted in the village.

awn slid back into the house, hoping no one had heard her talking to Martin. Ted had arrived home two hours after storming out the previous night, Harry with him. Harry, it seemed, had calmed him down.

Sarah had slunk back while he was out and crept up to bed. With Harry's help, Dawn had persuaded Ted to leave her to sleep, to wait until morning to punish her.

Poor girl. Dawn had no idea what she'd been through at the hands of those men, and her own father wanted to hurt her too.

And now this man, little more than a boy, was turning up on their doorstep, asking for her like he was a gentleman caller picking up his date.

His face had fallen when she'd told him about Sam. *Good*. Martin was bad for Sarah. Sam was what she needed.

She clicked the door shut. Someone was stirring upstairs; Sarah.

Dawn hurried to the kitchen and started slicing bread, anxious to look busy. As she sawed the bread knife to and fro, she heard Sarah's light steps cross to the living room behind her. The girl was holding her breath.

She paused in her slicing. The steps paused too. She continued slicing.

She heard the back door open. She spun round. Sarah was sliding it open, her eyes on Dawn. When she spotted her mother watching, she slammed the door open and threw herself outside.

Dawn ran to follow her. She pushed the door aside and reached out to grab her daughter's wrist.

"Where are you going?"

"I heard you. Talking to Martin." Sarah pulled away but Dawn's grip was strong.

"Stay here. Don't be stupid." She lowered her voice. "Your dad's livid as it is."

Sarah stopped pulling. "I want to know if they've decided to let him stay."

"Council can't have met yet, can it? Your dad's still in bed. He wouldn't miss that."

"I still need to speak to him."

Dawn tugged harder, pulling Sarah halfway through the open door. "Not yet. Wait. You need to be here when your dad wakes up."

Sarah looked towards the staircase. She curled her lip.

"Don't get on his bad side, love."

Sarah shook free of her grip. "I'll stay here, for you."

"Good."

Sarah stepped inside. She shivered and clasped her arms around herself. She was wearing a jumper Dawn had knitted for her last winter, and a striped scarf with unraveled ends.

"Come into the kitchen. I've got eggs boiling. Warm you up."

"Thanks."

Dawn gave her daughter a feeble smile then returned to the kitchen. Those eggs would be hard by now.

She heard Ted's heavy tread on the stairs and tensed. She carried on with her business, pretending she hadn't heard him.

"Morning," he said as he pulled back a chair. He'd lost the sling and was using his injured arm, his hands both on the table. Dawn stared at it: *so dirty*.

"Morning," muttered Sarah. She was at the chair opposite him, chewing a slice of bread.

Dawn smiled at her husband, trying to conceal her fear. She looked at Sarah; the girl had her head bowed, her almost-white hair brushing the table.

"Sit up straight, girl," Ted snapped. "That's unhygienic."

Dawn, her back to them as she lifted eggs out of the pan, heard Sarah's chair scrape on the floor as she shifted her weight. She waited, spoon in mid air.

"I've got council this morning," he muttered. "Getting rid of that bloody boy. I expect you to be here when I get back."

Silence. Dawn transferred one of the eggs to a plate and buttered some bread. Movement would calm her nerves.

"Speak to me!"

"Yes, Dad."

"Yes, Dad what?"

"I'll be here. When you get back."

"Good. Now, go up to your room. And stay there."

Dawn listened to Sarah retreat to the stairs and head up to her room. She closed her door just a touch more forcefully than she should have.

Ted grunted. "Where's those eggs?"

Dawn placed his plate on the table, her head bowed.

12

S arah opened the window again, wondering if she dared climb out in daylight. There were no houses behind theirs, nothing but the clifftop and the sea beyond. But Ted might come round this way for some reason, checking on her maybe. Or one of the neighbours might look out of their window.

Maybe she could slip out when Ted had gone, make sure she was back when he returned. Or maybe she should stay where she was. If Ted found her gone, he would only take his anger out on her mother.

She leaned out of the window, taking great gulps of air. Being in this house made her claustrophobic. It was as if the air pressure was two bars higher than outside, and the temperature five degrees hotter.

Dawn wanted her to fly the nest, to be with Sam. She couldn't do that. She couldn't leave her mother alone with him.

She pulled back, glad of the scarf, and listened to the birds wheeling above the clifftop. She envied them their freedom. To ride on the wind, only needing to land for food. That would be the life.

She frowned as she heard an unfamiliar sound. A car engine. No, two.

No one in this village had a car. There weren't the resources. Fuel was scarce and they didn't have a mechanic. Sam and Zack got a lift on a works truck down to the earthworks every morning.

So whose cars were they?

She leaned further out of the window, trying to see around the house and cursing the fact that her window was at the back.

This house had just one window facing the village; a high one over the stairs.

She eased her door open, listening for her parents' voices. They were quiet. She crept out, heading for the stairs. She leaned over the top steps, placing her palms on the windowsill.

At this angle, she couldn't see down to the road. But she could see lights reflecting off the buildings opposite.

Blue lights.

She shrank back, almost falling down the stairs. She leaped back towards her bedroom as her father crossed the bottom of the stairs and opened the front door.

She slid into her room and held the door open. Her heart felt like it might escape from her rib cage.

"Can I help you?" Ted sounded impatient. "I take it you've spoke to our steward."

She heard another voice; a woman. She couldn't make out the words. Something about *authority*?

"You got a warrant?"

More words. There were two voices now; the other a man, older.

"I think we should let them in." Her mother was behind her father, at the door. She had a tentative hand on his back.

Ted turned to his wife. "Leave it to me."

The woman took the opportunity to push the door further open. "Your wife's right, sir. It would be easier if we could come inside."

Sarah pushed her door further closed, leaving it open just a crack. How long before they summoned her?

And where was Martin?

"Thank you, Sir. Madam. Mr and Mrs Evans, is that correct?"

"Yes." Her father, his voice sharp.

"Can we all sit down, please?"

Dawn muttered something and there was the sound of feet shuffling into the living room. Sarah wondered how her mother would be feeling about all those shoes on her carpet.

She opened her door a fraction wider. The voices were muted now, further away.

She looked back at the window. If she climbed out, they would see her through the rear windows. She was trapped.

Movement again; the rustling of heavy jackets and footsteps muffled by carpet. Then more voices as the two police officers returned to the hallway.

"We would like to speak to everyone who was at the farm. To get a clear picture of what happened, and who was involved. I assume your injury was sustained there?"

"None of your business," said Ted.

"Of course," said Dawn.

"So when your daughter comes home, you'll be sure to let us know, won't you?"

"How?" Ted's voice.

'I'm sorry?"

"We don't have no phone. How will we contact you?"

"Oh, we'll be around the village for a while yet. House to house. You'll find us."

Ted grunted.

"Mr Evans?"

"Yes," said Ted. "We'll find you."

Sarah heard the door being opened and closed. She leaned back against the wall, her nerves on fire.

13

She waited five minutes – an agonising count to three hundred – then ran down the stairs.

"Sarah!" Her father was in the kitchen. He came towards her.

She turned to Dawn. "Where did he go, Mum? Where is he?"

Dawn cast Ted a worried look. "I don't know what you're talking about, love."

"We need a word," said her father. "The police want to talk to you."

"What's this about a murder?" Dawn asked.

She felt ice run down her back. "A murder?"

"They're making enquiries," said her father. "A murder investigation."

Her hands felt cold, and her feet leaden. "Not the kidnappings?"

"They said nothing about that. Murder, is what they said." He advanced on her. "You should never have brought him here."

She backed into the wall. "No! No, they've got it wrong. It was Robert. He took us. He got the others to..."

Her parents were staring at her. They were never going to believe what Martin had told her. She wasn't sure if she did herself.

But killing Robert hadn't been murder. It was self-defence. It was mercy.

She pulled open the door. "Mum? Which way? Which way did he go?"

Her mother shook her head at her. Tears rolled down her face. "Forget him, love. He's left."

Sarah shrieked in frustration then hurled herself through the door.

Outside, the blue lights still flashed off the house fronts, providing a contrast to the yellow-green clouds that hung over them. The air felt charged, as if electricity was running through her veins.

Two uniformed policemen stood in front of one of the houses, waiting. Clyde stood outside the JP, gawping. Clyde was the landlord and also the custodian of the village boat. It was he who had brought them all home.

A small crowd had gathered around him, watching.

She glared at them. This was supposed to be a community. They pulled together. They didn't stare at each others' troubles.

The road out of the village was blocked by a police car. Would Martin have gone that way? Would they have seen him?

She caught movement to her left. The door to Ruth and Ben Dyer's house opening. A woman in a grey suit walked out. The woman who'd been in her own living room, minutes before?

Behind her followed Ruth. Her head was bowed and she

wore a torn T-shirt over a pair of faded jeans. Her hair was dishevelled and she had no socks on under her thin shoes. A uniformed policewoman followed her, her hand on Ruth's shoulder.

An older man came after them, dressed in a dark suit and coat, and a tie that was far too bright for the circumstances. Ben trailed him, shouting.

Sarah collapsed to the ground. She watched, open mouthed, as they guided Ruth to one of the police cars. A door was opened – a rear door – and Ruth was ushered inside, a hand on her head. The door was closed behind her. Ben ran at it, pounding it with his fists.

The policewoman turned and pulled Ben away. The female detective spoke to him. He let out a groan then his body slumped, like a marionette with its strings cut.

The male detective got into the car. It headed up the Parade, passing Clyde and the shocked group of villagers.

She had to get to Martin. They had to be told the truth.

There were plenty of places to hide. Houses, trees, thickets of heather. He would have seen their lights before they could have seen him.

He *would* be hiding, though. He would have stopped moving.

Which meant she could catch up with him. She could find him.

14

Martin crouched behind a wooden hut at the edge of what seemed to be an allotment. Wooden and tin structures dotted the space, along with crates full of compost. Rows of perfectly arranged vegetables spread out around him; carrots, leeks, parsnips, cabbages. It reminded him of his childhood, his grandmother's insistence on self sufficiency. As if the 1953 floods, her obsession, hadn't taught her that crops could be wiped out in a heartbeat.

He'd spotted the police lights as he'd left the centre of the village behind. There were plenty of houses that would have sheltered him, but he didn't want to risk being seen by their inhabitants. The allotment was empty.

The village was quiet now, the police cars having passed him, heading towards the coast.

Had they gone to Sarah's house?

He stood up, not caring who saw him now. He picked his way across the rows of vegetables, careful not to trample them.

The Parade, the village's central artery, was two streets

away. He sprinted towards it, not stopping to consider what might happen when he got there. He had to keep Sarah out of trouble.

He passed a row of terraced houses and spotted a man watching him out of a downstairs window. The man was balding and wore a greying vest. He looked irritated.

Martin threw him a wave, hoping that might convince the man that he belonged here. He carried on running.

He rounded the houses and crashed into someone coming the other way.

It was a woman, slim and blonde. She was in a heap on the pavement, clutching her foot.

"Sarah?"

She looked up.

"Martin! You haven't left."

"No. Well, yes. But then I saw the police. I was coming back, to make sure they didn't…"

She stood up and brushed off her skirt. She poked her foot then shook it out, seemingly satisfied. "You thought they'd arrest me?" she said.

"No. I didn't know…"

"Why would they arrest me, Martin?"

"I don't know. I wasn't thinking straight. I…"

"They'd only arrest me if they thought I had some connection to you."

"D'you think they know? I mean, d'you think they'd think that?"

She sighed. "I don't know. I don't know anything anymore."

A car approached, heading out of the village. Martin grabbed Sarah's arm to pull her out of sight, then let go. She didn't acknowledge the contact.

They watched round the corner of the house. It felt as if

the car was going at one mile per hour, so long did it take to be out of sight. A man and a woman were inside, in the front seats. The back seat was empty.

Martin felt his stomach clench.

"Why have they gone?"

Sarah turned to him. "Didn't you see the last car?"

"No."

"They've arrested Ruth."

He pushed down memories of the encounter in the farmhouse kitchen. Robert holding a knife to Sarah's face. The fear in her eyes...

"Are you alright?" she asked.

He frowned. "Yes. Why?"

"You suddenly went very pale."

He fingered his cheeks. "Sorry. I've got to get back, tell them the truth."

"What truth?"

He eyed her. 'You know what truth. It's me they should be arresting."

"You were protecting me. All of us."

"Ruth doesn't deserve to get the blame."

"Even though she finished him off?"

He stepped back. "Sarah. It wasn't like that. You know that."

She pulled her hands through her hair. Martin wondered if that man would be watching again, from his window.

"I'm not myself," she said. "It's my dad."

"Has he hurt you?"

Her eyes went to his chin. The plaster had fallen off; he had no idea how the wound looked.

"No," she said. "There's been a lot of shouting, though. A lot of posturing."

"He's only trying to protect you."

"He's got a funny way of showing it."

He looked past her, towards the village centre. "Look, I don't think you should come with me."

"No."

"Good. You wait here, and I'll go on ahead. Unless you want to get safely home first?"

"I mean *no*. Don't go back. They'll kill you."

"I have to go to the police, Sarah. I can't be responsible for Ruth."

"That doesn't mean you have to face the village." She paused. "I've got a better idea. I'll talk to them. I'll tell them what he did to me. That Ruth was defending me. Jess will back me up."

"She wasn't there. Not for all of it."

"She'll back me up, Martin. I got the feeling she knew what Robert was like, better than any of us. And she'll want her sister-in-law home."

"And what about me? What will you tell them about me? They'll ask you about the abduction."

"It wasn't you who took me."

"This is dumb. You can't do this."

"I can, Martin. If you're a part of this, it'll make my dad so much worse. Trust me. Carry on walking. Get out of here."

She hesitated for a second, searching his face, then turned and ran. He watched until she was out of sight, hating himself. How could he let her do this?

He retreated into the shadow of the houses, not taking his eyes off the spot where Sarah had disappeared. Was she right? Was it better for everyone if he didn't get involved? Or was she lying, to protect him?

Don't be stupid. Why would she want to protect you?

He sighed and picked his way back across the allotment. At its far end was a wood, and then the road south.

He stopped next to a wooden shed, its door hanging open.

He couldn't leave her. Not like this. But he had to do what she told him.

He slid into the shed, checking no one had seen him. He closed the door and let himself slide to the ground, clutching his knees.

arah hurried back to the square. There was still a solitary police car: house to house. She scanned the buildings, trying to spot them. Would they go inside, or stay on doorsteps?

Maybe they were in one of the roads leading off the Parade, somewhere in the warren of streets and buildings.

"Sarah!"

Her father was standing outside their front door. He wore a shirt and thin trousers, and a frown so deep she felt it might eat her alive.

She looked behind him, into the doorway. *Mum?*

"Get in here, now!"

She took another look around the houses in hope of seeing the police officers. But the square was empty, fear having sent everyone indoors. She wondered what it had been like here after she and the others had been taken, how the village had reacted. Shocked, afraid, angry?

Did they blame her? Did they blame her family?

"I said, now!"

She took a deep breath and ran towards him. "No need to shout."

He raised his good arm as if to clip her round the head then thought better of it. She ducked past him into the house.

Inside, Dawn was sitting on the sofa, staring out to sea. The breakfast things had been washed up and cleared away and the kitchen table was as clean and empty as ever. Sarah felt a tug of guilt at not being around to help.

Ted slammed the door. "What the fuck are you thinking, running off like that!"

"Sorry." She cast a look at her mother, who continued staring ahead.

She felt a hand in her hair. She turned, flailing against it. Ted had her long hair by the roots and was pulling her towards the living room.

"Ow! Stop it! I'll come! I'll do what you want!"

Dawn turned, her mouth open. She inhaled but said nothing. Sarah threw her as reassuring a smile as she could manage. She tried not to look at the strands of hair on the carpet.

"Sit down." Ted jabbed his finger into her chest and pushed her onto the sofa, next to Dawn. She let herself fall.

Her mother's hands were clasped in her lap, her fingers twisting around each other. Ted gestured at them.

'Stop it, woman! It's bloody annoying!"

"Sorry." Dawn's voice was no more than a whisper.

Sarah looked up at her father. "You can't treat her like this. She's done nothing wrong."

Ted leaned forwards. He looked into Sarah's face. She stared back into his eyes, forcing herself not to blink.

Then he slapped her across the eyes.

She clapped a hand to her face and held in a shriek.

Dawn stood up. "Leave her!"

Dawn shifted to stand in front of Sarah. Sarah stared at her mother's back, trembling. Her father had never hit her before. He'd threatened to, plenty of times, but this was the first time he'd carried through.

She knew that the first time was like a locked door. Now it was open, she had no idea what to expect. She stood up, pushing Dawn out of the way.

The two women struggled, each vying to place herself between Ted and the other. He stood back and folded his arms across his chest, chuckling.

"What the fuck are you stupid women doing?"

He reached between them and shoved Dawn aside. She tumbled to a chair, her head hitting the wooden armrest. Sarah looked at her, panicked. Dawn raised her head. She wasn't cut, thank God.

Sarah swallowed the bile in her throat. "Please, Dad. I know I shouldn't have gone out. I'm sorry."

"Sorry?" his spit landed in her face and she resisted an ache to wipe it away. "Sorry is as sorry does, girl."

He jabbed at her again and sent her crashing onto the sofa. Then he grabbed her arm and yanked her off it and onto the floor. Her leg twisted beneath her and she landed on it awkwardly.

She fumbled on the floor. Her leg throbbed. She tried to move it, but it was stuck beneath her.

"Stop it!"

Dawn was in front of her again, her hands raised in front of her face. "You promised me you'd never touch her!"

He looked from Dawn to Sarah and back again. "That was before she decided to go gallivanting about with that bloody boy."

"She's not gallivanting, Ted. She went to see Sam."

"Sam?"

"Sam Golder. He's—"

"What the fuck has Sam Golder got to do with any of this?" He turned to Sarah, who was still twisted on the floor. She'd managed to get her leg out from under her and was trying to figure out how to pull herself upright. "And what are you doing seeing boys?"

"It's natural, Ted," pleaded Dawn. 'She deserves better than—"

"Better than what?" His eyes were blazing, bulging like they might explode. "Better than me?"

He balled his fist and struck Dawn across the jaw. She collapsed sideways, into the armchair. There was a crack as her head hit its arm.

"Mum!" Sarah shrieked. She was up on her feet, unaware of her own pain. "Mum!"

She turned to her father. She opened her mouth to speak. He cocked his head, challenging her. She closed her mouth.

Not now. Not yet.

She collapsed to the floor, muttering in her mother's ear. Ted cleared his throat loudly then slammed through the front door, leaving them in an aching silence.

16

Sarah was woken from her trance by someone pounding on the door.

"Is everything alright in there?"

She ushered their visitor inside: Jess.

"I heard shouting, then I saw Ted marching towards the JP. He looked like he'd swallowed a bee's nest. Are you OK?"

Sarah shook her head. She turned towards Dawn, lying crooked against the sofa.

"Oh my God." Jess went to Dawn's side. She lifted her arm and held her wrist, her eyes closed. "She's got a pulse."

Sarah's eyes widened. It hadn't occurred to her that she wouldn't.

Jess held Dawn's head in her lap. "But she's unconscious. What happened, Sarah?"

Sarah looked at her mother. How much should she say? What would Dawn say?

She took in a deep breath. "She fell."

"She fell? Just fell, like that?"

Sarah nodded. If she opened her mouth, she would scream until her lungs burst.

"What about the cut on her eyelid?"

Sarah squinted to look. Sure enough, Dawn had a small cut above her eye. It was starting to bleed. That was a good sign... wasn't it? Blood?

"I, I don't know. She must have got that earlier."

"Look, Sarah. It isn't for me to pry into your family's business. But you can talk to me, you know. You can trust me."

Sarah nodded, her lips clamped shut. The last thing her father would tolerate was for her to tell the steward their secrets.

Jess sighed. "Have it your way. But you might want to think of something to explain away the bruise you're going to have in the morning."

Sarah put her hand up to her face. The flesh to the side of her right eye stung. The pain in her ankle had come back now, but it didn't feel as if anything was broken. Just a twist, or a sprain.

Dawn blinked a few times, then opened her eyes. She looked at Jess, and her eyes widened. Her expression held more horror than when Ted had been attacking her.

"Jess," she murmured. "What are you doing here? Where's Ted?"

"He left. I'm just here to help Sarah get you to bed."

Dawn and Sarah exchanged glances. Dawn's face held remonstration, while Sarah tried to inject a plea into hers.

Jess stood up. "Come on then."

The two of them lifted Dawn to her feet. Her legs were weak and she could barely put weight on them. Sarah bit down on her lip, trying to shut out the pain in her ankle.

They half-dragged, half-carried Dawn to the stairs. Jess shifted Dawn's weight to take most of it.

"No," said Sarah. "Let me."

"She's light as air, and you're limping. I've got her."

Sarah trailed behind, taking Dawn's legs, as Jess hauled her mother up the stairs. Jess puffed out sharp breaths as she ascended, struggling in the confined space until they reached the top.

'Which room?"

"That one."

Jess backed into the door to Dawn and Ted's room. The room was gloomy and bare. They staggered through with Dawn between them. She made an involuntary noise every time she touched the doorframe, or the wall.

At last Dawn was on the bed. Sarah heaved the duvet out from under her and slid it over her. Dawn gave her a weak smile of thanks.

"Is she badly hurt?" asked Jess. "What did he do to her?"

Sarah lowered her eyes. "She isn't bleeding."

"That doesn't tell us anything. We need Ruth."

"Yes."

Jess closed her eyes. She looked tired. Sarah remembered that she'd walked forty miles to find her and the others who'd been taken, just a few days ago.

Jess eyed Sarah. "You know where she's gone?"

Sarah nodded. "I wanted to talk to you about that."

"I can imagine what you've got to say about things, but I don't want to hear it. I need to speak to the police, calm the village. It's not easy, being steward."

"Can I come and find you? I don't want to leave Mum right now, but I think I can help."

"Do you?" Jess replied.

"Yes."

"OK. Give me half an hour. I'll stall the police. If I can. You want to tell them something?"

"Yes."

"Right."

Jess gave Dawn one final worried look then left. Sarah listened as she hurried down the stairs and closed the door behind her.

"Mum? Can you hear me?"

Dawn opened her eyes. "Of course I can. Sit down here. Talk to your old mum."

"You're not so old."

"You know what I mean." She patted the bed next to her.

Sarah sat down, taking her mother's hand. "Does your head hurt?"

"Nothing that won't get better." She tried to smile. "Don't worry, love. I've had worse."

"I'm sorry."

"Don't be." Dawn closed her eyes. Sarah wondered if she was about to lose consciousness. She gripped her hand tighter.

"Ouch."

Sarah let go. Dawn opened her eyes.

"I'm sorry, love."

"It's not your fault."

"He's never hit you before."

Sarah lowered her eyes. He'd hit her mother, plenty of times.

Dawn continued. "I always promised myself that if he touched you..."

"Promised yourself what, Mum?"

Dawn closed her eyes. "Nothing. Things are too complicated, right now." She opened her eyes. "You need to stay out of trouble, love. Keep away from that boy."

"I know."

"And you need to get out of this house. You're a woman

now. You need a place of your own. I'm sure the council would give you and Sam that vacant flat."

Sarah dropped Dawn's hand. "Don't be ridiculous."

"Its not ridiculous, love. Sam's a good boy. Reliable, Even tempered. Safe. He's what you need."

"That's not what Dad thinks."

"He'll come round." Dawn looked into her eyes. "You know why you have to leave us. I can't have him hurting you again."

"Then why do you let him do it to you?"

"I don't have a lot of choice. Besides, your dad isn't as bad as all that."

"Mum."

"When you get to my age, you'll understand that life isn't all black and white." She paused. "I think you've had a bit of a taste of that lately, haven't you?"

Sarah felt herself blush.

"Well. Do the sensible thing. Talk to Sam. He's in love with you. He's got a job, of sorts, and a good family. He's what you need."

"I don't love him, Mum."

"And you do love this Martin boy?"

"That's not what I said."

"Stay away from him, Sarah." She squeezed her eyes shut. "He's a killer."

"No. No, he's not."

"I know his type, love. He's bad news."

"I'm not you."

Dawn's eyes sprang open. "That's not what I said."

Sarah held her gaze for a moment. Both women knew what her father was, but both were scared to give voice to it. But Martin wasn't Ted.

She stood up. She smoothed the duvet over her mother

then turned for the door. Jess had gone. The bedroom was entirely dark now; where had the day gone?

She walked into the hallway and looked at herself in the mirror. Her face was dimly lit from one side, through the window. Her hair was tangled and the skin under her eyes yellowing with a growing bruise. "He really isn't," she said to her reflection.

She closed the bedroom door and stumbled down the stairs. She needed to find Jess.

17

J ess was standing at the door to Ben and Ruth's house. She reached into her pocket and put a key in the lock. Sarah had never known Ben and Ruth lock their door before.

"Jess! Stop!"

She looked round. Sarah approached her, glad the square was quiet. She could hear the dim roll of thunder behind her, inland.

"Sarah. You had something to tell me."

"Yes. It wasn't Ruth's fault."

"I saw what she did, Sarah. I have no idea how she's going to defend herself. We can't exactly afford a lawyer."

"You didn't see what happened before that. You came bursting in after my dad, when he was on the floor, fighting Robert. Right?"

"You were kneeling over him."

"I hadn't been."

"What do you mean, you hadn't been?"

"When Dad saw me, from the yard. I was sitting at the

table. With Ruth. Robert had a knife against my cheek. He moved it to my forehead. He cut me."

She lifted her hair to show the scar that she knew zagged across her forehead.

"That was you. Not Ruth."

"I was in the cell next to her. I heard him visiting her."

Jess's eyes widened. "He raped her?"

"No. But he was going to. He threatened her with it, all the time. Kept going on about Ben and how he was going to steal her from him. None of it made any sense."

"They knew each other at school. Things happened."

"I gathered that."

"So you think she's got a defence? He was going to rape her?"

"When they brought me and Martin back, she appeared from upstairs. I think he'd forced her up to his room. He wanted her to live with him. It was sick."

Jess looked down at the ground. Sarah watched her, waiting. Was there something she didn't know about the Dyer family, and its history with Robert Cope? Something Jess knew, but wasn't revealing?

"You can try telling the police that," said Jess. "But Ruth's best chance is if they work out who really killed him."

"You think so?"

"Sarah, you know who grabbed that knife and went for him. Ruth only finished it off."

"Right." Jess had still been outside at that point, helping the other women escape. But she had to know...

This wasn't going to work. Martin was already far away, and Ruth was going to prison.

"I didn't see what Ted did," said Jess.

"Sorry?"

"Your dad. He went flying in through that door like he had wings. Did he see Robert hurt you?"

"I guess so. The first I knew, he was on top of him. He wasn't strong enough though."

"How is his shoulder?"

"Strong enough for him to do what he did tonight."

"Yes. Sorry."

"Don't be. You helped us."

Jess looked back at the house. "I need to get back in. I'm sure you can imagine the state Ben's in."

Sarah followed her gaze. Ben, Ruth's husband, was someone she'd never had cause to speak to. This was the first time she'd spoken to his sister Jess at any length. But in the last week his wife had been abducted and then arrested. He had five-year-old twins to think about. He must be breaking down.

"Sorry. I'll leave you to it. Maybe I can track Martin down."

Jess visibly relaxed. "That would be a huge help. For Ruth."

"Yes."

Jess put her hand on Sarah's arm. "He helped you get out, didn't he?"

"Yes."

"Is that why you wanted him to come back with us?"

Sarah blinked back tears. "It was a bad idea."

"Maybe not at the time. But now, maybe yes."

Sarah sniffed. "Go. Go to your brother. He needs you. I'll try to help."

"Thank you." Jess opened the door and went into the house. It flickered with the warm light of a log fire. She thought of her own house after power-down, the single candle allowed in each occupied room.

Jess closed the door behind her. Sarah watched it for a moment as if it might open again, then turned. She dragged herself across the square.

Ted was outside their house, elbowing the door open. She felt her heart pick up pace. What would he do, when he found Dawn upstairs in bed?

She peered towards the main road – *Martin, where are you?* – then clenched her fists and walked towards home.

She opened the door as quietly as she could. The house was quiet. She slid inside, her eyes on the staircase.

A shadow loomed at the top.

She squared her shoulders as he descended in silence.

"Hello, love."

"Hello." Why was he being so normal?

"Your mum's asleep."

"Yes." *She's not asleep, you bastard, she's half conscious because of what you did to her.*

"Best you go to bed too, eh."

She frowned at him. No apology. No anger. No continuation from where he left off.

Was this what he was like with Dawn, after he hit her?

She looked past him, up the stairs. "I'd like to see Mum."

"No, lass. She's fast asleep. She won't want you disturbing her."

She stared up the stairs. The faint light of a candle glowed from her parents' room. Did she dare stand up to him, barge past and insist on seeing Dawn? Would that make things worse for her mother?

"Right."

He smiled at her, then turned and started climbing. She followed, trying to shut out the sound of his heavy footsteps. His breathing was laboured; his shoulder would be giving him pain. She wanted to hit him, to knock him down the stairs and make him land crookedly against the sofa, like he'd done to Dawn.

But Dawn wouldn't want that. She wouldn't thank her.

She tiptoed up after him, keeping her breathing under control. It was an effort.

He stopped just past her door and turned. He gave her another smile.

"'Night, then."

She put her hand on the doorknob. "'Night."

He watched as she slipped inside. She closed the door behind her and let herself breathe again.

She sat down on the bed. The curtains were open and the moon shone weakly into the room. She stood to see it better, out beyond the clifftop. Maybe she should throw herself off. Maybe that would be better for everyone.

She heard a scratching sound at her door and spun towards it. A key, turning.

She ran to it, turning the handle. It didn't budge. She placed her hands on the wood, imagining him on the other side.

She wouldn't call out. Wouldn't give him the satisfaction.

She retreated to her bed. She'd only slept ten hours in the last five days.

She lay down and let sleep wash over her.

18
———

It had been dark for hours, and there was no sign of Sarah. Martin had watched the final police car pass along the Parade, empty expect for its driver and a detective in the passenger seat.

Had Sarah gone to them? Had she told them what she'd need to, to release Ruth?

It wouldn't work. The only thing that would lead to Ruth's release was his own arrest.

They would be looking for him. No one from the village had told them he'd come back with them, as far as he knew. So they'd go to the farm.

That was where he needed to be.

He pushed the shed door open. The night was damp, a faint moon shining through scudding clouds. He shivered in his thin shirt. He'd need more than this if he was going to make the walk past Withernsea.

He heard voices beyond the edge of the allotment. Men. He crouched down low and listened. The sky was lightening a little, over the sea. Sunrise, already?

"She's not what you think," said one of the men.

"Not as *old*!" the other joked.

"Don't."

"She was our *teacher*, Zack."

"*Was* being the operative word. That was years ago. We're men now, not boys. She knows that."

"So she likes you too?"

"I think so. There was something between us, when we were off looking for the women. Sorry."

"Don't."

"I didn't mean to—"

"I said it's alright. Tell me more about Jess. What's she like in the sack?"

Martin heard the sound of a fist hitting fabric.

"Oof. You didn't need to do that."

"Don't take the piss, little brother."

"Not so much of the little. I'm bigger than you now. I've been doing weights."

"Ten minutes, Sam. That's all I'm saying. It counts."

Martin held his breath, wishing the sky would stop brightening. He was behind a tiny shed in the middle of a featureless allotment. There was no way he could get away without them seeing him.

"So what about Sarah?"

"What about her?"

"Her mum's keen on you. Is *she*?"

"She will be."

"Don't. I've seen enough of that sort of talk with Robert Cope."

"I didn't mean it like that. But once that Martin geezer is out of the way, she'll come round."

"I hope so, mate. She's pretty."

"I know. That hair."

Martin closed his eyes and pictured Sarah's hair. Even

when matted and clogged with mud, it had an ethereal quality, strands of it wafting around her face like she was something out of a painting.

"Hang on. Here's Danny. Craig too."

"Better shut up about women then."

"Oh no, mate. We're getting all the mileage we can about you taking up with the steward."

Again, Martin heard flesh hitting cloth. Then a chuckle, followed by more voices.

He ducked inside the shed. He was going to have to wait it out.

19

Daylight was filtering through Sarah's thin curtains. She looked at the wind-up clock next to her bed: 9am.

She groaned. She'd slept over twelve hours, and her mother was out there alone.

She went to the door. It was still locked. She rattled the handle.

"Let me out! I need the toilet."

Footsteps hurried up the stairs. She heard breathing behind the door.

"I've brought you some breakfast, love."

"Mum? I need to get out. I'm bursting."

A pause. "You promise you won't try to run out again?"

She crossed her fingers. "Promise."

She stepped back as her mother unlocked the door. She had a bruise across her forehead and the beginnings of a black eye.

Sarah reached a hand towards her but Dawn shrank back.

"Where's Dad?"

"Out."

"Out where?"

"He didn't tell me. Here, take this."

Dawn pushed a bowl of porridge into Sarah's hands. Sarah put it on her bedside table.

"How are you?"

"I thought you needed the toilet."

"That can wait. You were in a bad way, last night."

Dawn looked at the carpet. It was pale blue, with stains where the sun had bleached it. "I'm fine."

"You don't look it."

Dawn looked up to make eye contact. "Do you need the toilet, or not?"

"Yes."

Sarah pushed past her mother to the bathroom. When she returned, Dawn was gazing out of her bedroom window.

"You can't keep me locked up in here."

Dawn nodded towards the porridge. "Eat."

"Where's Snowy? He needs to be let out."

"I've done it." Dawn crossed to the door. "Eat that. You need to regain your strength, after everything that's happened to you."

Everything that's happened to you. Was Dawn ever going to ask her about what happened? The abduction, the attempted rape, the escape? The killing.

"Mum? Can we talk, properly, please?"

There was a sound from downstairs. Dawn flung her head to one side, her nostrils flaring.

Silence. She looked back at Sarah and backed out of the room. "Eat."

Dawn closed the door and locked it. Sarah ran to it, hammering it with her fists.

"Mum! Please! You can't do this!"

"Your dad's orders."

"But he's not here."

Silence. Sarah hoped her mother wasn't leaving.

"You're going to let him imprison me?"

She heard movement against the door. Dawn was sliding down to the floor. Could she hear sobbing?

"I don't want to antagonise him, love. Not after he hit you. We need to keep the peace. Until we can get you out of here. With Sam."

"I'm not interested in Sam, for God's sake!"

"Don't blaspheme. You should be."

"Mum, why is Dad doing this? He's not normally this bad."

"He's scared, love."

"What the hell does *he* have to be scared of?"

Silence again. *Come back. Talk to me.*

The key clattered in the lock and Dawn opened the door. "Mind your language. You don't understand. This village is a place of refuge. It's safe. Or it was. It's not now. And you bringing that boy here hasn't helped."

"He helped me escape, Mum."

"He also took you. Or have you forgotten that?"

Sarah slumped onto her bed. "No." She looked at Dawn. "I'm confused, Mum. I don't know what's going on."

"I know." Dawn sat next to her and slid an arm around her shoulders. Her flesh was cold but the touch was welcome. Sarah leaned in, feeling her mother's breath on her cheek.

"Mum, I know how to help Ruth. I can tell them the truth. Tell them that it was Martin who killed Robert."

Dawn stopped stroking Sarah's hair. "You can?'

"Yes."

"You will?"

"Yes. I just need to find Jess. She must have a way of contacting the police."

Dawn stood up. Sarah stared ahead, her eyes on her mother's hands, red from household chores.

"Are you sure about this, love?"

Sarah looked up. "I'll be quick. I'll come straight back."

"Well..." Dawn glanced at the door. "I don't know when your father will be home. If you're not here..."

Sarah grabbed her hand. "I'll be quick. I'll run straight there and straight back."

"It's a fair way to Jess's house."

"She'll be at Ruth's. With Ben."

"Alright then." Dawn stood back. Her eyes were wide with fear. "But be quick, please."

20

M artin was woken by movement outside the shed. He sprang to his feet and grabbed the nearest weapon he could find. A trowel. Fat lot of good that would do.

There was a knock at the door. He frowned at it.

"Sarah?"

"It's Sam."

"I thought you'd gone out to work."

"I should have. But then I spotted them."

"Spotted who?"

"Just let me in, will you?"

Martin eyed the door. He'd tied it closed with a length of garden twine he'd found.

Could he trust Sam? He'd want Martin gone, with the way he felt about Sarah. He might have brought Ted with him.

"Are you alone?"

"Yes. Get a move on!"

He untied the twine and shoved it into his pocket. He

pushed the door open a crack, gripping its edge tightly so he could slam it into Sam if he needed to.

"What is it?"

"They're after you."

"Who?"

"Ted. Some others."

"How did they find me?"

"They must have spotted you. You need to move."

He leaned out of the shed and looked back towards the road. Sure enough, a small group of men was making its way towards them. Ted was at its head. His coat was draped over his bad shoulder; how did he have such strength, when he'd been stabbed?

"Shit."

"Exactly. Come on, I can get you out of here."

Martin let Sam pull him out of the shed and started running across the allotment. He muttered a silent apology each time his foot fell on something growing, but he didn't have time to be careful.

At the far edge of the allotment was a track. Martin looked back. The men were almost at the shed now, struggling across the heavy soil. Ted yelled something. Behind him was Harry and two other men Martin didn't recognise. They were all looking at Ted as if waiting for orders.

"Get back here, you little shit!"

"Run, now!" hissed Sam.

Martin ducked under a wire fence Sam was holding up and started to run. They sprinted along the track, dodging tree roots and potholes. He heard voices approaching from behind.

He looked round. They were coming under the fence now, Harry holding it up for the others to pass. Ted was yelling at them.

He felt Sam's hand on his sleeve and was pulled sideways into the hedge.

"Ow!"

"Sorry! They won't see us, this way."

Martin stared at Sam, who was shoving brambles and bracken aside. Thorns rebounded behind him, hitting Martin in the face. He held his arms up to shield himself.

"Where are we going?"

"The boat house. It's your only way out of here."

He stopped running. "I can't steal the boat!"

Sam turned. "I'll take you along the coast a couple of miles. That'll give you a head start. Now, run!"

Martin pushed down the questions and did as he was told. At last the undergrowth spat them out into a clearing. Ahead of them was a path leading to the boathouse. He looked at it, guilt eating at his insides.

"I can't…"

"You bloody well can. They'll kill you."

"Is this about Ruth?"

"They don't care about that. Ted doesn't, anyway. It's about Sarah."

He felt his heart drop inside his rib cage. "Is she alright?"

"She's fine. She's in there, getting the boat ready."

"What?" He ran ahead, careering through the door to the boathouse and almost falling into the boat.

Sarah was next to the boat, untying a rope.

"Hello."

"Sarah? What are you doing here?"

She shrugged. "Sam spotted me, when he was coming for you."

He stepped towards her. She took a step back. There was a bruise on her cheek.

"Did he hurt you?"

"Yes. But he won't do it again."

"How can you be sure?"

"Because I'll look after her," said Sam, closing the boathouse doors. Sarah flinched.

"Does she *need* you to look after her?" asked Martin.

"I didn't mean it like that. She just needs to get out of that house."

"Both of you, stop talking about me like I'm a child," said Sarah. "Help me with the boat."

Sam grabbed a rope off Sarah.

"I stole some food," she said. "From home. I thought you might need it."

"But you thought I'd left."

She shrugged. "I wasn't sure."

He smiled at her. She seemed to know his next move before he did. "Thank you."

Another shrug. "It's nothing."

"You know that's not true. You have rations here."

"My mum will cover for me."

"Let's hope so."

They opened the front doors of the boathouse and tugged the trailer onto the beach. Martin scanned the path behind the boathouse. Sure enough, the men were close.

They pulled the boat into the sea, cold water making him wince. Sam was unfastening it from the trailer. At last it was in the water, its hull lightly wedged against the sand.

Martin climbed into the boat. Sam was next to it, pushing it off. Sarah helped him on the other side.

"Good luck," she whispered.

He nodded. "I'll turn myself in. When I get to the farm. Get Ruth released."

She bit her lip; he knew she had to trust him.

There was a crashing sound as the door to the

boathouse flew open. Ted stumbled in, followed by Harry. Sam and Sarah started pushing harder.

Ted ran through the boathouse and onto the beach. "What the fuck? Stealing our boat again?"

"I'll bring it back!" Sam called back. "You want him gone, right?"

"Not like this."

Sam nodded at Martin. "We need to get going."

Martin nodded. He jumped out of the boat to help push, the water almost at his hips. Behind him, Sarah bent to push the boat, immersed up to her knees. She gave him a sad smile. He resisted the urge to ask her to come with him. Sam would be better for her.

"And as for you..." Ted ran onto the beach behind them, stumbling across the sand. He splashed into the shallows and made a lunge for Sarah. She shrieked and jumped into the boat. Martin felt it dip and touch the sand. He kept pushing.

Sam's face was red, his muscles straining. He stared at Sarah. "Get out!"

She looked back at Ted. He was level with Martin now, screaming at her. Martin pulled in towards the boat, desperate to avoid Ted's touch.

Ted turned to him and growled. Martin took a deep breath and jumped into the boat.

"You can get out now, Sarah!" he told her.

She took another look at her dad. His face was red with exertion and anger. Harry stood a few feet behind, water lapping at his feet.

Sarah turned to Martin. "I'm coming with you."

"What?" cried Sam. He stumbled against the side of the boat.

"Its fine, Sam," she said. "I'll take him. Drop him off a few miles south then bring the boat back."

"No you bloody won't!" Ted cried. She ignored him.

"Are you sure?" said Sam. "You know how to sail this thing?"

Sarah nodded. "How hard can it be?"

Sam gave the boat a final push. A wave caught it and dragged them back into shore. Martin cursed and grabbed an oar.

"Start rowing!" he told Sarah.

She fumbled for the other oar and they started pulling the boat out to sea. The coastline was steep along here and it wasn't long before they were deep enough to engage the outboard motor. Ted was behind them, screaming obscenities and waving madly despite the sling on his arm.

Martin took a look at Sarah. She was starring out to sea, her jaw set.

"You sure?" he asked.

She nodded, but didn't meet his eye. "Let's get going."

He pulled on the cord and started the motor.

21

D awn stared out of the kitchen window. It looked out to the side of the house and if she leaned over the sink, she could see the square, or at least part of it.

Sarah, where are you?

She'd been gone for nearly an hour now. How long did it take to get to Ruth's house four doors away and speak to Jess?

She washed her hands under the tap again, knowing she was wasting water but unable to resist. Her hands, like her home, were always scrubbed clean. Today they smarted, raw flakes peeling off between her fingers. She pulled at one of them then put it in her pocket. Better than letting it fall to the clean floor.

She heard a key turn in the front door. She rushed to it, ready to bundle the girl upstairs and back to her room.

The door opened, bringing a blast of fresh air inside. She pulled her cardigan tighter.

"What are you doing, lying in wait like that? Give a man a heart attack."

"Ted. Sorry."

"You look startled. Why do you look startled?"

"Sorry, I didn't mean to. The door, your coming back, it just..."

"Hmm. Put the kettle on."

She hurried to the kitchen and pulled the kettle out of a cupboard. She placed it on the stove and lit the gas. The blue flame warmed her hands; she held them close to it, glad of the metal heating up. This was the only time she used gas; it came from a bottle outside and was strictly rationed.

Ted was behind her, watching over her shoulder. "What's the matter?"

She stared at her reflection in the kettle. "Nothing."

"You're jumpy."

"No. No, I'm not."

"You let her out."

"No. I took her breakfast."

"Turn round when I'm talking to you, dammit."

His voice was low, calm. Dawn hated it when he spoke like this.

She turned, twisting her hands together against her apron. The knuckles were bleeding. Her head throbbed.

"Look at me."

She lifted her head and looked into his eyes, then looked quickly over his shoulder. He put a finger on her chin and pulled it down.

"I said, look at me."

She swallowed and did as she was told. Could she distract him, send him out again? Until Sarah came home?

"Why?" he asked.

"I'm sorry, I don't..."

He took a step backwards. She watched him pace into

the living room, angsty like a big cat. She stroked her knuckles, feeling blood on her fingertips.

He sat on the sofa, looking out of the window. The sky was white with cloud and the hedgerows at the top of the cliff were a dull, shadowless green.

She shrank back into the kitchen. The kettle whistled behind her, making her jump. She knocked it, spilling hot water onto her hand.

She yelped and thrust the hand into her mouth. She turned to run the tap, to soak it.

"Leave it. Come here."

She shoved her hand back in her mouth. She shuffled towards the living room, feeling her pulse running through her throbbing fingers.

"Sit with me." He patted the sofa next to him.

She shuffled in and lowered herself to sit, keeping to the end of the sofa.

"Closer. You're my wife, dammit."

She shifted a millimetre towards him. He sighed and turned to her.

"Why did you lie to me?"

She stopped sucking her hand. She felt her pulse pick up.

He leaned in. "I said, why did you lie to me?"

"I don't... I don't know what you mean."

He drew up his chest and she shrank back. Then he turned away from her, sinking into the sofa.

"She got away."

Dawn felt her body go heavy. She said nothing.

He turned to her. His face was softer now, less angry. She knew that meant nothing.

"How was she in the boat house, when you had her locked up here?"

Stupid girl. Sarah had promised that all she was going to do was to find Jess, then to hurry back.

Dawn shook her head.

"Well?"

"She told me she could help Ruth. She was going to find Jess."

"Well, she didn't, did she?"

Dawn shook her head. She lifted the tips of her fingers to her lips. The spot on her thumb where she'd spilt the water was throbbing.

"Take your bloody hand out of your mouth, woman."

She plunged her hand into her lap. She clasped the other one over it. It would be raw, later. Like the rest of her skin.

He stood up and crossed to the window. "She's out there somewhere."

"What?"

"She buggered off in the village boat. Took it."

He turned to face her, daring her to remind him of the time he'd stolen the village boat, with Harry's help. She said nothing.

"Is she alone?"

"No, of course she's not bloody alone! She's got Martin with her. Sam Dyer helped them."

"Sam?"

"Yes. Sam." He advanced to stand over her. "This is all your fault. You and your busybody matchmaking. She's nineteen. You've no right to go making some lad think he's got a chance with her."

"Nineteen is old enough to—"

"Are you not listening to a word I've said? She's gone off with that Martin, and Sam's helping them!"

Dawn looked at the window. The village boat was tiny,

just a leisure craft with a tiny cabin for the driver and open benches at the back. If they were out on the North Sea...

She stood up and pushed past Ted, not caring now what he did. She leaned on the glass, cupping her hands around her eyes.

She turned to him. "Why?"

"Why what?"

"Why did they go? Did you threaten her? Did you hurt her again?"

She'd promised herself. If he hit Sarah, she'd leave. But now it had happened, she was too scared.

His face clouded. She hurried past him to the front door, not stopping to grab her coat. She flung the door open and ran for the beach.

22

They travelled in silence, the only sound the hum of the boat's engine and the occasional bird swooping overhead. Sarah took the wheel after a few minutes, determined to accustom herself to this thing. Ahead of them the sky was dark, thick clouds pushing their way up the cliffs.

After perhaps twenty minutes, Martin broke the silence.

"Shall I go into shore now, carry on on foot?"

"What?"

"That was Sam's plan. He was going to let me off a few miles south then take the boat back."

"Oh." She thought of Ted, chasing her down the beach, into the waves. Sam's plan meant her steering the boat back home. Taking it back to him.

"We can push on a little further," she said. "So you don't have to walk as far."

"You sure?"

She nodded, staring ahead of them. The clouds were lowering now, scudding along the horizon like a threatening black army.

Martin shifted towards her. "Maybe we should pull ashore for a bit," he said. "Wait for that storm to pass."

"No."

"This boat is tiny. I know it's seen worse, but there's no point in—"

"I said no. We keep going. If it gets rough, then we head in to shore."

He sighed. "Let me take over for a bit. You'll need your strength for the trip back."

She let him take the wheel and shifted to the seat behind, careful to avoid physical contact. She stared at his back. Was he remembering the first time they'd been together on this boat? She'd been unconscious, but he would have known exactly what was going on.

She pulled her sweater more tightly around her. Spray hissed up from the water, coating the boat. The bottom was swilling with it. Should she bail it out?

She searched around for some sort of receptacle. A bucket, cup, anything.

All she could see in the bottom of the boat were ropes, and the food she'd brought for Martin. Bread and apples. The bread would be soggy.

She pulled it out of its paper bag. It was like a sponge, dripping and blue. She chucked it back to the bottom of the boat.

'What's that?'

"Bread. I brought you food, remember."

"Where did you get it?"

"We've got a bakery."

He watched her for a moment, calculating. She wondered what they ate on the farm. Oat biscuits were all she'd been given when she'd been imprisoned there. Stolen, probably.

"You grow wheat, up here?" he asked.

"We buy the flour. In Filey."

"How?"

She frowned. "Some of the men go out to work. At the reclamation works." She paused. "Sam's one of them."

Sam. She hoped her father wouldn't blame him.

Martin looked towards the shore. "I think you should drop me off now. It's getting choppy. There's a stretch of beach just there."

"It's still safe enough to continue."

He turned the boat. "I want you to go home."

She placed a hand on the wheel. "Not yet."

"Is it Ted? Are you scared of him?"

"Just keep going."

"No." He continued steering them in to shore. "You know how to sail this thing, don't you?"

"Please, carry on round that outcrop. Just a couple more miles."

"I'm worried about you going back in this weather."

They'd caught up with the clouds now and large drops of rain were falling on the boat. There was tarpaulin under Martin's feet; Sarah pulled it over as much of the boat as she could.

"Cover yourself," he said.

"I'll be fine."

"You don't have a coat. Here, have mine." He unzipped his coat.

"I'm fine." She shook her head at him. She was tired of people telling her what to do.

"At least use the tarp."

She shrugged and pulled it over her knees. She looked ahead; the sky was almost night-dark, and the waves were growing.

"We should get to shore," Martin said. She didn't argue this time. He pulled the boat hard to the right. As he did so, she heard a cracking sound.

"What was that?"

He was pale. "I don't know."

She lifted the tarpaulin and searched the bottom of the boat. Had something moved? Was it on the outside of the boat?

The boat lurched to one side. She grabbed the tarpaulin but it slid out of her hands and into the sea. She leaned over the side, her fingers brushing it.

She felt hands on her waist. Martin pulled her upright.

"What are you doing?" he shouted.

"Trying to save the tarp."

"I thought you were jumping in."

"Don't be daft!"

Rain was driving into her face now and she could barely hear her own voice. The boat listed to the left, bringing her dangerously close to the surface of the water. She scooted to the other side, hoping to balance it. It shifted a little but continued to list.

"We need to hurry," Martin shouted. His coat was soaked through and his face wet. He spat water out of his mouth as he tried to see over the boat's low windscreen and find somewhere to moor.

The boat lurched again and Sarah felt something scrape along the bottom.

"Oh my God!"

The boat ground to a halt. They were on the edge of a jagged pile of rocks, marooned.

"Help me push!" Martin leaned past her and over to the rocks. He placed his palms against them and pushed.

Sarah followed suit. The boat made some more ominous sounds and then dipped, as if going down in a lift.

"We need to get off!" she shouted.

"We can't leave it!"

"We have to! We'll drown!"

She eyed the rocks next to the boat. They were dark and slippery. To the other side was a beach, just a short swim away.

She tugged at Martin's arm. "Come on!"

"We need to save the boat!"

"We'll come back after the storm. Hurry!"

She climbed onto the side of the boat, her legs unsteady. It lurched again, almost tipping her into the water. Martin grabbed her round the waist.

"What are you doing?" he panted.

"We need to swim."

"You can't just jump in. You don't know how deep it is."

He was right. She ducked down to lean over the side of the boat, bringing her weight round so her legs dangled over the side. Martin shifted his hands to hold her under the arms.

She looked into his eyes then slithered down into the water. Her feet hit rock.

"It's not deep," she said. "But the rocks are sharp."

"Right." He climbed out after her. She felt her way along the rocks, placing each foot carefully in front of the other and holding her arms high for balance. As she walked, the rocks fell away.

"I'm going to swim." She pushed herself off towards the beach. A wave broke over her head, sending her down into the murky water.

She pushed herself up, spluttering. The water was freezing and she felt like her chest might explode.

Martin was behind her, gasping.

She had to ignore the pain. She had to focus.

She looked ahead of her, picking out a tree on the horizon. Her target.

She started to swim.

23

D awn ran out to the clifftop, her heart racing. She stumbled to a halt at the edge, glad of the scrubby hedge that kept her from falling.

The sea was hazy, shrouded in cloud, but she couldn't see any boats.

Sarah, why?

She ran for the path that led down to the beach, not stopping till the sand slowed her footsteps.

Down here it was cold, and lonely. A group of wading birds shifted in and out of the shallows, making hard, cackling sounds. The waves were low, thrumming into the sand like a bulldozer.

She slumped onto the sand, not caring about the damp through her skirt. She threw her hand over her eyes and scanned the sea. Nothing. Grey waves, birds bobbing on the surface. No boats. To the north, the rocks at Brigg End were white with sea spray, the water splitting dangerously over them.

She hoped they knew what they were doing. Sarah had never been out in the boat – at least not before she was taken... And Martin, well hadn't he fallen in the sea during Jess's misguided rescue, and given himself hypothermia?

She sniffed. *Don't cry*, she told herself. *Keep it together, like you always do.* Her daughter was lost, maybe drowned. *Stop it*, she told herself. *She'll come back, God willing.*

She took a ragged breath and pushed herself upwards. Watching the sea as she went, blindly hoping the boat would suddenly emerge, she picked her way back up the hill. She needed to get back to Ted. To calm him.

24

S arah dragged herself onto the sand, spluttering out sea water. Martin wasn't far behind. He lay next to her, pulling in breaths.

She sat up and turned back to the sea. Waves lapped at her feet. She'd lost a shoe.

Martin sat next to her, not touching. Not speaking.

They stared back at the boat, wedged on the rocks.

"We need to save it," she said.

"It's too dangerous."

"It's not ours to leave. It belongs to the village."

He stood up. "Let's work out where we are first. Come back for it, when the tide's gone out."

She eyed him, wondering if he had any intention of returning. She regretted jumping into the boat with him now, listening to the shrill voice in her head telling her to get away from her father.

She had to go home. Her mother needed her. And this escapade would only make her father more angry.

She shivered.

"You're soaked through," Martin said.

"So are you."

"At least we were close to shore."

She watched the water pushing at the boat. It shifted its weight on the rocks, looking as if it might capsize. Her throat felt tight.

"We can't leave it."

He turned to her. "You need to take it back."

She nodded, her lips trembling with the cold.

"Let's walk a bit, see where we are. If we're close to the farm, I can get them to help us with it."

A dark cloud passed through her mind at the thought of the farm. Even with Robert dead, those men were still there. Including Leroy, the man who'd attacked her.

What the hell had she been thinking? Why was she here?

She stood up. "I'm going out there."

"No. Please, not right now." He looked past her. "Wait, I think that's..."

He ran a short way along the beach, looking back at her from time to time. She watched, puzzled.

After a minute or so, he shouted something she couldn't make out. She shrugged exaggeratedly.

He waved his arms, beckoned her. She looked back at the boat. She shook her head.

Her skirt tugged at her, heavy with water. She lifted the front of it and wrung it out in her raw hands. She was shivering.

He ran back.

"The beach huts," he panted. "They're just out of sight. We came further than I thought."

She looked past him. The beach huts meant shelter. A

modicum of warmth, compared to this wind that was clawing at them.

They also meant that the farm was nearby. The farm where she'd been imprisoned. The farm where that man had tried to rape her. And Robert had held a knife to her face.

She put a hand to the wound on her forehead. She traced the thin red line where it had scabbed over. She hadn't noticed the plaster Ruth had given her falling off.

Her breath was catching in her throat and her skin felt tight. Her head span.

"The farm," she said.

His shoulders slumped. "We won't go back there."

She was shivering, her knees trembling. "I can't."

"We won't. I promise. Just the beach huts. We get shelter, then we work something out. I'll help you with the boat." He cocked his head. "Take you home, if it comes to it."

She shook her head. "No. I'll go back alone."

"Very well." He was smiling at her but his eyes looked sad.

She clenched and unclenched her fists, willing the nausea to subside.

"OK," she said. "But I go in one hut, and you have the other."

She needed to be alone, to work through her conflicting fears; returning here, versus the threat of what her father would do when she went home.

"That's fine. Come on."

He turned towards the huts.

She looked back at the boat. It was a little higher in the water now, the waves dropping. How long before the tide was out far enough for her to traverse those rocks?

In the meantime, she could use some shelter. Her feet

were numb, and her fingers felt like a thousand needles were jabbing at them. And if she tried to walk any distance, she would pass out.

Martin was almost out of sight. Reluctantly, she followed him.

25

He wasn't lying.

Around the curve of the beach was the spot where they'd taken shelter before, when they'd been running from the farm.

Were they really heading back to it? Was she that stupid?

Her hands felt clammy, her chest tight. She'd let him bring her back here. She had to get away, as soon as she could.

She'd rest here for an hour or so, get as dry as she could. Wait for the tide to drop. Then she'd go back to the boat. It had been damaged but it hadn't taken on water, at least not much. It was seaworthy. Martin would have to go on alone, as he should have all along.

The beach huts were much as they had been before; one without roofs and two of its walls, the other two intact. She pointed at one.

"I'll go in there. Alone."

He hardened his jaw but didn't argue.

She pushed open the door to the hut. In here the air was

cool but still; it smelled of wood, sand and salt. The wind, instead of beating at her, whistled outside in a way that reminded her of childhood summers. It felt calm.

She stripped down to her underwear, wringing out her skirt and blouse. She'd never known just how much water two garments could take on board. She kicked off her remaining shoe and tried to wring it out, but it was too stiff.

This was the hut where they'd spent the night, after fleeing the farm. Martin on the floor and her on a high shelf. It made a perfect drying rack. She arranged her clothes, stretching them out for maximum exposure.

She looked outside. The rain had stopped now; would her clothes dry quicker if she put them outside, took advantage of the wind? Or would they simply blow away?

Either way, she wasn't about to open the door dressed only in her underwear. She patted her clothes, trying to push the water out by sheer force of will.

She lifted herself up to sit next to them, feet dangling over the ledge. Outside, the beach was quiet. The hut next to her, Martin inside, was still.

She leaned against the wall, breathing in the musky scent of wood. Her toe throbbed from her fall last time she was here – was that really only two days ago? – and her back was sore where she'd scraped it on a rock during her swim. Every muscle in her body screamed at her, longing for sleep.

She didn't have time.

She leaned her face on the window, glad of the cool. Her face felt hot; she probably had a temperature. She knew from the warnings Ruth gave them that she shouldn't ignore a fever. It might be the first sign of infection, and with antibiotics so scarce it could be fatal.

She blinked her eyes open, cursing her feebleness. How

long had she been in here? The sky was darkening now and the sun had shifted in the sky. She'd been sleeping.

She pulled herself off the bench. Her clothes weren't much drier, but she had no choice. She dragged them on, wincing at the damp fabric rippling over her tingling flesh.

She padded to the door, abandoning the lone shoe, and pushed it open. She eyed the hut next to her. Would she tell him where she was going, or not?

He'd tell her it was dangerous. Warn her away from the rocks. Maybe try to go himself.

She couldn't go back to the farm.

She'd slip away, like she'd never been here.

She stepped down onto the sand and pushed the door closed. She sniffed the air, glad the wind had dropped.

She stepped away from the hut, turning for the direction they'd come. As she did so, she spotted someone next to the other hut.

Martin. He looked shrivelled and wet, his curly brown hair wild with water, sand and salt. He was talking to someone.

She felt her heart stop.

Run.

She turned and started to sprint across the beach, cursing the sand for dragging her down.

"Sarah?"

She forced herself not to stop, not to turn.

"Sarah! Come back!"

She heard footsteps behind her, heavy and quick. Martin's steps were lighter than that. She ignored the rising pulse in her throat and continued to run.

A hand grabbed her arm. She yanked it away, stumbling.

She righted herself and carried on running.

"Sarah, stop!"

She paused. She knew that voice.

Her chest was on fire now, her legs screaming at her to slow down. She ignored them.

The feet behind her kept coming. She could hear his breath now; short, sharp pants. A hand on her arm again.

She screamed as her legs buckled and she fell to the sand.

"Get off! Leave me alone!"

"I'm not going to hurt you."

She blinked up. Standing over her, blocking half the sky, was a man. He had dark, greasy hair that curled around his ears. He smelled of dirt, overlaid with mint. His face was weather-worn and ruddy and he had a tattoo that snaked up his right arm, under his shirt.

It was Bill. The man who'd taken her.

26

D awn eased open the front door, her senses sharp. The house was quiet, the only sound the ticking of the carriage clock on the mantelpiece. She'd found it in a cupboard upstairs, a week after moving into this house. Two weeks after Ted had been elected to the village council. She wondered who it had belonged to in a previous life and why they'd hidden it away.

She closed the door and leaned against it, trying to control her breathing. Her breaths were shallow and tight and her stomach ached.

She felt like a hole had been ripped out of her. Without Sarah, there was no reason to live.

She stepped from the doormat onto the wooden floor of the hallway, keeping her footsteps light. She glided to the kitchen. Outside, the sky was clearing, clouds shifting towards the south.

Had Sarah gone that way, with him? Had they gone back to that farm?

No. Dawn had been too scared to pry into what had happened to Sarah there. But she knew from the haunted look in her eyes that it was something to which her daughter never wanted to return.

She sat at the kitchen table; a chair was already pulled back so she didn't have to make a sound. She placed her arms on the table and leaned over them.

She caught movement from the corner of her eye. A shadow, shifting in the living room. She stilled her muscles.

He stood up from where he'd been sitting, concealed by the back of the sofa. His face was calm. Dawn pulled back in her chair.

"Where have you been?" His voice was little more than a whisper.

"Looking for Sarah."

"And?"

She shrugged.

He advanced. "And?"

She met his stare. "No sign of her."

He frowned and took the chair opposite her. She looked down at her hands, motionless on the table. She was scared to move.

She raised her head. "What happened? Why did she go off with him?"

"Because she's a stupid girl, that's why."

"But I don't understand. Why would she go off with him, when Sam was—"

"What's this about Sam?"

She swallowed. "Sam's a good boy. He's what she needs."

"Since when was that up to you?"

She blinked. "I—I don't know."

"She's too young. You shouldn't be putting daft ideas in her head."

"No."

He was right; if she hadn't filled Sam's head with hopes of Sarah, he wouldn't have helped them.

"Where is Sam?" she asked. "Is he alright?"

"I went to speak to his parents, while you were out."

She imagined Ted banging on the Golder family's door, demanding to be heard. Mack Golder, Sam's father, barring his way. Refusing to be cowed. Mack was a big man, as were his sons. His bulk had shifted from muscle to fat in middle age but he was still more than a match for Ted.

"What did they say?"

"They said nothing, woman. What do you imagine? They wouldn't let me see him."

"Why was he at the boathouse? What did he do?"

Ted shifted back in his chair. Dawn flinched.

"He got the boat ready, for that boy. Stupid idiot was going to go with him, or at least let him nick it. Typical."

Was Ted thinking of the time when *he'd* stolen the boat, taken it to go and find Sarah? Of the way Jess had been forced to take a rescue party south on foot, because of him?

Probably not.

"So why was she in the boat, and not Sam?"

He leaned in. "Because she's a fool, that's why. When she gets back here…"

"Please, Ted. If she comes back, go easy on her. We need to welcome her. To help her forget."

He stood up. "Welcome, my arse. That girl's going to get beaten to the back of beyond when I get my hands on her. She's made me look like a fool."

Dawn felt herself crumple. Sarah had gone again and all he cared about was how he looked to the village.

There was knock at the door. Ted glared at Dawn as if she'd invited the devil to come visiting. "Who's that?"

"I don't know."

She stood up. He put a hand on her shoulder to push her down.

"I'll go."

He ambled to the door, tensing as it knocked again. "Alright, alright, get some bloody patience."

Dawn rounded the kitchen table, anxious to see who it was. Could Sarah have come back?

"What do you want?" Ted's voice was hard.

"Sorry, Ted. Can I come in?"

"Whatever it is can be done on the doorstep."

Dawn advanced on him, her heart racing. Why was Jess here? Was there news?

"Very well," Jess said. She spotted Dawn over Ted's shoulder and threw her a tight smile. "Evening, Dawn."

"Evening." Ted turned to glare at her and she backed away, towards the kitchen. When he turned back to Jess she took a step forwards.

"What is it then?"

"It's the police. They're back."

"Jesus."

Dawn crossed herself. She hated the way he blasphemed.

"Why?" he asked.

"They still need to talk to people."

"About your sister-in-law?"

A pause. "They didn't tell me. I've got to go to Filey. They're going to talk to other villagers here. People who were there."

"I didn't see anything. I had a bloody knife sticking out of me shoulder."

"I told them that. It doesn't change anything."

"Jesus Christ." Ted leaned back to grab his coat.

"Don't go anywhere while I'm gone," he told Dawn, not looking at her as he slammed the door behind him.

Dawn slid to the floor. This was it. Ted was going to be arrested, and Sarah was gone. She was alone.

She heaved herself up, her limbs heavy. There was a rope in the loft.

She would get it down, and she would wait twenty-four hours. If neither of them returned, she'd use it.

27

M artin ran towards Bill and Sarah. He could only imagine how Sarah would be feeling, with one of the men chasing her across the sand. The very man who had grabbed her outside her house when she was barely awake, clamped a drug-soaked rag to her mouth and slung her over his shoulder.

Did she know it had been Bill?

He ground to a halt as he reached them. Bill gripped Sarah's arm and she was shouting into his face.

"Let me go, you bastard! I need to go home!"

"Not in that thing, you won't." Bill nodded towards the headland where the beach disappeared. "I saw your boat. It's washed up, further along."

Sarah's eyes widened. She pulled away from his grasp and resumed running.

"Sarah, stop!" Martin cried. "Let me help you!"

She skidded to a halt and looked back at him. Weighing up whether to believe him, no doubt. He hadn't lied to her, not once. Not unless he counted lying by omission.

He jogged to her. "Let's pull the boat in. Get some rest. Bill'll take us back to the farm."

"If you think I'm going back there…"

"When you jumped in the boat with me, you knew where I was going. I offered to get out, to let you go back, but you refused. Where exactly did you think we'd end up?"

"I don't know."

Bill caught up with them. He stopped a few paces away, and exchanged glances with Martin.

"It's alright," he said. "It's just me here now. The rest of them have gone."

"Gone?" said Sarah. "Where? Why?"

"They didn't like the police sniffing around."

"They came here?" asked Martin.

"Please, let's talk about this inside. I'll bring you up to speed. Things are very different around here now."

Sarah looked incredulous. "In two days?"

"A lot's happened."

Bill gave Martin a sideways glance. Martin wasn't sure what that look meant: blame for stabbing Robert, or relief that he'd ended the man's reign of terror.

Martin turned to Sarah. "I believe him, for what it's worth. We only need one night. We can get cleaned up, dried off."

"What about the boat?"

"Let's drag it further up the beach, for now. We can come back for it in the morning. You can. It's getting dark, there's no way you can sail it now."

She looked out to sea, then at Martin, then Bill, then the boat. Martin watched her, his chest tight.

"OK," she said.

"Thanks."

They walked towards the boat. The sand was damp and swallowed their feet.

"What happened to your shoes?"

"I lost one. It's easier with none."

"If you're sure."

She rounded on him, her hair flying out as she turned. "Yes, I'm sure. Stop trying to control me."

He raised his palms. "Sorry."

They reached the boat. He and Sarah grabbed a rope each and Bill pushed it from the back. They managed to get it halfway up the beach, to a spot where the sand was dry.

"It'll be OK here," said Bill. "I know this beach."

Martin looked at him. "You sure?"

"Sure."

Sarah stared at it for a moment then stepped away. Martin resisted the urge to take her hand. She looked cold, tired and dejected.

"Come on," he said. "Let's get you warm."

She scowled at him. *Don't control me.*

"You can't stay long," said Bill.

He felt his chest sink. "Why not?"

"The police, stupid. They're looking for you. You need to get away."

"They arrested Ruth."

"They did *what*?" Bill frowned then shook his head. "Makes sense."

"It wasn't her fault," said Martin.

"She did finish him off. Pushed the knife in harder, watched him die."

"It was me who put it there in the first place."

"Seems you're both as culpable as each other."

"It wasn't Ruth's fault," said Sarah. "I heard him with her, I know what he wanted from her."

A deep purple blush flushed up Bill's neck. How much did he recognise his own responsibility in all this?

How much do I recognise mine, thought Martin.

"I'll be off at first light," said Sarah. She looked at Bill. "Take us to the farm. You'd better be telling the truth."

She started walking along the beach, back to the huts.

"This way's quicker," Bill called after her.

She turned and gave him a wary look, then followed. They found a narrow path through some tall grasses, so dense that they had to fight their way through. The grass was stringy and wet and whipped Martin in the face as he passed.

At last they were spat out onto a road. Martin looked along it; no sign of life.

He pointed to the left. "This way, right?"

Bill nodded. Sarah shuddered. Her face was pale, the faint glow on her cheeks gone. She looked like a creature of the sea, or of the fairies. Martin remembered the stories his mum used to tell of spirit women, the way he'd hung off them as a child then laughed at them as a teenager.

They walked in silence. Martin listened to his and Bill's footsteps on the tarmac, wondering how long this road had been here. How long it would last. Sarah dragged behind, her footsteps slow. Her toe was bleeding and the bruise on her face was darkening. He stared at it and reminded himself not to offer help. *Don't control me.*

At last the farmhouse was ahead, staring out to sea. Bill unlocked the front door and ushered them into the kitchen. Martin's senses pricked for signs of habitation but there was nothing; no footsteps, no voices upstairs. No shouting.

The wooden floor had a dark patch near the back door where Robert's blood had been scrubbed away. He moved quickly to block it from Sarah's view.

The last time they'd been here, Robert had had her at knifepoint, and Bill had restrained Martin with twine round his wrists. He and two other men had dragged Martin and Sarah back here, and brought them to Robert. So much for his plan to rescue her.

Sarah sat carefully, her eyes ahead, glazed. She looked small, ten years younger than her nineteen years. Martin wanted to walk to her and give her a hug. He wanted to drag the sadness out of her and replace it with love.

He thought of Ben, clutching at Ruth in this kitchen. The way she'd shrugged him off. Was this all Ben's fault?

No. It was Robert's.

Bill filled the kettle from the tap. "There are spare clothes upstairs. Not the best fit, but better than what you're wearing. You need to get dry, both of you. Before you catch hypothermia."

"Thanks," said Martin.

"Have a cup of tea first. It's mint. Can't keep the stuff at bay, but at least it's useful."

"Thanks."

Bill handed him a mug and put one in front of Sarah. She looped her fingers around it and sipped. A hint of colour returned to her cheeks.

"How did they know about Robert?" he asked. "The police."

"They wouldn't tell me. But I've got a good idea." He gave Sarah a nervous look.

"Go on."

"Leroy. I couldn't find him after you left. Hadn't seen him for a few hours. I reckon he saw the whole thing and shopped us." A pause. "Shopped you."

"He never liked me."

Sarah's grip tightened on the mug; she almost spilled it.

Leroy had visited her in her cell, he knew. She'd refused to tell Martin what he'd done.

"It makes no sense," he said. "Leroy hated the cops."

Bill looked at Sarah. "Maybe he wanted to avoid getting into trouble himself."

Martin felt his face heat up. He needed to toughen up if he was going to be any help to Sarah.

"Where are the clothes?" asked Sarah.

"Upstairs," said Bill. "They're all men's, but Robert was smallest. And his clothes are clean."

"Right," she said. "Where?"

"Upstairs, big room at the back. There's a wardrobe. You can sleep there too. Both of you."

Sarah's eyes widened.

"No," said Martin. "I'll have my old room."

The room he had shared with Leroy and Mike. Thank God it would only be for one night. One night, and then he would never see Sarah again.

28

There was a key hanging on a peg outside the bedroom door. Sarah took it and closed the door behind her. She turned it. It worked.

She had no idea if there was another key. If she was safe.

She turned to search the room. It was sparse, just a high, lumpy bed, a wardrobe that looked at least a hundred years old and a wooden chair.

Flowers lay on the floor in front of a cast iron fireplace, dried and purple. She felt a cold shadow pass through her, imagining Ruth in here. She'd been coming down the stairs when Bill had brought them back to the house. She'd either escaped, or she'd never been locked up in the first place.

Escaped. Surely.

Sarah grabbed the chair and wedged it under the door handle, having no idea if this actually worked. It would at least topple if the door was opened, give her a warning.

She opened the wardrobe. Inside was a row of laundered and ironed shirts. She ran her hands over them; they were white and stiff with bleach. She took one out and lay it on the bed.

She felt sick; the sight of Bill, approaching them across the sand, kept flashing in her eyes. Followed by the recollection of turning outside her house and seeing him there, coming at her.

She took a few shaky breaths and tried to focus on the clothes. Next to the shirts hung blue jeans, also well cared-for. She took a pair. She could at least be clean and warm before she got away. And the door was locked.

Beyond the bed was another door. She pushed it open, hesitant, expecting it to lead onto the roof.

It didn't. There was a bathroom. It was clean and spartan, with a bar of soap by the sink and a heavy bathtub with a brown stain running from the tap to the plughole. She leaned over it and ran her finger through the stain; it came away clean.

She turned the taps, biting her lip. A bath. She hadn't taken a bath in years. The water was tepid, though; not hot.

She turned off the cold tap and let the hot tap fill the tub halfway. When the heat started to fade and the water spluttered, she closed the tap and turned towards the door. This one had a bolt; she would be safe in here.

She slid the bolt then peeled off her wet clothes. She left them in a bundle on the floor; she'd deal with them after she'd cleaned herself. She didn't want that bath cooling any more than it had to.

She lowered herself in, eyes closed. It felt good, like silk brushing against her skin. She lay still, her eyes closed, for a few moments.

She opened her eyes, wishing she'd thought to transfer the soap bar from the sink. She couldn't face getting out of this water, heaving herself over the side of the tub and splashing across the cold tiled floor.

She gasped in a breath and dipped under the water.

She'd learned to go without soap before, when the village supplies were low. The water was all she needed.

She rubbed herself as clean as she could, trying not to look at the bruises on her arms and the deep gash on her big toe. It stung in the water but at least it had stopped bleeding. She raised her fingers to her forehead; it was swollen next to the eye.

When she was clean, she gripped the sides of the bath and pushed herself up. She stepped out and put her foot down on the tiles, carefully so as not to slip.

There was a thin, greying towel on a hook by the sink. She grabbed it and towelled herself down.

She slid the bolt and eased the door ajar, peering through to check no one was in the bedroom. Her heart pounded against her ribcage. It was empty, the chair still wedged under the doorknob.

She opened the door and headed for the bed. She pulled the clothes on. They were large but not ridiculously so. If she tied a knot in the bottom of the shirt it fitted perfectly, and helped to hold the jeans up at the same time. She'd ask if there was a rope or something she could use to secure them.

In the bottom of the wardrobe were two drawers. She pulled one out, almost pulling it to the floor in her haste. It contained underpants and socks.

There was no way she was wearing Robert Cope's underpants but the socks would be welcome. She sat on the bed and pulled them on, wriggling her toes in reluctant pleasure. The sensation of being clean and dry, of wearing freshly laundered clothes, pulled at her. But her fear was still there. She couldn't let herself get comfortable.

She tried the other drawer. It held a wallet and a belt.

She tied the belt around her waist, glad not to have to worry about losing the jeans, and picked up the wallet.

It contained no money, unsurprisingly. Instead, there were a few scraps of paper with indecipherable writing, and a small pile of photos. They depicted a woman and two small boys. The woman was short, with thin brown hair and the drawn expression of someone accustomed to a hard life. The boys were toddlers, one of them little more than a baby. The photo was worn over their faces, where they'd been touched repeatedly.

She wondered if this was Robert Cope's family. Some poor woman, who he'd left behind when the flood hit. Or maybe she'd died, or preferred to stay behind. Sarah shuddered.

Missing this family didn't excuse what he'd done.

There was a knock at the door. She crammed the photos back into the wallet and shoved it under the bedspread.

She tiptoed to the door and put a hand on the handle. Her throat felt tight, her skin cold.

"Who is it?"

"Martin. I wanted to check you were alright."

"I'm fine."

"Can I come in?"

She frowned at the door then pushed the chair to one side. She pulled the door open, blocking the doorway with her body.

"What do you need?"

He looked embarrassed. "I just wanted to talk to you. Find out what your plans are."

"My plans are to get home, if I can."

"Can I come in?"

"I'd rather not."

He glanced towards the stairs and lowered his voice. "Will you come out then?"

She followed him into the hallway. It was chilly out here, and her previously warm skin started to shiver.

"I wish I understood you, Martin."

"Sorry?"

"You're being nice to me now. But you took me. You were one of them."

"I didn't want to."

"You told me that."

"Look," he said. "I don't think you should go back. Not yet. Wait till your dad's calmed down a bit."

"You can't stay here. You're a wanted man, remember. And I'm not staying on my own with Bill."

She felt a shiver run down her back. Bill had been quiet since they'd arrived, as if brooding on his own secrets. She wondered why he'd stayed here, when all the others had fled.

"I'll get the boat going," she said. "And if you know what's good for you, you'll get as far away from here as you can."

"You think I'm a monster."

"It doesn't matter what I think. Only you know what you're really like." She prodded his chest with a finger then quickly withdrew it. "In here."

"I'm not like them. Robert. My dad."

"Your dad?"

A nod. "He was a drunk. Violent. Made my life hell."

"And you think that excuses what you did?"

"That's not what I'm saying. But I'm not like them. I'm not going to be like them."

She was too tired for this. She longed for the soft bed

behind her, the heavy bedspread. But she needed to get away.

She retreated and started to push the door closed.

"Good luck, Martin. Whatever you've got planned. Just... be better. Don't fall in with people like Robert again."

"I'll try not to. I was planning—"

She held up a palm. "I don't want to know. If I don't know, I can't tell the police."

His eyes widened. "You don't want to tell them about me?"

"I know what you did. We all do. But Robert had it coming. The world's a better place without him. You shouldn't suffer for that. Nor should Ruth."

"Ruth. I need to go to the police, don't I?"

"You might only make it worse. Jess will vouch for her. You can't know what Ruth went through, why she did what she did."

"I know." He hung his head. "I'm sorry."

She heard sounds from downstairs; Bill, moving around in the kitchen. A door opened and closed. She stared towards the staircase, glad her door had a lock.

"I know." She pushed Martin back, but gently. "Now, goodnight."

29

D awn stood at the top of the ladder. She wished she'd thought to put shoes on; the rungs dug into her feet. She reached into the loft, feeling for the rope.

Her fingers landed on it and she tugged. There was a moment when she thought it might not budge, but then it came away, almost sending her toppling back.

Falling down the ladder; that would do the job. But she wasn't ready. Not yet.

She pushed the rope past her and watched as it went snaking to the floor below. It was stained and mottled, grey with age. Ted had carried it all the way here from Somerset, believing it to be useful. And he'd been right; they'd often used it to tie a tarpaulin over their belongings and some-times themselves, glad of the protection from the driving rain.

Since they'd arrived here, it had only come out once, when Harry had asked Ted to help him in the boathouse. Ted had come home disgruntled; it seemed Harry and Clyde had better ropes.

She lowered herself down the ladder, hand over hand, careful. As she was about to place a foot on the floor, there was a knock at the door.

She flinched, almost falling. She composed herself, then stepped down.

She looked at the ladder; did she have time to push it back up into the loft?

She grabbed the bottom rung and pulled it towards her, ducking out of the way as the ladder folded into itself.

The door knocked again; two short raps.

She gave a final heave and pushed the ladder up into the dark space of the loft. Brushing her hands together, she descended the stairs, wishing she'd stopped to look out of the upstairs window first.

As she reached the door the thought came to her that it might be Sarah. She flung the door open, her face bright.

"Oh."

"Hi Dawn." It was Jess.

"What can I do for you?"

"I just wanted a chat."

"A chat?" Chatting wasn't something Dawn did.

"While Ted's talking to the police."

Dawn put a hand on the doorframe. "They haven't taken him?"

"No. They just want to find out what happened, at the farm."

"Can't you tell them?"

"I didn't see it all. I burst in right at the end."

"Oh."

"And they'll want as many witnesses as they can get, I guess."

"Yes."

So Ted hadn't been arrested; that was a relief.

"Can I come in?"

Dawn squinted at Jess. Her thick red hair was unkempt. She looked flushed and harried.

"Go on. Be quick though."

As Jess slipped past her into the house, Dawn peered outside. Hopefully no one would see. Hopefully she would be gone before Ted returned.

Jess shrugged her shoulders a few times then peeled off her coat. Dawn watched her, alarmed. The hall felt cramped with a stranger in it.

"What can I do for you?"

"Like I said, just a chat. Can we sit down?"

Dawn ushered her through to the living room. Jess surveyed the twin sofas then chose one, perching as if she didn't want to crease it.

"Can I offer you a drink?"

"No. But thank you; that's kind."

Dawn never normally offered outsiders food and drink; they were strictly rationed and she had none to spare. She wondered if the other members of the village entertained each other, if they pooled their rations. She shuddered.

"So, what do you need to talk about?"

Jess sniffed. "I'm sorry about Sarah."

"Oh."

"I heard what happened, in the boat house."

"Yes."

Jess turned to her. "I also saw her, before that. She had a bruise." Jess raised a hand to her face. "Right here."

"Yes. She slipped."

"Really?"

"Would I be lying?"

Jess shuffled in her seat. Dawn perched on the edge of her own, her skin taut.

"Dawn, you can trust me."

"I know I can. You're the steward."

"That's not what I mean."

"Is this all you've come for?"

Jess put out a hand then stopped it in mid-air. "We can help you, you know. You and Sarah. This village doesn't exactly have a women's refuge but we can rehouse you, somewhere on the other edge. If needed, we can send Ted away."

"Why would you do that?"

"Because he hurts you."

Dawn stood up. "You have no evidence of that."

Jess looked uncomfortable. "I thought you trusted me, Dawn. After I left you those notes, when Sarah was taken?"

Dawn nodded. It was true that Jess had been the only member of the village with whom she'd had any communication at that time. Jess had left updates for her under her dustbin.

"I appreciate that. But if you don't mind, I've got jobs to be getting on with."

Jess heaved herself up and made for the door. As Dawn opened it, a man walked past the front of the house and Dawn felt her heart skip a beat. She closed the door again.

"I understand," said Jess. "But you can talk to me, if you need help. If he hurts Sarah again."

Dawn pushed her shoulders back; how dare Jess prod at her Achilles heel like that?

"I owe my life to my husband."

"Really?"

"He risked his neck for me and Sarah many times, on our way here. Without him, I'd be lying in a bush somewhere. And Sarah... well, the less said about that the better."

"I'm sorry. I didn't know."

Dawn remembered their journey to the village, the long walk north. Jess had no idea. She didn't have a daughter who'd been almost raped. A husband who had stopped it in the most forceful of ways.

Then she remembered. "We all had it hard. You had to bring your poor mother."

Jess's face darkened. Her mother, Sonia, had been ill on her journey here and had died not long after arriving at the village.

"I'm sorry," said Dawn. "I didn't mean to…"

Jess sniffed. "It's OK. I don't mind talking about her. But I mean it about Ted. We're here to protect you."

"As is my husband."

"Well." Jess sighed. "That's not how it always looks."

Dawn took a step forward, making Jess step back. "Don't talk about him like that. Don't come into his house, reject hospitality which would be impossible without his efforts, and then make insinuations about him. Please."

"That's not what I meant to—"

"My marriage is none of your concern. Now leave."

They met each others' gaze for a moment then Jess turned to the door. Her gaze caught on the wall next to it.

"Does that give you strength?"

Dawn looked past her at her crucifix. Wrapped in tissue paper, it had made its way here from Somerset. And before that, it had been her mother's and her grandmother's before her. It had survived two world wars; it would survive more.

As would she.

"It does. Strength to know my daughter will be coming back to me."

Jess stared at it. "I hope so."

"I know so." Dawn stepped past Jess and opened the

door. She stared at her visitor, urging her to leave with her eyes.

Jess gave her a sad smile. "It's been good to talk to you."

Dawn said nothing. She watched as Jess walked along the path that led to the village centre. She should be in her schoolroom, teaching those poor children. But instead here she was, throwing her weight around and poking her nose where it wasn't wanted.

Dawn pushed the door shut and closed her eyes. She leaned her forehead against the wood and trembled as tears ran down her face.

30

The moon was three-quarters full, clouds drifting across it like slow fingers of mist. Sarah picked her way through the long grass, heading back the way she'd arrived. Around her were the sounds of night; animals shooting through the grasses, an owl somewhere behind her, the sea ahead.

She reached the beach. It looked dirty and littered in the dark, piles of seaweed easily mistaken for washed-up debris.

The tide was on its way out and the sand was damp. She picked her way across it, glad not to be sinking into dry powder but troubled by the cold. She'd found a pair of trainers under Robert's bed; two sizes too big but she'd laced them tightly and stuffed a balled up sock in the toes of each one. They hung on, for now.

She sniffed the salty air and surveyed the shore, looking for the boat. Nothing. She walked closer to the shore, careful not to let the water touch her feet. The rocks where they had come to shore were to her left, dark and moody in the dim light. If the boat had been wrecked, the pieces would be there.

She withdrew from the shore, finding a firm patch of sand to make her way across. When she reached the rocks, she headed back out towards the water. She considered clambering across the rocks, but then remembered how slippery and encrusted with barnacles they were, dips and troughs catching the water and glinting every time the moon came out from behind a cloud.

Then she saw it at the edge of the water, lapped by the waves. A dark shape, listing heavily but still distinctly boat-shaped. She clenched her fists, hopeful. And angry; Bill had been wrong about leaving it on the beach.

She hurried to it and bent to put a hand on the hull. It was dirty but intact. She couldn't see what the underside was like.

She grabbed an edge and heaved. It wouldn't budge. She placed her feet up against the keel, leaning into it. It moved slightly then shuddered to a halt.

"Need a hand?"

She spun round to see Bill watching her. He wore a heavy black coat that made him look larger, and his outline against the pale sand was eerie. She felt her heart flutter.

"No thanks."

He approached her. She had nowhere to go; behind her, the sea, and to her side, the rocks.

"I said no thanks."

"I just want to help." He was closer now; she could smell tobacco on him and heard his coat rustle as he walked. He had a purple scar on the side of his neck; she wondered how he'd got it.

"I don't need any help."

"I can help you move it. Check it over. You want to take the boat home, yes?"

"Yes."

"Right, then. The quicker we get it fixed up, the quicker you can be back with your family."

She glared at him. What right did he have to talk about her family like that?

She turned to the boat and gave it another tug. He snorted.

"You'll never do it like that. It's wedged against that rock, see?"

She looked at the other side of the boat. Sure enough, it was wedged under an overhanging rock.

"We'll need to bring it out at an angle," Bill said.

She couldn't do this alone. "Go on then."

He chuckled. "That's better. Now, you take that end. Pull it upwards, just a little bit, and then angle it out. Like this."

She followed his lead. The boat shifted upwards on the side closest to them and downwards on the other, freeing itself from the rock.

"Now we pull it onto the beach," he said.

"I can take it from here."

He eyed her. "Maybe you can. But it's easier with two of us."

He was right. She said nothing but let him help her. They pulled the boat away from the rocks until there was space for him to slip around the other side. Then they each took one side and heaved it across the damp sand, stopping when it was a few feet over the high water line.

He leaned over and took some deep breaths. "Not as fit as I was. That thing's heavy."

"You told us it was safe before."

"Sorry. Tide's unpredictable, these days."

"Right."

He straightened. "I just want to help you. And Martin. I owe you that at least."

She felt her stomach hollow out and her head lighten. Here she was, miles from home, alone on a beach with the man who'd drugged her, slung her over his shoulder and abducted her.

"I'm sorry," he said.

"Huh?"

"For what I did to you. There's no excuse. Robert didn't coerce me. I just spotted you and thought you'd tell them about Ruth."

She pulled back. She shouldn't have let him help her. It was a mistake.

"I'd like you to leave."

He stared at her for a moment then nodded. "I don't blame you. But you can't take that thing out on your own. Not now."

"Why not?'

"Because you'll drown, out there in the dark."

"I didn't drown on the way here."

"The boat's damaged. I can tell by the way it leans on the sand. Even a slow leak is enough to sink a little thing like this. And you don't know what you're doing."

She turned to him. "How can you know that?"

"Do you have experience at sea?"

She thought of the times she'd sat on the beach in Somerset as a child, watching the other families with their inflatable dinghies and lilos. She'd always been alone, sitting at the spot where the sand began, an observer of these incomers on her territory. In winter they'd be gone and she'd have the beach to herself.

But she'd never gone out on the water. And she'd only been in the village boat three times.

"It's just a day boat," she said. "I can manage it."

He was crouching next to the boat, peering under it. It would be too dark to see properly.

"Please," he said. "Wait till daylight. Then I'll come down here with you, help you get it ready."

"I'd rather go now."

"Shall I tell you what it's like to think you're drowning?"

She shrugged.

"First there's the cold. Your limbs, legs first, drop a degree or two. Then there's the claustrophobia. You're out in the big wide ocean but you feel like you're being hemmed in to the tiniest room. Then there's the panic. You flail wildly, despite the fact that your brain's screaming at you to be still. You know how to be safe, but your body refuses to do it."

"Then?"

"Then you drown. I don't know what that bit feels like. But Martin came pretty close once."

"To drowning?"

"I watched him fall in. Ruth treated him for hypothermia."

"And then he repaid her by bringing her here, with you."

"Sarah, please come back to the farm. A good night's sleep will give you the energy you need for tomorrow. I'll help you get this thing fixed up."

"I don't believe you."

"Why would I lie? I could just walk away now and I'd be no worse off."

"Do you know boats? Can you help me?"

"I've got some experience with carpentry."

She pulled Robert's jacket tighter around her. The sky was lightening very slightly, dawn approaching. She could be back here in just a couple of hours.

"Alright."

"Good."

He turned and headed back for the farm. The darkness swallowed him up, making her wonder if he'd really gone or was just a few paces away.

"Bill?"

No response. Suddenly she didn't want to follow him, didn't want him jumping out at her from the grasses.

She turned back to the boat. It was safe now. This would have to wait until morning.

She looked back the way she had come. Was he there still, or had he left her behind?

Only one way to find out.

She pushed through the grasses, taking a different path, trying not to lose her bearings. When at last the grass let go of her, she was on the road a short way from the farm. She crept towards it, hoping the men were asleep.

She pushed the front door open. Silence. She eased off the damp trainers and crept upstairs, wondering if Bill was a man of his word.

31

M artin should have been on the move by now, heading as far away from here as he could get, but he'd stayed to help Sarah.

Early that morning they'd dragged the boat to the edge of the beach, where it met the grass. The hull was just scratched; no hole. But the propeller had been torn apart on the rocks, one of its blades flopping loosely onto the sand.

Even if they could get the thing started, Sarah would never be able to control it.

Bill had his arms crossed and his face contorted into a frown. "It's not good."

"Yes, but we can fix it, right?" Sarah asked.

"Not easily. If we had a welding torch, maybe... Anyone got a welding torch?"

Sarah looked at Martin.

"Course not," he muttered.

"What about at the farm? Is there one up there?" Sarah asked.

"Not that I know of," said Bill. He eyed Martin. "Shouldn't you be gone by now?"

"I'm not leaving Sarah here." He didn't add *with you*.

Bill shrugged. "The longer you stay here, the riskier for all of us."

Martin bristled. He didn't much care about putting Bill at risk. But Sarah...

"You're right," he said.

"No," said Sarah. She looked at Bill, then at Martin. "I'd rather you stayed. Just till we get this thing working."

"But what if the police turn up?"

"We'll hide you," said Bill.

"We'll lie," added Sarah. Her mouth turned up at the corners; he doubted she'd contemplated lying to the police before.

"Thanks. So, what about this boat?"

"I don't know," said Bill.

"Maybe you should come with me," said Martin. "You can't stay here."

She shook her head. "I want to go home."

He understood that. During the early weeks of his flight from the floodwater, he'd thought time and again about turning back for home, seeing his mum again. Not his dad. He'd promised her he'd return with help, that he'd get her rescued. He'd carried through on his promise; at the nearest town, he'd spoken to the guy co-ordinating the boats heading out across the flood-stricken Norfolk Broads and given them directions. But he'd been too scared of his dad to go back himself.

He'd spent six years haunted by the guilt at leaving his mum. He wasn't sure what was worse; leaving her to the floods, or leaving her to his dad.

"Well, you're not getting there in that," he said, gesturing at the boat.

"I could walk."

"You're not walking. It's forty miles."

"I could walk with you," said Bill.

"No," said Sarah. She shifted away from him, her eyes on the boat. "You sure you haven't got anything at the farm you can use to fix it?"

Bill fingered his chin. "We might have. Martin, do you know your way around a tractor engine?"

"I grew up on a farm."

"That doesn't answer my question."

"My dad's tractor was older than *he* was. We were constantly fixing it."

"Maybe you can work out some way to use the parts from one we've got in the barn."

"A tractor engine?"

"A whole bloody tractor. Hasn't moved for years. Pitted with rust, and the floor's gone. But there's an engine in there. It might have usable parts."

"What about fuel?"

"Robert was prepared on that score. He stole gallons of the stuff from a petrol station not long after we first got here. Enough to drive the farm's generator. And besides, there's still fuel in the boat. Isn't there?"

"Yes. Of course."

Sarah's face had brightened and she was looking from one man to the other. Martin thought she might burst with excitement. "I'll help," she said. "Fetching and carrying. Anything."

Martin smiled at her. "Come on. We've got work to do."

Martin was at the beach, fiddling with the parts he'd extracted from the tractor. Sarah had been struck by its bulk, the way it loomed at them in the empty barn. There'd been a family of mice nesting under the front seat and the bitter smell of droppings. There was also an acrid, nose-piercing smell that reminded her of her cat Snowy when he sprayed his territory.

She felt her chest tighten. Was Snowy being looked after? Would her mother remember him?

"We'll get this thing fixed soon, don't you worry," said Bill. He'd had a swing in his step since they'd started working on the engine, a lightness in his voice. He was enjoying it. She wondered what he'd do when they were gone. Then she remembered she didn't care. As long as he stayed away from her.

"I hope so," she said.

She was carrying a jagged piece of metal that looked like nothing useful to her, but it was one of the things Martin needed brought to him. He'd gone quiet since starting on the boat, not wanting to be disturbed.

Bill carried a toolbox he'd fished out from under the kitchen cupboard. The tools in it were rusted together, but they were all he had.

"I need to tell you something," he said. She shook her head; she didn't need his confession.

"You've already said sorry."

"It's not that."

They reached the edge of the grass. Martin was a few feet away, lying on his back next to the boat. He and Bill had overturned it so its keel was upwards. It looked vulnerable, like a pale marine creature stranded on land.

They handed him their prizes.

"Thanks." He yanked open the toolbox and picked out a spanner. "Is there a wire brush or something? I need to clean this stuff up."

"Maybe," said Bill. He looked at Sarah. "Come on."

She frowned at him but followed nonetheless, keeping her distance.

When they were in the middle of the tall grass, Bill called back to her.

"In the kitchen, when I had hold of Martin."

"You'd tied him up. With twine."

"I feel bad about that. But he seems to have forgiven me, so I hope you can too."

She continued walking.

He put a hand on her arm and she yanked it away.

"I let him go deliberately," he said.

She turned to face him. "He pulled himself away. He caught you unawares."

"I saw him looking at the knives. I knew what he was

thinking. I loosened my grip, in all the confusion when your dad burst in."

She felt a weight descend onto her shoulders at the mention of her father.

"You thought he was going to hurt you. You were saving yourself," she said.

"No. I saw the look on his face. The hatred. The love."

"Don't."

"Sorry. But it's true. The boy adores you."

"That's irrelevant."

"He'd do anything for you. Look at him, fixing up that boat so you can go home. The longer he stays here, the greater the chance of the police finding him. He knows that, but he's still here."

Her face felt hot. "He doesn't want to leave me alone with you."

"Maybe. But that's not why he's doing it. If that was his only motive, then surely he'd make you go with him."

"He can't make me do anything."

"He won't. He knows you've had enough of that. What with your dad, and what we did to you. He knows you need to make your own decisions."

"Good for him." She didn't see why Bill was so interested in this.

"All I'm saying is cut him some slack."

"Whatever."

They were at the road now. Dusk was descending; they weren't going to get the damn boat running tonight. And even if they did, maybe Bill was right about going out there on her own, at night.

"He loves you, Sarah," Bill said as he pushed open the farmhouse door. "And I think you love him too."

33

Martin's hands ached. His fingers were numb from fiddling with the boat engine in the cold. Luckily the rain had held off, but the damp air meant that his hands were red and swollen.

He stuffed them between his knees as he sat at the kitchen table. It was almost dark now and the night outside was still. No animals stirring, or at least none he could hear. And no police.

Bill put a plate of food in front of him; potatoes and carrots, steaming.

"Is this it?"

"Don't grumble. Without young Sammy, we've lost our hunter."

"Hunter?" asked Sarah. She was tucking into her potatoes, blowing on each and then placing it in her mouth as if it was a delicacy.

"Yeah," said Bill. He wiped his hands on his trousers and sat at the head of the table, between them. Martin wished he hadn't picked a chair opposite Sarah; she refused to meet his eye, and it made him nervous.

"He hunted rabbits for us," Bill continued. "Brought back a sheep once, God knows how he got that home. Only way of getting meat."

"And he disappeared with the others?" Sarah asked. She sounded casual, as if at a suburban dinner party discussing share prices, not the means of getting food when you were half-starved.

"Yep," said Bill. "They all buggered off at the same time. You not eating your veg, Martin?"

Martin pushed his plate away. "Not hungry."

"You need your strength, if you're planning on walking any distance."

Martin shrugged. He heard Sarah breathe out, a long whistling breath that spoke of irritation. That was all he was to her now. An irritation.

Well, if that was how she felt about him, she could sort the boat out herself.

"I'm heading out in the morning," he said.

Sarah dropped her knife. Bill placed his on his plate.

"You're what?" he asked.

Martin met his gaze. "You heard. You both keep telling me I need to get moving. Well, maybe you're right."

Sarah opened her mouth but then said nothing. Bill picked up his fork and shovelled a heap of potatoes into his mouth.

Martin stared at his plate, wishing now that he hadn't pushed it away. He couldn't pull it back now; he was too proud.

"You don't want this?" Bill asked. Martin shook his head.

Bill pulled the plate towards him. He shovelled half of its contents onto his plate and the other half onto Sarah's. It wouldn't be long before she was back at home, eating proper meals. He wandered what Dawn managed to cook with their rations. Better than carrots and potatoes.

Bill cleared his plate and pushed his chair back. He wiped his mouth with the back of his hand and looked between Martin and Sarah. Sarah was staring at her empty plate. So was Martin.

Bill picked up the plates and clattered to the sink.

Sarah stood up. "I'll do that."

"No," said Bill. "That's not right, after last time."

Sarah and the other women had been forced to do chores, when they were locked up here. Martin had supervised Ruth planting potatoes.

She pushed him to one side. Since when had she and Bill got so friendly?

"I know you're not forcing me to," she said. "And it doesn't matter what happened before. You cooked, I'm washing up."

Bill stepped back and gave her a tight smile. "Thanks." He looked at Martin. "In that case, I'm turning in. I want to be up at first light, try and get the boat running before you have to leave us, Martin."

Martin shrugged. It wasn't right that he was behaving like this. Bill had been good to him. And Sarah... well, Sarah was Sarah. He shouldn't abandon her.

"Night," he muttered.

He listened to Bill climbing the stairs. Sarah swilled water around the sink, intent on her task. It was taking longer than it should.

"I'd best be off to bed too," he said.

She turned round. "It can't be past eight. Don't be ridiculous."

"But Bill—"

"Bill nothing. I need to ask you something."

He sat down again. "Go on." He felt his stomach quiver.

She stacked the plates to dry and wiped her hands on her jeans – Robert's jeans. They were stained with rust and dried sand.

"Why can't you get the boat to work?" she said.

He frowned. "I told you. The engine..."

"You've been fiddling with it for hours. And it's just the propeller. I don't see why it won't run."

"I'm sorry, Sarah. I'm trying my best.'

"Are you?"

"What? Of course I am. Why wouldn't I?"

She didn't answer his question. Instead, she turned back to the dishes. She drained the sink and fished around in its depths, pulling out scraps and tossing them onto the newspaper that held food for the pigs. It seemed they, unlike the men, had stuck around.

He approached her. "Sarah, do you think I'm deliberately sabotaging the boat?"

"I didn't say that."

He stood behind her, close enough to smell the mustiness of Robert's aftershave on her shirt. It made him gag.

"I'm trying my best," he whispered. "I don't know anything about boats, that's all. It doesn't help."

She turned, making him back away. He almost toppled onto the table behind him then had a moment's light-headedness as he remembered when he'd last thrown himself onto that table, lunging at Robert, knife in hand.

"You don't want me to go," she said.

He swallowed down the dryness in his throat. "No. But that doesn't mean I'll stop you."

"Really?"

"We're not all like Ted."

She slapped him on the cheek. He threw his fingers up to it, suddenly delirious.

"You hit me!"

"I'll do it again, if you don't help me get that boat working."

"I heard about your dad, you know. When I was on the road. I didn't know it was him then, but I worked it out."

"You're lying."

He shook his head, remembering the long walk north. He'd encountered plenty of people on his way here, some friendly, others not so much. Robert had saved him from two lads who'd beaten him up and stolen his rucksack.

"I'm not," he said. "There were stories of a man with his wife and daughter, around the time I met Robert. What he did to people who crossed them."

She paled. "You told me that was near Lincoln."

He frowned. "Yeah."

"We passed that way too."

"I know. That's what I was saying. Your dad..."

"You don't know what you're talking about."

He was right, he could tell. They'd been near each other, on the road. He wondered what would have happened if they'd met.

She clenched her fists. "I need you to help me with the boat. In the morning."

"But you told me yourself. I need to get away from here. The police..."

"It's been two days. They're not coming."

She did have a point. He'd been wondering the same thing himself; it had been two days now since Ruth's arrest. This farm was less than an hour from Filey by car. Where were they?

Was he, maybe, safe?

"Don't talk like that about my dad," she snapped. Her voice was high, shaking. "You don't know him."

"I know he hit you." He struggled to keep his own voice steady. "I know the fear I saw on your face when you jumped into the boat. I understand, Sarah. My dad used to beat me."

A shadow crossed her face. "That's not— it's not— it's not what you think!"

She pushed past him towards the door. He wondered if Bill had heard them. Bill's room was at the far end of a corridor, possibly too far away.

"I'm sorry," he said. "I just wanted to help you."

"Well don't," she snapped as she threw the door closed behind her.

34

S arah stared up at the ceiling of Robert's bedroom. Her body felt numb, and her mind full of concrete.

Had she been too hard on Martin? He wasn't really trying to sabotage the boat, surely. Everything he'd done since leaving this farm last time, he'd been acting in her best interests.

And had he been right, about them being close to each other on the road? Could they have met? Could he have been one of the men who...?

No. He wasn't like that.

But he'd taken her from the village. He'd let Robert bring him along on his mission, taken advantage of Ruth's kindness.

Ruth, who was probably lying awake in a police cell.

She heaved her sore legs out of bed. Her feet throbbed from walking between the farm and the boat in ill-fitting shoes. She felt that if she did manage to sleep, she might never wake up. Her neck ached and her hands were raw and pink.

But maybe he was right about her father, when he'd said

that Ted was no better than him; worse in fact. No better than Robert.

She thought back to the look on Ted's face when he'd chased her down the beach, into the sea. The look when he'd hit her.

How was she going to face going home?

The thin blue curtains were torn and a draft made them shiver from time to time. She pulled them to one side to stare into the yard behind the farm. The outhouses, beyond it, were where they'd held her. Where she'd first encountered Martin. He'd been brought to her, shoved in by Robert, and told to *get on with it*.

But he hadn't. Instead, he'd told her where she was. He'd helped her escape.

She went to the bedroom door and turned the key. Outside, the house was still. She strained to hear Martin and Bill's breathing, but there was nothing, just the rhythmic tap tap of a tree hitting the window at the end of the corridor.

She turned towards the window, peering into each room in turn. They were dishevelled, clearly abandoned. Mattresses upended, curtains torn off their rails. No clothes, no valuables. The men had had time to pack up their belongings, then. If they had any.

She came to a door that was almost closed. She leaned towards it, listening. She could hear breathing.

Was it Martin, or Bill?

She pushed the door very slightly, holding her breath. It creaked. She stopped pushing, and counted to ten. There was no sound.

She gave the door another push, more gently this time. It gave way in silence.

The room was dark. She squinted to adjust her vision

and a mattress came into focus, a pale rectangular shape in the centre of a dark floor. On it was a single figure. Tall, thin.

Martin.

The figure moved. He was sitting up, reaching for something.

A weapon?

"It's me," she whispered.

"Sarah?"

35

"Are you alright?" he asked. "What's happened?"

"Nothing's happened. I just wanted to talk to you." She could feel the blood pulsing through her temples.

"In the middle of the night?"

"Sorry. I'll go." She backed away.

"No." He stood up, filling the room with his height. She could barely see where he ended and the shadows began.

"It's too dark," she said. "And it stinks."

"You want to go downstairs?"

She thought of the route they would have to take to get to the kitchen. Past Bill, no doubt.

"No. Come to my room." She had a bedside lamp. It worked, amazingly; the first time she'd used an electric lamp in years. She'd been so astounded by it that she'd only allowed herself to keep it on for a minute at a time, and then waited half an hour before lighting it again.

"Sure."

She turned into the hallway, half expecting to find Bill out there eavesdropping. But the corridor was quiet. The wind had picked up and the branch scraped more vigorously against the window pane. It needed pruning, she thought. In her village, such things were looked after, tended. If not by the inhabitants of the closest house, then by the gang that looked after the trees and shrubs that had been planted years ago, for the holidaymakers who'd once occupied the houses. Before they'd been allocated to refugees.

At her door she stopped to look back. Martin was padding silently behind her, his breathing regular.

She eased the door open then waited for him to follow her inside. She closed it again. She went to the bed and lit the lamp. She didn't sit down, but stayed upright, watching Martin scratch his neck. He stayed by the door.

"So this was Robert's room," he said.

"You never came in here?"

"No. What's that door?"

"A bathroom."

He whistled under his breath. "Lucky bastard." He reddened. "Sorry."

"Don't worry. I know I'm a lucky bastard. Hot water and electric light."

"I didn't mean..."

"I know you didn't."

"What did you want to talk about?"

She sat down on the bed. It bowed under her weight then rebounded a little. "About tonight. I shouldn't have said those things."

"It's alright."

"It's not. I'm scared. I'm—I'm confused. But that's no excuse."

"I don't blame you Sarah, really I don't. After all the things I've done..."

She patted the bed next to her, feeling her heart thud against her rib cage. "Sit down."

"Next to you?"

She nodded, feeling ice run down her back.

He walked slowly to the bed, his eyes not leaving hers for a second. He looked wary, as if expecting her to change her mind. To lash out at him.

He sat a foot or so away from her. The bed dipped further.

He bounced up and down. "Nice. Better than a mattress on the floor."

"Did you know he lived like this?"

A shrug. "I guessed as much. Never talked about it though. No point."

Her mouth was dry. "You didn't deserve it."

He looked at his fingers, which were twisting in his lap. "Oh, I think I did." He looked up. "I've done things. Bad things."

"We all had to, after the floods."

"Even you?"

"Well. Not me. But my dad did. To protect me and my mum."

"Hmm."

She could only imagine the thoughts going through his head, wild fictionalisations of Ted's behaviour on the road. She didn't feel like contradicting him.

She leaned towards him and put her hand over his. He stopped moving, holding it very still.

"Thank you," she said.

"You don't need to thank me."

"I do. You've looked after me. You're helping me get home."

He shrugged. His hand shifted and he stilled it quickly.

His skin was warm.

She twisted her hand to hold his. He moved his own so that they were holding hands in his lap. He placed his free hand over hers.

"I love you," he said.

She pushed down the fear that threatened to spill out of her. "I know."

He was looking at her. She stared ahead, at the window. The torn curtains. She counted the rips in them. Twenty-seven. He watched her in silence.

She turned to him. "Kiss me."

His eyes widened. "Sorry?"

"You heard." She gave him a nervous smile.

He licked his lips, then leaned towards her. She closed her eyes. His lips brushed hers then withdrew.

She found herself leaning forwards, holding onto the kiss. The only time she'd been kissed before was by Zack Golder, at the age of fourteen. It had been dry and horrible and neither of them had mentioned it again.

His eyes widened further then closed, and she felt him leaning in. The bed shifted as he moved to sit closer. He put a hand on the back of her neck and she felt her skin shiver.

His tongue was in her mouth now, exploring. But not pushing, like Zack had.

She thought of Jess and Zack; did he kiss her like that? She laughed into Martin's mouth.

He pulled back. "Have I done something wrong?"

She clapped her hand to her mouth. "I'm sorry! No, no you haven't. I was just thinking of... never mind." She swallowed. *Don't laugh.*

She grabbed his arm and pulled him to her. They kissed again, faster this time, deeper. She squeezed her eyes shut.

She carried on pulling, feeling his weight fall on her as

she toppled back onto the bed. She was lying down now, his weight half on her and half over the side of the bed.

She opened her eyes. He stopped kissing her to pull back, looking down at her.

"Are you sure about this?" he asked.

She nodded.

She shifted her weight, moving to the other side of the bed. He stroked her hair. She lay there, blinking up at him. So this was what bound her mother to her father. She'd heard them at night; his grunts and her moans.

She felt full and empty inside, both at the same time. She wanted him now, more than she'd ever wanted anything.

She grabbed the hand that was in her hair and brought it to her mouth. She kissed it. She smiled at him.

She reached up for his shoulder and pulled him down on top of her. He cupped her head in his hand and kissed her deeply. She pushed back with her tongue, losing herself.

His hand was on her arm, creeping towards her breast. She didn't stop it. She stiffened as she felt his hand rest there, and tried her hardest to keep breathing.

She reached down between them and unbuttoned her shirt. She squeezed her eyes shut, blocking out thoughts of Robert wearing this shirt.

For a second she thought she'd ruined the moment, that the memory of that bastard would get in the way. But she managed to push him away and now Martin's hand was inside the shirt, stroking her nipple.

She moaned.

His face was in her hair now, his mouth at her ear. "When you want me to stop, just say," he said.

She let out a long, shaky breath.

"Don't stop," she told him.

36

The room was dim when Sarah woke, sunlight just beginning to filter through the curtains.

She lay perfectly still, her eyes closed. Her fingers tingled and her body felt as if it had been filled with liquid fire.

And today, they were both leaving.

She blinked her eyes open, focusing on the wall next to the bed. There was a damp patch halfway up the wall, and the wallpaper was peeling at the edge. It was textured, painted in a shade of white that had yellowed with time.

She took a few slow breaths, not wanting to wake up. Not wanting the day to start.

At home, she'd have to face her father. Her mother—her mother would know, surely. She'd see it in Sarah's eyes. In the way her skin glowed. And Sam. Would she have to settle for Sam now? The safety, the dependability of Sam?

No, she wouldn't. Not if she convinced Martin to come with her.

She turned in the bed, ready to wake him, to tell him her plan. The bed shifted under her weight, springs squeaking.

Had they squeaked like that last night? Would Bill have been listening?

The bed next to her was empty.

She pushed herself up, clutching her arms around her chest. She was still naked, and suddenly cold.

She looked at the bathroom door. It was open, with no sound coming from beyond.

She turned towards the door to the corridor; it was closed.

She sat up to check the floor. His clothes would be there; she'd peeled them off him last night, letting them slide to the floor. He'd pulled her shirt off with his teeth.

The floor was empty.

She slumped back.

How could she be so stupid? So naive, and trusting, and *stupid*? He'd lied to her, had got what he wanted from her, and now he'd left. He was no better than Robert Cope.

How would she ever look her mother in the eye again? She should have listened to her. Should have chosen Sam.

Bill would be down there, pottering around the kitchen as he always did. He'd have seen Martin leave. It would be humiliating.

She couldn't face him. She would creep down the stairs and let herself out. If she couldn't get the boat to start, she'd walk home. She'd run. She'd swim if that was what it took.

She wanted her mother.

She crept to the wardrobe, aware that the kitchen was directly below, and took out another clean shirt. Her own skirt and blouse, the soaked clothes she'd arrived in, were nowhere to be seen.

Not to matter. Robert's clothes would be more practical anyway.

She flung on a shirt, then another one on top. It was cold

out there, and the coats were by the back door. She grabbed another and pulled it over the first two. It was tight now, but that was good. Tight meant no drafts.

She pulled on a pair of jeans then three pairs of socks. She picked up yesterday's jeans from the floor, blushing to think of how they'd been removed, and slid out the belt. She belted her clean jeans.

Shoes.

The sodden trainers were by the door. She'd lost one of her own, and the other was downstairs somewhere. With all these socks the trainers would fit better.

She slid them on and tied the laces tightly. It hurt, but she knew they mustn't move, mustn't rub. Tight was good.

She grabbed the door handle and turned it slowly. The door opened silently. She crept along the corridor to the stairs. There was a bend – she paused to listen before rounding it, afraid of bumping into Bill – but at last she was at the top of the stairs.

She held the bannister, trying to control her breathing. Her stomach felt as if it would expel its contents at any moment, and she couldn't be sure how. She swallowed. *Keep it down*.

The kitchen door, towards the back of the house, was closed. Thank God. She crossed herself, imagining how pleased Dawn would be to see her.

She placed a foot on the top step, gritting her teeth. It creaked slightly, but nothing that could be heard through a closed door. She took another step, and another, wishing she could tumble down and run through the front door.

As she neared the bottom of the stairs, she heard voices. She stopped, one foot hovering over the next step. She lowered it carefully, then turned to listen.

Bill; she knew his voice. The other was deeper, as if it

belonged to someone tall and broad. Not Martin. And was that a *woman*?

She felt her heart pick up pace. They couldn't hear her.

But then—

What if they'd taken more women? What if the other men had come back, with more captives? What if they were women from her village?

She slid to the bottom of the stairs, wishing she'd thought to wait before putting the shoes on. She stood next to the kitchen door, her chest rising and falling, her stomach growling. Her thighs smarted from last night. She hated them.

"So you're saying you haven't seen him since the incident?" The man, the one with the deep voice. Robert?

No. He's dead. One of the other men. There'd been another older man, like Bill. Robert's lieutenants.

"Sorry, but the last time I saw him was when he left here with the people from the village up the coast."

"The village you visited."

A pause. "We got into difficulties at sea. They came out for us. They were very kind."

"And you brought some of them back here with you?"

"There aren't a lot of people like us around here. Refugees. We wanted to make links with them."

Liar, she thought.

People like us. If he wasn't talking to his own men, who was he talking to? Newcomers? The owner of the farm?

"We need to speak to him in connection with a murder investigation."

Sarah held her breath. It was the police. Did they still have Ruth? And why hadn't Ruth or Jess told them about the abductions? Surely the villagers weren't that mistrustful of the authorities.

Then she remembered the time the village had been invaded by kids from the nearby estate. Their parents too, on the second night. The police had taken the side of the locals.

"Very well. We may have to take you in for questioning."

"Are you arresting me?"

"No."

"Then I don't have to go anywhere with you."

"Very well, Mr Peterson. I expect you to tell us if you see him or the girl."

Sarah clapped her hand to her mouth. The girl?

She backed away from the door. She looked at the front door. They could be out there, blue lights flashing. Waiting for her. For Martin.

She lifted a foot behind her, to the bottom step. She retreated backwards up the stairs, not taking her eyes off the kitchen door.

37

D awn was asleep when Ted returned. She'd hidden the rope under Sarah's bed, crossing herself and asking God for forgiveness as she did so. When she heard Ted slam the front door, felt the bed dip under his weight, she hadn't moved.

Now it was morning and she was in the kitchen, making breakfast. Fried eggs from the village hens, his favourite.

She knew he'd been awake when she got out of bed, but hadn't had the courage to turn and make eye contact. *Go easy on her*, she'd told him, referring to their daughter. But would he go easy on *her*?

He stumbled down the stairs, muttering under his breath, and slumped into a chair. He smelled of sweat, and teeth that hadn't been brushed. She pursed her lips, determined to put on a smile. But first, the eggs. She pushed them around the pan, focusing on their spitting, on the way they gradually changed colour as they solidified in the heat.

At last the eggs were cooked. Ted, behind her, was silent. Watching her, no doubt.

She scooped them onto a plate and added a hunk of bread. The bread was rough but satisfying, and always fresh. Although this was yesterday's; today, she couldn't face going to the village shop for her ration. The eyes, the questions. *Where is your daughter? Does your husband hit you?*

She pushed her shoulders back and took a shallow breath. She forced a smile onto her lips; she should be pleased, at least he hadn't been arrested.

She turned, holding the plate. Trying to still her hand.

"Morning love," she said, holding her voice steady.

He was looking past her, out of the window. It faced the side of their house, looking at Sanjeev's wall.

He said nothing.

She placed the plate in front of him and turned back to the bread. She sawed off a piece for herself, cursing her own clumsiness.

"What's this?"

She stopped cutting. "Eggs."

"Where's the bacon?"

She turned. He was holding the plate up at an angle, like it was something detestable. The eggs would slip to the floor if he wasn't careful.

"I haven't had a chance to go to the shop. We ran out—"

He dropped the plate. It clattered to the floor but didn't smash. She couldn't see if the eggs had stayed in place.

"I want bacon."

She hurried towards the hall, to fetch her coat. She would have to face them.

He put out a foot. She tripped over it, landing next to the eggs. Her fingers were in them. The yolks felt thick and viscous. She retched.

"Get up!"

She pulled her fingers out of the eggs and grabbed the plate. She stood, placing it on the table.

He pushed it to one side, sending it to the floor. This time, it smashed. She kept herself from crying out.

"I didn't tell you to leave."

"You wanted bacon."

He grabbed the fingers on her right hand, which were resting on the table, where the plate had been. He twisted a fingernail into her ring finger.

"You're not going out there."

"Right."

He stood up. "Clean up this mess. I'm going to find her."

She looked up from the floor where she was trying to collect pieces of egg white in her shaking fingers. "What?"

"You heard. I'll get some men together. We'll go after them."

"But it's been two days."

"So?"

"She'll be miles away."

He bent over her. She clasped her lips shut, trying not to gag at the smell of his breath combined with the egg.

"How would you know that, woman?"

She pulled away from him, her bottom landing on the cold floor. "The boat. It's fast. Isn't it?"

"How do you know she hasn't stopped somewhere? How do you know he hasn't taken her to that wretched farm?"

"I don't. But you tried this before and—"

He kicked the plate out of her hands. She yelped and shrank back. "Don't you remind me of that! This is different."

"Yes. This time she went willingly." She could hear herself contradicting him. She never did this. But Sarah's disappearance had banished Dawn's desire for self-preservation.

He froze, eyes boring into her. "You're right."

She chewed her lip, waiting for him to kick her again. Should she stand up, put the table between them? Or would movement provoke him?

"Don't do that, woman. Disgusting."

She stopped chewing. Slowly, she pulled herself up, using the table for support. He didn't stop her but instead stared out of the back window towards the sea.

When the table was safely between them she cleared her throat. "How do you mean, I'm right?"

He turned. His eyes bulged and his cheeks were inflamed. "She went willingly. That's what you said."

"Yes."

"She's going to let him do what he wants to her. Just like she did with those two lads back in Lincoln."

"She didn't and you know it! They would have—" she lowered her voice. "They would have raped her."

His eyebrows were knotted together and his mouth twisted. He sniffed at her.

"Yeah. Well, they won't be doing anything like that again. And nor will she, the little slag."

"Ted! That's our daughter you're—"

He leaned over the table. "She's my daughter and I'll say as I see it. I'll kill her for this."

"Don't say that…"

He spat at the floor. She stared at the globule of spit, anticipating cleaning it. That, and the remains of his breakfast. That left only one egg for the next two days.

"I'll say what I want. Just shut the fuck up and clean up that mess. You disgust me."

He yanked the kitchen door open and flew into the hall-way, slamming the front door behind him. Dawn ran up the stairs to watch him through the upstairs window. He sped towards the beach, shoulders hunched.

She slid down the wall, trembling. *Sarah, where are you?*

38

S arah stared at her bedroom door, waiting for it to open. For the police to come for her too.

She pulled the shirt tighter around her, tugging at the sleeve. She was hot, in all these layers.

At last there was a knock. She swallowed down the lump in her throat. She still didn't know what she was going to say to them.

"Come in."

"It's locked."

She crossed to the door and unlocked it. She pulled back to the bed again.

The door opened. It was Bill, alone.

She ran out and peered along the corridor. "Where are they?"

"So you heard."

"Yes. What did they want?"

"Martin." He gave her a look. He knew.

"I don't want you in here," she said. "Wait downstairs for me."

He shrugged. "You won't run off?"

She felt her cheeks redden. "No."

He nodded then left her. She watched him amble towards the stairs as if this was any other day. What would he do, now they were alone?

She felt a shiver run down her body.

She went back into the bedroom. On her first night, she'd cleared away the shards of pottery that lay on the floor, along with those blue flowers. Cornflowers. The flowers were a deep purple now, but the pottery remained. She picked up a sharp piece and wrapped it in between the layers of shirt. Then she took it out and wedged it in the back of her jeans.

She cast a last look around the room, trying not to stare at the bed, then headed downstairs.

Bill was sitting at the kitchen table, waiting for her. It was the stillest she'd seen him. He looked up. There were two mugs in front of him. He gestured to one of them.

She lifted her chin, determined not to let him humiliate her. "Did they take him?"

"No."

"Where is he then?"

"He went out the back. They were at the front."

"They didn't have people at the back, waiting for him?"

"Seems not. There were only two of them."

She grasped the mug and laced her fingers around it. She wanted to ask if Martin had said he was coming back.

"I think I should go home," she said.

"He had flowers."

She looked up. "Who?"

"Martin. He'd been out picking them. Soft lad. He was grabbing some breakfast for you both. An apple each. Crappy breakfast, but there you go."

On the table were two green apples. She glanced at them

then sipped at her drink, glad of the mug hiding her face. It tasted bitter.

"What's this?"

"Herbal tea. Not sure what herbs."

"It's vile."

"You get used to it."

She pushed the mug away. "What sort of flowers?"

"Yellow ones. I don't know much about flowers."

"Where are they now?"

"He took them. He had them in his hand, when the police arrived."

She looked towards the back door. Maybe he'd dropped them out there. Maybe he was still holding them, running with them.

It didn't matter now.

She stood up. "I'm going to the boat."

She turned towards the hallway and the front door. She turned back and grabbed a coat. Robert's. Martin's was still there, on its peg.

There was knock at the door. She stared at Bill, her heart racing.

Another knock, louder this time. Two more.

"Hide," Bill said.

39

Sarah was sure they would hear her breath echoing in the cramped confines of the cupboard. She shifted her weight, cramp already developing in one foot, then instantly regretted it as a tin shifted next to her, scraping on the floor. Her eyes darted to the door, but no one came.

She'd wanted to run up the stairs when Bill had gone to the door, but knew that they would hear her. That they would search the bedrooms. They might not think of this walk-in cupboard.

She heard movement upstairs, footsteps moving from room to room. She tried to remember how she'd left the bedroom. Was there evidence that a woman was here?

More noises upstairs, thuds and thumps. Drawers being opened, the smash of a lamp falling to the floor. The one in her room?

She held her breath, staring at the door. It smelt musty in here, and stale. There was the tang of pickled onions and the strong odour of feet. The air was dry. She wanted to cough.

Feet came down the stairs and she heard voices getting closer.

"You can't do this," said Bill. "Not without a warrant."

"You want us to arrest you too? Aiding and abetting? Obstruction? Not to mention squatting."

"No."

"Then let us do our job."

"Squatting doesn't really count, not any more."

"I'm sure the owner of this farm would see it differently."

"They haven't been back here in nearly five years. I doubt that they care."

"Are you always like this, Mr Peterson?"

"Like what?"

"Difficult."

Shut up, thought Sarah. *Don't wind them up.*

They were in the kitchen now. A shadow passed under the door. She clenched her fists, counting.

"We need to look in your outbuildings."

"Fine."

She heard keys being gathered, the back door opening. Was Martin hiding out there? Could he be in the very cell she'd been kept in, in the outhouse behind the farm?

She felt as if her insides might dissolve at any moment.

The voices receded but there was still someone in the room, moving around. A more junior officer maybe, prowling the kitchen. She shuffled further back in the vain hope she might be disguised by the empty boxes and tins.

Then the back door slammed. She held her breath and listened but there was no one in the kitchen, she was sure of it.

Unless they were sitting in silence, tempting her out.

No. If they were that clever, they'd have found her hiding place.

She took a hesitant step towards the door and gave it a tiny push. Light streamed in, illuminating the dust that danced in the confined space.

She waited. Nothing.

She pushed it a little more, to see the table. There was no one there. The only place for a person to hide would be right behind this door. And if they were there, it was too late anyway.

She eased the door open and lowered herself to a crouch, almost crawling along the floor. She looked at the door to the hall. It was open, but there were no shadows, no movement.

She crept to the back door, which was closed. She crouched behind it. Its lower half was solid but the top half had a pane of glass.

She glanced back at the other door then slid upwards, her hands on the wood. She had to see.

There were five people out in the yard, including Bill. A tall, broad-shouldered man in an ill-fitting suit and a younger woman wearing a bright blue jacket. The man talked to Bill while the woman watched the outhouse.

With them were two uniformed officers, both women. They prodded the piles of junk around the yard as if Martin might spring out from under them.

She could see shadows in the corridor at the front of the outhouse, that led to the four cells where she and the other women had been kept. She put her ear to the glass and heard the cell doors being opened and closed. She wondered again how much the police knew about what had happened to her, Ruth and the others. Why hadn't Ruth told them? Why wasn't Bill being arrested for taking her?

The shadows shifted and a shape appeared in the

doorway to the outhouse. Sarah ducked down, almost toppling in her haste.

"No sign of him."

She felt her breathing still. He'd be far away by now, running across fields. Maybe crawling through the muddy ditch they'd taken together, when he'd helped her run.

How many police would be looking for him? She knew police resources were stretched, had been since the floods and the economic collapse, so Filey would only have a handful of officers. They were probably all here.

"What's this?"

She peered over the doorframe to see one of the uniformed women standing at the side of the outhouse. There was a door there, behind which was the most unbelievable stink. Sarah had never had cause to open it, thankfully.

The detective turned to Bill. "Give us the key."

Bill took the keys from his pocket then stared at them. The detective snatched them from his hand.

"I suggest you help us. Better for you."

The detective tossed the keys to his colleague and she approached the uniformed officer, arm outstretched. They both disappeared round the corner of the outhouse.

Sarah held her breath. Her eyes prickled.

"Got him!"

She clutched her stomach, fighting nausea.

The two women emerged around the side of the outhouse. Between them, his head low and his jeans stained dark brown, was Martin.

Sarah bit her lip, ignoring the blood. She reached out for the door handle.

The male detective squared his shoulders. He turned to Bill. "Did you know he was there?"

"No idea." Bill had his head up, defiant.

"Hmm."

Martin was shoved in front of him. His face was streaked with dirt and he looked younger, like a boy being reprimanded by his parents. Sarah wanted to run out and grab him.

"Martin Walker?" the detective said. Sarah bit down on her lip, realising she'd never asked the surname of the man she'd slept with last night.

"Yes."

"Good. I'm arresting you for the murder of Jacob Cripps and Zahir Ali."

40

Martin stared up at the windows of the farmhouse as they bundled him into the back of the unmarked police car. This wasn't his first time; he'd been arrested for shoplifting as a teenager, had spent a night in the cells. His mum had arrived the next morning to collect him and he'd been released with a caution. His dad had been apoplectic when he arrived home; not at the crime, but at the fact he'd been caught. Martin had stood in front of his dad's faded armchair, head hung low, and taken the bollocking. He'd only moved when his dad had told him to stop blocking his view of the TV.

The door closed with a thud and the car dipped as two people got in the front. A uniformed woman in the driver's seat, and the man who'd arrested him next to her. He had a flat face with a scar that ran from his nose to his upper lip. Martin wondered how he'd got it, and hoped it was nasty.

The car started. They waited for the marked car to go ahead of them then sped off down the lane as if released from a catapult. He couldn't remember the last time he'd travelled at such speed; it had been six years since he'd been in a car.

He clung to the seat, muttering under his breath, hardly daring to look out of the window.

The detective turned in his seat. "Stop that."

Martin stared at him. He stopped muttering, but tightened his grip on the seat and dug his nails in.

His horror at being found had been almost matched by his relief at getting out of the toilet where he'd hidden. It was little more than a cesspit, a receptacle that the men who weren't privileged to live in the farmhouse had slung their slops into every morning. The smell had been solid, like an object hovering in the air. He could still taste it.

As they dragged him out he'd stared up at the back windows of the farmhouse, wondering if Sarah was awake. If she'd woken to find him gone. She would hate him for that. She would think he'd taken what he wanted, and then run.

Would Bill tell her he'd been arrested?

He screwed up his eyes, battling tears. But the thought of Sarah's pale face on the pillow was too much for him. She'd responded to his touch, her body quick and lithe. He'd gone slowly, waiting for her to say no at any moment. But she hadn't.

Now she would wish she had.

The detective was staring ahead, talking to his colleague in a low voice. Martin wondered if Ruth would still be at the police station, if he could help her. He would tell them that he killed Robert, that she bore no part of the blame.

But Robert's hadn't been the name they'd given him. *Jacob Cripps and Zahir Ali.*

Who were they?

No one he knew, that was for sure. Was this a red

herring, a pretext for getting him to the station, where they could poke and prod him, extract information about Robert's death?

If it was, he would tell them everything. Everything up to the point where Ruth stood over Robert and ground her foot into his chest. Martin had lunged for Robert, plunging a knife into his throat. That was what killed him.

Yes. That was what he would do. He would tell them he'd killed Robert, that he had no idea who the other two people were, and that Ruth was innocent. He would co-operate.

Maybe they'd be lenient. They didn't have the resources to hold him for long. Maybe they'd let him out after a couple of years. Sarah's family might accept him as the man that had saved Ruth.

But the thought kept nagging him, pushing its way above the surface. Who were Cripps and Ali? And how was he supposed to have killed them?

41

S arah threw herself out of the kitchen door. Bill was gone.

She ran around the side of the house, not caring who saw her now. Bill was standing at the front corner of the building, looking along the lane to the north. He turned towards her, his hands in his pockets. Casual.

When he saw her, his eyes widened.

"Why didn't you tell me?" she screamed. "Why?"

"Tell you what?"

"That he's a murderer!"

"Martin isn't a murderer. He was provoked. He was defending you."

"I'm not talking about Robert! Who the hell are Jacob Cripps and Zahir Ali?"

Bill's face darkened. "You heard."

"Yes, I heard."

"He didn't kill them. Look, Sarah—"

"That's not what the police say. You should have told me!"

She lurched at him, her hand whipping out to hit him.

He caught it, the two of them locked together. She glared at him.

"Let me go."

"You need to calm down. Martin didn't—"

"No. I just learned that the man I let into my bed last night is a double murderer."

Bill let go of her wrist, flinging it away. She brought it back up, but his look stopped her.

He turned to the back of the house. "Come inside."

She clattered into the kitchen and stood with her back to the door. He sat at the table. Their two mugs sat on it, cold. She wondered what the police would have made of them. Bill's and Martin's, they would have assumed.

"You're all as bad as each other," she said. Her voice was hoarse and her throat ached. She wanted to slide to the floor and let it swallow her up.

"No," said Bill. "They've got it wrong."

"I'm sick of your lies. I'm going home. Help me with the boat or don't. I can walk anyway."

She pushed the door open and stormed into the yard. Bill followed.

"Sarah, stop!"

"I'm not staying here with you."

"You'll never get that boat working. I don't know how to do it."

"Then I'll walk."

"It's forty miles."

"I don't care!"

There was a clap of thunder. She looked up, expecting to see lightning coming straight for her. Instead a faint flash echoed off the walls.

She was going to get wet. She might die of exposure.

She didn't care.

"At least wait till the storm's gone," said Bill. Rain was lashing down now, hammering into the corners of the yard and bouncing back at her. Her hair was already wet.

"No."

"You really want to go home?"

"I need to face my dad." She shuddered.

"He's not the monster you think he is, you know."

"He killed two people."

"Not Martin. Your dad."

"My dad is none of your business."

Her hair was stuck to her face, but she refused to push it away.

"I saw his face, when he found you. When he saw what Robert was doing to you. He was scared, Sarah. Terrified."

"So was I!"

"He saw his little girl with a knife to her face. He wanted blood. He loves you."

"He hits my mum."

A pause. "I didn't know that."

She stared at him. He stood in the doorway, only his chest wet. She ignored the water seeping into her shoes and through the layers of socks.

"There's a lot you don't know," she said.

He stepped down from the doorstep, squinting against the rain. "I'm sorry."

"Don't be. My mum's right."

"Right about what?"

"About Sam. He's safe, dependable. He hasn't killed anyone."

"Who's Sam?"

"Just a boy, at the village. A man. He loves me."

"Martin loves you."

The rain had worked its way through all her layers now.

It felt like it might permeate her skin. She shook the strands of wet hair out of her eyes. "Martin lied to me."

Bill stepped forwards. "He loves you. And you love him."

"No I don't."

He arched an eyebrow.

"I don't! How can you know how I feel?"

He stared at her, not speaking. She wanted to hit him.

"I don't care what you think. I'm going."

She turned away. She hoped there would be road all the way home, no muddy fields to traverse.

"Stop."

She carried on walking.

"I said stop. I have a better idea. For you to get home."

42

The lanes were narrow and winding until they reached the main road to Filey. Martin gazed out of the window, trying to imagine what it would have been like to walk this route, as Jess and her friends had done to find Sarah.

The car slowed as they reached a turning to the right, in the direction of the sea. He pulled himself up, his hand on the window.

They passed through a gateway and along a road that held no other cars. On either side, small houses stared out at them, their facades giving nothing away. The rain bounced off the car windows and no one was outside for a soaking.

They proceeded to an open area then took a right turn. Martin felt his stomach flip.

He knew this place. This wasn't Filey; it was Sarah's village.

He sank down in his seat, glad of the rain obscuring the windows. He wondered if they'd come here to arrest someone else, to take them to Filey too. Or maybe they would let him out here, give the villagers a chance to mete out whatever justice they deemed fit.

He felt a small noise leave his lips. For the first time in almost five years, he was scared.

The car pulled to a halt outside Ben and Ruth's house. The uniformed woman got out and knocked on the door, adjusting her cap to keep out the rain. Martin looked behind him; had the other car followed them? Yes. It was parked a few feet away, a marked police car like a beacon in this quiet, reclusive place.

The door opened to reveal a man in the doorway. The policewoman spoke to him and he leaned out to peer at the car.

Martin felt his chest stiffen: Ben. But where was Ruth?

Ben pointed along the road in the direction they'd come. The policewoman said something then returned to the car. Ben frowned after her and closed his door.

The policewoman brought cold and damp in with her. "She's at her house, guv."

"Where's that?"

"Back by the road."

"Shit. Turn round."

The woman swung the car around the open square, ignoring the ruts in the tarmac. They glided back towards the entrance to the village, the detective counting under his breath as they passed houses. Martin imagined the people inside, staring out, wondering what was happening. He sank further in his seat.

They turned left, then quickly right, and stopped in a cul-de-sac. It was neat and homely, and reminded Martin of the kinds of places his school friends had once lived. He'd envied them their narrow lives of TV and football at weekends, the fact they weren't expected to fix tractors and scrub concrete floors covered in pig shit.

The detective got out this time, leaving the uniformed woman with Martin. Once again, the other car stopped a short distance behind. Martin wondered who they were looking for. He still hadn't seen Ruth.

The door to a house opened and Jess emerged. He clenched his teeth, waiting for her to spot him.

The detective exchanged a few words with her. She stepped out into the rain and held her arm over her face, sheltering her eyes. She peered towards the car. The rain was easing now, sunlight making an effort to break through the clouds. He had nowhere to hide.

She said something to the detective. She looked animated, shocked. He put a hand on her arm and she shook it off. She raised her voice.

Martin stared at her, confused. Had they sought her out in her capacity as steward, or as a witness?

The detective shook his head and Jess closed the door in his face. Martin smiled, admiring her courage. He'd never dare do that, despite the attitude to the authorities he'd witnessed in his father. Maybe because of it.

The detective opened the car door and slid in. He wore a pinched expression.

"None of them are talking," he said. He turned to face Martin. "You should be pleased."

43

S arah paused for a moment, then carried on walking. He was stalling her. She had to leave, now.

"Wait!" he called after her. "There's a bike."

She turned. "A bike?"

"Ben brought it. When he came for Ruth."

"A *bike*?"

He nodded. "Easiest way for you to get home."

She approached him. "You had a bike here all along, and you didn't tell me about it?"

"You were intent on the boat..."

"You let me spend days fixing up that boat. You let Martin stay here, knowing the police might catch up with him, knowing that he could leave here on a bike?"

"Sorry."

"Why?" She raised a palm. "Don't tell me. Same reason you drugged me and dragged me onto that boat, I imagine."

"No. I saw you and Martin working together. I thought maybe you had a future."

"Martin's a murderer."

"No, he isn't. Sarah—"

"So where is this bloody bike?" She wondered what her mother would make of her language; it felt liberating, to swear.

He sighed. "Come with me."

She followed him to a door around the side of the house. It led to a shed of sorts, full of rusting tools and piled up junk. At the front, balancing precariously, was a blue mountain bike. It was scratched, and one of the tyres was low, but it would get her home.

"You bastard."

"I thought I was doing the right thing."

She pushed past him and grabbed the bike, hauling it out of the tangle. She lifted it up and heaved it out of the shed, not caring if she hit him.

"You weren't," she said.

"I'm sorry. Look, if you find Martin, I'd be grateful if you could—"

"I have no intention of going looking for Martin. I'm going to go back to my village to tell the police that it was him who killed Robert. Then they'll release Ruth."

"You know he did it for you."

She shook the bike at him, feeling stronger than she ever had. The clouds had cleared; she needed to get on the road while it remained light.

She realised she had no idea how to get home.

"Are there any maps here?"

"Sorry?"

"Maps. Of the area. I don't know the roads."

"Oh. Yes."

He dashed into the back of the house. She propped the bike against a wall and followed him inside. She stayed in the kitchen, suddenly uncomfortable being alone here with this man.

RACHEL MCLEAN

He was in a room deep inside the house, one she hadn't ventured into. She listened to him banging around and cursing under his breath. Eventually he emerged, brandishing a torn Ordnance Survey map. "Here."

She grabbed it, not stopping to examine it. She stuffed it inside her shirt and went outside.

He followed her out. "Don't you want to check it first?"

"I know which way the police went. I can start that way. I'll check the map when I'm safely away from here."

"Sarah, it's not like that. You know that."

"I don't know what I know anymore." She wiped a tear away. *Don't cry. Don't show your vulnerability.* "I just want to go home. Put all this behind me."

He nodded. "Good luck."

She sniffed at him. Another man was being kind to her one moment, then lying to her the next. It was worse than being at home.

She threw her leg over the bike and cycled away, ignoring the chill that pierced her clothes.

44

Ted threw the front door open and shot out of the house. Dawn hurried after him, wiping her hands on her apron. She'd almost dropped the plate she'd been washing in her shock at his sudden movement.

He ran towards the Parade. He was waving his arms, shouting. She watched, not daring to call after him. She scanned the surrounding houses; who would be watching?

He turned, his fist still clenched in the air. She slipped back inside, into the kitchen. She picked up the plate and began to scrub it, conscious of her heart pounding so hard she thought he'd hear it.

He slammed the front door and threw himself into a chair behind her. She flinched.

"What the fuck are they doing here?" he shouted.

She placed the plate on the draining board and inhaled.

"Who, love?"

She heard him shift in the chair. She could imagine him scowling at her back. Had she injected enough lightness into her voice?

"The police."

She felt her chest lift. She turned.

"Have they found her?" she asked.

"What? No. Of course they haven't."

"I thought…"

He stood up. "We didn't ask them to look for her, so why should they?"

"Oh." She hated that no one trusted the police anymore. But she couldn't go against Ted. Even if she dared to, how would she get to Filey on her own?

"They had someone," he said. "In the back seat."

"Oh."

He looked at her like she was an idiot. "You don't know what that means, do you?"

She shook her head. "Sorry."

"It means they've arrested someone. Put him in the back."

Maybe one of those men, she thought. But no one in the village would have trusted the police with enough information for them to come to any conclusions.

Perhaps Ruth had? It was her best defence.

"Could it be one of those men?"

He grunted. "Hopefully that little bastard Martin. I'd like to see him fester in a police cell."

"If they have him, they'll have found Sarah."

"Not necessarily." He balled his fists on his hips. "You haven't got a clue, have you?"

There was a knock at the door. Ted strode to it. Dawn watched, her hands shaking.

"Is everything alright?"

It was Sam.

Ted stepped forward, almost touching Sam. Dawn followed her husband into the hallway and looked past him at the boy. She gave him a weak smile.

"Are you alright, Mrs Evans?"

Ted stepped forward again, out of the house. Sam took a step back, his eyes still on Dawn.

"Why wouldn't she be?"

Sam looked back at Ted. "Sorry, that's not what I meant. It's just, I saw the police car. I thought they might have found Sarah?"

Ted drilled a finger into Sam's chest. "And what damn business is it of yours?"

"I was just concerned."

"She'd be fine and dandy if you hadn't stuck your oar in."

Sam's broad face paled. He was staring into Ted's eyes, his mouth wide. "I'm sorry. I shouldn't have done that."

Dawn stepped forward. "You were only trying to help."

"Trying to meddle, you mean!" Ted turned to glare at her. She shrank back.

"He wanted Martin out of the way as much as you did, love," she said. "He was trying to help Martin leave."

Ted turned back to Sam. "Fat lot of good he did."

"I'm sorry, Mr Evans. I just wanted the best for Sa—"

Ted raised an open hand. Sam clamped his lips shut. He lifted his chest. "You can't threaten me."

"Can't I?"

"I've done nothing wrong. I care about your daughter, that's all." He peered round Ted. "Mrs Evans, please can you tell me if she comes back?"

Ted's face turned from red to violet.

"Yes, Sam," Dawn said. "Now I think you should leave."

"Right." Sam gave Ted a last wary glance then hurried towards his own home.

Ted slammed the door shut. "What the fuck was he doing?"

"He was just concerned, that's all."

"Why would he be concerned?"

"He cares about Sarah."

Ted careered into the kitchen, pushing Dawn with him. She came to a stop against the stove, glad she'd turned the gas off.

"He's what she needs," she said. "Keep her away from that Martin."

"She needs to be with her family." He looked back towards the door. "Maybe that little runt knows more than he's letting on."

"Sam?"

"He helped her get away. He'll know where they were heading."

He pulled back. Her hips were sore where they'd been pressed into the stove.

"Don't follow me," he said, and grabbed his coat.

45

Dawn sat at the top of the stairs, watching the road through the small window. She'd been up and down the stairs for the last hour, alternating between watching for Ted's return and busying herself downstairs, distracting herself with polishing Ted's old golfing trophies that lived in a wooden cupboard. Trophies that he'd insisted on carrying all the way here, despite forcing Dawn to leave family photos behind.

She'd never been to Sam's house, but Ted had. He knew this village better than she did.

Sam's parents were good people who kept themselves to themselves and did more than their fair share of work to support the community. They'd sent their two oldest sons, Sam and Zack, out to work as soon as they were old enough, knowing the risks. Sam had told her that his mum liked Sarah, that she thought he'd be a good match for her son. And now she'd be punished for that by having Ted bowl up at her door.

It wasn't right. Sarah was nineteen; she needed to live her own life. She needed a boyfriend, a husband one day.

She couldn't stay here forever, picking her way through the tense atmospheres and stony silences.

Dawn's legs were numb. She stood up and stretched, her eyes on the road outside. A small team of men was working on the shrubs outside her house, pruning them. She wondered if they could hear through her front door; if they ever listened in.

She felt her chest cave in with the shame. Everyone knew about her, the quiet mouse who let her husband terrorise her.

She slid into Sarah's room. Like the rest of the house it was tidy, the bed made. A small cuddly toy sat against the pillow; a panda Sarah had brought north with her. Snuggled up next to it was her beloved cat Snowy. He'd been a stray who'd taken a liking to Sarah, refusing to leave and eventually being accepted as a member of the family, albeit one Ted wanted nothing to do with. Only the childhood toy was a link with home. Would they ever return home? She doubted it. This was home now, for all its failings.

She sat on the bed, stroking the cat between the ears. He purred in his sleep. It was warmer in here than in her own room, with the low sun slanting through the window. She stared out towards the sea, watching the distant waves.

She thought of the rope, hidden under Sarah's bed where Ted would never think to look. But Sarah might be coming home now. She would take it back up to the loft.

She couldn't stay here like this. She needed to be ready, when he came home. She returned to the top of the stairs and hesitated, her hand on the banister. More cleaning, to keep her busy? Once the trophies were gleaming she'd scrubbed the kitchen floor and swept under the cabinets, piling chairs onto the table to give it a proper job. Everything was back in its place now; neat, ordered, pristine. The

Lord looked down at her from his crucifix next to the door. She crossed herself and muttered a prayer for her family.

Her limbs tingled with nervous energy. She'd lost count of the days she'd spent like this, shut up in this house, hardly daring to emerge for fear of their stares. Waiting. Cleaning and tidying to distract herself. Cooking. She could make the rations stretch further than anyone else here, she was sure of it.

But today, she'd had enough.

She pursed her lips and stepped into the hall. She took her coat from its peg, questioning herself. He would be angry if she wasn't here when he returned. But she had to go after him, to still the waters.

She took a few breaths, her hand on the doorknob. What if he was outside already, coming home? She would pretend to have seen him from upstairs, to be welcoming him home.

She clenched and unclenched her free fist then pulled the door open.

The men pruning the shrubs looked up and nodded in greeting. She offered up a tight smile in return and they dipped their heads back to their work.

She looked past them, towards the Parade. Sam's family lived near the edge of the village, in a house that would barely contain two hulking sons and three younger siblings, as well as the parents. She thought of her own house, too big for the three of them. Maybe it would be the perfect size for a more lively family.

She caught movement from the corner of her eye and looked up. Something was rounding the bed, ahead of her. A bike?

She stepped onto the path, pulling the door behind her. Nobody had bikes here. They were too bulky for people to have carried them, and too expensive - too unnecessary to buy. Was it those boys again, from the estate? The ones who'd threatened those poor children?

She stood her ground, ready to tell them to leave, wondering where her strength had come from.

Then she realised it was a woman riding the bike, long white-blonde hair flying out behind her.

Sarah?

46

Her mother was at the front door, her arms wide, her jaw dropped.

"Sarah!"

Sarah brought the bike to a halt and threw it to the ground. Almost tripping over the wheel, she ran to her mother who gathered her up in a tight hug.

"You're safe! Oh dear Lord, I'm so glad to see you." Dawn drew back to push a stray hair out of Sarah's eyes. "Did he hurt you?"

"It wasn't like that."

Dawn frowned then looked towards a group of men who were tending the plants four houses along. "Come inside."

She pulled Sarah in, slamming the door behind her.

"The bike?" Sarah asked, her voice frail.

"We can worry about that later. Oh, come here. Let me hold you."

Sarah let her mother gobble her up again, feeling like a lost child. She felt tears run down her cheeks.

Dawn held her at arms length again and stroked her cheek. "You poor love. Here, you need warming up."

Sarah let her mother drag her into the kitchen and guide her to a chair. She was shivering, her layers of clothing soaked through.

"Can I get changed?"

"Of course! You go and clean yourself up while I warm you up some soup."

Sarah smiled in thanks and slid upstairs, listening for her father. He seemed to be out; causing trouble no doubt.

Her room had been tidied, her panda propped up on her bed like she was six. Snowy was on the windowsill, staring out at the sea. She gathered him up in her arms, sinking her face into his soft fur. He struggled against her and she put him gently back down, ruffling the fur behind his ears. He jumped off and slid downstairs. She watched him then crashed to the bed, exhausted.

Her mind felt full and empty at the same time. She couldn't quite believe she was home. Could things get back to normal now? Did she want them to?

She pushed herself up and went to her chest of drawers. One drawer held skirts, neatly folded. Another held blouses. She took one of each and some clean underwear. It felt good to have her own clothes next to her skin.

She sat heavily on the bed, thinking of the last time her clothes had been removed. Of Martin's touch on her. He'd been gentle, tender. How could a murderer be so considerate?

A deep longing to lie down was pulling her back to the bed. But she was hungry, and she'd promised her mother. She could smell pea soup. Her favourite.

She sat at the kitchen table and wrapped her chilled fingers around the mug. Next to it was a misshapen granary roll. She tore into it and dunked it into the soup, only now realising just how hungry she was.

"Thanks, Mum." She swallowed the soup in great, hungry gulps, smacking her lips when it was finished. She looked at the pan on the stove, hoping for more. But it was empty.

Dawn sat opposite her. Her face was pained, her forehead deeply lined. She smelt of the soap she made from seaweed and lavender.

Sarah looked down at her empty mug, hoping Dawn couldn't read the changes on her face. No one needed to know what had happened last night. The sooner she put it out of her own mind, the better.

"What happened?" her mother asked, her voice gentle. "Did he force you to go with him?"

Sarah shot her head up. "He's not like that." She felt her cheeks flush. "He's not."

Why was she lying? Martin was a murderer who had tricked her into bed.

She felt her stomach clench. What if she was pregnant?

"What is it, love? You look like you've got the cares of the world on your shoulders."

"I'm just tired."

"No surprise there. But you're home now, thank the Lord. We'll look after you. We'll help you recover."

"We?"

Dawn stiffened. "Your dad was worried about you."

"I bet he was."

"Now, Sarah. Don't go talking about him like that. He loves you, in his own way."

So does Martin, thought Sarah, then shook her head. "He's got a funny way of showing it." She pointed to the bruise on her forehead.

"I'm sorry about that, sweetheart. It won't happen again."

"How can you know?"

"Because I won't let it."

Sarah eyed her mother. Was she finding some courage at last? Was the sight of her daughter being hit by the man who'd dished out the same punishment to her time and time again enough to turn her?

"How?"

Dawn smiled. "Your dad's had a hard time, love. What with his injury, and that Martin causing trouble. He just needs a rest from all that."

"You don't think other people have had a hard time too?"

"He's different. I know how to look after him. I neglected him, for a while. I won't let it happen again."

Sarah slumped back in her chair. Dawn had it all wrong. It was she who needed to be treated better, not her husband.

She heard a key turning in the lock, and turned in her chair. Dawn pulled her hand off Sarah's. She stood up and put Sarah's mug and plate in the sink.

Ted pushed the door closed behind him, his face dark. Sarah held her breath.

"Hello Dad."

He spun round. "Sarah?"

She tried to smile. "I'm home."

He advanced on her. "Oh!" For a moment she thought he might hug her. Then his face fell. "What the hell were you doing, jumping into that boat?"

"I'm sorry, Dad. I was stupid."

"Fucking impetuous more like!"

"Ted," Dawn whispered. She was prepared to put up with violence but not with swearing. Sarah had never understood it.

Ted loomed over Sarah. She pulled herself up but he placed a hand on her shoulder, pushing her gently down.

"You shagged him, didn't you?"

Her eyes widened.

"Ted!" Dawn hissed. "Please don't talk like—"

Sarah recovered herself. "No," she said. "You've got no idea what you're talking about."

He grunted. "Well, you're grounded. No going running after him – and no seeing Sam Golder." At this his gaze flicked up to Dawn, who made an involuntary sound.

Sarah shrugged. "Fine with me."

"Good." He grabbed her shoulder and hauled her up. His own shoulder was free of its sling. "Get upstairs."

"Dad, I'm nineteen. You can't—"

"I said *go upstairs!*"

She looked at her mother, who nodded assent. She raised herself from the chair, leaning back to avoid making contact with him. She rounded him and made for the stairs.

"This is stupid," she said. "You can't lock me up."

"That's what you think," said Ted.

"You're no better than them."

He took a step towards her, his arm raised. Dawn's face crumpled. "No, Ted, please! She's been through enough!"

He lowered his hand, glaring at Sarah. His chin was trembling, his pupils dilated. She stared back at him.

She looked at her mother. She was close to tears.

"Like I say, you can't lock me up forever."

She ran upstairs and threw herself on the bed.

47

S arah woke to a grey room, sun seeping round the curtains. She yawned and sat up in bed, her limbs heavy.

For a moment she forgot everything that had happened over the last ten days; she was at home the way she'd been before Martin first came to the village. Before they'd taken her. But then the thought of it fell onto her, like lead cloaking her shoulders. She sighed and leaned back against the wall.

She was hungry. When was the last time she ate; twelve, fourteen hours ago? Her stomach growled as if in answer.

She flung her feet out of bed and found her slippers. She padded to the door.

It was locked. She rattled the handle, annoyed.

"Mum!" she called. "My door's stuck."

"No it isn't."

Her mother's voice was directly outside the door.

"Have you been sitting out there?"

"I wanted to make sure you were alright, when you woke."

"I'm fine. But I'm hungry, and I need the loo. Let me out."

"I can't."

She rattled the door again. "Of course you can. I need to eat."

"Look on your chest of drawers."

She looked at the chest of drawers. There was a plate on it, with some goats cheese, a hunk of bread and sliced up apple. The apple was starting to brown at the edges.

"You came in here? You left it?"

"I wanted to check on you. You were asleep."

"I still need to use the bathroom."

"You'll have to hold on. Wait till your dad gets home."

"I can't."

"I'm sorry, love."

She heard creaking and rustling outside as her mother stood up. There was a moment's silence; was she out there, looking at the door, coming to a decision?

"Let me out."

"You have to wait."

Sarah threw herself back onto the bed. Her stomach grumbled again. She went to the chest and picked up the plate. There was a glass of water next to it. She munched on the food. Maybe she shouldn't have come home after all.

She heard voices outside, below her window. She pulled the curtains aside and opened the window. Jess was on the grass below, running across the back of the houses that overlooked the cliffs.

"Jess?"

Jess stopped. "Sarah? Since when have you been back?"

"Yesterday afternoon. They've locked me in."

Jess looked towards the glass doors below Sarah's window. Was Dawn down there, discouraging her? Shooing her away?

"Sorry, I've got bigger things to deal with. I'm sure they'll let you out soon. Your mum's downstairs."

"It's her who's got me locked in. What is it you've got to deal with?"

Jess frowned. "Bill. From the farm."

"What about him?"

"He's turned up with the boat."

"What?"

"Sorry, Sarah. Got to dash."

Sarah ran to the door and hammered on it. "Let me out! I need to go out!"

The door handle turned.

"Stand back," her mother said through the wood. Sarah did as she was told.

Dawn pushed the door ajar. "Sit on the bed. Don't move."

Sarah sat on the bed, arranging her feet beneath her. She'd never seen her mother behave like this.

She watched as Dawn crossed the room, heading for the window. She reached into the pocket of her skirt and brought out a small key. She pulled the window shut then locked it.

"What are you doing?"

"I know you get out that way. When your dad grounds you."

"Why are you doing this?"

"It's for your own good. You need to see sense. Realise that I only want what's best for you."

"But I need the loo."

"Use the glass."

Sarah stared at Dawn. Her mother was the cleanest, most meticulous person she had ever known. The thought of peeing in a mug would be as unwelcome to her as peeling her own skin off.

"Mum? Are you alright?"

"I'm fine." Dawn looked tired, but there was colour in her cheeks and a determination in her eyes. "I'm going out. You stay quiet, and don't try talking to anyone again."

48

Dawn stood watching from the shadow of the house.

A hundred yards in front of her, Jess and some other council members were talking to a man. The man who'd come to the village with Martin. The man they called Bill.

He was solidly-built with greying hair that was thin on top, and he stood with a stoop. He wore a heavy black coat that stretched almost to his fingertips, with a pale stain running from collar to hem. He had a scar on his neck that made Dawn shudder. Apart from that he looked harmless enough, but that meant nothing. Martin had looked harmless too, with his open face and thick mousy hair.

She wished she could get closer. There was an open space ahead, with nothing to shield her. There were four of them other than the newcomer. Jess, her brother Ben, his friend Sanjeev, and Ted. She wondered what Bill wanted. Why he'd come here.

Ted looked angry. He was shouting at Jess, his arms waving. Ben was tense next to her, looking like he might throw himself at Ted any moment. He'd done it before, a couple of years ago. But Ted was stronger than he looked. As Dawn well knew.

Jess put a hand on Ted's shoulder and he jerked it away, shouting at her. Dawn winced; that would hurt. His words echoed off the buildings but were too muddled to make out. Bill watched them, his frown deepening. *You'll regret coming here now*, she thought. *As you should.*

She stared at him, horrified by his nerve. That he should cart her daughter off like that, imprison her on his farm, then come back here like he'd done nothing wrong. She had no idea why he'd chosen today to come here, but she could guess. He'd found the boat, washed up somewhere, and thought he could use it to inveigle his way into their trust again.

This time she wasn't going to stand by and watch.

She pulled back as Jess turned to glance in her direction. She was gesturing towards Dawn, towards the houses. Dawn crouched down, torn between running away and staying to hear more.

Then it hit her. If he had the boat, that meant he'd taken it from Sarah. He and Martin had worked together to convince her to leave with it, then attacked her and stolen it from her.

Good for her, escaping them. But where had she got that bike? She must have taken it from somewhere.

That wasn't good. *Thou shalt not steal.* But that was only one commandment that had been broken recently. The ones broken by the man she was watching, not to mention his friend who was where he belonged in a police cell; well, they were far worse.

The group turned to walk in Dawn's direction. She slipped through the shadows and darted to the side of

Sanjeev's house next to her own, hoping he wouldn't spot her. She crouched behind a side wall and peered out. Jess unlocked the door to the village hall and gestured for Bill to go in. Ted shouted something at her. She looked him in the eye and snapped something back. He growled but didn't reply.

Once Bill was inside, Jess locked the door. She spoke to Ted again then walked off towards the beach. Maybe she was going to check on the boat, talk to Clyde. She was friendly enough with him. Dawn disapproved; it wasn't right, a white woman and a black man. She'd never be as vociferous about it as her husband, but it still made her uncomfortable. It was enough that Sanjeev there had such a hold over Ben. Especially when it was Ben who had saved his life after the floods, so it should be the other way around.

She scurried across the square, stopping at the back of the JP. She leaned against the pub wall, looking around her. A woman passed with two small children; they looked sidelong at Dawn but didn't say anything. She gave them a nervous smile in return and hid behind the bins at the back of the pub.

She waited for footsteps. She heard three sets heading towards her: Ben and Sanjeev, followed by Ted's uneven gait a few paces behind. Ben and Sanjeev muttered as they passed her, but didn't spot her. She drew further back before Ted passed. She needed to be quick.

She slipped around to the other side of the pub, through the archway that linked it to the village hall. She went to the door of the hall and knocked gently.

"Who is it?"

"Let me in."

Bill came to the door. It was half-glazed and she could

see him staring out at her. His eyes were small and dark, pig-like.

"Who are you?"

"My name's Dawn. Let me in."

"The door's locked."

"They're keeping you prisoner?"

"Jess said it was for my protection. But yeah, I guess they are. D'you know where to find a key?"

"Even if I did, I wouldn't bring it."

He frowned. "Who are you? What have I done to you?"

"What did you do to my daughter?"

Recognition broke out on his face. "You're Sarah's mum."

"What did you do to her?"

"I'm so sorry."

"I don't want your apologies. I want to know what you did. Did you rape her?"

"What? No. Why would you think that?"

"Why else would you take her?"

He blew out a breath. "I don't know. Robert wanted Ruth. But he told us to take more women. I guess he thought it would give him bargaining power."

"Why is my daughter bargaining power?"

"I didn't say she was. Look, I'm really sorry. She's a good girl. She's forgiven me."

"Don't talk rubbish."

"We got to know each other. At the farm."

"After you captured her, and held her prisoner? I doubt it."

"No, I mean— you don't know, do you?"

"What don't I know? Enlighten me, please."

She looked behind her, towards the village square. Towards her house. If Ted got home and found her missing, would he come back here?

"I came here to tell you to leave," she said. "You and your friends are no good for this village."

"You mean Martin."

"I mean all of you. Don't entertain any notions of becoming part of this community."

"The other men left the farm, you know. I'm the only one there."

"Why should I care?"

He shrugged. "I'd rather be here."

She leaned on the glass, bringing her face close to it. Her fist was clenched, and she feared she might smash through it. "You get back to your farm. God wants us to be left alone, without any outside interference."

He cocked his head. He regarded her for a moment. "She's in love with Martin."

She felt her fist tighten. Was he not listening? "No she isn't. She's got Sam."

"Who's Sam?"

"It's none of your business!" she cried. She looked behind her; best to keep her voice down. "I have to go. If I hear you're still here this evening, I'll send my husband after you. And his friends."

"He doesn't scare me."

"He should. You and your friend Martin."

"He isn't a murderer. Martin. Tell Sarah that."

"What are you on about?"

"He was arrested. For murdering two boys. Young men. But he didn't do it."

"If she thinks he did it, she'll stay away from him."

"She deserves to know the truth."

"And why would you know the truth?"

"Because I was there. I know what happened."

49

Sarah heard the front door slam. Feet stamped up the stairs.

Those weren't Dawn's footsteps.

She pulled away from her door and sat on the bed, pushed up against the wall. If Bill was here, Ted might have got to him. Pounding up the stairs like that meant he was angry. Had Bill told him about her and Martin?

Her heart was pumping, her flesh shivering, as he threw the door open.

"Why is that man here?"

She wrapped her arms around herself. "What man?"

"You know what man. Bill Peterson. He brought the boat back. Did he take it from you? Was he working with Martin?"

"No!" She flung her arms aside, pushing up on the bed. "Martin's not what you think."

Ted stepped inside the room. It felt claustrophobic with him in here, his head inches away from the sloping ceiling. "So what is he? Your precious Martin?"

"He's not my precious anything."

Ted loomed over her, his face pale and his eyes bulging. She shrank back, folding her arms around herself in protection.

"I know men like that, girl. They're bad news."

She gritted her teeth.

"Are you listening to me?" he demanded, the colour returning to his cheeks.

She nodded.

"He left you, didn't he? He abandoned you. That's why you came back."

"It didn't happen like that."

"So why wasn't he with the other bastard?"

Her mouth felt dry, her tongue swollen. "He was arrested."

Ted blew out a long breath. "See? Bad news. Thank God you got away from him when you did."

She nodded, sniffing back a tear.

Ted went to the door. "So how come Ruth isn't back yet?"

"It wasn't Robert's death they arrested him for. Two others, names I didn't recognise."

Ted raised his hands to his temples, his fists clenched. "I'll kill him, the little shit. If he laid a hand on you—" He turned to her, his eyes questioning.

"No." She fought to keep her face under control. "No, Dad. He did nothing. He was arrested, and I came home. On Ben's bike."

"Ben doesn't have a bike. What are you on about?"

"I don't know. But Bill said he'd brought it to the farm."

Ted shook his head. "Fuck."

She stood up. "Can I come out now? I need the loo."

"No. I don't trust you."

"Please. I'm desperate."

He spun to face her. "I said no! Why doesn't anyone give me any fucking respect around here?"

He reached out and grabbed her hair. She screamed. He stared at her, nostrils flaring. She met his gaze. *Stop*, she thought. *Let go.*

He pushed her to the floor, spitting on the carpet.

"He's a killer. Stay away from him."

She said nothing but pulled herself up to sitting.

He took a step towards her. "You hear me?"

She nodded. "I heard you."

"And?"

She could feel her lungs tightening, her breath coming out in gasps. "You'd know about that though, wouldn't you?"

He let out a yell and hit her across the cheek with the back of his hand. She fell backwards, slamming into the bed.

"Respect, girl! You don't talk to me like that."

He turned and clattered down the stairs, his footsteps echoing in the empty house. She watched him, blinking away tears. Her cheek throbbed and her shoulder ached from where she'd hit the bed.

But he'd left the door open.

She ran down the stairs. She had no idea where he'd gone. He could be in the hall, waiting for her.

She had to risk it.

She stopped at the bottom of the stairs. Ted was in the living room, slumped on the sofa. Staring out at the growing dusk. His shoulders rose and fell heavily.

She grabbed the door handle, her eyes on him. He stood up. He rounded the sofa and sped to her, slamming the door shut, almost shutting her hand in it.

She grasped the door handle, pulling as hard as she could. He stared at her.

"Come into the living room," he said. "Talk to me."

His voice was low now, his cheeks had lost their colour. But she'd heard this tone of voice before.

He turned the key in the front door lock and pocketed it. "Living room. Now."

She bowed her head and hurried into the room, anxious to keep ahead of him, out of his reach. She perched on the arm of the sofa.

He sat in the armchair opposite her.

"Where's your mother?" he asked.

Sarah shrugged.

"Tell me."

She thought of Dawn, arriving home to this. "She told me she wouldn't be long. Maybe she had to go to the shop."

"It'll be closing soon."

"That means she'll be back soon."

He turned towards the window.

"It's beautiful, isn't it?" he said. "The sky. The sea."

She said nothing.

"Nearly losing you has made me appreciate what I should be grateful for." He leaned forward and grabbed her hand. She pulled on it but his grip was tight. Her heart rate picked up.

"Don't be scared, girl," he said. "I won't hurt you."

She stared out of the window, not making eye contact.

"I'm glad you're home," he said.

Yeah, she thought. *So you can lock me up. So you can hit me.* It wasn't much better than what they did to her at the farm.

She looked at him. She'd seen him do this before, with her mother. Go from ninety miles an hour to nothing in the blink of an eye. He wouldn't hit her again. Not tonight. "Can I ask you something?"

"You can ask."

She stared ahead. "After I left, in the boat. With Martin. You were worried about me."

"Of course I was."

"Did you tell the police I was gone?"

"The police?"

"Yes."

"That's not what I'd do. Not what any of us here would do."

"I don't mind, Dad. I understand you were concerned. You wanted me back. You'd do anything you thought might bring me home."

He tightened his grip on her fingers. "I never called the police, Sarah. How would I? We don't exactly have a phone."

"I just thought, maybe Jess..."

"Jess doesn't have a phone either."

"But they came here."

"They did."

"Did you speak to them?"

"Not about you."

"Are you sure, Dad?" She gathered her courage. "Did you tell them where to find Martin? So they could arrest him?"

He'd been grinding his teeth; she didn't notice until he stopped, plunging them into silence. "No."

"But somebody did."

"They did you a favour."

She didn't respond to that. "But if you didn't, then who did?"

"I did."

She spun round to see Dawn standing in the doorway. Her face was flushed with cold and she was peeling off a headscarf. Her lips were pinched together and her face had a tightness, a smooth hardness, that Sarah had never seen before. Sam was standing behind her, looking sheepish.

"I did, Sarah," she repeated. "I told them where to find him."

50

The police cell was cleaner than Martin had expected. Instead of being lined with filth, it smelt strongly of disinfectant. He wondered who had been here last, and if the disinfectant had been necessary for some reason.

He'd been in here for hours and still they hadn't told him why. When he'd arrived, there'd been a repetition of the charge – murder of Jacob Cripps and Zahir Ali – but when he asked when, or who they were, the detective had looked at him with irritation.

He counted the rows of bricks lining the walls, desperate to occupy his mind. When that was done, he counted the pockmarks on the tiled floor. Sixty-three. Just under twice as many as there were rows of bricks.

There was a high window in the corner, with obscured glass. He thought of Sarah in her cell back at the farm, the moss-hazed glass of the outhouse windows. He'd done that to her, played his part.

Whether he'd committed the crime he'd been arrested for or not, he deserved punishment.

He tried to push out the thought of her waking to find him gone, the deep sense of betrayal she would feel. She'd trusted him and he'd left her. Never mind that it hadn't been voluntary. He thought of the flowers he'd picked, tossed to the floor in his desperation to hide.

He heard footsteps outside his door and rushed to it, placing his mouth close to the cold metal.

"Hello?"

The footsteps stopped.

"Please, I need to speak to someone! I don't know why I'm here."

The footsteps grew closer. "Pull the other one, mate. I've heard 'em all." A female voice, edged with the harsh tones of a smoker.

"No, really. I've been arrested for murder, but I don't know who the people are I'm supposed to have killed."

"People? You're happy to shout around these cells that you're a serial killer, are you?"

"I'm not a serial killer. I'm not a killer at all."

He thought of Robert and felt his stomach churn.

"Is Ruth Dyer here?"

"Shut up."

"I need to know. She's a – a friend of mine. I need to know if she's OK."

The hatch slid open to reveal a pair of brown eyes. "Will you shut the bugger up?"

"What about Ruth Dyer?"

The eyes narrowed. They wore heavy mascara and blue eyeshadow that reminded him of his mum when she was going to the farmers' dances.

"She was released. This morning. I'm not telling you anything else."

The hatch slammed shut.

Martin slumped onto the bench at the back of the cell, wondering why Ruth had been released. Had she told them she'd been acting in self-defence, or something different?

He heard the rattling of keys and then the bang of the door opening. He sat straight.

The policewoman stood in the door, her head cocked to one side. "Come on then."

He stood up. "Where are you taking me?"

"To see your solicitor. That's what you want, isn't it?"

"I don't have a solicitor."

She shook her head: *another idiot.* "You've been allocated one. Lucky you: it normally takes longer than this. Come with me."

51

S arah rose to face her mother. Sam stood behind
Dawn, his mouth agape.

"Why?" she asked.

"For Ruth, of course. They needed someone else to
arrest. He was the best choice."

Sarah had told Dawn nothing about what had happened
in the farmhouse kitchen, about Martin throwing himself
on Robert. Ted had arrived right at the end, and couldn't
have seen it all.

"Why him?"

"It couldn't be anyone from the village. They needed
someone to blame. Two birds with one stone."

Ted was trembling. "How could you?"

Dawn looked at him, puzzled. "I thought you'd be
pleased with me."

"We don't talk to police. Not after the way they've
betrayed us in the past."

Dawn's face dropped. "I don't see it like that." She drew
herself up. "What would you rather I did, let Ruth go to
prison?"

"Co-operating with them... it's not what we do."

"Well, it worked."

"Did it?" asked Sarah. "Have you seen Ruth come back?"

"Give it time."

Sarah stared at her mother. "Did they tell you anything about why they were looking for him?"

"They didn't say anything like that. It was my idea."

"But they didn't...?"

Ted grabbed Sarah's wrist. "You're hiding something."

She looked at Sam. *Help me.* "No. I'm not."

Sam squinted at her. "You've got a bruise. On your cheek." He reached his hand out and Sarah shrank back.

Sarah looked at her father. He was glaring at her mother, his eyes full of warning.

"She fell," said Dawn. "I brought you here because it'll do her good." She gave Sarah a look that brooked no defiance.

Sam shrugged. "OK." He gave Sarah a nervous smile.

"Right," said Dawn, her voice sharper than Sarah had ever heard it. "Sarah, I think you and Sam should take a walk together."

"A walk?" cried Sarah. "A promenade, like an Edwardian lady and gentleman? I hardly think this is the time." She caught Sam's sigh. "Sorry, Sam. Nothing personal."

"You're not going anywhere," said Ted. "Sam, go home lad. Don't come back till I say you can. Alright?"

Sam nodded vigorously and turned for the door. Dawn reached round and grabbed his fingers. He was too polite to pull out of her grasp.

"No," she said. "I think Sarah needs some air. We can't trust her on her own. But we can trust young Samuel here."

Sam hunched his shoulders. Sarah felt for him; this was probably the most excruciating thing he'd ever experienced.

"Ted," said Dawn, "let her go. Just for half an hour. He'll take care of her, won't you Sam?"

"You know how I feel about all this," said Ted. "You got no business, leading young Sam on."

Dawn let go of Sam's fingers and took a step towards Ted. "If they go, you can deal with me."

Ted twisted his lips but said nothing.

"You're angry with me," said Dawn. "I'd rather you didn't tell me just how angry, not with the young people here."

Sarah felt like her mind was going to tear itself apart. "Mum, why are you doing this?"

Dawn smiled at her. "Like I say, a walk would do you good. And Sam here will keep you out of trouble. Go."

Sarah looked at her father. He looked from her to Dawn and back again. "Go," he muttered.

52

Sarah hurried out of the house, Sam alongside her. The door closed behind them and she looked back at it, confused. Scared.

What would her father do to her mother, after she'd stood up to him like that?

"Let's be quick," she told Sam. "Maybe down to the edge of the beach and back. Quick as we can."

She sped off, leaving him trailing in her wake.

"Sarah!" he called. "Stop. I don't need to walk. We can just talk."

She stopped. "Where?" It was cold out, and almost completely dark. The sky was clear, stars visible in the blackness of the night sky. She could barely make out the shapes of the houses, and was going more by memory than sight. Racing to the beach wouldn't be a wise idea.

"There's a bench, by the JP."

"That's a bit public."

"It's dark."

"Even worse. Someone could listen to us."

"OK. Where do you suggest?"

"Come with me."

She grabbed his sleeve and pulled him to the back of her own house. There were two garden chairs out there, to the side of the sliding doors. The doors were heavy and the curtains closed. Her parents would never think to look out here.

She lifted a chair from its position against the wall and unfolded it as quietly as she could. Sam followed suit with the other one. He sat down and blew on his hands.

"We could always go to my house," he said. "Mum's got a fire going."

She thought of his cosy home, full of people who loved each other. "No," she said. "This is better."

"Fair enough." He tugged on his coat sleeves, dragging them over his knuckles. The coat was a grey fleece, a size too small for him.

"What d'you want to talk about?" she asked.

"I don't know. Whatever you want. Martin?"

"Why would you want to talk about Martin?"

"Dunno. Understand the enemy, and all that." He grinned.

"He's not the enemy."

"I don't mean it like that. Just that he's my rival." He paused. "For you."

She leaned back, wanting to laugh. One man was a double murderer and the other was dull enough to satisfy her mother. He was kind though. Trustworthy. And he looked at her like she was some kind of minor deity.

"Did he really kill Robert Cope?" Sam asked.

She huddled into herself. "It's complicated."

"Well if he didn't, then who did? Not Ruth, surely."

"Like I say, it's complicated."

"Bill?"

She sat up. "What do you know about Bill?"

"Just that he's in the village hall. Jess locked him in there."

"Really?"

"Yup."

"Why would Jess do that?"

"Buys her time, I guess. Your dad's mad at her."

"My dad's mad at everyone." She paused. "Sam, tell me about your family."

"What about them?"

"Anything. The ordinary stuff. What irritates you about them. What you love about them."

He chuckled. "Zack's a nightmare since he got together with Jess."

"He did?"

"Yeah. While they were out looking for you."

"I thought she was with Clyde? Well, sort of."

"Nah. He fancies her, but she just laughs it off. Her and Zack are the real deal."

"Good for them."

"That's alright for you to say. Try having a brother who's going out with the steward."

She laughed. "You're pleased for him though, right?"

"Course."

She paused, listening to the sea beyond the headland. It was calm tonight, beating the drumroll of the waves. "What's it like, having brothers and sisters?"

"Difficult to say. I've never known any different. What's it like being an only child?"

"I've never known any different either. But sometimes I'd love a brother, to stand up to my dad. Or a sister, to share things with."

"Ain't as easy as that. Most of the time, they hate you."

"Yeah." She heard a door open and close somewhere. She stood up. "What was that?"

"Nothing."

"You didn't hear it?'

"Hear what?"

"Someone's around. They could be listening."

"We're just chatting about our siblings."

"Sam, d'you think Zack might be able to talk Jess into letting us into the village hall?"

"Why would he do that?"

"I want to talk to Bill."

Sam's voice dropped. "Why?"

"I just need to ask him some questions is all. Can you help me?"

"Alright," said Sam. "But you won't need to ask Jess."

"Why not?"

"Because Zack's got a key."

She almost cheered. "Brilliant!"

"He might not let us have it though."

"You can ask him though, can't you. Please?'

53

A woman sat alone at the table in the centre of the room, her loose skin and makeup-smudged eyes not flattered by the fluorescent light. She stood up as Martin entered.

He took the proffered hand and shook it limply. She was a woman of around fifty, with a tight-fitting blue suit and grey roots showing under her yellow-blonde hair. She looked tired, and eager to be done with this meeting.

"Evening, Mr..." she opened a file on the desk, stooping over it and placing a hand on her back. She looked up. "Mr Walker. My name's Judith Ramsay. I'm your solicitor."

"I don't have a solicitor."

"I've been appointed. Duty solicitor." She sat down, muttering *for my sins*. Martin wondered if he was supposed to hear.

She gestured at the seat opposite her. "Sit down."

Martin did as he was told. The seat was hard and cold but better than the bench in his cell.

"So," she said. She sat back, her eyes brightening. "It's not often I get a murder."

He frowned at her. He wasn't some sideshow, entertainment to brighten up her dull job. He shrugged. "They've got it wrong."

She huffed out a laugh. "If I had a pound for everyone who said that."

"I mean it. I don't even know who Jacob Cripps and Zahir Ali are."

She coughed and opened her file again. She looked up at the policewoman, who was still standing behind Martin. "I'll let you know when we're done."

Martin heard the door close behind him.

"Maybe this will jog your memory," Judith said. She pulled some photographs from her file and slid them in front of Martin.

The first one depicted a young Asian man. He was lying on a rutted tarmac surface in a skewed position. His eyes were closed and his skin pale. His clothes were covered in blood.

Martin felt his throat tighten. He pulled the other photo out from beneath the first. It depicted a white man, also young, with a shaved head. He was lying on his front, a pool of blood at his side.

Sweat broke out on his forehead. Was this what Robert's men had done to those two boys?

He hadn't actually seen the boys, not properly. They'd jumped him from behind, and they were wearing hoodies. But this had to be them.

His solicitor withdrew the photos and placed them back in the file. She took out a typed sheet and held it up to her face, squinting.

"Sorry," she said. "Don't carry my glasses in the evenings. I was out for a curry with my husband."

She didn't sound resentful of being dragged away from

her night out; despite the bags under her eyes and the dullness of her skin, she sounded excited, intrigued.

This was a game to her.

"I know who they are," he said.

"You do?"

"Yes. They attacked me. After the floods, when I was heading north. They beat me up and took my stuff."

"When exactly was this?"

"I can't be sure exactly. But it was February. March maybe."

"That tallies. What sort of stuff?"

He shrugged. "A rucksack. Food, and a tent I'd managed to—" he licked his lips. "I'd managed to steal. From a camping shop. Abandoned."

He twisted his hands in his lap. He was being accused of murder, but still wanted to account for stealing a tent from an abandoned store.

"They beat you up?"

"Yes. Left me for dead."

"So how did you do this?"

"I didn't."

She leaned back so far he thought her chair would tip. Her forehead caught the light as she did so, reflecting yellow off her skin. "The police think you did. They have your fingerprints on a knife that was found next to them."

"Fingerprints?"

"Mmm."

"But it was six years ago."

"Seems like they had it on file. But it's only now that they've caught up with you."

He nodded. Ruth would have given them his name.

"Is there a Ruth Dyer being held here?"

Her eyes darted up from the pad she'd been writing on. "Who?"

"Ruth Dyer. She's from the refugee village just south of here."

"I've got no idea. Why?"

"She's been arrested for killing the man who did this."

"Sorry?"

Martin sniffed. "His name's – was – Robert Cope. He was the leader of a group of men I was part of. They took me in after those kids attacked me. They retaliated."

"And what's that got to do with Ruth Dyer?"

"They abducted her, and some other women. A few days ago. Ruth was arrested for killing him."

"Whoah. You've been busy up here."

"It's not funny."

"Look, Martin, I'm not sure about your story or about this Robert Cope, but the police have got a pretty good case against you. How did your fingerprints get on that knife?"

"It was my knife."

"Your knife?"

"Yes. I took it with me when I left home. I used a boat, an inflatable dinghy. I lived with my parents in Norfolk. It was pretty bad there."

"But you're telling me that someone else used it to kill the men. Despite it being yours."

"It might have the killer's prints on it too."

"Robert Cope's."

"No."

She lifted her head to the ceiling, stretching her neck. She sighed. "You're making no sense, Martin. It's late. Just tell me what happened."

"Robert found me, unconscious. After they'd beaten me.

He and his men had captured the boys that did it. Then they killed them, and asked me to join their group."

"*They* killed them. Exactly who did it?"

He closed his eyes, trying to remember. He'd been woozy, delirious. It had happened out of his sight. He could remember their screams, though. "One of Robert's men. Maybe two. I don't know."

"You don't know."

"Sorry."

"That won't be good enough. Not in court."

"But—"

She stood up. "Look, Martin. It's late, and my husband's waiting for me. You say it was this Robert bloke, or his cronies, that killed the boys. But you don't know which one and you've got no evidence. And there's the prints."

Martin swallowed the lump in his throat.

"I'll talk to the CPS. But I doubt that it'll wash. Your best bet will be to plead guilty. Then I can get you a lower sentence."

She offered her hand again. Martin took it, his chest sinking. He'd planned on taking responsibility for Robert's death. At least that was something he'd done. But this... this was the last thing he'd expected.

54

Dawn stared at Ted as the door closed behind their daughter, feeling her stomach flutter. She'd never commanded him before, never told him what to do.

It felt good, and dreadful at the same time.

She clamped her teeth down on her bottom lip, waiting for him to start shouting. She wasn't sure which transgression he'd be most angry about; the police or the defiance.

"Stop that," he snapped.

"Sorry?"

"Biting your lip like that. It's ugly. Makes your lips swollen."

She released her lip and held her mouth as still as she could. It felt sore.

She stood by the door, watching him. He stared back at her, his nostrils flaring. She looked towards the kitchen. Could she put the table between them? Would that help?

He strode towards her. She shrank back but he didn't touch her. Instead he yanked his coat from the hook, sending Sarah's tumbling to the floor. She frowned; Sarah would be cold out there.

"I'm going to find Bill," he said.

"You're doing what?"

He pushed his face into hers. "You heard me. He's leaving. Tonight. I don't care what it takes."

"That might not be such a good idea."

"I'm sorry?" His tone was sarcastic.

"Maybe he knows something. About Robert Cope's death. About them taking Sarah. About what Martin really did. If he leaves here, you'll never know."

He pushed a hard breath out through gritted teeth. "Don't you get it, woman?"

She shrank back, waiting for him to raise his hand.

"I don't care what he really did," he breathed into her face. "It's irrelevant. He took our daughter. He raped her."

Dawn opened her eyes. "She told you that?"

"It's what men like him do."

"How would you know?"

He shook his head. "Don't you remember how I protected you on the road? Kept you and her safe? Those men, the ones who pretended to be her friends. The ones you so enjoyed sharing food with. I caught them slashing her tent with a knife. Grabbing her skirt. I stopped them."

"They were going to rape her?"

"Yes, they were going to rape her. But they didn't."

She felt hollow. How old had Sarah been then: twelve, thirteen?

She shivered. It was too much.

"Did you kill them?" she asked.

"Worse."

"What's worse than that?"

He grinned. "I sliced their dicks off with their own knife."

She felt faint. "Oh, sweet Jesus." She crossed herself.

"Yes. I imagine he was watching."

She slapped him. "Don't talk about the Lord like that!" She pulled back, horrified. "I'm sorry. I'm so sorry. I didn't mean—"

He rubbed his chin, where she had caught him. The slap had been a clumsy one, and only glanced off him. He looked pleased about it, vindicated.

"See?" he said. "We're all the same. Violent animals, when we need to be. Me, you. Martin. He'll have raped her, I'm sure of it. And if I can find him, I'll kill him."

"She'd have told me if—"

"You think that, do you? Had a lot of heart-to-hearts with her lately?"

"No."

"She hates you just as much as she hates me. Trying to force Sam on her. Ridiculous."

"He's what she needs."

He pulled back. "What she needs is her family! What she needs is her mother to stop meddling where she doesn't belong!"

She said nothing, but stared at him, feeling numb. She shouldn't have sent Sarah out there, without her mother to protect her.

"Did you hit her again?" she asked, her voice shaking.

He stared at her. He blinked. "Stop snivelling," Ted snapped. "I'm going to sort this once and for all."

"Ted, please—"

"Don't beg, woman. It's disgusting. You stay here. Send her to her room when she gets back. I'm going to break in the village hall and give that Bill bloke what for."

55

S arah wasn't used to being out at night. The shadows shifted every time the clouds moved, and it was as if there were living things here, things that only appeared once the human beings were safely in bed.

"What's that?" she whispered, grabbing Sam's arm.

"Ow. Just a fox or something. We're not the only things that call this home, you know."

She nodded as if to signal that she was reassured, but kept hold of his arm anyway.

They reached Sam's home. It was a squat semi-detached house, on the corner of the Parade. He turned to her.

"You wait out here. I'll get the keys."

She felt her eyes widen. "No. I'm coming with you."

"I can sneak in and get them. If you're with me, they'll want to know why."

"Can't I hide somewhere, in the house?"

"Stay here. I promise I'll be quick."

She clenched her teeth and pulled her arms around her. It was freezing out here, the kind of damp cold that permeated the skin. She wished she'd taken a coat.

He threw her an encouraging smile then eased the front door open with the assurance of someone who regularly let himself in unnoticed. She wondered what hours he worked, and whether everyone would be asleep when he came home from the gangs with his brother.

She approached the house to watch him but the curtains were drawn. Instead she shifted from foot to foot, blowing on her hands as quietly as she could.

When he re-emerged, he was patting his pocket.

"What took you so long?"

"I was only gone a minute. You OK?"

"I'm fine. Come on then."

They made their way towards the village hall, keeping to the shadow of the buildings along the Parade. When they reached the open space that had once been a traffic island, they darted across, hunched low.

The dark was like a blanket, a thick layer surrounding them and smothering the village in quiet. She heard scurrying in the bushes next to the road and stiffened, then forced herself to relax. Probably mice. Her cat Snowy had caught enough of them.

At the village hall, they hunched against the door, peering through the glass. It was black inside, no way of telling if Bill was in there. If he could see them, he wasn't showing it.

"Should we knock first?" asked Sam.

"Best to, I think."

She tapped gently on the door. There were noises from within, the sound of someone moving around. Bill's face appeared at the window, soft with sleep.

"What do you want?"

"Sorry," said Sarah. "Can we come in?"

"They locked me in."

"We've got a key."

"Then I haven't got much choice, have I?"

Sarah stifled an urge to apologise. She stood to one side as Sam unlocked the door and replaced the key in his inside pocket. She wondered how long it would be before Zack found it missing, and how much trouble Sam would be in.

They slipped inside and pulled the door closed. It was black in here, the only light the faint glow coming in at the front window. This had been a restaurant once, or a coffee shop, Sarah wasn't sure. Tables and chairs were piled in the corner; no longer used for serving coffee, they were put into service at village meetings.

"You got home OK then," Bill whispered.

"Yes. Thanks."

"Did they punish you?"

She didn't want to talk about it. "Why are you here?" she asked.

"I got the boat working. Thought I should bring it back."

"It would have been useful to you."

"I know that. But I felt bad, alright?" He coughed. "Wishing I hadn't bothered now."

"Why didn't you just dump it on the beach?"

"Because I've got no way of getting back to the farm now. Other than walking forty-odd miles. And I thought maybe I could live here."

"*Here*?"

"Fat chance, pal," said Sam. "After everything you've done."

"I know." Bill looked at Sarah. "But things have changed now, with Robert dead."

Sarah turned to Sam. "Bill helped me. Us. He helped me get the boat working, so I could come home."

"But you came back on a bike, your mum told me."

"Long story."

She turned to Bill. "I need your help again. I want to know why Martin was arrested."

Bill dragged a hand through his stubble. "I thought you knew."

"Yes. But who are Jacob Cripps and Zahir Ali?"

A shadow drifted across the back wall of the hall. They all shuffled to one side, afraid of being illuminated.

"What the—?" exclaimed Sam. A car passed outside, its headlights by far the brightest thing in the village.

"It's the police," Sarah said. She felt her heart quicken. "It has to be."

56

They shrank back to a side wall, hoping they hadn't been caught in the glare of the lights. Sarah stared at Bill.

"Are they here for you?"

He shrugged.

There was hammering at the door. It opened. Sarah cursed herself for not asking Sam to lock it again. Outside the lights had stilled, shining along the road towards the beach. Everything else was plunged into darkness, including the doorway.

"What the fuck are you doing here?" It was Ted.

Sam stepped forwards. "It was my idea, Mr Evans."

Sarah pulled him back. "Don't be stupid. It was me, Dad. I wanted to talk to Bill."

"You said you were going for a walk."

"I know."

She felt the air shift as he approached. She stood her ground, watching as his face materialised.

"Get home."

"No, Dad. I need to—"

He grabbed her chin in his fingers and pinched the skin. She lifted herself up, trying to move with him.

"I said get home. I'll deal with you later."

"It's me you want," said Bill. "Don't be so hard on the girl."

Ted dropped Sarah. She stumbled, catching her arm on the corner of a table. She raised a hand to it; it throbbed, but there was no blood.

Ted rubbed his shoulder. "Bloody girl, you made me hurt myself."

"It wasn't my fault," she said.

"Let her go," said Bill. "Deal with me instead."

"Oh I'll do that, mate. I will." He turned to Sarah and Sam. "Now – *go!*"

Sam pulled Sarah upright. He stepped towards Ted. Sarah slid in front of him.

"No, Dad. I came here to find out the truth."

"Oh, fucking Christ. The truth about what, exactly?"

"About Martin."

She felt his fingers brush her cheek as he made to slap her. Had it been a warning, or had he genuinely missed?

"Come on," said Sam. "I'll take you to my place."

"No. I need to find out if Martin really killed those people. I think Bill knows."

She felt another bite at her cheek, harder this time. Her father had caught her with the back of his hand. She resisted an urge to put her fingers to it.

"Forget your obsession with that snivelling turd. Get home."

Sam stepped between them. "You shouldn't have hit her, Mr Evans."

"*You shouldn't have hit her, Mr Evans.* Oh, listen to yourself. No wonder my wife loves you."

"He's right," said Bill. "You need to calm down."

"And who's going to stop me?"

"We are."

Sarah looked past her father to see Zack standing in the doorway. Jess was behind him.

"When I found my key missing, I guessed you were up to something, little brother."

"Not so much of the little."

"Ten minutes. It counts."

Sarah felt Sam slump beside her. All the fight had gone out of him. She wondered what Martin would do in this situation.

She knew what he'd do.

"You can't treat people like this, Dad. Bill's right."

"And how the fuck should you know?"

"Ted, please." Jess stepped around Zack. "Ruth's back. I need to deal with the police. Can all this wait until morning?"

The room went dark as the headlights outside were extinguished. Sarah felt hands at her side, grabbing her. She couldn't be sure who it was, but she dipped and sidestepped out of the way.

Then there was a voice in her ear. Bill.

"Come with me. I'll tell you everything."

He grabbed her hand. Together they ploughed through the confused bodies and ran out into the road.

57

M artin lay on the bench in his cell, staring at the ceiling. He would appear before the magistrates tomorrow, first thing, pleading Not Guilty. He didn't care what his solicitor said.

He ran through the months after the floods in his mind, trying to remember exactly when he'd met Robert. When he'd come across those boys. He hadn't killed them, but he wished he'd had the courage to do so.

He'd been walking for six weeks, maybe more. Winter was starting to turn into spring. He remembered snowdrops flowering alongside the road, a few daffodils emerging. The rain beat down on his shoulders some days, tiring him out. But it was better than the storms two months earlier. He'd spent days sheltering in old farm buildings, hiding out. He knew there were others on the road, people like him. But he heard shouts some nights, and screams. He kept himself to himself.

The last date he remembered was February 16th, when he'd broken into an empty supermarket, water up to his ankles, and stolen some food. There'd been a clock on the wall, one of the old-fashioned kind. It showed the time and the date, and had been ticking away unseen for weeks. 16th February. Two days before he'd been beaten up, and met Robert.

It fitted with what the solicitor told him.

His prints were on the knife. He'd been in the area at the time of the boys' deaths. Hell, that supermarket may even have had cameras.

And he didn't know which of Robert's men had killed the boys.

He had no chance.

It wasn't him who'd killed them, and it wasn't Robert. Robert had been in front of him the whole time, watching his face for a reaction as the boys had screamed.

But *who*?

There was only one person who knew, and Martin had a feeling he should be here in his place.

58

S arah stumbled out of the door, Bill dragging her along.

"Sam!" she cried.

"Here!"

"Come with us!"

She heard movement behind her; Sam pushing his way through the crowd.

"Oi, stop it."

She stopped, pulling Bill back with her. Sam was squaring up to his brother.

"No, Sam. This isn't your business."

"It isn't yours either."

Zack shrugged.

"Sarah needs me."

Zack shook his head as if marvelling at his brother's naivety. "Go on then."

She turned and jiggled Bill's arm, willing him to run. As she started to move, a foot flew out in front of her, sending her crashing to the ground.

"No, girl."

"Dad, please."

"He's right," said Jess. She pushed past Sam and Zack, Zack's eyes on her. "Bill needs to talk to the police. For Ruth's sake. If he knows something..."

"The bastard's gone," said Ted.

Sarah realised that her hand was empty. Bill, already out of the door when they'd stopped, had taken the opportunity to slip away.

"Bill!" she called. "Come back!"

He didn't know his way around the village and could have run towards the cliff edge. She turned back to Jess.

"We'll have to look for him in the morning," Jess said. "No point in this dark."

"We can get torches," said Ted.

"You have a bright enough torch to search the entire village?" said Jess.

"No."

"Exactly. And we don't want everyone waking up wondering what the hell's going on. I need to see Ruth."

"Is she alright?" asked Sarah.

Jess eyed her. Despite her air of command, she had dark circles under her eyes, and her thick hair was matted.

"She will be. No thanks to Martin."

"He was protecting me."

"I don't care what he was doing. He brought trouble to this village, and we shouldn't have let him come back with us."

"But you said—"

"I don't care what I said. I was wrong."

Ted was smiling, vindicated. "Go home, lass. I'll deal with you in the morning."

"I want to know what's going on."

"It's alright," said Jess. "I suggest you go home. Your

mum will be worrying about you." She turned to Sam. "Sam, can you walk her home?"

Sam nodded and smiled at Sarah. She felt herself slump. Everyone was against her. Ted was glaring at her, anger dancing on his face, and Jess clearly thought she was an idiot. Only Sam was on her side now.

"Alright," she said, and stepped outside with Sam.

The police car was still parked in the road, between the village hall and her house. Candles were lit in Ruth and Ben's house, flickering in a window. She wondered what sort of reconciliation they'd have; she'd seen the look on Ruth's face when she'd learned the truth about Ben and Robert. It had been all for Ben that this had happened; Robert's desire for revenge after Ben betrayed him so many years ago. Robert had killed a man, but he'd managed to convince himself it was all Ben's fault, just because he'd talked to the police. Now Robert was dead, and Ruth, of all people, was facing prison.

"Come on," said Sam. He laid a hand on her shoulder and she didn't shrug it away. Sam was a good man, like her mother said. He'd stood up to Ted.

They arrived at her house. Dawn would be inside, waiting. Was she sitting in the upstairs window as she often did, watching for her family?

"Thanks, Sam." She gave him a hug.

Clumsily, he pushed his face into hers and kissed her lips. It was a dry kiss, a cold one. She kissed him back. They stood there for a moment, kissing with closed mouths. She could feel his arousal.

She waited for her own heart rate to rise, for her skin to tingle. It didn't. She slid her face to one side, letting him kiss her neck, and looked up at the window.

Is this what you wanted, Mum?

She pulled away. "Thanks Sam." She smiled at him, feeling guilty.

He grinned. His face was flushed and his breathing heavy. She hated herself.

She turned and put her key in the lock, preparing to creep inside.

She closed the door behind her.

"So you've seen sense."

She started. "Mum?" She searched the dark rooms, her heart racing at last.

"In here." Her mother was in the kitchen, leaning against the cupboards.

"You saw us."

"You've made that boy very happy."

"I don't love him, Mum."

"Who said anything about love?"

"I did. That was the chastest, most unsatisfying kiss I've ever had."

Her mother pushed herself forward so she was standing straight. Sarah approached her, hoping she would understand.

"And you've had plenty of unchaste kisses, have you?"

She felt her skin flush, her fingers tingle. She could almost feel Martin's breath on her, his skin brushing hers. She closed her eyes.

Her mother was right in front of her when she opened them. "You little whore!" she screamed. "Get to your room!" Dawn crossed herself. "Dear God forgive me for raising such a sinful child."

"Mum, it's not sinful. Don't be ridiculous."

"You can shut up!" Dawn pushed her. Sarah stood her ground.

"Up! Now!"

She stared back at her mother. "Fair enough."

She backed away, reaching behind her in the darkness. She stopped at the bottom of the stairs, the coats hanging behind her. She had to be quick.

Dawn stayed where she was, a dark shadow in the dimly lit kitchen. "I said go! I can't look at you, you slut."

She moved her hands across the coats. Her own was woollen, and rough. Dawn's was made of a smooth manmade fabric. Her hand landed on it and she fumbled for the pocket. The key to her bedroom window might still be inside.

There.

But she'd had enough of stealth, of sneaking out of her room.

She turned for the door. She opened it, not stopping to look at her mother.

"What are you doing?"

She slammed the door behind her and ran out into the night.

59

S he leaned against the house wall, her chest rising and falling. Where to? The adrenaline was pumping through her veins, clogging her thoughts.

She could see shapes moving around in the dark ahead of her, hear voices. She squinted. People never came out at night here. It was too dark. What was happening.

She heard someone knocking at a door, followed by voices. She took a few steps forward, straining to hear.

"One of the men is here. The men what did the kidnappings. We're going to get 'im."

She put a hand to her chest. Her father. He was waking the villagers, assembling a mob.

She heard a door close and heard footsteps on the square. She shrank into the wall, her mind racing.

More knocks, more voices. She heard Harry's voice; her father had help.

She felt a hand on her arm, and almost screamed. She turned, expecting her father.

"Sam! What are you doing here?"

"I could ask the same of you. Why are you creeping around your own house?"

"I had to get away from my mum. And my dad. He's waking everyone up."

"I know."

She nodded. "Why are you here?"

"I came to tell you. I know where he is."

"Martin?"

His brow creased. "No. Bill."

"Where?"

"Come with me."

Sam pulled Sarah round the back of the house.

"Your mum's in there?" he asked her.

She thought of her mother, glaring at her. *Little whore.*

"Yes."

"Run, then!"

They ran across the grass at the back of the house. Sarah's chest felt tight and her skin tingled. She expected her mother to open the back doors at any moment, to call her in.

No one appeared.

They carried on running, past Sanjeev's house, Colin and Sheila's, then Ben and Ruth's, until they reached the end of the row of houses. Beyond it was a high fence, and a field. Beyond it the sky was lightening a little; was it almost morning already?

She stared at it. "We can't climb that."

"I'll give you a leg up." He pushed her towards the fence and bent down, his fingers entwined.

"Why are you doing this?" she asked.

"I want to help you."

She placed a foot in his hands. They gave but then stiffened.

"I don't get it," she said. He was helping her to find out the truth about Martin, so she could decide whether she trusted him or not.

Of course. Sam expected that the truth would pull her towards him.

She looked at the top of his head, stabbed by sympathy. He didn't deserve this. She pushed down and let him haul her up. She grabbed the fence and scrambled over, tumbling to the ground on the other side.

"Grab my hands," he said. His fingers appeared, gripping the fence. She grabbed them.

He lifted himself up so his face was visible. He was grinning and his eyes were sparkling. He shifted his weight forwards and onto the fence. She leaned back and pulled.

"Careful!" he cried. She kept hold but stopped leaning, letting him shift his weight himself. He was soon over and standing next to her, brushing down his already mud-crusted trousers and smiling triumphantly.

"He's in the shed. On the allotments."

"The same place that..."

"Yeah. I hid him there."

"Wow." Was there no end to what Sam would do to end all this? "Is he alright in there? Is he angry with you?"

"Why would he be angry with me?"

"Because you locked him in. Didn't you?"

"No. He didn't want to go anywhere. He wants to stay here, Sarah. He doesn't know that we won't let him, but he's not going anywhere, not yet."

She heard a commotion to her right. Behind the field, back in the village, there was shouting. Two men. Was that her father?

"Quick," she said.

They ran across the field, keeping low, until they came to

the edge of the allotments. They sank to the ground and surveyed the area. There was no one around, but people arrived early here. They would have to take care.

She heard voices to the left. Men shouting. She grabbed Sam's wrist.

"My dad. He's been knocking on doors. He's on the warpath."

"I know."

Two shapes approached across the rutted ground, their breathing heavy. Sarah and Sam shrank to the ground, their faces turned away.

The men passed, running towards the centre of the village. Sarah lifted her face from the soil and stared at Sam.

"Quick," she said. She lifted herself up to a crouch and made her way across the open space, glancing towards the village as she moved. It was difficult to run and stay low but at last she was at the shed.

She knocked on the wall of the shed. No answer.

"Bill!" she hissed. "Bill, its me! Sarah."

"And Sam." Sam fell to the ground next to her, breathing heavily. His bulk landing against the shed made it rattle.

Still no reply. She stared at Sam. "Are you sure he's still here?"

Sam shrugged.

She looked towards the village again and went to the shed door, which faced the village. She was vulnerable here but she had no choice.

She tugged on the handle. It didn't budge.

"Bill! Let us in. We're alone."

"There's no one watching you?"

She felt her chest empty at the relief of hearing him.

"Positive. Let us in, before someone comes."

He opened the door. His face was streaked with dirt and

his hair stood up in clumps. He'd cleared a space amongst the tools and junk, and looked like he'd tried to sleep.

"Sam says you can tell me the truth," she said.

Sam pulled the door closed and sat next to it, his hand on the doorknob.

Bill looked sheepish. "Yeah."

"Go on then."

"You're not going to like it."

"I just want to know. Who are Cripps and Ali? And did Martin kill them?"

"No." He frowned and looked into her eyes. "I did."

60

"Martin. Hello again."

He shifted his feet. He was due to appear before the Magistrate this morning, to give his plea. Not Guilty, despite his solicitor's advice.

"Sit down, will you," she said. She took a file from a shopping bag and placed it on the table between them. "Now, let me see..."

She bent to the file, yawning as she read. Martin stared at the ceiling, unconvinced that this woman would be able to help him.

"Right," she said. She slapped the file shut and leaned back in her chair. She smelled of a heavy musk perfume mixed with garlic. "So, I've spoken to the CPS lawyer."

"The who?"

"Sorry. Crown Prosecution Service. They're keen on plea bargaining these days."

He swallowed. "What does that mean?"

"It means you've got a chance to avoid a long prison sentence." She smiled at him, her brightly lipsticked lips crooked.

"How?"

"If you plead guilty when you go before the magistrates, then they'll give you – hang on." She licked her thumb and leafed through her file. "Twelve months inside then another year under curfew. Ankle bracelet, the usual."

"Sorry. If I plead guilty to what?"

"To killing those boys."

"You mean, they'll give me a year if I plead guilty to murder?"

"Well, no. It's been commuted to manslaughter. On the grounds that they supposedly attacked you first."

"Even so..."

"I know, I know. This would never have happened in the old days. But they've only got half as many prisons now, and twice as many people to lock up. They're keen to get rid of as many of you as they can." She put a hand on her chest. "And thanks to Judith here, you hit the jackpot."

She grinned at him. He felt sick.

"But I didn't kill them."

She waved a hand. "Whether you did it or not is pretty irrelevant."

"That makes no sense."

"Look, Martin. Can you produce any witnesses?"

"There's Bill."

She opened her file again. "Bill?"

"Bill Peterson. He was there. I think."

"And he'll vouch for you."

Martin let his limbs go numb. "No."

She raised an eyebrow. "You sure about that?"

"Yeah."

"So. Anyone else?"

He thought of the deserted farm, the disappeared men.

At first he'd thought Bill was lying, that they'd gone off on a foraging sortie. But all their gear was gone.

"No," he said.

"So you don't have a very strong case, do you?"

Stop talking to me like I'm a child, he thought. "No."

She stood up. "I'll let you think about it."

He looked up at her. She had at least two chins and a bead of sweat hanging at the end of her nose. "How long have I got?"

She checked her watch. "Half an hour. There'll be a copper in here, keeping an eye on you. I'll be back."

"Right."

"Seriously, Martin. I suggest you take the deal."

61

"You did what?" Sarah pulled away from Bill.

"Well, I didn't actually kill them. But it was me who gave the order."

"What the hell does that mean?" asked Sam. "This isn't the military."

Bill raised an eyebrow. "I think Robert had ambitions in that direction, at one time. He ran things on strict lines of authority. He would tell me to do things, and I would pass them on to one or more of the more junior men."

"Even murder?"

Bill lowered his eyes. "You have to understand. Those were hard times. We were all scared. Those lads were trouble."

Sarah thought of Martin, alone in a police cell. "The lads who attacked Martin?"

"What?"

"When he met you. He told me he'd been attacked, that Robert told your men to kill them."

Bill's brow was creased. "No. It's not them. I've no idea who those little fuckers were."

"Who were they then?"

Jacob and Zahir were part of our group."

She felt her jaw drop. "What?"

"Yeah. They attacked some girls. We told them to get packing."

"You didn't kill them?"

"We roughed them up a bit. Well, the lads did. I wasn't there. They told me it got nasty. Quite a lot of blood."

"They died?"

Bill shrugged. How could he be so calm about this?

"I guess so," he said. "Never thought about it till the police showed up."

"But why have they arrested Martin?"

"Ah."

"Ah what?"

"Yeah. Our lads. They nicked Martin's knife. I guess that's what they used on them."

Sam shifted his weight. Sarah felt as if the shed walls were pushing in on her. The dead men weren't even the ones she'd thought they were.

"Was Martin with you, when this happened? Was he a part of the group?"

"He'd been with us a couple days. Robert commented that it was fate, losing two bad 'uns and picking up a good 'un."

She stared at him, gathering her thoughts.

"We didn't mean to kill them," Bill said.

"Rubbish," she replied.

Bill's forehead creased. "What?"

"Surely you know if you've hurt someone badly enough to kill them."

"You wouldn't understand, you're— well, you're you. But you walked here too, with your parents. You know what it was like. You're telling me your dad didn't use violence at any point?"

She sensed Sam avoiding her eye. "He protected us," she said.

"He defended you, right?"

"Yes."

"He hurt people?"

She felt her head fill with clouds. "There were some men. They broke into my tent, tried to..." She swallowed. "They ran off."

Bill stared at her evenly. "Did you see them again?"

"No. I assumed they'd..." She straightened up. "This has nothing to do with it."

Bill arched an eyebrow.

"No," she said. "It doesn't. You killed those men. If you didn't do it, you told someone else to do it. Isn't that conspiracy?"

"Yes," said Sam. "Conspiracy to commit murder."

"What if we were defending ourselves?" said Bill.

The cramped shed seemed to shrink in on her, as if it would squeeze them in place. "Were you?"

"No. Not at that moment, no."

"So you murdered them."

A pause. She heard an animal scurry up the outside of the shed and land on the roof, its legs beating against the wood. Her breathing was heavy.

"Yes," said Bill. "We did. But Martin had nothing to do with it."

She stared at him. Why hadn't he told the police this, when they came to the farm? Did Martin know?

"You have to tell the police," she said.

Bill shook his head. "I can't do that. Those lads, the ones who did it, they're long gone. It's no use."

"Who was it?"

He eyed her, chewing his lip. He sniffed and lifted his head. "Leroy and Mike."

Leroy. She felt a shiver crawl down her back.

"But what about Martin?"

He eyed her. "He killed Robert, didn't he?"

"He was defending me."

"Was he? As I recall it, your dad had just dragged Robert off you when Martin pounced."

She clenched her fists. Her palms were clammy.

"I suggest you leave," said Sam.

Bill nodded at him. "Fair enough."

Sarah shrank back, almost leaning on Sam, as Bill clambered over the tools to the door of the shed. He hesitated, listening for anyone outside.

"Go," she said. He looked back at her then pushed the door open.

"Now," she said. She felt hot, her body steaming with anger. He stepped outside and let the door swung shut behind them, plunging her and Sam into the mist of the early morning.

She closed her eyes, listening. If there were people out there, they would stop him. What would they do to him? Would they know who he was? Would they take him to Jess?

Not if her father got to him first.

"Come on," she said to Sam. "I need to find my dad."

62

M artin allowed himself to be led up the narrow stairs into the dock. He could hear echoing voices above his head and smell disinfectant.

At the top, he turned to see his solicitor with two men beyond a panel of glass. Beyond them was a desk with a woman sitting at it. Another desk, to one side, held two more women. None of them looked at him.

Judith turned and gave him an encouraging smile. He didn't return it.

One of the women at the table to the side started speaking. The woman in the centre, the one he thought was the magistrate, stared at him with dark eyes. She was dressed in a neat grey suit and had hair pulled back in a severe bun. Her eyes weren't friendly.

"Can you state your name please?"

Martin turned to the woman who had spoken. She was almost his mother's age, with a thin face and greying hair. "Martin Walker," he said.

"And your address."

He looked at his solicitor. She cleared her throat. "Er, my client currently has no fixed address."

He looked down at his hands, ashamed. He'd tried so hard to find a home for himself, in the village. But it had been futile from the outset.

"Mr Walker, you are here today because you've been charged with the murder of Jacob Cripps and Zahir Ali on the first of March two thousand and—"

He leaned forwards. "What?"

His solicitor gave him a look. He wasn't supposed to speak.

"March?" he said. "March?"

The woman checked a sheet of paper on the desk in front of her and repeated the date. "March the first, two thousand and eighteen."

He shook his head. "No! No, it was the middle of February. I know that, because of the supermarket."

The magistrate raised a hand. "Mr Walker, you need to calm down please. We will tell you when it's your chance to speak."

"But you've got it wrong! It was February when it happened. Not March. How can you—"

Judith was leafing through her file, looking panicked. Martin heard footsteps behind him. He turned to see a policeman standing a foot away from him.

"You've got it wrong!" he shouted. "It's not me. The dates are wrong, you see!"

"Mr Walker." The magistrate stood up. The solicitors in front of her shuffled backwards. "If you can't keep calm, then I will hold you in contempt."

He stared at his solicitor. Her cheeks were red and her hair uncombed. "Tell them!" he shouted. "Tell them they've got it wrong."

"Remove him from the court, please," the magistrate said.

The policeman gripped Martin's arm and pulled him away.

63

The allotments were empty, the only life the crows pulling worms out of the rutted earth.

"Where did he go?" breathed Sam.

"I don't know," said Sarah. "Back to the farm, I hope."

Sam turned to her. "Are you alright?"

Her heart felt like it might burst and her legs felt hollow. "Yes."

"You look pale."

"I'll be fine."

What next? Did she have enough to take to the police herself? Bill hadn't told her which of his gang had actually killed those men. And without alternative suspects or a witness, Martin would have little chance.

She thought back to her own experiences on the road. Martin had been beaten up, but she'd faced worse. If it hadn't been for her father...

She felt the ground shift beneath her. She groaned and swayed a little, her head suddenly empty.

Sam grabbed her. "You're coming with me."

She blinked and leaned into him, gathering her breath. "No. I need to tell them. I need to talk to the police."

"What are you going to tell them?"

"That it wasn't Martin, of course." She swallowed.

"What about Robert's murder?" Sam said.

"That was different."

"They brought Ruth back, so they'll have charged Martin with that too."

She brought her fingertips to her forehead. It was beaded with sweat. Martin was under suspicion of three murders now.

"I have to talk to them," she croaked.

"You need to rest first."

She let Sam steer her towards his house, which was thankfully close to the allotments. She dreaded explaining herself to his family, but didn't have the strength to argue.

He propped her against him as he unlocked the door and pushed it open.

"Hello?" he called.

No reply. She felt a wave of relief flow over her, followed by nausea. She retched.

"Shit," Sam muttered. He grabbed a flowerpot next to the door and held it up to her face. She retched again but nothing came out.

"Sorry," she whispered.

"It's OK."

He guided her inside the house and onto the sofa. The house was cluttered and homely, dirty plates piled up next to the sink and books littering the floor between the sofa and the fire. There was another armchair, faded and green.

"I didn't take you for a reader," she said.

He held a book up. The cover featured a man with no

shirt on. He was tanned and muscled. "Not me," he said. "My mum. Escapism."

She smiled weakly. Plenty of people needed a dose of escapism, here. Her own was found in the folds at the back of her cat's neck, which she liked to nuzzle.

She blinked to clear her vision, focusing on each part of the room in turn. There were pictures on the walls, framed watercolours which probably dated from before the floods. Surrounding them were rougher, less polished pieces of art on scraps of paper. Crayon, coloured pencil and one or two in paint.

"My sister's work," Sam said, spotting her gaze. "She likes to paint."

"Where does she get the paints?'

"There were some in the shop, from before. No one had claimed them. Mum's friendly with Pam."

Pam was the stern-faced woman who presided over the village shop. It was less a shop, more a distribution point, with people being allowed their allocated rations and no more. Sarah knew that Pam liked to help the families of the men who went out to work, who brought cash in. Ted had complained about favouritism often enough.

"They're lovely," she said.

"You think so?"

She nodded.

She pulled herself forward in the chair. Sam had placed a glass of water on the table next to her and she drank from it eagerly, the water hitting her empty stomach like a hail-storm. She belched.

"Sorry."

"Don't apologise."

She nodded and pulled herself to her feet. She was better now; the lightness had gone from her head and her body felt solid again, not as if she might pass through the nearest object.

She remembered her mother, standing in the hallway, calling after her. How long before her father came home?

"I need to go home."

"Do you want me to come with you?"

She shook her head.

"Has it occurred to you to tell your mum the truth?"

She stared at him. He was looking away from her, at one of the crayon drawings. It depicted a family; two parents, four children.

"What truth?" Her heart was racing.

His lips tightened. "About Martin."

Her mouth fell open. Did she want to tell the truth? Did she even know what the truth was?

"If you can't tell her," he said, "what about the police?"

"I don't have any evidence." She tugged on his arm and he turned to her. His eyes were red. "I shouldn't have told Bill to leave."

"That wasn't you."

"No. But what he told us... I don't know, Sam."

"He killed them. If not that, he was responsible for their deaths."

"I don't know."

"Sarah," he said, standing up. "You need to do something. You'll never forgive yourself if you don't."

She let him pull her up to her feet.

"I have to go home," she said.

"You're going back to your mum."

"No. I'm going to get the bike."

64

T he house was still, no sign of her mother. She'd left the bike against the far wall after bringing it home the previous night, but would it still be there?

"Let's go round the back," she said. She gestured to Sam and he followed her round the side of Sanjeev's house, next door to her own. They flattened themselves against the back wall, feeling spray from the sea on their faces even this high above the waves. The sky was the washed-out grey of old towels.

She peered round the back window of Sanjeev's house. His younger brother was in the living room, crouched on the floor with what looked like a pack of cards spread out on the coffee table.

She smiled, wondering if she'd ever find normality like that.

She stepped out onto the grass and started to stroll towards her own house, past her neighbour's back windows. After a few paces she turned towards the boy. He was watching her, a card dropped to the floor.

She gave him a friendly wave and carried on walking.

Sam followed suit, hurrying to catch her up.

Anish was only sixteen years old; he wouldn't bother himself with the neighbours' business. She doubted he'd ever spoken to her mother.

At the corner of her own house, she stopped again. The bike was tucked under an overhang, right in front of a window.

"Do you want me to go?" asked Sam.

"No. I'll do it."

She reached forward and grabbed the rear wheel of the bike, which was closest to her. Gently, she pulled it towards her. She inched it to her slowly, until the handlebars were in her grasp.

There was no sign of her being spotted, no sign of the window being opened.

She turned to Sam. "Wish me luck."

He grinned. "Good luck. I'll be thinking of you."

"Thanks." She stood on tiptoe and kissed him on the cheek. He smelt of bread mixed with lavender and damp wood. "I appreciate your help."

He shrugged. "That's what friends are for."

She gave him a shrug in return, not meeting his eye.

She pulled the bike onto the path next to the house and swung herself into the saddle. The map was still where she'd left it in the bag tucked underneath.

"Can you pass me the map in the saddle bag?"

He rooted in the bag and brought out the map. Filey was only a couple of miles away; she'd do this in no time.

"Thanks." She folded the map and gave it to him to put back in its place.

She gave him a final smile and pushed off, clearing the front of the house. She glanced to her side to check if her mother had re-emerged; she hadn't. She let herself breathe again, aware that she had to focus on the bike now. She might be stopped on her way to the main road, challenged.

She considered. There was a field to the side of the village, leading to an old pathway. It snaked to the main road. It went in the wrong direction, but it would be safer than the public route of the Parade.

She turned into the side road leading to the beach, then pulled the bike onto the grass. It was a mountain bike so it coped with limited jolting and clattering.

She couldn't go fast; she had no experience with this sort of terrain. She'd had a bike back at home – at what had been home, once – but that had only been used on the road. Still, this couldn't be too hard.

"Sarah!"

She slammed on the brakes and scraped to a halt, almost skidding sideways. She turned to see her mother behind her, at the edge of the field.

"What are you doing?"

She stared back at Dawn. What could she tell her? What would she believe?

"Come back!"

She gritted her teeth. There wasn't time.

"Sorry, Mum!" she called. She turned the bike away and pushed off.

65

"What the hell was that about?" Judith stormed into the interview room, shoving the policeman out of her way. He frowned after her and closed the door, leaving them alone.

Martin stood up, kneading his fists on the table. "I met Robert and the others on the eighteenth of February. I know that because I was in a supermarket two days before, and the—"

"A supermarket?" She threw herself into the chair opposite him. "What does that have to do with anything?"

He sat down, trying to calm himself. "Look. They say I killed those men on the first of March. But it was February when it happened."

"You told me the dates tallied."

"I hadn't thought it through." He ran through their first meeting in his mind. "And you didn't tell me the exact date, anyway."

"They still have your prints on the knife."

"I know. I can't explain that. But I'm telling the truth. If

Cripps and Ali died in March, then they weren't the boys I was thinking of. I have no idea who they were."

"We just have your word for it."

"Wait." He stood up again, legs banging into the table. "Robert said something about losing two of their men. Kicking them out. I heard talk of it being rough. Maybe they killed them?"

"Was this in March?"

He slumped into the chair. "February. The day after I met them."

"So it doesn't help us."

"No."

"Alright. I'll talk to the CPS. We'll need to get your court appearance put back. But you didn't exactly do yourself any favours in there."

"Sorry."

"Don't apologise to me. It's not me who's looking at a jail sentence."

The door opened and Martin looked up. Judith turned in her chair. "Please, just a few more minutes. I have the right to meet my client in—"

Standing in the doorway was the detective who'd arrested Martin. Detective Sergeant Bryce. There were two uniformed officers behind him. No sign of his colleague.

"I said—" Judith began.

DS Bryce put a hand up. "That will have to wait. This concerns another case."

"Well, in that case you need to talk to me first."

"No. I don't."

Judith stood up. DS Bryce approached Martin. He gave him a wary look.

Martin looked back at him, his legs shaking. Had they found out who'd really killed those men?

"DS Bryce cleared his throat. "Martin Walker, I'm arresting you for the murder of Robert Cope."

66

Dawn watched Sarah recede into the distance, wishing she was young enough and fit enough to chase her. Sarah hated her now; she'd tried to imprison her in her room and prevent her from talking to Bill.

Maybe she was wrong. Maybe she should let the girl find out the truth for herself.

She turned to see Sam running towards her.

"Sam! What's going on?"

Sam stopped running. "Hello, Mrs Evans."

"Don't *hello* me, Samuel. Did you and Sarah take that bicycle?"

His face was blank. "No."

She approached him. "Then how come I just saw her riding it across the Meadows?"

He paled. "I don't know, Mrs Evans."

She resisted an urge to cuff him. "Don't lie to me."

He plunged his hands into the pockets of his fleece. It was grey, a rip in the shoulder. "She went to talk to the police."

"She did what?"

"She wanted to tell them the truth."

"What truth?" She stepped towards him. He clearly wanted to back away but was too polite, or scared, to do so. "What truth, Sam?"

"It wasn't Martin who killed those boys. It was someone else."

"Someone else." She felt her chest stiffen.

A nod.

She swallowed the lump in her throat. "Exactly which someone else?"

His Adam's apple bobbed up and down. "One of Bill's men. Robert's men."

"Who told you this? No. Don't tell me. It was Bill."

He didn't argue.

"Why would she believe him?" Dawn asked. "Why would she believe any of them?"

"For what it's worth, Mrs Evans, I believed him too."

She felt her shoulders slump. "Why, Sam? Why would you, of all people?"

"Because she deserves to know the truth. She deserves to be happy."

"You can make her happy."

He licked his lips. "I don't think I can."

She put a hand on his shoulder. It was solid, damp. "You underestimate yourself."

He shrugged.

He was looking over her shoulder. He stiffened, his face registering surprise.

She turned. There was someone in the field, running in the direction Sarah had gone.

"Stop him," she told Sam.

Sam nodded then started running. The man wasn't

expecting him so he caught up quickly. There were raised voices and waving arms, then the two men walked back to her.

"Bill Peterson," she said.

"Afternoon."

"My husband's got a lynch mob out after you."

His eyes widened. His face was heavily lined and he had a scar that snaked up from his wrist, disappearing under his heavy coat. He looked as if he'd seen pain, and loss. And death.

"You killed those boys," she said. "Didn't you?"

"No. But I know who did."

"I told him to leave," said Sam.

Dawn looked between them. "Why?"

Sam frowned. "We don't want killers here."

"He can help Sarah."

Sam made an involuntary noise. Dawn twisted her face at Bill.

"My daughter needs you."

"It wasn't me that killed them. It was two of the lads."

"Why?"

She felt herself shrink inside as Bill told her what had happened when they first came upon Martin. Such horror. She wanted to run home, to lock the doors and wait it out. That was what Ted would tell her to do.

If Ted found her out here, meddling, there would be consequences.

"You have to help her," she said. "She's gone off to the police, determined to protest Martin's innocence."

"What about Robert Cope? He killed him," said Bill.

"What kind of man was Robert Cope?"

"I think you know that."

"Not all of it."

"He had something deep in him, like a kernel of blackness. He enjoyed watching people suffer." A pause. "Including Ruth."

Dawn blinked back her horror. Her little girl had been caught in the crossfire.

"It sounds to me like Robert Cope was a man who deserved to die," she said.

"Possibly," said Bill.

"In which case Martin needs your help too."

67

Sarah passed a derelict supermarket as she rode into Filey. The petrol station forecourt next to it was overgrown and strewn with litter. The car park was crumbling into the ground.

She remembered these places; vast spaces full of food, household objects and a million things no one really needed. Pot pourri. Luxury chocolates. Dog food in little silver pouches. Such a waste.

She sped past it on her bike, trying to ignore the stench. It seemed that the local dogs used the place as a toilet; she could see a few of them now, chasing each other across the pitted tarmac.

She reached the edge of the town and slowed. This felt alien to her. Streets lined with houses, most of which looked occupied. Would the inhabitants know who she was, where she had come from? Would they run out of their front doors and chase her away? She'd heard her parents talking about the times the locals had invaded the village. Most recently it was just two teenagers scaring some of their kids and waving a misspelled banner. But four years ago it had been genuinely scary, villagers locking themselves up at night and the council sending guards out to patrol the edge of the village.

She hunched low on the bike, trying to be inconspicuous. She reached a traffic island and screeched to a halt. There was a sign, arrows pointing to the beach, the town centre, to Scarborough. But it had been torn from its moorings and lay on its side in the long grass at the centre of the roundabout.

She looked behind her, trying to gauge how many bends she'd turned. She was pretty sure the sea was to her right and slightly ahead. The road in that direction was wider than the others, with the houses set further back.

A car approached from behind and she pulled the bike off the road and behind a wall. The car crept past, its engine straining. It took the turning to the right. When it was out of sight she followed it.

The road sloped downwards now, giving her encouragement. She freewheeled along, enjoying the feel of the wind on her face. She'd been cold when she set off – bitterly cold, so cold she thought her bare hands might disintegrate – but the exertion had warmed her up. Her chest felt full and light at the same time. She was going to find Martin. She was going to get him released. What happened after that – she'd deal with that when the time came.

She reached another junction, traffic lights stopping her in her tracks. There was a sign to the civic centre, straight ahead. Maybe the police station would be there. She waited for the lights to change, despite there being no traffic other than herself on the road – it seemed her community wasn't the only one without access to fuel. When the light turned green, she pushed off, taking it slow so she could scan the buildings either side.

She came to a row of shops. Half of them were boarded up or in darkness. Half of what was left looked like they'd been closed for the day. Only a small few had dim lights on; a grocer's, a chip shop. The sea was approaching, in front of her down a steep hill. Maybe she'd gone too far.

She screeched to a halt as she came to the civic centre, almost losing the bike on the dip. In front of her was a vast beach, wider and shallower than the one at the village. She wanted to freewheel down the hill and explore, to see what such an expanse of unspoilt sand looked like.

But she had things to do. The sign for the civic centre also said Police. She leaned the bike against a wall. Thinking better of it, she pushed it towards the building and left it in front of a CCTV camera, making eye contact with the camera before leaving it. She had no idea if it would be working.

She pulled in a deep breath. Her chest felt tight and her stomach loose. She scanned the windows; was Martin behind one of them, or would he be deep inside, with no access to light? What rooms were lit looked more like offices than cells. And they wouldn't give prisoners a view of the street.

She dug her fingernails into her palm, ignoring the fact that they were ice-cold. She pushed the door open and went inside, trying to look as confident as she could.

She was in a generous hallway, with a potted plant in the corner and a few pictures of Filey on the walls. A woman sat at a long desk. She wore a green jumper and a pearl necklace that looked cheap. No uniform.

"Can I help you?" The woman smiled at her. She looked as if she rarely if ever saw people walk in here off the street.

"Yes."

Oh God. She should have prepared for this. She should

have planned what she was going to say. She didn't even know what they were holding Martin for now, and if he'd been charged. Should she have sought Ruth out, asked her about her own experience here? Or would that be too cruel?

"OK. How can I help you?" the woman asked. Her smile was dropping.

Sarah put a hand on the desk. It was trembling. "You've got someone I know here. His name's Martin Walker."

"I'm sorry, but I'm not able to talk to you about who we may or may not have in custody."

Custody. It sounded nurturing and safe. It wasn't.

The woman squinted at Sarah. She had blonde hair that fell stiffly to her shoulders, like it hadn't been washed in a while.

"Sorry," Sarah said. "I've got evidence. About Robert Cope's death. And the others too, Zahir Ali and Jacob Cripps. I know Martin didn't do it."

"And you are—"

"I'm not his girlfriend."

"I just need your name."

"Oh." *Damn*. Now they thought she *was* his girlfriend, and would expect her to lie for him. "My name's Sarah Evans."

The woman opened a pad. "Sarah Evans. Can you give me your address please?"

"Six Turnberry Drive."

The woman glanced up at her, surprised. It was rare people from their village came to Filey, let alone to the police station.

"I was there," Sarah continued. "When Robert Cope died. And I know who killed Zahir Ali and Jacob Cripps."

The women nodded. "You'll need to talk to someone from CID."

"Can I see them now, please?"

"Hold your horses. Wait there, and I'll see what I can do."

There was a row of threadbare chairs behind Sarah. She turned and took the centre one, still unsure exactly what she could tell them.

68

"Sarah Evans?"

She stood up, smoothing her skirt. A man had emerged from a door to the back of the lobby. He was tall with dark hair that curled round his ears and a faded scar that ran up to his ear. He carried himself like someone who was used to stooping to get through doors. She recognised him from the farm, but he would never have seen her before.

"That's me."

She looked out to where her bike was still leaning against a thick hedge. The sun had come out and was illuminating it: *steal me*. She wondered who its real owner was. Would the police be able to tell?

"Come with me, please."

He led her through a blue door next to the one he'd come through. A woman came with him, the one who'd been with him at the farm. Sarah flashed her a greeting but the woman only frowned in return.

The man motioned towards a chair, one of four around a bare wooden table. On it was a tape recorder and in the corner of the room, high up, was a camera. She tried not to stare at it, wondering if Martin had been brought here. If he'd sat in here with a lawyer, or if he hadn't been given one.

"My name is Detective Sergeant Bryce, and this is Detective Constable Paretska. Please take a seat."

She did as she was told. The chair was cold and hard and it hurt her back. Her bum was sore from the cycling.

The two detectives sat opposite her. DS Bryce put his hands on the table and clasped them together.

"I gather you're here in relation to two murder cases we've been working on."

She swallowed the bile in her throat. "I was there when Robert Cope was murdered."

He frowned. "I was told you were too ill to talk to us."

"Who told you that?"

"Your father is Ted Evans?"

"Yes."

He nodded but didn't answer the question.

"And what's your connection to the other case?"

"Jacob Cripps and Zahir Ali. I know who killed them."

He leaned back in his chair. He had a mole under his right eye, the other side from the scar. It throbbed ever so slightly. "Were you a witness to that as well?"

"No. But I know who did it."

"Go on then."

"It was two men. Their names were Leroy and Mike."

"Leroy and Mike?"

"Yes."

"Anything more specific?"

She dug a fingernail into the back of her hand: *idiot*.

"No. But I know someone who can tell you more."

"And what are your grounds for saying this?"

"I've spoken to someone who was there. Bill Peterson."

"We've already interviewed Mr Peterson."

"And he told you he didn't know anything, I know. He was lying."

"So he was lying and you aren't?"

"Yes."

"And why should we believe your second-hand account?"

She frowned. She wished she had brought Sam with her; he would give her strength. He would stop her running out of the room, which was what she wanted to do. "It was Bill who told me."

"Why would he tell you that?"

"He realised it was wrong that Martin should be arrested for it."

"Very well. DC Paretska has been taking notes. If we think there are sufficient grounds, we may speak to Mr Peterson again. Now the other matter. You say you were there when Robert Cope was killed?"

"Yes." She pulled her hands off the table and clasped them in her lap. She tugged on her thumb.

"You were one of the women they abducted?"

She stared at him. So the police had been told about that. In which case, Martin would be a suspect.

"I was there."

DC Paretska pushed away her pad. "How come no one from your village will tell us the truth about those abductions?"

Sarah shook her head. "That's not why I'm here."

"But why? Those men grabbed you in the middle of the night and took you. God knows what they did to you on that farm. But none of you will talk to us about it."

"We don't have the best history with the police."

DS Bryce coughed. "I think we've been very helpful to you. Everyone has."

"Have you seen the way people round here look at us? We have to keep our doors locked at night, for fear they'll turf us out of our beds."

"I think that's a bit extreme."

"Not for us, it isn't."

He sighed. "So. Tell us about Robert Cope's murder. You were at the farm?"

"Yes."

"And how did you get there?"

She hesitated. "On a bike."

"A bike."

"Yes. It's outside your police station now." She had to hope it hadn't been reported stolen. Maybe it *was* Ben's. Maybe it had been left behind by a holidaymaker, years ago.

"A bike." DC Paretska wrote in her pad. "How long did it take you to get there?"

"Four and a half hours."

The constable scribbled in her pad. She looked at her colleague. "It's about forty miles. That makes sense."

"And why did you go there?" asked DS Bryce.

"I didn't come here to answer questions about me. Just about the murders."

"We simply want to get a fuller picture," said DC Paretska. "Don't worry about it."

That was easy for them to say.

"So you were there on your bike. Why?" asked the sergeant.

"I was out hunting. For rabbits."

"Rabbits!"

She pulled at her thumb. That was stupid, lying to them.

"And you suddenly came across this farm and heard a commotion."

"No."

"No?"

"I was at the beach and some of the men grabbed me."

"Do you know which men?"

"I'm not sure, but I think it was Leroy and Mike."

"That's very convenient."

"They were the type."

"Was anyone else with them?"

"Yes. Bill Peterson."

"Not Martin Walker?"

"They caught up with him later. He tried to persuade them to let me go." She was digging herself in up to the neck now. They'd have asked Martin about this, and he'd have given a different story. "They took us both to Robert Cope."

"Where was Robert Cope when they took you to him?"

"In the kitchen. In the farmhouse."

"Which is where he was killed."

"Can I ask who told you about his death?"

DS Bryce smiled sardonically. "You can ask, but I'm afraid we can't tell you."

"Sorry," added his colleague.

She shrugged; worth a try.

"So what happened in the kitchen?"

"Robert Cope had a knife up to my face. He was threatening me with it."

"In what way was he threatening?"

"Twisting it against my skin." She brought her fingers to her cheek. "It dug in. He did it gently though, so as not to pierce the skin. Threatening."

"Then what?"

"He was shouting, arguing with Ben Dyer."

"Who'd got there how?"

Damn. It was Ben who'd used the bike.

"I didn't see him arrive."

"What were they arguing about?"

"Something that happened between them when they were teenagers. It didn't make a lot of sense."

"And Robert was holding the knife to your face while they did this?"

"Yes. He moved it to my forehead. He started to cut me. You can see the scar." She leaned forward to show them. DC Paretska drew a sketch in her pad.

"We'll need to photograph that," she said.

"No problem," said Sarah. Maybe they were believing her.

"And then what happened?"

"My father came running in."

"Your father?"

She felt an icy wave run down her back. "Yes. Ted Evans."

"And he'd come with you by bike?"

"No. He came on the boat. The village has a boat."

"What did Robert Cope do when your father came running in? What did your dad do?"

"They fought. Robert Cope let go of me and stabbed my dad's shoulder."

"We've seen that."

Good, she thought. Evidence. She needed more of that.

"And where was Martin Walker while all this was going on?"

"He was watching, from the other side of the room. They had him tied up."

"Did he manage to escape his bonds?"

"When my dad burst in, they let go of him. He threw himself in front of me, between me and Robert."

"Why would he do that?"

"I'm not sure." She could feel her cheeks flushing.

"You were a stranger to him, yet he leapt in front of a man he already knew – a man who had a knife and was clearly dangerous – to protect you?"

"I guess he's that kind of person." She allowed herself a quiet smile.

"What happened between your father and Mr Cope?"

"Like I said, Robert put a knife in his shoulder. Dad collapsed to the floor and I fell onto him, holding onto the wound. Martin had thrown himself towards Robert, to protect me. Then Robert started on him."

"What do you mean, started?"

She felt the blood pulsing through her wrists. "He started lunging at him with the knife."

"And Martin responded to that how?"

"I couldn't see it all, but I heard a struggle and then it went quiet. When I looked up, Robert was slumped against the wall with a kitchen knife in his neck."

"Martin put the kitchen knife in his neck?"

"Yes. In self defence."

DS Bryce leaned over the table. Sarah pulled away. She willed herself to hold his gaze.

"So you're saying that Robert attacked Martin and Martin defended himself."

"Yes."

"Not that Martin attacked Robert in anger at what he'd done to you and your father?"

"No."

The detective chewed on his lips. He peered sidelong at his colleague's pad.

"And what about Ruth Dyer? What did you see her do?"

"Nothing." She swallowed, her throat tight.

"Nothing at all?"

"She took a ring out of Robert's pocket, after he was dead. Before that she was sitting in the chair opposite me."

"And how did she get there?"

"I'm not sure."

"You're not sure."

"No." She lowered her eyes. She should be better than this at lying, with the home life she had.

"Very well. Do you have anything else to add?"

"Will you let Martin go now?"

"I'm sorry?"

"He didn't do any of the murders. You should let him go."

"It's not as simple as that. You've only given us hearsay evidence on the Cripps and Ali killings. And as for what happened in that farmhouse, it seems no one in your village can agree."

He stood up and extended his hand. "That's all we need from you, Miss Evans."

She pursed her lips. "Is he here?"

DS Bryce raised an eyebrow. "I'm sorry?"

"Can I see him?"

"If you're talking about Martin, as I assume you are, then the answer's no."

"No he's not here or no I can't see him?"

A sigh. "You can't see him. Do you have anything else for us?"

She frowned, wondering if she could reword some of what she'd told them. Make it sound better.

"No."

He stood up again. DC Paretska walked to the door and held it open.

"Thank you for coming to us," she said.

"Does this change anything?"

"We will consider what you've told us about Robert Cope's murder. But as for the others – you weren't there. It would be better if we could speak to someone who was."

"Didn't you talk to Bill, when you arrested Martin?"

"He wasn't exactly forthcoming," said Bryce. "Now, thank you once again." He gestured towards the door.

She shuffled through, feeling hollow. If anything, she'd made things worse for Martin. She traipsed to the main exit, spotting the bike through the glass doors. Once again she wondered where it had come from. Why had Bill not told her about it earlier?

She pushed back through the doors.

"Hello?" she called.

The woman at reception gave her a puzzled look. A door opened and DC Paretska emerged. She looked tired.

"I'll get him," Sarah told her.

"Sorry?"

"Bill. He'll tell you. Come to the village. He's there."

69

Sarah sped along the country roads, her legs going as fast as she could push them. How long ago had Sam told Bill to leave the village? Two hours? He'd only have got a few miles on foot.

She made for the village, wheels flying. She almost hit a man who was walking along the side of the road, keeping to the grass verge.

She flew past him then slammed on her brakes. Shouldn't Bill be going the other way?

She turned. The man had disappeared.

"Bill?"

Nothing. She dropped the bike and walked back to the spot where she'd passed him.

"It's me! Sarah. From the village."

He pushed his head over the hedge. "I know where you're from. What are you doing?"

"I've been to the police." She leaned over, balling her fists on her knees. She was out of breath. "They don't believe me."

"No surprise there then."

She gulped down a lungful of air and straightened up. "They've got Martin. We have to help him."

"We're no help to him now."

"That's not true! You can tell them what happened. How those boys died."

"And Robert's death?"

She clenched her jaw. "You can tell them Martin was defending himself."

"That's what you said?"

"Yes. Why were you walking this way? Were you following me?"

"I worked it out."

"Worked what out?" She felt the handlebars slacken in her grip.

"Who killed them. Zahir and Jacob."

"But you told me. It was your men."

He cocked his head. "They'll know you're lying. The police."

"Please, Bill. Martin's a good man. He deserves your help."

"And what makes you think I am?"

"What?"

"A good man. You've seen what I've done. It was me what took you."

"You apologised. You felt guilty."

He shrugged. "I still did it."

She stared at him, betrayal swirling around in her head alongside despair. "I don't care. People change."

"Like your dad?"

"Even my dad."

She heard a wailing sound in the distance. They both

turned towards it. It was faint but unmistakeable; police cars, approaching them.

Bill grabbed her arm and pulled her behind the hedge. She stumbled through and pushed him off, brushing herself down. The sound passed. She peered over the hedge to see three cars, two of them marked.

"Why did you do that?" she asked.

"Why the hell do you think?"

She breathed out through her nose. "Please, Bill. I told them to go to the village. They want to talk to you. You can set things straight."

"Straight?"

She nodded.

"What if I tell them the truth, about Jacob and Zahir?"

"That's what I need you to do."

"And then there's Robert. Martin stuck that knife in him—"

"He did it for me!" she cried. "And you've said yourself that Robert deserved it."

"That doesn't mean Martin should have—"

"Who else?" she cried. "You? Would you have defied him? No! But Martin did."

He raised a hand as if to push her back through the hedge and then thought better of it.

"I heard you talking to him," he said. "About Lincoln. How you and he almost met."

She stared at him. "You wouldn't."

"Why wouldn't I?"

"Please, Bill. He was defending me."

"That seems to happen a lot."

"Please."

He sighed. "You go back to the village. Tell them to wait for me. I'll catch up."

"It'll take you hours."

"I'll hurry."

She gave him one last look, her nostrils flaring, then mounted the bike and pushed off towards home.

70

Dawn had been busying herself with peeling potatoes and carrots. Ted had returned home briefly, stormed upstairs and then gone out again, carrying what looked like a lump of wood. She wondered how many people he'd talked into his way of thinking, how many of them were going after Bill.

He was gone now: they wouldn't find him. He'd told her he'd go back to the farm. But she didn't trust him.

She heard doors slamming outside. She tensed, expecting Ted to come barging through the front door. She crept upstairs and peered out of the front window, her heart racing. Could Sarah be back?

There were three cars parked in the square. Two police cars, and one unmarked. They stood quietly in the gloom, no one near them.

She pushed her face to the glass, trying to see along the row of houses. Where had they gone? Had they taken Sarah to Ruth?

Had they found Bill?

The door to the back of the village hall slammed and

three men ran out. Ted, Harry, and another man she didn't know. She put her hand to her chest and waited. If Ted came this way she would hurry downstairs and boil the kettle.

Instead, he headed for the police cars. He peered inside each of them in turn, hands against the glass. Either they were empty or their occupants weren't about to talk to him.

He turned back to Harry and spoke to him. Harry shook his head and put a hand on Ted's arm. Ted shook it off. He turned to the house, staring up at it.

Dawn froze. The house was in darkness but her face was close to the window. He didn't know she came up here, wouldn't expect to see her. But still.

She retreated as slowly as she could, hardly daring to blink. He frowned then looked towards Ben and Ruth's house. Dawn let out her breath again.

She slid down the stairs and into the kitchen. She lit the gas under the kettle and made a pot of tea. She placed it in the middle of the table, taking time to adjust it just so, then poured herself a cup. She sat down, closing her eyes as she drank. Her heart was racing and her skin felt like it had something crawling over it.

She heard another slamming door and muffled shouts. She put her mug down and went to the front door, where she leaned against the wood.

There was a rap at the door, almost knocking her to the ground. She smoothed her hands on her apron and opened it.

"Ted," she said. She wanted to berate him for forgetting his keys but didn't want to enflame his mood.

But it wasn't her husband.

"Mrs Evans?"

"Er, yes. That's me."

Two people stood on her doorstep. A short, chubby

policeman, the one who'd asked her name, and a taller, willowy man in a faded black suit. A detective, she assumed.

"We need to speak with your daughter, Sarah Evans."

Her lips were dry. "She's not here."

The detective turned away from her door. More police were out there; four more. Two of them were talking to Ted and Harry. She wanted to go to Ted's side, to calm him.

"She hasn't come back yet?"

But she was with you, Dawn thought. *Why haven't you got her?* She looked past him, towards the Parade. It would be getting dark soon. No time for a young girl to be out alone.

She pulled her cardigan tight around her. "I'm afraid not."

The man nodded. "We'll be here for a little while. Please tell her to find us when she arrives home."

"Yes."

"Have you seen a man called Bill Peterson?'

Dawn blinked back her surprise. "Not recently."

"When did you last see him?"

"About two hours ago. He was leaving the village."

The police officers exchanged glances.

"Do you know which way he was going?"

"I thought he might be coming to you."

"No."

"Sorry. That's all I know."

The detective gave her a stiff smile. "If you do see him, or if your daughter comes home, please let us know immediately."

"Err...yes."

They moved away, heading next door to Sanjeev's. No one answered the door so they continued along the row of houses, nearing Ruth's. Dawn hadn't seen Ruth since her return from Filey; she hoped she was all right. Ruth was a good doctor; kind, gentle. She didn't deserve any of this.

She looked towards the Parade again before closing the door. Ted had disappeared back into the village hall, with Harry. The angry mob he'd gathered earlier seemed to have dissipated.

She could make out movement in the distance. Two shapes, moving up and down. The shapes got larger and closer, and coalesced into two bright yellow shoes, pedalling a bike towards her.

Sarah.

71

Dawn ran out of the house towards her daughter. "Sarah!"

Sarah panted her way towards her. She was pale and her thin jacket was soaked through. The bike came to a stop and Dawn threw an arm around her.

"We haven't got time, Mum."

"Are you alright? What did they say?"

Sarah narrowed her eyes. "You didn't want me to go."

"That doesn't mean I didn't worry about you. Let's get inside."

Sarah looked towards the cars. "The police are here."

"Don't worry about that."

"Sarah!"

Dawn turned to see Ted running towards them from the village hall. He was alone. Sarah squared her shoulders.

"Where the fuck have you been?" he hissed.

"I went to Filey, Dad."

"I tried to stop her," said Dawn, "but she wouldn't—"

"What the hell are you playing at, girl?"

"I went to see the police."

"Why the hell would you do a stupid thing like that?"

"To tell them the truth about Martin."

He raised his hand to cuff her. Sarah threw her own arm up to stop him and he withdrew, muttering.

"Get inside," he said. "We don't want the whole bleedin' village listening in."

Dawn tugged Sarah towards her. She tried to push from her mind what Ted might do once they were hidden inside.

She glanced up and down the front of the houses as Ted opened their front door. The two police who'd spoken to her had gone into one of them; Sheila and Colin's, she thought. There was no sign of the others.

She and Sarah fought each other as they stumbled into the house, Dawn batting at her daughter in an attempt to smooth her hair and clothes, and Sarah desperate to pull away from her grip. At last Ted separated them.

"What's this about Bill Peterson and the police?" he said.

"He's got evidence, Dad," she said. "He can help."

"Rubbish. They want to arrest him."

"He didn't do it, Dad."

"Didn't do it? He slung you over his back and carted you off to that farm, the bastard. He should be in jail."

"I don't want to press charges."

"Of course you don't. But we can sort him out. The village. We look after our own."

Dawn looked between them, scared.

"Ted…" she said.

Ted batted a hand at her: *go away*. She frowned.

"Ted, you need to listen."

He turned to her. There were tight red circles high on his cheeks and his eyes sparked with anger. "What?"

"We don't know what he's going to tell the police," she said.

"So? They can all dig themselves into the shit for all I care."

"Ted. We need to make sure he tells them Robert's men did it."

"What are you on about, woman?"

Sarah stepped forward. "There were two boys. Zahir Ali and Jacob Cripps. They attacked Martin. The police think he killed them, but really it was Robert. His men, anyway."

Ted looked from Sarah to Dawn. His forehead was creased. "What were their names?"

"Zahir Ali and Jacob Cripps," Sarah said. "Did you hear anything about them, when you came after me, to the farm?"

"No." His eyes were on Dawn.

"I think you should let him," Dawn said, her voice tight.

Ted took a step towards her. His eyes were red-rimmed and his face pale. "Don't tell me what to do."

"Please, Ted..."

He hit her on the arm, one, twice, three times. She closed her eyes. He grabbed her other arm and started to pull her towards the living room.

"Dad! Stop!" Sarah cried. He ignored her.

Dawn threw her hands up in front of her face. He would be careful not to leave a mark, with the police sniffing around. But he was angry. Maybe scared.

He flung her onto the sofa. "Stay there! Don't go out and don't meddle in things that don't concern you again!"

Dawn drew her knees up to her chest. She lay still, waiting for more blows.

She saw Sarah above them. The girl grabbed her father's shoulder. He spun round. He pushed her to the ground.

"You!" he spat at her. "This is all your fault. If you hadn't brought that little shit here—"

There was a knock at the door.

"What now?" said Ted. He glared at Sarah, then Dawn. He marched towards the hallway. Dawn watched him, trembling.

72

"We've been told that your daughter has returned home."

Sarah stepped forwards, pushing past her father. "Hello, Detective Bryce."

"Hello again. Where is he?"

"Bill?"

"You said he was at the village. We've had various reports that he's left."

"That's because we drove him out," said Ted. "We could drive you out too, if you don't stop bothering us."

"Dad." Sarah turned back to the detective. "Let's go outside."

She stepped past her father onto their path. She looked towards the Parade; no sign of Bill.

Behind her, Ted was leaning against the door, glaring at the two police detectives. Sarah pulled the door closed, ignoring his complaints.

"Come with me," she said. She led them across the square to the JP. It was open but deserted, just Clyde behind the bar reading a book. He looked up as they entered and started busying himself behind the bar, looking flustered.

"Why have you brought us in here?" DC Paretska asked. "Is he here?"

Sarah shot Clyde a questioning look. He shook his head.

"I wanted to get away from my parents. And into somewhere warm. He's on his way."

"How do you know that?"

"He promised me. I saw him on my way back. He was on foot and I was on a bike. He said he'd catch up with me." She looked out of the window. It was dusk now, darkness descending. Lights-on would start soon and last for just an hour.

"You believed him?"

"Yes." Should she have trusted him? "He might have gone back to the farm though."

DS Bryce pulled a mobile phone out of his pocket. Sarah stared at it, and could sense Clyde doing the same. She'd never had a mobile, and he probably hadn't for years. She thought they'd disappeared.

"He's on the main road, either heading for Filey, or towards Scarborough. He won't be far away."

Sarah felt her hand tremble. "What will you do, when you catch up with him?"

"We'll ask him to corroborate your story."

She nodded. She'd been so sure Bill would help her. Back at the farm, after Martin had gone, he'd been good to her. He'd talked to her about her parents, reassured her about Martin. Given her the bike.

She'd been too trusting. Her parents were right; this was her weakness. She'd even trusted Martin, and she had no way of knowing if he really was innocent.

"We'll be off now then," said DC Paretska. "We'll let you know if we need to interview you again."

"Yes. Of course."

She watched them push through the door of the pub and disappear into the gloom outside. Then she had a thought.

She slammed into the door, banging her knee. They hadn't gone far.

"Wait!" She ran out, limping.

DC Paretska turned. Her colleague ignored her and continued walking to the cars.

"Wait!" she called again. "There's someone else you can talk to."

73

Ted stepped away from the door, eyeing Dawn. She met his stare.

"Does she know?" she said.

"Does she know what, woman?"

"That it was you who killed them."

He advanced on her. "Don't talk bollocks."

"I'm not, Ted. You know I'm not. Zahir and Jacob. Those were their names. Sarah didn't hear. But you did."

"I heard nothing of the sort."

"How many times have you hit her?"

He glared at her. "Don't you dare accuse me."

"How many, Ted?"

"Just the once."

"I saw that. But you pushed her, just now. I think that's not the only time."

She backed into the wall, next to the door. Her hair brushed against her crucifix. She reached behind her and pulled it off its hook.

"Put that damn thing down, woman."

"It gives me strength."

"Strength for what?"

"Just... strength."

His shoulders slumped. "You can't tell them. You can't tell her."

"I think she knows."

"Please, Dawn. What will you do without me? You won't be able to keep this house you're so proud of, for starters."

"I hate this house."

He puffed out his chest. "Dawn."

She felt for the door handle behind her. He would kill her, if he thought she was going to tell.

"I won't say anything."

He stepped towards her. He put a hand on her cheek. She stiffened but didn't push it away. "Really?"

She swallowed. "Really."

"Good."

There was banging at the door. "Dad! Mum! Let me in!"

She turned to the door and pulled it open, hoping Ted hadn't seen the lie in her eyes.

74

Sarah ran to her house, leaving the detectives behind her. She had no idea if they would follow. She slammed on the door, annoyed with herself for forgetting her key.

"Dad! Mum! Let me in!"

Her mother opened the door, her face grey and washed-out. She was clutching her crucifix. Sarah paused, wanting to ask her if everything was all right, but there wasn't time.

Her father was in the living room. He sat on the sofa, his hands on his knees. He looked awkward, sitting upright and staring into space.

She looked between her parents. Dawn had her shoulders pushed back and was looking more angry than Sarah had ever seen her.

"Dad, I need you to help me," she panted.

Ted blinked a few times as if coming out of a trance.

"Dad?" She sank to the floor in front of him, trying to make eye contact. "Dad, I need your help. With the police."

His face darkened. He looked at her steadily, his pupils dilated.

"Dad?"

She turned to her mother. "Is he alright? What's happened?"

"Nothing, dear." Dawn put a hand on her shoulder. "Nothing you need worry about."

Sarah frowned. Ted pushed himself up and walked past her. He stood by the back windows. "What's up?"

She stepped towards him, then stopped. He may be looking odd, frail even. But he was still Ted.

"You were with me," she breathed. "At the farm. In the kitchen."

He gave her a condescending look. "No I wasn't."

"You were. At the end. When Robert died. You saw it."

Ted put a hand to his shoulder. All his anger and bravado had made her forget he was injured. Was that it?

"Is your shoulder alright, Dad? It's not infected?"

Something passed across his face and he removed his hand. "No, love. No, I'm fine. Now what are you asking me again?"

"You saw what happened when Robert died. You saw what he was doing."

His features sharpened and he was the same rodent-like man again, raising his chest up and glaring at her.

"Don't talk bollocks, girl. I was bleeding on the floor, wasn't I?"

"The police don't know that."

Dawn gasped. Ted raised a corner of his mouth. "You want me to lie to the police."

"I want you to tell them Martin was defending us all. Including himself. You saw Robert with that knife. He was threatening me. He threatened Martin too."

Ted cocked his head. "He did?"

She nodded, her lips tight. She ignored Dawn's look of shock.

"He did," she whispered.

Ted stared at her for a moment. She held the stare, challenging him. Daring him. Ted had probably lied to the police before, but would he do it for her? For Martin?

"That's not the only thing you need to tell them," said Dawn.

Both Ted and Sarah span towards her.

"What?" said Ted.

"Mum, please," said Sarah.

"You know what I'm talking about, love," said Dawn. "It was going to catch up with us eventually."

Sarah looked at her father. He was staring at his wife with an expression she'd never seen before. It was fear.

He looked down at his hand and tugged at his wedding ring. For a moment Sarah thought he might pull it off.

"No," he said. "They deserved it."

There was a knock at the door. Ted turned to it. "Bastards," he muttered. He threw his shoulders back and went to it.

"What is it?"

DC Paretska was standing outside, raindrops beading her shoulders. She looked past Ted to Sarah.

"He's back," she said.

75

"Can we come in?"

"Of course," said Dawn. She headed into the kitchen and lit the stove. She was still reeling from what had happened between her and Ted.

She could escape him now. Armed with her knowledge. But if it didn't work, if they didn't believe her, what would he do?

Could she do this?

She crossed herself, muttering a short prayer. She needed guidance. What she was considering was wrong. *Till death us do part.* But what her husband had done was worse.

The two police detectives clattered into the house. The man was tall and gangly, with a permanent stoop. He wore a long black coat that made him look ill. The woman, younger, more nervous, wore a blue leather jacket that reminded Dawn of the times before the floods. The way Sarah had followed fashion.

"Would you like a cup of tea?" she asked.

The woman shook her head. The man hesitated for a moment them smiled. "That would be lovely."

They weren't alone. Behind them, looking dirty and awkward, was Bill. She'd told him to leave, and now here he was back again. She felt her chest rise and fall with the effort of not telling him how she felt about him.

She poured hot water into the kettle and rummaged in a cupboard for mugs. They only had three.

She met Sarah's eye. Sarah gave her a reassuring look. "Not for me, Mum."

Dawn smiled at her. All this horror, and she was still embarrassed not to be a proper hostess. What kind of woman was she?

They came into the kitchen, bulky coats and cold breath filling the space. They pulled out seats at the table and Ted joined them. Dawn looked at him, her mind ticking over. When he met her stare she looked away, her breath shallow. Sarah and Bill hovered behind them. Sarah was watching her father, looking puzzled.

The man looked at Ted. "My name's Detective Sergeant Bryce, this is Detective Constable Paretska. We just want to ask you all a few questions."

Ted grunted. Dawn busied herself with the teapot, relieved when the man refused milk; the goats here weren't made of the stuff.

"Sit down with us," the woman, DC Paretska, said. Dawn frowned then lowered herself into a seat opposite the man.

The man cleared his throat. "Bill, we need to ask you a few questions."

Bill shuffled forward. "About Robert Cope's death."

The detective turned in his chair. He motioned with his head for Bill to come closer. Bill shifted around the room until he was facing Dawn. He looked at the back of Ted's head. Ted stared ahead, glaring at Dawn.

"And two other murders," said the detective.

Sarah leaned forward. DC Paretska – nice looking girl, thought Dawn, couldn't be older than twenty-three – arched an eyebrow.

"Bill gave the order for them to be killed. Because Robert Cope told him to," said Sarah.

Bill eyed her. "Robert told lots of people to do lots of things. Do you want to know what he told Martin to do with you?"

Sarah flushed. Dawn lifted herself up in her seat, wishing she could comfort her daughter.

"Did he?" asked Bill.

Sarah glared at him. "Did he what?"

"Did he rape you?"

Ted roared and pushed his chair back. He grabbed Bill by the neck. DS Bryce was on his feet instantly, pulling Ted off. Dawn watched open-mouthed. When Ted had been bundled back into his seat, she looked at Sarah. Sarah was avoiding her eye.

"No," said Sarah. "He didn't."

Bill looked at her as if he knew something he wasn't telling. Dawn could feel her chest caving in. She felt a tear run down her face.

"Robert told Martin to hurt you, but he didn't. He helped you get away instead." Bill looked at Sarah. "If I was as strong as him, those boys would still be alive."

DS Paretska opened her pad. "Mr Peterson, can you tell us when it was you last saw Jacob Cripps and Zahir Ali?"

Bill twisted his mouth, thinking. "It was February. After the floods."

"Any idea of the date?"

"Yeh. The nineteenth. After Valentine's Day - that was when they got carried away."

"Carried away?"

"They went for some women. In a shelter. Tried to chat them up. It got nasty."

"In what way nasty?"

"One of the women had a can of mace. Don't worry, those lasses didn't get hurt."

"And then what?" DC Paretska was chewing her pen. Dawn glanced at Ted, who was shifting in his seat. Muttering.

"We roughed them up a bit. A lot. Kicked them out. They were in quite a bad way. But we didn't kill them."

DS Bryce rubbed his forehead. "None of this is making any sense."

Bill stared at him. "Tell me about it."

The detective looked at him. "Cripps and Ali were found almost three weeks after you say you kicked them out of your group. They'd only been dead a few days. They didn't die from what you did to them. They had other injuries. Severe ones. They'd bled out."

Bill gave a slow nod. Dawn let out a whimper. Sarah was staring at her, her eyes widening. Dawn shook her head at her daughter. If the girl touched her now, she would cave in.

"It was Ted," Dawn whispered.

"Mum..." Sarah muttered. Ted was glaring at Dawn, his face red.

She shifted away from her husband.

"They attacked Sarah. Broke into her tent. Outside Lincoln." She felt herself shaking. "Ted caught them. He – he hurt them."

DS Bryce turned to Ted. "Is this true, Mr Evans?"

"The little shits deserved everything they got," Ted muttered. Sarah gasped. Dawn held her breath.

"Go on," the detective said, his voice low.

Ted lifted his face to stare at the man. "They tried to rape

my girl. I wasn't going to let them do that. I defended her."
He turned to Sarah and sneered. "Like she says Martin did
for her."

"Mr Evans. Did they attack you? Did they provoke you?"

"Yes, they provoked me!" Ted stood up and his chair fell
to the floor. Dawn stared at it, chewing a fingernail.

"They attacked my bloody daughter. If that isn't provok-
ing, I don't know what is. I sliced their bloody dicks off."

DS Bryce nodded at his colleague. She stood up and
moved beside Ted. She put a hand on his shoulder.

"Ted Evans, I'm arresting you for murder."

Ted's eyes widened. "What?"

"What about Robert?" Sarah cried. "Bill, tell them the
truth about that. Please."

Dawn swallowed and looked across the table at Bill. "I
was holding Martin," he said. "I had him restrained, with
some electrical wire. I let him go when Robert attacked Ted
here. Then Robert went for Martin. He was going to stab
him, he had a flick knife. Martin grabbed a kitchen knife
and defended himself."

Sarah stood up. "I was there too. He's right."

She turned to Dawn. Dawn blinked back tears, staring at
Ted. She felt light, airy, like she might float away.

76

Sarah stood with her arms wrapped tightly around herself. Her father was just feet in front of her in the back of the police car, his eyes on the seat in front of him. In the front, the two detectives were muttering to each other.

They handled this wrong, Sarah thought. *They should never have let us all be in a room together.* Now they had no way of untangling what was a lie and what truth.

Her mother was behind her. Her face was grey, her jaw set. Sarah put a hand on her arm but Dawn shook it off.

She slapped the roof of the car to get DC Bryce's attention.

"How long before Martin's released?'

"It's not as simple as that," he said. "We'll need to speak to all the other witnesses. Jess and Ruth Dyer. And we're looking for the other men. The ones Bill was with in that farm."

"They're gone."

"We'll find them."

"If you don't, what happens?"

"That depends on the witnesses from the village."

She stiffened. She hardly knew the Dyers; what would they say? They'd do what they needed to to protect Ruth.

"But we'll be dropping charges against Martin on the murder of the two boys," said DS Paretska. She was looking at Dawn.

Dawn moved in behind her, her breath on her neck. "Don't worry," she whispered.

Sarah snapped round. "What?"

"I spoke to Jess. It's going to be alright."

"Are you alright, Mum?"

"No. But I will be."

"You were very brave."

Her mother's eyes hardened. "*Thou shalt not kill.*"

Sarah heard a door closing behind her and turned to see the Dyers coming out of their house. Ben, Ruth and Jess. Ruth looked pale, Ben angry. Jess stared at the police car, her jaw set.

The detectives were watching. Sarah looked back at them. DS Bryce turned and spoke to her father, while DC Paretska was beside him.

The cars drove off, rear lights receding to nothing at the top of the Parade. She realised that a crowd had gathered to see what was going on. The Dyers – Jess, Ruth, and Ben too – watched in silence. Sarah gave them a nod. Jess returned it.

77

"Here. I found you a saucepan."

Sarah opened the box she'd brought and lifted its contents into a cupboard. A saucepan, two plates and two bowls. Two sets of cutlery.

Martin watched her as she moved, his cheeks glowing. She knew what he was thinking.

She placed the empty box on the floor and kicked it towards the door. "What else?"

"Jess said she had some bits and bobs she could spare."

"Sonia's," Sarah said.

"Who's Sonia?"

"Jess's mum. She died not long after they got here. I never saw her much."

"Oh. Sorry."

She grabbed his hand. It was warm. "It's alright. You weren't to know."

"Hello? Anyone home?"

They turned to see Dawn at the top of the stairs leading up to the flat. She carried a teapot.

"Mum! You can't spare that."

"We've got two. Every new home needs a teapot."

Sam came out of the bedroom. "I've got your lamp working, mate. Right snug it is." He winked at Sarah. Then he spotted Dawn and blushed.

"Oh. Mrs Evans. I'm sorry."

Dawn laughed. "I was young once too, you know."

Sam's face went from pink to deep red.

"Welcome to our village, Martin," Dawn said. Sarah looked at him; she knew how nervous he was about getting to know her mother.

"Thank you, Mrs Evans."

"Please stop calling me that. You too, Sam Golder. Makes me feel old."

"Right. Yes," said Martin, looking even more clumsy and awkward than he had a moment before. Sarah knew it would take time for either Sam or Martin to call her mother by her first name.

Sarah grabbed the teapot. "Let's get the kettle on."

A few minutes later they were sitting on what seats they could find. Dawn occupied the sole armchair and Sarah was on its arm. Martin perched on a box while Sam leaned against the wall.

"Lovely brew," said Sam.

"I'm sorry about everything you went through," said Dawn, looking at Martin. "About what my husband did."

Martin looked at Sarah's mother, his cheeks flushing.

"Thank you," he said. "I appreciate what you did."

"It wasn't just for you. Sarah here, too."

"Why?" asked Martin.

"Because Sarah deserves better than I had. She loves you."

Sam was fidgeting by the door.

"Sorry, Samuel," said Dawn.

"'S alright, Mrs Evans."

Dawn raised her eyebrows at him. He said nothing.

Sarah exchanged glances with Martin. She thought of the way he'd kissed her when she'd gone to fetch him from the police station. They'd dropped charges on Robert's murder after Jess had corroborated Sarah's story. And Ted was awaiting his court appearance for the murder of Cripps and Ali. "How did you know, Mum?"

"A mother knows." Dawn tapped her nose. "And I had a tip-off from Sam here. You owe him."

Sam blushed. "No, it's not like that."

Sarah stood up, being careful not to walk into her mother's mug on the floor. She went to Sam. "Is it true, Sam?"

He shrugged and looked at her through lowered lashes. "I saw you together. You *worked*. And I could see the effect you have on him."

Sarah looked back at Martin, who was staring at Sam. "What effect?"

"You make him better." Sam sniffed. "If he hadn't met you, he'd still be one of Robert Cope's lackeys."

Martin paled. "He could be right. I owe you, Sam. And you, Sarah. All of you. This entire village. I'm so grateful for this flat."

Sarah looked at her mother. They had been offered another month in that big house, but Dawn had rejected it. They'd moved to a smaller cottage, away from the sea. Dawn had filled the surfaces with ornaments, flowers from the dunes, anything she could find. Sarah wondered how long she would stay there; her mother needed her, for now. But not forever.

Martin coughed. "Let's take a walk."

Sarah smiled up at him then looked at her mother. "We won't be long."

Dawn waved at her. "You go. We'll carry on making this place nice. Won't we, Samuel?"

"Well," said Sam. "My mum's expecting me home in—"

"I'm sure she won't mind waiting."

Sarah pulled Martin down the stairs and onto the street outside. He grabbed her hand and they walked towards the sea, their arms swinging between them. They passed people on the way; some said hello, while others looked wary. It would take time.

They stopped at the clifftop. She stared out to sea, thinking of their journey back here, from the farm, in separate boats. Then their journey back there, together. She hoped she'd never see that boat again.

She leaned her head on Martin's arm. He felt soft, and warm.

He wrapped his arm around her. "I love you."

"I know," she replied, her heart lifting. "I love you too."

FIND out what happens to the villagers next in the third book in the series, *One of Us*.

And you can join the Rachel McLean book club to read about the floods and how the Dyer family got to North Yorkshire at rachelmclean.com/underwater.

ONE OF US

PART 3 OF THE VILLAGE TRILOGY

1

"**Y**ou've *what*?"

Leah Golder stared at her son across the table. Beside him, Jess squirmed in her seat. She was a grown woman. She'd dealt with much worse than this; so why was she feeling scared?

"You heard, Mum," Zack replied. "I thought you'd be pleased."

Leah's gaze shifted from Zack to Jess. Jess gave her a nervous smile. In an instant, the woman had gone from beaming and friendly to shocked and hostile.

Jess looked down at the table between them. On it was a cake and a plate of biscuits. Leah had probably used a week's rations for this meal.

Next to her mother, Zack's youngest sister – was it Shirley or Rose? Jess struggled to remember – shovelled cake into her mouth, knowing she wouldn't get this opportunity again in a hurry. The girl was eleven years old, over ten years younger than her brother and his twin, Sam. Twenty years younger than Jess. Sam was currently stuffing the remains of a fish pie into his mouth. Crumbs slipped from his lips and rained onto the tablecloth. Jess wondered how often it got used.

"Well, I knew you were... close," said Leah, her stare moving back to Zack. "But I never thought it would come to..."

She put down her knife and picked up a napkin. She wiped her lips, her eyes closed.

Zack looked at his dad, Tim. Jess followed his gaze, hoping for some help.

Tim cleared his throat. "Don't get me wrong, Jess. This is nothing personal. And it's not because you're the steward, or anything like that. It's just – well – you're... it's the age difference."

"Don't be daft, Dad," said Zack. "Who cares about nine years? I love her."

He grabbed her hand under the table. She thought of the ring he'd slipped on her finger the previous night. Plastic, scavenged from a landfill site near his work, but it was the thought that counted. She recalled the rings she'd given to her sister-in-law Ruth six months ago, after Ruth had been kidnapped and Jess and Zack had gone to save her. Her mother Sonia's rings, kept safe in a tin for the previous five years. *I don't need them*, she'd said. She'd meant it at the time.

She took a deep breath and smiled at her prospective mother-in-law. "I'm sorry to have surprised you, Leah." She couldn't bring herself to call her Mrs Golder. Leah and Tim had been Leah and Tim before she'd got to know Zack. Maybe that was the problem.

"You taught him," Leah replied. "You were his teacher." She picked up the teapot and stared into it as if it would explain everything.

"For one year. Six years ago. And it's not as if our relationship started then."

"Hmm," said Tim. "Maybe she's got a... what was that?"

Jess felt a tremor ripple through her. She tightened her grip on Zack's hand and stood up.

The room went quiet. Rose-or-Shirley dropped her fork and squealed.

Leah put down the teapot. It was brown, chipped on the spout, its shine lost except for one patch on the side that reflected the light from the candles on the windowsill. It was almost completely dark now, the darkness exaggerated by the fact that lights-out was just fifteen minutes ago.

Maybe Jess had imagined it.

"Did you feel that?" she said.

"Yes," said Zack. He dropped her hand and went to the window. "Shit."

Jess ignored Leah's frown. "What?" She slid in behind him at the window, peering over his shoulder.

There it was again. Lower, this time, and less abrupt. A rumbling sound, and a low tremor running through them.

She turned to Zack's family. "I've got to go. Sorry."

She dashed towards the front door and yanked it open. The village was in darkness. Opposite, a door opened, the faint glow of a candle silhouetting a man, raising himself up to get a better view.

She didn't pause to check if Zack was behind her, but instead ran towards the centre of the village. As she approached the community centre, there was another bang, two beats and then a splintering sound. It was coming from the north.

She almost skidded to turn along the road that led to the northern edge of the village, wondering if any of the other council members had heard it. If they would be out too.

Doors were opening as she hurried past. People muttered as they stumbled out into darkness. Ahead of her, slowly gaining in intensity, a glow rose above the rooftops.

She felt her stomach lurch. *Oh no, please no.* Hadn't they been through enough? Her own sister-in-law had been kidnapped and then arrested, for God's sake. Ted Evans, her former neighbour, had been convicted of a double murder. They deserved some respite.

"Go back inside," she called as she passed the people emerging from their houses. "Stay indoors." They nodded at her, some muttering questions. But no one retreated. Instead, they followed.

She thundered to a halt as she reached the scrubby bushes that flanked this edge of the village. The road ended abruptly, giving way to potholed gravel and weeds as if someone had been interrupted while building it. Not unlikely, given that this place was still under construction when the flood hit six-and-a-half years ago.

Ahead of her, on the horizon, the glow was ballooning, mushrooming into the sky. She took a deep breath then coughed noisily.

Colin Barker was here already, the secretary to the village council.

"Jess." He stepped out from a crowd of villagers peppering him with questions. "There's been an explosion."

She pushed her ginger hair out of her eyes. The night was cold and still, the moon bright over the sea to her right.

"Where?" she asked.

"Not sure. Somewhere in Filey."

She swallowed. "Shit."

"At least it wasn't here."

She turned to look at him. "People could be hurt, Colin."

"Outsiders, Jess."

"Still." She felt a tremor run down her spine.

"Do you think they'd care if something like that happened to us?"

She said nothing. More villagers arrived, jostling her in their haste to get a good view.

"Exactly," Colin said. "They don't give a monkeys about us, so why should we about them?"

"Two wrongs don't make a right, Colin."

"Is that what you said when those men tried to kill Ruth?"

She glared at him. "Don't."

"I know what happened, Jess. I know why they came for her."

She tightened her jaw. Of course he knew. Despite her promise to her brother Ben to keep it secret.

"This isn't the time, Colin."

He grunted. She resisted the temptation to remind him that he wasn't exactly the innocent in all this. Not after he'd locked that boy from Filey up in the boat house – oh yes, she knew things too. Instead, she turned away from him and pushed through the crowd of villagers. Where were Ben and Ruth? Ben, surely, would be somewhere nearby, wanting to get involved.

"Ben." He was with Clyde and Sanjeev, muttering at the edge of the crowd. "Where's Ruth?"

"With the boys. What are you planning to do about this?"

"About what?"

He gestured towards the steadily brightening glow along the coast. "That."

"I can't exactly put it out, can I?"

"It'll be trouble."

"I don't see how. It's miles away."

He shook his head. She glanced at Sanjeev, Ben's best friend. He threw her a tight smile.

"It'll make its way here, sis," said Ben. "You can count on that."

She shook her head. Where was Zack? Had he continued with his little speech, his attempt to justify to his parents why he wanted to marry a woman who was not only the village steward, but nine years older than him?

"Let's get everyone inside," she said. "It might not be safe."

Ben shrugged, his eyes dark, and turned towards the crowd. With Sanjeev and Clyde's help, they started corralling everyone back to their homes.

2

Sarah sat down next to Martin, feeling the sofa dip beneath her weight.

"How was your mum?" he asked.

She smiled and blew on her mint tea. "Good." She sipped. "Very good."

"New job on the council suiting her?"

"I never knew she had it in her."

"Good for her."

She eyed him. "This is the woman who called you a bad influence. Who wanted you out of the village."

He shrugged. "She had her reasons. She changed her mind, remember."

"She changed her mind about a lot of things."

He said nothing. She drank the rest of her tea, thinking about her father. His trial had been and gone, with no one from the village attending. Now he was in a jail somewhere near Leeds. He hadn't received any visitors.

The sofa shook and she brought her hand up to steady her mug. "Hey, careful."

"I was about to say the same to you."

"That wasn't you?"

"No." He stood and crossed to the window. "Didn't you hear it?"

She placed her mug on the table and slipped in between him and the window, feeling him wind his arm around her waist. Outside was the usual darkness at this time of night. By day this self-sufficient refugee community was alive with activity: people tending the land, making food, keeping the place spick and span. But at night, they retreated. Electricity was permitted for the first hour of darkness, during which time many people sought comfort in the warmth of the JP, the community pub.

But now it was dark, and still.

"Oh my God." She felt her legs tremble. From outside there was a crashing sound, followed by something like the roar of a river.

Except there were no rivers near here.

She grabbed Martin's hand. "Come on."

She pulled him towards the door of the flat and they stumbled downstairs in the darkness. Candles weren't safe in the stairway and oil lighting was too dirty, so all they had to guide them was the dim light from beyond the windows. Tonight the sky was tinged with an unfamiliar shade of orange, reminding her of street lamps in the years before the floods.

She pushed open the outer door to the sound of voices passing.

"That way, look!"

"What was it?"

She peered out, failing to recognise faces. Two men ran past, shouting to each other. She shrank back, scared. They disappeared into the shadows, in the direction of the light. The sky above the rooftops glowed. It trembled and swayed, seeming to be alive with light. She stared at it, open-mouthed.

More people passed; a woman with a teenage boy and another woman with a man not far behind.

Sarah stepped forward, full of questions.

"Stay here." Martin's breath was hot on her neck. "Please."

She turned. "They won't bite."

"I know. But... well, we don't know what's happened. I don't want to be blamed."

"Why would they blame you?" She tried to push the irritation out of her voice. "That's ridiculous."

"I'm not popular. You know it. Please, Sarah. Just stay here. Just for now. Till we know what's going on."

"Skulking in the shadows will just make you look suspicious."

"Please."

His face was close to hers now, his eyes bright against his skin. He was staring into her face, his eyes flitting between hers.

She sighed. "Alright. Of course."

She should be more sympathetic, she knew. But six months ago she would have done what he'd said; or rather what her father had said. She would have stayed indoors, hiding away, never told what was going on outside.

Things had changed.

Martin shouldn't be so timid. He hadn't been like this before, when he had saved her from Robert Cope. When he had helped her understand the truth about her father.

She grasped his hand. It couldn't be easy, being the village's newest and most unwelcome resident. "Sorry. We can stay here. Of course."

She was interrupted by a deep-throated rumbling

coming from somewhere behind them. She turned, realising that she was holding her breath.

"What's happened?" she whispered. She turned to Martin, a finger on his lips. "Two seconds. I'll be back. I promise."

She stepped forwards. A man and a woman were passing, almost running but not quite daring to in the darkness. She recognised them from the school; they had a boy. Craig. Blond, cheeky. Clever.

"Hello," she said, her voice unsure.

The woman stopped. "Sarah. Did you hear?"

She nodded. "What is it?"

"An explosion, over towards Filey. That's what Pam said."

"Pam?"

Pam was the stern woman who presided over the village store. Sarah hated having to go to her to collect her rations every day, knowing that the woman was judging her, gossiping about her to the next person she encountered.

"She was walking home from the JP when it happened," Craig's mum said. "Half the council is out."

The woman peered round Sarah, no doubt looking for Martin. Sarah didn't enlighten her. She felt her breathing return to normal.

Was it bad, that she was relieved it hadn't been something closer? Something Martin might be blamed for? No one in Filey would care about him. At least, not anymore.

"Thanks." She turned back to the flat.

"You're not coming to see?"

"No." Why did people have to be so mawkish? "Thanks."

"Right. Goodnight."

The woman's words were followed by another rumble from the north. Sarah felt her heart hammering at her rib cage. She needed to get back to Martin. She needed to check on her mother.

"Have you seen Dawn?" Her voice was little more than a croak.

But the woman was gone, loping towards the glow over the rooftops, her hand gripping her companion's sleeve.

Should Sarah go looking for her mother? She was a grown woman after all, one who had suffered through much worse than a distant explosion.

"Sarah!" Martin hissed from the shadows. He'd ventured away from the wall of the building that contained his flat, and was in the shadow of an oak tree. Sarah looked at it, wondering what this land had been used for when it had been planted.

"Sorry." She slipped back to him. The April night was cold and crisp; it wasn't raining, for once.

"What happened?" he asked.

"An explosion, near Filey," she said. "Apparently."

"Blimey."

She drew closer to him, aware of his breathing in the quiet.

"What kind of explosion?" he asked.

She shrugged. "Dunno."

"Maybe I should help."

She put a hand on his arm. "A minute ago you wanted to hide away. Besides, what can you do? It's miles away."

"I don't know. But surely something."

"Please, Martin. Let's go back inside. I don't like it with everyone running around like this."

She patted his arm and he turned back towards the flat.

"Ow!"

"Shit, mate. Sorry."

Martin stumbled, hit by a man who'd appeared out of

the darkness, running the same way the first couple had been.

"It's OK." Martin stood up.

"Oh. It's you."

Sarah stepped between Martin and the man. He was young, about six feet tall. He smelt of wood smoke.

"This anything to do with you?" the man asked.

"No," said Sarah. "It's in Filey. Go to the northern edge of the village and you'll be able to see it."

The man stepped towards Sarah as if about to reach for her. She shrank back.

"You're alright, you are," he said. She felt her skin contract.

"Leave her alone," said Martin.

"It's fine," she said. "I can look after myself."

"Yeah," said the man. "She doesn't need you. None of us do."

Sarah narrowed her eyes. "What's your name?"

"What, going to tell on me to your mum?"

She felt her face flush. "No. You haven't got kids,, though."

"No, I haven't. Sorry, teacher."

"You're one of the lads who goes down to the earthworks, aren't you? With the Golder brothers."

"What's it to you?"

"Next time you want to lay into Martin, have a chat with Sam Golder first. Not everything is what you think."

The man snorted, gave Martin a gentle push on the chest, and ran off.

Sarah watched him melt into the night, her breathing shallow.

"You didn't have to do that," Martin said.

She gulped down the lump in her throat. "I don't know where it came from."

Martin put his arm round her and she leaned into him. "Don't put yourself at risk for me. Please."

She said nothing. Martin was the best thing that had ever happened to her, despite everything he'd done. He was worth the risk.

3

Ruth wiped her hand on the tea towel she'd stuffed into the waistband of her jeans, wondering when Sean and Ollie would become less messy at breakfast. She only had twenty minutes before she needed to be at the pharmacy; Sheila Barker had asked to see her at ten. She hoped it wasn't anything serious and wondered if Sheila had told her husband. At least Ruth could be discreet.

She wondered if it was Sheila at the door. Ruth wouldn't blame her; no one enjoyed passing through the village shop into the pharmacy, making it known that they were seeking medical help.

Ruth took a deep breath, pinned on her best smile, and pulled the door open. Outside it was grey, clouds scudding over the houses and a light drizzle beginning to form. In front of her stood a broad, dark-skinned woman she didn't recognise and a thin, pale man who looked as if he'd rather be anywhere but standing on her doorstep on a wet April morning.

Behind them was a police car. Two people sat inside it. Ruth felt her heart lurch.

She looked back into the house – *Ben, where are you?* – and put a hand on her chest. Her body felt light, as if she might float away.

She stared at the woman, waiting for her to speak. A new detective?

The woman smiled at her. *That won't help*, thought Ruth. She turned back to the house again, and croaked out Ben's name. Where was he?

"Ruth! Ruth, what's going on?" Ben rounded the corner of the house; he'd been out. Why hadn't he told her? She felt herself dip with relief.

"I don't know."

The woman turned. She had long dark hair tied back in a bun, the hair pulled so tight it made her look as if she'd had a face lift. The man next to her continued to stare at Ruth. She looked down at her hands; she hadn't realised she was wringing the tea towel.

"What's going on? What are you doing here? My wife was exonerated. You've got no business—"

The woman raised a hand. "We aren't here for your wife. We're looking for Jess Dyer. She isn't at her house. Am I right in thinking you're her brother?"

"What d'you want Jess for?"

"Village business. She is still the steward, yes?"

Ruth watched Ben's face drop a little as he stepped towards the woman. He still couldn't hide his disappointment at Jess taking over his old job.

"She lives two doors along now. In the house where the Evans family used to live. I imagine you know who they are."

Ted Evans was known to the authorities, and he would

certainly be known to the two shadows inside that police car. After Ruth had been released without charge, the police persuaded that she'd killed Robert Cope in self-defence, it had been Ted's turn to be taken away. Only in his case, it had been more permanent.

But why were they here now? Had they changed their minds? Was she about to be taken away from her boys again?

She put a hand on the doorframe.

"Ruth, get inside," Ben muttered. "You look pale."

She let out a shaky breath and took one last look at the police car. She recognised the woman in the driver's seat. PC Cregg. A plump young thing, she'd been nervous to find herself in the same room as a suspected murderer. They didn't get much of that round here.

She let herself almost fall back into the house and landed on a kitchen chair, feeling it shift beneath her as it took her weight. She could still hear Ben talking to them.

"She won't be in," he said. "At this time of day she's making her rounds."

"Rounds?"

"She likes to go round the village, visiting anyone who needs help with anything. Checking up on people."

"How long will she be?"

A pause. "No idea."

"In that case, can we come in, please? You may be able to help us."

Ruth stood up. She stared at Ben's back in the doorway. Her heart was racing and her skin felt damp. What did they want?

It had been six months since her arrest. Six months since Robert Cope and his men snatched her from her own home and imprisoned her in that godforsaken farmhouse with Sarah Evans, Roisin Murray and Sally Angus. Since Martin had helped Sarah escape, and come back to the village with Jess's blessing. Since Ruth had stood over Robert, watching blood splutter from his lips as she ground her heel into his chest, the pressure killing him as surely as the knife wound Martin had already inflicted.

He had imprisoned her in his bedroom. He'd touched her, in ways that made her want to climb out of her own skin. He'd intended to rape her.

He deserved everything he got.

She slipped across the kitchen behind Ben. On the staircase, she looped an arm around the bannister, trying not to remember the stairs she had thrown herself up when she had been fleeing Robert. She made her way to the top and stared at her bedroom door, and at the door to her boys' room. They were safely out at school, getting what passed for an education under the tutelage of Sheila Barker and her new apprentice Sarah Evans. She muttered thanks that they weren't at home to witness this.

She heard the rustling of coats and the creak of feet on the wooden floor as the two strangers followed Ben into the house. They stopped in the hallway. Ben didn't invite them in any further.

"Why are you here?" Ben glanced towards the kitchen, frowned, then looked up the stairs. Ruth pulled back, anxious not to be seen.

"We need some help," the woman said.

"What kind of help?"

"Did you see the explosion last night?"

Ruth clenched her fists. What did that have to do with them? Surely they weren't blaming the villagers?

"Yes." Ben's voice was clipped.

"It happened in a residential area."

"Oh." A pause. "I'm sorry to hear that."

"Mr Dyer, please can we come in further? The rain is getting in, your floor—"

"We'll be fine here. You already said it's Jess you want to see, not me."

"You're a member of the governing group in this community, though?"

"The village council. Yes."

"Good. We need your help."

"You already said that."

"Yes."

"What kind of help?"

"The explosion made twenty-six families homeless. With the damage to our infrastructure after the floods of 2017, well, we still haven't recovered."

"Who's we?"

"Filey. The town."

"Oh."

"Look, Mr Dyer. The fact is that you have these large properties here, in your village. They were allocated to you when you arrived here after the floods."

"Yes."

"My colleague here was one of the people you dealt with."

"Not me," said Ben. "I didn't come in the first wave."

"Anyway, it was the borough of Scarborough that generously let you people have these houses. We paid the holiday company handsomely for them."

The village had once been a holiday village, a place for wealthy southerners to spend their summers. Such things seemed ridiculous now, with over a million people being made homeless in 2017. Most of them Londoners, like Ruth and Ben.

Ruth shuffled forward to get a better view.

"Are you going to get to the point?" Ben looked as if he was about to push the woman out of the door.

"We need your houses, Mr Dyer. We need to house the people of Filey."

"You what?"

"You heard me."

Ruth put her hand to her lips. She couldn't see Ben's face, but she could hear his reaction in his voice.

Ben said nothing. Ruth heard movement and spotted the woman moving closer to him. She tensed.

Ruth thought back to four years earlier, when the people of Filey had attacked the village. They'd had to post guards; they'd feared for their lives. The boys were tiny babies and Ruth had barricaded herself into the nursery with them. It had been terrifying.

And now they wanted to house them here.

4

J ess's rounds took longer that morning. Everywhere she went, she was asked about the explosion. What had caused it, where it had been, who had done it. As if she knew. It hadn't taken place in their village, and didn't seem to have involved anyone from here. That was all she was going to let herself worry about.

But as steward she was expected to have answers. She wondered if people had looked at Ben so distrustfully. He'd served three years on the council before he'd actively pursued the steward job, glad-handing people who didn't even have a say in the election, then manoeuvring for the succession after Colin Barker's term had expired. And he'd loved the job. It had given him a purpose she'd never seen before: not when they were growing up, not when they'd been forced from their homes by the floods, and not on the journey here.

He seemed to have forgiven her now, but she couldn't be sure. She would have to content herself with doing her best and hoping it was enough. Would anyone ever forget she was the steward who had insisted on mounting a rescue mission at sea, who had brought those men to their village, who had offered to give them shelter? She'd been repaid by having her sister-in-law and three other women taken from them. They'd got them back, but at what price?

She would take half an hour's break, have a quick cup of tea and rest her feet. She'd gaze out of the window of her new house towards the sea, and try not to think about the things that had happened when its previous occupiers had been there. She knew some of it; she'd found Dawn slumped over the sofa she now forced herself to sit on every evening, and had helped Dawn's daughter Sarah carry her upstairs. Ted had been a controlling man, and a brutal one. But now he was gone, and Dawn had chosen to take a smaller house in the centre of the village.

The house felt more like home when Zack was with her. Jess felt a flood of warmth trickle through her at the thought of him. She was steward; she'd have to ask another member of the council to marry them. Colin would make the perfect candidate; after all, he'd done it for Ruth and Ben during his term as steward.

She left the Meadows behind and shook the mud off her boots, heading for the houses where she and most of the other council members lived. She stared at the ground as she walked, measuring her steps.

Something was different. A sound, overlaying the familiar repeating tones of a song thrush in the hedge and the waves behind the houses.

She stopped walking. It was a car engine, idling.

She picked up her pace and rounded the corner to her row of houses. A police car stood outside Ben and Ruth's house, with two shadowy figures inside.

She looked to her left, towards the entrance to the village. There were no other cars. Just this one police car.

Where were the others? When they'd come before, there had been at least two each time, sometimes four.

She dropped the bag of potatoes she'd been carrying, a gift from Flo Murray, and started to run. She ran into Ben and Ruth's door at full pelt, hammering on it.

The door flew open and she almost fell through.

"What's going on? Where's Ruth?" She was panting.

"It's alright, sis," said Ben. "It's the council."

"The council?"

"The local council. Not the police."

She flung an arm in the direction of the police car. "So what's that then?"

Ben screwed up his face. "Protection."

"Protection? For who?"

"For them. The council officers." He looked over her shoulder. "Come in. They want to talk to you."

She shook herself out and stepped inside, shucking her muddy boots off. Two strangers were in the living room, a large woman perched on the edge of the sofa and a balding man on the armchair.

She licked her lips and strode in, trying to project confidence.

"I'm Jess Dyer." She held out a hand. "What brings you here?"

The woman stood up. She smiled at Jess and shook her hand. As she did so she cast a wry look in Ben's direction.

"Glad to meet you, Ms Dyer."

"Who are you?"

"My name is Anita Chopra. I'm from Scarborough borough council."

Jess stiffened. Had they heard about Ruth's arrest, and Ted's? Did they know about Martin? She wondered if she had the authority to let him live here. Sarah would be devastated if he was evicted.

"Shall we take a seat, Ms Dyer?"

Jess glanced at Ben, feeling like a girl pulling faces at her brother behind their parents' back again. "No thanks, I'll stand."

"Oh. Of course."

The man, who had been perching on the armchair and staring out to sea, stood up and joined his colleague. Jess looked him up and down; he looked like he needed a good meal.

"Go on, then," Jess said.

"I've been explaining to your brother that we have a bit of a situation in Filey."

"A situation?"

"The explosion last night. It happened in a residential area."

"I'm sorry to hear that."

It was true. However little time Jess had for this woman and her pale sidekick, however little she trusted the authorities who had never lifted a finger to protect them from their tormentors. If people were hurt, it wasn't their fault.

"Is anyone hurt?" she asked.

"Five people have been taken to hospital in York. Plenty more have minor injuries. But it's the housing situation that I have to deal with."

"The housing situation."

"Twenty-six families have been made homeless. We need to bring them here."

"Here?"

"You have plenty of space."

"All our houses are occupied."

"Not fully occupied."

"That's hardly the fault of—"

"I'm told you've moved to the house two doors up, is that true?"

"Yes."

"A three-bedroomed house."

"Yes. We find that if council members live near the centre of the—"

"And you live alone?"

"With my – she hesitated at the word *fiancé* – my boyfriend."

"I'm sure you'd agree, Ms Dyer, that it seems unfair for a woman on her own to be living in such a large house when there are people sleeping on the floor of Filey church hall."

Jess narrowed her eyes. She'd slept on the floors of church halls herself, after the floods had wrecked her London flat. In London there had been sports halls and indoor stadiums, thronged with people. On the long walk north, they'd taken everything they could get. Including church halls.

"I'm sorry, Ms Chopra."

"Miss Chopra."

"Miss Chopra. It's not my decision."

"You're the steward."

Ben stepped towards them. "We run things democratically round here."

Miss Chopra pursed her lips at him. "I'm sure you do. But this is an urgent situation. Surely you can find space for these poor people now, and then decide whether you can offer them sanctuary for a longer period?"

Jess saw Ben stiffen. *Sanctuary.* That had only led to trouble, last time.

"No," said Ben.

Jess clenched her fists. "Ben, please. It's not up to us."

"You know what they'll say. They know what happens when we let outsiders in."

"We've let Martin back in."

"Have you seen the way people look at him?"

She turned to the council officer. "I want to help you, really I do." Was that the truth? "But like my brother says, we run things democratically. We'll have to consult with the other villagers, and let you know."

"There's no time for that."

"I'm sorry?"

The woman returned to the sofa and grabbed a bulging briefcase that was leaning against it. She drew out a file.

"If you don't cooperate, I can go to a judge. We gave you these houses, we can take them away again."

Jess closed her gaping mouth. "You wouldn't."

"I don't want to. Really, I don't. But we have people who need a place to live."

"Please," said Jess. "Give us twenty-four hours. I'm sure I can persuade—"

"No," said Ben. "She can't. No one is persuading anyone of anything. I always knew we couldn't trust you lot. Get out."

"Ben—"

Ben put a hand on Jess's forearm and squeezed. It hurt. She tried to shake him off but he wouldn't budge.

"Ben. Please. Let's be reasonable."

"No, Jess. This is my house – for now – and these people aren't welcome." He turned to their visitors. "Leave, please. Now."

5

The house shuddered as Ben slammed the door behind the two council officers. Ruth leaned into the wall, shrinking away from the voices that came up the stairs.

Ben stood with his back against the door, his chest rising and falling. Ruth watched him, wondering if he'd thought to consider the things that had happened to her.

"That was stupid." Jess's voice was jagged with anger.

"They can't kick us out."

"Can't they?"

"We've been here for six years. That counts for something."

Jess moved to the bottom of the stairs. Ruth considered going down to them, joining in. She shivered and decided to stay put.

"It counts for nothing, Ben," Jess said. "Have you read the housing agreement?"

"I was the steward. Of course I have."

"Then you'll know the eviction terms."

"They have to give notice."

"Unless…"

Ben glanced up the stairs. Ruth held her breath, confident he couldn't see her in the dark.

"Unless what?" he snapped.

"There are clauses about what happens if anyone from the village is convicted of a crime."

"Ted's gone. That can't affect us surely."

"Ben, don't be naive. They'll use it against us. If we don't cooperate, they could sling more of us out."

"They're already slinging us out!"

"They aren't. They just want to make better use of the housing stock available to them."

"Housing stock? Is that all this is to you? Has moving out of the house where Mum died made you so callous?"

"That was low, Ben," Jess said.

"This isn't housing stock. It's our homes. It's where Ruth and I are raising our boys."

Jess's shoulders slumped. "I know that. But I don't think we can just turn them down. It might—"

"Do you want them here? More outsiders, threatening us?"

"No, of course I—"

Ruth could feel her skin frosting over. She felt sick. She closed her eyes and leaned back. *Go, Jess, please. Leave us alone.*

"Don't you remember those boys," Ben said. "On your first day as steward? The way they threatened those children? Told us to *fuck off skum*?"

"They were just kids."

"They get it from their parents, and you know it."

Jess said nothing. Ruth heard her move into the kitchen. The tap ran and then there was a dull thud as the pipe cleared.

"Don't walk away from me when we're having a conversation." Ben's voice was fainter now; he'd followed his sister into the kitchen. Ruth slipped down a couple of steps, her guilt at eavesdropping cloaked by anxiety.

Outsiders. Last time they'd allowed outsiders into this village, it had been Robert and his men.

"There's no point," said Jess. "It'll have to go to a vote, anyway. This is too big for you and me to decide."

"OK. I'm sure the council will see it my way."

"Not the council. The whole village. This is too big. People could be made homeless."

"That's why we have to say no."

"I'm not so sure, Ben. If we refuse, it could be a lot worse."

6

Ben sat at the kitchen table, his fingers clenched around a mug. Ruth watched the rise and fall of his shoulders. His muscles were slack, his body slumped.

She picked her way across the room and placed a hand on his back. He flinched.

"Ben."

He turned, eyes dark. He looked tired. She felt her heart fill with concern and love.

"Are you alright, love?" she asked.

"Did you hear all that?"

She nodded.

"They don't get it. *She* doesn't get it."

Ruth dragged a chair out from under the table and positioned it to face him. He grabbed her hand and brought it onto his lap. He stroked the skin on the back of her knuckles. It tickled; she resisted the urge to pull it away.

"Have they gone?" she asked.

"Who? Those council officials? Bloody do-gooders."

She shook her head, feeling her chest tighten. "The police."

Ben's head jolted up. "Oh. Ruth, I'm so sorry."

She shrugged. *Don't say it. Don't mention it.*

Ben shifted his chair towards hers and leaned forward to put his arms around her. "I'm sorry, love. I didn't think."

She blinked, glad he couldn't see her face. "It's alright."

He pulled back. "You're so brave."

She bit her lower lip and nodded.

"You thought they'd come to arrest you again."

She frowned. There had been a moment, a fleeting moment, when that had passed through her mind. But no; that wasn't what she was scared of. Not really.

But he didn't need to know that. She pulled his hand up to her face and rubbed it against her chin. The skin on the back of his hand was rough; since losing his job as steward he'd started working on the allotments, and now he had gardener's hands. It felt real, comforting.

"I don't want them here," she said.

"Who? The police? The council?"

"Anyone."

"You mean the people they want to house here."

She swallowed.

"I'll do my best, Ruth." He pulled back, examining her face. "I thought you'd argue against me."

She frowned.

"After you helped Martin with his hypothermia. You let him stay here. Then you treated him, after he came back again. You've always been so generous. So welcoming."

"That was different."

"Was it?"

"Yes." She blinked, trying to push the thickening clouds

from her mind. *Don't think about it*, she told herself. *Forget. It's over.*

Except it wasn't. New people were coming here, people who hated them. People who'd attacked their community in the past, who'd told them to *go home*.

How could they possibly coexist, if those officials got their way? How could they survive?

"You're right," she said. "I used to think this place was a sanctuary. But now I know."

"What do you know?"

"It *is* a sanctuary. But only if we keep it safe. Only if we don't let anyone else in."

7

J ess hated listening to Pam. As the proprietor of the village shop and the keeper of rations and supplies, Pam was party to almost everything that went on in the village. Every family in the place came through her doors most days to pick up their rations. She never missed an opportunity to pry.

But Pam was powerful. She resented the council members and their privilege. The well-placed houses, the power over people's lives.

Jess often wondered if Pam would exercise her own power differently, the power she wielded over food, if they hadn't put checks and balances in place right from the start. Pam distributed rations. But Toni was in charge of getting food to the shop from the allotments, the smoke house and the bakery. She and Pam went over everyone's supply each day, checking and double checking that everything was shared fairly. The two women hated each other. But maybe that helped. Maybe that kept them from working together to abuse the system.

Jess had bumped into Toni on the way here; her friend

had been taciturn and gloomy. When Jess had asked her what was wrong, Toni had shaken her head; nothing for Jess to worry about. She'd muttered Roisin's name but said no more. Jess knew she shouldn't pry, but Toni had been distant lately. Jess was worried about her.

She needed to be more trusting, to worry less. But it was hard, after the way that woman had talked to her. Anita Chopra. Scarborough council, the body that had left them here to rot.

They'd adapted, partly thanks to this system that Pam and Toni presided over. But that didn't make it any easier.

Jess turned at the sound of the bell over the shop door, relieved to have some respite from Pam's voice. She knew she should listen when Pam gossiped. There might be information there that she needed to know. But there would also be information she most definitely did not need to know. It wasn't the steward's place to delve into people's intimate lives. So whenever she had to come to the shop, she drowned it out with her own thoughts. Mainly of Zack.

The door opened and Ruth entered. She flinched as she spotted Jess, then put on a smile.

"Hello."

"Hi, Ruth. I've been looking for you."

"Oh."

Ruth's eyes wore dark circles and her cheeks were puffy. She looked as if she hadn't washed her normally thick, dark hair for days.

"Has Ben told you about the council officials who came round earlier?" Jess asked.

Jess sensed Pam prick up her ears.

"Come into the pharmacy," Ruth said.

Jess gave Pam a brusque nod and followed Ruth through.

Inside, the pharmacy was still and quiet. Boxes were arranged neatly on the shelves and the table in the centre of the space had been wiped clean. The walls held two posters on first aid and the floor was clean and free of footprints. There was a faint smell of vinegar and elderflower.

Ruth waited for Jess to close the door. "Go on."

"Sorry about this. I know you don't need me asking more of you."

"I'm not busy right now."

"I know, but—"

"Please. Tell me what it is you need."

"OK. It's the explosion last night. They need medical help."

"Oh."

"They asked if we had a doctor."

"We don't."

"Ruth. You may not be trained as a doctor, but you're the closest we've got."

"They don't need me. I'm just a veterinary nurse."

"I think the last few years have qualified you for more than that. You're an expert at practising medicine without traditional supplies."

"I wouldn't say that."

"You are, Ruth. I can smell it, in this room. I know you struggle to source medicines. I know you go down to the beach, and into the fields. You use herbs, and minerals from the rocks. It's impressive."

Ruth shrugged. "It's not medicine."

"Try telling that to all the people you've treated."

"It's not. They'll have hospitals, and real doctors. They don't need me."

"They need all the help they can get. There are a lot of

people with injuries. They need to stem infection, and they have as much problem accessing antibiotics as we do."

"Antibiotics that still work, you mean."

"Yes." Jess could feel her pulse rising. This wasn't like Ruth. "Can you help?"

"I think I'd do more harm than good."

Jess's shoulders slumped. Ruth turned her back, shifting boxes from one shelf to another; something Jess was sure she didn't need to do. She'd probably move them back again after Jess had gone.

"Please, Ruth."

Ruth kept her back to her sister-in-law. "I don't think it would be wise."

There was a knock on the door behind Jess. Ruth pushed past her and opened it. "Sheila. Good to see you." She turned to Jess. "I need you to leave, please."

8

S arah listened to the voices outside; friends and neighbours, all heading for the same place. A child shouted something and a woman laughed. She went to the window and looked out. A family had stopped below, waiting for a little boy to catch up. Ezra Clarke: she knew him from the school. He shrieked something unintelligible and then ran to catch up. His mum ruffled his hair and continued walking.

"I think we should go," she said, still looking out.

"I'd rather not," Martin replied.

"Mum will be wondering why we're not there."

"She'll be too busy."

Sarah turned and sat on the sofa next to Martin. "You're part of this community now. You'll be with me. You shouldn't let them scare you."

He shifted away from her. "They don't scare me."

"Why won't you go, then?"

He took a deep breath. "I didn't tell you what happened this morning."

"This morning?"

"Yes."

"Go on."

She kept her smile on, not wanting to make him any more worried. This wouldn't be the first time Martin had been met with hostility.

"It was Mark Palfrey," he said.

"Who?"

"Sally Angus's boyfriend."

"Oh. How is Sally?" Sarah felt a pang of guilt; she hadn't spoken to Sally more than twice since they'd been kidnapped.

Martin eyed her. "I don't bloody know, do I? Sorry, that sounded callous. Mark's not exactly going to tell me, though. He made it pretty clear how he feels about me."

"What did he say?"

Martin pursed his lips and let out a whistling breath. "I'd rather not say."

"You were the one who wanted to tell me about it."

A pause. "Alright. He told me to go back to the farm. Said no one was safe with me here."

She put a hand on his arm. "I'm sorry."

"It's no more than I deserve."

"It's not. Robert made you do what you did. And you rescued me, didn't you? You stopped Robert."

He was chewing his lower lip, saying nothing. She squeezed his arm, feeling the muscle tense beneath her hand.

"That's not you. I know what you're like. My mum does. Jess, and the other council members."

He wiped his face. "They're not what counts though."

She felt suddenly irritated. She let go of his arm and stood up.

"Come on. You have to face them. You have to show them you're not what they think you are."

"Not tonight."

"Why on earth not?"

"Because this meeting is about bringing outsiders into the village. People like me, as far as they're concerned."

"People who've been made homeless. Just like we were. Families."

"They won't see it like that."

She was at the door now. Her coat was on the hook next to it. Should she go without him, support her mother?

"Martin, there's only one way to know for sure, and that's to come."

He shook his head.

"Please." Her hand was on her coat. She tightened her grip around it but didn't pull it down.

He looked up. "You go. Be with your mum."

"I don't want to go without you."

"I don't mind." But he did; she could tell from the way he was holding himself, turned away from her and stiff.

She let go of her coat and returned to the sofa. "I'm staying with you."

"No. You go. You don't need me holding you back."

"Come with me."

He crossed to the door and yanked her coat down from its place. He threw it into her lap. She grabbed it, irritated.

She stood up. "Alright then."

She headed for the door and clattered down the stairs without looking back. There were just a few stragglers passing now, people who in all likelihood would be late for the meeting, like her. She hoped they hadn't shut the doors.

She ran to the village hall, grabbing her skirt in her fist so as not to trip. A fine drizzle was beginning to fall and dusk was descending. Somewhere in a hedge, a dunnock was calling its mate. A few windows glowed into the night. Not many though; no one here would leave electricity on while they were at a meeting.

Sanjeev was just closing the doors. She squeezed through, shooting him an out-of-breath smile. He looked past her, clearly wondering where Martin was.

Inside, the room was full. People stood behind the rows of chairs, jostling to get a view. She slipped between two men and found a space at the side of the room from where she could see her mother. Dawn was sitting in the front row, right at the end. She had a notebook in her lap and looked pleased with herself, as if proud of her role here.

Until six months ago, Dawn had been a ghost to the other villagers, someone who they rarely glimpsed and hardly ever emerged out of her own front door. But now Sarah's father was in prison, and Dawn was an active member of the village council.

Someone jostled Sarah and she looked round. It was Zack Golder, Sam's twin. She looked past him to see if her friend was with him.

"Hi Sarah."

"Hi Zack."

"No Martin?"

"No. Where's Sam?"

"Can you close the doors please Sanjeev?" called Jess Dyer from the front. "I'm worried it's getting overcrowded."

The doors closed with a thud and the room grew quiet. The woman in front of Sarah shifted a little, giving her a better view. Jess was perched on a table at the front, facing the rest of the village. Colin sat next to her, looking uncomfortable; he'd rather use a chair, she imagined. But there wasn't space.

Sarah liked Jess. She trusted her to come up with the right solution to this. Their community was wary of outsiders, and rightly so. But surely the people of Filey deserved the same refuge they'd enjoyed here?

"Right," said Jess. "I imagine you all know why we're here. I know how quickly news spreads."

There was muttering around Sarah. Colin put his hand up for quiet.

"You saw the explosion in Filey the night before last. It was a gas main, in a residential area. Two people were killed, and more injured. Twenty-six households have been made homeless.

The muttering rose.

"You all know how this village started. Every one of you was displaced by the floods. You had nowhere to go, and this place took you in. I think we should continue that tradition. What does it make us, if we turn them away?"

"Would they do the same for us?" A voice at the front.

"I don't think that's the issue," replied Jess.

"They hate us!" Another voice, closer to Sarah.

"Why should we be as bad as them?" That was Zack, standing right next to her. Sarah threw him a grin. Maybe if they took in a few more newcomers, Martin would be less noticeable.

"Where would they live, if we said yes?" Ben Dyer was standing up at the front, flanked by his two boys, their blonde hair bright in the dimness of the room. Beyond one of them – Sean, Sarah thought – Ruth sat, her back straight.

Jess pursed her lips. "We would need to make more efficient use of the space we have."

"Kick people out of their homes, you mean," he replied.

"No. There is the option of asking for volunteers."

"Volunteers? How many people do you think will voluntarily leave their home, after everything we've all suffered?"

Jess dipped her head as Colin whispered something in her ear. She frowned.

"I won't!" cried a woman behind Sarah.

"Nor me!"

"Me neither!"

"*You* should!"

Jess's head whipped up.

The same voice came again. "The steward lives in a big house, on her own. She should give that up. Maybe for some of us. We've got six people in our house. It's hardly fair."

Jess nodded. "You're right." She looked at Zack. He nodded. "I can give up my house," she continued.

Ben was on his feet again. He turned to the crowd. "Can't you hear what they're asking us to do?" he cried. "It's ridiculous!"

9

J ess stared at her brother's back, her breath shallow.

Not again, Ben.

She knew he didn't agree with her on this. She knew he was scared of outsiders, not that he would ever admit it. But to override her like this, in a village meeting...

"Ben, please..." she began. He ignored her.

"I want to remind you all of something," he said. His voice was low and flat. He didn't make the effort to raise it, and in return, the room descended into a hush so they could hear him.

"Do you remember the twenty-eighth of October last year?"

He paused, his head moving from left to right as he scanned the room. There were a few mutters of *yes*. Flo Murray, three rows back, let out a gasp.

"Of course you do," he continued. "That was the day I did the most stupid, regrettable thing I've ever done."

Silence. At the time, he had blamed her. After all, she had convinced him to answer that distress call at sea.

"I allowed those men to come to our village. Robert Cope and his friends."

He looked round at Jess. She stiffened. He turned back.

"Thank you, Ben," she began. "Can we please get on with the—"

He raised a hand to dismiss her. She gritted her teeth. How dare he?

"I take responsibility. I let Jess persuade me to send villagers out to answer that rescue call. I sat in a council meeting where we agreed to give the men shelter. I took one of them into my home."

Jess noticed Sarah Evans, standing just behind Zack. She wondered if Martin was with her. Sarah's face was a deep shade of pink.

"And I will regret those decisions till the day I die."

You're not telling them the rest of it, she thought. *How it was revenge for what you did to him when you were young that brought Robert here. How you helped him kill a man.* She wondered how many people here knew. Sarah, and Zack. Ben and Ruth, of course. Sanjeev. Dawn? Would Sarah have told her? She'd probably not even heard them talk about it, at the time.

"So I'm urging you now," Ben continued. "Don't make that mistake twice."

"This is different," she interrupted. "Families. Who have been genuinely displaced. They aren't faking it, like the men were with their boat."

He kept his back to her. "That doesn't matter. They're outsiders. Outsiders are trouble. They hate us. Don't you all remember four years ago, when we had to place guards on the village perimeter? They would have murdered us in our sleep. They've always resented us being here, and they always will. And if we let them come here, they'll find a way to turf us out. That is, if we're still alive to *be* turfed out."

In the front row, Ruth leaned over Sean and put her hands over his ears. Ollie, his twin brother, let out a sob.

Ben, thought Jess. *Can't you see what you're doing? Fomenting panic. Exaggerating the risk.*

She stood up. The crowd was pushing in on her now, and she could barely see past the front row. Sarah Evans had disappeared into the melee. She hoped the girl was all right.

This will never work, she thought. She climbed onto the table she'd been perching on. Below her, voices were raised. Someone screamed. Jess could smell fear: the acrid smell of sweat.

"Everyone!" she shouted. "Calm down, please. Ben is exaggerating."

Ben turned to her. "Am I? Am I really?"

She glared at him. "Yes. Sit down, please."

"You sit down."

This was starting to remind her of her childhood, the way the two of them had bickered at every opportunity, both of them insisting to Sonia that the other was in the wrong.

"Alright," she breathed. She squatted on the table then lowered herself so she was sitting on it. Ben returned to his seat. Ruth was staring ahead, her jaw set. She'd gathered both boys onto her lap and was stroking their hair, not noticing their protests as her fingers caught in the tangles.

Ben shifted his chair to face sideways, with a view of both Jess and the room. He was enjoying this. Ruth clearly wasn't.

Colin cleared his throat. In all the commotion, Jess had forgotten that he was still standing beside her.

"I think we can have a reasonable conversation about this," he said. He had a pencil in his hand and he was twisting the tip into the flesh of his thumb. He hated outsiders too. When two youths had invaded their village six months ago, he'd locked one of them in the boathouse.

"Thanks, Colin," she said. She scanned the crowd. Surely there was someone who would support her. Her eye caught on Zack. No, too obvious. She didn't want this looking like a setup.

Sanjeev was right at the back. He tended to be reasonable. But he was loyal to Ben.

Then she remembered. The woman who'd let Martin come to the village to be with her daughter. She turned towards Dawn, sitting with her hands in her lap at the end of the front row.

"I'd like other members of the council to have their say," Jess said. "Dawn, what do you think?"

Dawn reddened. "Well..."

"Remember we're talking about families here. Children, who've lost their homes just like we did." Did she dare try a Bible reference? They appealed to Dawn. But then, she'd probably get whatever quote she tried to drag up from her memory wrong.

"Dawn?"

Dawn nodded. "The poor little mites. They're innocents."

"Exactly."

"But what about their parents? Who's to say they aren't the people who tried to have us evicted four years go?"

Jess sighed. Ben stood up. He turned away from her again.

"Dawn's right," he said. "If we let those people live among us, what will they do to us? It's all very well thinking of their children. What about *ours*?"

He grabbed Sean's hand. Sean grinned and threw his

arms around his dad. Older than Ollie by a full hour and always the confident one, he looked up to his dad. Ollie, on the other hand, was Ruth's baby. He shrank towards her, almost as if he were trying to burrow inside her. *Don't single him out too, Ben*, Jess thought.

But Ben knew his boys better than she gave him credit for. He threw Ollie a smile and lifted Sean onto his shoulders. Sean giggled.

"It's up to you all," Ben said. "But I speak as someone who almost lost his family the last time this happened." He paused. Sean grabbed his hair where it was thinning at the top. "Let's not allow it to happen again."

Colin motioned for Ben to sit down. Ben swung Sean down onto his lap and gave the boy a noisy kiss. He looked at Ruth but she was staring ahead, her eyes bright.

Jess watched her. Was Ruth OK? Had something happened between them?

"Right," said Colin. "It's only fair to ask if anyone else wants to speak."

Jess cleared her throat.

"Anyone else," Colin muttered in her ear. She clenched her fist.

No one spoke. A few people looked at Dawn, then at Sanjeev. But neither of them had anything to say.

"Right," said Colin. "In that case, let's put it to a vote."

10

"We won't let it happen, sis."

Jess stared at him. *How can you be so naive, after everything that's happened to you?*

"They're going to get a court order," she told him.

Ben snorted. "That'll go nowhere. By the time they've done that, those people will have all found somewhere else to live."

"Don't be so sure."

He shook his head. "You'll see. We made the right decision."

"We didn't make any decision. You talked the village into making the wrong choice."

"Hi, Jess. What's happening?"

Jess looked past Ben to see Ruth coming down the stairs.

"Why didn't you say anything, Ruth?"

Ruth shook her head but said nothing.

"You're the most generous, decent, tolerant person I know. You treated Martin after he kidnapped you. Even Ted. You—"

"I don't want to get involved, Jess."

Jess felt herself deflate. "Why not?"

"You don't understand."

Jess bit her lip. Her sister-in-law was right. How could Jess understand everything Ruth had suffered?

Ruth hadn't spoken about her arrest since she'd returned from Filey. As far as Jess was aware, she hadn't even told Ben what she'd been through.

There was a wail from upstairs. Ruth tensed. "See you, Jess. We need to be alone, right now."

Jess blanched; the rejection was like a slap in the face. The three of them had walked here together from London. They'd cared for Sonia together. They'd shared everything. And now Sonia was dead, and Jess wasn't wanted.

She eyed Ben. He said nothing.

"I hope you know what you've done," she said.

He shrugged and opened the front door. She retreated through it, feeling empty. He'd told her he was happy for her to be steward now, that he wanted to focus on his family. But his ambition, his need to be in control, was strong.

Outside, the night was cold. Not many people ventured outdoors in the dark, there being no street lamps. And the winds could blow you right off the cliff edge if you weren't careful. But Jess only lived two doors away and besides, her eyes had grown accustomed; she could see by the starlight. This would be what life had been like centuries ago, before electric light was a glint in anyone's eye.

She dragged her feet towards her own house, reluctant to go inside. Zack was with his parents tonight – they hadn't reacted well to the news of the engagement, and he was trying to placate them – and her house would be dark and cold. She'd got used to being on her own, even in her last house with its memories of Sonia. But here, in this gloomy house with the sea never far away and the wind whistling in the eaves, she experienced an emptiness that felt like it could never be filled.

It didn't help that she could only imagine things that had happened in the house before her tenancy. She'd been a witness once, picking Dawn up from her position slumped against the sofa and helping Sarah to carry her upstairs. How many times had Ted beaten Dawn, behind the door she now called hers? How many times had he terrorised Sarah?

She opened the door and peered inside, half expecting Ted to rush out at her. She shivered and fumbled in the chest of drawers behind the door, searching for a match. She lit the candle she kept on the chest and instantly regretted it. It threw long, flickering shadows across the wall and up the stairs, the kind of shadows that were more at home in ghost stories.

Zack would be back in an hour or two. Maybe she'd go for a walk, to occupy herself.

She grabbed her heavy coat – Sonia's coat – from behind the door and shrugged it onto her shoulders. The weight of being steward felt like an animal draped across her back. Anita Chopra had barely disguised her anger this afternoon, when she'd arrived at Jess's door and been told their decision. She'd left in a flurry of hissed accusations and threats. One way or the other, this wasn't going to be good.

The sky was clear enough now for her to make her way down to the beach safely, and the rain had subsided. She knew where she was going; she'd be careful.

She shuffled along the road that led to the cliff path, imagining what this would have been like when it was a holiday village. Windows would have been lit, people would have been lighting barbecues, cars coming and going. And children. This was the kind of place that would have had children everywhere. At least the children who lived here now could enjoy some sort of innocence. They were allowed to roam the village in a way she'd certainly never been allowed to roam the streets around her mother's London house; and they'd never known twenty-four-hour electricity, the internet, or computer games. But then, who knew what the future held for them? Tending the land and maybe working down in Hull on the earthworks, if those still existed? Not the greatest of prospects.

She heard a yell from somewhere behind her and stopped walking. She listened, breathing in the sea air. Was someone calling her?

She turned back towards the village centre, peering into the night.

Then she heard them. Footsteps, coming from behind her, the direction of the beach. Not just one set, but two; three; more.

She span to face the beach. Who was out there?

"Hello?"

No one replied. Instead, the footsteps grew until she couldn't tell how many pairs of feet they belonged to. They sounded chaotic, like the rumble of feet in a running race. She felt her breath catch.

"Hello? Who is it?"

"Go!"

She frowned and shrank back. "Zack?"

There was a time when Zack and his bother Sean might have played a practical joke on her, back then they were young men. But Zack wasn't stupid; he knew how intimidating the night could be.

"Who is it? Stop it, now!"

An individual set of footsteps approached, echoing off

the darkened buildings. Suddenly overcome by dread, she darted into the gap between two houses.

She stared out onto the road. Dark figures rushed past, feet hammering on the tarmac. Torches flamed in people's hands, raised into the night air.

She stumbled. No one here used torches like that. It was a waste of resources.

Should she make herself known, challenge them? Or not?

The shapes passed, flames flickering off the buildings and the blank windows. She wondered if there were people in there, staring out, hearts hammering in their chest like hers was.

When the light had receded she dragged herself out on to the tarmac. A dimly-lit crowd of people moved in the direction of the village centre. None of them spoke.

She thumped on the door of the house closest to her. A man opened the door, wearing a vest and a pair of patched-up tracksuit bottoms.

"Jess?"

"We're under attack," she panted. "We have to defend ourselves."

11

"What was that?"

Ruth flinched as Ben jumped up from his place on the sofa and ran to the window in the kitchen. They'd been gazing at the stars through the window in silence. The boys had just gone to sleep and she had no energy for anything more than slumping on the sofa and staring out at the sky. She felt so tired, she wished she could close her eyes and find herself in her bed.

"What was what?" she repeated.

"There's people out there."

She drew a breath and pushed herself up from the sofa. Ollie would be awake again at five. She needed her bed.

Ben was leaning over the kitchen sink, peering sideways out of the window. Ruth could make out dim lights, dancing in the gloom.

"What's that?"

"No idea." Ben turned and stared into her face for a moment. His eyes were full of excitement.

"Careful," she said, as he hurried to the front door. "Please, love."

"It's fine." He pulled on his coat and eased the door open. Light came through the gap, illuminating a slice of the wall. She gasped.

"Who is it?"

"I'll find out. You stay here." He looked up the stairs, the boyish anticipation falling from his face. "Look after the boys."

She nodded; as if she needed asking.

He looked back at her as he stood in the open doorway. "Don't open the door."

She frowned; why not? But then she nodded, swallowing her fear. "I love you."

"You too."

He eased the door closed and was gone. She hurried to the kitchen window but there was nothing to see. Vague figures flashed past in the direction of the square, but the view from here was of the side of Colin and Sheila's house, not of the street.

She hurried to the stairs and took them two at a time. At the top was a window; the one window that faced the road. The building had been designed to make the most of the sea views and so it felt isolated from the life of the village sometimes, with its aspect over the cliffs and the crashing waves beyond.

Outside, lights reflected off walls and windows and there was shouting. She heard a crash and a scream. She pulled her fist to her chest and glanced at the door to her sons' room.

She leaned forward to see better. People were running around in the square. A shape was moving over by the JP, the village pub. She couldn't tell if it was one person lying on the ground, or several people wrestling.

She looked down at the front door. If she bolted it, Ben

wouldn't be able to get back in. But if she didn't, her boys were at risk.

Don't open the door, he'd said. *Look after the boys*. There was roaring in her ears that was nothing to do with the noise outside. Her palms were sweaty. Her stomach felt like it was being scrubbed from inside.

She descended the stairs slowly, one at a time, and reached out for the bolt. She slid it closed, then checked it. She pushed against the door, then tugged it.

It was firm.

She retreated up the stairs, not taking her eyes off the door. Soon she was by the window again. Something was on fire out there, but she couldn't make out what. It was at the back of the JP: the composting bins?

She flinched as a knock sounded at her door. She shrank back and stared at it.

Another knock. And another. She stared at it, confused. Could it be Ben?

She stumbled down the stairs. She crouched behind the door, wishing there was a spy hole.

"Who is it?" she croaked.

No answer. The knocking had stopped. She put a hand on the bolt, considering opening it. *No*. She had to stay safe. She had to keep them out.

She pulled herself back up the stairs, sliding up like Ollie had when he was too little to walk. At the top, the first door was the one to her sons' room. She had to protect them.

She pulled herself up and turned the knob, slowly. She eased the door open.

The curtains were open and shapes danced on the walls. Dim, red shapes. She stumbled to the window and pulled the curtains closed, not pausing to look out. No one could know her children were in here.

She lowered herself to the floor between their beds, thinking of the night Martin had slept here, in the room beyond the wall that ran next to Sean's bed. She'd been worried about their safety, wary about the newcomers. So she'd slept in here, on the floor. And he'd taken her from here.

She lay down on the floor and stared up at the ceiling. Her mistake that time had been to fall asleep. If she was unconscious, she couldn't protect her children. She would keep her eyes open until the morning came, or until the noise outside stopped. Whichever came first.

12

Jess ran to the village square. The houses were dark, the night chilly. She looked back at the council members' houses; she needed to alert them. Why had she run past them?

"Jess!"

She span to see Toni running towards her.

"Toni! Have you heard?"

"Heard what?"

"We're under attack. People from Filey, I think. Wasn't that why you were out here?"

Toni leaned over, her fists balled on her thighs. She was out of breath.

"It's complicated."

"Oh." Jess wasn't sure she had time for Toni's problems right now. "Everything OK?"

"Not really. But look, tell me what's happening. What can I do?"

"Toni!"

Jess looked past her friend to see a pale figure running towards them: Roisin Murray.

Toni turned. "Get back inside, Roi. Your mum can't see you out here."

"I don't care about my mum." She fell on Toni and threw her arms around her. Her face was pale, reminding Jess of how she'd looked when they got her out of her cell at the kidnappers' farm.

"Roisin," she said. "You OK?"

"I will be." Roisin stared into Toni's eyes. "I'm sorry. I shouldn't have let my mum tell me what to do. She's got no idea."

Toni kissed her briefly, then looked towards where Roisin had come from. "Does she know where you are?"

"I snuck out."

Toni nodded. Her lips were tight and her face pale. Jess heard sounds behind them.

"Damn," she said. "Come on, you two, we need to sound the alarm."

"Why?" asked Roisin. She shrank into Toni's side.

"There are people here from Filey. We need to tell everyone to get indoors."

"No you bloody don't," said Toni. "We fight back."

"Toni, please..."

Toni pushed Jess out of the way and watched the advancing crowd. She turned to Jess. "It's not like you to run and hide."

"I'm not saying run and hide," said Jess. "But they've got weapons. We aren't prepared. We should sit it out, wait until morning."

"What, and let them loot and vandalise our village, and God knows what else? Sod that."

Toni grabbed Roisin's shoulder. "Can you bring me the garden spade, from the cupboard in my kitchen?"

"What are you keeping garden tools in your flat for?" asked Jess.

Toni eyed her. "I never knew when I might need to defend myself."

"This isn't about you. It's about those idiots, and about the council trying to take our houses."

"All the more reason to stand up to them. Jess, don't worry. I'll knock some people up. It'll be fine."

Roisin was sobbing. "I'm not fetching it."

Toni wrapped an arm around her. "Please, Roi. I'm no use without a weapon."

"No, Toni. Please. Just come home with me. Keep out of it."

"Home? Back to your mum's, where I'm despised?"

Roisin blushed. "No. Back to your flat."

"And what will your mum do if she finds you there?"

"We can deal with that when we come to it."

Toni kissed her again. "That's very brave of you. But I have to help. We've got to fight. They aren't doing this to us again." She pushed Roisin gently away. Roisin wiped her cheek and started running towards the flats.

Around them, doors were opening and people were emerging.

"Get inside!" Jess shouted. "It isn't safe."

No one paid any attention. A group of people was forming behind her. The invaders had stopped moving now. They were in a line, between Jess and her house.

She ran to the growing crowd of villagers. Colin was at the head of them.

"This isn't like you," she said.

"They can't do this."

"We can't fight them," she said. "I've seen them up close. They've got better weapons than us."

"We're more determined than they are."

She shook her head. This was going nowhere. "Keep this lot under control, will you?" she told him. "I'm going to find Zack."

13

Martin stood at the door to the street, his chest rising and falling. Sarah had her hand on his arm, trying to hold him back.

"I don't understand," she said. "You didn't want to go to the village meeting. Why do you want to get involved in this?"

He turned to her. "Don't you get it?"

"No. I really don't." She scratched her arm; it itched, the skin raw.

"This is my fault. I have to help make it right."

"How is it your fault?"

"This all started with me and Robert."

"Robert would have found someone else to do his dirty work."

He shrugged her hand off. His skin was hot, like it might set her on fire. "But he didn't," he said. "He found me."

"If he hadn't persuaded you to do it, you wouldn't be here now. With me. Have you ever thought about that?"

His face softened. "You really see it like that?"

She wasn't sure how she saw it. Mostly, she tried not to think about the circumstances of their meeting.

"You think it was a good thing I did, because it brought us together?" he asked.

"No. Of course not. But it's complicated, isn't it?"

He leaned in and kissed her forehead. "I love the way you see the good in everything."

"Thank you. So don't go."

"I have to. I'm one of you now, I have to prove myself. I can't let outsiders take over this village."

"You're talking like you've lived here all your life."

"Not yet, I haven't." His eyes were boring into hers; she felt a shiver run down her spine. She didn't dare think about the future. When her father had been at home, the future represented getting through the next day without him losing his temper. Now the future was a looming wall she couldn't imagine scaling.

"You'll get hurt."

"People are already getting hurt. You think I should be any different?"

He was right, of course. If there ever was logic in getting involved in a fight, his was solid enough. She grabbed his arm. "Keep safe," she muttered.

He pulled her to him and kissed her, long and hard. She savoured the taste of his lips, the smell of his skin, hoping she would feel this again.

She pushed him away. "Go. Before I change my mind."

Behind him, two people ran past. She couldn't tell if they were from the village, or not. She felt her eyes widen, her skin bristle. "Be safe," she whispered.

"I will. You go inside. You're too fragile to be out there."

She put her hands on her hips. "I'm a lot less fragile than I look. And my mum's out there. I'm going to check on her."

"Please, Sarah…"

"You can't tell me what to do. That's what my father did."

"It's not safe."

"She needs me. I'll come with you as far as the corner, then I'll head to her house. I can take side routes, I know my way."

"I don't want you risking it."

She took a breath. "You don't tell me what to do."

"You know that's not what I…"

"Whatever. I'm going."

He opened his mouth as if to speak, then shifted his weight, seeming to deflate. She knew what he was thinking.

"Be careful," he muttered.

"I will."

She gripped his hand and together they ran the first hundred yards. Up ahead, torches blazed and men were shouting. They passed a woman who was slumped over another figure, talking incoherently. Sarah shuddered.

"Wait." She approached the woman. "What's happened?"

The woman looked up at her. She was bent over a man, unconscious on the ground.

Sarah fell to the ground and put a hand on the man's back. There was no sign of injury. The man shifted under her hand, his back moving against her skin.

"What happened to him?" She looked up at the woman; she didn't know her. She was as sure as she could be that this woman didn't have children. Had they ever met?

The woman said nothing.

"I'll get help," Sarah said. "I'll find Ruth."

The woman stared at her, her eyes wide. Then looked at Martin. Her eyes narrowed and she shook her head. "He'll be fine."

"He's not moving."

"I can deal with it."

"But that's ridiculous."

The woman moved forward to grab Sarah's arm. Sarah winced; her grip was tight. "Why won't you let me help?"

The woman stiffened. "Go, please. We'll be fine."

Martin whispered in Sarah's ear. "Your mum, remember."

She waved a hand in his direction. "This is more important."

"Please," said the woman. "We'll be fine. You have somewhere you need to be, clearly."

She felt her chest tighten. She looked into the woman's face, trying to determine the reason for her mistrust.

She remembered her mother. Alone, in that cottage. "I'll see if I can find someone from the council. My mum." She shook off the woman's hand.

The woman nodded.

"Please, Sarah," said Martin. "I don't want you out here any longer than you need to be. I'll find Ruth."

The woman was watching them, not bothering to disguise her interest. The man on the ground was sitting up now, rubbing his forehead. Sarah moved away from them, towards Martin. She lowered her voice.

"I said, don't tell me what to do."

"Sorry. But please. I love you, Sarah. I don't want you to get hurt."

"I know." She forced out a smile then stood on her tiptoes and kissed him lightly on the cheek. She took one last glance at the woman, who was leaning into the man, pulling him up to standing. Her mother would know what to do.

She pulled away and ran towards a narrow gap in the

houses opposite. These cut-throughs were dark, and difficult to spot. She'd be safe.

14

The route to Jess's house was blocked. Someone had pushed a tangle of fallen branches into the alleyway that led to it, and in the darkness she'd failed to find a way through. She headed back for the village square, where villagers and attackers were tearing into each other.

The attackers had weapons: basic ones, but enough. Baseball bats, a scythe, the glint of knives. They wore heavy, dark clothing, bundled up against the night.

Some of the villagers were in pyjamas; a few had thrown coats over their day clothes. One or two had knives but others fought with kitchen utensils. This was not going to end well.

Jess ran towards two young men who she'd taught as teenagers. They were fighting three strangers, men with hoods hiding their faces. She pushed through the crowd, feeling the air stir as a garden fork passed her head.

"Stop it! Stop it, now! We all have to get inside!"

The young men ignored her. Instead, they pushed the hooded men aside and waded into the crowd of torch-bearing attackers, wielding garden tools. Once of them held a hoe and the other a garden fork and a hammer. Jess felt herself blanch at the thought of what damage it might inflict.

There was a crash off to one side and a flash of light from behind the houses close to her. She ran towards it, not stopping to consider if this was wise.

She stopped in the village square, panting. Ahead of her, the JP was ablaze, flames pouring out of an open window. She stared at it, unable to move.

Clyde ran out of the main door, shouting.

"Help! We need water!"

Jess ran towards him. "There are buckets in the boathouse."

"That's too far away. We don't have time."

She tried to focus. The flames were thickening; she could feel heat in the air. People ran towards them: Colin and three other men.

She span round. "Where can we find buckets?"

"The village hall, the storage room," replied Colin.

She frowned. "That's just school supplies."

"The space in the roof. It's full of junk. There are a dozen buckets up there, God knows why."

People were already running towards the village hall, Colin behind them. She sped after them; she had a key. Colin caught up.

"It's alright," he called to her. "I can get in. You go and check on people. Make sure no one's hurt."

She stared then nodded at him, her mind awash. Running away, she could hear sounds behind her; shouting and the crackle of the flames. Someone was chanting something. Were more people coming out to confront them, or would they stay safe in their houses? Could she blame them, if they did fight back?

But if they won this, if they repelled the invaders, the authorities would never forgive them. Anita Chopra would be back here in the morning, court order miraculously expedited, ready to evict them all. And worse.

She turned to see the torchlight brighten behind her as it rounded the houses. It was accompanied by a crowd, at least twenty-strong. She felt her stomach sink.

Ahead of her, a group of villagers approached, young men employed at the earthworks. Was Zack with them?

She ran towards them. "Stop!" she screamed. "Can't you see this is what they want?"

But no one could hear her. Between the roaring of the torches, the shouts that came from all round, and the whistling of the wind, her voice was drowned out. She clenched her fists at her sides, summoning more energy.

"Stop!" she yelled.

One of them turned towards her: Sam, Zack's brother. "Sorry, Jess!" he called. "We can't let this happen."

She stared at him, her arms wide. He shrugged and carried on his way, picking up pace. She had to get back to the JP, to check it was empty. But the way was blocked by fighting.

The two crowds met in the middle of the village square. They blurred into one. The noise rose: shouts, and screams. The clash of weapons.

She collapsed to the ground. "Stop, everyone. Just *stop*."

This wasn't going to work. Diplomacy, politics, negotiation. None of it was worth anything in the face of the blind rage she could see on the faces around her.

A man came out of the throng and shoved past her,

blood oozing from a cut on his forehead. She knew him;
Mark Palfrey, Sally's fiancé.

Where was Ruth? People would need her help.

She took a side route to Ben and Ruth's house. Ben
would be out here somewhere; not like him to avoid a fight.
But Ruth; Ruth would be in there, with her boys.

She hammered on the door. No answer. She knocked
again. She put her face to the door and tried to shout. But
there was smoke in her lungs, and her voice was hoarse.

This was useless. If Ruth was in there, alone with her
boys, there was no way she would come to the door.

Jess ran back to the village square. Their attackers
consisted of twenty, maybe thirty men. They carried
torches and weapons. Axes, hammers, knives. Her own
side, the villagers, numbered more, but had been caught
unawares. Some of them were attempting to fight with
their bare hands. Others wielded kitchen knives, or garden
tools.

This had to stop.

She waded into the crowd, throwing her arms out in an
attempt to protect herself.

"Jess! What the fuck are you doing?" Ben grabbed her by
the arm and dragged her out. She stumbled then managed
to catch herself, thumping his arm to push him off. He held
a length of metal piping; his eyes were bright.

"You have to stop!" she yelled at him. "Can't you see,
we'll lose this either way!"

"We have to defend ourselves."

He disappeared back into the crowd. She stared after
him, her heart pounding in her ears. She could feel something warm on her cheek. She raised a hand and looked at it
to see blood on her fingers. Hers, or someone else's? She
licked it, feeling as if she was watching herself licking her

own bloody fingers; not inside her body but somewhere outside, observing from a safe distance.

"Arrrrgh!" A man threw himself at her. She pushed him off, her fingers clumsy against the rough wool of his coat. He was one of hers.

"It's me, Jess! Don't hurt me!"

It was dark, and windy. The sea pounded in her ears. She was confused, and scared. She didn't have a weapon. These men were just as terrified: who knew who they might stab?

"Stop," she croaked. "You all have to stop."

They could retreat to their homes. The houses were solidly built, with brick or stone walls and heavy windows to keep out the cold. They would be safe. Anita Chopra would have nothing to accuse them of.

But no one was listening.

She half-ran, half-fell from the crowd and towards the tree that sat on the corner of the road leading out of the village. This tree had been here before them, before this holiday village was built. It would outlast them.

She staggered into it and let herself slide to the ground, glad of the solidity of the wood at her back.

She watched the crowd morph and sway in front of her. Blood dripped into her eyes; where had that come from? She blinked, and felt the world blur in front of her.

She wasn't up to this. The steward's role was to protect the village, and she'd failed. She didn't have the mental strength to convince them what was right, or the physical strength to stop this.

She'd failed.

A man ran past. Large, nimble, but heavily built.

"Zack, stop!"

He hadn't heard her.

She pushed herself upright. "Zack, wait!"

If she could persuade him to stop, then the others might follow his lead. Zack loved her. He was going to marry her. They'd talked about the future, about children. The thought terrified her, but she was prepared to give in to it. It was the only way to build a future, after all.

She thought of Ruth and Ben's wedding, out there on the beach five years earlier. It had rained. Everyone had been relieved when the ceremony was over, and they could retreat to the JP.

Would the whole village turn out for her wedding, as they had for Ben and Ruth? Or would they shun her? The woman who couldn't protect them. The steward who couldn't keep their children safe.

She had to find him. She stumbled forward. "Zack!"

A shape at the edge of the crowd stopped moving. Was it him? She couldn't tell. Her eyes hurt.

She picked up her pace. She had to get to him before he melted into the crowd.

She was almost on him when she heard the shout; loud, high-pitched, terrible.

"Zack!"

She started running. The shape she'd been aiming for swayed and fell to the ground. Maybe it wasn't him. Surely it wasn't him. It couldn't be him. They were getting married.

She almost tripped over a mound on the tarmac.

"Zack?"

She fell to the ground. It was him, covered in blood.

She raised her face to the night and screamed.

15

D awn's house was dark, the curtains closed against the night. Sarah shifted from foot to foot as she waited for her mother to come to the door, glancing around to check no one had followed her.

She leaned against the door and knocked again, listening for movement inside. There was nothing.

She looked up and down Dawn's road. Dawn lived in a semi-detached cottage, near the Meadows. Not far from Martin's flat. The front window was dark, no sign of movement or flicker of a candle.

Was her mother out there, in all this? She felt her chest sink.

She looked back towards the centre of the village.

"Mum!" she called. "Mum! Dawn!"

She caught movement from the corner of her eye. In a window opposite, a curtain moved.

Don't shout, she told herself. *Don't panic.*

She ran back towards the centre of the village. She could see people moving in the village square. Torches lit the shapes that advanced on each other then receded. Someone screamed and she threw a hand to her chest.

Mum, where are you?

She started towards the fighting, wondering if this was the right thing to do. Her mother wouldn't be here, surely? Dawn knew when to stay away from trouble.

Martin's flat was off to the left, closer now than her mother's house. Maybe Dawn had been in there all along, but just too afraid to open the door. That would be the sensible thing to do.

Someone was running towards her. She ducked into the shadows, unsure if it was a villager or a stranger. She watched as a woman sped past.

"Mum?"

The woman stopped. "Sarah?"

She stepped out of the shadows. "What are you doing?"

"Helping."

"Helping with what? Not fighting, surely?"

"Don't be silly. I was with Pam. We were making sure the village hall was properly locked, and checking the shop."

Sarah didn't know her mother was friendly with Pam. "Why?"

"Because we don't want anyone getting in there, of course. There's a lot of food in that shop. If it was stolen, we'd go hungry."

"Can't someone else do that?"

"No, love. Someone had to step up."

"I think you should be at home."

Dawn raised an eyebrow. "Do you now? Is that why you're out here, running around like a banshee?"

"I was looking for you. I wanted to check you were safe."

"I'm fine, sweetheart. You need to be indoors."

"It's alright. I'm going back to Martin."

Dawn clutched her upper arm. "He's not in the middle of all that then?"

"I talked him out of it."

"He'd be vulnerable."

Sarah swallowed the lump in her throat. Behind her, she heard a shout, and glass shattering.

"Go home to your young man," Dawn said. "He needs you, tonight."

"I'll walk you home first."

"I'm perfectly fine."

"I don't mind."

The eyebrow went up again. "Sarah. I can look after myself."

"I'm worried about you."

Dawn flapped a hand. "I've faced worse than this."

Sarah tightened her jaw. She didn't know if Dawn was referring to the years of domestic abuse, or to what had happened on the walk here from Somerset, after the floods. To the young men Ted had killed, defending his daughter's honour.

"Go," Dawn said. "Make sure he's alright. I wouldn't want him getting hurt, for your sake."

Sarah kissed her mother gently on the forehead – something she'd never done when their father was around – and started running.

16

J ess slumped to the ground, her skin tight. Zack had fallen against her, his weight heavy on her legs.

She looked up.

"Help! Someone, help!"

But there was too much noise. A man ran past, maybe fifty yards away, oblivious to her.

She leaned over Zack, pawing at him, pulling him.

"Zack. Zack, talk to me! Are you hurt?"

Zack said nothing. His eyes were blinking, his face pale, only his left side visible.

She tugged at him, wondering why he'd never felt this heavy before. His jacket felt matted with something.

As she turned him on his back, his weight caught and he continued moving until his face was against her stomach.

There was a knife in his neck. Its dark handle stared at her.

She grabbed it and tugged. A spurt of blood covered her fingers, making her yelp. She threw the knife to one side and clutched his neck, pushing against a wound she couldn't see for the blood.

She looked up again. People were running towards her. She had no idea if they were villagers, or attackers. No torches.

"Help! Help me!"

Someone broke free of the group and sprinted towards her. He almost crashed into her, then clattered to the ground, kneeling in front of her.

"Ben! Where's Ruth?"

Ben looked from her face down at Zack. "What happened?"

"He's been stabbed."

"What?"

"Where's Ruth?"

"She's at home."

"Jess. Zack. Oh my— Zack!" Sam was behind Ben, blocking out what little light there was. He pushed Ben to one side. "Get Ruth. I'm taking him to the pharmacy."

Sam crouched and placed his arms beneath his brother. Zack grunted. That was good, wasn't it? At least he was making sounds.

Sam groaned and lifted Zack, hauling him onto his shoulder. Jess stared at him, her chest full of ice.

Sam started towards the pharmacy. His steps were slow and uneven, but he wasn't going to drop Zack. Jess could be sure of that. She threw her hands over her face and peered through her fingers, as if blocking it out could make it go away, could undo the last few minutes.

"You OK, sis?"

She nodded. "Ruth," she croaked.

"Yes. Course." Ben put a hand on her shoulder. "Are you OK to get to the pharmacy? I'm sure I can find someone..."

She shook her head, her eyes closed. "No. Yes. Just go. Get Ruth. I'll make it."

Ben squeezed her shoulder and ran off towards his house.

Jess pulled herself up to standing, ignoring the damp that soaked her jeans. Around her people were running, shouting. She heard a cry. A woman.

Stop it, she whispered. *Just stop it, all of you.*

Sam was out of sight now, the darkness having swallowed him up. She forced herself to take a step forward, swaying as she moved. She had to go with him. Zack needed her.

She clenched her fists, then pummelled them against her thighs. Her mind felt full and empty at the same time, like she was floating in a vacuum.

She wiped her eyes and looked at her fist. It was smeared with blood. She put her fingers on her eyebrow; it stung.

It was nothing.

"Zack! Sam!" she cried, and made for the pharmacy.

17

Ruth ran to the pharmacy, Ben calling after her.

"Stay!" She looked round to see him standing in the doorway. "Stay with the boys!"

When Ben had got home, she'd been lying on the floor between the boys' bed, staring at the blank ceiling. She had no idea how long she'd been there. Ben had almost battered the door down to rouse her.

Ahead of her, shapes loomed out of the darkness. Someone shouted, off to her right. She felt her hair shift as someone ran past. She turned; who was it? But they were gone.

She set her jaw and focused on the route to the pharmacy. It may be dark, with the streets blocked, but she walked this route every day of her life.

The village shop had its door hanging open. She grabbed the doorframe and pulled herself in, preparing herself for what she might find inside.

Jess was in the doorway to the pharmacy, slumped against the doorframe, her body shaking. Ruth put a hand on her arm.

"You OK?"

"I'm fine." Jess wiped her face. Her hand came away bloody.

Jess nodded towards the table in the centre of the space. Sam stood over it, his back to Ruth, blocking her view. Behind him she could see the lower half of Zack's body. The lights were on; someone had made an exception to the energy conservation rules.

"Sam. Excuse me, please."

He turned to face her. His face was pale, streaked with dirt, eyes dark and wide, his pupils huge. He seemed to have lost the six years she'd seen him grow since arriving at the village, despite his bulk.

"Help him," he said.

She nodded. "I will."

Sam shifted to one side, his eyes on Zack. She slid past him to inspect her patient.

Zack's feet hung over the edge of the table closest to her. He wore jeans and a heavy coat. Blood soaked the collar of the coat and covered his neck. His face was pale and his eyes closed.

She felt her stomach shift. She stared at his neck, at the blood. It pulsed once, twice. She held her breath.

"We need to get his coat off." Her voice was thin and low.

Sam stepped forward and started taking his brother's coat off. He was gentler than she expected.

"Here." She took the sleeve, the one on the opposite side to the wound. Jess stepped in. Together, they managed to remove the coat without disturbing Zack too much. Ruth stared at the fabric of the coat the whole time, not wanting to look at the wound.

The coat dropped to the floor. Jess grabbed Zack's hand.

"I'm here, sweetie. Ruth's here. She's going to make you better."

Ruth turned to stare at Jess, horrified. This was impossible. She turned back to Zack, her stomach full of lead.

Zack's eyelids flickered, just slightly. Ruth gulped down the bile that was rising in her throat.

She blinked. Sweat was pouring into her eyes. She wiped the back of her sleeve across her face and muttered to herself: *you can do this*.

She opened her eyes to see Robert Cope in front of her, lying on the table. A knife in his throat, blood pouring onto the kitchen floor.

She heard a whimper.

"Ruth?" Jess's voice was sharp in her ear. She shook her head to banish it.

She squeezed her eyes shut then looked back down, prising her eyes open as slowly as she could. Zack's inert figure lay on the table, his eyes closed. She felt a long breath flicker through her lips.

"Oh thank God," she breathed.

"What? Is he going to be alright?" Jess sounded shocked.

"I don't know."

Ruth kept her eyes on Zack's face. If she looked away again, he would be replaced by Robert. She heard Robert's voice in her ear: *Mrs Dyer*. She shuddered.

"Leave me alone!"

"Ruth? What's going on?"

Jess pulled at Ruth's shoulder. Ruth stared at Zack: she mustn't take her eyes off him. She had to treat him, try and save him. She could do this.

"Sam, grab me a pair of gloves. Up there, on the shelf."

Sam fumbled with the gloves and got them into Ruth's

hand. She put them on blindly, staring at Zack's closed eyes. His face was turning from white to grey.

"Stethoscope," she said, pointing towards the hook where she knew it was hanging. The cold metal landed in her palm and she placed the earpieces in her ears without once taking her eyes off Zack.

She placed the chest piece on his chest, fumbling with the buttons on his shirt. Nothing. She moved the instrument around, desperately searching for a pulse. She raised a hand for silence. Sam was breathing heavily beside her, Jess's breath fluttering in her ear.

The door clattered open. "Zack! Oh my Zachary!"

A tall woman with her hair in a severe ponytail pushed past them and threw herself over Zack. Sam grabbed her.

"Mum, leave him. Let Ruth do her job."

Ruth shook her head. Zack's face looked cold and small now, nothing like the strong face that had so charmed Jess. She heard Jess sob behind her.

"I'm so sorry. There was nothing I could do."

She allowed her eyes to travel away from Zack's face and down to his wound. She should clean it. She couldn't face that.

"I'm sorry," she repeated. She'd taken her eyes off his face; she couldn't risk looking again.

She turned to Jess. Their eyes tore into each other, Jess's searching her own for some sign that she was wrong, that she might change her mind.

She shook her head, the motion frantic, and pushed past Jess and into the shop. She stumbled towards the counter, almost hitting her head on it as she fell to the ground. She leaned around it and vomited onto Pam's clean floor.

18

F og had descended over the village, casting the houses in a dense shroud. Sarah picked her way along the streets, aware of how easy it would be to miss a turning.

The streets were quiet now, with the shouting and yells from earlier having died down. Up ahead, something was on fire. She approached it hesitantly, afraid there might still be people there. It was surrounded by villagers, a chain of people with buckets attempting to put out a fire in the composting bin at the back of the JP. The stench of burning plastic rent the air, making her gag.

She scanned the chain of people for Martin. No sign of him. Was he somewhere else, still fighting? Or had he gone home? Maybe he'd been told to go home, that this wasn't his fight.

She swallowed. When would Martin be made to feel he belonged here?

She'd wanted to stay with Dawn, to spend the night in the cottage she'd made so homely. In the house Dawn had shared with Ted, there had been no adornments. Only the crucifix on the wall. But here, the house was full of objects. Drawings Sarah had done as a young girl, smoothed-over pebbles from the beach, anything that was shiny or beautiful. She no longer had to worry about any of these objects being used as a weapon against her.

Go home to your young man, Dawn had said. *I wouldn't want him getting hurt, for your sake.*

But what about Dawn's sake?

Now she was on the main road which ran from the village centre to the outside world, parallel to the coast. Buildings loomed at her through the mist. She counted them. Theirs – Martin's – was the third block of flats on the left.

The building was still and dark, no candles flickering at the windows. She turned her key in the lock and slipped inside, her ears alert for the sounds of people. Martin might be back, or their neighbours might be inside, listening. She knew the two of them were an object of interest.

She hurried up the stairs, her breath short, and knocked gently on Martin's door. She rubbed her hands together against the cold and waited.

No answer. She tried again, but he wasn't in.

She pulled her keys back out of her pocket. She didn't like letting herself in when he was out, it still felt like trespassing. But she wasn't about to go back to Dawn, not in this fog.

She pushed the door open and blinked as a draught hit her face. They would never have left the window open, not on a night like this.

She crossed to it, muttering in irritation. She reached out for the handle but it was already closed. She froze.

In the middle pane was a jagged hole, not much bigger

than her fist. She stared at it, then walked to it and touched the rough edge with her fingertip.

Had the attackers come this far? Had they been breaking windows? She hadn't seen any evidence of that on any of the other buildings she'd passed.

She stepped back, aware of the crunch of glass beneath her feet. Hundreds of tiny shards littered the carpet. It would be impossible cleaning them all up in the dark. She'd have to warn Martin, tell him to steer clear until the morning.

She stepped backwards, shaking out her feet. Then she saw it. At the edge of the glass, a dark object. She frowned and bent to it. Anxious not to lose her balance.

She picked it up between her fingertips, carefully in case it had glass stuck to it. It was hard, and rectangular. A brick.

A length of string was wrapped around it, and beneath that was a piece of paper.

She almost dropped it in her shock. She glanced up at the door, wondering again where Martin was, if he was safe.

She retreated to the kitchen and placed the brick on the worktop. She reached into a drawer and lit a candle, taking care not to bring it too close to the paper. She unravelled the string and placed it carefully in her pocket. Good string couldn't go to waste.

She glanced at the door again, wishing she'd closed it. Then she unfolded the paper. She squinted to make out the rough black letters in the candlelight.

Leave, or die.

19

Ruth headed for the clifftop, half running, half staggering. Her chest felt like it might burst and her stomach ached. Her legs were weak and a sharp pain worked its way up her body, threatening to overwhelm her.

Her mind was thick with images. Robert's face, in that cell. The bedroom he'd locked her in. The vase of flowers she'd knocked to the floor. Then there were the smells. His aftershave, heavy and cloying. The institutional smell of the cooking in that kitchen. The toilet she'd been forced to sling her waste into, from a bucket.

She collapsed to the ground, not sure if she'd reached the beach or was still on the clifftop. Or was she on the path between the two? She couldn't tell. It wasn't dark now; her eyes were filled with light, green-filtered light like she'd had in that cell with its algae-encrusted window.

She let herself slide to the ground, resting her head on the grass next to the path. The sky was dull, only a few stars visible now. She thought she could remember being brought down here, brought to the boat. Thrown over someone's shoulder: was it Robert's, or Martin's?

That was wrong. She'd woken up in her cell, not knowing where she was or who had taken her. She had remembered nothing from falling asleep in her son's room, to waking up almost two days later.

But she could see it. She could feel the rhythm of his steps beneath her, the sensation of her body shifting as he carried her. She could hear the voices, men muttering to each other. Congratulating each other.

She let out a cry. Was she remembering, or imagining? Was her mind filling in the blanks? And why couldn't she get it to stop?

Above, a star flickered. There was a break in the fog cover, just big enough to make out a patch of clear sky. It felt bright, brighter than the sun, so bright she might burn.

She rolled over, whimpering into the grass. She shoved her hands into the ground and pushed herself up. She didn't know why, but she had to get to the sea.

She stumbled down the path, not stopping until her feet were slowed by sand. The fog had thickened now and she could see nothing; not the stars, not the sea, not the waves that lashed at her feet.

They'd brought her here, and taken her. She'd come back this way, after – after...

Robert's head flashed in front of her eyes. The way his eyes had bulged as she'd twisted her foot into his chest. The way the blood had eased its way out of his lips, like he was regurgitating red wine. She felt her insides hollow out. She needed the toilet.

She reached behind a rock and yanked her trousers down. She relieved herself noisily, tears rolling down her face. She pulled her trousers back up, not caring about cleaning herself.

She crawled towards the water. If she went out there, if she went back to the farm, would it all go away? Maybe if she saw for herself, could know for sure that he was dead. She hadn't even seen them bury him.

"Ruth!"

She wailed. Sheila Barker was behind her, her hands looping under Ruth's armpits. She dragged her up, repeating her name.

"Ruth, are you alright?" her neighbour's voice was loud.

"Leave me. Please."

"Ruth, please. I'll take you home. It's not safe out here."

She felt a shudder rip through her body. She turned to see Sheila looking down at her, eyes full of worry.

What was she doing? Why was she here, kneeling at the edge of the sea? She couldn't even swim.

"Oh my God."

"It's alright, Ruth sweetheart. They've gone now."

"What? Who?"

"The attackers. They've gone."

Ruth frowned. "Don't tell Ben."

"Don't tell Ben what, sweetheart?"

"This. About this."

Sheila smiled. "Don't worry. I'll take you home."

20

"What's that?"

Sarah crumpled the note between her fingers and pushed it into the palm of her hand. Her skin was damp and hot. She could feel heat rising to her cheeks.

"A brick. It got thrown through the window. Did you see anything?"

Martin closed the door to the flat behind him. His face was smudged with dirt, his hair dishevelled.

"Are you alright?" Sarah asked. "You didn't get hurt?"

"I'm fine. No one could see who I was in the dark so they let me help."

"How is it?"

"Bad."

"Tell me."

He took a step towards her. "We managed to fight them off, but not without..." his shoulders rose and fell. "Not without casualties."

Sarah thought of her mother, of her pale face as Sarah had run off into the night. She shouldn't have left her.

"Who?"

He put a hand on her shoulder. "Who?" she repeated.

"Zack. He was one of the people who came to the—"

"I know who he is," she snapped. "Sorry."

"Sam's brother," Martin whispered.

Sarah nodded. "How is he?"

"Not good. They took him to the pharmacy."

She nodded again.

"You were reading something," he said.

"What?" She crunched the note even tighter in her hand.

"You had something in your hand. Was it from your mum?"

"No. Why would it be—?"

He put his hand out. "You're pale."

"I'm fine."

"If you don't want to show me, that's fine. I respect your—"

"It's not that."

"What, then?" He pulled a hand through his hair, catching on the knots. He wiped his cheek; a clear patch appeared.

"You need a shower," she said.

"There's not enough water till the morning. I'll have a wash. I tried checking on your mum's cottage, Sarah. But there was no answer."

"I told her not to answer the door."

"When?"

"After you left. I went to see her, remember?"

His brow furrowed. "Yes. Sorry."

She sat down on the sofa, pulling him down next to her. "Was it awful?"

He nodded.

"Are they really gone?"

"For now."

She swallowed the lump that had risen in her throat. As she lifted her hand to wipe her eyes, the note fell onto her lap.

She looked down at it. The word *die* was clearly visible.

"What's that?" Martin asked. "Something about dying." He looked from the note to her face. She closed her eyes. She didn't want him to know about it; but did she have the right to hide it from him? To lie to him?

There'd been enough lies.

She picked it up and unfolded it. She held it out, her fingers loose.

He took it, his eyes not leaving hers. He brushed her face with his fingertips then lowered his gaze to the note.

She watched his eyes travel quickly across the page, then the look of shock register on his face.

"I'm sorry," she said.

"Don't be." He stared at the note. "When?"

"It was here when I got back from Mum's."

He looked behind him at the window. He shrugged off her hand and walked to it. He fingered the edges of the hole as if that would tell him something.

"Wait here." He hurried out of the door and clattered down the stairs. She followed him, lingering in the doorway. Whoever it was might still be out there.

She stumbled down the stairs. "Martin! Come back! What if they're there?"

Outside, he was standing on the grass at the front of the building, staring up at the window. He bent to examine the ground, peering around him. He ruffled through the neatly tended shrubs that separated the grassed area from the road.

"It might not be for you," she said.

"*Leave, or die.* It's not for you."

"You don't know."

"Sarah, you've lived here since the beginning. I've been here six months. It's for me."

"But who?"

He pursed his lips. "I don't know. It could be anyone. It could be one of the women we took."

"Ruth?"

"No. Not Ruth. And she was in the pharmacy, anyway."

"Ben?"

He said nothing.

"You think it was Ben?" she asked. Again he said nothing.

After a few more moments staring up at the window, he shivered. "It can't have been. He's Jess's brother. If he felt that strongly, I wouldn't be here."

"I don't think he and Jess get on."

He shook his head, then looked up and down the road as if expecting someone to appear out of the shadows. "Let's get inside."

She held out her hand and he took it. Together they closed the door and retreated upstairs. They passed the other three flats in the block and she stared at the doors, suspicious. Who was it who hated them this much that they were prepared to send death threats?

In the flat, Martin went to the sink and gulped down a glass of water. He refilled it and emptied it again.

"You're not safe here," he said.

"I'm fine."

He turned and slumped against the sink. "I'm putting you at risk."

"You don't know it was for you."

"Sarah," he cried. "You're being naive. Of course it was for me!"

"Maybe."

"Someone wants me dead. I don't want you getting caught up in it."

"I'm not leaving you alone."

She leaned against him. He gripped the sink behind him, not touching her. His breathing was ragged. "You have to, Sarah."

"I'm not leaving you."

He pushed her off and held her at arm's length. "You know I love you. You know I don't want to push you away. But you can't be hurt because of me, not again. Please, I'll take you to your mum's. You should sleep there."

"You can come too."

"I'm not putting your mum in danger."

Sarah couldn't argue with that. "Let me stay here."

"Please, Sarah. I'll lock the door. I'll barricade the window. But I don't want you here."

"No."

"What if they take it out on your mum? Who's to say she hasn't had a brick through *her* window?"

"I'd know."

"How?"

She felt her stomach tighten. "I would."

"Not in the middle of everything that's been going on tonight. No one would know. Go and check on her, please. Stay with her. We can work out what we're going to do in the morning."

"I don't see what we can do."

He slid down the front of the kitchen units coming to a stop with his legs splayed on the floor in front of him. "I'll think of something. D'you want me to walk with you?"

She thought of her mother, alone in that cottage. Peering through the curtains, watching the fighting outside. Would it remind her of Ted? Would she stand too close to the window?

"I'll go on my own," she said. "I'm not scared of this village."

He stood up. "Please, let me."

"No." She walked to the door, then remembered herself and returned to him. She kissed him on the chin. He bowed his head to return the kiss and they stood there, locked together, for a few seconds. Tears ran down her face.

"I'll see you tomorrow," she said. "Stay safe."

As she left the flat, she didn't turn back. Looking at him again would mean she'd never manage to get out.

21

Jess stared at the deep trench that had been dug before the sun even came up. It ran alongside the one they had dug for Sonia five years ago.

Sonia's grave was covered in lush grass now, wildflowers in a chipped vase at its head. The vase was new; the last one had been lost to the weather. Jess had been meaning to create something more permanent, to plant flowers, but the position on the exposed land to the north of the village meant she'd never been able to persuade anything to grow.

The wind whipped at them today. It tugged at Jess's hair, threatening to pull her off the hillside and over the cliffs. Ahead of her stood Zack's family, opposite the trench. Leah was leaning on her husband Tim, her eyes dry but her body overcome with shaking. Next to her Zack's three younger sisters. Behind them Sam, his face blotched with red and white, a cut which snaked down his right cheek. His clothes were dirty and dishevelled and he looked like he hadn't been home since the previous night.

Jess didn't know where Sam had been when Zack was

stabbed. She didn't know if he'd been close, or if he was off somewhere else fighting another group. She wished they'd been together. They would have protected each other.

She felt something push up from the pit of her stomach into her throat, like a gust of wind or an almighty heave of breath. She turned to the side, expecting to be sick, but nothing came.

Zack's body lay beside the trench, not more than a metre from Jess's feet. He was wrapped in a greying sheet. He looked smaller than he had in life.

She'd stayed with him for as long as she could, hunched over the table in Ruth's pharmacy. No one had seen Ruth since. She'd caught a glimpse of Ben on her way here this morning but he'd been hurrying somewhere and had ignored her when she called out to him.

Clyde stood next to her. He'd helped Tim and Sam carry Zack here, Colin trailing behind. Colin stood a few metres away, a respectful distance. Jess wished he would get closer. They all needed to gather together now, to support each other. Everyone here had suffered loss in one form or another.

She felt her legs weaken, and clenched her feet inside her boots in an effort to keep her balance. She was the steward; she had to maintain control. And the family opposite her had more right to be grieving than she.

They all stared at Zack's body in silence. She wondered what, or who, they were waiting for. Ben? Ruth? The rest of the council?

No. At Sonia's funeral, there'd only been five people. Herself, Ruth and Ben, Clyde who'd dug the grave, and Murray, the steward at the time. He'd conducted the ceremony.

Her head snapped up. They were waiting for her.

She opened her mouth to speak, then felt a wave of nausea. This was impossible. Just twelve hours ago, she'd been laughing with Zack. He'd told her a funny story about something Sam had said to him about weasels. She felt her eyes well up.

She looked at Colin. He was staring down at his feet, his face pale.

"Colin?"

As the council secretary, he was the next most senior person here.

Colin looked up. "You need me to do the honours?"

She nodded, grateful that he understood.

Colin stepped forward. Leah looked up at him, then at Jess. A dark shadow crossed over her face, then dropped as Sam clutched her elbow.

Colin took a breath. "We are here this morning to bury our son, brother and friend, Zack."

And fiancé, Jess thought. But Colin didn't even know they were engaged. Only his family did. And hers.

Where were her family? Had Ben been hurt, and she didn't even know it?

No. Ben had gone home to watch the boys, when Ruth had been summoned out for Zack.

She turned and scanned the route back to the village, wondering who knew they were here. Should they have told more people, given them the opportunity to come?

But this was how they did things here. There were no undertakers, no coffins, no embalming. Just the elements to take the dead back to the earth. Burials were done quickly so that the body could be safely in the ground and not presenting an infection risk.

Colin was looking at her. Not just Colin: Leah and Tim too. Sam gave her a sad smile over his mother's head.

"Sorry," she said.

Leah shook her head. Sam nodded at Jess. "Are you alright?" he asked.

She felt uncomfortable. She looked at Leah and Tim, their swollen eyes. How would it feel, to lose a child?

"Yes," she muttered. "Sorry. Carry on."

Colin licked his lips. "Zack was a valuable and productive member of the village. He earned funds for his neighbours by going out to work outside our community, and he was always a willing volunteer when we needed someone to undertake a dangerous or difficult task."

Leah sobbed. Jess felt tears wash her cheeks. She listened to Colin's low voice, pierced by Leah's sobs, as he remembered what the man she loved had meant to the rest of them.

22

J ess's feet felt numb as she tried to pick her way across the rutted field. Behind her, a mound of earth marked the spot where the man she had been supposed to marry now lay. Ahead of her, his parents walked, huddled together.

Above them, seagulls wheeled, shrieking at them from a pale blue sky. From time to time their cries would be accompanied by a moan from Leah.

The custom after any ceremony at the village was to go to the JP. Weddings, namings, funerals: all of them were marked by the community coming together afterwards. She hoped more people would be there, that she wouldn't have to face the onslaught of Leah's raw grief alone.

They reached the path back to the village and her feet began to feel secure. Colin caught up with her and fell into step.

"Thanks," she said.

"Of course," he replied.

Colin would be thinking of his brother, who died on the journey here. He, like so many others, hadn't been afforded the dignity of a funeral. At least Sonia had managed to make it here, to spend her last months in peace and warmth. At least she hadn't died violently at the hands of other refugees, or of people reluctant to welcome refugees to their homes.

"Do you think they'll come back?" she said.

"Hmm?"

"The people from last night. They'll be back, I'm sure of it."

Colin sighed. Could she take it, if they were besieged again? Could she stand to sit inside and watch the violence, or – even worse – to go out there and play her part, without Zack next to her?

"I don't know," Colin said.

But he did. They all did. No one was safe anymore.

They rounded the first pair of houses, identical beach houses that had once been designed to provide a touch of New England glamour for holiday makers, but whose wooden frames were now disintegrating. They had never tried to house anyone in these structures; the storms six years ago had battered them, exposing the short-sightedness of the construction company in not making everything out of brick or stone. Suddenly the story of the three little pigs came to mind and she stifled a laugh.

"You alright?" Colin asked.

"Yes. Sorry."

"I know how it can hit you. Sometimes it can feel like your reactions are... inappropriate."

"But I can't be inappropriate in front of his parents."

Colin looked ahead to where the Golder family had disappeared around a corner. "It can't be easy."

"We were getting married."

Colin stopped walking. "That was quick."

"Six months. Not that quick."

"No. I'm so sorry, Jess."

She sniffed, wishing she'd thought to bring a handkerchief. But she'd spent only a few hours at home since the fighting had stopped.

"Thank you."

They rounded the corner where the Golders had disappeared, and almost crashed into them.

Jess grunted. Why hadn't they carried on walking? Why weren't they in the JP?

Then she saw. Up ahead of them, outside the back of the JP. Two police cars, and two others. One long and dark, the other small and blue.

She pushed through the grieving family, ignoring Leah's trembling hand on her shoulder, and called out.

"Not today! You can't be here today!"

She ran towards the cars. She peered inside the first one; it was empty. She ran between them all, pulling on the handles, shouting through the windows. But no one was inside.

She heard a bang behind her. She turned to see the door to Ben and Ruth's house closing. Ben was outside, marching towards her.

"Where were you?" she breathed. "We just buried Zack."

"What are they doing here?" he hissed. "We said no!"

"Have they spoken to you?"

He marched past her and slapped the side of one of the police cars. He turned and looked round the square. Behind her, Colin, Clyde and the Golder family stared. She could sense their breath being drawn in.

"Ben, please. We're in the middle of a funeral."

"Where are you? Why have you come here again?" Ben was ignoring her, pushing her out of the way in his haste to reach the centre of the village. He stared wildly around him as he moved, as if expecting someone to appear in the shadow of the houses.

She followed him. "Did you see them arrive?"

He didn't reply, but carried on walking. She kept pace, her legs heavy.

They passed the JP. Either side of them, people emerged from their front doors, asking questions. Ahead was Sarah Evans. She'd been walking away from them, towards Martin's flat. She looked scared.

"Jess? What's happened?"

"Have you seen any police come past?"

Sarah blanched. "No."

"We're here."

A woman emerged from a side road.

"You! What are you doing here?" Ben ran at her.

"Ben, stop!" Jess called. They couldn't afford to antagonise her.

"Miss Chopra," she said. "What are you doing here? Why so many cars?"

"We've brought you some new residents."

"But we didn't agree."

"We don't need you to agree. Read this."

Anita pulled a grey folder out of her battered brown leather bag. She opened it and pulled a sheet of paper out, handing it to Jess.

Jess scanned it, the words dancing in front of her. *Courts - order - mandatory.*

"I don't get it."

Ben snatched the paper off her and read it. He threw it to the floor.

"It says the council can move residents in and out of the village at any time, if the housing need is sufficiently acute."

"Do you know what they did to us?" Ben yelled. "Have you heard what happened last night?"

"You gave as good as you got, I hear." Anita Chopra had her arms folded across her chest. Jess realised this woman had never been on her side. She'd never intended to negotiate.

"But we've been here six years!" Jess cried. "Surely that counts for something."

"Sorry."

Jess felt her chest hollow out. She took a step towards Anita. The other woman stared back at her, her face calm.

How dare you, Jess thought. Heat rose from her stomach into her chest. She felt sick.

She felt her arm come up, not aware of having decided to lift it. Her fist clenched. She gritted her teeth and thumped Anita, catching her with a glancing blow to the jaw.

Anita stumbled back, her eyes wide. She glared at Jess and clutched her face. Jess stared back at her, her heartbeat deafening in her ears.

"I just buried my fiancé," Jess said. "Surely you could have waited."

23

S arah stared at Jess, her mouth falling open.

Had she really seen the steward punch someone?

The woman was sitting on the grass. A man stood behind her, writing in a notebook. DS Bryce, from Filey police station. She eyed him, hoping he wouldn't start asking questions about Martin.

Jess stood over the woman. Her body was tense, quivering almost. Colin Barker put a hand on her arm.

"Jess?" Sarah whispered. "Are you alright?" Stupid question.

Jess turned to her. Her face was pale and her features hard. "Zack's dead."

"I know." The Golders were standing behind Jess. Sam looked at Sarah, his face soft. His sister was sobbing into her mother's shirt.

Sarah smiled at Leah Golder, who gave her a tight nod.

"I'm so sorry," Sarah said. Holding her voice steady was a struggle. Other people were going through worse than she was.

"What about me?" The woman on the ground was dabbing her chin with a grubby handkerchief. There was blood, but not a lot of it.

The woman stood up. She raised a finger, was about to jab it into Jess's chest. She stopped herself.

"You can't do this. I have every right."

"Don't you know what happened here last night?" Jess replied.

"I imagine you're about to enlighten me."

Ben stepped forward. "People from Filey. They attacked us. My sister's fiancé is dead."

The woman frowned. "What people from Filey?"

DS Bryce cleared his throat. "Are you saying he was murdered?"

"Yes." Leah Golder. Her voice was thin. She put an arm around Jess, who sank into her. "My son. He was going to marry Jess. You robbed us of his future."

"I didn't do anything," the woman said. Sarah knew she was from outside, that she was an authority figure. Jess had talked about her at the village meeting.

"We'll need to speak to witnesses," said DS Bryce. Leah glared at him.

"Bit late for that."

"I was there," Jess said. The woman was fingering her nose. It didn't look broken. Sarah wondered if she should offer to find Ruth.

"What did you see?" asked the detective.

"Nothing," Jess sighed. "It was dark. Chaotic."

"Maybe someone else will have…"

"No one will talk to you," Ben interjected. Jess frowned at him. But he was right. The police; the council; the attackers. They were all the same, as far as the villagers were concerned.

"Do you want to report a crime?" DS Bryce said.

"Yes," said Jess.

"No," said Leah. She looked at Tim, her husband. He nodded agreement.

DS Bryce shook his head. He plunged his notebook back into the inside pocket of his jacket.

"This doesn't change anything," the woman said to Jess. "We're still appropriating those houses. I could report a crime myself. Assault."

Jess stared at her. Her chest was rising and falling; would she do it again?

"But I won't," the woman continued. "Just leave me alone to do my job. Or you'll find yourself under arrest."

24

R uth stared at the sea, letting its ebb and flow fill her mind. She focused on the waves, approaching and receding; the hiss and crash of the water as it hit the rocks to her left. The sea washed over them, splashing her every few seconds. She was wet, and cold.

She didn't care.

She focused on the horizon, trying to drag the memories back, to remember what it had been like to be taken out there. Somehow, if she could remember being taken, if she could recall the trip to the farm on the tiny village boat, she would feel better. She had to know that there was nothing she could have done, that she didn't bring it all on herself.

But her mind was blank. From the moment she'd lain down on the boys' floor, to walking up in that cell, there was nothing.

Every time she closed her eyes, she saw his face. Robert Cope, smiling at her. Threatening her. Touching her. *Mrs Dyer*, he'd called her, as if her marriage was more important than she was. To him, it turned out, it was. If it hadn't been for Ben, for that stupid thing he'd done as a teenager, none of this would have happened. He'd told Ruth nothing about it, not until the confrontation in the farmhouse kitchen, when Robert had accused him.

Ruth had to believe Ben had told the truth. She had to believe he'd never meant to kill that man, that it had been an accident, and really Robert's fault. Of course it was Robert's fault; he was the type. But it was Ben who had struck the fatal blow. Ben who had followed Robert blindly like he had no mind of his own. Ben who'd lied to the police.

She stared at the grey water, willing the images out of her mind. She'd woken this morning to find a spray of wild flowers on the kitchen table. Had she put them there, or had Ben? An image of the cornflowers Robert had picked for her sprang to mind, falling to the floor as she'd thrown them off the mantelpiece in his bedroom.

Then there was the feel of fabric against her skin. Everything she wore was the shirt he'd made her wear. The stiff white cotton, neatly pressed and tighter than a straightjacket around her.

She drew her lower lip into her mouth and bit down, hard. The pain helped to bring her back to the here and now. Maybe she should find something sharp, something she could hurt herself with, to remember where she was. That would be something Robert hadn't done to her, a new sensation.

Still biting down, she pushed herself up to standing. Her boys had been asleep when she'd left the house. Ben was out somewhere; he'd rushed out when she was sitting at the kitchen table trying to keep her breakfast down. She'd sat in the silence of the house for one hour, maybe two, not moving, hardly daring to breathe. The day was still young; she'd woken just as dawn was sending its tendrils around the bedroom curtains. Unable to lie next to Ben and listen to him breathing, she'd crept downstairs, and felt herself slump when he'd come down right after her.

Eventually, she couldn't take it anymore. She'd stood up and walked out of the house without even taking her coat off the peg. It had started to rain: a hard, cold rain that seemed to bite her through the skin. She didn't care. The cold was good, it reminded her she was alive.

But her boys had been alone for over an hour now. She had to go back. She pulled in a breath. The thought of going through the motions, of making their breakfast, sending them off to school, of going to the pharmacy, filled her with lead.

The pharmacy. She couldn't go back there. She couldn't even remember if she'd returned to clean up after Zack's death. She'd rushed out, unable to contain herself, desperate not to intrude on the Golders' grief. If she hadn't, would someone else have cleaned up? Jess, maybe?

People would understand if she didn't go in to work today. But then, they'd need her. Zack wouldn't be the only one injured. They might be waiting for her already, lining up in the shop under Pam's hard stare.

She had to do it. Duty could pull her through the day. And her love for her children.

She dragged her feet though the sand – was she still wearing slippers? – and headed for the village. She could do this.

At the top of the cliff path, she slowed. She couldn't bear for anyone to see her like this.

The roads were quiet, the rain sending everyone indoors. The houses were dark, people inside not looking through their windows she hoped. Nevertheless, she kept to the shadows.

"Ruth?"

She looked up to see a woman approaching her. She took a step back, horrified.

"Ruth are you alright? It's just me, Sheila. I'm with Benji, he needed the toilet."

Ruth heard the snuffling of Sheila's dog in the undergrowth. She withdrew from it, scared of the dog suddenly coming at her.

She said nothing.

"I'm on my way home, if you'd like to walk with me," Sheila said. She was wearing a long raincoat and a hat. She didn't comment on Ruth's attire. This wasn't the first time they'd met out here; was Sheila watching her?

Ruth couldn't refuse. Sheila lived right next door, with her husband Colin. If she told the other woman she wasn't heading home, then Sheila would want to know where she was going. And why she was soaked through.

"Thanks," she muttered. She fell into step with Sheila, who talked to her dog as they walked and didn't ask questions. Ruth shivered as she trudged towards the houses, every muscle in her body on edge.

They came to her house first and Sheila stopped, grabbing the dog by the scruff of the neck. He was a small dog, a mongrel she'd found lost on the cliffs just over a year ago. He was tubby and spoiled, the darling of the children Sheila taught.

"Thanks," whispered Ruth. She scuttled towards her front door, not looking back.

She clattered through the door and shook herself off. *Please, let the boys be safe upstairs*, she thought.

She froze. The boys were sitting at the kitchen table, Ben between them. Ollie sniffed out a sob when he saw her and Sean pushed his chair back and started to approach her.

"No," said Ben. He put a hand on his son's arm. Sean's face crumpled and he sat down in his chair.

"Finish your breakfast for Daddy."

Sean nodded and picked up his fork. Eggs and bread. Was that what she would have given them, if she'd been here?

Ben sidled towards her. "What were you thinking?" he hissed.

"I wasn't long. I needed some air."

"I got back here and found them alone. Anything could have happened to them."

"You weren't here either."

"I left them with you. Not alone."

She ran her tongue across her lips; they were calloused. "You ran out without saying anything. I was looking for you."

"I was with Jess. Zack's funeral."

She felt herself crumple. "I'm sorry."

She pushed down the wave of emotion rising from her stomach. She wanted to lash out at Ben, to pummel his chest until he bled. She wanted to shout at her boys, to demand why they hadn't covered for her.

How could she think about her family like this? Her family, who loved her?

She met Ben's gaze, unable to think of anything to say. After a few long moments, she felt a whimper escape her lips.

She couldn't let them see how she was feeling. She couldn't let it go.

She ran up the stairs and slammed the bedroom door behind her, throwing herself onto the bed.

25

"We can't take them."

"We don't have much choice, Ben."

Jess pushed her fingertips into her forehead, fighting off a headache. She'd convened a meeting of the village council, to discuss how they were going to respond to the actions of Anita Chopra. Not to mention the attack last night. She wondered how many of them had been talking about her punching Anita. There had been more than one muttered *well done* or *you told her* when they arrived.

"Come on," said Toni. "Let's not argue among ourselves. We have to work out a plan. Where are the people who've been evicted going to live?"

Ben turned to Jess, facing away from Toni. "They go back to their homes."

"And then what happens to the families they've put in those houses?" Jess asked.

"Not our problem."

Jess sat back in her chair. She didn't need this. She hadn't even had a chance to speak to Leah Golder.

"Look," she sighed. "I'm in that big house that used to be Dawn's." She ignored Dawn's blushes. "It's just me, with three bedrooms. I'll move out, and they can have my house."

"But where will you live?" asked Dawn. She looked agitated, as if expecting to be sent back to the house where she'd suffered Ted's cruelty.

Jess turned to her brother. "Ben?"

He frowned and scrunched up his mouth. "If you leave your house, you're just saying they've won."

"I know, Ben. And I don't want them to kick us out of our homes any more than you do. But there are nine people currently sitting in the JP surrounded by all their belongings. They need a place to go."

"You can come in with me," said Toni.

"Really?"

"Yes. I've got one of the flats. It's only one bedroom, but I'll take the sofa."

"No, I will."

"Whatever."

Jess considered. Ben and Ruth had a spare room. But they also had a house with two young boys in, that felt a lot fuller than it really was. Toni was out most of the time, and wouldn't expect much of her.

"OK. Thanks, Toni. I'll go and tell them."

"Wait," said Colin.

Jess wanted to sleep. She wanted to lie down on her bed – or Toni's sofa, it seemed – and remember Zack. She wanted to process her guilt about not conceding to Anita Chopra's demands. If she had, the attack would never have happened.

"What?" she replied. Colin glared at her. "Sorry, Colin. Is there something else?"

"The attack. Who's to say it won't happen again tonight? We need to agree how we're going to defend ourselves."

"I think we'll be safe," said Dawn.

"What makes you think that?" snapped Ben. Jess shot him a look.

Dawn sniffed. "They've won, haven't they? When someone thinks they've won, there's not much point in attacking again."

The room fell silent, no doubt each person processing their own understanding of Dawn's experience with aggressive behaviour.

"We can't assume that, though," Colin said. "We need to be ready."

"Too right," muttered Ben.

Jess looked past him and out of the window. It was growing dark, the April evening descending. They shouldn't stay here any longer than they needed to.

"Any suggestions?" she asked.

"Quite a few people have weapons," suggested Clyde.

Jess shook her head. "That's not the answer. We need to keep our people safe, not let things escalate. I saw what happened last night. I saw how useful our so-called weapons were."

Clyde dipped his head. "Sorry, I didn't mean to..."

"It's alright."

"We have to defend ourselves," said Ben.

"No, Ben," said Jess. "We have to keep our people safe."

He glared at her. "How about we use those newcomers as human shields?"

"Ben! You don't mean that."

"If they think they might be attacking their own, maybe they'll be put off."

"That's barbaric. I'll pretend you didn't say it."

She looked round the others. Dawn was staring at Ben, her cheeks pale. Dawn's only prior contact with Ben was when he had fallen apart after Ruth's disappearance. She was used to men like Ted. Bitter, aggressive men. Maybe that was what Ben was turning into.

Jess shook herself out. Ben was no Ted. She saw him with his sons every day. He loved them more than she'd ever seen a man love anyone.

"I suggest we batten down the hatches," she said.

"I agree," said Toni.

"You think that'll work?" asked Colin.

"I don't know what will and won't work," Jess replied. "But these houses are solidly built. And they have had a small victory. I don't think they'll be as desperate this time. We should tell everyone to stay safe, to stay indoors."

"We need to post guards, at least," said Sanjeev. Ben threw him a nod. Jess looked between Sanjeev and Toni. Each of she and Ben had their own ally on this council; why did it all have to be so confrontational?

"OK. Any volunteers?" If she was giving up her house, she wasn't about to give up her night as well.

"I'll go," said Toni. "Give you some space."

"Thanks. Anyone else?"

"Me," said Sanjeev.

"Don't you need to stay with Navi?"

"My brother is eighteen now. He can take care of himself."

Jess thought of Sanjeev and his brother, who also lived in one of the large houses on the clifftop. Maybe they should volunteer to share, as well.

She wasn't about to start forcing people out of their homes. Sanjeev's parents and sister had died in a fire after the floods; they'd suffered enough.

"OK," she sighed. "But two people isn't enough."

"I'm pretty sure Martin will do it," suggested Dawn.

"Martin?"

"He wants to prove himself."

"Makes sense. Anyone else?" She looked at Ben.

"I'll go," said Clyde. He threw Jess a smile that reminded her of the way he used to flirt with her, before she'd grown close to Zack.

"Thanks." She stood up. "Right, it'll be getting dark soon, and we've got things to do. You all know the cascade system. I'll cover my share. Just make sure everyone knows to stay indoors, and bolt their doors. OK?"

26

The school had been quiet today. All but five of the children had been kept home by their parents, scared after the attacks of the previous night.

But Sheila had insisted that they owed it to those children who had turned up to provide them with a semblance of normality. She'd tasked Sarah with running a history lesson. Sarah had forced herself through it, impatient for the day to end so she could talk to Martin.

Coming out of the village hall after tidying up, she saw Dawn going past with a group of council members. Toni, Sanjeev and Clyde, people Dawn had never spoken to until six months ago. Now they were her friends. Sarah felt a rush of pride.

"Mum!"

Dawn paused in her conversation. She put a hand on Toni's arm and said something to her, then hurried across the damp grass to her daughter.

"Hello, love. Everything alright?"

Sarah hadn't told Dawn about the note. She'd explained her agitation by saying that she and Martin had had an argument. *Don't worry, love*, Dawn had said. *It's perfectly normal.* After an awkward pause, Dawn had asked if Martin had hurt her. Sarah had bit back the urge to snap that not all men were like that, but managed to keep it inside.

She'd spent a restless night staring at the grey ceiling of her bedroom, listening to her mother's snoring through the wall. She'd never noticed it before. After finally falling asleep at three am, she'd slept late and had to rush straight to the school when she woke. So she hadn't seen Martin since he'd told her to leave.

"I'm fine," she said. "Have you been at a council meeting?"

"We needed to agree what to do about the new people."

"What new people?"

"You haven't heard? They've forced us to take in some people from Filey."

"They're here already?"

"They got two of the cottages next to the Meadows. The Argyrises and Snellings were forced out, told they weren't using their homes to full capacity."

Sarah frowned. "Where will they go?"

"Jess is going to move out."

Sarah felt a shiver run down her back. "Where will...?"

"Toni's."

"Right." Sarah barely knew Toni. She'd gone south with Jess to rescue her and the others, but her focus had been on Roisin Murray, not Sarah. "I need to speak to Martin," she said. "Will you be alright without me tonight?"

"They're imposing a curfew."

"A what?"

"We're all to stay indoors once it gets dark. Apart from the people who'll be keeping guard. I thought Martin might volunteer."

"You did?"

"He's always saying how he wants to play his part. Helping to protect us is a good way to do that, don't you think?"

Sarah thought of the note. *Leave, or die.* Could helping to guard the village convince them that Martin belonged here now?

"I'll tell him."

"Thanks. He's to assemble at the JP, as soon as it's dark. Which will be soon. You come straight home after you've seen him, yes?"

Sarah looked into her mother's eyes. They were pale, and hooded. Was she scared?

"Of course."

The two of them hurried towards Dawn's house. The sky was showing the first signs of dusk. Sarah insisted on walking Dawn home and when she'd heard her mother bolt the door behind her, she went to Martin's flat.

The outside door was locked. That was unusual, but then these were unusual times. She supposed one of the neighbours had learned about the curfew. She fished in the pocket of her skirt for her key and slid the door open as quietly as she could, making sure to lock it behind her.

At the top of the stairs, Martin's door was open. He was hunched over, scrubbing the floor just inside the doorway.

"What are you doing?" she asked.

He looked up. His hair was greasy and he looked like he'd barely slept. He wore a pair of pink rubber gloves; she had no idea where they'd come from.

"What does it look like I'm doing?"

"OK." Why was he being so tetchy? "Are you scrubbing the floor?"

He blinked at her then returned to his task, his hair bobbing as he moved.

"You're scrubbing the floor, at nine o'clock at night."

He didn't look up. "Yes."

She felt cold. She looked at the carpet beneath him. It was shaded by his body. "Why?"

He stopped scrubbing. After a moment's hesitation, he looked up at her. His face was pale.

"Because someone thought it would be fun to post a pile of shit through my letterbox."

27

J ess stared at the row of cottages. Four of them huddled into each other, their backs to the Meadows, the field to the south of the village which would have been for walking dogs back when this was a holiday village. Now, it was a wasteland. To one edge sat the rubbish dump for the village, and at the other was the pit into which they dug any rubbish that couldn't be reused or recycled. They'd learned to be creative with their waste: having no access to the disposable conveniences of the world before the floods had concentrated minds, and now the amount of waste that went into that pit each month was less than she had thrown out in just one bin bag every week.

The two houses closest had been appropriated for the newcomers. She had no idea why Anita Chopra had chosen these: perhaps there was some logic behind it, perhaps it was random. These certainly weren't the only houses the authorities would deem under-occupied. There was her own for starters, now the home of the two couples who'd been turfed out of these two houses, and plenty of other two-bedroom cottages with only two adults living in them. The flats had one bedroom but there were only sixteen of those in total. Holidaymakers liked large houses, with light and space and sea views.

If Anita Chopra was planning on continuing with her quest to rehome all the people affected by that explosion, they'd all be doubling up. It would be like the journey here all over again. Like the spell they had spent in Leeds at her Aunt Liz's house. Six adults in one two-bedroom flat. No wonder Liz and her wife Val hadn't complained too much when they said they were heading north.

Standing here would do no one any good. They were probably watching her from behind the mesh curtains that adorned the windows of the two cottages. Or if they weren't, their neighbours beyond would be. Watching her, discussing the way she'd betrayed them all.

She walked to the first door and knocked on it, trying to project confidence. She heard movement behind the door.

"Who is it?"

"My name's Jess. I'm the village steward. I've come to welcome you, help you settle in."

There was muttering behind the wood. She tried to remember which of the two families had been given this house: was it the Asian family with their three kids, or the white couple and their hulking teenage sons? She wondered if those boys would be prepared to go to the earthworks with the other lads and earn money for their new community.

The thought of it made her think of Zack. She fought down a wave of emotion and focused on the door knocker. It was brass, and shaped like a lion. Dark patches of dirt surrounded it.

"Hello?" she called, standing closer to the door. She didn't want the neighbours listening in.

"We don't need settling in, thanks."

"I just want to help you feel more at home in your new house."

"We won't be staying for long. You can leave us now."

"I don't want to intrude."

"You already are."

More muttering.

"One question."

"Go on," she said.

"The electricity isn't working."

She frowned. From what she'd been told, electricity was rationed in Filey as much as it was here. Maybe that was a lie, designed to keep the villagers from wanting to move there.

"It only works for an hour a day. The first hour after sunset."

"How am I supposed to know when that is?"

She looked at the sky. It was darkening, the pale white clouds turning grey at the edges.

"It should be in the next fifteen minutes or so."

"What time?"

"I don't have a watch. Sorry."

"How do you know?"

"I just do. You learn. Can you let me in?"

"No. Leave us alone."

She stared at the door for a moment longer, aware that the person – woman? – she'd been speaking to would be watching her through the peephole. Then she nodded and gave a small, awkward wave.

"OK. You can find me in the first block of flats on the

Parade. Or I'm normally out and about around the village. Ask anyone for Jess, they can usually find me."

"That won't be necessary."

She resisted the urge to pull a face at the door. "OK. Well, I hope you have a pleasant evening."

No response. She backed up the path and went to the next door.

This time, it was opened immediately. A plump woman in a headscarf stood in the doorway, one child in her arms and another leaning against her leg. She gave Jess a nervous smile.

"You're the steward."

"Yes. How did you know?"

The woman looked towards the house Jess had been outside before. "They don't like us."

"Sorry?"

"It's just us, and them, and all you lot. But they hate us just as much as you do."

"We don't hate you. Whatever made you—"

The woman shook her head. "Who lived here before?"

"Mary and Hugo Snelling. They're an elderly couple."

"And now they're homeless, because of us. Of course you hate us."

"They aren't homeless. They're living in my house now."

"So where are you?"

"With a friend."

Why was she telling the woman all this?

"Look," she said. "This village took us all in after the floods. That's what happens here. You'll be made to feel welcome, once things have died down."

A man appeared behind the woman.

"Aabida. I told you not to answer the door."

The woman turned to her husband. "She's friendly enough."

"How do you know she's genuine?"

Jess extended a hand. "I'm sorry. They didn't tell me your names. I'll Jess Dyer. You are...?"

"Mohammed Bagri," replied the man. "This is my wife, Aabida."

Jess gave him a smile. He didn't drop his frown. "Pleased to meet you. I'm the village steward. If you have any questions or concerns, please come and find me. Or if anyone behaves inappropriately towards you."

"You're trying to tell me you'd take our side, over that of your own people?" the man said.

"It's not like that."

He grunted. He tapped his wife on the shoulder and ushered her back into the house.

"We'll be keeping our doors locked tonight," he said. "We didn't ask to be sent here."

Jess nodded. Keeping their doors locked was a good idea; the rest of the village would be doing the same thing. "You don't know if anyone from Filey is planning to come here tonight, do you?"

"We had nothing to do with that."

"I'm not saying you did. But if you heard anything, you'd tell me, I hope. Your family would be just as much at risk as anyone else."

Another grunt. "Unless we daub our house in blood. Like the Jews at Passover."

Jess had no idea what he was talking about. "Please don't daub your house in anything. Just stay inside. You'll have electricity for an hour, starting very soon. Have you been given your food rations?"

"If you call this stuff food."

"It's the best we can do. You'll get used to it."

He sighed. "I guess we'll have to."

She nodded again. "Anyway. I need to get home, before it's dark. Don't forget, if you need anything, ask for Jess.

He closed the door without saying anything. Biting down her anger, she turned and made for Toni's flat.

28

"You have to report it," said Sarah.

"There's no point."

She stared at the dark patch on the doormat where he had cleaned it up. The smell was in her nostrils, sharp and hard. It felt as if it would never leave the flat.

"Who do you think it was?" she asked.

"Same person who threw that brick through the window."

She looked towards the window. He'd patched it up with a piece of rough wood while she'd been at the school. It didn't look as if it would withstand much.

"I hope so."

"Why?"

"Because if it isn't, that means there's two people victimising you."

"It could be anyone," he said. "They all want rid of me."

"No they don't. Stop talking like that."

He stared at her. "I'm putting you at risk."

When he'd first said this, it had been endearing. It had shown how much he cared about her. But now, she was beginning to tire of his paranoia. If her mother had integrated herself into the community after all they'd been through, why couldn't Martin?

"Stop saying that. We just need to go to the council, that's all. Find out who it was, and make sure they're punished."

"You think they will be? How can you be sure it isn't someone off the council?" He twisted his lips into a sneer. "Ben, for one, hates me."

She said nothing; Ben would take longer than most to accept Martin's presence here. After all, Martin had accepted the man's hospitality and then stolen his wife away in the middle of the night.

"Look," she said. "Let's lock the door tonight. Cover up the letterbox. We can deal with this in the morning."

"I can't stand to keep the windows closed. It stinks."

"It stinks of vinegar more than anything."

"I can still smell it."

"I know. I can too." She looked at the dark patch again, and shuddered. Who would do such a thing? And was it human excrement, or from an animal? The village kept pigs, but it hadn't smelt like it came from them.

"We haven't got much choice," she said, trying to breathe through her mouth. "I'll go and see Mum, see if she can help."

"I don't want her to know."

"She's part of the council."

"I know." His brow was creased. "But it's so humiliating."

She wrapped her arms around him. "I know. I'm sorry."

They stood like that for a while. She tried to ignore the smell that engulfed the flat, but it was impossible. She had to tell someone. He couldn't let them treat him like this.

"Look," she said. "I told Mum I'd spend some time with her tonight. I won't be long."

"OK." He glanced towards the door. "Don't tell her about this. Not yet."

"She might be able to help."

"I just want to keep it private."

"Martin—"

"Please?"

She sighed. "Alright. Not tonight. But you can't keep this secret forever. What if they hurt you?"

He said nothing.

"You need to accept help." She put a hand on his arm. It was stiff.

"I'll lock the door. You go to your mum."

"I'll be back soon. Before lights-out."

"Be careful. Please."

"Sure." She kissed him on the cheek, then let him pull her to him and fold her in a hug. His body was tense, and he smelled of vinegar.

She was careful to avoid the damp patch as she left, and crept down the stairs. There was a chance that one of their neighbours had done this.

She hesitated at the bottom of the stairs. Maybe she could sit outside, watch them? If anything else arrived at their flat and no one entered or left, then she would know it was one of them. Or she might see them.

No. Nothing else would happen tonight. They'd made their point.

She needed help. She understood why Martin wanted to keep this quiet, why he didn't want to draw attention to himself, but she knew there was one person she could trust.

She ran to her old house, where Jess lived now. The house looked as forbidding as it always had; Jess's presence hadn't affected the way it looked from the outside. She didn't know what she'd been expecting; Jess was too busy to change the house. But somehow she was disappointed that as she walked up the path, she felt like she was coming home instead of visiting the home of a friend, the familiar dread rising in her chest.

She knocked on the door and a young woman she didn't recognise opened it.

"Yes?" The woman looked tired. Her hands were damp and she wore a threadbare apron Sarah recognised as Dawn's.

"Oh. Is Jess here?"

"She moved out." The woman wiped her hands on the apron. "Just until we get our place back. You looking for her?"

"I don't understand." She didn't know why, but the idea of strangers moving into this house annoyed her somehow.

"They kicked us out of our cottage." *Of course*, thought Sarah. Dawn had told her; she hadn't expected it to be so quick. "Me and George," the woman continued, "and the Snellings too. Jess said this place was big enough for all of us. It is, too. Want to come in? I'll give you the tour."

Sarah felt her skin prickle. Did this woman not know that she had lived here until six months ago? Had she been that anonymous?

"I just need to find Jess."

"She said if anyone came looking for her, she'd be at Toni's."

All Sarah knew was that Toni lived in one of the flats. "Do you know where that is?"

"Hang on." The woman disappeared then returned with a slip of paper. She grinned at Sarah. "I know. Colin gave it to me. I haven't used paper in years. Anyway, it says thirty-six on here. So I guess that's the number of the flat. Does that help?"

Not much, thought Sarah. But she smiled and thanked the woman anyway.

Flat thirty-six was in the block next to Martin's. She approached it carefully, not wanting Martin to see her. It had turned dark now, and lights shone from the windows of the ground floor flat. She examined the numbers on the front of the building, and compared them to the numbers on Martin's in her head. By her reckoning, the flat with the lights on would be Toni's.

She pushed the outer door. It was locked. She felt herself deflate. Of course it was locked; they were all subject to curfew in about thirty minutes. She tried the doorbell, but knew it would long since have stopped working. Then she rapped on the wood. She waited. No one came.

She went to the edge of the illuminated window to her right. If there was someone inside, they might not react kindly to her face appearing at their window. But she had no choice. She peered round, hoping the growing darkness would give her some camouflage.

Toni was in the kitchenette beyond the living room, washing dishes. Jess was nowhere to be seen.

She pulled back, disappointed. Jess was probably out somewhere, doing steward work. Maybe if she went looking around the village...

That was pointless. This village was a warren of roads and alleyways. She'd never find her.

"Sarah?"

She opened her eyes to see Jess standing at the door next to her.

"Are you looking for me?"

She nodded, aware that she was blushing. "Sorry."

"Don't be." Jess glanced towards the lit window. "Walk with me."

They started towards the allotments. Jess walked fast and Sarah struggled to keep up.

"Everything OK?" asked Jess.

"Yes. I mean no."

Jess didn't break stride. "Go on."

"It's not easy to talk about."

"You can tell me anything, you know." Jess slowed momentarily, and looked at Sarah. Then she picked up the pace again. Her voice was low, as was Sarah's. Sarah was relieved that Jess no more wanted them to be overhead than she did.

"Is your mum OK?" Jess asked.

"It's not my mum."

They were at the allotment. Jess led her to a bench at its edge. Clay pots stood in a precarious pile at its feet. The bench had been patched up a few times over the years, and the wood of its back didn't match its base. Sarah lowered herself onto it. She scanned the allotment, hoping no one was around.

"They'll all have gone home," said Jess. "Don't worry."

"Right."

"So are you going to tell me what's going on? I assume this is related to Martin?"

Jess was smiling, her voice encouraging. Sarah stared back at her: what was the steward expecting her to tell her?

"You can't tell him I told you."

Jess frowned. The life fell from her face. "Why not?"

"Because I told him I wouldn't."

"Is that wise?"

Sarah said nothing. She stared at a bush ahead of them. It overflowed with small yellow flowers.

"Lying to him isn't a good idea. Not with your relationship having the history it does."

Again, Sarah said nothing.

"Sorry. I shouldn't have said that." Jess sighed. "Go on, tell me."

Sarah looked at her friend and mentor. Jess had puffy eyes, and her skin was pale. Her cheeks were clothed with red.

"I'm so sorry about Zack," she blurted.

Jess seemed to shrink, as if Sarah had hit her with a hammer. "Thank you," she muttered. She pulled her shoulders up. "Please, tell me what you need to. It's getting dark."

Sarah took a breath. "He's been getting death threats."

She felt the bench shift as Jess stiffened. "Death threats?"

"A note. And something... unpleasant... posted through the door."

"What kind of unpleasant?"

"Human excrement."

"Seriously?" Jess kneaded her fists into her thighs. "Sarah, I'm so sorry. Do you have any idea who it was?"

"No. It could be anyone."

"What makes you say that?"

"He's not exactly popular."

Jess didn't contradict her. Sarah appreciated that; she hated having to lie to Martin herself, to convince him that he was being accepted. Last night's attack had highlighted how isolated this community was, and she knew that plenty of people saw him as part of the problem.

"When did this happen?" asked Jess.

Sarah told her.

"You weren't at the flat?"

"No. The first time, I was with mum and the second, at

the school."

"Hmmm."

"Do you think he's making it up?" Sarah felt defensive.

"No." Jess shook her head. "No, that's not what I'm saying. But other people might."

Sarah felt cold. She needed to get back to Martin. God only knows what else might have happened while she was away.

"Can you help us?" she asked.

"Of course. That's my job." But Jess didn't sound convinced. "Look, you keep an eye out. See if you spot anyone watching your flat. If you get anything else, tell me."

"Will you ask around, see if you can find who did it?"

"I don't think that'll help."

"Why not?"

Jess raked her hands through her hair, picking at the tangles. "There are two hundred people in this village. Finding the person who did this won't be achieved by asking all of them, and hoping people tell the truth."

Sarah felt bile rise in her throat. "But what if they hurt him? Leave, or die, it said."

"People who do things like that rarely follow through."

"How do you know?"

Jess said nothing. "Come on. Let's get you home." She grabbed Sarah's hand and pulled her up from the bench. "I'll do everything I can. But I can't promise much. Meanwhile, stay vigilant."

"Of course."

"But I really don't think they'll carry through with it. Martin isn't at risk."

Sarah stared at the steward. Jess was always right. She always knew what to do, what was best for Sarah.

But this time, Sarah didn't believe her.

29

S arah made her way back towards Martin's flat. The most direct route was across the Meadows and past the cottages at the southern edge of the village.

She hesitated at the edge of the allotment, peering into the darkness. *Stop it*, she told herself. She could skirt around the edge and be home in a few minutes. The dark didn't matter; she knew her way.

Nevertheless, she went faster than she normally would, hoping the extra speed wouldn't make her more likely to trip on the undergrowth or crash into a tree. Before long, she was at the gap in the hedge that led to the village centre.

She walked quickly but lightly along the middle of the road, not wanting to appear suspicious. If anyone was following her, they would have to show themselves if they wanted to approach.

There was someone up ahead; a man, overweight and balding. He leaned on the wall of a house. Was he smoking? No one smoked here.

She pulled back to watch him, ducking down behind a bush. The door of the house opened. Candlelight spilled out. She could hear voices inside: loud conversation, and someone singing. She wondered which family lived there.

Two people approached the man. One of them brought something out of his pocket and then bent towards the first man's outstretched hand. A second cigarette sparked between them. She held her breath. They must be the newcomers, the people from Filey.

But how many of them were there? A family, Dawn had told her. With teenage sons.

She clenched her fists and forced herself to relax. The three men over there could very well be the father and his sons. She had nothing to worry about.

But she didn't move.

Their voices rose, loud in the still of the night. They were talking over each other, their words indecipherable. They had strong accents she struggled to follow.

The door to the house opened again. Inside were more people: at least four as far as she could tell. She frowned.

One of the people inside gestured towards the smoking men.

"Get back in here!" they hissed. "You don't want them seeing you."

Sarah felt cold sweat trickle down her back. She watched the men withdraw into the house. One of them leaned out of the door and peered up and down the road. Sarah crouched behind the hedge, as still as possible.

The man closed the door. She waited, wondering if they would be watching if she walked past their house. But she knew her way around this village. She ducked behind one of the houses opposite and sped around the back of it, running for Martin's flat.

30

"Just when I thought things might finally calm down around here," said Jess. She was sitting in a threadbare armchair in Toni's flat, sipping strong mint tea.

"I don't think this place ever gets easy," Toni replied. She was on the floor in front of the single log that sufficed for a fire, her arms wrapped around her knees.

"We had six years of peace, before I got lumbered with the steward job."

Toni turned to her. "Is that really how you'd describe it?"

Jess yawned. "OK, maybe not."

"There were attacks before, remember. And it was ages before the authorities left us alone."

"No one died then."

Toni stiffened. "I'm sorry, Jess. That was heartless of me."

Jess sighed. "No. I'm being self-obsessed. You were right."

Toni slid backwards along the pine boards to lean against Jess's legs. The sensation was good; it made Jess feel grounded.

"I can't even mourn him properly."

Toni reached round to rub Jess's calf. "You can here."

"Not like his parents are doing. I missed the wake because of that bloody Anita Chopra. And they won't come near me. It's like I'm tainted."

"None of this is your fault."

There was a knock on the door. Toni flinched and drew away from Jess, inching back towards the fire.

"Come in," she said. Jess wondered who might be visiting this late.

The door inched open – Toni had insisted on not locking it, not until later – and a face appeared in the gap between the door and the frame.

"Tone?" came a whisper.

Toni stood up and threw Jess a nervous smile. "It's Roisin."

She opened the door and ushered the visitor in. Roisin started when she saw Jess. "Oh."

"It's OK, it's only Jess. She's cool." Toni had a hand on Roisin's cheek. She was staring into the other woman's face, her eyes dark. Jess remembered the way she had softened when they got Roisin out of her cell at the farm, traumatised and covered in blood.

Jess sat up straighter. "Hi, Roisin."

"Hi." Roisin looked from her to Toni, her expression puzzled.

"She's staying here for a bit," said Toni. "She gave her big house to the Snellings and the Argyrises."

"Oh. That was kind."

"I rattle around in that big old thing," said Jess. "I was happy to get out."

She thought of the last night she had spent there with Zack. The night before the attack. He'd grilled some fish that he'd brought up from the smokehouse; extra rations, a perk of being one of the people who went out and earned money for the village. It had been burnt and bitter and she'd probably been unappreciative of his efforts. Now she remembered it as a delicacy.

"I'll go out for a bit," Jess said. "Leave you two in peace."

"It's OK, Jess," said Toni. She turned to Roisin. "How long have you got?"

"Mum thinks I've gone to drag Dad back from the JP. If he gets home before I do, I'll be in trouble."

Toni slumped. She'd told Jess about the problems she had gaining the acceptance of Roisin's family, when they were walking south to rescue her. The Murrays looked down on Toni, and kept pushing Roisin in the direction of Zack's cousin, John.

"It's fine," Jess said. "I need some fresh air anyway." And she needed to speak to Ben. After rescuing Ruth, she'd been under the impression she and her brother would be working as a team from now on; it seemed he had other ideas. She needed to bring him into line.

"You sure?" Toni wasn't looking at Jess, but at Roisin. Jess thought of Zack looking at her like that, and a pellet of something hard lodged in her stomach.

She nodded, unable to speak, and pushed past the two women.

Outside, the night was clear. Stars pulsed down from a dark sky, and she could hear the sea in the distance. Toni's flat was further away from the water than her own house, but not as far as the house she'd shared with Sonia, from which they'd very rarely heard the sea. But tonight she could not only hear the sea; she could smell it. Heavy and dank and salty, reminding her of the journey back here with Ruth. Of the rescue mission she'd made with Zack, when he was just another young man from the village.

She shouldn't be out here. The guards would be assembling soon and she had no way of knowing if they'd be enough. They could be invaded at any moment. She'd told the rest of the village to stay indoors, to lock themselves in, but here she was. Strolling down the Parade like it was a sunny afternoon.

Suddenly self-conscious, she slipped into the shadow of the houses to her left, and kept to the shadows as she made her way towards Ruth and Ben's. She hurried across the open space in front of the JP and peered inside the pub. It was empty, probably had been for some time. She could see Clyde inside, polishing the bar in the dark. She considered knocking on the window and giving him a wave but then thought better of it.

She crept past the pub windows and came into view of Ben's house. It stood in a row of almost identical houses, all of them built to the same design but with differences in the surface details. Ben and Ruth's, for example, was painted blue, while her own was clad in local stone. Sanjeev's house, between them, was surfaced in red brick. She wondered if it was built of brick, or if that was just cladding to hide featureless concrete.

As she prepared to step out of the shadow of the pub, she caught movement opposite. Ruth and Ben's door was opening. She pulled back and watched, wondering where Ben was going when there was a curfew on. She'd follow him; maybe she could talk to him more easily if Ruth wasn't in earshot.

But it wasn't her brother. Instead. Ruth slid backwards out of the door, peering into the house as if worried someone might see her. At last she drew away from the door and pulled it gently closed. She glanced up at the window above her and shrank into herself before walking away from Jess, towards the cliff path.

Jess stared at her, wondering if she should follow. Ruth had surprised her, creeping out of her own house like that. Sure, there was the curfew to consider, but it looked as if she was sneaking out behind Ben's back. Why?

Did she owe it to Ruth to go after her and help her, to warn her about the danger of attack? The first wave of invaders had come from the beach last night; who was to say they wouldn't come the same way again?

Or did she owe it to Ben to tell him what she'd seen? If she let Ben know that she'd seen Ruth leaving the house, then they could sort this out between themselves. But she'd already involved herself in their relationship more than she felt comfortable with.

Ruth was out of sight now. She was a grown woman; Jess had no place telling her what to do. She'd be back soon, surely.

She hurried across the road, peering in the direction Ruth had gone, and knocked quietly on the door. She turned the doorknob and pushed. It wasn't locked. Was no one observing this curfew?

She stepped into the dark house and closed the door behind her.

"Ben?"

A muffled sound came from upstairs. She stood at the bottom of the stairs and whispered her brother's name as loudly as she dare.

Ben appeared at the top of the stairs.

"Jess? What the fuck? You gave me a scare."

"Sorry. Your door was open."

"It was what?" He shuffled down the stairs and grabbed a key from its hook.

"Ruth's out there. She might not have her key."

"What?" Ben put his fingertips to his cheeks and pulled the skin down, dragging his eyes into long ovals. "What are you talking about? Ruth's in with the boys. Ollie couldn't sleep."

"I just saw her. She was heading for the beach."

"Don't be daft."

"I wouldn't lie to you."

"Look. She's upstairs. I promise you." He clattered up the stairs and opened a door. There was a pause during which Jess could hear his breath rising, then he slid back down again.

"She's not there."

"No."

"Did you speak to her?"

"She didn't see me."

Ben said nothing. Instead, he stared at Jess, his eyes hooded.

"Has she done this before?"

Ben shrugged. "I'm not sure." He gritted his teeth. "Yes. Yes, she has."

"Don't you think we'd best go after her?"

"What? Oh, yes. Yes, of course."

Jess narrowed her eyes at her brother. What had happened between him and Ruth, that he wasn't immediately hurling himself down to the beach in pursuit of his wife?

"Is everything OK?" she asked.

"It's fine." His voice was terse.

"I'll go, if you want. You stay with your boys."

"No. I need to find her. Can you…?"

"Of course." She smiled. Looking after two five-year-olds

was the last thing she felt like right now, but they were her nephews. And they'd be unlikely to wake. She nodded.

Ben reached for the door. "Thanks."

As he opened the door, something fell against it on the other side. He yanked it open.

"Ruth?"

A woman was leaning against the door, her head bowed. She had shoulder-length blonde hair and she was slight. It wasn't Ruth.

"What?" exclaimed Ben.

The woman looked up. It was Sally Angus. One of the women who'd been kidnapped with Ruth.

"Sally," said Jess. "You should be indoors. There's a curfew."

Sally's nostrils were flaring. Her cheeks were flushed, and she was missing a shoe. "You have to come quickly," she panted.

"Can't this wait until the morning?"

"No. You have to come now. And Ruth. Mark needs her."

"Mark?" Mark was Sally's fiancé. An annoying, wheedling man who they'd stopped from coming along on the rescue mission. "Have they come back?" Jess felt a fist clutch at her chest. "Is it happening again?"

Sally shook her head. "No. It's that Martin. He's attacked my Mark."

31

J ess stared at Sally.

"What?"

"You heard me. He attacked him. Mark's face is a state. He'll get infected if Ruth doesn't help him."

Ben's voice was low. "I told you he was trouble."

As Jess recalled, Ben had done no such thing. She gave him a warning look then turned to Sally. "Did you see this attack?"

Sally straightened her shoulders. "Yes. It was when Mark was coming home from the shop. He'd picked up our rations, ready for the curfew. Then he was walking across the grass outside our house and Martin jumped out at him. He covered him in scratches." She wrinkled her nose. "He fights like a woman."

"You're sure it was Martin?"

"Of course I'm bloody sure. What are you accusing me of?"

"I'm not accusing you of anything. But *you* are. You're accusing Martin of a serious offence. If he really attacked another villager..."

"What do you mean, *if he really attacked a villager*? Are you saying I'm lying?"

Jess stared up at the ceiling for a moment, pulling together all of her strength. She looked at Ben. She wanted to urge him to go after Ruth, but she didn't want Sally to know what was going on.

"Sally. There's a curfew on, like you just said. I think it's best if you stay here for now, keep indoors. We can sort this out in the morning."

"I'm not staying here." Sally gave Ben a look of disgust, as if she might catch a communicable disease if she took shelter in his house.

"I'll stay too," said Jess.

"Mark needs me. He needs you to talk to him. To hear what happened. Every minute that Martin stays here is a minute we're all at risk."

Jess stared at Sally. Did she really think like this? Then it occurred to her how little effort she'd taken to talk to Sally after the kidnappings, to find out how she was recovering.

But still.

"It's not as simple as that," she said.

"He attacked my husband."

"I'd need to hear both sides of the story."

"It's not a story."

Jess looked at Ben. He was staring at Sally, his jaw firm. "It'd be easier if we just kicked him out," he said.

"No," said Jess. "He faces the same justice as anyone else. We need to find out the truth, and then we can decide if there's punishment to be meted out."

"Oh, this is ridiculous," snapped Sally. "I'm going to tell him what we think of him."

She turned and started running away from the house.

"Sally, no!" Jess called.

"I have to go after her," she told Ben.

"What about Ruth?"

She let out a long, shaky breath. "I'll see if I can find her, after I've stopped Sally. If Martin's locked his door, there shouldn't be any trouble."

"Be quick."

She squeezed his arm. "I'll be as quick as I can," she said, and started running after Sally.

S arah hammered on the door to Martin's flat. It flew open.

"What is it?" Martin's face shifted from fear to irritation. "Oh. Didn't you have your key?"

"It's not that. It's the people."

"What people?"

She pushed inside and bolted the door behind her. She was hot, despite the drizzle she'd run through. "From Filey."

He paled. "They're back."

She nodded. "I have to go back to Jess."

"What do you mean, go back?"

She cursed herself. "Nothing. I'll go and tell her."

"You're soaked. I'll go."

A shout came from outside.

"Oi!"

Sarah frowned at Martin, her eyes widening. He'd paled.

"Who is it?" she whispered. "Is it them?"

He put his fingers to his lips and crept to the window, bending over so as not to be seen. He crouched beneath it and lifted his head slowly to see out.

"Who?" she hissed.

He raised a hand behind him. "There's a woman out there."

"Martin! Get out here now!"

"Is it the attackers? Oh God, they saw me."

"They would hardly know my name," said Martin.

She felt her stomach dip. He was right. It had to be the same person who'd left them the note, and the 'present'.

She followed him to the window and looked out, not bothering to hide.

"Sarah! Get down."

"It's only Sally Angus. What's she doing here?'

"Your bloke attacked my husband!"

Sarah frowned down at the other woman. Sally had been on the other side of the wall, in the farmhouse. She had no recollection of a wedding.

"What are you on about?"

"What's all that shouting?" A man's voice this time, from directly beneath them. Keith, who lived in the flat below.

"Your neighbour's a monster!" Sally cried.

"Go away," came the reply. "Get indoors."

Martin was at Sarah's side now, the two of them looking out at Sally.

"Have you seen Mark Palfrey today?" she whispered.

"I don't even know who Mark Palfrey is."

She pointed at Sally. "Do you remember her? She was at the farm."

Martin nodded.

"Mark is her fiancé. Husband, if you believe what she's saying."

"I've never set eyes on the man."

She eyed him. Martin had no reason to lie. If he said he didn't know who Mark Palfrey was, then that was the truth.

"Sally, go home!" she called. "You need to get indoors. Martin doesn't know what you're talking about."

"You can't fob me off like that."

Sally disappeared. Sarah heard thumping on the door downstairs, the outside door to their block. She grimaced, thinking of Keith downstairs. "Why won't she just go away?"

"Maybe if I speak to her, she will," Martin said.

"I don't think that's wise."

"We can't have her out there disturbing the neighbours all night. And what if it kicks off again? She won't be safe."

"Leave it. You have to report to the JP anyway. Mum volunteered you to be one of the guards tonight."

But he hadn't heard her. He'd opened the door to the flat and disappeared down the stairs. Sarah followed.

"Stay upstairs," he said, shooing her away. It's safer up there."

"Don't mollycoddle me."

He said nothing, but let her stay close to him as he opened the outer door. Sally was outside, yelling obscenities. Jess was with her now.

"Jess? I was just heading to the JP. Guard duty." Martin sounded shocked, and not a little embarrassed. Sarah thought of their conversation earlier, of the look on Jess's face when she'd mentioned Zack.

"It's not that," Jess said. "Sally says you attacked Mark."

Martin sighed. "I don't even know who Mark is."

"Liar!" Sally screamed. She launched herself at Martin, grabbing the collar of his shirt. Sarah gasped as it tore. Martin stared down at Sally, but did nothing. Sally was tiny; not much more than five feet tall, and slim. If he retaliated, he would hurt her.

"Right," said Jess. "I don't need this, tonight. Martin, Sarah, I want you back indoors. We'l get someone to cover for you, Martin. Sally, I'll take you home. You can show me any injuries Mark might have, but I'm not going to follow this up until the morning."

"That's ridiculous," said Sally. "By the morning, he'll—"

"I wasn't inviting debate," said Jess. "Now, are you coming with me, or not?"

Sally seemed to shrink into herself. Sarah allowed herself a smile at Jess. Not everyone knew what Jess was capable of, but Sarah knew how strong she was. If it hadn't been for Jess, Sarah would have nothing. No family, no boyfriend, no job.

Jess turned to her. She didn't return Sarah's smile. "You two, get indoors. Now."

Sarah pulled Martin inside. She bolted the door then dragged him up to the flat. They locked the door then leaned a chair against it. After a moment staring at it, Martin pulled the chair away and dragged a chest of drawers over to take its place.

"Happy?" Sarah asked.

"No."

She slipped her arms around him from behind. "It's nothing," she reassured him. "God knows what Sally's got into her head, but Jess will see that Mark's got no injuries, and it'll all be over in the morning."

"I hope so." He was looking at the door, no doubt wondering how someone had got inside the block to post anything through their door in the first place. "Thanks for not telling her about the notes, and the shit."

She nodded, feeling her chest tighten. She hated lying to him. She'd spotted Jess looking at the hole in the window. But true to her word, she'd said nothing.

Then she remembered. "Oh my God."

"What?"

"I didn't tell her. About the people from Filey. I have to go out."

He grabbed her hand. "You can't go out there."

"What if they attack again?"

"What did you see?"

She shook her head. She didn't know everyone in this village; she'd spent too much of her life shut indoors. But they'd been smoking. And they'd talked about not being seen.

"They were in one of the houses. By the Meadows. It looked – I'm not sure – it looked suspicious."

He tightened his grip. "What was suspicious?"

"They were standing, smoking, outside one of the houses. That's why I noticed them. No one smokes here."

"No. What else?"

"There were people inside. More than Jess said. Six of them, I think. Maybe more. Plotting something, it looked like. They talked about not being seen. It felt wrong." She turned to him. "It could be nothing."

"Doesn't sound like nothing." His grip slackened. "Wait here. I'll go."

33

R uth sat on the damp sand, her limbs numb.

She'd checked on the boys before leaving and she knew they were asleep. So was Ben.

Lying in bed next to him, all she could hear was the sound of Robert's breath, heavy in the confines of his neat bedroom at the farm. Every time she looked at her husband, she saw him. The way he stared into her face like he was trying to worm his way into her brain. The way he had stroked her skin, making her want to climb out of it.

This afternoon, Ben had come into the pharmacy. He'd seen how pale and tired she looked and tried to give her a hug. She'd felt like she would suffocate. She pushed him off, moaning, and then been pricked by guilt when she saw the hurt on his face. How could she tell him that every time he came near her, it wasn't him there but his childhood friend? And that it was all his fault?

The only people she could bear to touch were her sons. She'd approached them hesitantly this morning, after her reaction to Zack's death, believing herself to be a monster. She'd killed a man. She felt angry and confused every time someone showed her affection. Could she hurt her children too?

But to her great relief, holding them in her arms had quietened the rage that churned inside her, not ignited it as she'd feared. But when they spoke to her, when they asked her questions or looked to her for reassurance, she knew she was found wanting. She'd lost the ability to gauge their reactions to anything she said, the skill she'd had for reading between the lines of their smooth faces and understanding what they weren't asking from her, but needed nonetheless.

She couldn't tell anyone how she felt. Jess was too full of grief over Zack. Ben was the enemy now, someone she had to avoid, and keep at a distance. And everyone else needed her. Six people had been injured in last night's attack. Six people who'd had to wait all night and much of the morning before she could bring herself to treat them. Treating minor wounds without making skin contact wasn't easy. She'd worn a pair of woollen gloves from home, making excuses about having an allergic reaction to something or other, and hoped the fibres wouldn't get into any of the cuts she was treating.

The village didn't know that Ruth had gone. They didn't know that she'd been replaced by this woman who wanted to kill everyone who came near her. Who wanted to blank it all out.

She stood up and waded into the shallows, ignorant of the cold. Ruth had grown up near the coast, and had always had a healthy respect for the sea. She wasn't a strong swimmer. If she went out there, she wouldn't come back.

Would her boys survive without her? Would they be better off without a mother who was incapable of feeling warmth?

She was up to her knees in the dark water now. It lapped

around her legs, splashing at her as if trying to get inside her skin. It felt light and heavy at the same time, cold and oddly warm. She bent to run her fingers through it, shuddering at the movement against her hand. She took a step forwards.

"Ruth?"

She froze, her eyes piercing the darkness.

"Ruth!"

The voice grew louder. She heard stumbling behind her, the sound of someone running across the damp sand.

It was Ben.

"Ruth, what are you doing?"

She took a deep breath. She couldn't turn around. She couldn't see that look on his face. He would be looking at her like this was her fault. Like she was the one in the wrong, the one whose mind was lost.

When would he take responsibility for what he'd done to her?

He was at the edge of the water now, just feet away. She could hear his clumsy movements in the shallows.

She raised a hand to stop him.

"Ruth, I don't know what you're doing. Jess said she'd find you. But I couldn't wait."

Wait for what? For her to walk into the sea like it would swallow up her rage and bewilderment?

"Ruth. Please, come home. It's not safe. The boys need you."

There was panic in his voice, and could she hear guilt?

"I need you."

There it was. His need, bigger than her own. Looming in his mind like there was nothing else that mattered.

"You never ask what I need," she muttered.

"What? Did you say something, love?"

She felt her face crease at the 'love'. *Don't call me that. You have no idea what love is.*

His hand brushed against her arm. She yanked it away.

"Ruth love, you're scaring me. Come home, please."

The cold was seeping up her body now. It gnawed at her organs, and trickled into her arms. She shivered violently. She felt something land on her shoulders. A coat. She went to throw it off then stopped herself. It was just a coat. Ben's coat. But still, it couldn't hurt her.

She turned to him, her eyes lowered. "Don't touch me."

"What's wrong? What did I do?"

She said nothing.

He advanced and she shook her head, pulling her neck back. "No."

He nodded. He looked like he might cry. She thought of their sons, their tousled heads on their pillows as she'd left the house. She wiped a tear from her cheek.

"Alright," she said. She lifted her feet high to walk through the water, feeling the damp sand suck at her shoes.

She didn't look at Ben as she passed him. He reached towards her but then thought better of it and pulled his hand back. It was shaking.

She could hear dim sounds ahead. Footsteps. Voices?

Had Jess come to find her after all?

"Alright," she repeated. She would go home. To her boys.

She made for the coastal path towards the house, not caring if he was behind her or not. As long as he didn't touch her.

34

M ark Palfrey sat on a hard-backed chair, rubbing a red mark on his skin. For all Jess knew, it was caused by the rubbing, not by any alleged attack.

He sat side-on to Jess and refused to meet her eye. Sally hovered behind him, her fingertips fluttering over the fabric of his T shirt.

"So what happened then?" asked Jess. She considered whether she should have brought another member of the council with her. No, that was ridiculous. This was a minor alleged assault, not the Old Bailey.

"That Martin attacked him," said Sally. "He's bad news."

Jess fought down the irritation. "I was asking Mark."

Sally gave her a hard look. "Tell her, Mark." Her voice was clipped, her West Country accent stronger than usual. Jess realised she knew nothing about this couple's history. Had they been together before they came here, or had they met in the village? And did it matter?

"Mark?" Jess said. "I don't have long, so I'd be grateful if you could fill me in."

He sniffed. "You need to hold a village meeting."

"I don't see what that's got to do with anything."

He turned to her. There was a red line snaking over his right eye. It looked swollen.

"Have you been to see Ruth for that?" she asked.

"Didn't you hear me? You need to show everyone what he's like. You let him in."

She placed a hand on the back of the chair next to Mark's. She was standing over him, having not been invited to sit. "You still haven't told me what happened."

"I think it looks pretty obvious, don't you?"

"Martin attacked him," Sally interrupted.

"You've already said that. But I need more details. When? What was the weapon? And why?"

"Why? Because he's no good," said Sally. Jess narrowly avoided rolling her eyes.

"You have to understand. You've clearly been hurt, Mark, but before I can accuse another member of our community"—she ignored Sally's huff — "I need more information. I need evidence. You say Martin did this to you. Can you tell me what he used, and when it happened?"

"His nails, of course," said Sally.

"Mark?"

Mark nodded. Jess bent over him to look more closely at the wounds. They did indeed look thin and ragged, like they'd been created with fingernails. She glanced at Mark's fingers; his nails were neatly trimmed, almost down to the quick. Sally's were longer, and a couple of them looked as if they'd been bitten.

"OK," she said. "I've got other things to attend to. You come and find me when you've got more to say. OK?"

Mark said nothing. Was this the same man who'd found it impossible to shut up when his girlfriend had been kidnapped? Was it the effect of the alleged attack, or something else, that was making him taciturn?

"OK?" she repeated.

"Don't worry," said Sally. "We'll find you."

"Good."

She let herself out and made for the centre of the village. She passed Martin's flat and looked up, wondering if Sarah and Martin were up there, looking at her. But the window was dark.

Ahead of her, two figures were moving up the hill form the beach. She stiffened; another raid? But then the one at the front spoke: it was Ben, with Ruth. He'd found her. She allowed herself a relieved smile and decided to leave them to it.

She sighed. It felt more like being back in the schoolroom than running a community of adults, with people accusing each other of things and launching petty attacks. Maybe she should sit them all in separate corners for a day until they learned to behave themselves.

She approached Toni's flat. The curtains were drawn. She crept upstairs, anxious not to disturb Toni and Roisin.

Btu the flat was dark, and quiet. She shuffled around the kitchen and poured herself a glass of water.

Toni emerged from her bedroom, yawning.

"Hey."

"Hey," replied Jess. "Everything OK with Roisin?"

"Yeah." Toni rubbed the back of her hand across her eyes. "Just don't tell anyone she was here, huh?"

"None of my business."

"Thanks. You can have the bedroom, if you want."

"It's fine."

"You sure?"

Jess's head was full: of Mark and Sally, of Ben and Ruth.

Of Zack. Sleeping on a sofa would be easier; a bed would feel so empty.

"Sure. See you in the morning."

Toni slipped back into the bedroom. Within moments, Jess could hear snoring. She found the pile of blankets Toni had left out for her and arranged them on the sofa. She settled down, fidgeting.

She heard rattling coming from the window. The wind was picking up; she had no idea Toni's windows were so loose. She'd ask the maintenance team to fix them tomorrow.

There it was again. Rattling. She pushed the blankets to the floor and opened the curtains.

She flinched as a hail of pebbles hit the glass in front of her.

"What the hell?"

She opened the window. "Sally? I told you I'd deal with it in the morning."

"It's not Sally." Martin's voice.

She sighed. "You want to know what happened with Sally and Mark."

"No. I came to warn you."

"Warn me about what?" Not more people posting things through letterboxes, she hoped.

"It's the people from Filey. We think they're starting something."

This was all she needed. "I'll be right down."

They hurried towards the road where the newcomers had been housed. Drizzle still filled the air and the wind gusted off the sea. Jess longed for her bed, even if that bed was just Toni's sofa.

They rounded the road where the newcomers had been billeted and stopped to look at the houses. They blinked back, impassive. She wondered if the occupants were watching.

"Are you sure?" she whispered.

"Sarah said she saw people. More than just the people who should be here."

"How many?"

"She wasn't sure."

This was ridiculous. "There's nothing here. They're asleep."

She grabbed his arm and guided him away from the houses. "Tell me what she saw."

"There were people standing outside one of the houses smoking. And more people inside."

"They could have been visiting each other."

Martin shrugged. The sense of purpose seemed to have left him.

"I can't wake them up in the middle of the night without a good reason," she said. "I'll come back in the morning."

She started walking. Martin stayed where he was, staring at the houses. She ignored him and hurried to Toni's. She had no idea who to believe anymore.

35

T he morning was dull and cold, a biting wind scudding in from the north. Jess headed for the newcomers' houses, feeling uneasy.

She would knock on their door, pretend to be checking they were settling in.

She rounded the JP. Her legs felt heavy and her mind numb. Being in charge of a village full of people she'd known for years was bad enough, but now there were strangers to contend with. Would they trust her, or would they be as wary of her as she was of them?

As the first house came into view, she stopped walking. Its dark grey-painted facade was daubed in graffiti.

She looked along the road – no one around – and hurried over to the house. Across the front wall, in large, ragged letters, were the words *Go Home*.

She put a hand on the *e* of *Home*. It was dry, painted in a bright white that gleamed against the grey. This wasn't fresh. But it hadn't been here last night.

She thought of Martin, standing behind her, staring up at the houses. Surely not?

She looked along the row of houses again. Would anyone have seen?

She scratched at a patch of dry skin on the back of her hand. Goosebumps pricked her arms; the cold was deepening.

Should she knock on the door, let the inhabitants know what had happened? She stepped back and stared at it, trying to sense whether people were moving around inside. The two windows facing the road had their curtains closed.

She looked along the row of houses, towards the flats. Surely Martin wouldn't have done this? He was angry, and scared. But graffiti?

The people inside should be told. They probably needed to be protected. She heaved a deep breath at the irony. She had no idea who would help with that.

But the village had one person who could be relied upon to follow the rule of law, or at least of the village rulebook, and push his feelings down. That person was Colin.

She strode to the Barkers' house and rapped on the door three times. Sheila opened the door, her eyes wide.

"Oh, Jess, it's you. I thought you were Ruth."

"Is Colin in?"

"He's just eating his bacon. Come in."

Jess smiled and let Sheila usher her in.

"I'm heading to the school. I'll leave you two to it." Sheila tugged on a bright pink hat and stepped out into the morning.

"Sheila."

Sheila turned. "Yes?"

"Which way do you walk, to the school?"

A frown. Sheila pointed in the direction of the coastal path. "I take the long route. Give Benji some exercise."

"Good." That meant she wouldn't pass the grafittied

house. Even so, this needed to be dealt with quickly. People would be starting the day soon. "I mean, good for you." Jess gave Sheila a tight smile. "See you later."

Sheila shrugged and trudged off towards the beach, humming under her breath. Jess turned back towards Colin. He was sitting at the kitchen table, cutting a slice of bacon into neat squares.

"You're not going to like this."

He forked two squares into his mouth and swallowed. "I thought as much. Bit early for a social call."

"Sorry."

"Did we miss another attack?"

"No. It's the house. The one we put the people from Filey in."

"The Snellings want it back?"

"No."

"What, then?"

"Finish your breakfast, then come and look."

Colin grabbed a slice of heavy brown bread and put the bacon squares into it. He palmed the sandwich he'd created. "Come on. I can tell you're in a hurry."

When they reached the house, he whistled. "Oh, no."

"Oh, no. Is that all?"

"I was expecting worse."

"Like what?"

"A fight, or something. I guess."

"What are we going to do?"

"Clean it off would make sense."

"That's not what I mean."

He stared at the letters. "I don't know, Jess. I really don't. This is no worse than what their lot have been giving us for the last six years. They should be glad it wasn't worse."

"That doesn't make it right."

The front door of the house opened a crack. A man looked out, his movement wary. When he caught sight of Jess and Colin, he stiffened.

"Who are you?"

"I'm Jess Dyer. Village steward. I met your wife yesterday. This is Colin Barker, secretary of our council."

"What are you doing here?"

"I'm afraid your house has been vandalised."

"It's not my house."

"I'm sorry. But you need to see."

He stepped outside and stood next to her. He was wearing a blue sweater that looked home-knitted, and heavy brown cords. His eyes roamed over the words on the wall of the house he'd slept in.

"Bastards," he said. "I'll fucking kill them."

"It won't come to that," said Jess. "But we will find out who did it, and in the meantime we'll help clean it up."

"Like hell you will."

"Sorry?"

"This is evidence."

He ducked back into the house and emerged holding a mobile phone. He started taking photos.

Colin tried to take it off him. "Mr Haywood. I really don't think this is a—"

"Get your filthy hands off me! That's assault."

"Please. We can help with this."

"Colin," Jess muttered. He withdrew his hand and stopped trying to take the phone. Better to let the man take his photographs than to risk a fight.

When he'd taken his fill of photos, the man turned to them. "Now leave us alone."

He retreated inside and slammed the door.

Jess knocked on it. There was no response.

"Let's just leave it," said Colin. "They can clean it up themselves."

"You're kidding. What will happen when everyone sees this?"

"Why do you care?"

"Because however obnoxious that man is, he's part of this village now. We don't want things getting any worse."

Colin sniffed. "Let's try the other house. You said they were friendly."

Jess knocked on the door of the Bagris. She hopped from foot to foot, wishing she'd put on a warmer coat.

Once again, there was no response. She stood back to look up at the upstairs window. The curtains were open. The downstairs window was open and there was no sign of life inside.

"This makes no sense," she said.

"Maybe they're asleep."

"No. This smells wrong."

"How?"

"Sarah saw suspicious activity here last night, and now the Bagris have gone, by the looks of it."

"We don't know that."

"You need to fetch the master key," she said. "We have to get inside."

36

"I don't like that idea," said Colin.

"I knew you'd say that," replied Jess, "but we need to know if they're OK."

"Why wouldn't they be?"

"I spoke to Mrs Bagri earlier. Aabida. And her husband. She seemed scared. Said the people next door hated them."

"That doesn't give us a reason to break into their house."

"We've knocked three times. They're either gone, or they aren't coming out for some reason."

"Isn't that their business?"

"Sarah Evans said she saw suspicious activity here last night. I'm worried."

"What kind of suspicious activity?"

"People. More of them than there should be."

"OK."

Jess heard a voice from the other house, the Haywoods'. She put a hand up to listen, but there was nothing more.

"Colin, please. I'll take responsibility. I just want to go in there and check that everything's OK."

Colin looked at the Bagris' front door again and sighed. "If there's any trouble, or anybody asks, you coerced me."

"That's fine."

Ten minutes later, Colin had returned with the key. Jess watched the houses while she waited for him, backing away to stand on the opposite side of the road. The Haywoods' house was silent, the curtains unmoving. The Bagris' was just as quiet but with the curtains open. It felt wrong.

"Here." Colin handed her the key. "You can do it."

"Right." She unlocked the Bagris' front door, glad of the original cleaners' master key.

She pushed the door open a short way.

"Hello? Mr and Mrs Bagri?"

No answer. She stepped inside.

The hallway was empty. No sign of the toys she'd seen behind those children yesterday. The hooks were empty of coats and there were no shoes on the floor, as there always were in Ben and Ruth's house.

She went into the living area. "Hello?"

It too was empty. The tired sofa that sat in the middle of the space looked as if it hadn't been sat on for months, even though another couple had been here until very recently.

The kitchen too was bare. No food on the worktops. No sign of the rations they had provided for the Bagris.

"Where the hell are they?" asked Colin.

"Shh." She raised a finger to her lips. She could hear voices through the wall. Men. She couldn't make out what they were saying but there was definitely more than one man in there. Even if she accounted for the teenage sons, there were too many voices.

Then she heard a baby crying, followed by a woman shouting for it to shut up.

Colin's eyes were wide. "What's going on in there?"

He hurried out of the house and started pounding on the front door of its neighbour.

"Let us in!"

Jess stood behind him. "Calm down, Colin."

He turned to her, a stray lock of hair bobbing over his eyes. "We allocated that house to one family. They can't start moving more people in. It's against the rules."

"I think we're past the rules now."

"What do you think they're doing in there?"

She thought back to the night of the attack. She hadn't seen the faces of any of the invaders; she had no way of knowing if the Haywoods were among them.

Surely Anita Chopra wouldn't have brought people here who'd attacked them?

But maybe Anita didn't know. Or didn't care.

Colin pounded on the door again.

"Open it," Jess said.

"It's occupied. I can't."

"Colin, please. Forget the rules for once."

He pulled the key out of his pocket and handed it to her. Then he pushed her hand down.

"No." He held onto her hand. "I have to believe that someone is in danger before I let you break in."

"I already said we're not breaking in. We've got a key."

"You know what I mean. If you do this, I'll have to report you. You'll be kicked off the council."

She dragged a hand through her hair. Why did Colin have to be like this?

"Can I overrule you?" she said. She pocketed the key, frustrated.

"You'll have to call an emergency meeting of the council."

37

The room that had once been a coffee shop but now did double duty as school by day and village hall by night was dull in the early morning light. Jess watched as the council members filed in. Normal conversation that accompanied the beginning of council meetings was absent. Today, people were withdrawn and slow-moving. Faces were pale and eyes were dark-rimmed or bloodshot. Ben, opposite Jess, stared at his hands. He twisted them together in front of him, muttering. They were all standing, or perched on the edges of tables; there hadn't been time to rearrange the furniture.

"You OK, Ben?" she whispered.

He looked up. "Let's get this over with, huh?"

She nodded. "How is she?"

He shrugged. "I don't know, sis. She won't talk to me. Won't let me anywhere near her."

"She's been through a lot."

"We all have."

"Would it help if I spoke to her?"

He shook his head. He opened his mouth to speak but stopped as Colin called the meeting to order.

"Thanks for coming at short notice, everyone. We've got a problem."

Heads turned towards him and the silence thickened. Jess wiped her damp palms on her jeans.

"Jess?" Colin prompted.

She nodded. The council members stared at her, waiting.

"The people who've been housed in the cottages over by the Meadows," she said. "The ones from Filey."

"We know who they are," said Ben.

She glared at him. "I think there's more of them in there."

Ben tensed. He stared at her, his cheeks red. He would be angry that she hadn't told him first.

"What's happened?" asked Dawn.

Jess stood up. She swallowed. "An hour ago, I spotted something on one of the houses. Graffiti." She surveyed the room, wondering if anyone here knew who had done it. Or if it mattered. "But they wouldn't let me and Colin in. The Haywoods. I think there are more people in there. And the other house, the Bagris. It's empty."

"Empty?" asked Sanjeev.

"I knocked on the door and no one answered. We were worried, so Colin got a key."

She glanced at Colin. He was holding himself very still.

"There was no one in there," she said. "But we could hear the other house through the wall. There seemed to be a lot of people inside."

"Maybe the Bagris had gone next door to be with the Haywoods?" suggested Dawn.

"They hated each other. I spoke to Mrs Bagri. She was scared."

She leaned on the table behind her. "I have no idea what 's happened to them."

"What about all these other people?" asked Ben. His eyes were bloodshot and he was wearing the same shirt she'd seen him in last night.

"I don't know," she sighed. "All the curtains were closed and the deadbolt was closed. You know the rules about letting ourselves into an occupied house."

Colin sniffed.

"We have to go there," said Ben. "Right now."

"Let's not be hasty," said Jess. She surveyed the group. "Where's Toni?"

Sanjeev looked towards the empty seat where Toni normally sat. "Working, maybe."

Toni worked on the allotments, bakery and smoke house, overseeing the production of food. Jess frowned; it would be good to have the support of her friend today. But she couldn't afford to wait.

"Who's to know they aren't plotting something?" said Harry. Harry was one of the older members of the council. He'd been an ally of Ted Evans, Dawn's husband. He'd mainly kept himself to himself since Ted's arrest.

"Why would they be doing that?" asked Jess.

"The graffiti could have been a diversion," said Ben. "Keep us busy while they tell their friends from Filey about the layout of the village. Our weak points."

She frowned at her brother. "You're being paranoid."

He shrugged. "I'm being careful."

"The reason I brought this up wasn't to discuss your conspiracy theories. It was to ask for the council's permission to go into that house. And to start the process of identifying whoever did the graffiti. I don't care who the victims were; it's not acceptable for anyone to deface another villager's house."

"They aren't villagers," said Ben.

She said nothing.

"I'll see what I can find out," said Dawn. "They're neighbours of mine. I've spoken to Mary once or twice."

"We don't have time for that," said Ben.

"Ben, please—" began Jess.

He stood up. "No. If they've brought more people, who knows what they're up to. Your friend Anita Chopra said nothing about more people."

"She isn't my friend."

"Whatever. Come on. I'm going over there now."

Jess approached him. She lowered her voice. "Is Ruth at home?"

He paled. "Yes."

"Don't you think you should be with her, instead of careering around the village? I'm worried about her."

"You think I'm not?"

"That's not what I said."

Colin cleared his throat.

"Sorry," said Jess.

"I'm going over there," said Ben.

"Not just yet," said Jess. "There's a second agenda item. An alleged attack."

"The people from Filey?" asked Dawn.

Jess shook her head. "Mark Palfrey was assaulted, yesterday, he claims. His girlfriend, Sally Angus, says that she knows who did it. But so far there's no evidence. And Mark himself won't say anything about it."

"Who did it?" asked Sanjeev.

"I can't be sure."

"Who does Sally say did it then?" asked Colin.

She threw him a glance. She should have talked to Colin about this beforehand, but they'd been too caught up in the graffiti incident.

"Martin Walker," she said.

"What?" Ben was standing by the door. He looked as if he might laugh.

"She *claims* it was him. He denies it, and as I say, Mark hasn't said anything himself."

"Well it's hardly surprising, is it?" replied Ben.

"Ben," warned Colin.

"No." Ben stood up. "Look, I was taken in by him last time. I let him sleep in my house. You all know how that turned out. We should never have let him back here."

Dawn moved away from the chair she'd been leaning against. She looked from Jess to Ben. Her eyes were bright and her chest rose and fell conspicuously.

"Dawn?" said Jess. If Martin did attack Mark, she realised, then Sarah might not be safe. "I should have told you about this.".

Dawn shook her head. "I don't believe them."

"Sorry?"

Dawn stood. "When Martin came here, I was scared. I knew what he did." She looked at Ben. "To your lovely wife. I'm not denying that. But he was coerced. He's not like that. I've seen him with my daughter. He's kind, and tender. He wants to stay here, and to prove himself."

"He's not doing a very good job of that," said Ben.

"Did you see him when we were attacked?" asked Dawn, her cheeks pink. "He fought those people off as bravely as anyone who's been here all along. He's one of us. I know it."

Jess bit her lower lip. It was swollen, and tasted metallic. If Martin hadn't attacked Mark, then who had?

"Did anyone see Mark during the attacks?" she asked.

Heads shook all round.

"We need to find out if he was hurt then. Ben, do you know if Ruth treated him yesterday morning?"

Ben shook his head. "Mark Palfrey is one of us. Don't we trust our own anymore?"

"Martin is one of us, too. If one villager accuses another of attacking them, we owe it to both of them to find out the truth. We can't take sides."

"Bloody naive."

Colin coughed. "Now, Ben. This is a council meeting."

"I don't care if it's the palace of bleeding Versailles. Martin took my Ruth, and now he's assaulting our people. He's no better than those murderous bastards from Filey."

This was going nowhere. "I'll talk to them all again," Jess said. "Mark and Sally, Martin and Sarah." She noticed Dawn shrinking into herself. "If you want to be with your daughter, Dawn, that's fine."

"Thank you."

"I'll get to the bottom of it."

"We all know what you'll find," said Ben. His eyes were small and dark and his shoulders hunched.

"Let's not make assumptions," she replied.

"I'll come with you," said Colin.

"Sorry?"

"That's a good idea," said Sanjeev. He was watching Ben. "We don't want Jess being accused of bias."

I'm not biased, she wanted to snap. But Sanjeev was right. An impartial observer like Colin would protect her from any accusations.

"Fine," she said. "Colin, I'll see you back here in an hour. But we need to go to those cottages first." She tried to face the other council members. "Do Colin and I have your permission to use the master key, if they still won't let us in?"

Mutters of assent. As she turned for the door, it flew open. She shrank back.

Toni stood in the doorway, out of breath. "Sorry I'm late," she said. "Did I miss anything?"

Jess stared at her. "You could say that."

Toni was flushed and her coat was in disarray. She blinked at Jess a few times, as if not entirely present.

"Get back here!"

Toni stumbled into the room as someone barrelled through the door behind her. The council members shrank back.

Jess stepped forward. One of the newcomers? But no, it was Flo Murray. Roisin's mum.

Flo barged into the room and looked quickly around. Her gaze landed on Toni.

"What in heaven do you think you've been playing at?" she shouted.

38

Toni barged past Flo and into the square. The council members followed, suddenly quiet.

"Flo, please," Toni said. "This isn't the time."

"I don't care if it's the time or not," Flo replied. "My daughter has been through enough. And now she's lying to me, because of you."

Jess took a step forward. "Flo, I'm sure this isn't as bad as you—"

Flo turned on her, her eyes wild. "You've been helping them, haven't you? And you the steward too."

"I don't know what you're talking about."

Jess looked at Toni. "Where's Roisin?"

"At home. She's been grounded. Like a kid," she muttered.

Jess nodded. "Please, Flo. We're in the middle of a village meeting right now. Can this wait?"

Flo ignored her and advanced on Toni.

"Leave her alone, you hear me? She's still recovering from what those awful men did to her. Do you have any idea?"

Jess saw a shadow pass over Toni's face. She probably knew better than anyone what Roisin had been through.

"She needs peace and quiet," Flo continued. "Not—this!" She waved a hand in dismissal of Toni.

"Is this because I'm a woman?" accused Toni.

"Woman, man, whatever! She doesn't need you. She told me she wasn't going to see you anymore, and now I find out she's been sneaking about behind my back."

"She's a grown woman. She's allowed to—"

Flo jabbed a finger into Toni's face. "She's twenty. She still lives in my house. Don't you go filling her head with nonsense."

Jess pulled Toni away from Flo. "Maybe if I can sit down with you all later, and we can work something out?"

"There's nothing to work out," spat Flo. "You keep that woman away from my girl, or I'll tell people the truth about your family."

Jess felt the air behind her move. The entire village council was standing in the square now, seemingly oblivious to the cold. Someone muttered.

"What truth?" she asked.

"I know why he did it. That Robert Cope."

Jess narrowed her eyes at the other woman. For herself, she didn't care who knew about Ben and Robert, and their past. She didn't care on Ben's behalf; he'd made that bed years ago. But Ruth...

She approached Flo. "Please, for Ruth's sake. Let's just calm things down a bit, eh? I'm sure we can find a solution."

"Help!"

Jess span round at the voice. Sheila stood behind them, her cheeks pale and her breathing laboured. Colin stepped towards his wife, looking perturbed. Flo stared at Sheila, angry that her thunder had been stolen.

"Sheila? What's wrong?" Jess asked. "Is it the school?"

Sheila shook her head. Her normally tidy if coarse hair was haloed around her head, curls sticking up in all directions.

"Where are the children?"

"On their way back. Sarah's with them."

"Way back from where?"

Sheila looked at Ben. "Oh my God."

Colin strode to his wife. "Sheila love, tell us. What is it?"

Sheila swallowed. She looked from Colin to Ben, and then back to Jess. "It's Ruth. We just found her, on the beach."

"What's she doing there?"

Sheila scanned the room again. She opened her mouth but nothing came out.

Ben stood up. "Sheila, tell us." He pushed past her, almost knocking Sanjeev over in his haste.

"We found her, on the beach," Sheila echoed. "Little Paul Murchison, he was paddling." She threw her hands to her face.

Jess tried to keep her voice steady. "Sheila, please. What do you mean?"

"Ruth. She was in the water." She dragged her fingers down her pale skin, pulling the flesh out of shape. Colin put an arm around her. She ignored it. "I— I think she's dead."

39

Martin was in the flat when Sarah came home from school.

"Back early?" she asked, trying to inject levity into her voice.

"Akash sent me home." Akash was Martin's supervisor on the allotment.

"Why?"

"Said there wasn't enough work to do."

"That makes no sense."

He was in the kitchen, making tea. He poured her a mug and placed it in front of her. "He didn't want me there. Someone's got to him."

"You think so?"

She hugged him; he smelt of sweat and dirt. Normally he changed out of the clothes he used for work as soon as he came home.

"But you're going back tomorrow, right?" She sipped at her tea, realising how thirsty she was after a day using her voice.

He shrugged. "He said he'd let me know in the morning."

"What?"

He stroked her cheek. "I have to stop this," he said."

"How?"

"I don't know. But I'm one of you now. I can't be here and not work."

"I'll talk to Mum."

"No. You can't go running to your mum every time I have a problem. I'll sort this out myself."

She heard a slam in the corridor outside the flat. They both stiffened and watched the door to the flat. Sarah could feel Martin's heartbeat against her chest.

Silence. They let themselves breathe again.

Martin slid towards the door and pulled it open a little.

"No one out here. Probably just Gloria getting home." Gloria lived in the other first floor flat.

Sarah nodded; should she knock on Gloria's door, to check?

No. She was being paranoid.

"We can't carry on like this," Martin said. "I'm going out."

"Where? You're going to confront them?"

"No. Something else."

"What?"

"It might not work."

"Martin, tell me what's going on."

He kissed her forehead. "It'll be fine. I won't be long."

40

Jess ran after Ben towards the beach. Sam Golder was staggering up the hill, carrying Ruth. She was pale, the colour of a dead fish. Jess stifled a cry.

Ben ran forward. "Ruth! Oh my God, is she—?"

"She's breathing," said Sam. "I don't want to drop her."

Ben grabbed her feet and struggled with Sam to the village hall. Jess ran with them, pushing open the door to let them through.

They laid Ruth on a table. Her mouth was partly open and her eyes were closed.

Jess looked around the other council members. Ruth was the only thing close to a doctor here. Who would treat her?

"Does anyone know what to do?" she asked, feeling helpless.

Colin pushed past her. "She's cold. Best get her wrapped up. And we should put her in a warm bath."

Jess nodded. Ben hauled Ruth up from the table and struggled with her to his house. Jess ran ahead to open the front door. Inside, Ben stared at the stairs.

"I can't carry her up there."

"I'll help."

Together they manoeuvred Ruth up the stairs. Ben had her under the shoulders and Jess under the knees. Colin ran in after them and flung blankets over her. Jess stared at Ruth, waiting for her to stir, to come to life.

At the top of the stairs, they laid her on the floor, gently.

"The boys," said Jess. "Where are they?"

Ben looked back at her, his eyes wide. "I don't know."

"They're down here!" called Colin. "Playing cards." His voice disappeared as he retreated into the living room to speak to the boys. How long had they been alone?

Ben was in the bathroom, running the taps.

"When did she go out?" Jess asked.

Ben said nothing. His mouth was tight and he was looking between the bath and his wife. He kept dipping his hands into the water, testing it.

"How warm should it be?" he asked.

Jess tried to remember back to when Martin had fallen in the sea, when Ruth had nursed him. "Not too hot," she said. "It'll shock her, or something. Just warm."

Ben nodded. He turned on the cold tap. Jess wondered when this bath had last been used: baths were banned, due to the shortage of hot water. She turned back to Jess and pulled the blanket tighter around her. She rubbed her through the rough fabric, willing her to be warm.

At last the bath was half-full. Ben looked at Ruth, his eyes empty.

"We can do this," she said. "Same way we got her up here."

They lifted her again, Ben at her head and Jess her feet. They shuffled into the bathroom, careful not to knock Ruth into the doorframe or the walls. Gently, they lowered her into the bath. Ben held her shoulders as she slipped in, holding her head upright. He stared into her face.

"Ruth," he whispered. "Ruth, sweetheart. Come back to me."

Ruth gasped, making Ben almost tumble backwards. Jess held her breath. She counted inside her head, not sure why she felt the need.

Ruth's eyes opened. She stared at Ben, her eyes full of fear. Ben blinked back at her. He forced a smile. "It's alright, love. I'm here. Jess is with me."

Ruth said nothing. She blinked at Ben, ignoring Jess. Then she closed her eyes again.

Ben turned to Jess. "I don't know what to do."

"Keep the water warm. Talk to her."

Ben nodded.

"Ruth, it's me, Ben. I'm here with you, in our bathroom. The boys are downstairs, with Colin. Everyone's safe. What happened, Ruth? What happened to you?"

"Don't," said Jess. "You'll agitate her."

"What happened, Jess? How did Ruth end up in the sea? She never goes to the beach."

"She does," corrected Jess. "She has been, recently. You said so yourself."

"Are you suggesting she did this? That she tried to..." Ben sobbed.

Jess put a hand on his arm, anxious that he not let go of Ruth. "I'm sure there's a perfectly reasonable explanation. She couldn't swim, could she?"

He shook his head, tears dripping onto Ruth's arm. "She grew up in Suffolk. I don't know why she never learned."

"We just need to look after her now. Don't think about all that. Keep her warm. I'll go and get help."

"Who? Ruth's our doctor. She's the only person who knows what to do."

"I'll go to Filey."

His face fell. "No."

"Yes. They can help us."

"They can't."

"I have to try."

"I forbid it."

She shrank back, knowing that he couldn't follow her. "I have to try."

She hurried to the landing. Below, she could hear Colin trying to chat to the boys. His voice was stilted.

"They'll help her, Ben," she said. "I know they will."

"No!" he yelled, stuck in the bathroom.

She ran down the stairs.

"Colin."

Colin looked up from his huddle with Sean and Ollie. He muttered something to them, then hurried to Jess.

"How is she?" His voice was low.

"She opened her eyes. She's getting warmer. But we don't know what to do."

"Can I help?"

"I'm going to Filey."

"Is that wise?"

"What else do you suggest?"

"I don't know." He looked back at the boys. Sean was pulling Ollie's hair. "Mum!" Ollie shrieked.

"Go," said Colin. "Get help."

41

S arah ran to Dawn's cottage. She knocked on the door, shifting from foot to foot. No answer.

She pulled out her key and let herself in. The house was quiet. Dawn's knick-knacks stared at her from the shelves and countertops. Sarah liked seeing Dawn's personality on display like this. It was like peeling away a layer of skin and finding a new woman underneath. A woman who could show warmth, and wasn't constantly scared.

"Mum?" she called. But it was useless. Dawn was out.

She ran towards the village hall. Dawn would be there, she'd said something about a council meeting.

As she reached the square, Dawn was walking towards her, her head down.

"Mum!"

Dawn looked up and smiled. "Hello, dear."

"I need your help."

A shadow crossed over Dawn's face. "Yes, dear."

"It's Martin."

"What about him?" A pause, during which the colour fell from Dawn's face. "He hasn't hurt you, has he?"

"No. They sent him home from the allotment."

Dawn folded her arms across her chest. "Why do you need my help with that?"

"He got a letter."

"No one gets letters here. No post. Love, I need to get back to Ruth."

"Why?"

"You don't know?"

Sarah shook her head.

"They found her on the beach."

Sarah felt her stomach drop. She teared up. Dawn reached out and pulled her daughter to her chest.

"She's alive. But she's in a bad way. Hypothermia, by the looks of it. They need help with her little boys."

Sarah nodded. "I can help. They know me."

"Sheila's there. I don't think they need any more people, right now. But can this letter of Martin's wait?"

"Someone threw a brick through his window. There was a death threat wrapped round it."

"Oh Lord." Dawn crossed herself. "Is he hurt?"

"No. It happened a few days ago. During the riot."

"Oh. That's good." She frowned. "Sorry, love. It's not good. But it's not urgent. I need to help Ruth now. We'll talk about this later, yes? You want me to talk to the council?"

"I already told Jess."

"Well you don't need my help then. I need to fetch some food. Seems Ruth's house hasn't been stocked up for a few days."

"Can't you go to the store?"

"What, and face Pam? No thanks, I'd rather give those boys my own rations."

Sarah kissed her mother on the cheek. "Give them my love. Ruth's a good woman."

"She is that." Dawn returned the kiss and hurried towards her cottage.

Sarah stared after her. Her heart was heavy in her chest and she couldn't stop thinking of Martin's face when he'd told her what had happened on the allotment. So grey, as if the life had gone out of him.

She thought of another face, one that hadn't been grey at all. She felt a rush of energy.

She turned and started running.

42

J ess left the house, her heart pounding. Which way?

The coast road was the most direct route. But a storm was threatening, and she had no idea how safe it was. And even then, she didn't know where in Filey she needed to go.

She hurried to the Haywoods' house. She could hear footsteps behind her; was she being followed?

She carried on, not looking round. All that mattered was getting help for Ruth.

At the house, she stopped to hammer on the door.

"I need your help! We have a sick woman. I need to get to Filey."

She could hear voices inside. They stilled at the sound of her voice.

"Please!" she called. She wanted to cry.

She fingered the key in her pocket. The council had been about to give her permission to do this, when Flo and Toni had interrupted.

Not allowing herself the time to change her mind, she plunged the key into the lock and shoved the door open.

Inside was a crowd of men. They turned as one, staring at her. She counted them: one, two, three… six of them here, just in the hallway. How many more inside?

And where had they come from?

She resisted the urge to retreat, to alert the council.

"I need to find a hospital!"

They stared at her, blinking. They were like a wall of muscle in the confined space. The house smelt of cigarettes and boiled vegetables. She wondered if they had used the rations they'd been given.

"You shouldn't be here," she said. "Where's Mr Haywood?"

"That's me," one of them said. He was the smallest of the men, about five-foot-six with a bald patch and teeth that looked as if they hadn't seen a dentist for some years. "These are my sons, and two of my nephews."

Nephews? No one had said anything about nephews.

"I need your help," she said, swallowing the urge to ask questions, to make accusations. Did they know what had happened to the Bagris? Could the other family be here?

The men parted and a woman pushed though. "What's going on?"

It was the woman she'd met yesterday. She wore a threadbare dressing gown and a pair of slippers with rabbit teeth on the front.

"Oh. You again. How did you get in here?"

"Sorry. I need a hospital. Is there one in Filey?"

"Hah!" the woman spat. She smelled of gin. "You've got to be kidding."

"So where is the nearest one?"

"Fuck knows," the woman replied. "Leeds, for all I know. Wouldn't trust them even if I knew where it was."

"Please," breathed Jess. "My sister is dying. I need to get help for her."

"I thought you had a doctor."

"She *is* the doctor."

"That's unfortunate."

The men sniggered. Jess stared at them, her chest tight. She should leave; this was useless.

"Go to the police," the woman said. "They've got cars. They can get her to the hospital."

"The police?" Jess felt a shudder run through the group of men; she suspected they didn't have a friendly relationship with the local police force.

"Yeah. You'll find them overlooking the beach. Bastards, the lot of them. But they'll help the likes of you."

"Thanks."

The woman jabbed a finger into her chest. "Now get out of here, before we notice the way you broke in."

43

Whan Jess left the Haywoods' house, there was a growing crowd of villagers outside. They were staring at the house, as if daring its occupants to come out. The graffiti stared back at them.

Clyde was at the back. "What's going on?" she asked.

"They've got wind of what's happening in there."

"Nothing's happening in there." *Not yet*.

"How many of them are in there?" he asked.

"You know that. I saw you outside the council meeting. But how do all this lot know?"

More people arrived at the edge of the crowd. Clyde shrugged.

"I can't deal with this right now," she said. "I have to get help for Ruth. But you're the most responsible person here, so it's your job to disperse this crowd."

"I can't do that."

"You can. We can't have any more trouble. Keep an eye on the house, but don't let anyone attack it."

"What else do you suggest?"

She sighed. "I don't have time, Clyde. Sort it, OK?'

She'd never spoken to him like this before. Clyde and she had an easy relationship, a flirtatious one, at least on his side. Or they had before she'd fallen in love with Zack.

It was dark now, and starting to rain. The quickest way to Filey was along the coastal path. But in the dark, that would be foolish. The roads would be quiet, and possibly lit once she got closer to the town, although she doubted it.

She gave Clyde a look that she hoped meant business then headed for her old house. There was a bike round at the back, one she'd occasionally used to get around the village. Sarah had taken it to Filey when Martin was under arrest. And Ben had cycled to the farm in search of Ruth.

She ran to her own house, hoping the new occupants wouldn't see her. Two days ago it had still been propped up behind Jess's bin.

She ducked and slid around the side of the house. There was a window here, to the side of the living room, but it was high in the wall. There was no sound from within, and no light. Lights-out had been and gone. She thought of Ben and Ruth, in their house with no light and no heat. She should have lit a fire.

She should go back. She didn't know the specifics of how to override the power settings, but she had the authority to make it happen. At this time of night, the generator would be switched off. Only an hour's power per day, and that just after dusk.

But with Ruth almost drowned, no one would say no to Ben if he asked the same thing. She just had to hope he'd have the presence of mind. Or that Colin would.

Focus, she told herself. *Get help.* She dragged the bike out from its hiding place, wishing that she'd ridden it at some point while she'd been living here. It was pitted with scraps of rust from being left out in the rain, and there was mud etched onto the frame. But it would be usable.

She pulled it onto the road, keeping as quiet as possible, then mounted it. She hadn't ridden a bike in years and unlike her brother, she'd never been a champion racer. He'd told her how good it had felt speeding to the farm, feeling the wind on his face and catching a moment when he forgot why he was riding and just enjoyed the freedom of it.

She picked up pace and sped to the edge of the village, past the house she'd lived in with Sonia. No one was about; the village was quiet. Those villagers who weren't outside the newcomers' houses were locked away indoors.

At the road, she hesitated. She had no idea how frequently this road was used now. When she'd lived out on this edge of the village she'd listened to the occasional vehicle passing at night, and wondered where they got the fuel from.

She had to risk it. If she heard something coming, she could dive into a hedge.

She started cycling. The road led up a slight gradient and she felt the muscles in her thighs tense with the effort. After a while, the road levelled out. She swept past a gloomy hulk on the left, what might have been an abandoned petrol station or small supermarket, and took a right turn when the road forked. She just had to keep turning towards the sea, surely, and she would find it.

Filey announced itself with a smattering of houses, some with dim light inside and others clearly ruined. She could smell the residue of the explosion: an acrid smell that coated the insides of her nostrils, and a heaviness to the air that made her gag.

She pulled her shirt up, trying to cover her face, and pedalled on. The road went uphill and then steeply down-

RACHEL MCLEAN

hill again. At the bottom of the hill was the sea. She stopped, wary of the steepness of the hill and the fact that she couldn't see where the road ended and the water began.

She looked around her. The police station overlooked the beach, she knew that much.

The only sound was of the wind ahead of her, blowing in from the sea, and the cry of a single seagull somewhere to her right. Next to her, a large building was set back from the road. She approached it. A pole in front of it had long since lost the sign that would have sat on top.

Then she saw the police sign by the door. She allowed herself a shiver of relief and hurried to it.

S arah knocked on the door, trying not to hammer too hard. She shifted from foot to foot; it was cold.

The door opened. A gust of warm air blew out.

"You."

"Let me in," Sarah said.

"What do you want?"

"I want to talk to you. I want to know why you lied."

Sally shrugged. She pushed Sarah out of the way and looked past her. "Where's your boyfriend?"

"Martin's at home. I'm on my own."

Sally crossed her arms and cocked her head. "You should have left him. After what he did."

"They made him."

"*They made him.* You are so stupid."

"Please, let me in. It's freezing out here. And we're letting the rain in."

Sally pursed her lips and looked Sarah up and down. "Alright then." She pulled the door wider and let Sarah pass.

The living room of Sally and Mark's house was lit by just

two candles. They flickered into the corners, sending long shadows up the walls. Sarah wondered why they didn't have any more.

"Where's Mark?"

"In bed."

Sarah glanced up the stairs. No sound came from above. There was no reason to assume Sally was lying; where else would he be?

She walked further into the room and turned to face the other woman. Sally was right behind her, her breath hot on Sarah's cheeks as she turned. Alarmed, Sarah took a step back and almost tripped over a low table.

"Better be quick," Sally said. She sat down on a threadbare sofa. She didn't invite Sarah to do the same. "You've come to apologise, I hope."

"Why would I do that?"

"Because of what Martin did to my Mark. Have you seen his face?"

"Yes. But there's no evidence it was Martin."

Sally rolled her eyes. "He kidnapped us. He got himself arrested. Who else would it have been?"

Sarah shrugged. "It wasn't Martin."

"What's going on?"

Both women turned to see a man coming down the stairs. He was short and slim, with dark, curly hair and a scruffy beard. Sarah tried to remember if she'd ever seen him before.

"Mark darling, I thought you were asleep." Sally's voice had changed; it was no longer sharp, but honeyed.

He rubbed his eyes. "I heard voices. Everything OK?"

"Sarah's just leaving."

Mark looked at her. "Good."

Sarah stepped towards him. "Can I look at your face?"

He put his hand up to his cheek and cast Sally an anxious look. "I'd rather you didn't."

"Please. I want to see what happened to you."

Again he looked at Sally. "Your boyfriend attacked me, is what happened." His voice was low.

Sarah leaned towards him. He looked at Sally again and she nodded. Slowly, he dropped his hand.

He had a thin line running diagonally across his cheek, and another over his eyebrow. The skin around his eye was purpling, with yellow tinges at the edges.

"You say Martin did this?" she asked.

"He did." Mark didn't meet her eye.

"Why?"

"What do you mean, why?"

"Why would he attack you? Why you, in particular?"

He shrugged. "Who's to know I'm the only one?"

"Leave him alone." Sally rose. She placed herself between Sarah and Mark. Her face was in darkness. "Stop harassing us."

"I'm not harassing anyone. I just want to know the truth. Why would Martin attack your boyfriend?"

"Husband."

"I don't remember any wedding."

"That's none of your business."

"Look, just tell me why you think he did it, and I'll leave you alone."

Sally and Mark exchanged glances. They said nothing.

"It couldn't be because you threw a brick through our window, could it? Or because you posted shit through our door?"

Sarah listened to herself. What would Dawn say, if she heard her saying *shit*?

Mark flinched. His eyes darted to Sally's face. She was staring back at him, her back to Sarah now.

"I'm right, aren't I? It was you who did those things. Why do you want him dead?"

"He's trouble," said Sally.

"You don't know what you're talking about," said Mark. "I didn't do anything of the sort."

"No, but maybe your *wife* did."

Sally turned. "Get out," she spat into Sarah's face. Sarah shrank back.

"Happily. I don't want to stay in this sick household any longer than I have to."

Sally came after her into the night. "If you think we did that, then you know why he attacked Mark. You can't deny it!"

Sarah ignored her and walked away. Sally had a point. But there was something about those injuries that didn't add up.

45

The door to the police station was unlocked. Jess pushed it open and felt the warm air hit her. She hadn't realised how cold she'd been.

Inside was a bare waiting room, two threadbare chairs against one wall and a long desk on the other side. There was no one sitting at it.

She walked to the desk and looked for a bell. There was nothing. A paperweight sat in the middle of the desk, two manila files one on top of the other and a pencil case that bulged with pens. She thought of the way writing materials were rationed in the village. Paper and pens couldn't be grown, they had to be bought with what limited money they had, and took low priority beneath medicines and food that couldn't be grown.

She put her hand back in her pocket; she was no thief.

A man emerged from the door at the back of the space. When he saw Jess, he stopped.

"Can I help you?"

"I'm Jess Dyer. From the refugee village down the coast. We need help."

He frowned. "You're not the only one."

"Sorry?"

"We've got another one of you here."

She frowned. "Who?"

"Can't tell you. Sorry."

"I'm the steward. The leader of the village council. If one of our people needs help, then I should know."

"You don't have any jurisdiction here. You do know that your little council means nothing, don't you?"

She sniffed. "Not to us. It keeps our community stable."

"I'm sure it does. I remember you. Your sister-in-law was arrested. And you assaulted Anita Chopra."

She shifted her feet. "My sister-in-law is the person I've come about. She needs an ambulance."

He raised an eyebrow. "This is a police station."

"Is there a hospital in Filey?"

"Of course not."

"But can you request an ambulance for Ruth?"

"I thought you looked after your own? You didn't even want us to investigate the alleged murder of your fiancé."

His tone made her feel like she had when she'd hit Anita. This was a bad idea; the police would never help them. But she had to try.

"Ruth is the village doctor. She almost drowned today."

The eyebrow rose further. "Really?"

"Don't you believe me?"

"Look. Wait here. I've got things to deal with. I'll be back shortly."

"She can't wait. What if she—?"

But he was gone.

Jess threw herself into one of the chairs. The space felt musty and institutional, taking her back to dentists' surgeries and hospital waiting rooms before the floods. A solitary lightbulb hung from the ceiling, casting a dull yellow glow over the space.

Should she wait, or was there somewhere else she could go?

It was late. Even if Anita Chopra had an office in Filey, it would be long since closed. And there was no hospital. The police were her only hope.

She went to the glazed door that the man had disappeared into and peered through. Beyond it was a dim corridor. Someone moved at its opposite end, too indistinct for her to make out.

She grabbed the door handle and tugged. It was locked. She went back to the reception desk, wondering if those files would help her.

She picked one of them up, then heard movement behind her. A young woman emerged from the other door. She eyed Jess, then went through the same door as the man. Jess held the files behind her back. When the woman was out of site, she dropped them back onto the desk.

Her heart was pounding. Every time she thought of Ruth, she felt a vice grip her chest. She had to help her, and fast.

46

S arah ran home, her senses alert and her feet light. She felt nothing more than anger: bright, energetic anger, lifting her up and throwing her along the roads.

Sally and Mark were lying, she knew it. There was something about the tone of Mark's voice, the way he looked at his girlfriend. And he'd been careful not to actually say that Martin had put those marks on his face. Sure, Sally had repeated her accusations, but Mark himself had not.

So if Martin hadn't attacked Mark, who had? Why? And why would he lie about it?

Maybe Martin could provide some answers. Someone had to.

She reached Martin's flat. She divided her life between his home and her mother's, never really thinking of either as her own. At some point, she would have to choose. Her mother was independent now, a member of the village council. But Sarah's urge to protect her, at least to be with her if she couldn't shield her, was strong.

She unlocked the outer door, slid inside so as not to

disturb the neighbours, and locked it behind her. She took the stairs as quietly as she could and unlocked the door to the flat.

"Martin?"

No response. Was he in bed? She felt irritation wash over her.

"Martin?" She pushed open the door to the bedroom.

The bed was empty. The duvet was piled in its centre. Martin's jeans, which had been folded over a chair, were gone.

She turned back to the living room. "Martin? I'm back." But he wasn't there.

She opened the door to the bathroom; also empty. She stepped back, suddenly scared.

She went to the sink and poured a glass of water. She gulped it down and wiped the spillage from her shirt.

She went to the window and looked out. The village was dark now, and silent. Not even the sound of wildlife. It was as if she'd been plunged into a thick soup of blackness.

She tore off the piece of wood that Martin had used to cover the broken window. A blast of cold air blew into her face, making her blink. She resisted the urge to call his name out into the night.

Martin, where are you? He knew as well as anyone that there was a curfew. And he also knew that someone in this village wanted to kill him.

She went to the door, hesitating before opening it. He could be anywhere. Maybe they'd been attacked again and he'd gone to help. But she hadn't heard anything.

She looked around the room. His coat was gone, and his shoes. There was a mug next to the sink which had been washed out. She was sure it hadn't been there before.

So he'd meant to leave. He'd had the time to grab his

coat, and wash his mug. He hadn't been snatched. That was something.

There was a piece of paper in the seat of the armchair next to the window. She picked it up. It was the same paper that had been thrown through the window: *Leave, or die.* Any normal person would throw a note like this away. But maybe Martin thought it held a clue.

She turned it over. There was writing on it, in faint pencil. She pulled it up to her face, but it was too dark to read.

She went into the kitchen and lit a candle. She held it near the note, careful not to make contact.

Wait here. M xxx

She felt her limbs weaken. Where had he gone? Was he going to confront his attacker? And should she stay here, like he asked, or go looking for him?

47

"Ruth. Ruth, it's me, Ben. You're at home. You're safe."

Ruth felt as if her chest would explode. She reached inside herself to identify the source of the pressure, but could feel nothing. She gulped in air and coughed, feeling like she might choke on her own breath.

She felt a hand on hers, tight and hot. She tried to move her arm away but it was too heavy.

She moaned.

She felt lips brush her cheek. She blinked, frozen. Where was she? Who was this person, touching her? *Leave me alone*, she thought. *Let me go.*

She clenched her eyes shut. Maybe if they thought she was unconscious, or even asleep, they would go.

She focused on her breathing, keeping it calm and steady. *Don't draw attention to yourself.*

The hand loosened on hers. She felt herself lighten.

The pain in her chest was hard and rough. It extended from deep inside and rasped its way up her windpipe to her lips, feeling like it might tear through her flesh. Her legs felt heavy and dull, her skin hot.

She worked her mind over the parts of her body, trying to regain sensation, to take control of herself. Feet first; aching and sore. Then her legs, heavy and loose. Her torso; she skipped that, overwhelmed by pain. Her arms felt hot and light, totally unlike her legs. She felt as if they might fly up into the air if she let go of them.

She moved up to her neck. It was stiff and cold. Her head felt as if it was packed full of burning cotton wool. Pain jabbed at her eyes and ears, threatening to pierce right into her, to tear her head apart.

She moaned again.

"Ruth?"

This person was never going to leave. Not until she told them to.

She fluttered her eyes open. Above her was a dim space, light flickering off to one side. A shape hovered over her. She blinked and the shape came into focus; it was a person.

She gasped, trying to pull herself down and into the bed. Robert! She had to get away.

She felt her legs convulse, as if trying to run from the bed. That was it. She had to run.

She let her legs fall to one side, feeling for the edge of the bed. At last she felt the mattress fall away. She shifted her weight, knowing that if she wasn't careful, she would fall. And then she would be powerless.

"Ruth? What are you doing?"

She muffled a scream. He put a hand on her chest and she tried to pull her muscles in, to create a cave of her flesh so he couldn't touch her.

She pushed air up onto her mouth in an attempt to speak. Nothing but a hoarse croak came out.

She opened her eyes again. The figure had pulled back and the hand was off her chest.

"She's scared, Ben. Maybe we should leave her alone for a bit."

"I can't leave her alone. I have to watch her."

She felt that icy fist clutch at her stomach again. Robert Cope was in here, watching her. He wasn't going to let her go. Not ever.

She pushed out a shaky breath. "Get off me," she whispered.

He leaned over her. "Ruth love, it's good to hear your voice. What happened?"

"You took me," she whispered. "You know what happened."

"I didn't take you anywhere, love. I brought you home."

The back of her throat rasped. She coughed.

A hand looped around her back and pulled her up. She felt herself being raised in the bed, horrified. Her legs kicked out and she screamed.

The hand pulled back and she dropped to the bed again. *Thank God.*

"It's me, Ben. I've got you."

"We want to get you better." Another voice, female. Who were the other women they were holding? She couldn't remember.

"Leave me," she croaked.

"Come on, Ben. Let's leave her for a bit. She needs time. Maybe the cold did something to her senses."

"I'm scared, Sheila."

"I know, sweetheart. But we're scaring her. You go downstairs to those boys, and I'll keep an eye on her from the door."

Ruth felt her breath become more steady. If one of the

other women was watching over her, then maybe she'd be safe.

48

J ess paced the room. From time to time, she stopped
at one of the doors and tried to open it. She pushed
her face against the glass and peered into the dimly
lit space, leaving a mark where her breath hit it.

She wondered if there was supposed to be a receptionist
of some sort at the front desk. She examined the items on
the desk; the paperweight was dusty but the pencil case and
file looked recently used. It seemed like the desk had been
abandoned, or maybe that it had been left temporarily by
someone who had decided – or been told – not to return.

Would Ruth have woken up yet? She tried to imagine
how Ben would be when his wife came round. She hoped
he could keep control of his emotions.

"Ms Dyer?"

She span round to see a woman standing in the open
doorway behind her. It was the young woman who'd passed
her before.

She hurried to her.

"I'm Detective Constable Paretska," she said.

"I remember you. You were there when…"

The woman nodded.

"Has he told you what's happened?"

"Yes. We called the hospital. But there's a complication."

Jess felt her heart sink to her shoes. "What kind of complication? Is Ruth alright?"

DC Paretska blinked and looked away. "I'm sorry, but I don't know. You don't have phones in your village."

"Of course we don't." *Because we're only allowed a certain amount of power. Because we don't have the money. Because people like you think it's inappropriate for refugees to have luxuries like phones, and confiscated them when we arrived.*

"Have they sent an ambulance?"

"Come with me."

Jess pushed down her anger and impatience and followed the woman through the door and along the corridor she'd been spying on. She began to wonder if she'd made the right decision coming here; this was getting them nowhere.

DC Paretska stopped at a closed door. She opened it and ushered her through.

Inside were three people. The man she'd spoken to before, who she remembered as the Detective Sergeant who'd arrested Ruth before. Anita Chopra, wearing a crumpled jacket and with mascara rimming her eyes. And Martin.

49

R uth sat up in the bed, wincing as Sheila plumped cushions behind her.

"Here you go," Sheila said in her sing-song voice. "Let's make you comfy."

"Where am I?" asked Ruth.

Sheila stopped moving. "Why, you're in your own bed of course. Don't you recognise it?"

Ruth looked around. The room was a blur, dancing shapes and patterns of light and dark. She squinted to try to make out details, but all she could see was a white mist.

"I don't feel so well."

Sheila wheezed as she lowered Ruth to the pillows. Ruth felt the softness of them hit the back of her head. She tensed, feeling as if she might be sucked into the bed.

Sheila's hand was on her cheek. "You look peaky, love."

Ruth tried to move her head but it wouldn't cooperate.

"Ruth? Sheila, is it alright to come in?"

Ruth squeezed her eyes shut. It was him again.

The room filled with hazy figures, people moving around. She tightened her eyes and tried to shut it out. She could just about cope with Sheila here; the older woman had a confidence that made Ruth feel more solid than she had, as if she could cling onto the edge of the world and not fall off. But now there were more people: moving, swaying, talking.

Sheila bent to her. "It's just Ben, love. Your husband, remember? And your kiddies. Little Sean and Ollie." Her voice dipped to a whisper. "They're scared."

Ruth felt fear grip at her. What were her boys doing in a house with Robert Cope in it? She needed to get them to safety, quickly.

"Take them away, get them away. They aren't safe!" she whimpered.

"It's fine, Ruth. They're with me." A man, on the other side of the bed. Sheila had said it was Ben. He smelled familiar, of soap and cooking fat. She tried to remember Robert's smell: aftershave, wasn't it?

She sniffed. She couldn't smell any aftershave. Maybe this wasn't him. Maybe her boys would be safe, after all. She opened her eyes.

A man bent over the bed, his eyes boring into her. She raised her hand to shield herself from his gaze, and shifted her head to the side.

The sight of two small boys snagged on her vision. She gasped. Blonde hair; one neat, the other tousled. She knew them.

She felt a tear roll down her cheek. "Boys."

The boy on the right – Sean, she was sure of it – nodded. His brother turned away. She felt her stomach dip.

"Ollie. Ollie, come to Mummy."

The boy turned back to her. His lip was trembling, and his eyes were red. He shouldn't be here.

"Take them away," she said. She wanted to pull them to

her, to clutch them so tightly that none of them would be able to breathe. But she didn't trust herself with them. She didn't trust that in this room, Robert wouldn't return. That he wouldn't come back for them.

She fell back against the pillow, raked with sobs. Sheila muttered something and the man she hoped was Ben bent over her again. He laid a kiss on her forehead. She stiffened, holding herself still. He grabbed the two boys by the hand and led them out.

Sheila stroked her arm. "Well done, sweetheart. How did it feel, to see your boys again?"

Numbness was creeping up her legs. There was a deep pain inside her abdomen, growing and threatening to spill out of her. She scratched at her skin, frightened.

She stared up at Sheila, willing her to come for her, to come inside the hole Ruth had fallen down. *Save me*, she thought.

The pain jabbed at her, then spread up her chest, bringing numbness behind it. She felt herself sway against the pillows and then the world went black.

50

"Martin?"

Martin stood up and gave Jess a nervous smile. "Hi, Jess."

"What are you doing here? Where's Sarah?"

She looked from him to the two detectives and the council officer. Had they brought him here?

"Have you been arrested?" she asked him.

He shook his head. "No. I came here myself."

"Why?"

Martin bowed his head. "I wanted to help."

Anita Chopra stepped forward. "He's offered to do an exchange."

"What sort of exchange?"

"I gather he's been allocated a flat, in your village. He says we can house people in it. He'll move to the hostel we've established, here in Filey."

Jess stared at Martin. "That flat isn't yours to give them. I worked bloody hard to get you—"

"Nobody wants me there," he said. "I've been getting death threats."

"I know. It doesn't mean anything."

"I can't put Sarah at risk."

"Does she know you've done this?"

A blush. "No."

"And is she going to live here with you, or go back to Dawn?"

"She officially lives with Dawn still. But I hope we can work something out."

"She won't move here."

He shrugged. "I had to protect her."

She gritted her teeth. She'd fought to protect this young man's rights, to persuade the other council members and then villagers to allow him to live among them. She'd thought his acceptance showed something about the village, and what it stood for. But now, at the slightest perceived threat, he was running away. Maybe she was wrong about him.

"I haven't got time for this," she said. She turned to Anita Chopra. "Ruth needs help. She almost drowned today. I left her at home, I have no idea if she's going to be alright."

A shadow crossed Anita Chopra's face. "You haven't come here to assault me again?"

"I'm sorry about that. I was grieving. I was angry. I took it out on you."

"You did."

"So?" asked Jess. "Can you help her? I've already asked the police if they'll call an ambulance." She turned to the detectives. "Have you?"

Anita stepped towards her. Jess gave her a *back off* look, but she ignored it. She flicked her gaze to the woman's chin; there was no scar.

"I thought you looked after your own," Anita said.

"The only doctor we have can't treat herself. We need help."

She stared back at the official. She hated having to come to them like this, to admit weakness. But Ruth's life was at stake.

"We can help you, yes."

Jess let out the breath she had been holding. "Thank God. She's at home. Tell them to hurry."

"But we need something from you in return."

"What kind of people are you? There's a woman who could be dying, and you won't send her an ambulance?"

"You don't pay taxes. You don't contribute to the wider community."

"We pay our way. We send men out to work on the earthworks."

"Casual labour. Hardly a full role in society, would you say?"

"I don't see what that has to do with Ruth!"

Anita sat down. She gestured for Jess to do the same. Jess ignored her.

"Jess – can I call you Jess?"

Jess nodded, holding in her anger and frustration. She wanted to claw this woman's eyes out.

"Jess, you know how society works. You make what contribution you can, and the state helps you out when you need it. Medical help, housing, that sort of thing."

Jess narrowed her eyes. "You left us to survive alone."

"No. You chose to. Don't you remember what that village was in the early days?"

"I don't know what you're talking about."

"Hmm." Anita raised her eyes to the ceiling, as if calculating something. "No. You arrived just as we were leaving. You missed the worst of it."

"I still don't know what you're talking about. Or why it means you can't help Ruth. The village needs her."

"The place was lawless. People who'd spent months living rough, eking out a living on the road. People get used to different standards in those conditions, I imagine. We let you stay, on the understanding you would govern yourselves, and that you wouldn't cause us any trouble. That you wouldn't be a drain on resources."

"That was six-and-a-half years ago."

"Just under six, to be precise. But yes. And now you expect us to help you, but you won't help us."

"Is this why you sent more people, without telling us?"

Anita frowned. "I'm sorry?"

"There are almost twenty people in those houses, that shouldn't be there. They say they're just looking for shelter, but"—she glanced at Martin—"how can we be sure?"

Anita licked her lips. "If there are people squatting, then we'll deal with it."

Jess thought of the little girl she'd seen, sitting on the stairs of the house. How old had she been – four, five? She remembered the children she'd seen sleeping on the floors of church halls and sheltering in hedgerows after the floods.

The anger left her.

"You will?"

"Of course. We want to make sure everyone is looked after, not just those who are prepared to break the law."

Jess looked at Martin again. He was blinking at her, nodding. Nothing was what it seemed.

"Tell me what you need," she said.

Anita stood up. "At last. We understand each other." She scratched her chin. "It's simple, Jess. You let us make better use of the hosting stock in that village, and we help your sister-in-law. Say the word, and I'll make a call."

Jess thought of Ben, adamant that they weren't taken over by outsiders. Of Ruth, and her fear of everyone who wasn't familiar. Jess had failed to notice Ruth's deterioration before her eyes.

Then she thought of Zack, lying in her arms, bleeding to death. Of the people who'd invaded their village.

"They killed him," she whispered.

"I'm sorry?"

"My fiancé. Zachary Golder. He was murdered by people from your so-called civilisation."

"When was this?"

"Two nights ago."

"And what did you do about it?" Anita looked towards the police officers. They shook their heads.

"Of course we didn't tell the police," Jess said. "They never would have listened."

"Don't you see why?" Anita said. "You can break this deadlock. You can get medical help for your sister-in-law. Justice for your boyfriend, maybe. Just say the word."

She thought of the village meeting, the way she'd been trampled on, ignored. The helplessness she felt.

This wasn't her decision to make. The council was a democratic body, with clear processes. The village had survived all this time by allowing everybody to have their say.

But Ruth could die. Ben would see that this had to be done. Wouldn't he?

"Alright," she muttered.

"Sorry?"

She jerked her head up. "I said yes. Send her an ambulance. Ask these two to help find Zack's killer. We'll work with you on the housing."

51

S arah ran out into the night. She turned wildly from side to side, knowing that expecting to find him nearby was just wishful thinking.

How long had she been gone? It had turned dark since she'd arrived at Sally and Mark's house almost an hour ago. And it had been dusk when she'd left Martin. He'd been lying in bed feeling sorry for himself. It hadn't occurred to her for a moment that he'd go, much less that he'd do something stupid.

She ran back to Sally and Mark's house, her agitation rising the closer she came to it. If he'd gone to confront them, who knows what recklessness might have come over him?

She stopped in her tracks, almost falling over in her shock.

What if Sally had been right? What if Martin *had* discovered that it was Mark who'd targeted him? What if he'd decided to retaliate? Martin could be violent; she'd seen him hurl himself at Robert Cope. He'd claimed to be protecting her, but what if it had really been revenge that motivated him?

If he could plunge a knife into a man who'd once saved his life, what was he capable of doing to a man who'd posted human shit through his letterbox?

She was slumped on the ground, grass scratching at her bare legs. She hadn't even pulled the door to the flats closed behind her. Their neighbours wouldn't forgive her.

She had to know. She had to face him.

She squared her shoulders and pointed herself in the direction of the house. The buildings around her all looked the same; dark, squat lumps of stone or brick, looming around her. Which way had she come from? And which way did she need to go?

She closed her eyes for a moment, waiting for the dizziness to recede. When she opened them, she was back in the familiar village. She knew where she had to go. She started running.

At Sally and Mark's house, she hammered on the door, not caring this time about being subtle. The door flew open almost instantly.

"I've told you to fuck off!" Sally's eyes were blazing.

"Is Martin here?"

"No. Why the hell would he be?"

"I just thought he might have come here."

Sally pushed the door against her. Sarah caught it with her foot. "Please. He's disappeared."

"Good."

Sarah dug her fingernail into the flesh of her palm, anxious to conceal her panic and frustration. "If you see him, will you let me know?"

"What's going on?" Mark was behind Sally, his face shadowed in the dim light of the candles.

"It's this bitch again."

"I'm looking for Martin. I thought he might have come here."

Mark and Sally exchanged glances. "No," said Mark. "He's buggered off, hasn't he? Like he should have in the first place."

Sally reached round to touch Mark's face. "It was worth it, then."

Mark gave her a look and retreated inside. Sally took advantage of Sarah's surprise and slammed the door on her, narrowly avoiding her toes.

Sarah stood and stared at the house, confused. What was going on with that pair? And where was Martin?

She looked back towards the village centre. Her chest was heaving now, her breaths shallow and fast. She didn't know if she was thinking straight, or if panic had taken over. Martin had left the village before, when he thought she was at risk from his presence. She'd gone with him that time, defying her father. But this was different. He'd lived here for six months. He had a job on the allotments. He came home at night talking to her about the chicken pens they'd built, about the personalities of the different chickens. It was almost as if he saw them as pets; she'd worried he might baulk at eating them when the time came.

He had everything to stay here for, and nowhere to go. He'd never go back to that farm, and Filey just held memories of his arrest for Robert's murder.

She pulled at the skin on her face, berating herself. Maybe he was hiding out on the allotments like he had when her father had been searching for him after he'd first arrived.

She turned towards them.

She picked her way between the rows of vegetables,

anxious not to trample the precious food. There were two sheds in these allotments: one on this side and another at the far edge. She hurried to the closest one, and tore the door open.

It was empty. A spade leaned against the wall, a pile of flowerpots teetered in a corner, and cobwebs strewed the ceiling. She shuddered and closed the door again.

The other shed was equally deserted.

Maybe if she tried her mother's house. Dawn and Martin had grown closer over the last six months. He hadn't wanted Dawn to know about the threats, but maybe he'd changed his mind.

She considered going back to the flat, just in case. But it was in the opposite direction from the clifftops. And she needed Dawn's reassurance that she wasn't going mad.

She made for the cottage.

She started to run.

52

J ess sat in the back of the car, feeling uncomfortable. The rough fabric of the seat scratched through her thin jeans and the stale air jabbed at her nostrils. She realised this was the smell of civilisation, and she didn't miss it.

They swept along the main road down the coast, headlights picking out bushes and crumpled road signs as they careered round the bends. She gripped the seat front with her ragged fingernails, fighting nausea.

Martin was beside her in the back. In the front was Anita Chopra, and a uniformed police officer. He stared ahead in silence, all his senses focused on the road ahead.

At last they reached the entrance to the village. The car slowed and took the corner steadily. She turned to see the car behind follow them. The two detectives were in there, along with another uniformed policewoman. And there was a dark van behind that; she'd asked Anita what it was for, but had got no response.

She stared out at the houses as they glided along the Parade. People inside would be coming to their windows, wondering why two cars were arriving at the village at this time of night. Both cars were unmarked: she'd managed to persuade the senior detective that the villagers didn't need the shock of police cars descending on them two days after a vicious attack, and that Ruth in particular didn't need to be reminded of the last time they'd been here.

They reached the circle of grass that marked this edge of the village centre. She stared at the oak tree on its opposite side, her vision clouded. She'd seen Zack run out in front of that tree, heard him cry out her name. Then, nothing. Could she have saved him? Even if she hadn't been able to stop the attack itself, could she have been in the right place, at the right time?

She closed her eyes. She had to focus on Ruth. She didn't need to be grieving for two people she loved.

"You know the way?" she asked, superfluously. Of course they did. Every time the authorities came to this village, they made straight for Ben and Ruth's house.

The car stopped outside the house. The front door opened and Ben emerged. Jess climbed out of the back of the car and steeled herself. The van had gone; where was it?

"What did you do?" he cried.

"Is the ambulance here?"

"What ambulance?'

"They called an ambulance. Has it arrived yet?"

'I don't know what you're talking about, sis. Why did you bring the police here?"

She grabbed his wrists. He pulled against her grip but she held tight.

"Listen to me, Ben. I persuaded them to send help. An ambulance will be here any minute. How is she?"

"You've been gone for hours."

Not hours, she thought. *But too long.* She felt panic rise in her throat. "How is she?"

He stared into her face. "Not good."

"Is she conscious?"

"She has been. But she's asleep. I think. I hope."

Jess looked towards the house. "Can I see her?"

They both turned at the sound of advancing sirens. Blue lights reflected off the windows and glowed through the gaps between buildings. This would escape no one's attention, thought Jess. They'd want to know how she'd persuaded them to help.

The ambulance pulled up next to the car. Two paramedics jumped out. One of them, a grey-haired woman, spotted DS Bryce and hurried to him. The detective pointed at Ben and Ruth's open door and the two paramedics hurried inside.

Jess wondered what it would have been like if they'd had access to professional medical care when Sonia had been sick. When Zack had been stabbed. Why hadn't she gone to the authorities years ago?

Ben ran after the paramedics, calling instructions.

"Leave them to do their job," Jess called. He ignored her.

Sheila came out of the house, her eyes wild.

Jess stepped forward. "Thanks for looking after her. How is she?"

"Not good. Ben thinks she's asleep but it didn't look like that to me."

Jess felt the blood leave her face. "She's not—?"

Sheila put a hand on her arm. "No, love. She's still with us. But she's going in and out of consciousness, like she's struggling to hold on. At one point she started shouting a name."

"A name?"

Sheila leaned in towards her. "Robert."

Jess stiffened. "Are you sure?"

Sheila nodded. Jess looked back at the house. Why was Ruth shouting Robert's name? Did she think he was there with her, in the house? Did she think Ben was him?

She shivered. "Where are the boys?"

Sheila sighed. "Asleep, on the sofa. Little loves."

"I'll look after them now."

"Surely you need to deal with all these people."

"They can wait."

Sheila smiled. "You're right, love. Family first."

Jess strode towards the house. She was halted in her tracks by the paramedics, pushing Ruth out on a trolley. She stood aside to let them pass, then watched as they loaded her onto the ambulance. Ben trailed behind them, climbing up into the ambulance to be with his wife.

"Where will they take her?" she called out, not sure if anyone who might know was listening.

"I'll ask them, love," said Sheila. "You go in to those kiddies."

Jess nodded and stepped into the house.

53

R uth stared out of the window. All she could see was a pale sky, and the tip of a mast on the building opposite. She wondered how far they were from the sea.

A nurse bustled in, carrying a clipboard. "Hello, love. How are you feeling?"

Ruth said nothing, but gave her the best smile she could muster.

"Your husband's here."

Ruth felt her skin constrict. This hospital was so anonymous, so removed from everything that had happened to her. None of these people knew her or what she had done, what had been done to her. She could dissolve in the anonymity of it, the routine. She could let herself be carried on it until maybe, just maybe, she came out the other side.

"I don't want to see him."

The nurse stopped in her tracks. "You sure?"

Ruth nodded. Her chest felt heavy and there was a stillness behind her eyelids that felt like her head had been filled with glass.

"I can't."

The nurse perked up. "We won't force anything on you. I'll tell him to wait."

Ruth slumped against the pillows. "No. It's alright."

If she didn't see Ben, then she wouldn't be able to see Sean and Ollie. They needed to know she was getting better.

The nurse smiled and went away while Ruth took deep breaths and ran her fingers through her hair repeatedly until Ben appeared. He was smiling sheepishly.

"Hey, love."

"Where are the boys?"

"They're at home, with Jess. I thought this would be too much for them."

She closed her eyes. She shouldn't have let him come. She couldn't stand it.

She opened her eyes again. She forced herself to explore his face, to take in every aspect of him. *He's not Robert*, she reminded herself. *He won't hurt you.*

But it was all his fault.

"I want to see the boys."

"I can bring them tomorrow."

She nodded, her body feeling as if it was full of nail filings. She forced out a smile.

"How are you?" he asked.

"I'm fine," she lied.

"Good."

She widened her eyes. Did he believe her? Was he that insensitive?

"How did I get here?"

He shuffled his orange plastic chair towards her. She gave him a warning look and he stopped moving.

"Jess went to the police, in Filey. She found out where

the station was from those people they moved into the village."

She swallowed. Her throat was sore and her stomach felt like it had been turned inside out. "Are they still there?"

"Who?"

"The new people."

"No. Turns out they were hiding some family members, who were wanted by the police. They arrested some of them, and threw the others out."

She felt fatigue wash over her.

"Good riddance," Ben said. "We don't need outsiders."

"They won't all be like that."

Ben sat upright. "What? You didn't want them here any more than I did."

She swallowed down her distaste. *You never listen.*

"The explosion. They were all made homeless. Just like us, with the floods."

Her voice was hoarse; she needed to protect it. She grabbed his hand.

"Come back tomorrow, with the boys. And tell Jess she needs to do what that council officer says. It'll be worse, if she doesn't."

54

"You had no authority."

Ben glared at Jess. His sons were still asleep. Anita Chopra sat at the third kitchen table, perfume surrounding her like a cloud.

Ben had spent the night at the hospital with Ruth. This morning, Anita had brought him back to the village. Ruth was awake and responsive. She was calling him Ben instead of Robert. But she didn't want him there. So here he was, losing his rag with Jess again.

She leaned over the table, staring him down. "I had no choice."

He looked from her to Anita. True to the promise she'd given Jess last night, she'd said nothing of their deal on the way here with Ben. That had been left for Jess to do.

"We'll overturn it," he said.

"You can't."

"We can. We will. Ruth is in that hospital because of what happened the last time we welcomed outsiders into this village."

"She's in that hospital because we were too busy fighting

to see how sick she was. *And* because of what you and Robert Cope did when you were teenagers."

He reddened. "How dare you."

"You know what you did." She glanced towards Anita. "You said it yourself. And it brought Robert Cope here. Look at what you've done to Ruth."

"I didn't do that."

She felt as if he'd punched her. "Is that the best you can come up with?"

"I looked after her, Jess. While you buggered off looking for help."

"From what I hear, it was Sheila we have to thank."

He reddened. "What do you expect me to say?"

She tried to drag some energy out of her body. She was tired. She missed Zack.

"We need to accept help. Whatever the terms. The people from Filey, they're just like we were once. People who've lost their homes because of a disaster. Don't you remember what it was like to feel like that?"

"They attacked us. They've victimised us for the last six years."

"I know. But why does that mean we have to be as bad as them? Can't we be the ones to forgive?"

"Have you met them? Do they want to make friends?"

She thought of the men in that hallway. The way they'd crowded around her.

But they were gone now. The Bagris were also gone, too scared of the neighbours who'd been forced on them. She wondered if they had family to stay with in Filey.

But new families would soon arrive in their place. Families who weren't intent on trouble. More than two of them.

"What does Ruth think?" she asked.

"About what?"

"About us letting new people come here. About this village opening itself up to the outside world."

He reddened. "You know what she thinks."

"Tell me."

"She's Ruth. She wants to help them, of course."

"Don't you think she's right?"

"She's not a council member. It isn't up to her."

She felt her mouth drop open. "She's your wife, Ben. And she's the most sensible person I know."

His shoulders dropped. "I feel like I've lost her, sis."

"Well, you have to win her back then. She's been through a lot. She's been very sick. It's not going to be easy, and you have to be patient."

"I know."

"And not just with Ruth."

"Huh?"

"The new people. If we make them feel welcome, they'll behave themselves."

"How do you know that?"

"Because I know what this place was like, before we arrived. Anita told me." She exchanged glances with the council officer. "It calmed down. It can again."

He shook his head, staring at her like she was an imbecile.

"Without this, Ruth would still be upstairs. She needs help, Ben. Not just for the hypothermia, and her lungs. She's messed up."

Ben's face darkened. She knew how hard it was for him to accept that his solid, steadfast wife was losing her grip on reality. But he needed to find some courage.

"Ruth is strong, Ben. She's been there for all of us when we needed her. I don't know what Mum would have done without her."

Her voice tailed off. Ruth had nursed Sonia on the journey north, had stayed with her all day and all night. She'd done things for Sonia that Jess hadn't been able to face. Jess had spent the last six years coming to terms with the fact that Ruth had been like a daughter to Sonia, and maybe a better one than she had been. She would have to make her peace with it, and teach herself to be less possessive of her mother's memory.

"But right now, she needs help. She's got further to fall than people like you and me. She must be terrified."

"You think she... you think she tried to drown herself?"

Anita sat up straighter in her chair. Jess swallowed. "We can't know that. Not without Ruth here to tell us. But it doesn't matter. What matters is that she gets better."

"Am I such a terrible husband, sis?"

Jess felt a sob leave her lips. She went to Ben's chair and folded herself over him from behind. He was shaking.

"No, Ben. You really aren't."

Ben looked at Anita. "You promise you'll help her. That we'll have access to proper healthcare?"

"Healthcare, and education, and more."

Jess caught herself before she protested at the mention of education. She'd been about to defend the village school where she'd worked for so many years. They'd tried to provide the children with an education. But of course, it hadn't been enough.

"We think there are things we can teach you," she said.

"You do?"

"Yes. We've learned to live off the land. We grow our own food. We share everything. We make good use of limited resources. I imagine the people you work with would benefit from some of that."

"They probably would. But what they need most are places to live."

Ben bristled. Jess nodded. "We'll have to work out the logistics of that. I'll put together a group, one or two of the villagers who can work with you."

Anita frowned. *She's about to override me*, thought Jess. *She's going to exert her authority.*

Then Anita seemed to catch the look on Jess's face. "Very well," she said. "We'll see what we can do."

55

"It was the night of the riot."

Sarah stood as still as she could, clutching her hands together. The village council surrounded her.

Jess smiled at her. "Go on."

Sarah licked her lips. "I was out checking on my mum." She looked at Dawn, who gave her an encouraging smile. The two of them had spent the whole of yesterday preparing for this. It didn't make it any easier.

"I got back to the flat – Martin's flat – and there was a hole in the window. I found a brick on the floor. It was wrapped in a piece of paper."

"A note?" asked Colin.

Sarah nodded. "Yes."

"What did it say?"

She reached into her pocket, her fingers trembling. She held it out to him.

He took it, his fingers brushing hers.

"Thank you," said Jess. "And then you found something else, posted through the letterbox?"

"Not me."

"Who then?"

"It was Martin who found it." She lowered her voice. "Human excrement." She avoided her mother's eye.

"How do you know it was human?" asked another man. Sanjeev; she knew him from when he had been their neighbour.

"The smell," she said. "Martin works with the chickens, and the pigs. He knows the smell of their – of their waste. It's different."

"It couldn't have been from a dog?"

Jess leaned across the other councillors. "Does that really matter? It's still just as offensive."

Sanjeev shrugged. "Guess so."

Jess turned to Sarah. "And who do you believe did this?"

Sarah glanced at Dawn, who gave her an encouraging nod. "I think it was Sally Angus."

Jess raised an eyebrow. "But it was Mark Palfrey, Sally's fiancé, who accused Martin of attacking him. If the two of them had some sort of disagreement..."

"Martin had never met Mark before. There was no disagreement. Sally wanted him gone. She hated that he'd been part of the group that took us, and that he was here."

Colin cleared his throat. "I don't think it's appropriate to speculate on motive."

"Sorry," Sarah whispered.

"How do you feel about him being here? After what he did to you, and the others?" Colin asked.

Sarah heard a clatter behind her. The council members looked past her, towards the doors. She turned.

Sally Angus was pushing towards Sarah, the doors swinging behind her. Sarah shrank back.

"She's lying!" Sally screeched.

Colin stood up. "Please! You'll have your turn."

Sally pointed at Sarah. Sanjeev and Ben had hurried to Sally and were holding her by the shoulders, keeping her away from Sarah.

"Have you seen the scars on my Mark's face?"

Sarah felt the skin on her arms prickle. She'd seen those scars. She'd seen Sally's nails. She'd put two and two together.

But why?

The doors opened again and Mark walked in. He had less energy than his girlfriend, and less colour in his cheeks.

Colin sighed loudly. "Please, everybody. We'll be taking evidence from one person at a time."

Mark shook his head. "She's lying."

"We've already heard Miss Angus say that."

"Mrs Palfrey!" Sally cried. He's my husband."

Mark stepped towards her. "No, love. We're not married. Not yet." He put an arm around her, resisting Sanjeev who was trying to keep them apart.

"Please," he said. "She's not well."

Jess motioned for everyone to sit down. Someone Sarah didn't know pulled more chairs over, and Mark guided Sally into one. Mark placed himself between Sarah and Sally. It reminded her of the way Sally had put herself between Sarah and Mark when she'd gone to their house.

"This is very irregular," said Colin.

"It's alright," said Jess. "Maybe we can get to the bottom of this more easily, with everyone here. This isn't a court of law, after all."

Sarah felt her muscles relax a little. She trusted Jess. She wasn't so sure about Colin. But he was Sheila's husband; he couldn't be all bad.

She thought of Mark, waiting outside alone. He'd already given his evidence; what had he said?

"Someone ask Martin to come in," said Jess. She ignored Colin's remonstrations.

Martin was given a chair next to Sarah. Sally scowled at him as he sat, but he kept his gaze ahead. He looked nervous.

Sarah grabbed his hand and pulled it into her lap.

"Right," said Jess. She leaned back in her chair. "Mark, carry on."

Mark stood up.

"It's alright. You can stay seated."

Mark sat down. Sally started making small animal-like sounds.

"Thanks," said Mark. He lowered his voice. "I'm sorry, Sally."

The room quietened.

"Please," said Colin. "Say what you barged in here to tell us." Jess frowned at him.

"Sally isn't well. Since the kidnapping."

Sarah felt Martin's hand tense in hers; she held onto it.

"I think she's got PTSD," continued Mark. "She doesn't always know what's real, and what isn't."

"Go on," said Jess, her voice soft.

"She did this to me." Mark pointed at his face. There was a scar running down one cheek. "She was suicidal. I hid all the knives in the house, and she was desperate for me to give them to her. Afterwards, she was insistent that Martin had done it."

Martin's hand loosened in Sarah's. It was damp.

"And the death threat? The parcel through the letter-box?" asked Jess.

"Sally again. I don't think she knew what she was doing." A pause. Sally sniffed. "I'm sorry," continued Mark. "I should have told someone."

"You should," said Colin.

Sally was silent. Sarah risked peering round Mark to look at her. She stared straight ahead, her face stiff. Tears ran down her cheeks.

Poor woman.

"She blamed him," said Mark. "He was a constant reminder. But she went too far. She's not a bad person. She just needs help."

"There's a psychiatrist in Filey," Jess said. "It might be best if the two of you move there."

Mark stood, pushing his chair back. "Is this some kind of punishment?"

"She sent death threats to another member of the village. She made us go through all this."

"She didn't mean to."

Sarah squeezed Martin's hand.

"It's alright," Martin said. Sarah looked at him. How could he be so forgiving?

"We'll move to Filey," Martin continued. He looked at Sarah. "I think it's what we need."

She looked back at him. They'd already discussed this. It was the best way to build their own life together. They wouldn't be far from Dawn, after all. She nodded.

"Very well," said Jess. "But I think Sally owes you an apology, at the very least."

After a moment's silence, Mark spoke. "I'm sorry."

Sally said nothing.

56

"It's hard not being with my boys."

Ruth thought of the conversation she'd had with Sean and Ollie the previous day, when they'd been brought to Filey to visit her. Ollie had wanted to know why they hadn't moved out of the village with her. Sean had put on a brave face, telling his brother to shut up.

But for now, she felt more secure on her own. She'd been given a tiny studio flat in Filey, over a chip shop. She was putting on weight, but the fact that she didn't need to cook or look after anyone was helping her to regain control of her sanity. And using money had been a revelation.

"How do they feel about that?" the therapist asked.

"Confused. They veer from sad to bitter, when I see them. Two hours a week isn't much, but it's all I can take right now."

"That's understandable." The woman leaned forward over the low table. She was white-haired and thin; Ruth wondered if she'd been brought out of retirement for this.

"But I don't feel as if I might hurt them anymore."

"No?"

"No. I can touch them. I can hold them. I just can't be a mother to them. Not properly. Does that make me a bad person?"

"It makes you a person who's unwell. It won't be permanent."

Ruth nodded; it was difficult to believe that, no matter how many times the counsellor said it.

"How are you finding your new accommodation?"

"I like the quiet. No one bothers me."

"Go on."

Ruth frowned. "I don't know. What do you want me to say?"

"Why don't you want people to bother you?"

"That's pretty obvious, I'd have thought."

"I just want to hear it from you."

"I need space. I need time. I want to be back with my boys some day. When I'm... when I'm better."

She swallowed the lump in her throat.

"And your husband?"

Ruth pulled herself inwards. "I don't know."

"Your boys are with him still, in the village."

"Yes."

"You don't have to push yourself too hard, you know. If the thought of being with your boys helps you, then that's great. But it's fine to just focus on yourself right now. Your husband can wait."

Ruth nodded. He would have to. She still didn't know if it would be worth his while, but she knew he would.

"Yes," she said.

The counsellor straightened in her chair. "Our hour is up, I'm afraid. I'll see you next week, same time?"

"Yes. Thanks."

Ruth hated the way their sessions ended so abruptly. It

didn't matter where she was in her train of thought, how much she'd managed to come to terms with: the hour was sacred. She shuffled out of the room and down the dark stairs to the street.

The counsellor's office was just two streets away from her own flat, closer to the sea front. She passed a couple in the street. They nodded at her; she had no idea who they were. Was Filey friendly, or was it just that they all knew her, the mad woman from down the coast who'd tried to drown herself?

Jess was standing outside the chippy. It was closed, but the smell of cooking oil still wafted onto the street.

"Hey."

"Hey," replied Ruth. "What brings you to Filey?"

"You do. I came to check up on you."

Ruth didn't believe her sister-in-law. She knew she had business here; she and Anita Chopra were working out the terms of the village being reintegrated into society.

"Come on up."

"Thanks."

Ruth led Jess up the narrow staircase to her flat. She knew it was dirty, with yellow stains on the walls, and that it stank of chips. But she didn't care.

"Coffee?"

Jess pulled a face. "No thanks."

Ruth smiled and put the kettle on. Using electrical appliances again had been a revelation. And she'd rediscovered the addiction to coffee she'd enjoyed in her youth. It probably didn't help her troubled sleep.

"So," she said. "How are Sean and Ollie?"

Jess smiled to herself. "Ollie has lost a tooth."

"Did the tooth fairy come?"

"Of course."

"Ben?"

A blush. "Me. They've been staying with me some of the time."

"Oh." She didn't want to know why. If Ben was falling apart, that was his problem.

"I'll be back soon," she said. "I'm doing well. Making progress."

Jess lowered herself into a chair. "I can see."

Ruth sat next to her. "Thank you."

"What for?"

"You did that deal with Anita Chopra, so I could have help."

"Not just you. Turns out Sally Angus will be visiting the psychiatrist too."

"Oh. Not surprising, I guess."

Ruth sipped at her coffee and stared through the window. Beyond it, seagulls wheeled.

"When I come back," she asked, "will I have to live with Ben?"

"Of course not. You can live wherever you want."

"I want to be with my boys."

"They want to be with you."

"And I might want to be with Ben in time. But not yet. I can't forgive him just yet."

A seagull squawked. "That's fine," said Jess. "He'll understand.

Ruth stiffened. "Will he?"

Jess turned to her. "I'll make sure of it. We'll look after you, Ruth. And I'll look after Ben."

"Thanks. I miss the boys."

"They miss you too."

Ruth smiled. "Give them a hug from me. Tell them Mummy will be home soon."

57

J ess left the coastal path and headed into the village. Seeing Ruth always made her feel better and worse, at the same time. It was good to see that Ruth was getting better, but heartbreaking to see her alone.

She passed her old house on the clifftop. It had a family living in it now: four kids under the age of ten. Sheila would have her work cut out, at least until they started sending all the kids to the school in Filey. She wondered how it would feel, to let all those children leave the village. She had visions of the parents following them up the coast, standing outside the school building until they emerged at the end of the day.

Two boys were ahead of her; young men, maybe. She didn't know them. One wore a grey hoody and the other a sweatshirt with Adidas on the back.

She stopped walking. These were the same boys she'd confronted on her first day as steward, seven months ago. They'd mounted the climbing frame, waving a banner between them: *go home skum.*

Did they live here now? Or were they causing trouble?

"Boys!" she called to them. They turned.

She felt herself deflate. These boys were too young. They were no more than thirteen, and their faces were smoother. They exchanged glances then ran off between the houses, calling to each other good-naturedly.

She would have to get used to this. The village wasn't what it was. They had more people to deal with, more mouths to feed. But they had help. There was a doctor in Filey now, and a school. And there was money. The men who went to Hull to work on the earthworks, Sam still among them, earned a proper wage. Sam was a team leader, earning five times what he had. It wouldn't be long before they were expected to have bank accounts.

She stopped walking. Sometimes, the grief hit her like a bullet. She thought of Zack, strolling through the village with her, towards his family's house. On the night they'd told them about the engagement. They'd held hands, swinging their arms between them. For the first time in over six years, her mind had been on the future.

What now? Stay here, try to steer this village into an uncertain future? Or move to Filey, where she wouldn't be reminded of her fiancé every time she turned a corner?

Filey was still a ghost town; that much had been clear from this last visit. The area where the gas explosion had taken place was hazardous, the wreckage of buildings being hastily blocked off by the authorities. But some of the villagers had chosen to live in the town. And it was giving the place a new lease of life. Toni and Roisin were among them. She hoped they'd be happy there. Toni had told her Flo was coming round to the idea gradually, but it could take a while.

Ben emerged from his house as she passed.

"Did you see her?"

She stopped walking, irritated. "Yes."

Be patient, Ben. That was what she'd said to him, on the day she'd done the deal with Anita Chopra.

"How was she?"

"She was drinking coffee."

"Coffee?"

"She offered me a mug. I said no."

"Is that a good thing?"

"I guess so." She didn't tell him Ruth wanted to come back to her boys, but not her husband. *Cross that bridge when we come to it.*

He said nothing, but fell into step beside her. They were heading for the village hall, for the council's final meeting. The group was to be disbanded. Next month the villagers would be voting in local elections. She tried to muster enthusiasm for electing members of Filey town council, but couldn't bring herself to. Maybe that would change. Maybe she would stand herself.

"Give her time, Ben."

"I want her back."

"If you push her, you'll lose her for good."

"Put a good word in for me, will you? I haven't seen her for weeks."

She grabbed his hand. "I know, bruv. I'll do what I can."

They pushed open the door to the village hall and she steeled herself for her last meeting as steward.

A HOUSE DIVIDED, PART 1 OF THE DIVISION BELL TRILOGY

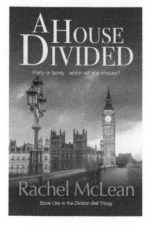

Jennifer Sinclair is many things: loyal government minister, loving wife and devoted mother.

But when a terror attack threatens her family, her world is turned upside down. When the government she has served targets her Muslim husband and sons, her loyalties are tested. And when her family is about to be torn apart, she must take drastic action to protect them.

A House Divided is a tense and timely thriller about political extremism and divided loyalties, and their impact on one woman.

Available from Amazon in paperback and e-book.

READ THE PREQUEL

Find out how Jess, Ben and Ruth arrived at the village in the prequel, *Underwater*.

'Hurricane Victoria, they called it. Such a British name. So full of history, and patriotism, and shades of Empire.'

Little did they know it would devastate London and send an exodus of refugees north.

In this companion set of prequel stories to *The Village*, discover how Sonia, Jess, Ben and Ruth Dyer are forced to leave London as it descends into chaos. **Will they reach Leeds and their eventual coast destination safely?**

To read *Underwater* as well as *Torn in Two*, the companion stories to my novel *A House Divided*, join my book club at rachelmclean.com/underwater.

Thanks,
Rachel McLean